THADDEUS OF WARSAW.

BY

MISS JANE PORTER

AUTHOR OF "THE SCOTTISH CHIEFS," ETC.

"Loin d'aimer la guerre, il l'abhorre
En triomphant même il déplore
Les désastres qu'elle produit
Et couronné par la victoire,
Il gémit de sa propre gloire,
Si la paix n'en est pas le fruit."

A NEW AND REVISED EDITION,

WITH THE ADDITION OF NEW NOTES, ETC., BY THE AUTHOR

WILDSIDE PRESS

THE AUTHOR

TO

HER FRIENDLY READERS.

Written for the new edition of "Thaddeus of Warsaw," forming one of the series called "The Standard Novels."

To such readers alone who, by the sympathy of a social taste, fall in with any blameless fashion of the day, and, from an amiable interest, also, in whatever may chance to afford them innocent pleasure, would fain know something more about an author whose works have brought them that gratification than the cold letter of a mere literary preface usually tells: to such readers this—something of an egotistical—epistle is addressed.

For, in beginning the republication of a regular series of the novels, or, as they have been more properly called, biographical romances, of which I have been the author, it has been considered desirable to make certain additions to each work, in the form of a few introductory pages and scattered notes, illustrative of the origin of the tale, of the historical events referred to in it, and of the actually living characters who constitute its personages, with some account, also, of the really local scenery described; thus giving, it is thought, a double zest to the entertainment of the reader, by bringing him into a previous acquaintance with the persons he is to meet in the book, and making him agreeably familiar with the country through which he is to travel in their company. Indeed, the social taste of the times has lately fully shown how advantageous the like conversational disclosures have proved to the recent republications of the celebrated "Waverley Novels," by the chief of novel-writers; and in the new series of the admirable naval tales by the distinguished American novelist, both of whom paid to the mother-country the gratifying tribute of making it their birthplace.

Such evidences in favor of an argument could not fail to

persuade me to undertake the desired elucidating task; feeling, indeed, particularly pleased to adopt, in my turn, a successful example from the once Great Unknown—now the not less great avowed author of the Waverley Novels, in the person of Sir Walter Scott, who did me the honor to adopt the style or class of novel of which "Thaddeus of Warsaw" was the first,—a class which, uniting the personages and facts of real history or biography with a combining and illustrative machinery of the imagination, formed a new species of writing in that day, and to which Madame de Staël and others have given the appellation of "an epic in prose." The day of its appearance is now pretty far back: for "Thaddeus of Warsaw" (a tale founded on Polish heroism) and the "Scottish Chiefs" (a romance grounded on Scottish heroism) were both published in England, and translated into various languages abroad, many years before the literary wonder of Scotland gave to the world his transcendent story of Waverley, forming a most impressive historical picture of the last struggle of the papist, but gallant, branch of the Stuarts for the British throne.*

"Thaddeus of Warsaw" being the first essay, in the form of such an association between fact and fancy, was published by its author with a natural apprehension of its reception by the critical part of the public. She had not, indeed, written it with any view to publication, but from an almost resistless impulse to embody the ideas and impressions with which her heart and mind were then full. It was written in her earliest youth; dictated by a fervent sympathy with calamities which had scarcely ceased to exist, and which her eager pen sought to portray; and it was given to the world, or rather to those who might feel with her, with all the simple-hearted enthusiasm which saw no impediment when a tale of virtue or of pity was to be told.

In looking back through the avenue of life to that time, what events have occurred, public and private, to the countries and to the individuals named in that tale! to persons of even as lofty names and excellences, of our own and other lands, who were mutually affected with me in admiration and regret for the virtues and the sorrows described! In sitting down now to my retrospective task, I find myself writing this, my second preface to the story of "Thaddeus of Warsaw," just thirty years from the date of its first publication. Then, I wrote

* It was on the publication of these, her first two works, in the German language that the authoress was honored with being made a lady of the Chapter of St. Joachim, and received the gold cross of the order from Wirtemburg.

when the struggle for the birthright independence of Poland was no more; when she lay in her ashes, and her heroes in their wounds; when the pall of death spread over the whole country, and her widows and orphans travelled afar.

In the days of my almost childhood,—that is, eight years before I dipped my pen in their tears,—I remember seeing many of those hapless refugees wandering about St. James's Park. They had sad companions in the like miseries, though from different enemies, in the emigrants from France; and memory can never forget the variety of wretched yet noble-looking visages I then contemplated in the daily walks which my mother's own little family group were accustomed to take there. One person, a gaunt figure, with melancholy and bravery stamped on his emaciated features, is often present to the recollection of us all. He was clad in a threadbare blue uniform great coat, with a black stock, a rusty old hat, pulled rather over his eyes; his hands without gloves; but his aspect was that of a perfect gentleman, and his step that of a military man. We saw him constantly at one hour, in the middle walk of the Mall, and always alone; never looking to the right nor to the left, but straight on; with an unmoving countenance, and a pace which told that his thoughts were those of a homeless and hopeless man—hopeless, at least, of all that life might bring him. On, on he went to the end of the Mall; turned again, and on again; and so he continued to do always, as long as we remained spectators of his solitary walk: once, indeed, we saw him crossing into St. Martin's Lane. Nobody seemed to know him, for he spoke to none; and no person ever addressed him, though many, like ourselves, looked at him, and stopped in the path to gaze after him. We often longed to be rich, to follow him wherever his wretched abode might have been, and then silently to send comforts to him from hands he knew not of. We used to call him, when speaking of him to ourselves, *Il Penseroso;* and by that name we yet not unfrequently talk of him to each other, and never without recurrence to the very painful, because unavailing, sympathy we then felt for that apparently friendless man. Such sympathy is, indeed, right; for it is one of the secondary means by which Providence conducts the stream of his mercies to those who need the succor of their fellow-creatures; and we cannot doubt that, though the agency of such Providence was not to be in our hands, there were those who had both the will and the power given, and did not, like ourselves, turn and pity that interesting emigrant in vain.

Some time after this, General Kosciusko, the justly celebrated hero of Poland, came to England, on his way to the United States; having been released from his close imprisonment in Russia, and in the noblest manner, too, by the Emperor Paul, immediately on his accession to the throne. His arrival caused a great sensation in London, and many of the first characters of the times pressed forward to pay their respects to such real patriotic virtue in its adversity. An old friend of my family was amongst them; his own warm heart encouraging the enthusiasm of ours, he took my brother Robert to visit the Polish veteran, then lodging at Sablonière's Hotel, in Leicester Square. My brother, on his return to us, described him as a noble looking man, though not at all handsome, lying upon a couch in a very enfeebled state, from the effects of numerous wounds he had received in his breast by the Cossacks' lances after his fall, having been previously overthrown by a sabre stroke on his head. His voice, in consequence of the induced internal weakness, was very low, and his speaking always with resting intervals. He wore a black bandage across his forehead, which covered a deep wound there; and, indeed, his whole figure bore marks of long suffering.

Our friend introduced my brother to him by name, and as "a boy emulous of seeing and following noble examples." Kosciusko took him kindly by the hand, and spoke to him words of generous encouragement, in whatever path of virtuous ambition he might take. They never have been forgotten. Is it, then, to be wondered at, combining the mute distress I had so often contemplated in other victims of similar misfortunes with the magnanimous object then described to me by my brother, that the story of heroism my young imagination should think of embodying into shape should be founded on the actual scenes of Kosciusko's sufferings, and moulded out of his virtues!

To have made him the ostensible hero of the tale, would have suited neither the modesty of his feelings nor the humbleness of my own expectation of telling it as I wished. I therefore took a younger and less pretending agent, in the personification of a descendant of the great John Sobieski.

But it was, as I have already said, some years after the partition of Poland that I wrote, and gave for publication, my historical romance on that catastrophe. It was finished amid a circle of friends well calculated to fan the flame which had inspired its commencement some of the leading heroes of the British army just returned from the victorious fields of Alexandria and St. Jean d'Acre; and, seated in my brother's little study, with the war-dyed coat in which the veteran Abercrombie breathed his last grateful sigh, while, like Wolfe, he gazed on the boasted invincible standard of the enemy, brought to him by a British soldier,—with this trophy of our own native valor on one side of me, and on the other the bullet-torn vest of another English commander of as many battles,—but who, having survived to enjoy his fame, I do not name here,—I put my last stroke to the first campaigns of Thaddeus Sobieski.

When the work was finished, some of the persons near me urged its being published. But I argued, in opposition to the wish, its different construction to all other novels or romances which had gone before it, from Richardson's time-honored domestic novels to the penetrating feeling in similar scenes by the pen of Henry Mackenzie; and again, Charlotte Smith's more recent, elegant, but very sentimental love stories. But the most formidable of all were the wildly interesting romances of Anne Radcliffe, whose magical wonders and mysteries were then the ruling style of the day. I urged, how could any one expect that the admiring readers of such works could consider my simply-told biographical legend of Poland anything better than a dull union between real history and a matter-of-fact imagination?

Arguments were found to answer all this; and being excited by the feelings which had dictated my little work, and encouraged by the corresponding characters with whom I daily associated, I ventured the essay. However, I had not read the sage romances of our older times without turning to some account the lessons they taught to adventurous personages of either sex; showing that even the boldest knight never made a new sally without consecrating his shield with some impress of acknowledged reverence. In like manner, when I entered the field with my modern romance of Thaddeus of Warsaw, I inscribed the first page with the name of the hero of Acre. That dedication will be found through all its successive editions, still in front of the title-page; and immediately following it is a second inscription, added, in after years, to the memory of the magnanimous patriot and exemplary man, Thaddeus Kosciusko, who had first filled me with ambition to write the tale, and who died in Switzerland, A. D. 1817, fuller of glory than of years. Yet, if life be measured by its vicissitudes and its virtues, we may justly say, "he was gathered in his ripeness."

After his visit to old friends in the United States,—where, in his youth, he had learned the art of war, and the science of a noble, unselfish independence, from the marvel of modern times, General Washington,—Kosciusko returned to Europe, and abode a while in France, but not in its capital. He lived deeply retired, gradually restoring his shattered frame to some degree of health by the peace of a resigned mind and the occupation of rural employments. Circumstances led him to Switzerland; and the country of William Tell, and of simple Christian fellowship, could not but soon be found peculiarly congenial to his spirit, long turned away from the pageants and the pomp of this world. In his span he had had all, either in his grasp or proffered to him. For when nothing remained of all his military glory and his patriotic sacrifices but a yet existing fame, and a conscious sense within him of duty performed, he was content to "eat his crust," with that inheritance alone; and he refused, though with an answering magnanimity of acknowledgment, a valuable property offered to him by the Emperor of Russia, as a free gift from a generous enemy, esteeming his proved, disinterested virtues. He also declined the yet more dazzling present of a crown from the then master of the continent, who would have set him on the throne of Poland—but, of a truth, under the vassalage of the Emperor of the French! Kosciusko was not to be consoled for Poland by riches bestowed on himself, nor betrayed into compromising her birthright of national independence by the casuistry that would have made his parental sceptre the instrument of a foreign domination.

Having such a theme as his name, and the heroes his copatriots, the romance of "Thaddeus of Warsaw" was no sooner published than it overcame the novelty of its construction, and became universally popular. Nor was it very long before it fell into General Kosciusko's hands, though then in a distant land; and he kindly and promptly lost no time in letting the author know his approbation of the narrative, though qualified with several modest expressions respecting himself. From that period she enjoyed many treasured marks of his esteem; and she will add, though with a sad satisfaction, that amongst her several relics of the Great Departed who have honored her with regard, she possesses, most dearly prized, a medal of Kosciusko and a lock of his hair. About the same time she received a most incontestable proof of the accuracy of her story from the lips of General Gardiner, the last British minister to the court of Stanislaus Augustus. On his reading the book, he was so sure that the facts it represented could only have been learned on the spot, that he expressed his surprise to several persons that the author of the work, an English lady, could have been at Warsaw during all the troubles there and he not know it. On his repeating this observation to the late Duke of Roxburgh, his grace's sister-in-law, who happened to overhear what was said, and knew the writer, answered him by saying, "The author has never been in Poland." "Impossible!" replied the general; "no one could describe the scenes and occurrences there, in the manner it is done in that book, without having been an eye-witness." The lady, however, convinced the general of the fact being otherwise, by assuring him, from her own personal knowledge, that the author of "Thaddeus of Warsaw" was a mere school-girl in England at the time of the events of the story.

How, then, it has often been asked, did she obtain such accurate information with regard to those events? and how acquire her familiar acquaintance with the palaces and persons she represents in the work? The answer is short. By close questioning every person that came in her way that knew anything about the object of her interest; and there were many brave hearts and indignant lips ready to open with the sad yet noble tale. Thus every illustrious individual she wished to bring into her narrative gradually grew upon her knowledge, till she became as well acquainted with all her desired personages as if they were actually present with her; for she knew their minds and their actions; and these compose the man. The features of the country, also, were learned from persons who had trodden the spots she describes: and that they were indeed correct pictures of their homes and war-fields, the tears and bursting enthusiasm of many of Poland's long expatriated sons have more than once borne testimony to her.

As one instance, out of the number I might repeat, of the inextinguishable love of those noble wanderers from their native country, I shall subjoin the copy of a letter addressed to me by one of those gallant men, then holding a high military post in a foreign service, and who, I afterwards learned, was of the family of Kosciusko, whose portrait he sent to me: for the letter was accompanied with a curiously-wrought ring of pure gold, containing a likeness of that hero. The letter was in French, and I transcribe it literally in the words of the writer:—

"Madame!

"Un inconnu ose addresser la parole à l'auteur immortel de Thaddeus de Warsaw; attaché par tent de liens à l'héros que vous avez chanté, je m'enhardis à distraire pour un moment vos nobles veilles.

"Qu'il me soit permis de vous offrir, madame, l'hommage

de mon admiration la plus exaltée, en vous présentant la bague qui contient le buste du Général Kosciusko:—elle a servi de signe de ralliment aux patriots Polonois, lorsque, en 1794, ils entreprirent de sécouer leur joug.

"Les anciens déposoient leurs offrandes sur l'autel de leurs divinités tutélaires ;—je ne fais qu'imiter leur exemple. Vous êtes pour tous les Polonois cette divinité, qui la première ait élevée sa voix, du fond de l'impériale, Albion, en leur faveur.

"Un jour viendra, et j'ose conserver dans mon cœur cet espoir, que vos accens, qui ont retenti dans le cœur de l'Europe sensible, produiront leur effêt célestial, en ressuscitant l'ombre sanglante de ma chère patrie.

"Daignez agréer, madame, l'hommage respectueuse d'un de vos serviteurs le plus dévoué, &c. &c."

Probably the writer of the above is now returned to his country, his vows having been most awfully answered by one of the most momentous struggles she has ever had, or to which the nations around have ever yet stood as spectators; for the balance of Europe trembles at the turning of her scale.

Thus, then, it cannot but be that in the conclusion of this my, perhaps, last introductory preface to any new edition of "Thaddeus of Warsaw," its author should offer up a sincerely heart-felt prayer to the King of kings, the Almighty Father of all mankind, that His all-gracious Spirit may watch over the issue of this contest, and dictate the peace of Poland!

ESHER, *May*, 1831.

Dedication to the First Edition.

THADDEUS OF WARSAW

IS INSCRIBED TO

SIR SIDNEY SMITH;

IN THE HOPE THAT, AS

SIR PHILIP SIDNEY

DID NOT DISDAIN TO WRITE A ROMANCE,

SIR SIDNEY SMITH

WILL NOT REFUSE TO READ ONE.

SIR PHILIP SIDNEY CONSIGNED HIS EXCELLENT WORK TO THE AFFECTION OF A SISTER.

I CONFIDE MY ASPIRING ATTEMPT TO THE URBANITY OF THE BRAVE; TO THE MAN OF TASTE, OF FEELING, AND OF CANDOR;

TO HIM WHOSE FRIENDSHIP WILL BESTOW THAT INDULGENCE ON THE AUTHOR WHICH HIS JUDGMENT MIGHT HAVE DENIED TO THE BOOK;

TO HIM OF WHOM FUTURE AGES WILL SPEAK WITH HONOR, AND THE PRESENT TIMES BOAST AS THEIR GLORY!

TO

SIR SIDNEY SMITH,

I SUBMIT THIS HUMBLE TRIBUTE OF THE HIGHEST RESPECT WHICH CAN BE OFFERED BY A BRITON OR ANIMATE THE HEART OF HIS SINCERE FRIEND,

THE AUTHOR.

PREFACE TO THE FIRST EDITION.

HAVING attempted a narrative of the intended description, but written, in fact, from the mere impulse of sympathy with its subject still fresh in my own and every pitying memory, it is natural that, after having made up my mind to assent to its publication, in which much time and thought has been expended in considering the responsibility of so doing, from so unpractised a pen, I should feel an increase of anxiety respecting its ultimate fate.

Therefore, before the reader favors the tale itself with his attention, I beg leave to offer him a little account of the principles that actuated its composition, and in regard to which one of the most honored heads in the author's family urged her "not to withhold it from the press;" observing, in his persuasions, that the mistakes which many of my young contemporaries of both sexes continually make in their estimates of human character, and of the purposes of human life, require to have a line of difference between certain splendid vices and some of the brilliant order of virtues to be distinctly drawn before them. "And," he remarked, "it appeared to be so done in the pages of my Polish manuscript. Therefore," added he, "let Thaddeus of Warsaw speak openly for himself!"

This opinion decided me. Though with fear and trembling, yet I felt an encouraging consciousness that in writing the manuscript narrative for my own private enjoyment only, and the occasional amusement of those friends dearest around me, I had wished to portray characters whose high endowments could not be misled into proud ambitions, nor the gift of dazzling social graces betray into the selfish triumphs of worldly vanity,—characters that prosperity could not inflate, nor disappointments depress, from pious trust and honorable action. The pure fires of such a spirit declare their sacred origin; and such is the talisman of those achievements which amaze everybody but their accomplisher. The eye fixed on it is what divine truth declares it to be "single!" There is no double purpose in it; no glancing to a man's own personal aggrandizement on one side and on professing services to his fellow-creatures on the other; such a spirit has only one aim—Heaven! and the eternal records of that wide firmament include within it "all good to man."

What flattered Alexander of Macedon into a madman, and perverted the gracious-minded Julius Cæsar into usurpation and tyranny, has also been found by Christian heroes the most perilous ordeal of their virtue; but, inasmuch as they are Christian heroes, and not pagan men, worshippers of false gods, whose fabled examples inculcated all these deeds of self-absorbing vain-glory, our heroes of a "better revelation" have no excuse for failing under their trial, and many there be who pass through it "pure and undefiled." Such were the great Alfred of England, Gustavus Vasa of Sweden, and his greater successor in true glory, Gustavus Adolphus,—all champions of immutable justice and ministers of peace. And though these may be regarded as personages beyond the sphere of ordinary emulations, yet the same principles, or their opposites, prevail in every order of men from the prince to the peasant; and, perhaps, at no period of the world more than the present were these divers principles in greater necessity to be considered, and, according to the just conclusion, be obeyed. On all sides of us we see public and private society broken up, as it were by an earthquake: the noblest and the meanest passions of the human bosom at contention, and the latter often so disguised, that the vile ambuscade is not even suspected till found within the heart of the fortress itself. We have, however, one veritable touchstone, that of the truest observation, "ye shall know a tree by its fruits." Let us look round, then, for those which bear "good fruits," wholesome to the taste as well as pleasant to the sight, whether they grow on high altitudes or in the humbler valleys of the earth; let us view men of all degrees in life in their actions, and not in their pretensions,—such men as were some of the Sobieski race in Poland, in every change of their remarkable lives. When placed at the summit of mortal fame, surrounded by greatness and glory, and consequent power, they evinced neither pride to others nor a sense of self-aggrandizement in themselves; and, when under a reverse dispensation, national misfortunes pursued them, and family sorrows pierced their souls, the weakness of a murmur never sunk the dignity of their sustaining fortitude, nor did the firmness of that virtue harden the amiable sensibilities of their hearts.

To exhibit so truly heroic and endearing a portrait of what

every Christian man ought to be,—for the law of God is the same to the poor as to the rich,—I have chosen one of that illustrious and, I believe, now extinct race for the subject of my sketch; and the more aptly did it present itself, it being necessary to show my hero amidst scenes and circumstances ready to exercise his brave and generous propensities, and to put their personal issues to the test on his mind. Hence Poland's sadly-varying destinies seemed to me the stage best calculated for the development of any self-imposed task.

There certainly were matters enough for the exhibition of all that human nature could suffer and endure, and, alas! perish under, in the nearly simultaneous but terrible regicidal revolution of France; but I shrunk from that as a tale of horror, the work of demons in the shapes of men. It was a conflict in which no comparisons, as between man and man, could exist; and may God grant that so fearful a visitation may never be inflicted on this world again. May the nations of this world lay its warnings to their hearts!

It sprung from a tree self-corrupted, which only could produce such fruits: the demon hierarchy of the French philosophers, who had long denied the being of that pure and Almighty God, and who, in the arrogance of their own deified reason, and while in utter subjection to the wildest desires of their passions, published their profane and polluted creed amongst all orders of the people, and the natural and terrible consequences ensued. Ignorant before, they became like unto their teachers, demons in their unbelief,—demons in one common envy and hatred of all degrees above them, or around them, whose existence seemed at all in the way of even their slightest gratification: mutual spoliation and destruction covered the country. How often has the tale been told me by noble refugees, sheltered on our shores from those scenes of blood, where infamy triumphed and truth and honor were massacred; but such narratives, though they never can be forgotten, are too direful for the hearer to contemplate in memory.

Therefore, when I sought to represent the mental and moral contest of man with himself, or with his fellow-men, I did not look for their field amongst human monsters, but with natural and civilized man; inasmuch as he is seen to be influenced by the impulses of his selfish passions—ambition, covetousness, and the vanities of life, or, on the opposite side, by the generous amenities of true disinterestedness, in all its trying situations; and, as I have said, the recent struggle in Poland, to maintain her laws and loyal independence, against the combined aggressions of the three most powerful states in Europe, seemed to afford me the most suitable objects for my moral aim, to interest by sympathy, while it taught the responsible commission of human life.

I have now described the plan of my story, its aim and origin.

If it be disapproved, let it be at once laid aside; but should it excite any interest, I pray its perusal may be accompanied with an indulgent candor, its subjects being of so new, and therefore uncustomary, a character in a work of the kind. But if the reader be one of my own sex, I would especially solicit her patience while going through the first portion of the tale, its author being aware that war and politics are not the most promising themes for an agreeable amusement; but the battles are not frequent, nor do the cabinet councils last long. I beg the favor, if the story is to be read at all, that no scene may be passed over as extraneous, for though it begin like a state-paper, or a sermon, it always terminates by casting some new light on the portrait of the hero. Beyond those events of peril and of patriotic devotedness, the remainder of the pages dwell generally with domestic interests; but if the reader do not approach them regularly through the development of character opened in the preceding troubled field, what they exhibit will seem a mere wilderness of incidents, without interest or end; indeed I have designed nothing in the personages of this narrative out of the way of living experience. I have sketched no virtue that I have not seen, nor painted any folly from imagination. I have endeavored to be as faithful to reality in my pictures of domestic morals, and of heroic duties, as a just painter would seek to be to the existing objects of nature, "wonderful and wild, or of gentlest beauty!" and on these grounds I have steadily attempted to inculcate "that virtue is the highest proof of understanding, and the only solid basis of greatness; that vice is the natural consequence of grovelling thoughts, which begin in mistake and end in ignominy."

POSTCRIPT TO A SUBSEQUENT EDITION.

After so many intervening years have passed since the author of Thaddeus of Warsaw wrote the foregoing preface, to introduce a work so novel in its character to the notice and candid judgment of the British public, it was her intention to take the present occasion of its now perfectly new republication, at the distance of above forty years from its earliest apperance and so continued editions, to express her grateful sense of that public's gratifying sympathies and honoring testimonies of approbation, from its author's youth to age; but even in the hour she sits down to perform the gracious task, she feels a present incapability to undertake it. The very attempt has too sensibly recalled to her heart events that have befallen her since she lived amongst the models of her tale; and she has also more recently been in many of the places it describes; and circumstances, both of joys and sorrows, having occurred to her there to influence the whole future current of her mortal life, she finds it impossible to yet touch on those times and scenes connected with the subjects of her happy youth, which would now only reverberate notes of sadness it is her duty to repress. Hence, though while revising the work itself she experiences a calm delight in the occupation, being a kind of parting duty, also, to the descendants of her earliest, readers, she would rather defer any little elucidations she may have met with regarding the objects of her pen to a few pages in the form of an Appendix at the end of the work; all, indeed, bringing her observations, whether by weal or woe, to the one great and guiding conclusion, "Man is formed for two states of existence—a mortal and an immortal being;" in the Holy Scriptures authoritatively declared, "For the life that now is, and for that which is to come."

JANE PORTER.

Bristol, *November*, 1844.

CONTENTS.

THADDEUS OF WARSAW.

CHAPTER I.

THE large and magnificent palace of Villanow, whose vast domains stretch along the northern bank of the Vistula, was the favorite residence of John Sobieski, King of Poland. That monarch, after having delivered his country from innumerable enemies, rescued Vienna and subdued the Turks, retired to this place at certain seasons, and thence dispensed those acts of his luminous and benevolent mind which rendered his name great and his people happy.

When Charles the Twelfth of Sweden visited the tomb of Sobieski, at Cracow, he exclaimed, "What a pity that so great a man should ever die!" * Another generation saw the spirit of this lamented hero revive in the person of his descendant, Constantine, Count Sobieski, who, in a comparatively private station, as Palatine of Masovia, and the friend rather than the lord of his vassals, evinced by his actions that he was the inheritor of his forefather's virtue as well as of his blood.

He was the first Polish nobleman who granted freedom to his peasants. He threw down their mud hovels and built comfortable villages; he furnished them with seed, cattle, and implements of husbandry, and calling their families together, laid before them the deed of their enfranchisement; but before he signed it, he expressed a fear that they would abuse this liberty of which they had not had experience, and become licentious.

"No," returned a venerable peasant; "when we were ignorant men, and possessed no property of our own except these staffs in our hands, we were destitute of all manly motives for propriety of conduct; but you have taught us to read out of

* In the year 1683, this hero raised the siege of Vienna, then beleagured by the Turks; and driving them out of Europe, saved Christendom from a Mohammedan usurpation.

the Holy Book, how to serve God and honor the king. And shall we not respect laws which thus bestow on us, and ensure to us, the fruits of our labors and the favor of Heaven!"

The good sense and truth of this answer were manifested in the event. On the emancipation of these people, they became so prosperous in business and correct in behavior, that the example of the palatine was speedily followed by the Chancellor Zamoiski * and several of the principal nobility. The royal Stanislaus's beneficent spirit moved in unison with that of Sobieski, and a constitution was given to Poland to place her in the first rank of free nations.

Encircled by his happy tenantry, and within the bosom of his family, this illustrious man educated Thaddeus, the only male heir of his name, to the exercise of all the virtues which ennoble and endear the possessor.

But this reign of public and domestic peace was not to continue. Three formidable and apparently friendly states envied the effects of a patriotism they would not imitate; and in the beginning of the year 1792, regardless of existing treaties, broke in upon the unguarded frontiers of Poland, threatening with all the horrors of a merciless war the properties, lives, and liberties of the people.

The family of Sobieski had ever been foremost in the ranks of their country; and at the present crisis its venerable head did not hang behind the youngest warrior in preparations for the field.

On the evening of an anniversary of the birthday of his grandson, the palatine rode abroad with a party of friends, who had been celebrating the festival with their presence. The countess (his daughter) and Thaddeus were left alone in the saloon. She sighed as she gazed on her son, who stood at some distance, fitting to his youthful thigh a variety of sabres, which his servant a little time before had laid upon the table. She observed with anxiety the eagerness of his motion, and the ardor that was flashing from his eyes.

"Thaddeus," said she, "lay down that sword; I wish to speak with you." Thaddeus looked gayly up. "My dear Thaddeus!" cried his mother, and tears started to her eyes. The blush of enthusiasm faded from his face; he threw the sabre from him, and drew near the countess.

"Why, my dear mother, do you distress yourself? When I

* This family had ever been one of the noblest and most virtuous in Poland. And had its wisdom been listened to in former years by certain powerful and wildly ambitious lords that once great kingdom would never have exchanged its long line of hereditary native princes for an elective monarchy—that arena of all political mischiefs.

am in battle, shall I not have my grandfather near me, and be as much under the protection of God as at this moment?"

"Yes, my child," answered she, "God will protect you. He is the protector of the orphan, and you are fatherless." The countess paused—"Here, my son," said she, giving him a sealed packet, "take this; it will reveal to you the history of your birth and the name of your father. It is necessary that you should know a painful fact, which has hitherto been concealed from you by the wish and noble judgment of your grandfather." Thaddeus received it, and stood silent with surprise. "Read it, my love," continued she, "but go to your own apartments; here you may be interrupted."

Bewildered by the manner of the countess, Thaddeus, without answering, instantly obeyed. Shutting himself within his study, he impatiently opened the papers, and soon found his whole attention absorbed in the following recital:

"TO MY DEAR SON, THADDEUS CONSTANTINE SOBIESKI.

"You are now, my Thaddeus, at the early age of nineteen, going to engage the enemies of your country. Ere I resign my greatest comfort to the casualties of war; ere I part with you, perhaps forever, I would inform you who your father really was—that father whose existence you have hardly known and whose name you have never heard. You believe yourself an orphan, your mother a widow; but, alas! I have now to tell you that you were made fatherless by the perfidy of man, not by the dispensation of Heaven.

"Twenty-three years ago, I accompanied my father in a tour through Germany and Italy. Grief for the death of my mother had impaired his health, and the physicians ordered him to reside in a warmer climate; accordingly we fixed ourselves near the Arno. During several visits to Florence, my father met in that city with a young Englishman of the name of Sackville. These frequent meetings opened into intimacy, and he was invited to our villa.

"Mr. Sackville was not only the most interesting man I had ever seen, but the most accomplished, and his heart seemed the seat of every graceful feeling. He was the first man for whose society I felt a lively preference. I used to smile at this strange delight, or sometimes weep; for the emotions which agitated me were undefinable, but they were enchanting, and unheedingly I gave them indulgence. The hours which we passed together in the interchange of reciprocal sentiments, the kind beaming of his looks, the thousand sighs that he breathed, the half-uttered sentences, all conspired to rob me of myself.

"Nearly twelve months were spent in these delusions. During the last three, doubts and anguish displaced the blissful reveries of an infant tenderness. The attentions of Mr. Sackville died away. From being the object of his constant search, he then sedulously sought to avoid me. When my father withdrew to his closet, he would take his leave, and allow me to walk alone. Solitary and wretched were my rambles. I had full leisure to compare my then disturbed state of mind with the comparative peace I had enjoyed in my own country. Immured within the palace of Villanow, watching the declining health of my mother, I knew nothing of the real world, the little I had learned of society being drawn from books; and, uncorrected by experience, I was taught to believe a perfection in man which, to my affliction, I since found to be but a poet's dream. When my father took me to Italy, I continued averse to public company. In such seclusion, the presence of Sackville, being almost my only pleasure, chased from my mind its usual reserve, and gradually and surely won upon the awakened affections of my heart. Artless and unwarned, I knew not the nature of the passion which I cherished until it had gained an ascendancy that menaced my life.

"On the evening of one of those days in which I had been disappointed of seeing this too-dearly-prized companion, I strolled out, and, hardly conscious of my actions, threw myself along the summit of a flight of steps in our garden that led down to the Arno. My head rested against the base of a statue which, because of its resemblance to me, Sackville had presented to my father. Every recollected kindness of his now gave me additional torment; and clinging to the pedestal as to the altar of my adoration, in the bitterness of disappointment I addressed the insensible stone: 'O! were I pale as thou art, and this breast as cold and still, would Sackville, when he looked on me, give one sigh to the creature he had destroyed? My sobs followed this adjuration, and the next moment I felt myself encircled in his arms. I struggled, and almost fainting with shame at such utter weakness, implored to be released. He did release me, and, in an agony of emotion, besought my pardon for the misery I had endured. 'Now, Therese,' cried he, 'all is as it ought to be! you are my only hope. Consent to be mine, or the world has no hold on me!' His voice was hurried and incoherent. Raising my eyes to his, I beheld them wild and bloodshot. Terrified at his look, and overcome by my own distracted thoughts, my head sunk on the marble. With increased violence he exclaimed, 'Have I deceived myself here too? Therese, did you not prefer me? Did you not love me? Speak now, I conjure you, by your own happiness and mine! Do you reject me?' He clasped my hands with a force that made me tremble, and I hardly articulated, 'I will be yours.' At these words he hurried me down a dark vista, which led out of the gardens to the open country. A carriage stood at the gate. I fearfully asked what he intended. 'You have given yourself to me,' cried he; 'and by that vow, written in heaven, no power shall separate us until you are mine beyond the reach of man!' Unnerved in body and weak in mind, I yielded to his impetuosity, and suffering him to lift me into the chariot, was carried to the door of the nearest monastery, where in a few minutes we were married.

"I am thus particular in the relation of every incident, in the hope that you, my dear son, will find some excuse for my great imprudence,—in the circumstances of my youth, and in the influence which a man who seemed all excellence had gained over my heart. However, my fault went not long unpunished.

"The ceremony past, my husband conducted me in silence back to the carriage. My full bosom discharged itself in abundance of tears, while Sackville sat by me, without any movement, and mute. Two or three times I raised my eyes, in hopes of discerning in his some consolation for my hasty compliance. But no; his gaze, vacant and glaring, was fixed on the window, and his brow became heavily clouded, as if he had been forced into an alliance with one he hated, rather than had just made a voluntary engagement with the woman he loved. My soul shuddered at this commencement of a contract which I had dared to make unsanctioned by my father's consent. At length my sighs seemed to startle my husband; and suddenly turning round, he cried, 'Therese, this marriage must not be told to the palatine. I have been precipitate. It would ruin me with my family. Refrain, only for one month, and then I will publicly acknowledge you.' The agitation of his features and the feverish burning of his hand, which then held mine, alarmed me. Trembling from head to foot, I answered, 'Sackville! I have already erred enough in consenting to this stolen marriage. I will not transgress further by concealing it. I will instantly throw myself at my father's feet, and confess all.' His countenance darkened again. 'Therese,' said he, 'I am your husband. You have sworn to obey me, and till I allow you, divulge this marriage at your peril!' This last stern sentence, and the sterner look that accompanied it, pierced me to the heart, and I fell senseless on the seat.

"When I recovered, I found myself at the foot of that statue beneath which my unfortunate destiny had been fixed. My husband was leaning over me. He raised me with tenderness from the ground, and conjured me, in the mildest accents, to be comforted; to pardon the severity of those words, which had arisen from a fear that, by an imprudent avowal on my part, I should risk both his happiness and my own. He informed me that he was heir to one of the first families in England; and before he set out for the continent, he had pledged his honor to his father never to enter into any matrimonial engagement without first acquainting him with the particulars of the lady and her family. Should he omit this duty, his father declared that, though she were a princess, he would disinherit him, and never again admit him to his presence.

"'Consider this, my dear Therese,' continued he; 'could you endure to behold me an outcast, and stigmatized with a parent's curse, when a little forbearance on your part would make all right? I know I have been hasty in acting as I have done, but now I cannot remedy my error. To-morrow I will write to my father, describe your rank and merits, and request his consent to our immediate union. The moment his permission arrives, I will cast myself on the palatine's friendship, and reveal what has passed. The tenderness of my husband blinded my reason, and with many tears, I sealed his forgiveness and pledged my faith on his word.

"My dear deceived parent little suspected the perfidy of his guest. He detained him as his visitor, and often rallied himself on the hold which this distinguished stranger's accomplishments had taken on his heart. Sackville's manner to me in public was obliging and free; it was in private only that I found the tender, the capricious, the unkind husband. Night after night I have washed the memory of my want of duty to my father with bitter tears; but my husband was dear to me—he was more precious than my life! One affectionate look from him, one fond word, would solace every pain, and make me wait the arrival of his father's letter with all the sanguine anticipations of youth and love.

"A fortnight passed away. A month—a long and lingering month. Another month, and a packet of letters was presented to Sackville. He was conversing with us. At sight of the superscription, he tore open the paper, ran his eyes over a few lines, and then, flushed and agitated, started from his seat and left the room. My emotions were almost uncontrollable. I had already half risen from my chair to follow him, when the palatine exclaimed, 'What can be in that letter? Too plainly I see some afflicting tidings.' And without observing me, or waiting for a reply, he hurried out after him. I hastened to my chamber, where, throwing myself on my bed, I tried, by all the delusions of hope, to obtain some alleviation from the pangs of my suspense.

"The dinner-bell roused me from my reverie. Dreading to excite suspicion, and anxious to read in the countenance of my husband the denunciation of our fate, I obeyed the summons and descended to the dining-room. On entering it, my eyes irresistibly wandered round to fix themselves on Sackville. He was leaning against a pillar, his face pale as death. My father looked grave, but immediately took his seat, and tenderly placed his friend beside him. I sat down in silence. Little dinner was eaten, and few words spoken. As for myself, my agitation almost choked me. I felt that the first words I should attempt to pronounce must give them utterance, and that their vehemence would betray our fatal secret.

"When the servants had withdrawn, Sackville rose, and said, in a faltering voice, 'Count, I must leave you.' 'Nay,' replied the palatine; 'you are unwell—disturbed—stay till to-morrow.' 'I thank your excellency,' answered he, 'but I must go to Florence to-night. You shall see me again before to-morrow afternoon; all will then, I hope, be settled to my wish.' My husband took his hat. Motionless, and incapable of speaking, I sat fixed to my chair, in the direct way that he must pass. His eye met mine. He stopped and looked at me, abruptly snatched my hand; then as abruptly quitting it, darted out of the room. I never saw him more.

"I had not the power to dissemble another moment. I fell back into the arms of my father. He did not, even by this imprudence, read what I almost wished him to guess, but, with all the indulgence of perfect confidence, lamented the distress of Sackville, and the sensibility of my nature, which sympathized so painfully with his friend. I durst not ask what was the distress of his friend. Abashed at my duplicity to my father, and overwhelmed with a thousand dreads, I obtained his permission to retire to my chamber.

"The next day I met him with calmness, for I had schooled my heart to endure the sufferings it had deserved. He did not remark my recovered tranquillity, so entirely was his generous heart occupied in conjecturing the cause of Sackville's grief, who had acknowledged having received a great shock, but would not reveal the occasion. This double reserve to my father surprised and distressed me, and to all his suppositions I said little. My soul was too deeply interested in the subject to trust to the faithfulness of my lips.

"The morning crept slowly on, and the noon appeared to stand still. I anxiously watched the declining sun, as the signal for my husband's return. Two hours had elapsed since his promised time, and my father grew so impatient that he went out to meet him. I eagerly wished that they might miss each other. I should then see Sackville a few minutes alone, and by one word be comforted or driven to despair.

"I was listening to every footstep that sounded under the colonnade, when my servant brought me a letter which had just been left by one of Mr. Sackville's grooms. I broke open the seal, and fell senseless on the floor ere I had read half the killing contents."

Thaddeus, with a burning cheek, and a heart all at once robbed of that elastic spring which till now had ever made him the happiest of the happy, took up the letter of his father. The paper was worn, and blistered with his mother's tears. His head seemed to swim as he contemplated the handwriting, and he said to himself, "Am I to respect or to abhor him?" He proceeded in the perusal.

"To Therese, Countess Sobieski.

"How, Therese, am I to address you? But an attempt to palliate my conduct would be to no purpose; indeed it is impossible. You cannot conceive a viler opinion of me than I have of myself. I know that I forfeit all claim to honor, in the most delicate point of your noble and trusting heart!—that I have sacrificed your tenderness to my distracted passions; but you shall no more be subject to the caprices of a man who cannot repay your innocent love with his own. *You* have no guilt to torture you; and you possess virtues which will render you tranquil under every calamity. I leave you to your own purity, and, therefore, peace of mind. Forget the ceremony which has passed between us; my wretched heart disclaims it forever. Your father is happily ignorant of it; pray spare him the anguish of knowing that I was so utterly unworthy of his kindness; I feel that I am more than ungrateful to you and to him. Therese, your most inveterate hate cannot more strongly tell me than I can tell myself that to you I have been a villain. But I cannot retract. I am going where all search will be vain; and I now bid you an eternal farewell. May you be happier than ever can be the self-abhorring.

"R. S——.

"FLORENCE."

Thaddeus, after a brief pause, went on with his mother's narrative.

"When my senses returned, I was lying on the floor, holding the half-perused paper in my hand. Grief and horror had locked up the avenues of complaint, and I sat as one petrified to stone. My father entered. At the sight of me, he started as if he had been a spectre. His well-known features opened at once my agonized heart. With fearful cries I cast myself at his feet, and putting the letter into his hand, clung, almost expiring, to his knees.

"When he had read it, he flung it from him, and dropping into a chair, covered his face with his hands. I looked up imploringly, for I could not speak. My father stooped forward, and raising me in his arms, pressed me to his bosom. 'My Therese,' said he, 'it is I who have done this. Had I not harbored this villain, he never could have had an opportunity of ruining the peace of my child.' In return for the unexampled indulgence of this speech, and his repeated assurances of forgiveness, I promised to forget a man who could have had so little respect for truth and gratitude, and his own honor. The palatine replied that he expected such a resolution, in consequence of the principles my exemplary mother had taught me; and to show me how far dearer to him was my real tranquillity than any false idea of impossible restitution, he would not remove even from one principality to another, were he sure by that means to discover Mr. Sackville and to avenge my wrongs. My understanding assented to the justice and dignity of all he said; but long and severe were my struggles before I could erase from my soul the image of that being who had been the lord of all my young hopes.

"It was not until you, my dear Thaddeus, were born that I could repay the goodness of my father with the smiles of cheerfulness. And he would not permit me to give you any name which could remind him or myself of the faithless husband who knew not even of your existence; and by his desire I christened you Thaddeus Constantine, after himself, and his best beloved friend General Kosciusko. You have not yet seen that illustrious Polander; his prescient watchfulness for his country keeps him so constantly employed on the frontiers. He is now with the army at Winnica, whither you must soon go; and in him you may study one of the brightest models of patriotic and martial virtue that ever was presented to mankind. It is well said of him 'that he would have shone with distinguished lustre in the ages of chivalry.' Gallant, generous, and strictly just, he commands obedience by the reverence in which he is held, and attaches the troops to his person by the affability of his manners and the purity of his life. He teaches them discipline, endurance of fatigue, and contempt of danger, by his dauntless example, and inspires them with confidence by his tranquillity in the tumult of action and the invincible fortitude with which he meets the most adverse stroke of misfortune. His modesty in victory shows him to be one of the greatest among men, and his magnanimity under defeat confirms him to be a Christian hero.

"Such is the man whose name you share. How bitterly do I lament that the one to which nature gave you a claim was so unworthy to be united with it, and that of my no less heroic father!

"On our return to Poland, the story which the palatine related, when questioned about my apparently forlorn state, was simply this:—'My daughter was married and widowed in the course of two months. Since then, to root from her memory as much as possible all recollection of a husband who was only given to be taken away, she still retains my name; and her son, as my sole heir, shall bear no other.' This reply satisfied every one; the king, who was my father's only confidant, gave his sanction to it, and no further inquiries were ever made.

"You are now, my beloved child, entering on the eventful career of life. God only knows, when the venerable head of your grandfather is laid in dust, and I, too, have shut my eyes upon you in this world, where destiny may send you! perhaps to the country of your father. Should you ever meet him—but that is unlikely; so I will be silent on a thought which nineteen years of reflection have not yet deprived of its sting.

"Not to embitter the fresh spring of your youth, my Thaddeus, with the draught that has poisoned mine: not to implant in your breast hatred of a parent whom you may never behold, have I written this; but to inform you in fact from whom you sprung. My history is made plain to you, that no unexpected events may hereafter perplex your opinion of your mother, or cause a blush to rise on that cheek for her, which from your grandfather can derive no stain. For his sake as well as for mine, whether in peace or in war, may the angels of heaven guard my boy! This is the unceasing prayer of thy fond mother,

"THERESE, COUNTESS SOBIESKI.

"VILLANOW, *March*, 1792."

When he finished reading, Thaddeus held the papers in his hand; but, unable to recover from the shock of their contents, he read them a second time to the end; then laying them on the table, against which he rested his now aching head, he gave vent to the fulness of his heart in tears.

The countess, anxious for the effect which her history might have made on her son, at this instant entered the room. Seeing him in so dejected an attitude, she approached, and pressing him to her bosom, silently wept with him. Thaddeus, ashamed of his emotions, yet incapable of dissembling them, struggled a moment to release himself from her arms. The countess, mistaking his motive, said in a melancholy voice, "And do you, my son, despise your mother for the weakness which she has revealed? Is this the reception that I expected from a child on whose affection I reposed my confidence and my comfort?"

"No, my mother," replied Thaddeus; "it is your afflictions which have distressed me. This is the first unhappy hour I ever knew, and can you wonder I should be affected? Oh! mother," continued he, laying his hand on his father's letter, "whatever were his rank, had my father been but noble in mind, I would have gloried in bearing his name; but now, I put up my prayers never to hear it more."

"Forget him," cried the countess, hiding her eyes with her handkerchief.

"I will," answered Thaddeus, "and allow my memory to dwell on the virtues of my mother only."

It was impossible for the countess or her son to conceal their agitation from the palatine, who now opened the door. On his expressing alarm at a sight so unusual, his daughter, finding herself incapable of speaking, put into his hand the letter which Thaddeus had just read. Sobieski cast his eye over the first lines; he comprehended their tendency, and seeing the countess had withdrawn, he looked towards his grandson. Thaddeus was walking up and down the room, striving to command himself for the conversation he anticipated with his grandfather.

"I am sorry, Thaddeus," said Sobieski, "that your mother

has so abruptly imparted to you the real country and character of your father. I see that his villany has distressed a heart which Heaven has made alive to even the slightest appearance of dishonor. But be consoled, my son! I have prevented the publicity of his conduct by an ambiguous story of your mother's widowhood. Yet notwithstanding this arrangement, she has judged it proper that you should not enter general society without being made acquainted with the true events of your birth. I believe my daughter is right. And cheer yourself, my child! ever remembering that you are one of the noblest race in Poland! and suffer not the vices of one parent to dim the virtues of the other."

"No, my lord," answered his grandson; "you have been more than a parent to me; and henceforward, for your sake as well as my own, I shall hold it my duty to forget that I draw my being from any other source than that of the house of Sobieski."

"You are right," cried the palatine, with an exulting emotion; "you have the spirit of your ancestors, and I shall live to see you add glory to the name!" *

The beaming eyes and smiling lips of the young count declared that he had shaken sorrow from his heart. His grandfather pressed his hand with delight, and saw in his recovered serenity the sure promise of his fond prophecy.

CHAPTER II.

THE MILL OF MARIEMONT.

The fearful day arrived when Sobieski and his grandson were to bid adieu to Villanow and its peaceful scenes.

The well-poised mind of the veteran bade his daughter farewell with a fortitude which imparted some of its strength even to her. But when Thaddeus, ready habited for his journey, entered the room, at the sight of his military accoutrements she

* John Sobieski, King of Poland, was the most renowned sovereign of his time. His victories over the Tartars and the Turks obtained for him the admiration of Europe. Would it might be said, "the gratitude also of her posterity!" For his signal courage and wondrous generalship on the field of Vienna, against the latter Mohammedan power, rescued Austria, and the chief part of Christendom at that time, from their ruinous grasp. Where was the memory of these things, when the Austrian emperor marched his devastating legions into Poland, in the year 1793?

shuddered ; and when, with a glowing countenance, he advanced, smiling through his tears, towards her, she clasped him in her arms, and riveted her lips to that face the very loveliness of which added to her affliction. She gazed at him, she wept on his neck, she pressed him to her bosom. "Oh! how soon might all that beauty be mingled with the dust! how soon might that warm heart, which then beat against hers, be pierced by the sword—be laid on the ground, mangled and bleeding, exposed and trampled on!" These thoughts thronged upon her soul, and deprived her of sense. She was borne away by her maids, while the palatine compelled Thaddeus to quit the spot.

It was not until the lofty battlements of Villanow blended with the clouds that Thaddeus could throw off his melancholy. The parting grief of his mother hung on his spirits; and heavy and frequent were his sighs while he gazed on the rustic cottages and fertile fields, which reminded him that he was yet passing through the territories of his grandfather. The picturesque mill of Mariemont was the last spot on which his sight lingered. The ivy that mantled its sides sparkled with the brightness of a shower which had just fallen; and the rays of the setting sun, gleaming on its shattered wall, made it an object of such romantic beauty, that he could not help pointing it out to his fellow-travellers.

Whilst the eyes of General Butzou, who was in the carriage, followed the direction of Thaddeus, the palatine observed the heightening animation of the old man's features ; and recollecting at the same time the transports which he himself had enjoyed when he visited that place more than twenty years before, he put his hand on the shoulder of the veteran, and exclaimed, "General, did you ever relate to my boy the particulars of that mill?"

"No, my lord."

"I suppose," continued the palatine, "the same reason deterred you from speaking of it, uncalled for, as lessened my wish to tell the story? We are both too much the heroes of the tale to have volunteered the recital."

"Does your excellency mean," asked Thaddeus, "the rescue of our king from this place?"

"I do."

"I have an indistinct knowledge of the affair," continued his grandson, "from I forget who, and should be grateful to hear it clearly told me, while thus looking on the very spot."

"But," said the palatine, gayly, whose object was to draw

his grandson from melancholy reflections, "what will you say to me turning egotist?"

"I now ask the story of you," returned Thaddeus, smiling; "besides, as soldiers are permitted by their peaceful hearth to 'fight their battles o'er again,' your modesty, my dear grandfather, cannot object to repeat one to me on the way to more."

"Then, as a preliminary," said the palatine, "I must suppose it is unnecessary to tell you that General Butzou was the brave soldier who, at the imminent risk of his own life, saved our sovereign."

"Yes, I know that!" replied the young count, "and that you too had a share in the honor: for when I was yesterday presented to his majesty, amongst other things which he said, he told me that, under Heaven, he believed he owed his present existence to General Butzou and yourself."

"So very little to me," resumed the palatine, "that I will, to the best of my recollection, repeat every circumstance of the affair. Should I err, I must beg of you, general" (turning to the veteran), "to put me right."

Butzou, with a glow of honest exultation, nodded assent; and Thaddeus bowing in sign of attention, his smiling grandsire began.

"It was on a Sunday night, the 3d of September, in the year 1771, that this event took place. At that time, instigated by the courts of Vienna and Constantinople, a band of traitorous lords, confederated together, were covertly laying waste the country, and perpetrating all kinds of unsuspected outrage on their fellow-subjects who adhered to the king.

"Amongst their numerous crimes, a plan was laid for surprising and taking the royal person. Casimir Pulaski was the most daring of their leaders; and, assisted by Lukawski, Strawenski, and Kosinski, three Poles unworthy of their names, he resolved to accomplish his design or perish. Accordingly, these men, with forty other conspirators, in the presence of their commander swore with the most horrid oaths to deliver Stanislaus alive or dead into his hands.

"About a month after this meeting, these three parricides of their country, at the head of their coadjutors, disguised as peasants, and concealing their arms in wagons of hay, which they drove before them, entered the suburbs of Warsaw undetected.

"It was about ten o'clock P. M., on the 3d of September, as I have told you, they found an apt opportunity to execute their scheme. They placed themselves, under cover of the night, in those avenues of the city through which they knew his majesty must pass in his way from Villanow, where he had been dining with me. His carriage was escorted by four of his own guards, besides myself and some of mine. We had scarcely lost sight of Villanow, when the conspirators rushed out and surrounded us, commanding the coachman to stop, and beating down the serving men with the butt ends of their muskets. Several shots were fired into the coach. One passed through my hat as I was getting out, sword in hand, the better to repel an attack the motive of which I could not then divine. A cut across my right leg with a sabre laid me under the wheels; and whilst in that situation, I heard the shot pouring into the coach like hail, and felt the villains stepping over my body to finish the murder of their sovereign.

"It was then that our friend Butzou (who at that period was a private soldier in my service) stood between his majesty and the rebels, parrying many a stroke aimed at the king; but at last, a thrust from a bayonet into his gallant defender's breast cast him weltering in his blood upon me. By this time all the persons who had formed the escort were either wounded or dispersed, and George Butzou, our friend's only brother, was slain. So dropped one by one the protectors of our trampled bodies and of our outraged monarch. Secure then of their prey, one of the assassins opened the carriage door, and with shocking imprecations seizing the king, discharged his pistol so near his majesty's face, that he felt the heat of the flash. A second villain cut him on the forehead with a sabre, whilst the third, who was on horseback, laying hold of the king's collar, dragged him along the ground through the suburbs of the city.

"During the latter part of this murderous scene, some of our affrighted people, who had fled, returned with a detachment, and seeing Butzou and me apparently lifeless, carried us to the royal palace, where all was commotion and distraction. But the foot-guards followed the track which the conspirators had taken. In one of the streets they found the king's hat dyed in blood, and his pelisse also. This confirmed their apprehensions of his death; and they came back filling all Warsaw with dismay.

"The assassins, meanwhile, got clear of the town. Finding, however, that the king, by loss of blood, was not likely to exist much longer by dragging him towards their employer, and that delay might even lose them his dead body, they mounted him, and redoubled their speed. When they came to the moat, they compelled him to leap his horse across it. In the attempt the horse fell and broke its leg. They then ordered his majesty, fainting as he was, to mount another and spur it over. The conspirators had no sooner passed the ditch, and saw their king fall insensible on the neck of his horse, than they tore from his breast the ribbon of the black eagle, and its diamond cross. Lukawski was so foolishly sure of his prisoner, dead or alive, that he quitted his charge, and repaired with these spoils to Pulaski, meaning to show them as proofs of his success. Many of the other plunderers, concluding that they could not do better than follow their leader's example, fled also, tired of their work, leaving only seven of the party, with Kosinski at their head, to remain over the unfortunate Stanislaus, who shortly after recovered from his swoon.

"The night was now grown so dark, they could not be sure of their way; and their horses stumbling at every step, over stumps of trees and hollows in the earth, increased their apprehensions to such a degree, that they obliged the king to keep up with them on foot. He literally marked his path with his blood; his shoes having been torn off in the struggle at the carriage. Thus they continued wandering backward and forward, and round the outskirts of Warsaw, without any exact knowledge of their situation. The men who guarded him at last became so afraid of their prisoner's taking advantage of these circumstances to escape, that they repeatedly called on Kosinski for orders to put him to death. Kosinski refused; but their demands growing more imperious, as the intricacies of the forest involved them completely, the king expected every moment to find their bayonets in his breast.

"Meanwhile," continued the palatine, "when I recovered from my swoon in the palace, my leg had been bound up, and I felt able to stir. Questioning the officers who stood about my couch, I found that a general panic had seized them. They knew not how to proceed; they shuddered at leaving the king to the mercy of the confederates, and yet were fearful, by pursuing him further, to incense them through terror or revenge to massacre their prisoner, if he were still alive. I did all that was in my power to dispel this last dread. Anxious, at any rate, to make another attempt to preserve him, though I could not ride myself, I strenuously advised an immediate pursuit on horseback, and insisted that neither darkness nor apprehension of increasing danger should be permitted to impede their course. Recovered presence of mind in the nobles restored hope and animation to the terrified soldiers, and my orders were obeyed. But I must add, they were soon disappointed, for in less than half an hour the detachment returned in despair, showing me his majesty's coat, which they had found in the fosse. I sup pose the ruffians tore it off when they rifled him. It was rent in several places, and so wet with blood that the officer who presented it to me concluded they had murdered the king there, and drawn away his body, for by the light of the torches the soldiers could trace drops of blood to a considerable distance.

"Whilst I was attempting to invalidate this new evidence of his majesty's being beyond the reach of succor, he was driven before the seven conspirators so far into the wood of Bielany, that, not knowing whither they went, they came up with one of the guard-houses, and, to their extreme terror, were accosted by a patrol. Four of the banditti immediately disappeared, leaving two only with Kosinski, who, much alarmed, forced his prisoner to walk faster and keep a profound silence. Notwithstanding all this precaution, scarce a quarter of an hour afterwards they were challenged by a second watch; and the other two men taking flight, Kosinski, full of indignation at their desertion, was left alone with the king. His majesty, sinking with pain and fatigue, besought permission to rest for a moment; but Kosinski refused, and pointing his sword towards the king, compelled him to proceed.

"As they walked on, the insulted monarch, who was hardly able to drag one limb after the other, observed that his conductor gradually forgot his vigilance, until he was thoroughly given up to thought. The king conceived some hope from this change, and ventured to say 'I see that you know not how to proceed. You cannot but be aware that the enterprise in which you are engaged, however it may end, is full of peril to you. Successful conspirators are always jealous of each other. Pulaski will find it as easy to rid himself of your life as it is to take mine. Avoid that danger, and I will promise you none on my account. Suffer me to enter the convent of Bielany: we cannot be far from it; and then, do you provide for your own safety.' Kosinski, though rendered desperate by the circumstances in which he was involved, replied, 'No; I have sworn, and I would rather sacrifice my life than my honor.'

"The king had neither strength nor spirits to urge him further, and they continued to break their way through the bewildering underwood, until they approached Mariemont. Here Stanislaus, unable to stir another step, sunk down at the foot of the old yew-tree, and again implored for one moment's rest. Kosinski no longer refused. This unexpected humanity encouraged his majesty to employ the minutes they sat together in another attempt to soften his heart, and to convince him that the oath which he had taken was atrocious, and by no means binding to a brave and virtuous man.

"Kosinski heard him with attention, and even showed he was affected. 'But,' said he, 'if I should assent to what you propose, and reconduct you to Warsaw, what will be the consequence to me? I shall be taken and executed.' 'I give you my word,' answered the king, 'that you shall not suffer any injury. But if you doubt my honor, escape while you can. I shall find some place of shelter, and will direct your pursuers to take the opposite road to that which you may choose.' Kosinski, entirely overcome, threw himself on his knees before his majesty, and imploring pardon from Heaven for what he had done, swore that from this hour he would defend his king against all the conspirators, and trust confidently in his word for future preservation. Stanislaus repeated his promise of forgiveness and protection, and directed him to seek refuge for them both in the mill near which they were discoursing. Kosinski obeyed. He knocked, but no one gave answer. He then broke a pane of glass in the window, and through it begged succor for a nobleman who had been waylaid by robbers. The miller refused to come out, or to let the applicants in, expressing his belief that they were robbers themselves, and if they did not go away he would fire on them.

"This dispute had continued some time, when the king contrived to crawl up close to the windows and spoke. 'My good friend,' said he, if we were banditti, as you suppose, it would be as easy for us, without all this parley, to break into your house as to break this pane of glass; therefore, if you would not incur the shame of suffering a fellow-creature to perish for want of assistance, give us admittance.' This plain argument had its weight upon the man, and opening the door, he desired them to enter. After some trouble, his majesty procured pen and ink, and addressing a few lines to me at the palace, with difficulty prevailed on one of the miller's sons to carry it, so fearful were they of falling in with any of the troop who they understood had plundered their guests.

"My joy at the sight of this note I cannot describe. I well remember the contents; they were literally these:—

"'By the miraculous hand of Providence I have escaped from the hands of assassins. I am now at the mill of Mariemont. Send immediately and take me hence. I am wounded but not dangerously.'

"Regardless of my own condition, I instantly got into a carriage, and followed by a detachment of horse, arrived at the mill. I met Kosinski at the door, keeping guard with his sword drawn. As he knew my person, he admitted me directly. The king had fallen into a sleep, and lay in one corner of the hovel on the ground, covered with the miller's cloak. To see the most virtuous monarch in the world thus abused by a party of ungrateful subjects pierced me to the heart. Kneeling down by his side, I took hold of his hand, and in a paroxysm of tears, which I am not ashamed to confess, I exclaimed, 'I thank thee, Almighty God, that I again see our true-hearted sovereign still alive!' It is not easy to say how these words struck the simple family. They dropped on their knees before the king, whom my voice had awakened, and besought his pardon for their recent opposition to give him entrance. The good Stanislaus soon quieted their fears, and graciously thanking them for their kindness, told the miller to come to the palace the next day, when he would show him his gratitude in a better way than by promises.

"The officers of the detachment then assisted his majesty and myself into the carriage, and accompanied by Kosinski, we reached Warsaw about six in the morning."

"Yes," interrupted Butzou; "I remember my tumultuous joy when the news was brought to me in my bed that my brave brother had not died in vain for his sovereign; it almost deprived me of my senses; and besides, his majesty visited me, his poor soldier, in my chamber. Does not your excellency recollect how he was brought into my room on a chair, between two men? and how he thanked me, and shook hands with me, and told me my brother should never be forgotten in Poland? It made me weep like a child."

"And he never can!" cried Thaddeus, hardly recovering from the deep attention with which he had listened to this recital.* "But what became of Kosinski? For doubtless the king kept his word."

"He did indeed," replied Sobieski; "his word is at all times sacred. Yet I believe Kosinski entertained fears that he would not be so generous, for I perceived him change color very often

* The king had his brave defender buried with military honors, and caused a noble monument to be raised over him, with an inscription, of which the following is a translation:—

"Here lieth the respected remains of George Butzou, who, on the 3d of September, 1771, opposing his own breast to shield his sovereign from the weapons of national parricides, was pierced with a mortal wound, and triumphantly expired. Stanislaus the king, lamenting the death of so faithful a subject, erects this monument as a tribute to him and an example of heroic duty to others."

while we were in the coach. However, he became tranquillized when his majesty, on alighting at the palace in the midst of the joyous cries of the people, leaned upon his arm and presented him to the populace as his preserver. The great gate was ordered to be left open; and never whilst I live shall I again behold such a scene! Every loyal soul in Warsaw, from the highest to the lowest, came to catch a glimpse of their rescued sovereign. Seeing the doors free, they entered without ceremony, and thronged forward in crowds to get near enough to kiss his hand, or to touch his clothes; then, elated with joy, they turned to Kosinski, and loaded him with demonstrations of gratitude, calling him the 'saviour of the king.' Kosinski bore all this with surprising firmness; but in a day or two, when the facts became known, he feared he might meet with different treatment from the people, and therefore petitioned his majesty for leave to depart. Stanislaus consented; and he retired to Semigallia, where he now lives on a handsome pension from the king."

"Generous Stanislaus!" exclaimed the general; "you see, my dear young count, how he has rewarded me for doing that which was merely my duty. He put it at my option to become what I pleased about his person, or to hold an officer's rank in his body-guard. Love ennobles servitude; and attached as I have ever been to your family, under whom all my ancestors have lived and fought, I vowed in my own mind never to quit it, and accordingly begged permission of my sovereign to remain with the Count Sobieski. I did remain; but see," cried he, his voice faltering, "what my benefactors have made of me. I command those troops amongst whom it was once my greatest pride to be a private soldier."

Thaddeus pressed the hand of the veteran between both his, and regarded him with respect and affection, whilst the grateful old man wiped away a gliding tear from his face." *

"How happy it ought to make you, my son," observed Sobieski, "that you are called out to support such a sovereign! He is not merely a brave king, whom you would follow to battle, because he will lead you to honor; the hearts of his people acknowledge him in a superior light; they look on him as their patriarchal head, as being delegated of God to study what is their greatest good, to bestow it, and when it is attacked, to de-

* Lukawski and Strawenski were afterwards both taken, with others of the conspirators. At the king's entreaty, those of inferior rank were pardoned after condemnation; but the two noblemen who had deluded them were beheaded. Pulaski, the prime ring-leader, escaped, to the wretched life of an outlaw and an exile, and finally died in America, in 1779.

fend it. To preserve the life of such a sovereign, who would not sacrifice his own?"

"Yes," cried Butzou; "and how ought we to abhor those who threaten his life! How ought we to estimate those crowned heads who, under the mask of amity, have from the year sixty-four, when he ascended the throne, until now, been plotting his overthrow or death! Either calamity, O Heaven, avert! for his death, I fear, will be a prelude to the certain ruin of our country."

"Not so," interrupted Thaddeus, with eagerness; "not whilst a Polander has power to lift an arm in defence of a native king, and an hereditary succession, can she be quite lost! What was ever in the hearts of her people that is not now there? For one, I can never forget how her sons have more than once rolled back on their own lands legions of invaders, from those very countries now daring to threaten her existence!"

Butzou applauded his spirit, and was warmly seconded by the palatine, who (never weary of infusing into every feeling of his grandson an interest for his country) pursued the discourse, and dwelt minutely on the happy tendency of the glorious constitution of 1791, in defence of which they were now going to hazard their lives. As Sobieski pointed out its several excellences, and expatiated on the pure spirit of freedom which animated its revived laws, the soul of Thaddeus followed his eloquence with all the fervor of youth, forgetting his late domestic regrets in the warm aspirations of patriotic hopes; and at noon on the third day, with smiling eyes he saw his grandfather put himself at the head of his battalions and commence a rapid march.

CHAPTER III.

THE OPENING OF THE CAMPAIGN.

The little army of the palatine passed by the battlements of Chelm, crossed the Bug into the plains of Volhinia, and impatiently counted the leagues over those vast tracts until it reached the borders of Kiovia.

When the column at the head of which Thaddeus was stationed descended the heights of Lininy, and the broad camp of his countrymen burst upon his sight, his heart heaved with an emotion quite new to him. He beheld with admiration the regular disposition of the intrenchments, the long intersected tented streets, and the warlike appearance of the soldiers, whom he could descry, even at that distance, by the beams of a bright evening sun which shone upon their arms.

In half an hour his troops descended into the plain, where, meeting those of the palatine and General Butzou, the three columns again united, and Thaddeus joined his grandfather in the van.

"My lord," cried he, as they met, "can I behold such a sight and despair of the freedom of Poland!"

Sobieski made no reply, but giving him one of those expressive looks of approbation which immediately makes its way to the soul, commanded the troops to advance with greater speed. In a few minutes they reached the outworks of the camp, and entered the lines. The eager eyes of Thaddeus wandered from object to object. Thrilling with that delight with which youth beholds wonders, and anticipates more, he stopped with the rest of the party before a tent, which General Butzou informed him belonged to the commander-in-chief. They were met in the vestibule by an hussar officer of a most commanding appearance. Sobieski and he having accosted each other with mutual congratulations, the palatine turned to Thaddeus, took him by the hand, and presenting him to his friend, said with a smile,

"Here, my dear Kosciusko, this young men is my grandson; he is called Thaddeus Sobieski, and I trust that he will not disgrace either of our names!"

Kosciusko embraced the young count, and with a hearty pressure of his hand, replied, "Thaddeus, if you resemble your grandfather, you can never forget that the only king of Poland who equalled our patriotic Stanislaus was a Sobieski; and as becomes his descendant, you will not spare your best blood in the service of your country." *

As Kosciusko finished speaking, an aid-de-camp came forward to lead the party into the room of audience. Prince

* Kosciusko, noble of birth, and eminently brave in spirit, had learnt the practice of arms in his early youth in America. During the contest between the British colonies there and the mother country, the young Pole, with a few of his early compeers in the great military college at Warsaw, eager to measure swords in an actual field, had passed over seas to British America, and offering their services to the independents, which were accepted, the extraordinary warlike talents of Kosciusko were speedily honored by his being made an especial aid-de-camp to General Washington. When the war ended, in the peace of mutual concessions between the national parent and its children on a distant land, the Poles returned to their native country, where they soon met circumstances which caused them to redraw their swords for her. But to what issue, was yet behind the floating colors of a soldier's hope.

Poniatowski welcomed the palatine and his suite with the most lively expressions of pleasure. He gave Thaddeus, whose figure and manner instantly charmed him, many flattering assurances of friendship, and promised that he would appoint him to the first post of honor which should offer. After detaining the palatine and his grandson half an hour, his highness withdrew, and they rejoined Kosciusko, who conducted them to the quarter where the Masovian soldiers had already pitched their tents.

The officers who supped with Sobieski left him at an early hour, that he might retire to rest; but Thaddeus was neither able nor inclined to benefit by their consideration. He lay down on his mattress, shut his eyes, and tried to sleep; but the attempt was without success. In vain he turned from side to side; in vain he attempted to restrict his thoughts to one thing at once: his imagination was so roused by anticipating the scenes in which he was to become an actor, that he found it impossible even to lie still. His spirits being quite awake, he determined to rise, and to walk himself drowsy.

Seeing his grandfather sound asleep, he got up and dressed himself quietly; then stealing gently from the marquée, he gave the word in a low whisper to the guard at the door, and proceeded down the lines. The pitying moon seemed to stand in the heavens, watching the awaking of those heroes who the next day might sleep to rise no more. At another time, and in another mood, such might have been his reflections; but now he pursued his walk with different thoughts: no meditations but those of pleasure possessed his breast. He looked on the moon with transport; he beheld the light of that beautiful planet, trailing its long stream of glory across the intrenchments. He perceived a solitary candle here and there glimmering through the curtained entrance of the tents, and thought that their inmates were probably longing with the same anxiety as himself for the morning's dawn.

Thaddeus walked slowly on, sometimes pausing at the lonely footfall of the sentinel, or answering with a start to the sudden challenge for the parole; then lingering at the door of some of these canvas dwellings, he offered up a prayer for the brave inhabitant who, like himself, had quitted the endearments of home to expose his life on this spot, a bulwark of liberty. Thaddeus knew not what it was to be a soldier by profession; he had no idea of making war a trade, by which a man may acquire subsistence, and perhaps wealth; he had but one motive for appearing in the field, and one for leaving it,—to repel invasion and to establish peace. The first energy of his mind was a desire to maintain the rights of his country; it had been inculcated into him when an infant; it had been the subject of his morning thoughts and nightly dreams; it was now the passion which beat in every artery of his heart. Yet he knew no honor in slaughter: his glory lay in defence: and when that was accomplished, his sword would return to its scabbard, unstained by the blood of a vanquished or invaded people. On these principles, he was at this hour full of enthusiasm; a glow of triumph flitted over his cheek, for he had felt the indulgences of his mother's palace, had left her maternal arms, to take upon him the toils of war, and risk an existence just blown into enjoyment. A noble satisfaction rose in his mind; and with all the animation which an inexperienced and raised fancy imparts to that age when boyhood breaks into man, his soul grasped at every show of creation with the confidence of belief. Pressing the sabre which he held in his hand to his lips, he half uttered, "Never shall this sword leave my arm but at the command of mercy, or when death deprives my nerves of their strength."

Morning was tinging the hills which bound the eastern horizon of Winnica before Thaddeus found that his pelisse was wet with dew, and that he ought to return to his tent. Hardly had he laid his head upon the pillow, and "lulled his senses in forgetfulness," when he was disturbed by the drum beating to arms. He opened his eyes, and seeing the palatine out of bed, he sprung from his own, and eagerly inquired the cause of his alarm.

"Only follow me directly," answered his grandfather, and quitted the tent.

Whilst Thaddeus was putting on his clothes, and buckling on his arms with a trembling eagerness which almost defeated his haste, an aid-de-camp of the prince entered. He brought information that an advanced guard of the Russians had attacked a Polish outpost, under the command of Colonel Lonza, and that his highness had ordered a detachment from the palatine's brigade to march to its relief. Before Thaddeus could reply, Sobieski sent to apprise his grandson that the prince had appointed him to accompany the troops which were turning out to resist the enemy.

Thaddeus heard this message with delight; yet fearful in what manner the event might answer the expectations which this wished distinction declared, he issued from his tent like a youthful Mars,—or rather like the Spartan Isadas,—trembling at the dazzling effects of his temerity, and hiding his valor and his blushes beneath the waving plumes of his helmet. Kosciusko, who was to head the party, observed this modesty with pleasure, and shaking him warmly by the hand, said, "Go, Thaddeus; take your station on the left flank; I shall require your fresh spirits to lead the charge I intend to make, and to ensure its success." Thaddeus bowed to these encouraging words, and took his place according to order.

Everything being ready, the detachment quitted the camp, and dashing through the dews of a sweet morning (for it was yet May), in a few hours arrived in view of the Russian battalions. Lonza, who, from the only redoubt now in his possession, caught a glimpse of this welcome reinforcement, rallied his few remaining men, and by the time that Kosciusko came up, contrived to join him in the van. The fight recommenced. Thaddeus, at the head of his hussars, in full gallop bore down upon the enemy's right flank. They received the charge with firmness; but their young adversary, perceiving that extraordinary means were necessary to make the desired effect, calling on his men to follow him, put spurs to his horse and rushed into the thickest of the battle. His soldiers did not shrink; they pressed on, mowing down the foremost ranks, whilst he, by a lucky stroke of his sabre, disabled the sword-arm of the Russian standard-bearer and seized the colors. His own troops seeing the standard in his hand, with one accord, in loud and repeated cries, shouted victory. Part of the reserve of the enemy, alarmed at this outcry, gave ground, and retreating with precipitation, was soon followed by some of the rear ranks of the centre, to which Kosciusko had penetrated, while its commander, after a short but desperate resistance, was slain. The left flank next gave way, and though holding a brave stand at intervals, at length fairly turned about and fled across the country.

The conquerors, elated with so sudden a success, put their horses on full speed; and without order or attention, pursued the fugitives until they were lost amidst the trees of a distant wood. Kosciusko called on his men to halt, but he called in vain; they continued their career, animating each other, and with redoubled shouts drowned the voice of Thaddeus, who was galloping forward repeating the command. At the entrance of the wood they were stopped by a few Russian stragglers, who had formed themselves into a body. These men withstood the first onset of the Poles with considerable steadiness; but after a short skirmish, they fled, or, perhaps, seemed to fly, a second time, and took refuge in the bushes, where, still regardless of orders, their enemies followed. Kosciusko, foreseeing the consequence of this rashness, ordered Thaddeus to dismount a part of his squadron, and march after these headstrong men into the forest. He came up with them on the edge of a heathy tract of land, just as they were closing in with a band of the enemy's arquebusiers, who, having kept up a quick running fire as they retreated, had drawn their pursuers thus far into the thickets. Heedless of anything but giving their enemy a complete defeat, the Polanders went on, never looking to the left nor to the right, till at once they found themselves encompassed by two thousand Muscovite horse, several battalions of chasseurs, and in front of fourteen pieces of cannon, which this dreadful ambuscade opened upon them.

Thaddeus threw himself into the midst of his countrymen,and taking the place of their unfortunate conductor, who had been killed in the first sweep of the artillery, prepared the men for a desperate stand. He gave his orders with intrepid coolness —though under a shower of musketry and a cannonade which carried death in every round—that they should draw off towards the flank of the battery. He thought not of himself; and in a few minutes the scattered soldiers were consolidated into a close body, squared with pikemen, who stood like a grove of pines in a day of tempest, only moving their heads and arms. Many of the Russian horse impaled themselves on the sides of this little phalanx, which they vainly attempted to shake, although the ordnance was rapidly weakening its strength. File after file the men were swept down, their bodies making a horrid rampart for their resolute brothers in arms, who, however, rendered desperate, at last threw away their most cumbrous accoutrements, and crying to their leader, "Freedom or death!" followed him sword in hand, and bearing like a torrent upon the enemy's ranks, cut their way through the forest. The Russians, exasperated that their prey should not only escape, but escape by such dauntless valor, hung closely on their rear, goading them with musketry, whilst they (like a wounded lion closely pressed by the hunters, retreats, yet stands proudly at bay) gradually retired towards the camp with a backward step, their faces towards the foe.

Meanwhile the palatine Sobieski, anxious for the fate of the day, mounted the dyke, and looked eagerly around for the arrival of some messenger from the little army. As the wind blew strongly from the south, a cloud of dust precluded his view; but from the approach of firing and the clash of arms, he was led to fear that his friends had been defeated, and were retreating towards the camp. He instantly quitted the lines to call out a reinforcement; but before he could advance, Kosciusko and his squadron on the full charge appeared in flank of the enemy, who suddenly halted, and wheeling round, left the harassed Polanders to enter the trenches unmolested.

Thaddeus, covered with dust and blood, flung himself into his grandfather's arms. In the heat of action his left arm had been wounded by a Cossack.* Aware that neglect then might disable him from further service, at the moment it happened he bound it up in his sash, and had thought no more of the accident until the palatine remarked blood on his cloak.

"My injury is slight, my dear sir," said he. "I wish to Heaven that it were all the evil which has befallen us to-day! Look at the remnant of our brave comrades."

Sobieski turned his eyes on the panting soldiers, and on Kosciusko, who was inspecting them. Some of them, no longer upheld by desperation, were sinking with wounds and fatigue; these the good general sent off in litters to the medical department; and others, who had sustained unharmed the conflict of the day, after having received the praise and admonition of their commander, were dismissed to their quarters.

Before this inspection was over, the palatine had to assist Thaddeus to his tent; in spite of his exertions to the contrary, he became so faint, it was necessary to lead him off the ground.

A short time restored him. With his arm in a sling, he joined his brother officers on the fourth day. After the duty of the morning, he heard with concern that, during his confinement, the enemy had augmented their force to so tremendous a strength, it was impossible for the comparatively slender force of the Poles to remain longer at Winnica. In consequence of this report, the prince had convened a council late the preceding night, in which it was determined that the camp should immediately be razed, and removed towards Zielime.

This information displeased Thaddeus, who in his fairy dreams of war had always made conquest the sure end of his battles; and many were the sighs he drew when, at an hour before dawn on the following day, he witnessed the striking of

* Cossacks. There are two descriptions of these formidable auxiliaries: those of clear Tartar race, the other mixed with Muscovites and their tributaries. The first and the fiercest are called Don Cossacks, because of their inhabiting the immense steppes of the Don river, on the frontiers of Asia. They are governed by a hetman, a native chief, who personally leads them to battle. The second are the Cossacks of the Crimea, a gallant people of that finest part of the Russian dominions, and, by being of a mingled origin, under European rule, are more civilized and better disciplined than their brethren near the Caucasus. They are generally commanded by Russian officers.

the tents, which he thought too like a prelude to a shameful flight from the enemy. While he was standing by the busy people, and musing on the nice line which divides prudence from pusillanimity, his grandfather came up, and bade him mount his horse, telling him that, owing to the unhealed state of his wound, he was removed from the vanguard, and ordered to march in the centre, along with the prince. Thaddeus remonstrated against this arrangement, and almost reproached the palatine for forfeiting his promise, that he should always be stationed near his person. The veteran would not be moved, either by argument or entreaty; and Thaddeus, finding that he neither could nor ought to oppose him, obeyed, and followed an aid-de-camp to his highness.

CHAPTER IV.

THE PASS OF VOLUNNA.

AFTER a march of three hours, the army came in sight of Volunna, where the advanced column suddenly halted. Thaddeus, who was about a half mile to its rear, with a throbbing heart heard that a momentous pass must be disputed before they could proceed. He curbed his horse, then gave it the spur, so eagerly did he wish to penetrate the cloud of smoke which rose in volumes from the discharge of musketry, on whose wing, at every round, he dreaded might be carried the fate of his grandfather. At last the firing ceased, and the troops were commanded to go forward. On approaching near the contested defile, Thaddeus shuddered, for at every step the heels of his charger struck upon the wounded or the dead. There lay his enemies, here lay his friends! His respiration was nearly suspended, and his eyes clung to the ground, expecting at each moment to fasten on the breathless body of his grandfather.

Again the tumult of battle presented itself. About an hundred soldiers, in one firm rank, stood at the opening of the pass, firing on the now vacillating steadiness of the enemy. Thaddeus checked his horse. Five hundred had been detached to this post; how few remained! Could he hope that Sobieski had escaped so desperate a rencontre? Fearing the worst, and dreading to have those fears confirmed, his heart sickened when he received orders from Poniatowski to examine the extent of the loss. He rode to the mouth of the defile. He could nowhere see the palatine. A few of his hussars, a little in advance, were engaged over a heap of the killed, defending it from a troop of Cossacks, who appeared fighting for the barbarous privilege of trampling on the bodies. At this sight Thaddeus, impelled by despair, called out, "Courage, soldiers! The prince with artillery!" The enemy, looking forward, saw the information was true, and with a shout of derision, took to flight. Poniatowski, almost at the word, was by the side of his young friend, who, unconscious of any idea but that of filial solicitude, had dismounted.

"Where is the palatine?" was his immediate inquiry to a chasseur who was stooping towards the slain. The man made no answer, but lifted from the heap the bodies of two soldiers; beneath, Thaddeus saw the pale and deathly features of his grandfather. He staggered a few paces back, and the prince, thinking he was falling, hastened to support him; but he recovered himself, and flew forward to assist Kosciusko, who had raised the head of the palatine upon his knee.

"Is he alive?" inquired Thaddeus.

"He breathes."

Hope was now warm in his grandson's breast. The soldiers soon released Sobieski from the surrounding dead; but his swoon continuing, the prince desired that he might be laid on a bank, until a litter could be brought from the rear to convey him to a place of security. Meantime, Thaddeus and General Butzou bound up his wounds and poured some water into his mouth. The effusion of blood being stopped, the brave veteran opened his eyes, and in a few moments more, whilst he leaned on the bosom of his grandson, was so far restored as to receive with his usual modest dignity the thanks of his highness for the intrepidity with which he had preserved a passage which ensured the safety of the whole army.

Two surgeons, who arrived with the litter relieved the anxiety of the bystanders by an assurance that the wounds, which they re-examined, were not dangerous. Having laid their patient on the vehicle, they were preparing to retire with it into the rear, when Thaddeus petitioned the prince to grant him permission to take the command of the guard which was appointed to attend his grandfather. His highness consented; but Sobieski positively refused.

"No, Thaddeus," said he; "you forget the effect which

this solicitude about so trifling a matter might have on the men. Remember that he who goes into battle only puts his own life to the hazard, but he that abandons the field, sports with the lives of his soldiers. Do not give them leave to suppose that even your dearest interest could tempt you from the front of danger when it is your duty to remain there." Thaddeus obeyed his grandfather in respectful silence; at seven o'clock the army resumed its march.

Near Zielime the prince was saluted by a reinforcement. It appeared very seasonably, for scouts had brought information that directly across the plain a formidable division of the Russian army, under General Brinicki, was drawn up in order of battle, to dispute his progress.

Thaddeus, for the first time, shuddered at the sight of the enemy. Should his friends be defeated, what might be the fate of his grandfather, now rendered helpless by many wounds! Occupied by these fears, with anxiety in his heart, he kept his place at the head of the light horse, close to the hill.

Prince Poniatowski ordered the lines to extend themselves, that the right should reach to the river, and the left be covered by the rising ground, on which were mounted seven pieces of ordnance. Immediately after these dispositions, the battle commenced with mutual determination, and continued with unabated fury from eight in the morning until sunset. Several times the Poles were driven from their ground; but as often recovering themselves, and animated by their commanders, they prosecuted the fight with advantage. General Brinicki, perceiving that the fortune of the day was going against him, ordered up the body of reserve, which consisted of four thousand men and several cannon. He erected temporary batteries in a few minutes, and with these new forces opened a rapid and destructive fire on the Polanders. Kosciusko, alarmed at perceiving a retrograde motion in his troops, gave orders for a close attack on the enemy in front, whilst Thaddeus, at the head of his hussars, should wheel round the hill of artillery, and with loud cries charge the opposite flank. This stratagem succeeded. The arquebusiers, who were posted on that spot, seeing the impetuosity of the Poles, and the quarter whence they came, supposed them to be a fresh squadron, gave ground, and opening in all directions, threw their own people into a confusion that completed the defeat. Kosciusko and the prince were equally successful, and a general panic amongst their adversaries was the consequence. The whole of the Russian army now took to flight, except a few regiments of carabineers, which were entangled between the river and the Poles. These were immediately surrounded by a battalion of Masovian infantry, who, enraged at the loss their body had sustained the preceding day, answered a cry for quarter with reproach and derision. At this instant the Sobieski squadron came up, and Thaddeus, who saw the perilous situation of these regiments, ordered the slaughter to cease, and the men to be taken prisoners. The Masovians exhibited strong signs of dissatisfaction at such commands; but the young count charging through them, ranged his troops before the Russians, and declared that the first man who should dare to lift a sword against his orders should be shot. The Poles dropped their arms. The poor carabineers fell on their knees to thank his mercy, whilst their officers, in a sullen silence, which seemed ashamed of gratitude, surrendered their swords into the hands of their deliverers.

During this scene, only one very young Russian appeared wholly refractory. He held his sword in a menacing posture when Thaddeus drew near, and before he had time to speak, the young man made a cut at his head, which a hussar parried by striking the assailant to the earth, and would have killed him on the spot, had not Thaddeus caught the blow on his own sword; then instantly dismounting, he raised the officer from the ground, and apologized for the too hasty zeal of his soldier. The youth blushed, and, bowing, presented his sword, which was received and as directly returned.

"Brave sir," said Thaddeus, "I consider myself ennobled in restoring this weapon to him who has so courageously defended it."

The Russian made no reply but by a second bow, and put his hand on his breast, which seemed wet with blood. Ceremony was now at an end. Thaddeus never looked upon the unfortunate as strangers, much less as enemies. Accosting the wounded officer with a friendly voice, he assured him of his services, and bade him lean on him. Overcome, the young man, incapable of speaking, accepted his assistance; but before a conveyance could arrive, for which two men were dispatched, he fainted in his arms. Thaddeus being obliged to join the prince with his prisoners, unwillingly left the young Russian in this situation; but before he did so he directed one of his lieutenants to take care that the surgeons should pay attention to the officer, and have his litter carried next to the palatine's during the remainder of the march.

When the army halted at nine o'clock, P. M., preparations

were made to fix the camp; and in case of a surprise from any part of the dispersed enemy which might have rallied, orders were delivered for throwing up a dyke. Thaddeus, having been assured that his grandfather and the wounded Russian were comfortably stationed near each other, did not hesitate to accept the command of the intrenching party. To that end he wrapped himself loosely in his pelisse, and prepared for a long watch. The night was beautiful. It being the month of June, a softening warmth still floated through the air, as if the moon, which shone over his head, emitted heat as well as splendor. His mind was in unison with the season. He rode slowly round from bank to bank, sometimes speaking to the workers in the fosse, sometimes lingering for a few minutes. Looking on the ground, he thought on the element of which he was composed, to which he might so soon return; then gazing upward, he observed the silent march of the stars and the moving scene of the heavens. On whatever object he cast his eyes, his soul, which the recent events had dissolved into a temper not the less delightful for being tinged with melancholy, meditated with intense compassion, and dwelt with wonder on the mind of man, which, whilst it adores the Creator of the universe, and measures the immensity of space with an expansion of intellect almost divine, can devote itself to the narrow limits of sublunary possessions, and exchange the boundless paradise above for the low enjoyments of human pride. He looked with pity over that wide tract of land which now lay betwixt him and the remains of those four thousand invaders who had just fallen victims to the insatiate desires of ambition. He well knew the difference between a defender of his own country and the invader of another's. His heart beat, his soul expanded, at the prospect of securing liberty and life to a virtuous people. He *felt* all the happiness of such an achievement, while he could only *imagine* how that spirit must shrink from reflection which animates the self-condemned slave to fight, not merely to fasten chains on others, but to rivet his own the closer. The best affections of man having put the sword into the hand of Thaddeus, his principle as a Christian did not remonstrate against his passion for arms.

When he was told the fortifications were finished, he retired with a tranquil step towards the Masovian quarters. He found the palatine awake, and eager to welcome him with the joyful information that his wounds were so slight as to promise a speedy amendment. Thaddeus asked for his prisoner. The palatine answered that he was in the next tent, where a surgeon closely attended him, who had already given a very favorable opinion of the wound, which was in the muscles of the breast.

"Have you seen him, my dear sir?" inquired Thaddeus.

"Yes," replied the palatine; I was supported into his marquée before I retired to my own. I told him who I was, and repeated your offers of service. He received my proffer with expressions of gratitude, and at the same time declared he had nothing to blame but his own folly for bringing him to the state in which he now lies."

"How, my lord?" rejoined Thaddeus. "Does he repent of being a soldier? or is he ashamed of the cause for which he fought?"

"Both, Thaddeus; he is not a Muscovite, but a young Englishman."

"An Englishman! and raise his arm against a country struggling for loyalty and liberty!"

"It is very true," returned the palatine; "but as he confesses it was his folly and the persuasions of others which impelled him, he may be pardoned. He is a mere youth; I think hardly your age. I understand that he is of rank; and having undertaken a tour in whatever part of Europe is now open to travellers, under the direction of an experienced tutor, they took Russia in their route. At St. Petersburg he became intimate with many of the nobility, particularly with Count Brinicki, at whose house he resided; and when the count was named to the command of the army in Poland, Mr. Somerset (for that is your prisoner's name), instigated by his own volatility and the arguments of his host, volunteered with him, and so followed his friend to oppose that freedom here which he would have asserted in his own nation."

Thaddeus thanked his grandfather for this information; and pleased that the young man, who had so much interested him, was a brave Briton, not in heart an enemy, he gayly and instantly repaired to his tent.

A generous spirit is as eloquent in acknowledging benefits as it is bounteous in bestowing them; and Mr. Somerset received his preserver with the warmest demonstrations of gratitude. Thaddeus begged him not to consider himself as particularly obliged by a conduct which every soldier of honor has a right to expect from another. The Englishman bowed his head, and Thaddeus took a seat by his bedside.

Whilst he gathered from his own lips a corroboration of the

narrative of the palatine, he could not forbear inquiring how a person of his apparent candor, and who was also the native of a soil where national liberty had so long been the palladium of its happiness, could volunteer in a cause the object of which was to make a brave people slaves?

Somerset listened to these questions with blushes; and they did not leave his face when he confessed that all he could say in extenuation of what he had done was to plead his youth, and having thought little on the subject.

"I was wrought upon," continued he, "by a variety of circumstances: first, the predilections of Mr. Loftus, my governor, are strongly in favor of the court of St. Petersburg; secondly, my father dislikes the army, and I am enthusiastically fond of it—this was the only opportunity, perhaps, in which I might ever satisfy my passion; and lastly, I believe that I was dazzled by the picture which the young men about me drew of the campaign. I longed to be a soldier; they persuaded me; and I followed them to the field as I would have done to a ball-room, heedless of the consequences."

"Yet," replied Thaddeus, smiling, "from the intrepidity with which you maintained your ground, when your arms were demanded, any one might have thought that your whole soul, as well as your body, was engaged in the cause."

"To be sure," returned Somerset, "I was a blockhead to be there; but when there, I should have despised myself forever had I given up my honor to the ruffians who would have wrested my sword from me! But when *you* came, noble Sobieski, it was the fate of war, and I confided myself to a brave man."

CHAPTER V.

THE BANKS OF THE VISTULA.

Each succeeding morning not only brought fresh symptoms of recovery to the two invalids, but condensed the mutual admiration of the young men into a solid and ardent esteem.

It is not the disposition of youthful minds to weigh for months and years the sterling value of those qualities which attract them. As soon as they see virtue, they respect it; as soon as they meet kindness, they believe it; and as soon as a union of both presents itself, they love it. Not having passed through the disappointments of a delusive world, they grasp for reality every pageant which appears. They have not yet admitted that cruel doctrine which, when it takes effect, creates and extends the misery it affects to cure. Whilst we give up our souls to suspicion, we gradually learn to deceive; whilst we repress the fervors of our own hearts, we freeze those which approach us; whilst we cautiously avoid occasions of receiving pain, at every remove we acquire an unconscious influence to inflict it on those who follow us. They, again, meet from our conduct and lips the lesson that destroys the expanding sensibilities of their nature; and thus the tormenting chain of deceived and deceiving characters may be lengthened to infinitude.

About the latter end of the month, Sobieski received a summons to court, where a diet was to be held on the effect of the victory at Zielime, to consider of future proceedings. In the same packet his majesty enclosed a collar and investiture of the order of St. Stanislaus, as an acknowledgment of service to the young Thaddeus; and he accompanied it with a note from himself, expressing his commands that the young knight should return with the palatine and other generals, to receive thanks from the throne.

Thaddeus, half wild with delight at the thoughts of so soon meeting his mother, ran to the tent of his British friend to communicate the tidings. Somerset participated in his pleasure, and with reciprocal warmth accepted the invitation to accompany him to Villanow.

"I would follow you, my friend," said he, pressing the hand of Thaddeus, "all over the world."

"Then I will take you to the most charming spot in it?" cried he. "Villanow is an Eden; and my mother, the dear angel, would make a desert so to me."

"You speak so rapturously of your enchanted castle, Thaddeus," returned his friend, "I believe I shall consider my knight-errantry, in being fool enough to trust myself amidst a fray in which I had no business, as one of the wisest acts of my life!"

"I consider it," replied Thaddeus, "as one of the most auspicious events in mine."

Before the palatine quitted the camp, Somerset thought it proper to acquaint Mr. Loftus, who was yet at St. Petersburg, of the particulars of his late danger, and that he was going to Warsaw with his new friends, where he should remain for several weeks. He added, that as the court of Poland, through the intercession of the palatine, had generously given him his liberty, he should be able to see everything in that country worthy of investigation, and that he would write to him again, enclosing letters for England, soon after his arrival at the Polish capital.

The weather continuing fine, in a few days the party left Zielime; and the palatine and Somerset, being so far restored from their wounds that they could walk, the one with a crutch and the other by the support of his friend's arm, they went through the journey with animation and pleasure. The benign wisdom of Sobieski, the intelligent enthusiasm of Thaddeus, and the playful vivacity of Somerset, mingling their different natures, produced such a beautiful union, that the minutes flew fast as their wishes. A week more carried them into the palatinate of Masovia, and soon afterwards within the walls of Villanow.

Everything that presented itself to Mr. Somerset was new and fascinating. He saw in the domestic felicity of his friend scenes which reminded him of the social harmony of his own home. He beheld in the palace and retinue of Sobieski all the magnificence which bespoke the descendant of a great king, and a power which wanted nothing of royal grandeur but the crown, which he had the magnanimity to think and to declare was then placed upon a more worthy brow. Whilst Somerset venerated this true patriot, the high tone his mind acquired was not lowered by associating with characters nearer the common standard. The friends of Sobieski were men of tried probity—men who at all times preferred their country's welfare before their own peculiar interest. Mr. Somerset day after day listened with deep attention to these virtuous and energetic noblemen. He saw them full of fire and personal courage when the affairs of Poland were discussed; and he beheld with admiration their perfect forgetfulness of themselves in their passion for the general good. In these moments his heart bowed down before them, and all the pride of a Briton distended his breast when he thought that such men as these his ancestors were. He remembered how often their chivalric virtues used to occupy his reflections in the picture-gallery at Somerset Castle, and his doubts, when he compared what is with what was, that history had glossed over the actions of past centuries, or that a different order of men lived then from those which now inhabit the world. Thus, studying the sublime characters of Sobieski and his friends, and enjoying the endearing kindness of Thaddeus and his mother, did a fortnight pass away without his even recollecting the promise of writing to his governor. At the end of that period, he stole an hour from the countess's society, and enclosed in a short letter to Mr. Loftus the following epistle to his mother :—

To Lady Somerset, Somerset Castle, Leicestershire.

"Many weeks ago, my dearest mother, I wrote a letter of seven sheets from the banks of the Neva, which, long ere this time, you and my dear father must have received. I attempted to give you some idea of the manners of Russia, and my vanity whispers that I succeeded tolerably well. The court of the famous Catharine and the attentions of the hospitable Court Brinicki were then the subjects of my pen.

"But how shall I account for my being here ? How shall I allay your surprise and displeasure on seeing that this letter is dated from Warsaw ? I know that I have acted against the wish of my father in visiting one of the countries he proscribes. I know that I have disobeyed your commands in ever having at any period of my life taken up arms without an indispensable necessity ; and I have nothing to allege in my defence. I fell in the way of temptation, and I yielded to it. I really cannot enumerate all the things which induced me to volunteer with my Russian friends ; suffice it to say that I did so, and that we were defeated by the Poles at Zelime : and as Heaven has rather rewarded your prayers than punished my imprudence, I trust you will do the same, and pardon an indiscretion I vow never to repeat.

"Notwithstanding all this, I must have lost my life through my folly, had I not been preserved, even in the moment when death was pending over me, by a young officer with whose family I now am. The very sound of their title will create your respect ; for we of the patrician order have a strange tenacity in our belief that virtue is hereditary, and in this instance our creed is duly honored. Their patronymic is Sobieski ; the family which bears it is the only remaining posterity of the great monarch of that name ; and the count, who is at its head, is Palatine of Masovia, which, next to the throne, is the first dignity in the state. He is one of the warmest champions of his country's rights ; and though born to command, has so far transgressed the golden adage of despots, 'Ignorance and subjection,' that throughout his territories every man is taught to worship his God with his heart as well as with his knees. The understandings of his peasants are opened to all useful knowledge. He does not put books of science and speculation into their hands, to consume their time in vain pursuits: he gives them the Bible, and implements of industry, to afford them the means of knowing and of practising their duty. All Masovia around his palace blooms like a garden. The cheerful faces of the farmers, and the blessings which I hear them implore on the family when I am walking in the field with the young count (for in this country the sons bear the same title with their fathers *), have even drawn a few delighted drops from the eyes of your thoughtless son. I know that you think I have nothing sentimental about me, else you would not so often have poured into my not inattentive ears, 'that to estimate the pleasures of earth and heaven, we must cultivate the sensibilities of the heart. Shut our eyes against them, and we are merely nicely-constructed speculums, which reflect the beauties of nature, but enjoy none.' You see, mamma, that I both remember and adopt your lessons.

"Thaddeus Sobieski is the grandson of the palatine, and the sole heir of his illustrious race. It is to him that I owe the preservation of my life at Zielime, and much of my happiness since; for he is not only the bravest but the most amiable young man in the kingdom; and he is my friend! Indeed, as things have happened, you must think that out of evil has come good. Though I have been disobedient, I have repented my fault, and it has introduced me to the knowledge of a people whose friendship will henceforward constitute the greatest pleasure of my days. The mother of Thaddeus is the only daughter of the palatine; and of her I can say no more than that nothing on earth can more remind me of you; she is equally charming, equally tender to your son.

"Whilst the palatine is engaged at the diet, her excellency, Thaddeus, and myself, with now and then a few visitors from Warsaw, form the most agreeable parties you can suppose. We walk together, we read together, we converse together, we sing together—at least, the countess sings to us, which is all the same; and you know that time flies swiftly on the wings of harmony. She has an uncommonly sweet voice, and a taste which I never heard paralleled. By the way, you cannot

* *Prince*, (ancient *Kniaz*,) and *Boyard*, (which is equivalent in rank to our old English Baron,) are titles used by Russians and Polanders, both nations being descended from the Sclavonians, and their languages derived from the same roots. *Prince* indicates the highest rank of a subject; *Boyard* simply that of *Nobleman*. But both personages must be understood to be of hereditary power to raise forces on their estates for the service of the sovereign, to lead them in battle, and to maintain all their expenses. The title of *Count* has been adopted within a century or two by both nations, and occasionally appended to the ancient heroic designation of *Boyard*. The feminine to these titles is formed by adding *gina* to the paternal title; thus *Kniazgina Olgæ*, means Princess Olga; also, *Boyarda*, Lady. The titles of *Palatine*, *Vaivode*, *Starost* and the like belong to civil and military offices.

imagine anything more beautiful than the Polish music. It partakes of that delicious languor so distinguished in the Turkish airs, with a mingling of those wandering melodies which the now-forgotten composers must have caught from the Tartars. In short, whilst the countess is singing, I hardly suffer myself to breathe; and I feel just what our poetical friend William Scarsdale said a twelvemonth ago at a concert of yours, 'I feel as if love sat upon my heart and flapped it with his wings.'

"I have tried all my powers of persuasion to prevail on this charming countess to visit our country. I have over and over again told her of you, and described her to you; that you are near her own age, (for this lovely woman, though she has a son nearly twenty, is not more than forty;) that you are as fond of your ordinary boy as she is of her peerless one; that, in short, you and my father will receive her and Thaddeus, and the palatine, with open arms and hearts, if they will condescend to visit our humbler home at the end of the war. I believe I have repeated my entreaties, both to the countess and my friend, regularly every day since my arrival at Villanow, but always with the same issue: she smiles and refuses; and Thaddeus 'shakes his ambrosial curls' with a 'very god-like frown' of denial; I hope it is self-denial, in compliment to his mother's cruel and unprovoked negative.

"Before I proceed, I must give you some idea of the real appearance of this palace. I recollect your having read a superficial account of it in a few slight sketches of Poland which have been published in England; but the pictures they exhibit are so faint, they hardly resemble the original. Pray do not laugh at me, if I begin in the usual descriptive style! You know there is only one way to describe houses and lands and rivers; so no blame can be thrown on me for taking the beaten path, where there is no other. To commence :—

"When we left Zielime, and advanced into the province of Masovia, the country around Praga rose at every step in fresh beauty. The numberless chains of gently swelling hills which encompass it on each side of the Vistula were in some parts checkered with corn-fields, meadows, and green pastures covered with sheep, whose soft bleatings thrilled in my ears and transported my senses into new regions, so different was my charmed and tranquillized mind from the tossing anxieties attendant on the horrors I had recently witnessed. Surely there is nothing in the world, short of the most undivided reciprocal attachment, that has such power over the workings of the human heart as the mild sweetness of nature. The most ruffled temper, when emerging from the town, will subside into a calm at the sight of a wide stretch of landscape reposing in the twilight of a fine evening. It is then that the spirit of peace settles upon the heart, unfetters the thoughts and elevates the soul to the Creator. It is then that we behold the Parent of the universe in his works; we see his grandeur in earth, sea, and sky: we feel his affection in the emotions which they raise, and, half mortal, half etherealized, forget where we are, in the anticipation of what that world must be of which this earth is merely the shadow.*

"Autumn seemed to be unfolding all her beauties to greet the return of the palatine. In one part the haymakers were mowing the hay and heaping it into stacks; in another, the reapers were gathering up the wheat, with a troop of rosy little gleaners behind them, each of whom might have tempted the proudest Palemon in Christendom to have changed her toil into 'a gentler duty.' Such a landscape intermingled with the little farms of these honest people, whom the philanthropy of Sobieski has rendered free (for it is a tract of his extensive domains I am describing), reminded me of Somerset. Villages repose in the green hollows of the vales, and cottages are seen peeping from amidst the thick umbrage of the woods which cover the face of the hills. The irregular forms and thatched roofs of these simple habitations, with their infant inhabitants playing at the doors, compose such lovely groups, that I wish for our dear Mary's pencil and fingers (for, alas! that way mine are motionless!) to transport them to your eyes.

"The palace of Villanow, which is castellated, now burst upon my view. It rears its embattled head from the summit of a hill that gradually slopes down towards the Vistula, in full view to the south of the plain of Vola, a spot long famous for the election of the kings of Poland.† On the north of the

* This description of the banks of the Vistula was given to me with smiles and sighs. The reality was once enjoyed by the narrator, and there was a delight in the retrospection "sweet and mournful to the soul." At the time these reflections arose on such a scene, I often tasted the same pleasure in evening visits to the beautiful rural environs of London, which then extended from the north side of Fitzroy Square to beyond the Elm Grove on Primrose Hill, and forward through the fields to Hampstead. But most of that is all streets, or Regent's Park; and the sweet Hill, then the resort of many a happy Sunday group, has not now a tree standing on it, and hardly a blade of grass, "to mark where the primrose has been."

† It was from this very assumption by the nation, on the extinction of the male line of the monarchs of the house of Jaghellon, that all their subsequent political calamities may be dated. The last two sovereigns of this race were most justly styled good and great kings—father and son—Sigismund I. and II. But on the death of the last, about the middle of the sixteenth century, certain nobles of the nation, intoxicated with their wealth and privileges, ran wild for dictation in all things; and as the foundation for such rule, they determined to make the succession of their future kings entirely dependent on the free vote of

building, the earth is cut into natural ramparts, which rise in high succession until they reach the foundations of the palace, where they terminate in a noble terrace. These ramparts, covered with grass, overlook the stone outworks, and spread down to the bottom of the hill, which being clothed with fine trees and luxuriant underwood, forms such a rich and verdant base to the fortress as I have not language to describe: were I privileged to be poetical, I would say it reminds me of the God of war sleeping amid roses in the bower of love. Here the eye may wander over the gifts of bounteous Nature, arraying hill and dale in all the united treasures of spring and autumn. The forest stretches its yet unseared arms to the breeze; whilst that breeze comes laden with the fragrance of the tented hay, and the thousand sweets breathed from flowers, which in this delicious country weep honey.

"A magnificent flight of steps led us from the foot of the ramparts up to the gate of the palace. We entered it, and were presently surrounded bv a train of attendants in such sumptuous liveries, than I found myself all at once carried back into the fifteenth century, and might have fancied myself within the courtly halls of our Tudors and Plantagenets. You can better conceive that I can paint the scene which took place between the palatine, the countess, and her son. I can only repeat, that from that hour I have known no want of happiness but what arises from regret that my dear family are not partakers with me.

"You know that this stupendous building was the favorite residence of John Sobieski, and that he erected it as a resting-place from the labors of his long and glorious reign. I cannot move without meeting some vestige of that truly great monarch. I sleep in his bed chamber: there hangs his portrait, dressed in the robes of sovereignty; here are suspended the arms with which he saved the very kingdoms which have now met together to destroy his country. On one side is his library; on the

public suffrage; and the plain of Vola was made the terrible arena. So it may be called; for, from the time of the first monarch so elected, Henry of Valois, a stranger to the country, and brother to the execrable Charles IX. of France, bribery or violence have been the usual keys to the throne of Poland. For the doors of the country being once opened by the misguided people themselves to the influence of ambition, partiality, and passion, and shut against the old tenure of a settled succession, foreign powers were always ready to step in, with the gold or the sword; and Poland necessarily became a vassal adjunct to whatever neighboring country furnished the new sovereign. Thus it was, with a few exceptions (as in the case of the glorious John Sobieski), until the election of Stanislaus Augustus, who, though nominated by the power of the Empress of Russia, yet being, like Sobieski, a native prince of the nation, determined to govern the people of Poland in the spirit of his and their most glorious ancestors; and true to the vow, treading in the steps of the last of the Jaghellons, he gave to Poland the constitution of 1791, which, with the re-enaction of many wise laws, again made the throne hereditary. Hence the devoted struggles of every arm in the country in loyal defence of such a recovered existence.

other, the little chapel in which he used to pay his morning and evening devotions. Wherever I look, my eye finds some object to excite my reflections and emulation. The noble dead seem to address me from their graves; and I blush at the inglorious life I might have pursued had I never visited this house and its inhabitants. Yet, my dearest mother, I do not mean to insinuate that my honored father and brave ancestors have not set me examples as bright as man need follow. But human nature is capricious; we are not so easily stimulated by what is always in our view as with sights which, rising up when we are removed from our customary associations, surprise and captivate our attention. Villanow has only awakened me to the lesson which I conned over in drowsy carelessness at home. Thaddeus Sobieski is hardly one year my senior; but, good heaven! what has he not done? what has he not acquired? Whilst I abused the indulgence of my parents, and wasted my days in riding, shooting, and walking the streets, he was learning to act as became a man of rank and virtue; and by seizing every opportunity to serve the state, he has obtained a rich reward in the respect and admiration of his country. I am not envious, but I now feel the truth of Cæsar's speech, when he declared 'The reputation of Alexander would not let him sleep.' Nevertheless, I dearly love my friend. I murmur at my own demerits, not at his worth.

"I have scribbled over all my paper, otherwise I verily believe I should write more; however, I promise you another letter in a week or two. Meanwhile I shall send this packet to Mr. Loftus, who is at St. Petersburg, to forward it to you. Adieu, my dear mother! I am, with reverence to my father and yourself,

"Your truly affectionate son,

"PEMBROKE SOMERSET.

"VILLANOW, *August*, 1792."

CHAPTER VI.

SOCIETY IN POLAND.

"To Lady Somerset, Somerset Castle, England.

[Written three weeks after the preceding.]

"You know, my dear mother, that your Pembroke is famous for his ingenious mode of showing the full value of every favor he confers! Can I then relinquish the temptation of telling you what I have left to make you happy with this epistle?

"About five minutes ago, I was sitting on the lawn at the feet of the countess, reading to her and the Princess Poniatowski the charming poem of 'The Pleasures of Memory.' As both these ladies understand English, they were admiring it, and paying many compliments to the graces of my delivery, when the palatine presented himself, and told me, if I had any commands for St. Petersburg, I must prepare them, for a messenger was to set off on the next morning, by daybreak.' I instantly sprang up, threw my book into the hand of Thaddeus, and here I am in my own room scribbling to you!

"Even at the moment in which I dip my pen in the ink, my hurrying imagination paints on my heart the situation of my beloved home when this letter reaches you. I think I see you and my good aunt, seated on the blue sofa in your dressing-room, with your needle-work on the little table before you; I see Mary in her usual nook—the recess by the old harpsichord—and my dear father bringing in this happy letter from your son! I must confess this romantic kind of fancy-sketching makes me feel rather oddly: very unlike what I felt a few months ago, when I was a mere coxcomb—indifferent, unreflecting, unappreciating, and fit for nothing better than to hold pins at my lady's toilet. Well, it is now made evident to me that we never know the blessings bestowed on us until we are separated from the possession of them. Absence tightens the strings which unites friends as well as lovers: at least I find it so; and though I am in the fruition of every good on this side the ocean, yet my very happiness renders me ungrateful, and I repine because I enjoy it alone. Positively, I must bring you all hither to pass a summer, or come back at the termination of my travels, and carry away this dear family by main force to England.

"Tell my cousin Mary that, either way, I shall present to her esteem the most amiable and accomplished of my sex; but I warn her not to fall in love with him, neither in *propriâ personâ*, nor by his public fame, nor with his private character. Tell her 'he is a bright and particular star,' neither in her sphere nor in any other woman's. In this way he is as cold as 'Dian's Crescent;' and to my great amazement too, for when I throw my eyes over the many lovely young women who at different times fill the drawing-room of the countess, I cannot but wonder at the perfect indifference with which he views their (to me) irresistible charms.

"He is polite and attentive to them all; he talks with them, smiles with them, and treats them with every gentle complacency; but they do not live one instant in his memory. I mean they do not occupy his particular wishes; for with regard to every respectful sentiment towards the sex in general, and esteem to some amiable individuals, he is as awake as in the other case he is still asleep. The fact is, he has no idea of appropriation; he never casts one thought upon himself; kindness is spontaneous in his nature; his sunny eyes beam on all with modest benignity, and his frank and glowing conversation is directed to every rank of people. They imbibe it with an avidity and love which makes its way to his heart, without kindling one spark of vanity. Thus, whilst his fine person and splendid actions fill every eye and bosom, I see him moving in the circle unconscious of his eminence and the admiration he excites.

"Drawn by such an example, to which his high quality as well as extraordinary merit gives so great an influence, most of the younger nobility have been led to enter the army. These circumstances, added to the detail of his bravery and uncommon talents in the field, have made him an object of universal regard, and, in consequence, wherever he is seen he meets with applause and acclamation: nay, even at the appearance of his carriage in the streets, the passengers take off their hats and pray for him till he is out of sight. It is only then that I perceive his cheek flush with the conviction that he is seated in their hearts.

"'It is this, Thaddeus,' said I to him one day, when walking together we were obliged to retire into a house from the crowds that followed him; 'it is this, my dear friend, which shields your heart against the arrows of love. You have no place for that passion; your mistress is glory, and she courts you.'

"'My mistress is my country,' replied he; 'at present I desire no other. For her I would die; for her only would I wish to live.' Whilst he spoke, the energy of his soul blazed in his eye. I smiled.

"'You are an enthusiast, Thaddeus,' I said.

"'Pembroke!' returned he, in a surprised and reproachful tone.

"'I do not give you that name opprobriously,' resumed I, laughing; 'but there are many in my country, who, hearing these sentiments, would not scruple to call you mad.'

"'Then I pity them,' returned Thaddeus. 'Men who cannot ardently feel, cannot taste supreme happiness. My grandfather educated me at the feet of patriotism; and when I forget his precepts and example, may my guardian angel forget me!'

"'Happy, glorious Thaddeus!' cried I, grasping his hand; 'how I envy you your destiny! to live as you do, in the lap of honor, virtue and glory the aim and end of your existence!'

"The animated countenance of my friend changed at these words, and laying his hand on my arm, he said, 'Do not envy me my destiny. Pembroke, you are the son of a free and loyal country, at peace with itself; insatiate power has not dared to invade its rights. Your king, in happy security, reigns in the confidence of his people, whilst our anointed Stanislaus is baited and insulted by oppression from without and ingratitude within. Do not envy me: I would rather live in obscurity all my days than have the means which calamity may produce of acquiring celebrity over the ruins of Poland. O! my friend, the wreath that crowns the head of conquest is thick and bright; but that which binds the olive of peace on the bleeding wounds of my country will be the dearest to me.'

"Such sentiments, my dear madam, have opened new lights upon my poor mistaken faculties. I never considered the subject so maturely as my friend has done; victory and glory were with me synonymous words. I had not learned, until frequent conversations with the young, ardent, and pious Sobieski taught me, how to discriminate between animal courage and true valor —between the defender of his country and the ravager of other states. In short, I see in Thaddeus Sobieski all that my fancy hath ever pictured of the heroic character. Whilst I contemplate the sublimity of his sentiments and the tenderness of his soul, I cannot help thinking how few would believe that so many admirable qualities could belong to one mind, and that mind remain unacquainted with the throes of ambition or the throbs of self-love."

Pembroke judged rightly of his friend; for if ever the real disinterested *amor patriæ* glowed in the breast of a man, it animated the heart of the young Sobieski. At the termination of the foregoing sentence in the letter to his mother, Pembroke was interrupted by the entrance of a servant, who presented him a packet which had that moment arrived from St. Petersburg. He took it, and putting his writing materials into a desk, read the following epistle from his governor:

"To Pembroke Somerset, Esq.

"My dear sir,

"I have this day received your letter, enclosing one for Lady Somerset. You must pardon me that I have detained it, and will continue to do so until I am favored with your answer to this, for which I shall most anxiously wait.

"You know, Mr. Somerset, my reputation in the sciences; you know my depth in the languages; and besides, the Marquis of Inverary, with whom I travelled over the Continent, offered you sufficient credentials respecting my knowledge of the world, and the honorable manner in which I treat my pupils. Sir Robert Somerset and your lady mother were amply satisfied with the account which his lordship gave of my character; but with all this, in one point every man is vulnerable. No scholar can forget those lines of the poet:—

> 'Felices ter, et amplius,
> Quos irrupta tenet copula; nec malis
> Divulsus quærimoniis,
> Supremâ citius solvet amor die.'

It has been my misfortune that I have felt them.

"You are not ignorant that I was known to the Brinicki family, when I had the honor of conducting the marquis through Russia. The count's accomplished kinswoman, the amiable and learned widow of Baron Surowkoff, even then took particular notice of me; and when I returned with you to St. Petersburg, I did not find that my short absence had obliterated me from her memory.

"You are well acquainted with the dignity of that lady's opinions on political subjects. She and I coincided in ardor for the consolidating cause of sovereignty, and in hatred of that levelling power which pervades all Europe. Many have been the long and interesting conversations we have held together on the prosecution of the grand schemes of the three great contracting monarchs.

"The baroness, I need not observe, is as handsome as she is ingenuous; her understanding is as masculine as her person is desirable; and I had been more or less than man had I not understood that my figure and talents were agreeable to her. I cannot say that she absolutely promised me her hand, but she went as far that way as delicacy would permit. I am thus circumstantial, Mr. Somerset, to show you that I do not proceed without proof. She has repeatedly said in my presence that she would never marry any man unless he were not only well-looking, but of the profoundest erudition, united with an acquaintance with men and manners which none can dispute. 'Besides,' added she, 'he must not differ with me one tittle in politics, for on that head I hold myself second to no man or woman in Europe.' And then she has complimented me, by declaring that I possessed more judicious sentiments on government than any man in St. Petersburg, and that she should consider herself happy, on the first vacancy in the imperial college, to introduce me at court, where she was 'sure the empress would at once discover the value of my talents; but,' she continued, 'in such a case, I will not allow that even her majesty shall rival me in your esteem.' The modesty natural to my character told me that these praises must have some other source than my comparatively unequal abilities; and I unequivocally found it in the partiality with which her ladyship condescended to regard me.

"Was I to blame, Mr. Somerset? Would not any man of sensibility and honor have comprehended such advances from a woman of her rank and reputation? I could not be mistaken; her looks and words needed no explanation which my judgment could not pronounce. Though I am aware that I do not possess that *lumen purpureum juveniæ* which attracts very young, uneducated women, yet I am not much turned of fifty; and from the baroness's singular behavior, I had every reason to expect handsomer treatment than she has been pleased to dispense to me since my return to this capital.

But to proceed regularly—(I must beg your pardon for the warmth which has hurried me to this digression): you know, sir, that from the hour in which I had the honor of taking leave of your noble family in England, I strove to impress upon your rather volatile mind a just and accurate conception of the people amongst whom I was to conduct you. When I brought you into this extensive empire, I left no means unexerted to heighten your respect not only for its amiable sovereign, but for all powers in amity with her. It is the characteristic of genius to be zealous. I was so, in favor of the pretensions of the great Catherine to that miserable country in which you now are, and to which she deigned to offer her protection. To this zeal, and my unfortunate though honorable devotion to the wishes of the baroness, I am constrained to attribute my present dilemma.

"When Poland had the insolence to rebel against its illustrious mistress, you remember that all the rational world was highly incensed. The Baroness Surowkoff declared herself frequently, and with vehemence she appealed to me. My veracity and my principles were called forth, and I confessed that I thought every friend to the Tzaritza ought to take up arms against that ungrateful people. The Count Brinicki was then appointed to command the Russian forces preparing to join the formidable allies; and her ladyship, very unexpectedly on my part, answered me by approving what I said, and added that of course I meant to follow her cousin into Poland, for that even she, as a woman, was so earnest in the cause, she would accompany him to the frontiers, and there await the result.

"What could I do? How could I withstand the expectations of a lady of her quality, and one who I believed loved me? However, for some time I did oppose my wish to oblige her; I urged my cloth, and the impossibility of accounting for such a line of conduct to the father of my pupil? The baroness ridiculed all these arguments as mere excuses, and ended with saying, Do as you please, Mr. Loftus. I have been deceived in your character; the friend of the Baroness Surowkoff must be consistent; he must be as willing to fight for the cause he espouses as to speak for it: in this case, the sword must follow the oration, else we shall see Poland in the hands of a rabble.'

"This decided me. I offered my services to the count to attend him to the field. He and the young lords persuaded you to do the same; and as I could not think of leaving you, when your father had placed you under my charge, I was pleased to find that my approval confirmed your wish to turn soldier. I was not then acquainted, Mr. Somerset (for you did not tell me of it until we were far advanced into Poland), with Sir Robert's and my lady's dislike of the army. This has been a prime source of my error throughout this affair. Had I known their repugnance to your taking up arms, my duty would have triumphed over even my devotion to the baroness; but I was born under a melancholy horoscope; nothing happens as any one of my humblest wishes might warrant.

"At the first onset of the battle, I became so suddenly ill that I was obliged to retire; and on this unfortunate event, which was completely unwilled on my part (for no man can command the periods of sickness), the baroness founded a contempt which has disconcerted all my schemes. Besides, when I attempted to remonstrate with her ladyship on the promise which, if not directly given, was implied, she laughed at me; and when I persisted in my suit, all at once, like the rest of her ungrateful and undistinguishing sex, she burst into a tempest of invectives, and forbade me her presence.

"What am I now to do, Mr. Somerset? This inconsistent woman has betrayed me into conduct diametrically opposite to the commands of your family. Your father particularly desired that I would not suffer you to go either into Hungary or Poland. In the last instance I have permitted you to disobey him. And my Lady Somerset (who, alas! I now remember lost both her father and brother in different engagements), you tell me, had declared that she never would pardon the man who should put military ideas into your head.

"Therefore, sir, though you are my pupil, I throw myself on your generosity. If you persist in acquainting your family with the late transactions at Zielime, and your present residence in Poland, I shall finally be ruined. I shall not only forfeit the good opinion of your noble father and mother, but lose all prospect of the living of Somerset, which Sir Robert was so gracious as to promise should be mine on the demise of the present incumbent. You know, Mr. Somerset, that I have a mother and six sisters in Wales, whose support depends on my success in life; if my preferment be stopped now, they must necessarily be involved in a distress which makes me shudder.

"I cannot add more, sir; I know well your character for generosity, and I therefore rest upon it with the utmost confidence. I shall detain the letter which you did me the honor to enclose for my Lady Somerset till I receive your decision; and ever, whilst I live, will I henceforth remain firm to my old and favorite maxim, which I adopted from the glorious epistle of

Horace to Numicius. Perhaps you may not recollect the lines? They run thus :—

Nil admirari, prope res est una, Numici,
Solaque, quæ possit facere et servare beatum.

"I have the honor to be,
"Dear sir,
"Your most obedient servant,
"ANDREW LOFTUS.

"ST. PETERSBURG, *September*, 1792."

"P. S. Just as I was about sealing this packet, the English ambassador forwarded to me a short letter from your father, in which he desires us to quit Russia, and to make the best of our way to England, where you are wanted on a most urgent occasion. He explains himself no further, only repeating his orders in express commands that we set off instantly. I wait your directions."

This epistle disconcerted Mr. Somerset. He always guessed the Baroness Surowkoff was amusing herself with his vain and pedantic preceptor; but he never entertained a suspicion that her ladyship would carry her pleasantry to so cruel an excess. He clearly saw that the fears of Mr. Loftus with regard to the displeasure of his parents were far from groundless; and therefore, as there was no doubt, from the extreme age of Dr. Manners, that the rectory of Somerset would soon become vacant, he thought it better to oblige his poor governor, and preserve their secret for a month or two, than to give him up to the indignation of Sir Robert. On these grounds, Pembroke resolved to write to Mr. Loftus, and ease the anxiety of his heart. Although he ridiculed his vanity, he could not help respecting the affectionate solicitude of a son and a brother, and as that plea had won him, half angry, half grieved, and half laughing, he dispatched a few hasty lines.

"TO THE REVEREND ANDREW LOFTUS, ST. PETERSBURG.

"What whimsical fit, my dear sir, has seized my father, that I am recalled at a moment's notice? Faith, I am so mad at the summons, and at his not deigning to assign a reason for his order, that I do not know how I may be tempted to act.

"Another thing, you beg of me not to say a word of my having been in Poland; and for that purpose you have withheld the letter which I sent to you to forward to my mother!

You offer far-fetched and precious excuses for having betrayed your own wisdom, and your pupil's innocence, into so mortal an offence. One cause of my being here, you say, was your 'ardor in the cause of insulted Russia, and your hatred of that levelling power which pervades all Europe.'

"Well, I grant it. I understood from you and Brinicki that you were leading me against a set of violent, discontented men of rank, who, in proportion as each was inflated with his own personal pride, despised all of their own order who did not agree with them, and, coalescing together under the name of freedom, were introducing anarchy throughout a country which Catharine would graciously have protected. All this I find to be in error. But both of you may have been misled: the count by partiality and you by misrepresentation; therefore I do not perceive why you should be in such a terror. The wisest man in the world may see through bad lights; and why should you think my father would never pardon you for having been so unlucky?

"Yet to dispel your dread of such tidings ruining you with Sir Robert, I will not be the first to tell him of our quixoting. Only remember, my good sir,—though, to oblige you, I withhold my letters to my mother, and when I arrive in England shall lock up my lips from mentioning Poland,—that positively, I will not be mute one day longer than that in which my father presents you with the living of Somerset; then you will be independent of his displeasure, and I may, and will, declare my everlasting gratitude to this illustrious family.

"I am half mad when I think of leaving them. I must now tear myself from this mansion of comfort and affection, to wander with you in some rumbling old barouche 'over brake and through briar!' Well, patience! Another such upset to your friends of the Neva, and with 'victory perched like an eagle on their laurelled brows,' I may have some chance of wooing the Sobieskis to the banks of the Thames. At present, I have not sufficient hope to keep me in good-humor.

"Meet me this day week at Dantzic: I shall there embark for England. You had best not bring the foreign servants with you; they might blab. Discharge them at St. Petersburg, and hire a courier for yourself, whom we may drop at the seaport.

"I have the honor to remain,
"Dear sir,
"Your most obedient servant,
PEMBROKE SOMERSET

"VILLANOW. *September*, 1702."

When Somerset joined his friends at supper, and imparted to them the commands of his father, an immediate change was produced in the spirits of the party. During the lamentations of the ladies and the murmurs of the young men, the countess tried to dispel the effects of the information by addressing Pembroke with a smile, and saying, "But we hope that you have seen enough at Villanow to tempt you back again at no very distant period? Tell Lady Somerset you have left a second mother in Poland, who will long to receive another visit from her adopted son."

"Yes, my dear madam," returned he; "and I shall hope, before a very distant period, to see those two kind mothers united as intimately by friendship as they are in my heart."

Thaddeus listened with a saddened countenance. He had not been accustomed to the thought of a long separation, and when he met it now, he hardly knew how to proportion his uneasiness to the privation. Hope and all the hilarities of youth flushed in his soul; his features continually glowed with animation, whilst the gay beaming of his eyes ever answered to the smile on his lips. Hence the slightest veering of his mind was perceptible to the countess, who, turning round, saw him leaning thoughtfully in his chair, whilst Pembroke, with increasing vehemence, was running through various invectives against the hastiness of his recall.

"Come, come, Thaddeus!" cried she; "let us think no more of this parting until it arrives. You know that anticipation of evil is the death of happiness; and it will be a kind of suicide should we destroy the hours we may yet enjoy together in vain complainings that they are so soon to terminate."

A little exhortation from the countess, and a maternal kiss which she imprinted on his cheek, restored him to cheerfulness, and the evening passed more pleasantly than it had portended.

Much as the palatine esteemed Pembroke Somerset, his mind was too deeply absorbed in the condition of the kingdom to attend to less considerable cares. He beheld his country, even on the verge of destruction, awaiting with firmness the approach of the earthquake which threatened to ingulf it in the neighboring nations. He saw the storm lowering; but he determined, whilst there remained one spot of vantage ground above the general wreck, that Poland should yet have a name and a defender. These thoughts possessed him; these plans engaged him; and he had not leisure to regret pleasure when he was struggling for existence.

The empress continued to pour her armies into the heart of the kingdom. The King of Prussia, boldly flying from his treaties, marched to bid her colors a conqueror's welcome; and the Emperor of Germany, following the example of so great a prince, did not blush to show that his word was equally contemptible.

Dispatches daily arrived of the villages being laid waste; that neither age, sex, nor situation shielded the unfortunate inhabitants, and that all the frontier provinces were in flames.

The Diet was called,* and the debates agitated with the anxiety of men who were met to decide on their dearest interests. The bosom of the benevolent Stanislaus bled at the dreadful picture of his people's sufferings, and hardly able to restrain his tears, he answered the animated exordiums of Sobieski for resistance to the last with an appeal immediately to his heart.

"What is it that you urge me to do, my lord?" said he. "Was it not to secure the happiness of my subjects that I labored? and finding my designs impracticable, what advantage would it be to them should I pertinaciously oppose their small numbers to the accumulated array of two empires, and of a king almost as powerful as either. What is my kingdom but the comfort of my people? What will it avail me to see them fall around me, man by man, and the few who remain bending in speechless sorrow over their graves? Such a sight would break my heart. Poland without its people would be a desert, and I a hermit rather than a king."

In vain the palatine combated these arguments, showing the vain quiet such a peace might afford, by declaring it could only be temporary. In vain he told his majesty that he would purchase safety for the present race at the vast expense of not only the liberty of posterity, but of its probity and happiness.

"However you disguise slavery," cried he, "it is slavery still. Its chains, though wreathed with roses, not only fasten on the body but rivet on the mind. They bend it from the loftiest virtue to a debasement beneath calculation. They disgrace honor; they trample upon justice. They transform the legions of Rome into a band of singers. They prostrate the sons of Athens and of Sparta at the feet of cowards. They make man abjure his birth right, bind himself to another's will, and give that into a tyrant's hands which he received as a deposit from Heaven—his reason, his conscience, and his soul. Think on this, and then, if you can, subjugate Poland to her enemies."

* The constitutional Diet of Poland nearly answers in principle to the British three estates in Parliament—King, Lords, and Commons.

Stanislaus, weakened by years and subdued by disappointment, now retained no higher wish than to save his subjects from immediate outrage. He did not answer the palatine, but with streaming eyes bent over the table, and annulled the glorious constitution of 1791. Then with emotions hardly short of agony, he signed an order presented by a plenipotentiary from the combined powers, which directed Prince Poniatowski to deliver the army under his command into the hands of General Brinicki.

As the king put his signature to these papers, Sobieski, who had strenuously withstood each decision, started from his chair, bowed to his sovereign, and in silence left the apartment Several noblemen followed him.

These pacific measures did not meet with better treatment from without. When they were noised abroad, an alarming commotion arose among the inhabitants of Warsaw, and nearly four thousand men of the first families in the kingdom assembled themselves in the park of Villanow, and with tumultuous eagerness declared their resolution to resist the invaders of their country to their last gasp. The Prince Sapieha, Kosciusko, and Sobieski, with the sage Dombrowski, were the first who took this oath of fidelity to Poland ; and they administered it to Thaddeus, who, kneeling down, inwardly invoked Heaven to aid him, as he swore to fulfil his trust.

In the midst of these momentous affairs, Pembroke Somerset bade adieu to his Polish friends and set sail with his governor from Dantzic for England.

CHAPTER VII.

THE DIET OF POLAND.

THOSE winter months which before this year had been at Villanow the season for cheerfulness and festivity, now rolled away in the sad pomp of national debates and military assemblies.

Prussia usurped the best part of Pomerelia, and garrisoned it with troops ; Catharine declared her dominion over the vast tract of land which lies between the Dwina and Borysthenes ; and Frederick William marked down another sweep of Poland, to follow the fate of Dantzic and of Thorn, while watching the dark policy of Austria regarding its selecting portions of the dismembering state.

Calamities and insults were heaped day after day on the defenceless Poles. The deputies of the provinces were put into prison, and the provisions intended for the king's table interrupted and appropriated by the depredators to their own use. Sobieski remonstrated on this last outrage; but incensed at reproof, and irritated at the sway which the palatine still held, an order was issued for all the Sobieski estates in Lithuania and Podolia to be sequestrated and divided between four of the invading generals.

In vain the Villanow confederation endeavored to remonstrate with the empress. Her ambassador not only refused to forward the dispatches, but threatened the nobles "if they did not comply with every one of his demands, he would lay all the estates, possessions, and habitations of the members of the Diet under an immediate military execution. Nay, punishment should not stop there; for if the king joined the Sobieski party (to which he now appeared inclined), the royal domains should not only meet the same fate, but harsher treatment should follow, until both the people and their proud sovereign were brought into due subjection."

These menaces were too arrogant to have any other effect upon the Poles than that of giving a new spur to their resolution. With the same firmness they repulsed similar fulminations from the Prussian ambassador, and, with a coolness which was only equalled by their intrepidity, they prepared to resume their arms.

Hearing by private information that their threats were despised, next morning, before daybreak, these despotic envoys surrounded the building where the confederation was sitting with two battalions of grenadiers and four pieces of cannon, and then issued orders that no Pole should pass the gates without being fired on. General Rautenfeld, who was set over the person of the king, declared that not even his majesty might stir until the Diet had given an unanimous and full consent to the imperial commands.

The Diet set forth the unlawfulness of signing any treaty whilst thus withheld from the freedom of will and debate. They urged that it was not legal to enter into deliberation when violence had recently been exerted against any individual of their body; and how could they do it now, deprived as they were of five of their principal members, whom the ambassadors well knew they had arrested on their way to the Senate? Sobieski and four of his friends being the members most inimical to the oppression going on, were these five. In vain their liberation was required; and enraged at the pertinacity of this opposition, Rautenfeld repeated the former threats, with the addition of more, swearing that they should take place without appeal if the Diet did not directly and unconditionally sign the pretensions both of his court and that of Prussia.

After a hard contention of many hours, the members at last agreed amongst themselves to make a solemn public protest against the present tyrannous measures of the two ambassadors; and seeing that any attempt to inspire them even with decency was useless, they determined to cease all debate, and kept a profound silence when the marshal should propose the project in demand.

This sorrowful silence was commenced in resentment and retained through despair; this sorrowful silence was called by their usurpers a consent; this sorrowful silence is held up to the world and to posterity as a free cession by the Poles of all those rights which they had received from nature, ratified by laws, and defended with their blood.*

The morning after this dreadful day, the Senate met at one of the private palaces; and, indignant and broken-hearted, they delivered the following declaration to the people:—

"The Diet of Poland, hemmed in by foreign troops, menaced with an influx of the enemy, which would be attended by universal ruin, and finally insulted by a thousand outrages, have been forced to witness the signing of a submissive treaty with their enemies.

"The Diet had strenuously endeavored to have added to that treaty some conditions to which they supposed the lamentable state of the country would have extorted an acquiescence, even from the heart of a conqueror's power. But the Diet were deceived: they found such power was unaccompanied by humanity; they found that the foe, having thrown his victim to the ground, would not refrain from exulting in the barbarous triumph of trampling upon her neck.

"The Diet rely on the justice of Poland—rely on her belief that they would not betray the citadel she confided to their keeping. Her preservation is dearer to them than their lives;

* Thus, like the curule fathers of Rome, they sat unyielding, awaiting the threatened stroke. But the dignity of virtue held her shield over them; and with an answering silence on the part of the confederated ambassadors, the Diet-chamber was vacated.

but fate seems to be on the side of their destroyer. Fresh insults have been heaped upon their heads and new hardships have been imposed upon them. To prevent all diliberations on this debasing treaty, they are not only surrounded by foreign troops, and dared with hostile messages, but they have been violated by the arrest of their prime members, whilst those who are still suffered to possess a personal freedom have the most galling shackles laid upon their minds.

"Therefore, I, the King of Poland, enervated by age, and sinking under the accumulated weight of my kingdom's afflictions, and also we, the members of the Diet, declare that, being unable, even by the sacrifice of our lives, to relieve our country from the yoke of its oppressors, we consign it to our children and the justice of Heaven.

"In another age, means may be found to rescue it from chains and misery; but such means are not put in our power. Other countries neglect us. Whilst they reprobate the violations which a neighboring nation is alleged to have committed against rational liberty, they behold, not only with apathy but with approbation, the ravages which are now desolating Poland. Posterity must avenge it. We have done. We accede in silence, for the reasons above mentioned, to the treaty laid before us, though we declare that it is contrary to our wishes, to our sentiments, and to our rights."

Thus, in November, 1793, compressed to one fourth of her dimensions by the lines of demarcation drawn by her invaders, Poland was stripped of her rank in Europe; her "power delivered up to strangers, and her beauty into the hands of her enemies!" Ill-fated people! Nations will weep over your wrongs; whilst the burning blush of shame, that their fathers witnessed such wrongs unmoved, shall cause the tears to blister as they fall.

During these transactions, the Countess Sobieski continued in solitude at Villanow, awaiting with awful anxiety the termination of those portentous events which so deeply involved her own comforts with those of her country. Her father was in prison, her son at a distance with the army. Sick at heart, she saw the opening of that spring which might be the commencement only of a new season of injuries; and her fears were prophetic.

It being discovered that some Masovian regiments in the neighborhood of Warsaw yet retained their arms, they were ordered by the foreign envoys to lay them down. A few, thinking denial vain, obeyed; but bolder spirits followed

Thaddeus Sobieski towards South Prussia, whither he had directed his steps on the arrest of his grandfather, and where he had gathered and kept together a handful of brave men, still faithful to their liberties. His name alone collected numbers in every district through which he marched. Persecution from their adversary as well as admiration of Thaddeus had given a resistless power to his appearance, look, and voice, all of which had such an effect on the peasantry, that they eagerly crowded to his standard, whilst their young lords committed themselves without reserve to his sole judgment and command. The Prussian ambassador, hearing of this, sent to Stanislaus to command the grandson of Sobieski to disband his troops. The king refusing, and his answer being communicated to the Russian envoy also, war was renewed with redoubled fury.

The palatine remained in confinement, hopeless of obtaining release without the aid of stratagem. His country's enemies were too well aware of their interest to give freedom to so active an opponent. They sought to vex his spirit with every mental torture; but he rather received consolation than despair in the reports daily brought to him by his jailers. They told him "that his grandson continued to carry himself with such insolent opposition in the south, it would be well if the empress, at the termination of the war, allowed him to escape with banishment to Siberia." But every reproach thus levelled at the palatine he found had been bought by some new success of Thaddeus; and instead of permitting their malignity to intimidate his age or alarm his affection, he told the officer (who kept guard in his chambers) that if his grandson were to lose his head for fidelity to Poland, he should behold him with as proud an eye mounting the scaffold as entering the streets of Warsaw with her freedom in his hand. "The only difference would be," continued Sobieski, "that as the first cannot happen until all virtue be dead in this land, I should regard his last gasp as the expiring sigh of that virtue which, by him, had found a triumph even under the axe. But for the second, it would be joy unutterable to behold the victory of justice over rapine and violence! But, either way, Thaddeus Sobieski is still the same—ready to die or ready to live for his country, and equally worthy of the sacred halo with which posterity would encircle his name forever."

Indeed, the accounts which arrived from this young soldier, who had formed a junction with General Kosciusko, were in the highest degree formidable to the coalesced powers. Having gained several advantages over the Prussians, the two victorious battalions were advancing towards Inowlotz, when a large and fresh body of the enemy appeared suddenly on their rear. The enemy on the opposite bank of the river, (whom the Poles were driving before them,) at sight of this reinforcement, rallied; and not only to retard the approach of the pursuers, but to ensure their defeat from the army in view, they broke down the wooden bridge by which they had escaped themselves. The Poles were at a stand. Kosciusko proposed swimming across, but owing to the recent heavy rains, the river was so swollen and rapid that the young captains to whom he mentioned the project, terrified by the blackness and dashing of the water, drew back. The general, perceiving their panic, called Thaddeus to him, and both plunged into the stream. Ashamed of hesitation, the others now tried who could first follow their example; and, after hard buffeting with its tide, the whole army gained the opposite shore. The Prussians who were in the rear, incapable of the like intrepidity, halted; and those who had crossed on their former defeat, now again intimidated at the daring courage of their adversaries, concealed themselves amidst the thickets of an adjoining valley.

The two friends proceeded towards Cracow,* carrying redress and protection to the provinces through which they marched. But they had hardly rested a day in that city before dispatches were received that Warsaw was lying at the mercy of General Brinicki. No time could be lost; officers and men had set their lives on the cause, and they recommenced their toil of a new march with a perseverance which brought them before the capital on the 16th of April.

Things were in a worse state than even was expected. The three ambassadors had not only demanded the surrender of the national arsenal, but subscribed their orders with a threat that whoever of the nobles presumed to dispute their authority should be arrested and closely imprisoned there; and if the people should dare to murmur, they would immediately order General Brinicki to lay the city in ashes.

The king remonstrated against such oppression, and to "punish his presumption," his excellency ordered that his majesty's garrison and guards should instantly be broken up and dispersed. At the first attempt to execute this mandate, the people flew in crowds to the palace, and, falling on their knees, implored Stanislaus for permission to avenge the insult

* Cracow is considered the oldest regal city in Poland; the tombs of her earliest and noblest kings are there, John Sobieski's being one of the most renowned. It stands in a province of the same name, about 130 miles south-west of Warsaw, the more modern capital of the kingdom, and also the centre of its own province.

offered to his troops. The king looked at them with pity, gratitude, and anguish. For some time his emotions were too strong to allow him to speak; at last, in a voice of agony, wrung from his tortured heart, he answered, "Go, and defend your honor!"

The army of Kosciusko marched into the town at this critical moment; they joined the armed people; and that day, after a dreadful conflict, Warsaw was rescued from the immediate grasp of the hovering Black Eagle. During the fight, the king, who was alone in one of the rooms of his palace, sunk in despair on the floor; he heard the mingling clash of arms, the roar of musketry, and the cries and groans of the combatants; ruin seemed no longer to threaten his kingdom, but to have pounced at once upon her prey. At every renewed volley which followed each pause in the firing, he expected to see his palace gates burst open, and himself, then indeed made a willing sacrifice, immolated to the vengeance of his enemies.

While he was yet upon his knees petitioning the God of battles for a little longer respite from that doom which was to overwhelm devoted Poland, Thaddeus Sobieski, panting with heat and toil, flew into the room, and before he could speak a word, was clasped in the arms of the agitated Stanislaus.

"What of my people?" asked the king.

"They are victorious!" returned Thaddeus. "The foreign guards are beaten from the palace; your own have resumed their station at the gates."

At this assurance, tears of joy ran over the venerable cheeks of his majesty, and again embracing his young deliverer, he exclaimed, "I thank Heaven, my unhappy country is not bereft of all hope! Whilst a Kosciusko and a Sobieski live, she need not quite despair. They are thy ministers, O Jehovah, of a yet longer respite!"

CHAPTER VIII.

BATTLE OF BRZESC—THE TENTH OF OCTOBER.

THADDEUS was not less eager to release his grandfather than he had been to relieve the anxiety of his sovereign. He hastened, at the head of a few troops, to the prison of Sobieski, and gave him liberty, amidst the acclamations of his soldiers.

The universal joy at these prosperous events did not last many days: it was speedily terminated by information that Cracow had surrendered to a Prussian force, that the King of Prussia was advancing towards the capital, and that the Russians, more implacable in consequence of the late treatment their garrison had received at Warsaw, were pouring into the country like a deluge.

At this intelligence the consternation became dreadful. The Polonese army in general, worn with fatigue and long service, and without clothing or ammunition, were not in any way, excepting courage, fitted for resuming the field.

The treasury was exhausted, and means of raising a supply seemed impracticable. The provinces were laid waste, and the city had already been drained of its last ducat. In this exigency a council met in his majesty's cabinet, to devise some expedient for obtaining resources. The consultation was as desponding as their situation, until Thaddeus Sobieski, who had been a silent observer, rose from his seat. Sudden indisposition had prevented the palatine attending, but his grandson knew well how to be his substitute. Whilst blushes of awe and eagerness crimsoned his cheek, he advanced towards Stanislaus, and taking from his neck and other parts of his dress those magnificent jewels it was customary to wear in the presence of the king, he knelt down, and laying them at the feet of his majesty, said, in a suppressed voice, "These are trifles; but such as they are, and all of the like kind which we possess, I am commanded by my grandfather to beseech your majesty to appropriate to the public service."

"Noble young man!" cried the king, raising him from the ground; "you have indeed taught me a lesson. I accept these jewels with gratitude. Here," said he, turning to the treasurer, "put them into the national fund, and let them be followed by my own, with my gold and silver plate, which latter I desire may be instantly sent to the mint. Three parts the army shall have; the other we must expend in giving support to the surviving families of the brave men who have fallen in our defence." The palatine readily united with his grandson in the surrender of all their personal property for the benefit of their country; and, according to their example, the treasury was soon filled with gratuities from the nobles. The very artisans offered their services gratis; and all hands being employed to forward the preparations, the army was soon enabled to take the field, newly equipped and in high spirits.

The countess had again to bid adieu to a son who was now

become as much the object of her admiration as of her love. In proportion as glory surrounded him and danger courted his steps, the strings of affection drew him closer to her soul; the "aspiring blood" of the Sobieskis which beat in her veins could not cheer the dread of a mother, could not cause her to forget that the spring of her existence now flowed from the fountain which had taken its source from her. Her anxious and watching heart paid dearly in tears and sleepless nights for the honor with which she was saluted at every turning as the mother of Thaddeus: that Thaddeus who was not more the spirit of enterprise, and the rallying point of resistance, than he was to her the gentlest, the dearest, the most amiable of sons. It matters not to the undistinguishing bolt of carnage whether it strike common breasts or those rare hearts whose lives are usually as brief as they are dazzling; this leaden messenger of death banquets as greedily on the bosom of a hero as if it had lit upon more vulgar prey; all is levelled to the seeming chance of war, which comes like a whirlwind of the desert, scattering man and beast in one wide ruin.

Such thoughts as these possessed the melancholy but prayerful reveries of the Countess Sobieski, from the hour in which she saw Thaddeus and his grandfather depart for Cracow until she heard it was retaken, and that the enemy were defeated in several subsequent contests.

Warsaw was again bombarded, and again Kosciusko, with the palatine and Thaddeus, preserved it from destruction. In short, wherever they moved, their dauntless little army carried terror to its adversaries, and diffused hope through the homes and hearts of their countrymen.

They next turned their course to the relief of Lithuania; but whilst they were on their route thither, they received intelligence that a division of the Poles, led by Prince Poniatowski, having been routed by a formidable body of Russians under Suwarrow, that general, elated with his success, was hastening forward to re-attack the capital.

Kosciusko resolved to prevent him, prepared to give immediate battle to Ferfen, another Russian commander, who was on his march to form a junction with his victorious countrymen. To this end Kosciusko divided his forces; half of them to not only support the retreat of the prince, but to enable him to hover near Suwarrow, and to keep a watchful eye over his motions; whilst Kosciusko, accompanied by the two Sobieskis, would proceed with the other division towards Brzesc.

It was the tenth of October. The weather being fine, a

cloudless sun diffused life and brilliancy through the pure air of a keen morning. The vast green plain before them glittered with the troops of General Ferfen, who had already arranged them in order of battle.

The word was given. Thaddeus, as he drew his sabre* from its scabbard, raised his eyes to implore the justice of Heaven on that day's events. The attack was made. The Poles kept their station on the heights. The Russians rushed on them like wolves, and twice they repulsed them by their steadiness. Conquest declared for Poland. Thaddeus was seen in every part of the field. But reinforcements poured in to the support of Ferfen, and war raged in new horrors. Still the courage of the Poles was unabated. Sobieski, fighting at the head of his cavalry, would not recede a foot, and Kosciusko, exhorting his men to be resolute, appeared in the hottest places of the battle.

At one of these portentous moments, the commander-in-chief was seen struggling with the third charger which had been shot under him that day. Thaddeus galloped to his assistance, gave him his horse, mounted another offered by a hussar, and remained fighting by his side, till, on the next charge, Kosciusko himself fell forward. Thaddeus caught him in his arms, and finding that his own breast was immediately covered with blood, (a Cossack having stabbed the general through the shoulder,) he unconsciously uttered a cry of horror. The surrounding soldiers took the alarm, and "Kosciusko, our father, is killed!" was echoed from rank to rank with such piercing shrieks, that the wounded hero started from the breast of his young friend just as two Russian chasseurs in the same moment made a cut at them both. The sabre struck the exposed head of Kosciusko, who sunk senseless to the ground, and Thaddeus received a gash near his neck that laid him by his side.

The consternation became universal; groans of despair seemed to issue from the whole army, whilst the few resolute Poles who had been stationed near the fallen general fell in mangled heaps upon his breast. Thaddeus with difficulty extricated himself from the bodies of the slain; and, fighting his way through the triumphant troops which pressed around him, amidst the smoke and confusion soon joined his terror-stricken comrades, who in the wildest despair were dispersing under a

* The sabre (like the once famed claymore of Scotland) was the characteristic weapon of Poland. It was the especial appendage to the sides of the nobles;—its use, the science of their youth, their ornament and graceful exercise in peace, their most efficient manual power of attack or defence in war. It is impossible for any but an eye-witness to have any idea of the skill, beauty, and determination with which this weapon was, and is, wielded in Poland.

heavy fire, and flying like frighted deer. In vain he called to them—in vain he urged them to avenge Kosciusko; the panic was complete, and they fled.

Almost alone, in the rear of his soldiers, he opposed with his single and desperate arm party after party of the enemy, until a narrow stream of the Muchavez stopped his retreat. The waters were crimsoned with blood. He plunged in, and beating the blushing wave with his left arm, in a few seconds gained the opposite bank, where, fainting from fatigue and loss of blood, he sunk, almost deprived of sense, amidst a heap of the killed.

When the pursuing squadrons had galloped past him, he again summoned strength to look round. He raised himself from the ground, and by the help of his sabre supported his steps a few paces further; but what was the shock he received when the bleeding and lifeless body of his grandfather lay before him? He stood for a few moments motionless and without sensation; then, kneeling down by his side, whilst he felt as if his own heart were palsied with death, he searched for the wounds of the palatine. They were numerous and deep. He would have torn away the handkerchief with which he had stanched his own blood to have applied it to that of his grandfather; but in the instant he was so doing, feeling the act might the next moment disable himself from giving him further assistance, he took his sash and neck-cloth, and when they were insufficient, he rent the linen from his breast; then hastening to the river, he brought a little water in his cap, and threw some of its stained drops on the pale features of Sobieski.

The venerable hero opened his eyes; in a minute afterwards he recognized that it was his grandson who knelt by him. The palatine pressed his hand, which was cold as ice: the marble lips of Thaddeus could not move.

"My son," said the veteran, in a low voice, "Heaven hath led you hither to receive the last sigh of your grandfather." Thaddeus trembled. The palatine continued: "Carry my blessing to your mother, and bid her seek comfort in the consolations of her God. May that God preserve you! Ever remember that you are his servant; be obedient to him; and as I have been, be faithful to your country."

"May God so bless me!" cried Thaddeus, looking up to heaven.

"And ever remember," said the palatine, raising his head, which had dropped on the bosom of his grandson, "that you are a Sobieski! it is my dying command that you never take any other name."

"I promise."

Thaddeus could say no more, for the countenance of his grandfather became altered; his eyes closed. Thaddeus caught him to his breast. No heart beat against his; all was still and cold. The body dropped from his arms, and he sunk senseless by its side.

When consciousness returned to him, he looked up. The sky was shrouded in clouds, which a driving wind was blowing from the orb of the moon, while a few of her white rays gleamed sepulchrally on the weapons of the slaughtered soldiers.

The scattered senses of Thaddeus gradually returned to him. He was now lying, the only living creature amidst thousands of the dead who, the preceding night, had been, like himself, alive to all the consciousness of existence! His right hand rested on the pale face of his grandfather. It was wet with dew. He shuddered. Taking his own cloak from his shoulders, he laid it over the body. He would have said, as he did it, "So, my father, I would have sheltered thy life with my own!" but the words choked in his throat, and he sat watching by the corpse until the day dawned, and the Poles returned to bury their slain.

The wretched Thaddeus was discovered by a party of his own hussars seated on a little mound of earth, with the cold hand of Sobieski grasped in his. At this sight the soldiers uttered a cry of dismay and sorrow. Thaddeus rose up. "My friends," said he, "I thank God that you are come! Assist me to bear my dear grandfather to the camp."

Astonished at this composure, but distressed at the dreadful hue of his countenance, they obeyed him in mournful silence, and laid the remains of the palatine upon a bier, which they formed with their sheathed sabres; then gently raising it, they retrod their steps to the camp, leaving a detachment to accomplish the duty for which they had quitted it. Thaddeus, hardly able to support his weakened frame, mounted a horse and followed the melancholy procession.

General Wawrzecki, on whom the command had devolved, seeing the party returning so soon, and in such an order, sent an aid-de-camp to inquire the reason. He came back with dejection in his face, and informed his commander that the brave Palatine of Masovia, whom they supposed had been taken prisoner with his grandson and Kosciusko, was the occasion of this sudden return; that he had been killed, and his body was now approaching the lines on the arms of the soldiers. Wawrzecki, though glad to hear that Thaddeus was alive and at liberty, turned to conceal his tears; then calling out a guard, he marched at their head to meet the corpse of his illustrious friend.

The bier was carried into the general's tent. An aid-de-camp and some gentlemen of the faculty were ordered to attend Thaddeus to his quarters; but the young count, though scarcely able to stand, appeared to linger, and holding fast by the arm of an officer, he looked steadfastly on the body. Wawrzecki understood his hesitation. He pressed his hand. "Fear not, my dear sir," said he; "every honor shall be paid to the remains of your noble grandfather." Thaddeus bowed his head, and was supported out of the tent to his own.

His wounds, of which he had received several, were not deep; and might have been of little consequence, had not his thoughts continually hovered about his mother, and painted her affliction when she should be informed of the lamentable events of the last day's battle. These reflections, awake or in a slumber, (for he never slept,) possessed his mind, and, even whilst his wounds were healing, produced such an irritation in his blood as hourly threatened a fever.

Things were in this situation, when the surgeon put a letter from the countess into his hand. He opened it. and read with breathless anxietv these lines:

"To Thaddeus, Count Sobieski.

"Console yourself, my most precious son, console yourself for my sake. I have seen Colonel Lonza, and I have heard all the horrors which took place on the tenth of this month. I have heard them, and I am yet alive. I am resigned. He tells me you are wounded. Oh! do not let me be bereft of my son also! Remember that you were my dear sainted father's darling; remember that, as his representative, you are to be my consolation; in pity to me, if not to our suffering country, preserve yourself to be at least the last comfort Heaven's mercy hath spared to me. I find that all is lost to Poland as well as to myself! that when my glorious father fell, and his friend with him, even its name, as a country, became extinct. The allied invaders are in full march towards Masovia, and I am too weak to come to you. Let me see you soon, very soon, my beloved son. I beseech you to come to me. You will find me feebler in body than in mind; for there is a holy Comforter that descends on the bruised heart, which none other than the unhappy have conceived or felt. Farewell, my dear, dear Thaddeus! Let the memory that you have a mother check your too ardent courage. God forever guard you! Live for your mother, who has no stronger words to express her affection for you than she is thy mother—thy

"THERESE SOBIESKI.

"VILLANOW, *October*, 1794."

This letter was indeed a balm to the soul of Thaddeus. That his mother had received intelligence of the cruel event with such "holy resignation" was the best medicine that could now be applied to his wounds, both of mind and body; and when he was told that on the succeeding morning the body of his grandfather would be removed to the convent near Biala, he declared his resolution to attend it to the grave.

In vain his surgeons and General Wawrzecki remonstrated against the danger of this project; for once the gentle and yielding spirit of Thaddeus was inflexible. He had fixed his determination, and it was not to be shaken.

Next day, being the seventh from that in which the fatal battle had been decided, Thaddeus, at the first beat of the drum, rose from his pallet, and, almost unassisted, put on his clothes. His uniform being black, he needed no other index than his pale and mournful countenance to announce that he was chief mourner.

The procession began to form, and he walked from his tent. It was a fine morning. Thaddeus looked up, as if to upbraid the sun for shining so brightly. Lengthened and repeated rounds of cannon rolled along the air. The solemn march of the dead was moaning from the muffled drum, interrupted at measured pauses by the shrill tremor of the fife. The troops, preceded by their general, moved forward with a decent and melancholy step. The Bishop of Warsaw followed, bearing the sacred volume in his hands; and next, borne upon the crossed pikes of his soldiers, and supported by twelve of his veteran companions, appeared the body of the brave Sobieski. A velvet pall covered it, on which were laid those arms with which for fifty years he had asserted the loyal independence of his country. At this sight the sobs of the men became audible. Thaddeus followed with a slow but firm step, his eyes bent to the ground and his arms wrapped in his cloak; it was the same which had shaded his beloved grandfather from the dews of that dreadful night. Another train of solemn music succeeded; and then the squadrons which the deceased had commanded dismounted, and, leading their horses, closed the procession.

On the verge of the plain that borders Biala, and within a few paces of the convent gate of St. Francis, the bier stopped. The monks saluted its appearance with a requiem, which they continued to chant till the coffin was lowered into the ground. The earth received its sacred deposit. The anthems ceased; the soldiers, kneeling down, discharged their muskets over it; then, with streaming cheeks, rose and gave place to others. Nine volleys were fired, and the ranks fell back. The bishop advanced to the head of the grave. All was hushed. He raised his eyes to heaven; then, after a pause, in which he seemed to be communing with the regions above him, he turned to the silent assembly, and, in a voice collected and impressive, addressed them in a short but affecting oration, in which he set forth the brightness of Sobieski's life, his noble forgetfulness of self in the interests of his country, and the dauntless bravery which laid him in the dust. A general discharge of cannon was the awful response to this appeal. Wawrzecki took the sabre of the palatine, and, breaking it, dropped it into the grave. The aids-de-camp of the deceased did the same with theirs, showing that by so doing they resigned their offices; and then, covering their faces with their handkerchiefs, they turned away with the soldiers, who filed off. Thaddeus sunk on his knees. His hands were clasped, and his eyes for a few minutes fixed themselves on the coffin of his grandfather; then rising, he leaned on the arm of Wawrzecki, and with a tottering step and pallid countenance, mounted his horse, which had been led to the spot, and returned with the scattered procession to the camp.

The cause for exertion being over, his spirits fell with the rapidity of a spring too highly wound up, which snaps and runs down to immobility. He entered his tent and threw himself on the bed, from which he did not raise for the five following days.

CHAPTER IX.

THE LAST DAYS OF VILLANOW.

At a time when the effects of these sufferings and fatigues had brought his bodily strength to its lowest ebb, the young Count Sobieski was roused by information that the Russians had planted themselves before Praga, and were preparing to bombard the town. The intelligence nerved his heart's sinews again, and rallied the spirits, also, of his depressed soldiers, who energetically obeyed their commander to put themselves in readiness to march at set of sun.

Thaddeus saw that the decisive hour was pending. And as the moon rose, though hardly able to sit his noble charger, he refused the indulgence of a litter, determining that no illness, while he had any power to master its disabilities, should make him recede from his duty. The image of his mother, too, so near the threatened spot, rushed on his soul. In quick march he led on his troops. Devastation met them over the face of the country. Scared and houseless villagers were flying in every direction ; old men stood amongst the ashes of their homes, wailing to the pitying heavens, since man had none. Children and woman sat by the waysides, weeping over the last sustenance the wretched infants drew from the breasts of their perishing mothers.

Thaddeus shut his eyes on the scene.

"Oh, my country ! my country ! " exclaimed he ; "what are my personal griefs to thine ? It is your afflictions that barb me to the heart ! Look there," cried he to the soldiers, pointing to the miserable spectacles before him ; "look there, and carry vengeance into the breasts of their destroyers. Let Praga be the last act of this tragedy."

Unhappy young man ! unfortunate country ! It was indeed the last act of a tragedy to which all Europe were spectators—a tragedy which the nations witnessed without one attempt to stop or to delay its dreadful catastrophe ! Oh, how must virtue be lost when it is no longer a matter of policy even to assume it." *

After a long march through a dark and dismal night, the morning began to break ; and Thaddeus found himself on the southern side of that little river which divides the territories of Sobieski from the woods of Kobylka. Here, for the first time, he endured all the torturing varieties of despair.

The once fertile fields were burnt to stubble ; the cottages were yet smoking from the ravages of the fire ; and in place of smiling eyes and thankful lips coming to meet him, he beheld the dead bodies of his peasants stretched on the high roads,

* To answer this, we must remember that Europe was then no longer what she was a century before. Almost all her nations had turned from the doctrines of "sound things," and more or less drank deeply of the cup of infidelity, drugged for them by the flattering sophistries of Voltaire. The draught was inebriation, and the wild consequences burst asunder the responsibilities of man to man. The selfish principle ruled, and balance of justice was then seen only aloft in the heavens!

mangled, bleeding, and stripped of that decent covering which humanity would not deny to the vilest criminal.

Thaddeus could bear the sight no longer, but, setting spurs to his horse, fled from the contemplation of scenes which harrowed up his soul.

At nightfall, the army halted under the walls of Villanow. The count looked towards the windows of the palace, and by a light shining through the half-drawn curtains, distinguished his mother's room. He then turned his eye on that sweep of building which contained the palatine's apartments; but not one solitary lamp illumined its gloom: the moon alone glimmered on the battlements, silvering the painted glass of the study window, where, with that beloved parent, he had so lately gazed upon the stars, and anticipated with the most sanguine hopes the result of the campaign which had now terminated so disastrously for his unhappy country.

But these thoughts, with his grief and his forebodings, were buried in the depths of his determined heart. Addressing General Wawrzecki, he bade him welcome to Villanow, requesting at the same time that his men might be directed to rest till morning, and that he and the officers would take their refreshment within the palace.

As soon as Thaddeus had seen his guests seated at different tables in the eating-hall, and had given orders for the soldiers to be served from the buttery and cellars, he withdrew to seek the countess. He found her in her chamber, surrounded by the attendants who had just informed her of his arrival. The moment he appeared at the room door, the women went out at an opposite passage, and Thaddeus, with a bursting heart, threw himself on the bosom of his mother. They were silent for some time. Poignant recollection stopped their utterance; but neither tears nor sighs filled its place, until the countess, on whose soul the full tide of maternal affection pressed, and mingled with her grief, raised her head from her son's neck, and said, whilst she strained him in her arms, "Receive my thanks, O Father of mercy, for having spared to me this blessing!"

Thaddeus Sobieski (all that now remained of that beloved and honored name!) with a sacred emotion breathed a response to the address of his mother, and drying her tears with his kisses, dwelt upon the never-dying fame of his revered grandfather, upon his preferable lot to that of their brave friend Kosciusko, who was doomed not only to survive the liberty of his country, but to pass the residue of his life within the dungeons of his enemies. He then tried to reanimate her spirits with hope. He spoke of the approaching battle, without any doubt of the valor and desperation of the Poles rendering it successful. He talked of the resolution of their leader, General Wawrzecki, and of his own good faith in the justice of their cause. His discourse began in a wish to cheat her into tranquillity; but as he advanced on the subject, his soul took fire at its own warmth, and he half believed the probability of his anticipations.

The countess looked on the honorable glow which crimsoned his harassed features with a pang at her heart.

"My heroic son!" cried she, "my darling Thaddeus! what a vast price do I pay for all this excellence! I could not love you were you otherwise than what you are; and being what you are, oh, how soon may I lose you! Already has your noble grandfather paid the debt which he owed to his glory. He promised to fall with Poland; he has kept his word; and now, all that I love on earth is concentrated in you." The countess paused, and pressing his hand almost wildly on her heart, she continued in a hurried voice, "The same spirit is in your breast; the same principle binds you; and I may be at last left alone. Heaven have pity on me!"

She cast her eyes upward as she ended. Thaddeus, sinking on his knees by her side, implored her with all the earnestness of piety and confidence to take comfort. The countess embraced him with a forced smile. "You must forgive me, Thaddeus; I have nothing of the soldier in my heart: it is all woman. But I will not detain you longer from the rest you require; go to your room, and try and recruit yourself for the dangers to-morrow will bring forth. I shall employ the night in prayers for your safety."

Consoled to see any composure in his mother, he withdrew, and after having heard that his numerous guests were properly lodged, went to his own chamber.

Next morning at sunrise the troops prepared to march. General Wawrzecki, with his officers, begged permission to pay their personal graditude to the countess for the hospitality of her reception; but she declined the honor, on the plea of indisposition. In the course of an hour, her son appeared from her apartment and joined the general.

The soldiers filed off through the gates, crossed the bridge, and halted under the walls of Praga. The lines of the camp were drawn and fortified before evening, at which time they found leisure to observe the enemy's strength.

Russia seemed to have exhausted her wide regions to people the narrow shores of the Vistula; from east to west, as far as the eye could reach, her arms were stretched to the horizon. Sobieski looked at them, and then on the handful of intrepid hearts contained in the small circumference of the Polish camp. Sighing heavily, he retired into his tent; and vainly seeking repose, mixed his short and startled slumbers with frequent prayers for the preservation of these last victims to their country.

The hours appeared to stand still. Several times he rose from his bed and went to the door, to see whether the clouds were tinged with any appearance of dawn. All continued dark. He again returned to his marquée, and standing by the lamp which was nearly exhausted, took out his watch, and tried to distinguish the points; but finding that the light burned too feebly, he was pressing the repeating spring, which struck five, when the report of a single musket made him start.

He flew to his tent door, and looking around, saw that all near his quarter was at rest. Suspecting it to be a signal of the enemy, he hurried towards the intrenchments, but found the sentinels in perfect security from any fears respecting the sound, as they supposed it to have proceeded from the town.

Sobieski paid little attention to their opinions, but ascending the nearest bastion to take a wider survey, in a few minutes he discerned, though obscurely, through the gleams of morning, what appeared to be the whole host of Russia advancing in profound silence towards the Polish lines. The instant he made this discovery, he came down, and lost no time in giving orders for the defence; then flying to other parts of the camp, he awakened the commander-in-chief, encouraged the men, and saw that the whole encampment was not only in motion, but prepared for the assault.

In consequence of these prompt arrangements, the assailants were received with a cross-fire of the batteries, and case-shot and musketry from several redoubts, which raked their flanks as they advanced. But in defiance of this shower of bullets, they pressed on with an intrepidity worthy of a better cause, and overleaping the ditch by squadrons, entered the camp. A passage once secured, the Cossacks rushed in by thousands, and spreading themselves in front of the storming party, put every soul to the spear who opposed them.

The Polish works being gained, the enemy turned the cannon on its former masters, and as they rallied to the defence of what remained, swept them down by whole regiments. The noise of artillery thundered from all sides of the camp; the smoke was so great, that it was hardly possible to distinguish friends from foes; nevertheless, the spirits of the Poles flagged not a moment; as fast as one rampart was wrested from them, they threw themselves within another, which was as speedily taken by the help of hurdles, fascines, ladders, and a courage as resistless as it was ferocious, merciless, and sanguinary. Every spot of vantage position was at length lost; and yet the Poles fought like lions; quarter was neither offered to them nor required; they disputed every inch of ground, until they fell upon it in heaps, some lying before the parapets, others filling the ditches and the rest covering the earth, for the enemy to tread on as they cut their passage to the heart of the camp.

Sobieski, almost maddened by the scene, dripping with his own blood and that of his brave friends, was seen in every part of the action; he was in the fosse, defending the trampled bodies of the dying; he was on the dyke, animating the few who survived. Wawrzecki was wounded, and every hope hung upon Thaddeus. His presence and voice infused new energy into the arms of his fainting countrymen; they kept close to his side, until the victors, enraged at the dauntless intrepidity of this young hero, uttered the most fearful imprecations, and rushing on his little phalanx, attacked it with redoubled numbers and fury.

Sobieski sustained the shock with firmness; but wherever he turned his eyes, they were blasted with some object which made them recoil; he beheld his companions and his soldiers strewing the earth, and their triumphant adversaries mounting their dying bodies, as they hastened with loud huzzas to the destruction of Praga, whose gates were now burst open. His eyes grew dim at the sight, and at the very moment in which he tore them from spectacles so deadly to his heart, a Livonian officer struck him with a sabre, to all appearance dead upon the field.

When he recovered from the blow, (which, having lit on the steel of his cap, had only stunned him,) he looked around, and found that all near him was quiet; but a far different scene presented itself from the town. The roar of cannon and the bursting of bombs thundered through the air, which was rendered livid and tremendous by long spires of fire streaming from the burning houses, and mingling with the volumes of smoke which rolled from the guns. The dreadful tocsin, and the hurrahs of the victors, pierced the soul of Thaddeus. Springing from the ground, he was preparing to rush towards the gates, when loud cries of distress issued from within. They were burst open, and a moment after, the grand magazine blew up with a horrible explosion.

In an instant the field before Praga was filled with women and children, flying in all directions, and rending the sky with their shrieks. "Father Almighty!" cried Thaddeus, wringing his hands, "canst thou suffer this?" Whilst he yet spake, some straggling Cossacks near the town, who were prowling about, glutted, but not sated with blood, seized the poor fugitives, and with a ferocity as wanton as unmanly, released them at once from life and misery.

This hideous spectacle brought his mother's defenceless state before the eyes of Sobieski. Her palace was only four miles distant; and whilst the barbarous avidity of the enemy was too busily engaged in sacking the place to permit them to perceive a solitary individual hurrying away amidst heaps of dead bodies, he flew across the desolated meadows which intervened between Praga and Villanow.

Thaddeus was met at the gate of his palace by General Butzou, who, having learned the fate of Praga from the noise and flames in that quarter, anticipated the arrival of some part of the victorious army before the walls of Villanow. When its young count, with a breaking heart, crossed the drawbridge, he saw that the worthy veteran had prepared everything for a stout resistance; the ramparts were lined with soldiers, and well mounted with artillery.

"Here, thou still honored Sobieski," cried he, as he conducted Thaddeus to the keep; "let the worst happen, here I am resolved to dispute the possession of your grandfather's palace until I have not a man to stand by me!" *

Thaddeus strained him in silence to his breast; and after examining the force and dispositions, he approved all with a cold despair of their being of any effectual use, and went to the apartments of his mother.

The countess's women, who met him in the vestibule, begged him to be careful how he entered her excellency's room, for she had only just recovered from a swoon, occasioned by alarm at hearing the cannonade against the Polish camp. Her son waited for no more, but not hearing their caution, threw open the door of the chamber, and hastening to his mother's couch, cast himself into her arms. She clung round his neck, and for a while joy stopped her respiration. Bursting into tears, she wept over him, incapable of expressing by words her

* It was little more than just a century before this awful scene took place that the invincible John Sobieski, King of Poland, acting upon the old mutually protecting principles of Christendom, saved the freedom and the faith of Christian Europe from the Turkish yoke. And in this very mansion he passed his latter years in honored peace. He died in 1694—a remarkable coincidence, the division of Poland occurring in 1794.

tumultuous gratitude at again beholding him alive. He looked on her altered and pallid features.

"O! my mother," cried he clasping her to his breast; "you are ill; and what will become of you?"

"My beloved son!" replied she kissing his forehead through the clotted blood that oozed from a cut on his temple; "my beloved son, before our cruel murderers can arrive, I shall have found a refuge in the bosom of my God."

Thaddeus could only answer with a groan. She resumed. "Give me your hand. I must not witness the grandson of Sobieski given up to despair; let your mother incite you to resignation. You see I have not breathed a complaining word, although I behold you covered with wounds." As she spoke, her eye pointed to the sash and handkerchief which were bound round his thigh and arm. "Our separation will not be long; a few short years, perhaps hours, may unite us forever in a better world."

The count was still speechless; he could only press her hand to his lips. After a pause, she proceeded—

"Look up, my dear boy! and attend to me. Should Poland become the property of other nations, I conjure you, if you survive its fall, to leave it. When reduced to captivity, it will no longer be an asylum for a man of honor. I beseech you, should this happen, go that very hour to England: that is a free country; and I have been told that the people are kind to the unfortunate. Perhaps you will find that Pembroke Somerset hath not quite forgotten Poland. Thaddeus! Why do you delay to answer me? Remember, these are your mother's dying words!"

"I will obey them, my mother!"

"Then," continued she, taking from her bosom a small miniature, "let me tie this round your neck. It is the portrait of your father." Thaddeus bent his head, and the countess fastened it under his neck-cloth. "Prize this gift, my child; it is likely to be all that you will now inherit either from me or that father. Try to forget his injustice, my dear son; and in memory of me, never part with that picture. O, Thaddeus! From the moment in which I first received it until this instant, it has never been from my heart!"

"And it shall never leave mine," answered he, in a stifled voice, "whilst I have being."

The countess was preparing to reply, when a sudden volley of firearms made Thaddeus spring upon his feet. Loud cries succeeded. Women rushed into the apartment, screaming,

"The ramparts are stormed!" and the next moment that quarter of the building rocked to its foundation. The countess clung to the bosom of her son. Thaddeus clasped her close to his breast, and casting up his petitioning eyes to heaven, cried, "Shield of the desolate! grant me a shelter for my mother!"

Another burst of cannon was followed by a heavy crash, and the most piercing shrieks echoed through the palace. "All is lost!" cried a soldier, who appeared for an instant at the room door, and then vanished.

Thaddeus, overwhelmed with despair, grasped his sword, which had fallen to the ground, and crying, "My mother, we will die together!" would have given her one last and assuring embrace, when his eyes met the sight of her before-agitated features tranquillized in death. She fell from his palsied arms back on the couch, and he stood gazing on her as if struck by a power which had benumbed all his faculties.

The tumult in the palace increased every moment; but he heard it not, until Butzou, followed by two or three of his soldiers, ran into the apartment, calling out "Count, save yourself!"

Sobieski still remained motionless. The general caught him by the arm, and instantly covering the body of the deceased countess with the mantle of her son, hurried his unconscious steps, by an opposite door, through the state chambers into the gardens.

Thaddeus did not recover his recollection until he reached the outward gate; then, breaking from the hold of his friend, was returning to the sorrowful scene he had left, when Butzou, aware of his intentions, just stopped him in time to prevent his rushing on the bayonets of a party of the enemy's infantry, who were pursuing them at full speed.

The count now rallied his distracted faculties, and making a stand, with the general and his three Poles, they compelled this merciless detachment to seek refuge among the arcades of the building.

Butzon would not allow his young lord to follow in that direction, but hurried him across the park. He looked back, however; a column of fire issued from the south towers. Thaddeus sighed, as if his life were in that sigh, "All is indeed over;" and pressing his hand to his forehead, in that attitude followed the steps of the general towards the Vistula.

The wind being very high, the flame soon spread itself over the roof of the palace, and catching at every combustible in its way, the invaders became so terrified at the quick progress of a fire which threatened to consume themselves as well as their plunder, that they quitted the spot with precipitation. Descrying the count and his soldiers at a short distance, they directed their motions to that point. Speedily confronting the brave fugitives, they blocked up a bridge by a file of men with fixed pikes, and not only menaced the Polanders as they advanced, but derided their means of resistance.

Sobieski, indifferent alike to danger and to insults, stopped short to the left, and followed by his friends, plunged into the stream, amidst a shower of musket-balls from the enemy. After hard buffeting with the torrent, he at last reached the opposite bank, and was assisted from the river by some of the weeping inhabitants of Warsaw, who had been watching the expiring ashes of Praga, and the flames then devouring the boasted towers of Villanow.

Emerged from the water, Thaddeus stood to regain his breath; and leaning on the shoulder of Butzou, he pointed to his burning palace with a smile of agony. "See," said he, "what a funeral pile Heaven has given to the manes of my unburied mother!"

The general did not speak, for grief stopped his utterance; but motioning the two soldiers to proceed, he supported the count into the citadel.

CHAPTER X.

SOBIESKI S DEPARTURE FROM WARSAW.

From the termination of this awful day, in which a brave and hitherto powerful people were consigned to an abject dependence, Thaddeus was confined to his apartment in the garrison.

It was now the latter end of November. General Butzou, supposing that the illness of his young lord might continue some weeks, and aware that no time ought to be lost in maintaining all that was yet left of the kingdom of Poland, obtained his permission to seek its only remaining quarter. Quitting Warsaw, he joined Prince Poniatowski, who was yet at the head of a few troops near Sachoryn, supported by the undaunted Niemcivitz, the bard and the hero, who had fought by the side of the then imprisoned Kosciusko in the last battle in which that general fell.*

Meanwhile the young count, finding himself tolerably restored, except in those wounds of the heart which time only can heal, was enabled to leave his room, and breathe the fresh air on the ramparts. His appearance was greeted by the officers with melancholy congratulations; but their replies to his anxious questions displaced the faint smile which he tried to spread over his countenance, and with a contracted brow he listened to the following information:—

"Praga was not only razed to the ground, but upwards of three thousand persons had perished by the sword, the river, and the flames. All the horrors of Ismail had been re-enacted by its conqueror on the banks of the Vistula. The citizens of Warsaw, intimidated by such a spectacle, assembled in a body, and, driven to desperation, repaired to the foot of the throne. On their knees they implored his majesty to forget the contested rights of his subjects, and in pity to their wives and children, allow them, by a timely submission, to save those dear relatives from the ignominy and cruelty which had been wreaked upon the inhabitants of Praga. Stanislaus saw that opposition would be fruitless. The walls of his capital were already surrounded by a train of artillery, ready to blow the town to atoms; the fate of Poland seemed inevitable, and with a deep sigh, the king assented to the petition, and sent deputies to the enemy's camp.

"General Suwarrow, the commander-in-chief," continued the officer, "demands that every man in Warsaw shall not only surrender his arms, but sue for pardon for the past. This is his reply to the submission of the king, and these conditions are accepted."

"They never shall be by me," said Sobieski; and turning from his informer, hardly knowing what were his intentions, he walked towards the royal palace.

When his majesty was apprised that the young Count Sobieski awaited his commands in the audience-chamber, he left his closet and entered the room. Thaddeus, with a swelling

* Niemcivitz had been a fellow collegian with Kosciusko. But being of a more literary disposition, his pen rather than his sword took part in the early struggles between Poland and her enemies; and in this light he was regarded as the *Tyrtæus* of his country. But at length he joined the army in person, and, as above noticed, fought in some of the decisive fields of Poland. In one of these, he also was taken prisoner, and put into the same prison with the friend of his youth, the severely-wounded General Kosciusko. When the Emperor Paul, on his succession to the imperial throne, generously, and with signal marks of respect, released the captive chief, the liberty of Niemcivitz was likewsie given to him. And both together shortly afterwards proceeded to the United States, on a warm invitation from the President. They took England, for a brief visit, on their way.

heart, would have thrown himself on his knee, but the king prevented him, and pressed him with emotion in his arms.

"Brave young man!" cried he, "I embrace in you the last of those Polish youth who were so lately the brightest jewels in my crown."

Tears stood in the monarch's eyes while he spoke. Sobieski, with hardly a steadier utterance, answered, "I come to receive your majesty's commands. I will obey them in all things but in surrendering this sword (which was my grandfather's) into the hands of your enemies."

"I will not desire it," replied Stanislaus. "By my acquiescence with the terms of Russia, I only comply with the earnest petitions of my people. I shall not require of you to compromise your country; but alas! you must not throw away your life in a now hopeless cause. Fate has consigned Poland to subjection; and when Heaven, in its mysterious decrees, confirms the chastisement of nations, it is man's duty to submit. For myself, I am to bury my griefs and indignities in the castle of Grodno."

The blood rushed over the cheek of Thaddeus at this declaration, to which the proud indignation of his soul could in no way subscribe, and with an agitated voice he exclaimed, "If my sovereign be already at the command of our oppressors, then indeed is Poland no more! and I have nothing to do but to perform the dying will of my mother. Will your majesty grant me permission to set off for England, before I may be obliged to witness the last calamity of my wretched country?"

"I would to Heaven," replied the king, "that I, too, might repose my age and sorrows in that happy kingdom! Go, Sobieski; your name is worthy of such an asylum; my prayers and blessings shall follow you."

Thaddeus pressed his hand in silence to his lips.

"Believe me, my dear count," continued Stanislaus, "my soul bleeds at this parting. I know the treasure which your family has always been to this nation; I know your own individual merit. I know the wealth which you have sacrificed for me and my subjects, and I am powerless to express my gratitude."

"Had I done more than my duty in that," replied Thaddeus, "such words from your majesty would have been a reward adequate to any privation; but, alas! no. I have perhaps performed less than my duty; the blood of Sobieski ought not to have been spared one drop when the liberties of his country perished!" Thaddeus blushed while he spoke, and almost repented the too ready zeal of his friends in having saved him from the general destruction at Villanow.

The voice of the venerable Stanislaus became fainter as he resumed—

"Perhaps had a Sobieski reigned at this time, these horrors might not have been accomplished. That resistless power which has overwhelmed my people, I cannot forget is the same that put the sceptre into my hand. But Catherine misunderstood my principles, when assisting in my election to the throne; she thought she was planting merely her own viceroy there. But I could not obliterate from my heart that my ancestors, like your own, were hereditary sovereigns of Poland, nor cease to feel the stamp the King of kings had graven upon that heart —to uphold the just laws of my fathers! and, to the utmost, I have struggled to fulfil my trust."

"Yes, my sovereign," replied Thaddeus; "and whilst there remains one man on earth who has drawn his first breath in Poland, he will bear witness in all the lands through which he may be doomed to wander that he has received from you the care and affection of a father. O! sire, how will future ages believe that, in the midst of civilized Europe, a brave people and a virtuous monarch were suffered, unaided, and even without remonstrance, to fall into the grasp of usurpation!—nay, of annihilation of their name!"

Stanislaus laid his hand on the arm of the count.

"Man's ambition and baseness," said the king, "are monstrous to the contemplation of youth only. You are learning your lesson early; I have studied mine for many years, and with a bitterness of soul which in some measure prepared me for the completion. My kingdom has passed from me at the moment you have lost your country. Before we part forever, my dear Sobieski, take with you this assurance—you have served the unfortunate Stanislaus to the latest hour in which you beheld him. That which you have just said, expressive of the sentiments of those who were my subjects, is indeed a balm to my heart, and I will carry its consolations to my prison."

The king paused. Sobieski, agitated, and incapable of speaking, threw himself at his majesty's feet, and pressed his hand with fervency and anguish to his lips. The king looked down on his graceful figure, and pierced to the soul by the more graceful feelings which dictated the action, the tear which stood in his eye, rolled over his cheek, and was followed by another before he could add—

"Rise, my young friend. Take from me this ring. It contains my picture. Wear it in remembrance of a man who loves you, and who can never forget your worth or the loyalty and patriotism of your house."

The Chancellor Zamoyisko at that moment being announced, Thaddeus rose from his knee, and was preparing to leave the room, when his majesty, perceiving his intention, desired him to stop.

"Stay, count!" cried he, "I will burden you with one request. I am now a king without a crown, without subjects, without a foot of land in which to bury me when I die. I cannot reward the fidelity of any one of the few friends of whom my enemies have not deprived me; but you are young, and Heaven may yet smile upon you in some distant nation. Will you pay a debt of gratitude for your poor sovereign? Should you ever again meet with the good old Butzou, who rescued me when my preservation lay on the fortune of a moment, remember that I regard him as once the saviour of my life! I was told to-day that on the destruction of Praga this brave man joined the army of my brother. It is now disbanded, and he, with the rest of my faithful soldiers, is cast forth in his old age, a wanderer in a pitiless world. Should you ever meet him, Sobieski, succor him for my sake."

"As Heaven may succor me!" cried Thaddeus; and putting his majesty's hand a second time to his lips, he bowed to the chancellor and passed into the street.

When the count returned to the citadel, he found that all was as the king had represented. The soldiers in the garrison were reluctantly preparing to give up their arms; and the nobles, in compassion to the cries of the people, were trying to humble their necks to the yoke of the dictator. The magistrates lingered as they went to take the city keys from the hands of their good king, and with sad whispers anticipated the moment in which they must surrender them, and their laws and national existence, to the jealous dominion of three despotic foreign powers.

Poland was now no place for Sobieski. He had survived all his kindred. He had survived the liberties of his country. He had seen the king a prisoner, and his countrymen trampled on by deceit and usurpation. As he walked on, musing over these circumstances, he met with little interruption, for the streets were deserted. Here and there a poor miserable wretch passed him, who seemed, by his wan cheeks and haggard eyes, already to repent the too successful prayers of the deputation.

The shops were shut. Thaddeus stopped a few minutes in the great square, which used to be crowded with happy citizens, but now, not one man was to be seen. An awful and painful silence reigned over all. His soul felt too truly the dread consciousness of this utter annihilation of his country, for him to throw off the heavy load from his oppressed heart, in this his last walk down the east street towards the ramparts which covered the Vistula.

He turned his eyes to the spot where once stood the magnificent towers of his paternal palace.

"Yes," cried he, "it is now time for me to obey the last command of my mother! Nothing remains of Poland but its soil—nothing of my home but its ashes!"

The victors had pitched a detachment of tents amidst the ruins of Villanow, and were at this moment busying themselves in searching amongst the stupendous fragments for what plunder the fire might have spared.

"Insatiate robbers!" exclaimed Thaddeus; "Heaven will requite this sacrilege." He thought on his mother, who lay beneath the ruins, and tore himself from the sight, whilst he added, "Farewell! forever farewell! thou beloved, revered Villanow, where I was reared in bliss and tenderness! I quit thee and my country forever!" As he spoke, he raised his hands and eyes to heaven, and pressing the picture his mother had given him to his lips and bosom, turned from the parapet, determining to prepare that night for his departure the next morning.

He arose by daybreak, and having gathered together all his little wealth, the whole of which was compressed within the portmanteau that was buckled on his gallant horse, precisely two hours before the triumphal car of General Suwarrow entered Warsaw, Sobieski left it. As he rode along the streets, he bedewed its stones with his tears. They were the first that he had shed during the long series of his misfortunes, and they now flowed so fast, that he could hardly discern his way out of the city.

At the great gate his horse stopped, and neighed with a strange sound.

"Poor Saladin!" cried Thaddeus, stroking his neck; "are you so sorry at leaving Warsaw that, like your unhappy master, you linger to take a last lamenting look!"

His tears redoubled; and the warder, as he closed the gate after him, implored permission to kiss the hand of the noble Count Sobieski, ere he should turn his back on Poland, never to return. Thaddeus looked kindly round, and shaking hands with the honest man, after saying a few friendly words to him, rode on with a loitering pace, until he reached that part of the river which divides Masovia from the Prussian dominions.

Here he flung himself off his horse, and standing for a moment on the hill that rises near the bridge, retraced, with his almost blinded sight, the long and desolated lands through which he had passed; then involuntarily dropping on his knees, he plucked a tuft of grass, and pressing it to his lips, exclaimed, "Farewell, Poland! Farewell all my earthly happiness!"

Almost stifled by emotion, he put this poor relic of his country into his bosom, and remounting his noble animal, crossed the bridge.

As one who, flying from any particular object, thinks to lose himself and his sorrows when it lessens to his view, Sobieski pursued the remainder of his journey with a speed which soon brought him to Dantzic.

Here he remained a few days, and during that interval the firmness of his mind was restored. He felt a calm arising from the conviction that his afflictions had gained their summit, and that, however heavy they were, Heaven had laid them on him for a trial of his faith and virtue. Under this belief, he ceased to weep; but he never was seen to smile.

Having entered into an agreement with the master of a vessel to carry him across the sea, he found the strength of his finances would barely defray the charges of the voyage. Considering this circumstance, he saw the impossibility of taking his horse to England.

The first time this idea presented itself, it almost overset his determined resignation. Tears would again have started into his eyes, had he not by force repelled them.

"To part from my faithful Saladin," said he to himself, "that has borne me since I first could use a sword; that has carried me through so many dangers, and has come with me even into exile—it is painful, it is ungrateful!" He was in the stable when this thought assailed him; and as the reflections followed each other, he again turned to the stall. "But, my poor fellow, I will not barter your services for gold. I will seek for some master who may be kind to you, in pity to my misfortunes."

He re-entered the hotel where he lodged, and calling a waiter, inquired who occupied the fine mansion and park on the east of the town. The man replied, "Mr. Hopetown, an eminent British merchant, who has been settled at Dantzic above forty years."

"I am glad he is a Briton!" was the sentiment which succeeded this information in the count's mind. He immediately took his resolution, but hardly had prepared to put it into execution, when he received a summons from the vessel to be on board in half an hour, the wind having set fair.

Thaddeus, somewhat disconcerted by this hasty call, with an agitated hand wrote the following letter:—

"To John Hopetown, Esq.

"Sir,

"A Polish officer, who has sacrificed everything but his honor to the last interests of his country, now addresses you.

"You are a Briton; and of whom can an unhappy victim to the cause of loyalty and freedom with less debasement solicit an obligation?

"I cannot afford support to the fine animal which has carried me through the battles of this fatal war; I disdain to sell him, and therefore I implore you, by the respect that you pay to the memory of your ancestors, who struggled for and retained that liberty in defence of which we are thus reduced—I implore you to give him an asylum in your park, and to protect him from injurious usage.

"Perform this benevolent action, sir, and you shall ever be remembered with gratitude by an unfortunate

"Polander.

"Dantzic, *November*, 1794."

The count, having sealed and directed this letter, went to the hotel yard, and ordered that his horse might be brought out. A few days of rest had restored him to his former mettle, and he appeared from the stable prancing and pawing the earth, as he used to do when Thaddeus was about to mount him for the field.

The groom was striving in vain to restrain the spirit of the animal, when the count took hold of the bridle. The noble creature knew his master, and became gentle as a lamb. After stroking him to or three times, with a bursting heart Thaddeus returned the reins to the man's hand, and at the same time gave him a letter.

"There," said he; "take that note and the horse directly to the house of Mr. Hopetown. Leave them, for the letter requires no answer."

This last pang mastered, he walked out of the yard towards the quay. The wind continuing fair, he entered the ship, and within an hour set sail for England.

CHAPTER XI.

THE BALTIC.

SOBIESKI passed the greater part of each day and the whole of every night on the deck of the vessel. He was too much absorbed in himself to receive any amusement from the passengers, who, observing his melancholy, thought to dispel it by their company and conversation.

When any of these people came upon deck, he walked to the head of the ship, took his seat upon the cable which bound the anchor to the forecastle, and while their fears rendered him safe from their well-meant persecution, he gained some respite from vexation, though none from misery.

The ship having passed through the Baltic, and entered on the British sea, the passengers, running from side to side of the vessels, pointed out to Thaddeus the distant shore of England, lying like a hazy ridge along the horizon. The happy people, whilst they strained their eyes through glasses, desired him to observe different spots on the hardly-perceptible line which they called Flamborough Head and the hills of Yorkshire. His heart turned sick at these objects of their delight, for not one of them raised an answering feeling in his breast. England could be nothing to him ; if anything, it would prove a desert, which contained no one object for his regrets or wishes.

The image of Pembroke Somerset, indeed, rose in his mind, like the dim recollection of one who has been a long time dead. Whilst they were together at Villanow, they regarded each other warmly, and when they parted they promised to correspond. One day, in pursuit of the enemy, Thaddeus was so unlucky as to lose the pocket-book which contained his friend's address ; but yet, uneasy at his silence, he ventured two letters to him, directed merely at Sir Robert Somerset's, England. To these he received no answer ; and the palatine evinced so just a displeasure at such marked neglect and ingratitude, that he would not suffer him to be mentioned in his presence, and indeed Thaddeus, from disappointment and regret, felt no inclination to transgress the command.

When the young count, during the prominent interests of the late disastrous ca[illegible]mbered these things, he found little comfort in recollecting the name of his young English guest; and now that he was visiting England as a poor exile, with indignation and grief he gave up the wish with the hope of meeting Mr. Somerset. Sensible that Somerset had not acted as became the man to whom he could apply in his distress, he resolved, unfriended as he was, to wipe him at once from his memory. With a bitter sigh he turned his back on the land to which he was going, and fixed his eyes on the tract of sea which then divided him from all that he had ever loved, or had given him true happiness.

"Father of mercy!" murmured he, in a suppressed voice, "what have I done to deserve this misery? Why have I been at one stroke deprived of all that rendered existence estimable? Two months ago, I had a mother, a more than father, to love and cherish me; I had a country, that looked up to them and to me with veneration and confidence. Now, I am bereft of all. I have neither father, mother, nor country, but I am going to a land of utter strangers."

Such impatient adjurations were never wrung from Sobieski by the anguish of sudden torture without his ingenuous and pious mind reproaching itself for such faithless repining. His soul was soft as a woman's; but it knew neither effeminacy nor despair. Whilst his heart bled, his countenance retained its serenity. Whilst affliction crushed him to the earth, and nature paid a few hard-wrung drops to his repeated bereavements, he contemned his tears, and raised his fixed and confiding eye to that Power which poured down its tempests on his head. Thaddeus felt as a man, but received consolation as a Christian.

When his ship arrived at the mouth of the Thames, the eagerness of the passengers increased to such an excess that they would not stand still, nor be silent a moment; and when the vessel, under full sail, passed Sheerness, and the dome of St. Paul's appeared before them, their exclamations were loud and incessant. "My home! my parents! my wife! my friends!" were the burden of every tongue.

Thaddeus found his calmed spirits again disturbed; and, rising from his seat, he retired unobserved by the people, who were too happy to attend to anything which did not agree with their own transports. The cabin was as deserted as himself. Feeling that there is no solitude like that of the heart, when it looks around and sees in the vast concourse of human beings not one to whom it can pour forth its sorrows, or receive the answering sigh of sympathy, he threw himself on one of the lockers, and with difficulty restrained the tears from gushing from his eyes. He held his hand over them, while he contemned himself for a weakness so unbecoming his manhood.

He despised himself: but let not others despise him. It is difficult for those who lie morning and evening in the lap of domestic indulgence to conceive the misery of being thrown out into a bleak and merciless world; it is impossible for the happy man, surrounded by luxury and gay companions, to figure to himself the reflections of a fellow-creature who, having been fostered in the bosom of affection and elegance, is cast at once from all society, bereft of home, of comfort, of "every stay, save innocence and Heaven." None but the wretched can imagine what the wretched endure from actual distress, from apprehended misfortune, from outraged feelings, and ten thousand nameless sensibilities to offence which only the unfortunate can conceive, dread and experience. But what is it o be not only without a home, but without a country? Thaddeus unconsciously uttered a groan like that of death.

The noise redoubled above his head, and in a few minutes afterwards one of the sailors came rumbling down the stairs.

"Will it please your honor," said he, "to get up? That be my chest, and I want my clothes to clean myself before I go on shore. Mother I know be waiting me at Blackwall."

Thaddeus rose, and with a withered heart again ascended to the deck.

On coming up the hatchway, he saw that the ship was moored in the midst of a large city, and was surrounded by myriads of vessels from every quarter of the globe. He leaned over the railing, and in silence looked down on the other passengers, who where bearing off in boats, and shaking hands with the people who came to receive them.

"It is near dark, sir," said the captain; "mayhap you would wish to go on shore? There is a boat just come round, and the tide won't serve much longer: and as your friends don't seem to be coming for you, you are welcome to a place in it with me."

The count thanked him; and after defraying the expenses of the voyage, and giving money amongst the sailors, he desired that his portmanteau might be put into the wherry. The honest fellows, in gratitude to the bounty of their passenger, struggled who should obey his commands, when the skipper, angry at being detained, snatched away the baggage, and flinging it into the boat, leaped in after it, and was followed by Thaddeus.

The taciturnity of the seamen and the deep melancholy of his guest were not broken until they reached the Tower stairs.

"Go, Ben, fetch the gentleman a coach."

The count bowed to the captain, who gave the order, and in a few minutes the boy returned, saying there was one in waiting. He took up the portmanteau, and Thaddeus, following him, ascended the Tower stairs, where the carriage stood. Ben threw in the baggage and the count put his foot on the step.

"Where must the man drive to?"

Thaddeus drew it back again.

"Yes, sir," continued the lad; "where be your honor's home?"

"In my grave," was the response his aching heart made to this question. He hesitated before he spoke. "An hotel," said he, flinging himself on the seat, and throwing a piece of silver into the lad's hat.

"What hotel, sir?" asked the coachman.

"Any."

The man closed the door, mounted his box, and drove off.

It was now near seven o'clock, on a dark December evening. The lamps were lighted; and it being Saturday-night, the streets were crowded with people. Thaddeus looked at them as he was driven along. "Happy creatures!" thought he; "you have each a home to go to; you have each expectant friends to welcome you; every one of you knows some in the world who will smile when you enter; whilst I, wretched, wretched Sobieski where are now all thy highly-prized treasures, thy boasted glory, and those beloved ones who rendered that glory most precious to thee? Alas! all are withdrawn; vanished like a scene of enchantment, from which I have indeed awakened to a frightful solitude."

His reflections were broken by the stopping of the carriage. The man opened the door.

"Sir, I have brought you to the Hummums, Covent Garden; it has as good accommodations as any in the town. My fare is five shillings.

Thaddeus paid the amount, and followed him and his baggage into the coffee-room. At the entrance of a man of his figure, several waiters presented themselves, begging to know his commands.

"I want a chamber."

He was ushered into a very handsome dining-room, where one of them laid down the portmanteau, and then bowing low, inquired whether he had dined.

The waiter having received his orders, (for the count saw that it was necessary to call for something,) hastened into the kitchen to communicate them to the cook.

"Upon my word, Betty," cried he, "you must do your best to-night; for the chicken is for the finest-looking fellow you ever set eyes on. By Jove, I believe him to be some Russian nobleman; perhaps the great Suwarrow himself! and he speaks English as well as I do myself."

"A prince, you mean, Jenkins!" said a pretty girl who entered at that moment. "Since I was borne I never see'd any English lord walk up and down the room with such an air; he looks like a king. For my part, I should not wonder if he is one of them there emigrant kings, for they say there is a power of them now wandering about the world."

"You talk like a fool, Sally," cried the sapient waiter. "Don't you see that his dress is military? Look at his black cap, with its long bag and great feather, and the monstrous sword at his side; look at them, and then if you can, say I am mistaken in deciding that he is some great Russian commander, —most likely come over as ambassador!"

"But he came in a hackney-coach," cried a little dirty boy in the corner. "As I was running up stairs with Colonel Leson's shoes, I see'd the coachman bring in his portmanteau."

"Well, Jack-a-napes, what of that?" cried Jenkins; "is a nobleman always to carry his equipage about him, like a snail with its shell on its back? To be sure, this foreign lord, or prince, is only come to stay here till his own house is fit for him. I will be civil to him."

"And so will I, Jenkins," rejoined Sally, smiling; "for I never see'd such handsome blue eyes in my born days; and they turned so sweet on me, and he spoke so kindly when he bade me stir the fire; and when he sat down by it, and throwed off his great fur cloak, I see'd a glittering star on his breast, and a figure so noble, that indeed, cook, I do verily believe he is, as Jenkins says, an enthroned king!"

"You and Jenkins be a pair of fools,"cried the cook, who, without noticing their description, had been sulkily basting the fowl. "I will be sworn he's just such another king as that palavering rogue was a French duke who got my master's watch and pawned it! As for you, Sally, you had better beware of hunting after foreign men-folk: it's not seemly for a young woman, and you may chance to rue it."

The moralizing cook had now brought the whole kitchen on her shoulders. The men abused her for a surly old maid, and the women tittered, whilst they seconded her censure by cutting sly jokes on the blushing face of poor Sally, who stood almost crying by the side of her champion, Jenkins.

Whilst this hubbub was going forward below stairs, its unconscious subject was, as Sally had described, sitting in a chair close to the fire, with his feet on the fender, his arms folded, and his eyes bent on the flames. He mused; but his ideas followed each other in such quick confused succession, it hardly could be said he thought of anything.

The entrance of dinner roused him from his reverie. It was carried in by at least half a dozen waiters. The count had been so accustomed to a numerous suite of attendants, he did not observe the parcelling out of his temperate meal: one bringing in the fowl, another the bread, his neighbor the solitary plate, and the rest in like order, so solicitous were the male listeners in the kitchen to see this wonderful Russian.

Thaddeus partook but lightly of the refreshment. Being already fatigued in body, and dizzy with the motion of the vessel, as soon as the cloth was withdrawn, he ordered a night candle, and desired to be shown to his chamber.

Jenkins, whom the sight of the embroidered star confirmed in his decision that the foreigner must be a person of consequence, with increased agility whipped up the portmanteau and led the way to the sleeping-rooms. Here curiosity put on a new form; the women servants, determined to have their wishes gratified as well as the men, had arranged themselves on each side of the passage through which the count must pass. At so strange an appearance, Thaddeus drew back; but supposing that it might be a custom of the country, he proceeded through this fair bevy, and bowed as he walked along to the low curtesies which they continued to make, until he entered his apartment and closed the door.

The unhappy are ever restless; they hope in every change of situation to obtain some alteration in their feelings. Thaddeus was too miserable awake not to view with eagerness the bed on which he trusted that, for a few hours at least, he might lose the consciousness of his desolation, with its immediate suffering.

CHAPTER XII.

THADDEUS'S FIRST DAY IN ENGLAND.

When he awoke in the morning, his head ached, and he felt as unrefreshed as when he had lain down; he undrew the curtain, and saw, from the strength of the light, it must be mid-day. He got up; and having dressed himself, descended to the sitting-room, where he found a good fire and the breakfast already placed. He rang the bell, and walked to the window, to observe the appearance of the morning. A heavy snow had fallen during the night; and the sun, ascended to its meridian, shone through the thick atmosphere like a ball of fire. All seemed comfortless without; and turning back to the warm hearth, which was blazing at the other end of the room, he was reseating himself, when Jenkins brought in the tea-urn.

"I hope, my lord," said the waiter, "that your lordship slept well last night?"

"Perfectly, I thank you," replied the count, unmindful that the man had addressed him according to his rank; "when you come to remove these things, bring me my bill."

Jenkins bowed and withdrew, congratulating himself on his dexterity in having saluted the stranger with his title.

During the absence of the waiter, Thaddeus thought it time to examine the state of his purse. He well recollected how he had paid at Dantzic; and from the style in which he was served here, he did not doubt that to defray what he had already contracted would nearly exhaust his all. He emptied the contents of his purse into his hands; a guinea and some silver was all that he possessed. A flush of terror suffused itself over his face; he had never known the want of money before, and he trembled now lest the charge should exceed his means of payment.

Jenkins entered with the bill. On the count's examining it, he was pleased to find it amounted to no more than the only piece of gold his purse contained. He laid it upon the tea-board, and putting half-a-crown into the hand of Jenkins, who appeared waiting for something, wrapped his cloak round him as he was walking out of the room.

"I suppose, my lord," cried Jenkins, pocketing the money with a smirk, and bowing with the things in his hands, "we are to have the honor of seeing your lordship again, as you leave your portmanteau behind you?"

Thaddeus hesitated a few seconds, then again moving towards the door, said, "I will send for it."

"By what name, my lord?"

"The Count Sobieski."

Jenkins immediately set down the tea-board, and hurrying after Thaddeus along the passage, and through the coffee-room, darted before him, and opening the door into the lobby for him to go out, exclaimed, loud enough for everybody to hear, "Depend upon it, Count Sobieski, I will take care of your lordship's baggage."

Thaddeus, rather displeased at his noisy officiousness, only bent his head, and proceeded into the street.

The air was piercing cold; and on his looking around, he perceived by the disposition of the square in which he was that it must be a market-place. The booths and stands were covered with snow, whilst parts of the pavement were rendered nearly impassable by heaps of black ice, which the market-people of the preceding day had shoveled up out of their way. He recollected it was now Sunday, and consequently the improbability of finding any cheaper lodgings on that day.*

Thaddeus stood under the piazzas for two or three minutes, bewildered on the plan he should adopt. To return to the hotel for any purpose but to sleep, in the present state of his finances, would be impossible; he therefore determined, inclement as the season was, if he could not find a chapel, to walk the streets until night. He might then go back to the Hummums to his bed chamber; but he resolved to quit it in the morning, for a residence more suitable to his slender means.

The wind blew keenly from the north-east, accompanied with a violent shower of sleet and rain; yet such was the abstraction of his mind, that he hardly observed its bitterness, but walked on, careless whither his feet led him, until he stopped opposite St. Martin's church.

"God is my only friend!" and in any house of His I shall surely find shelter!"

He turned up the steps, and was entering the porch, when he met the congregation thronging out of it.

"Is the service over?" he inquired of a decent old woman

* Those who remember the terrible winter of 1794, will not call this description exaggerated. That memorable winter was one of mourning to many in England. Some of her own brave sons perished amidst the frozen dykes of Holland and the Netherlands, vainly opposing the march of the French anarchists. How strange appeared then to him the doom of nations!

who was passing him down the stairs. The woman started at this question, asked her in English by a person whose dress was so completely foreign. He repeated it. Smiling and curtseying, she replied—

"Yes, sir; and I am sorry for it. Lord bless your handsome face, though you be a stranger gentleman, it does one's heart good to see you so devoutly given!"

Thaddeus blushed at this personal compliment, though it came from the lips of a wrinkled old woman; and begging permission to assist her down the stairs, he asked when service would begin again.

"At three o'clock, sir, and may Heaven bless the mother who bore so pious a son!"

While the poor woman spoke, she raised her eyes with a melancholy resignation. The count, touched with her words and manner, almost unconsciously to himself, continued by her side as she hobbled down the street.

His eyes were fixed on the ground, until somebody pressing against him, made him look round. He saw that his aged companion had just knocked at the door of a mean-looking house, and that she and himself were surrounded by nearly a dozen people, besides boys who through curiosity had followed them from the church porch.

"Ah! sweet sir," cried she, "these folks are staring at so fine a gentleman taking notice of age and poverty."

Thaddeus was uneasy at the inquisitive gaze of the bystanders; and his companion observing the fluctuation of his countenance, added, as the door was opened by a little girl,

"Will your honor walk in out of the rain, and warm yourself by my poor fire?"

He hesitated a moment; then, accepting her invitation, bent his head to get under the humble door-way, and following her through a neatly-sanded passage, entered a small but clean kitchen. A little boy, who was sitting on a stool near the fire, uttered a scream at the sight of the stranger, and running up to his grandmother, rolled himself in her cloak, crying out,

"Mammy, mammy, take away that black man!"

"Be quiet, William; it is a gentleman, and no black man. I am so ashamed, sir; but he is only three years old."

"I should apologize to you," returned the count, smiling, "for introducing a person so hideous as to frighten your family."

By the time he finished speaking, the good dame had pacified the shrieking boy, who stood trembling, and looking askance at the tremendous black gentleman stroking the head of his pretty sister.

"Come here, my dear!" said Thaddeus, seating himself by the fire, and stretching out his hand to the child. He instantly buried his head in his grandmother's apron.

"William! William!" cried his sister, pulling him by the arm, "the gentleman will not hurt you."

The boy again lifted up his head. Thaddeus threw back his long sable cloak, and taking off his cap, whose hearse-like plumes he thought might have terrified the child, he laid it on the ground, and again stretching forth his arms, called the boy to approach him. Little William now looked steadfastly in his face, and then on the cap, which he had laid beside him; whilst he grasped his grandmother's apron with one hand, he held out the other, half assured, towards the count. Thaddeus took it, and pressing it softly, pulled him gently to him, and placed him on his knee. "My little fellow," said he, kissing him, "you are not frightened now?"

"No," said the child; "I see you are not the ugly black man who takes away naughty boys. The ugly black man has a black face, and snakes on his head; but these are pretty curls!" added he, laughing, and putting his little fingers through the thick auburn hair which hung in neglected masses over the forehead of the count.

"I am ashamed that your honor should sit in a kitchen," said the old lady; "but I have not a fire in any other room."

"Yes," said her granddaughter, who was about twelve years old; "grandmother has a nice first-floor up stairs, but because we have no lodgers, there be no fire there."

"Be silent, Nanny Robson," said the dame; "your pertness teases the gentleman."

"O, not at all," cried Thaddeus; "I ought to thank her, for she informs me you have lodgings to let; will you allow me to engage them!"

"You, sir!" cried Mrs. Robson, thunderstruck; "for what purpose? Surely so noble a gentleman would not live in such a place as this?"

"I would, Mrs. Robson: I know not where I could live with more comfort; and where comfort is, my good madam, what signifies the costliness or plainness of the dwelling?"

"Well, sir, if you be indeed serious; but I cannot think you are; you are certainly making a joke of me for my boldness in asking you into my poor house."

"Upon my honor, I am not, Mrs. Robson. I will gladly

be your lodger if you will admit me; and to convince you that I am in earnest, my portmanteau shall this moment be brought here."

"Well, sir," resumed she, "I shall be honored in having you in my house; but I have no room for any one but yourself, not even for a servant."

"I have no servant."

"Then I will wait on him, grandmother," cried the little Nanny; "do let the gentleman have them; I am sure he looks honest."

The woman colored at this last observation of the child, and proceeded:

"Then, sir, if you should not disdain the rooms when you see them, I shall be too happy in having so good a gentleman under my roof. Pardon my boldness, sir; but may I ask? I think by your dress you are a foreigner?"

"I am," replied Thaddeus, the radiance which played over his features contracting into a glow; "if you have no objection to take a stranger within your doors, from this hour I shall consider your house my home?"

"As your honor pleases," said Mrs. Robson; "my terms are half-a-guinea a week; and I will tend on you as though you were my own son! for I cannot forget, excellent young gentleman, the way in which we first met."

"Then I will leave you for the present," returned he, rising, and putting down the little William, who had been amusing himself with examining the silver points of the star of St. Stanislaus which the count wore on his breast. "In the meanwhile," said he, "my pretty friend," stooping to the child, "let this bit of silver," was just mounting to his tongue, as he put his hand into his pocket to take out half-a-crown; but he recollected that his necessities would no longer admit of such gifts, and drawing his hand back with a deep and bitter sigh, he touched the boy's cheek with his lips, and added, "let this kiss remind you of your new friend."

This was the first time the generous spirit of Sobieski had been restrained; and he suffered a pang, for the poignancy of which he could not account. His had been a life accustomed to acts of munificence. His grandfather's palace was the asylum of the unhappy—his grandfather's purse a treasury for the unfortunate. The soul of Thaddeus did not degenerate from his noble relative: his generosity, begun in inclination, was nurtured by reflection, and strengthened with a daily exercise which had rendered it a habit of his nature. Want never appeared before him without exciting a sympathetic emotion in his heart, which never rested until he had administered every comfort in the power of wealth to bestow. His compassion and his purse were the substance and shadow of each other. The poor of his country thronged from every part of the kingdom to receive pity and relief at his hands. With those houseless wanderers he peopled the new villages his grandfather had erected in the midst of lands which in former times were the haunts of wild beasts. Thaddeus participated in the happiness of his grateful tenants, and many were the old men whose eyes he had closed in thankfulness and peace. These honest peasants, even in their dying moments, wished to give up that life in his arms which he had rescued from misery. He visited their cottage; he smoothed their pillow; he joined in their prayers; and when their last sigh came to his ear, he raised the weeping family from the dust, and cheered them with pious exhortations and his kindest assurances of protection. How often has the countess clasped her beloved son to her breast, when, after a scene like this, he has returned home, the tears of the dying man and his children yet wet upon his hand! how often has she strained him to her heart, whilst floods of rapture have poured from her own eyes! Heir to the first fortune in Poland, he scarcely knew the means by which he bestowed all these benefits; and with a soul as bounteous to others as Heaven had been munificent to him, wherever he moved he shed smiles and gifts around him. How frequently he had said to the palatine, when his carriage-wheels were chased by the thankful multitude, "O my father! how can I ever be sufficiently grateful to God for the happiness he hath allotted to me in making me the dispenser of so many blessings! The gratitude of these people overpowers and humbles me in my own eyes; what have I done to be so eminently favored of Heaven? I tremble when I ask myself the question." "You may tremble, my dear boy," replied his grandfather, "for indeed the trial is a severe one. Prosperity, like adversity, is an ordeal of conduct. Two roads are before the rich man—vanity or virtue; you have chosen the latter, and the best: and may Heaven ever hold you in it! May Heaven ever keep your heart generous and pure! Go on, my dear Thaddeus, as you have commenced, and you will find that your Creator hath bestowed wealth upon you not for what you have done, but as the means of evincing how well you would prove yourself his faithful steward."

This *was* the fortune of Thaddeus; and *now*, he who had

scattered thousands without counting them drew back his hand with something like horror at his own injustice, when he was going to give away one little piece of silver, which he might want in a day or two, to defray some indispensible debt.

"Mrs. Robson," said he, as he replaced his cap upon his head, "I shall return before it is dark."

"Very well, sir," and opening the door, he went out into the lane.

Ignorant of the town, and thanking Providence for having prepared him an asylum, he directed his course towards Charing Cross. He looked about him with deepened sadness; the wet and plashy state of the streets gave to every object so comfortless an appearance, he could scarcely believe himself to be in that London of which he had read with so much delight. Where were the magnificent buildings he expected to see in the emporium of the world? Where that cleanliness, and those tokens of greatness and splendor, which had been the admiration and boast of travellers? He could nowhere discover them; all seemed parts of a dark, gloomy, common-looking city.

Hardly heeding whither he went, he approached the Horse-Guards; a view of the Park, as it appears through the wide porch, promised him less unpleasantness than the dirty pavement, and he turned in, taking his way along the Bird-Cage Walk.*

The trees, stripped of their leaves, stood naked, and dripping with melten snow. The season was in unison with the count's fate. He was taking the bitter wind for his repast, and quenching his thirst with the rain that fell on his pale and feverish lips. He felt the cutting blast enter his soul, and shutting his eyelids to repel the tears which were rising from his heart, he walked faster; but in spite of himself, their drops mingled with the wet that trickled from his cap upon his face. One melancholy thought introduced another, until his bewildered mind lived over again, in memory, every calamity which had reduced him from happiness to all this lonely misery. Two

* The young readers of these few preceding pages will not recognize this description of St. Martin's Lane, Charing Cross, and St. James's Park, in 1794, in what they now see there in 1844. St. Martin's noble church was then the centre of the east side of a long, narrow, and somewhat dirty lane of mean houses, particularly in the end below the church. Charing Cross, with its adjoining streets, showed nothing better than plain tradesmen's shops; and it was not till we saw the Admiralty, and entered the Horse-Guards, that anything presented itself worthy the great name of London. The Park is almost completely altered. The lower part of the lane has totally disappeared; also its adjunct, the King's Mews, where now stands the royal National Gallery, while the church of St. Martin's rears its majestic portico and spire, no longer obscured by its former adjacent common buildings; and the grand naval pillar lately erected to the memory of Britain's hero, Nelson, occupies the centre of the new quadrangle now called Trafalgar Square.

or three heavy convulsive sighs followed these reflections; and quickening his pace, he walked several times quite round the Park. The rain ceased. But not marking time, and hardly observing the people who passed, he threw himself down upon one of the benches, and sat in a musing posture, with his eyes fixed on the opposite tree.

A sound of voices approaching roused him. Turning his eyes, he saw the speakers were two young men, and by their dress he judged they must belong to the regiment of a sentinel who was patrolling at the end of the Mall.

"By heavens! Barrington," cried one, "it is the best shaped boot I ever beheld! I have a good mind to ask him whether it be English make."

"And if it be," replied the other, "you must ask him who shaped his legs, that you may send yours to be mended."

"Who the devil can see my legs through that boot?"

"Oh, if to veil them be your reason, pray ask him immediately."

"And so I will, for I think the boot perfection."

At these words, he was making towards Sobieski with two or three long strides, when his companion pulled him back.

"Surely, Harwold, you will not be so ridiculous? He appears to be a foreigner of rank, and may take offence, and give you the length of his foot!"

"Curse him and rank too; he is some paltry emigrant, I warrant! I care nothing about his foot or his legs, but I should like to know who made his boots!"

While he spoke he would have dragged his companion along with him, but Barrington broke from his arm; and the fool, who now thought himself dared to it, strode up close to the chair, and bowed to Thaddeus, who (hardly crediting that he could be the subject of this dialogue) returned the salutation with a cold bend of his head.

Harwold looked a little confounded at this haughty demeanor; and, once in his life, blushing at his own insolence, he roared out, as if in defiance of shame.

"Pray, sir, where did you get your boots?"

"Where I got my sword, sir," replied Thaddeus, calmly; and rising from his seat, he darted his eyes disdainfully on the coxcomb, and walked slowly down the Mall. Surprised and shocked at such behavior in a British officer, while he moved away he distinctly heard Barrington laughing aloud, and ridiculing the astonished and set-down air of his impudent associate.

This incident did not so much ruffle the temper of Thaddeus as it amazed and perplexed him.

"Is this a specimen," though he, "of a nation which on the Continent is venerated for courage, manliness, and generosity? Well, I find I have much to learn. I must go through the ills of life to estimate myself thoroughly; and I must study mankind in themselves, and not in reports of them, to have a true knowledge of what they are."

This strange rencontre was of service to him, by diverting his mind from the intense contemplation of his situation; and as the dusk drew on, he turned his steps towards the Hummums.

On entering the coffee-room, he was met by the obsequious Jenkins, who, being told by Thaddeus that he wanted his baggage and a carriage, went for the things himself, and sent a boy for a coach.

A man dressed in black was standing by the chimney, and seemed to be eyeing Thaddeus, as he walked up and down the room, with great attention. Just as he had taken another turn, and so drew nearer the fireplace, this person accosted him rather abruptly—

"Pray, sir, is there any news stirring abroad? You seem, sir, to come from abroad."

"None that I know of, sir."

"Bless me, that's strange! I thought, sir, you came from abroad, sir; from the Continent, from Poland, sir? at least the waiter said so, sir."

Thaddeus colored. "The waiter, sir?"

"I mean, sir," continued the gentleman, visibly confused at the dilemma into which he had brought himself, "the waiter said that you were a count, sir—a Polish count; indeed the Count Sobieski! Hence I concluded that you are from Poland. If I have offended, I beg pardon, sir; but in these times we are anxious for every intelligence."

Thaddeus made no other reply than a slight inclination of his head, and walking forward to see whether the coach had arrived, he thought, whatever travellers had related of the English, they were the most impertinent people he had ever met with.

The stranger would not be contented with what he had already said, but plucking up new courage, pursued the count to the glass door through which he was looking, and resumed:

"I believe, sir, I am not wrong? You are the Count Sobieski; and I have the honor to be now speaking with the bravest champion of Polish liberty!"

Thaddeus again bowed. "I thank you, sir, for the compliment you intend me, but I cannot take it to myself; all the men of Poland, old and young, nobles and peasants, were her champions, equally sincere, equally brave."

Nothing could silence the inquisitive stranger. The coach drew up, but he went on:

"Then I hope that many of these patriots, besides your excellency, have taken care to bring away their wealth from a land which they must now see is abandoned to destruction?"

For a moment Thaddeus forget himself, indignation for his country, and all her rights and all her sufferings rose in his countenance.

"No, sir! not one of those men, and least of all would I have drawn one vital drop from her heart! I left in her murdered bosom all that was dear to me—all that I possessed; and not until I saw the chains brought before my eyes that were to lay her surviving sons in irons did I turn my back on calamities I could no longer avert or alleviate."

The ardor of his manner and the elevation of his voice had drawn the attention of every person in the room upon him, when Jenkins entered with his baggage. The door being opened, Sobieski sprang into the coach, and gladly shut himself there, from a conversation which had awakened all his griefs.

"Ah, poor enthusiast!" exclaimed his inquisitor, as the carriage drove off. "It is a pity that so fine a young man should have made so ill a use of his birth, and other natural advantages!"

"He appears to me," observed an old clergyman who sat in an adjoining box, to have made the best possible use of his natural advantages; and had I a son, I would rather hear him utter such a sentiment as the one with which that young man quitted the room, than see him master of millions."

"May be so," cried the questioner, with a contemptuous glance; "'different minds incline to different objects!" His has decided for 'the wonderful, the wild;' and a pretty finale he has made of his choice!"

"Why, to be sure," observed another spectator, "young people should be brought up with reasonable ideas of right and wrong, and prudence; nevertheless, I should not like a son of mine to run harum-scarum through my property, and his own life; and yet one cannot help, when one hears such a brave speech as that from yonder Frenchman just gone out,—I say one cannot help thinking it very fine."

"True, true," cried the inquisitor; "you are right, sir; very fine indeed, but too fine to wear; it would soon leave us acreless, as it has done him; for it seems, by his own confession, he is penniless; and I know that a twelvemonth ago he was an heir to a fortune which, however incalculable, he has managed, with all his talents, to see the end of."

"Then he is in distress!" exclaimed the clergyman, "and you know him. What is his name?"

The man colored at this unexpected inference; and glad the company had not attended to that part of the dialogue in which the name of Sobieski was mentioned, he stammered some indistinct words, took up his hat, and looking at his watch, begged pardon, having an appointment, and hurried out of the room without speaking further; although the good clergyman, whose name was Blackmore, hastened after him, requesting to know where the young foreigner lived.

"Who is that spectacled coxcomb?" cried the reverend doctor, as he returned from his unavailing application.

"I don't know, sir," replied the waiter; "I never saw him in this house before last night, when he came in late to sleep; and this morning he was in the coffee-room at breakfast, just as that foreign gentleman walked through; and Jenkins bawling his name out very loud, as soon as he was gone, this here gentleman asked him who that count was. I heard Jenkins say some Russian name, and tell him he came last night, and would likely come back again; and so that there gentleman has been loitering about all day till now, when the foreign gentleman coming in, he spoke to him."

"And don't you know anything further of this foreigner?"

"No, sir; I forget what he is called; but I see Jenkins going across the street; shall I run after him and ask him?"

"You are very obliging," returned the old clergyman; "but does Jenkins know were the stranger lives?"

"No, sir; I am sure he don't."

"I am sorry for it," sighed the kind questioner; "then your inquiry would be of no use; his name will not do without his direction. Poor fellow! he has been unfortunate, and I might have befriended him."

"Yes, to be sure, doctor," cried the first speaker, who now rose to accompany him out; "it is our duty to befriend the unfortunate; but charity begins at home; and as all's for the best, perhaps it is lucky we did not hear any more about this young fellow. We might have involved ourselves in a vast deal of unnecessary trouble; and you know people from outlandish parts have no claims upon us."

"Certainly," replied the doctor, "none in the world, excepting those which no human creature can dispute,—the claims of nature. All mankind are born heirs of suffering; and as joint inheritors, if we do not wipe away each other's tears, it will prove but a comfortless portion."

"Ah! doctor," cried his companion, as they separated at the end of Charles-street, "you have always the best of an argument: you have logic and Aristotle at your finger ends."

"No, my friend; my arguments are purely Christian. Nature is my logic, and the Bible my teacher."

"Ah, there you have me again. You parsons are as bad as the lawyers; when once you get a poor sinner amongst you, he finds it as hard to get out of the church as out of chancery. However, have it your own way; charity is your trade, and I won't be in a hurry to dispute the monopoly. Good-day! If I stay much longer, you will make me believe that black is white."

Dr. Blackmore shook him by the hand, and wishing him good-evening, returned home, pitying the worldliness of his friend's mind, and musing on the interesting stranger, whom he could not but admire, and compassionate with a lively sorrow, for he believed him to be a gentleman, unhappy and unfortunate. Had he known that the object of his solicitude was the illustrious subject of many a former eulogium from himself, how increased would have been his regret—that he had seen Count Thaddeus Sobieski, that he had seen him an exile, and that he had suffered him to pass out of the reach of his services!

CHAPTER XIII.

THE EXILE'S LODGINGS.

MEANWHILE the homeless Sobieski was cordially received by his humble landlady. He certainly never stood in more need of kindness. A slow fever, which had been gradually creeping over him since he quitted Poland, soon settled on his nerves, and reduced him to such weakness, that he possessed neither strength nor spirits to stir abroad.

Mrs. Robson was sincerely grieved at this illness of her guest. Her own son, the father of the orphans she protected, had died of consumption, and any appearance of that cruel disorder was a certain call upon her compassion.

Thaddeus gave himself up to her management. He had no money for medical assistance, and to please her he took what little medicines she prepared. According to her advice, he remained for several days shut up in his chamber, with a large fire, and the shutters closed, to exclude the smallest portion of that air which the good woman thought had already stricken him with death.

But all would not do; her patient became worse and worse. Frightened at the symptoms, Mrs. Robson begged leave to send for the kind apothecary who had attended her deceased son. In this instance only she found the count obstinate; no arguments, nor even tears, could move him to assent. When she stood weeping, and holding his burning hand, his answer was constantly the same.

"My excellent Mrs. Robson, do not grieve on my account; I am not in the danger you think; I shall do very well with your assistance."

"No, no; I see death in your eyes. Can I feel this hand and see that hectic cheek without beholding your grave, as it were, opening before me?"

She was not much mistaken; for during the night after this debate Thaddeus grew so delirious that, no longer able to subdue her terrors, she sent for the apothecary to come instantly to her house.

"Oh, doctor!" cried she, while he ascended the stairs, "I have the best young gentleman ever the sun shone on dying in that room! He would not let me send for you; and now he is raving like a mad creature."

Mr. Vincent entered the count's humble apartment, and undrew the curtains of the bed. Exhausted by delirium, Thaddeus had sunk senseless on his pillow. At this sight, supposing him dead, Mrs. Robson uttered a shriek, which was echoed by the cries of the little William, who stood near his grandmother.

"Hush! my good woman," said the doctor; "the gentleman is not dead. Leave the room till you have recovered yourself, and I will engage that you shall see him alive when you return."

Blessing these words she quitted the room with her grandson.

On entering the chamber, Mr. Vincent had felt that its hot and stifling atmosphere must augment the fever of his patient;

and before he attempted to disturb him from the temporary rest of insensibility, he opened the window-shutters and also the room-door wide enough to admit the air from the adjoining apartment. Pulling the heavy clothes from the count's bosom he raised his head on his arm and poured some drops into his mouth. Sobieski opened his eyes and uttered a few incoherent words; but he did not rave, he only wandered, and appeared to know that he did so, for he several times stopped in the midst of some confused speech, and laying his hand on his forehead, strove to recollect himself.

Mrs. Robson soon after re-entered the room, and wept out her thanks to the apothecary, whom she revered as almost a worker of miracles.

"I must bleed him, Mrs. Robson," continued he; "and for that purpose shall go home for my assistant and lancets; but in the meanwhile I charge you to let every thing remain in the state I have left it. The heat alone would have given a fever to a man in health."

When the apothecary returned, he saw that his commands had been strictly obeyed; and finding that the change of atmosphere had wrought the expected alteration in his patient, he took his arm without difficulty and bled him. At the end of the operation Thaddeus again fainted.

"Poor gentleman!" cried Mr. Vincent, binding up the arm. "Look here, Tom," (pointing to the scars, on the count's shoulder and breast;) "see what terrible cuts have been here! This has not been playing at soldiers! Who is your lodger, Mrs. Robson?"

"His name is Constantine, Mr. Vincent; but for Heaven's sake recover him from that swoon."

Mr. Vincent poured more drops into his mouth; and a minute afterwards he opened his eyes, divested of their feverish glare, but still dull and heavy. He spoke to Mrs. Robson by her name, which gave her such delight, that she caught his hands to her lips and burst again into tears. The action was so abrupt and violent, that it made him feel the stiffness of his arm. Casting his eyes towards the surgeon's, he conjectured what had been his state, and what the consequence.

"Come, Mrs. Robson," said the apothecary, "you must not disturb the gentleman. How do you find yourself, sir?"

As the deed could not be recalled, Thaddeus thanked the doctor for the service he had received, and said a few kind and grateful words to his good hostess.

Mr. Vincent was glad to see so promising an issue to his proceedings, and soon after retired with his assistant and Mrs. Robson, to give further directions.

On entering the parlor, she threw herself into a chair and broke into a paroxysm of lamentations.

"My good woman, what is all this about?" inquired the doctor. "Is not my patient better?"

"Yes," cried she, drying her eyes; but the whole scene puts me so in mind of the last moments of my poor misguided son, that the very sight of it goes through my heart like a knife. Oh! had my boy been as good as that dear gentleman, had he been as well prepared to die, I think I would scarcely have grieved! Yet Heaven spare Mr. Constantine. Will he live?"

"I hope so, Mrs. Robson. His fever is high; but he is young, and with extreme care we may preserve him."

"The Lord grant it!" cried she, "for he is the best gentleman I ever beheld. He has been above a week with me; and till this night, in which he lost his senses, though hardly able to breath or see, he has read out of books which he brought with him; and good books too: for it was but yesterday morning that I saw the dear soul sitting by the fire with a book on the table, which he had been studying for an hour. As I was dusting about, I saw him lay his head down on it, and put his hand to his temples. 'Alas! sir,' said I, 'you tease your brains with these books of learning when you ought to be taking rest.' 'No, Mrs. Robson,' returned he, with a sweet smile, 'it is this book which brings me rest. I may amuse myself with others, but this alone contains perfect beauty, perfect wisdom, and perfect peace. It is the only infallible soother of human sorrows.' He closed it, and put it on the chimney-piece; and when I looked at it afterwards, I found it was the Bible. Can you wonder that I should love so excellent a gentleman?"

"You have given a strange account of him," replied Vincent. "I hope he is not a twaddler;* if so, I shall despair of his cure, and think his delirium had another cause besides fever."

"I don't understand you, sir. He is a Christian, and as good a reasonable, sweet-tempered gentleman as ever came into a house. Alas! I believe he is most likely a papist;

* A term of derision, forty years ago, amongst unthinking persons, when speaking of eminently religious people.

though they say papists don't read the Bible, but worship images."

"Why, what reason have you to suppose that? He's an Englishman, is he not?"

"No, he is an emigrant."

"An emigrant! Oh, ho!" cried Mr. Vincent, with a contemptuous twirl of his lip. "What, a poor Frenchman! Good Lord! how this town is overrun with these fellows!"

"No, doctor," exclaimed Mrs. Robson, greatly hurt at this scorn to her lodger, whom she really loved; "whatever he be, he is not poor, for he has a power of fine things; he has got a watch all over diamonds, and diamond rings, and diamond pictures without number. So, doctor, you need not fear you are attending him for charity; no, I would sell my gown first."

"Nay, don't be offended, Mrs. Robson; I meant no offence," returned he, much mollified by this explanation; "but, really, when we see the bread that should feed our children and our own poor eaten up by a parcel of lazy French drones—all *Sans Culottes* * in disguise, for aught we know, who cover our land, and destroy its produce like a swarm of filthy locusts—we should be fools not to murmur. But Mr. ——, Mr. ——, what do you call him, Mrs. Robson? is a different sort of body."

"Mr. Constantine," replied she, "and indeed he is; and no doubt, when you recover him, he will pay you as though he were in his own country."

This last assertion banished all remaining suspicion from the mind of the apothecary; and, after giving the good woman what orders he thought requisite, he returned home, promising to call again in the evening.

Mrs. Robson went up stairs to the count's chamber with other sentiments to her sapient doctor than those with which she came down. She well recollected the substance of his discourse, and she gathered from it that, however clever he might be in his profession, he was a hard-hearted man, who would rather see a fellow-creature perish than administer relief to him without a reward. She had paid him to the uttermost farthing for her poor son.

But here Mrs. Robson was mistaken. She did him justice in esteeming his medical abilities, which were great. He had made medicine the study of his life, and not allowing any other occupation to disturb his attention, he became master of

* The democratic rabble were commonly so called at that early period of the French Revolution; and certainly some of their demagogues did cross the Channel at times, counterfeiting themselves to be loyal emigrants, while assiduously disseminating their destructive principles wherever they could find an entrance.

that science, but remained ignorant of every other with which it had no connection. He was the father of a family, and, in the usual acceptation of the term, a very good sort of a man. He preferred his country to every other, because it was his country; he loved his wife and his children; he was kind to the poor, to whom he gave his advice gratis, and letters to the dispensary for drugs; and when he had any broken victuals to spare, he desired that they might be divided amongst them; but he seldom caught his maid obeying this part of his commands without reprimanding her for her extravagance, in giving away what ought to be eaten in the kitchen: "in these times, it was a shame to waste a crumb, and the careless hussy would come to want for thinking so lightly of other people's property."

Thus, like many in the world, he was a loyal citizen by habit, an affectionate father from nature, and a man of charity because he now and then felt pity, and now and then heard it preached from the pulpit. He was exhorted to be pious, and to pour wine and oil into the wounds of his neighbor; but it never once struck him that piety extended further than going to church, mumbling his prayers and forgetting the sermon, through most of which he generally slept; and his commentaries on the good Samaritan were not more extensive, for it was so difficult to make him comprehend who was his neighbor, that the subject of the argument might have been sick, dead and buried before he could be persuaded that he or she had any claims on his care. Indeed, his "charity began at home;" and it was so fond of its residence, that it stopped there. To have been born on the other side of the British Channel, spread an ocean between every poor foreigner and Mr. Vincent's purse which the swiftest wings of charity could never cross. "He saw no reason," he said, "for feeding the natural enemies of our country. Would any man be mad enough to take the meat from his children's mouths and throw it to a swarm of wolves just landed on the coast?" "These wolves" were his favorite metaphor when he spoke of the unhappy French, or of any other penniless strangers that came in his way.

After this explanation, it may appear paradoxical to mention an inconsistency in the mind of Mr. Vincent which never permitted him to discover the above Cainish mark of outlawry upon a wealthy visitor, of whatever country. In fact, it was with him as with many: riches were a splendid and thick robe that concealed all blemishes; take it away, and probably the poor stripped wretch would be treated worse than a criminal.

That his new patient possessed some property was sufficient to ensure the respect and medical skill of Mr. Vincent; and when he entered his own house, he told his wife he had found "a very good job at Mrs. Robson's, in the illness of her lodger —a foreigner of some sort," he said, "who, by her account, had feathered his nest well in the spoils of battle (like Moore's honest Irishman) with jewels and gold." So much for the accuracy of most quotations adopted according to the convenience of the speaker.

When the Count Sobieski quitted the Hummums, on the evening in which he brought away his baggage, he was so disconcerted by the impertinence of the man who accosted him there, that he determined not to expose himself to a similar insult by retaining a title which might subject him to the curiosity of the insolent and insensible; and, therefore, when Mrs. Robson asked him how she should address him, as he was averse to assume a feigned name, he merely said Mr. Constantine.

Under that unobtrusive character, he hoped in time to accommodate his feelings to the change of fortune which Providence had allotted to him. He must forget his nobility, his pride, and his sensibility; he must earn his subsistence. But by what means? He was ignorant of business; and he knew not how to turn his accomplishments to account. Such were his meditations, until illness and delirium deprived him of them and of reason together.

At the expiration of a week, in which Mr. Vincent attended his patient very regularly, Sobieski was able to remove into the front room; but uneasiness about the debts he had so unintentionally incurred retarded his recovery, and made his hours pass away in cheerless musings on his poor means of repaying the good widow and of satisfying the avidity of the apothecary. Pecuniary obligation was a load to which he was unaccustomed; and once or twice the wish almost escaped his heart that he had died.

Whenever he was left to think, such were his reflections. Mrs. Robson discovered that he appeared more feverish and had worse nights after being much alone during the day, and therefore contrived, though she was obliged to be in her little shop, to leave either Nanny to attend his wants or little William to amuse him.

This child, by its uncommon quickness and artless manner, gained upon the count, who was ever alive to helplessness and innocence. Children and animals had always found a friend and protector in him. From the "majestic war-horse, with his neck clothed in thunder," to "the poor beetle that we tread upon"—every creature of creation met an advocate of mercy in his breast: and as human nature is prone to love what it has been kind to, Thaddeus never saw either children, dogs, or even that poor slandered and abused animal, the cat, without showing them some spontaneous act of attention.

Whatever of his affections he could spare from memory, the count lavished upon the little William. The child hardly ever left his side, where he sat on a stool, prattling about anything that came into his head; or, seated on his knee, followed with his eyes and playful fingers the hand of Thaddeus, while he sketched a horse or a soldier for his pretty companion.

CHAPTER XIV

A ROBBERY AND ITS CONSEQUENCES.

By these means Thaddeus slowly acquired sufficient strength to allow him to quit his dressing-gown, and prepare for a walk.

A hard frost had succeeded to the chilling damps of November; and looking out of the window, he longed, almost eagerly, to inhale again the fresh air. After some tender altercations with Mrs. Robson, who feared to trust him even down stairs, he at length conquered; and taking the little William by his hand, folded his pelisse round him, and promising to venture no further than the King's Mews, was suffered to go out.

As he expected, he found the keen breeze act like a charm on his debilitated frame; and with braced nerves and exhilarated spirits, he walked twice up and down the place, whilst his companion played before him, throwing stones, and running to pick them up. At this moment one of the king's carriages, pursued by a concourse of people, suddenly drove in at the Charing-Cross gate. The frightened child screamed, and fell. Thaddeus darted forward, and seizing the heads of the horses which were within a yard of the boy, stopped them; meanwhile, the mob gathering about, one of them raised William, who continued his cries. The count now let go the reins, and for a few minutes tried to pacify his little charge; but finding that his alarm and shrieks were not to be quelled, and that his own figure, from its singularity of dress, (his high cap and plume adding to its height,) drew on him the whole attention of the people, he took the trembling child in his arms, and walking through the Mews, was followed by some of the by-standers to the very door of Mrs. Robson's shop.

Seeing the people, and her grandson sobbing on the breast of her guest, she ran out, and hastily asked what had happened. Thaddeus simply answered, that the child had been frightened. But when they entered the house, and he had thrown himself exhausted on a seat, William, as he stood by his knee, told his grandmother that if Mr. Constantine had not stopped the horses, he must have been run over. The count was now obliged to relate the whole story, which ended with the blessings of the poor woman, for his goodness in risking his own life for the preservation of her darling child.

Thaddeus in vain assured her the action deserved no thanks.

"Well," cried she, "it is like yourself, Mr. Constantine: you think all your good deeds nothing; and yet any odd little thing I can do, out of pure love to serve you, you cry up to the skies. However, we won't fall out; I say, heaven bless you! and that is enough. Has your walk refreshed you? But I need not ask; you have got a fine color."

"Yes," returned he, rising and taking off his cap and cloak, "it has put me in a glow, and made me quite another creature." As he finished speaking, he dropped the things from the hand that held them, and staggered back a few paces against the wall.

"Good Lord! what is the matter?" cried Mrs. Robson, looking in his face, which was now pale as death; "what is the matter?"

"Nothing, nothing," returned he, recovering himself, and gathering up the cloak he had let fall; "don't mind me, Mrs. Robson; nothing:" and he was leaving the kitchen, but she followed him, terrified at his look and manner.

"Pray, Mr. Constantine!"

"Nay, my dear madam," said he, leading her back, "I am not well; I believe my walk has overcome me. Let me be a few minutes alone, till I have recovered myself. It will oblige me."

"Well, sir, as you please!" and then, laying her withered hand fearfully upon his arm, "forgive me, dear sir," said she, "if my attentions are troublesome. Indeed, I fear that sometimes great love appears like great impertinence; I would always be serving you, and therefore I often forget the wide difference between your honor's station and mine."

The count could only press her hand gratefully, and with an emotion which made him hurry up stairs to hide. When in his own room, he shut the door, and cast a wild and inquisitive gaze around the apartment; then, throwing himself into a chair, he struck his head with his hand, and exclaimed, "It is gone! What will become of me?—of this poor woman, whose substance I have consumed?"

It was true; the watch, by the sale of which he had calculated to defray the charges of his illness, was indeed lost. A villain in the crowd, having perceived the sparkling of the chain, had taken it unobserved from his side; and he knew nothing of his loss until, feeling for his watch to see the hour, he discovered his misfortune.

The shock went like a stroke of electricity through his frame; but it was not until the last glimmering of hope was extinguished, on examining his room where he thought he might have left it, that he saw the full horror of his situation.

He sat for some minutes, absorbed, and almost afraid to think. It was not his own, but the necessities of the poor woman, who had, perhaps, incurred debts on herself to afford him comforts, which bore so hard upon him. At last, rising from his seat, he exclaimed,

"I must determine on something. Since this is gone, I must seek what else I have to part with, for I cannot long bear my present feelings!"

He opened the drawer which contained his few valuables.

With a trembling hand he took them out one by one. There were several trinkets which had been given to him by his mother; and a pair of inlaid pistols, which his grandfather put into his belt on the morning of the dreadful 10th of October; his miniature lay beneath them: the mild eyes of the palatine seemed beaming with affection upon his grandson. Thaddeus snatched it up, kissed it fervently, and then laid it back into the drawer, whilst he hid his face with his hands.

When he recovered himself, he replaced the pistols, believing that it would be sacrilege to part with them. Without allowing himself time to think, he put a gold pencil-case and a pair of brilliant sleeve-buttons into his waistcoat pocket.

He descended the stairs with a soft step, and passing the kitchen-door unperceived by his landlady, crossed through a little court; and then anxiously looking from right to left, in quest of some shop where he might probably dispose of the trinkets, he took his way up Castle Street, and along Leicester-Square.

When he turned up the first street to his right, he was impeded by two persons who stood in his path, the one selling, the other buying a hat. The thought immediately struck Thaddeus to ask one of these men (who appeared to be a Jew, and a vender of clothes) to purchase his pelisse. By parting with a thing to which he annexed no more value than the warmth it afforded him, he should possibly spare himself the pain, for this time at least, of sacrificing those gifts of his mother, which had been bestowed upon him in happier days, and hallowed by her caresses.

He did not permit himself to hesitate, but desired the Jew to follow him into a neighboring court. The man obeyed; and having no ideas independent of his trade, asked the count what he wanted to buy.

"Nothing: I want to sell this pelisse," returned he, opening it.

The Jew, without any ceremony, inspected its covering and its lining of fur.

"Ay, I see: black cloth and sable; but who would buy it of me? An embroidered collar! nobody wears such things here."

"Then I am answered," replied Thaddeus.

"Stop, sir," cried the Jew, pursuing him, "what will you take for it?"

"What would you give me?"

"Let me see. It is very long and wide. At the utmost I cannot offer you more than five guineas."

A few months ago, it had cost the count a hundred; but glad to get any money, however small, he readily closed with the man's price; and taking off the cloak, gave it to him, and put the guineas into his pocket.

He had not walked much further before the piercing cold of the evening, and a shower of snow, which began to fall, made him feel the effects of his loss; however, that did not annoy him; he had been too heavily assailed by the pitiless rigors of misfortune to regard the pelting of the elements. Whilst the wind blew in his face, and the sleet falling on his dress, lodged in its lappels, he went forward, calculating whether it were likely that this money, with the few shillings he yet possessed, would be sufficient to discharge what he owed. Unused as he had been to all kinds of expenditure which required attention, he supposed, from what he had already seen of a commerce with the world, that the sum he had received from the Jew was not above half what he needed; and with a beating heart he walked towards one of those shops which Mrs. Robson had described, when speaking of the irregularities of her son, who had nearly reduced her to beggary.

The candles were lit. And as he hovered about the door, he distinctly saw the master through the glass, assorting some parcels on the counter. He was a gentleman-like man, and the count's feelings took quite a different turn from those with which he had accosted the Jew, who, being a low, sordid wretch, looked upon the people with whom he trafficked as mere purveyors to his profit. Thaddeus felt little repugnance at bargaining with him: but the sight of a respectable person, before whom he was to present himself as a man in poverty, as one who, in a manner, appealed to charity, all at once overcame the resolution of a son of Sobieski, and he debated whether or not he should return. Mrs. Robson, and her probable distresses, rose before him; and fearful of trusting his pride any further, he pulled his cap over his face, and entered the shop.

The man bowed very civilly on his entrance, and requested to be honored with his commands. Thaddeus felt his face glow; but indignant at his own weakness, he laid the gold case on the counter, and said, in a voice which, notwithstanding his emotion, he constrained to be without appearance of confusion, "I want to part with this."

Astonished at the dignity of the applicant's air, and the nobility of his dress, (for the star did not escape the shop-keeper's eye), he looked at him for a moment, holding the case in his hand. Hurt by the steadiness of his gaze, the count, rather haughtily, repeated what he had said. The man hesitated no longer. He had been accustomed to similar requests from the emigrant French *noblesse*: but there was a loftiness and aspect of authority in the countenance and mien of this person which surprised and awed him; and with a respect which even the application could not counteract, he opened the case, and inquired of Thaddeus what was the price he affixed to it.

"I leave that to you," replied he.

"The gold is pure," returned the man, "but it is very thin; I cannot give more than three guineas. Though the workmanship is fine, it is not in the fashion of England, and will be of no benefit to me till melted."

"You may have it," said Thaddeus, hardly able to articulate, while the gift of his mother was passing into a stranger's hand.

The man directly paid him down the money, and the count, with a bursting heart, darted out of the shop.

Mrs. Robson was shutting up the windows of her little parlor, when he hastily passed her and glided up the stairs. Hardly believing her senses, she hastened after him, and just got into the room as he drank off a glass of water.

"Good lack! sir," where has your honor been? I thought you were all the while in the house, and I would not come near, though I was very uneasy; and there has been poor William crying himself blind, because you desired to be left alone."

Thaddeus was unprepared to make an answer. He was in hopes to have gotten in as he had stolen out, undiscovered; for he determined not to agitate her too kind mind by the history of his loss. He would not allow her to know anything of his embarrassments, from a sentiment of justice, as well as from that sensitive pride which all his sufferings and philosophy could not wholly subdue.

"I have been taking a walk, Mrs. Robson."

"Dear heart! I thought when you staggered back, and looked so ill, after you brought in William, you had over-walked yourself."

"No; I fancy my fears had a little discomposed me; and I hoped that more air might do me good; I tried it, and it has: but I am grieved for having alarmed you."

This ambiguous speech satisfied his worthy landlady; and, fatigued by a bodily exertion, which, in the present feeble state of his frame, nothing less than the resolution of his mind could have carried him through, Thaddeus went directly to bed, where tired nature soon found temporary repose in a profound sleep.

CHAPTER XV.

THE WIDOW'S FAMILY.

NEXT morning Sobieski found himself rather better than worse by the exertions of the preceding day. When Nanny appeared as usual with his breakfast and little William, (who always sat on his knee, and shared his bread and butter,) the count desired her to request her grandmother to send to Mr. Vincent with his compliments, and to say her lodger felt himself so much recovered as to decline any further medical aid, and therefore wished to have his bill.

Mrs. Robson, who could not forget the behavior of the apothecary, undertook to deliver the message herself, happy in the triumph she should enjoy over the littleness of Mr. Vincent's suspicions.

After the lapse of a quarter of an hour, she re-appeared in the count's rooms, accompanied by the apothecary's assistant, who, with many thanks, received the sum total of the account, which amounted to three guineas for ten days' attendance.

The man having withdrawn, Thaddeus told Mrs. Robson, he should next defray the smallest part of the vast debt he must ever owe to her parental care.

"Oh, bless your honor, it goes to my heart to take a farthing of you! but these poor children," cried she, laying a hand on each, and her eyes glistening, "they look up to me as their all here; and my quarter-day was yesterday, else, dear sir, I should scorn to be like Doctor Vincent, and take your money the moment you offer it."

"My good madam," returned Sobieski, giving her a chair, "I am sensible of your kindness: but it is your just due; and the payment of it can never lessen your claim on my gratitude for the maternal care with which you have attended me, a total stranger."

"Then, there, sir," said she, looking almost as ashamed as if she were robbing him, when she laid it on the table; "there is my bill. I have regularly set down everything. Nanny will bring it to me." And quite disconcerted, the good woman hurried out of the room.

Thaddeus looked after her with reverence.

"There goes," thought he, "in that lowly and feeble frame, as generous and noble a spirit as ever animated the breast of a princess! "Here, Nanny," said he, glancing his eye over the paper, "there is the gold, with my thanks; and tell your grandmother I am astonished at her economy."

This affair over, the count was relieved of a grievous load; and turning the remaining money in his hand, how he might replenish the little stock before it were expended next occupied his attention. Notwithstanding the pawnbroker's civil treatment, he recoiled at again presenting himself at his shop. Besides, should he dispose of all that he possessed, it might not be of sufficient value here to subsist him a month. He must think of some source within himself that was not likely to be so soon exhausted. To be reduced a second time to the misery which he had endured yesterday from suspense and wretchedness, appeared too dreadful to be hazarded, and he ran over in his memory the different merits of his several accomplishments.

He could not make any use of his musical talents; for at public exhibitions of himself his soul revolted; and as to his literary acquirements, his youth, and being a foreigner, precluded all hopes on that head. At length he found that his sole dependence must rest on his talents for painting. Of this art he had always been remarkably fond; and his taste easily perceived that there were many drawings exhibited for sale much inferior to those which he had executed for mere amusement.

He decided at once; and purchasing, by the means of Nanny, pencils and Indian ink, he set to work.

When he had finished half-a-dozen drawings, and was considering how he might find the street in which he had seen the print-shops, the recollection occurred to him of the impression his appearance had made on the pawnbroker. He perceived the wide difference between his apparel and the fashion of England; and considering the security from impertinence with which he might walk about, could he so far cast off the relics of his former rank as to change his dress, he rose up with an intention to go out and purchase a surtout coat and a hat for that purpose, when catching an accidental view of his uniform, with the star of St. Stanislaus on its breast, as he passed the glass, he no longer wondered at the curiosity which such an appendage, united with poverty, had attracted. Rather than again subject himself to a similar situation, he summoned his young messenger; and, by her assistance, furnished himself with an English hat and coat, whilst with his penknife he cut away the embroidery of the order from the cloth to which it was affixed.

Thus accoutred, with his hat flapped over his face and his great-coat wrapped round him, he put the drawings into his bosom, and about eight o'clock in the evening walked out on his disagreeable errand. After some wearying search, he at last found Great Newport Street, the place he wanted; but as he advanced, his hopes died away, and his fears and reluctance re-awakened. He stopped at the door of the nearest print-shop. All that he had suffered at the pawnbroker's assailed him with redoubled violence. What he presented there possessed a fixed value, and was at once to be taken or refused; but now he was going to offer things of mere taste, and he might meet not only with a denial, but affronting remarks.

He walked to the threshold of the door, then as hastily withdrew, and hurried two or three paces down the street.

"Weak, contemptible that I am!" said he to himself, as he again turned round; "where is all my reason, and rectitude of principle, that I would rather endure the misery of dependence and self-reproach than dare the attempt to seek support from the fruits of my own industry?"

He quickened his step and started into the shop, almost fearful of his former irresolution. He threw his drawings instantly upon the counter.

"Sir, you purchase drawings. I have these to sell. Will they suit you?"

The man took them up without deigning to look at the person who had accosted him, and turning them over in his hand, "One, two, three, hum; there is half-a-dozen. What do you expect for them?"

"I am not acquained with the prices of these things."

The printseller, hearing this, thought, by managing well, to get them for what he liked, and throwing them over with an air of contempt, resumed—

"And pray, where may the views be taken?"

"They are recollections of scenes in Germany."

"Ah!" replied the man, "mere drugs! I wish, honest friend, you could have brought subjects not quite so threadbare, and a little better executed; they are but poor things! But every dauber nowadays sets up for a fine artist, and thinks we are to pay him for spoilt paper and conceit."

Insulted by this speech, and, above all, by the manner of the printseller, Thaddeus was snatching up the drawings to leave the shop without a word, when the man, observing his design, and afraid to lose them, laid his hand on the heap, exclaiming—

"Let me tell you, young man, it does not become a person in your situation to be so huffy to his employers. I will give you a guinea for the six, and you may think yourself well paid."

Without further hesitation, whilst the count was striving to subdue the choler which urged him to knock him down, the man laid the gold on the counter, and was slipping the drawings into a drawer; but Thaddeus, snatching them out again, suddenly rolled them up, and walked out of the shop as he said—

"Not all the money of all your tribe should tempt an honest man to pollute himself by exchanging a second word with one so contemptible."

Irritated at this unfeeling treatment, he returned home, too much provoked to think of the consequences which might follow a similar disappointment.

Having become used to the fluctuations of his looks and behavior, the widow ceased altogether to tease him with inquiries, which she saw he was sometimes loath to answer. She now allowed him to walk in and out without a remark, and silently contemplated his pale and melancholy countenance when, after a ramble of the greatest part of the day, he returned home exhausted and dispirited.

William was always the first to welcome his friend at the threshold, by running to him, taking hold of his coat, and asking to go with him up stairs. The count usually gratified him, and brightened many dull hours with his innocent caresses.

This child was literally his only earthly comfort; for he saw that in him he could still excite those emotions of happiness which had once afforded him his sweetest joy. William ever greeted him with smiles, and when he entered the kitchen, sprang to his bosom, as if that were the seat of peace, as it was of virtue. But, alas! fate seemed adverse to lend anything long to the unhappy Thaddeus which might render his desolate state more tolerable.

Just risen from a bed of sickness, he required the hand of some tender nurse to restore his wasted vigor, instead of being reduced to the hard vigils of poverty and want. His recent disappointment, added to a cold which he had caught, increased his feverish debility; yet he adhered to the determination not to appropriate to his own subsistence the few valuables he had assigned as a deposit for the charges of his rent. During a fortnight he never tasted anything better than bread and water; but this hermit's fare was accompanied by the resigned thought that if it ended in death, his sufferings would then be over, and the widow amply remunerated by what little of his property remained.

In this state of body and mind he received a most painful shock, when one evening, returning from a walk of many hours, in the place of his little favorite, he met Mrs. Robson in tears at the door. She told him William had been sickening all the day, and was now so delirious, that neither she nor his sister could keep him quiet.

Thaddeus went to the side of the child's bed, where he lay gasping on the pillow, held down by the crying Nanny. The count touched his cheek.

"Poor child!" exclaimed he; "he is in a high fever. Have you sent for Mr. Vincent?"

"O, no; I had not the heart to leave him."

"Then I will go directly," returned Thaddeus; "there is not a moment to be lost."

The poor woman thanked him. Hastening through the streets with an eagerness which nearly overset several of the foot-passengers, he arrived at Lincoln's-Inn-fields; and in less than five minutes after he quitted Mrs. Robson's door he returned with the apothecary.

On Mr. Vincent's examining the pulse and countenance of his little patient, he declared the symptoms to be the small-pox, which some casualty had repelled.

In a paroxysm of distress, Mrs. Robson recollected that a girl had been brought into her shop three days ago, just recovered from that frightful malady.

Thaddeus tried to subdue the fears of the grandmother, and at last succeeded in persuading her to go to bed, whilst he and Nanny would watch by the pillow of the invalid.

Towards morning the disorder broke out on the child's face, and he recovered his recollection. The moment he fixed his eyes on the count, who was leaning over him, he stretched out his little arms, and begged to lie on his breast. Thaddeus refused him gently, fearing that by any change of position he might catch cold, and so again retard what had now so fortunately appeared; but the poor child thought the denial unkind, and began to weep so violently, that his anxious friend believed it better to gratify him than hazard the irritation of his fever by agitation and crying.

Thaddeus took him out of bed, and rolling him in one of the blankets, laid him in his bosom; and drawing his dressing-gown to shield the little face from the fire, held him in that situation asleep for nearly two hours.

When Mrs. Robson came down stairs at six o'clock in the morning, she kissed the hand of the count as he sustained her grandson in his arms; and almost speechless with gratitude to him, and solicitude for the child, waited the arrival of the apothecary.

On his second visit, he said a few words to her of comfort, but whispered to the count, while softly feeling William's pulse, that nothing short of the strictest care could save the boy, the infection he had received having been of the most malignant kind.

These words fell like an unrepealable sentence on the heart of Thaddeus. Looking on the discolored features of the patient infant, he fancied that he already beheld its clay-cold face, and its little limbs stretched in death. The idea was bitterness to him; and pressing the boy to his breast, he resolved that no attention should be wanting on his part to preserve him from the grave. And he kept his promise.

From that hour until the day in which the poor babe expired in his arms, he never laid him out of them for ten minutes together; and when he did breathe his last sigh, and raised up his little eyes, Thaddeus met their dying glance with a pang which he thought his soul had long lost the power to feel. His heart seemed to stop; and covering the motionless face of the dead child with his hand, he made a sign to Nanny to leave the room.

The girl, who from respect had been accustomed to obey his slightest nod, went to her grandmother in the shop.

The instant the girl quitted the room, with mingled awe and grief the count lifted the little corpse from his knee; and without allowing himself to cast another glance on the face of the poor infant, now released from suffering, he put it on the bed, and throwing the sheet over it, sunk into a chair and burst into tears.

The entrance of Mrs. Robson in some measure restored him; for the moment she perceived her guest with his handkerchief over his eyes, she judged what had happened, and, with a piercing scream, flew forward to the bed, where, pulling down the covering, she uttered another shriek, and must have fallen on the floor had not Thaddeus and little Nanny, who ran in at her cries, caught her in their arms and bore her to a chair.

Her soul was too much agitated to allow her to continue long in a state of insensibility; and when she recovered, she would again have approached the deceased child, but the count withheld her, and trying by every means in his power to soothe her, so far succeeded as to melt her agonies into tears.

Whilst she concealed her venerable head in the bosom of her granddaughter, he once more lifted the remains of the little William; and thinking it best for the tranquillity of the unhappy grandmother to take him out of her sight, he carried him up stairs, and laid him on his own bed.

By the time he returned to the humble parlor, one of the female neighbors, having heard the unusual outcry, and suspecting the cause, kindly stepped in to offer her consolation and services. Mrs. Robson could only reply by sobs, which were answered by the loud weeping of poor Nanny, who lay with her head against the table.

When the count came down, he thanked the worthy woman

for her benevolent intentions, and took her up stairs into his apartments. Pointing to the open door of the bedroom, "There, madam," said he, "you will find the remains of my dear little friend. I beg you will direct everything for his interment that you think will give satisfaction to Mrs. Robson. I would spare that excellent woman every pang in my power."

All was done according to his desire; and Mrs. Watts, the charitable neighbor, excited by a kindly disposition, and reverence for "the extraordinary young gentleman who lodged with her friend," performed her task with tenderness and activity.

"Oh! sir," cried Mrs. Robson, weeping afresh as she entered the count's room, "Oh, sir, how shall I ever repay all your goodness? and Mrs. Watt's? She has acted like a sister to me. But, indeed, I am yet the most miserable creature that lives. I have lost my dearest child, and must strip his poor sister of her daily bread to bury him. That cruel Dr. Vincent, though he might have imagined my distress, sent his account late last night, saying he wanted to make up a large bill, and he wished I would let him have all, or part of the payment. Heaven knows, I have not a farthing in the house; but I will send poor little Nanny to pawn my silver spoons, for, alas! I have no other means of satisfying the cruel man."

"Rapacious wretch!" cried Thaddeus, rising indignantly from his chair, and for a moment forgetting how incapable he was to afford relief: "you shall not be indebted one instant to his mercy. I will pay him."

The words had passed his lips; he could not retract, though conviction immediately followed that he had not the means; and he would not have retracted, even should he be necessitated to part with everything he most valued.

Mrs. Robson was overwhelmed by this generous promise, which, indeed, saved her from ruin. Had her little plate been pledged, it could not have covered one half of Mr. Vincent's demand, who, to do him justice, did not mean to cause any distress. But having been so readily paid by Thaddeus for his own illness, and observing his great care and affection for the deceased child, he did not doubt that, rather than allow Mrs. Robson a minute's uneasiness, her lodger would defray his bill. So far he calculated right; but he had not sufficient sagacity to foresee that in getting his money this way, he should lose the future business of Mrs. Robson and her friend.

The child was to be buried on the morrow, the expenses of which event Thaddeus saw he must discharge also; and he had engaged to pay Mr. Vincent that night! He had not a shilling in his purse. Over and over he contemplated the impracticability of answering these debts; yet he could not for an instant repent of what he had undertaken; he thought he was amply recompensed for bearing so heavy a load in knowing that he had taken it off the worn-down heart of another.

CHAPTER XVI.

THE MONEY-LENDER.

SINCE the count's unmannerly treatment at the printseller's, he had not sufficiently conquered his pride to attempt an application to another. Therefore, he had no prospect of collecting the money he had pledged himself to Mrs. Robson to pay but by selling some more of his valuables to the pawnbroker.

For this purpose he took his sabre, his pistols, and the fated brilliants he had brought back on a similar errand. He drew them from their deposit, with less feeling of sacrilege, in so disposing of such relics of the sacred past, than he had felt on the former occasion. They were now going to be devoted to gratitude and benevolence—an act which he knew his parents, were they alive, would warmly approve; and here he allowed the end to sanctify the means.

About half-past six in the evening, he prepared himself for the task. Whether it be congenial with melancholy to seek the gloom, or whether the count found himself less observed under the shades of night, is not evident; but since his exile, he preferred the dusk to any other part of the day.

Before he went out, he asked Mrs. Robson for Mr. Vincent's bill. Sinking with obligation and shame, she put it into his hand, and he left the house. When he approached a lighted lamp, he opened the paper to see the amount, and finding that it was almost two pounds, he hastened forward to the pawnbroker's.

The man was in the shop alone. Thaddeus thought himself fortunate; and, after subduing a few qualms, entered the door. The moment he laid his sword and pistols on the counter, and declared his wish, the man, even through the disguise of a large coat and slouched hat, recollected him. This honest money-lender carried sentiments in his breast above his occupation. He did not commiserate all who presented themselves before him, because many exhibited too evidently the excesses which brought them to his shop. But there was something in the figure and manner of the Count Sobieski which had struck him at first sight, and by continuing to possess his thoughts, had excited so great an interest towards him as to produce pleasure with regret, when he discerned the noble foreigner again obliged to proffer such things.

Mr. Burket (for so this money-lender was called) respectfully asked what he demanded for the arms.

"Perhaps more than you would give. But I have something else here," laying down the diamonds; "I want eight guineas."

Mr. Burket looked at them, and then at their owner, hesitated and then spoke.

"I beg your pardon, sir; I hope I shall not offend you, but these things appear to have a value independent of their price; they are inlaid with crests and ciphers."

The blood flushed over the cheeks of the count. He had forgotten this circumstance. Unable to answer, he waited to hear what the man would say further.

"I repeat, sir, I mean not to offend; but you appear a stranger to these transactions. I only wish to suggest, in case you should ever like to repossess these valuables—had you not better pledge them?"

"How?" asked Thaddeus, irresolutely, and not knowing what to think of the man's manner.

At that instant some other people came into the shop; and Mr. Burket, gathering up the diamonds and the arms in his hand, said, "If you do not object, sir, we will settle this business in my back-parlor."

The delicacy of his behavior penetrated the mind of Thaddeus, and without demurring, he followed him into a room. While Mr. Burket offered his guest a chair, the count took off his hat and laid it on the table. Burket contemplated the saddened dignity of his countenance with renewed interest; entreating him to be seated, he resumed the conversation.

"I see, sir, you do not understand the meaning of pledging, or pawning, for it is one and the same thing; but I will explain it in two words. If you leave these things with me, I will give you a paper in acknowledgment, and lend on them the guineas you request; for which sum, when you return it to me with a stated interest, you shall have your deposit in exchange."

Sobieski received this offer with pleasure and thanks. He

had entertained no idea of anything more being meant by the trade of a pawnbroker than a man who bought what others wished to sell.

"Then, sir," continued Burket, opening an escrutoire, "I will give you the money, and write the paper I spoke of."

Just as he put his hand to the drawer, he heard voices in an adjoining passage; and instantly shutting the desk, he caught up the things on the table, threw them behind a curtain, and hastily taking the count by the hand, said, "My dear sir, do oblige me, and step into that closet; you will find a chair. A person is coming, whom I will dispatch in a few seconds."

Thaddeus, rather surprised at such hurry, did as he was desired; and the door was closed on him just as the parlor door opened. Being aware from such concealment that the visitor came on secret business, he found his situation not a little awkward. Seated behind a curtained window, which the lights in the room made transparent, he could not avoid seeing as well as hearing everything that passed.

"My dear Mr. Burket," cried an elegant young creature, who ran into the apartment, "positively without your assistance, I shall be undone."

"Anything in my power, madam," returned My. Burket, with a distant, respectful voice; "will your ladyship sit down?"

"Yes; give me a chair. I am half dead with distraction Mr. Burket, I must have another hundred upon those jewels."

"Indeed, my lady, it is not in my power; you have already had twelve hundred; and, upon my honor, that is a hundred and fifty more than I ought to have given."

"Pshaw! who minds the honor of a pawnbroker!" cried the lady, laughing; "you know very well you live by cheating."

"Well, ma'am," returned he, with a good-natured smile, "as your ladyship pleases."

"Then I please that you let me have another hundred. Why, man, you know you let Mrs. Hinchinbroke two thousand upon a case of diamonds not a quarter so many as mine."

"But consider, madam; Mrs. Hinchinbroke's were of the best water."

"Positively, Mr. Burnet," exclaimed her ladyship, purposely miscalling his name, "not better than mine! The King of Sardinia gave them to Sir Charles when he knighted him. I know mine are the best, and I must have another hundred. Upon my life, my servants have not had a guinea of board wages these four months, and they tell me they are starving.

Come, make haste, Mr. Burnet: you cannot expect me to stay here all night; give me the money."

"Indeed, my lady, I cannot."

"Heavens! what a brute of a man you are! There," cried she, taking a string of pearls from her neck, and throwing it on the table; "lend me some of your trumpery out of your shop, for I am going immediately from hence to take the Misses Dundas to the opera; so give me the hundred on that, and let me go."

"This is not worth a hundred."

"What a teasing man you are!" cried her ladyship, angrily. "Well, let me have the money now, and I will send you the bracelets which belong to the necklace to-morrow."

"Upon those conditions I will give your ladyship another hundred."

"Oh, do; you are the veriest miser I ever met with. You are worse than Shylock, or,—Good gracious! what is this?" exclaimed she, interrupting herself, and taking up the draft he had laid before her; "and have you the conscience to think, Mr. Pawnbroker, that I will offer this at your banker's? that I will expose myself so far? No, no; take it back, and give me gold. Come, dispatch! else I must disappoint my party. Look, there is my purse," added she, showing it; "make haste and fill it."

After satisfying her demands, Mr. Burket handed her ladyship out the way she came in, which was by a private passage; and having seated her in her carriage, made his bow.

Meanwhile the Count Sobieski, wrapped in astonishment at the profligacy which the scene he had witnessed implied, remained in concealment until the pawnbroker returned, and opened the closet-door.

"Sir," said he, coloring, "you have, undesignedly on your part, been privy to a very delicate affair; but my credit, sir, and your honor——"

"Shall both be sacred," replied the count, anxious to relieve the poor man from his perplexity, and forbearing to express surprise. But Burket perceived it in his look; and before he proceeded to fulfill the engagement with him, stepped half way to the escrutoire, and resumed.

"You appear amazed, sir, at what you have seen. And if I am not mistaken, you are from abroad?"

"Indeed, I am amazed," replied Sobieski; "and I am from a country where the slightest suspicion of a transaction such as this would brand the woman with infamy."

"And so it ought," answered Burket; "though by that assertion I speak against my own interest, for it is by such as Lady Hilliars we make our money. Now, sir," continued he, drawing nearer to the table, "perhaps, after what you have just beheld, you will not hesitate to credit what I am going to tell you. I have now in my hands the jewels of one duchess, of three countesses, and of women of fashion without number. When these ladies have an ill run at play, they apply to me in their exigencies; they bring their diamonds here, and as their occasions require, on that deposit I lend them money, for which they make me a handsome present when the jewels are released."

"You astonish me!" exclaimed Thaddeus; "what a degrading system of deceit must govern the lives of these women!"

"It is very lamentable," returned Burket; "but so it is. And they continue to manage matters very cleverly. By giving me their note or word of honor, (for if these ladies are not honorable with me, I know by what hints to keep them in order,) I allow them to have the jewels out for the birth-days, and receive them again when their exhibition is over. As a compensation for these little indulgences, I expect considerable additions to the *douceur* at the end."

Thaddeus could hardly believe such a history of those women, whom travellers mentioned as not only the most lovely but the most amiable creatures in the world.

"Surely, Mr. Burket," cried he, "these ladies must despise each other, and become contemptible even to our sex."

"O, no," rejoined the pawnbroker; "they seldom trust each other in these affairs. All my fair customers are not so silly as that pretty little lady who just now left us. She and another woman of quality have made each other confidants in this business. And I have no mercy when both come together! They are as ravenous of my money as if it had no other use but to supply them. As to their husbands, brothers, and fathers, they are usually the last people who suspect or hear of these matters; their applications, when they run out, are made to Jews and professed usurers, a race completely out of our line."

"But are all English women of quality of this disgraceful stamp?"

"No; Heaven forbid!" cried Burket; "if these female spendthrifts were not held in awe by the dread of superior characters, we could have no dependence on their promises.

Oh, no; there are ladies about the court whose virtues are as eminent as their rank; women whose actions might all be performed in mid-day, before the world; and them I never see within my doors."

"Well, Mr. Burket," rejoined Thaddeus, smiling; "I am glad to hear that. Yet I cannot forget the unexpected view of the famous British fair which this night has offered to my eyes. It is strange!"

"It is very bad, indeed, sir," returned the man, giving him the money and the paper he had been preparing; "but if you should have occasion to call again upon me, perhaps you may be astonished still further."

The count bowed; and thanking him for his kindness, wished him a good evening and left the shop.*

It was about seven o'clock when Thaddeus arrived at the apothecary's. Mr. Vincent was from home. To say the truth, he had purposely gone out of the way. For though he did not hesitate to commit a shabby action, he wanted courage to face its consequence; and to avoid the probable remonstrances of Mrs. Robson, he commissioned his assistant to receive the amount of the bill. Without making an observation, the count paid the man, and was returning homeward along Duke Street and the piazzas of Drury Lane Theatre, when the crowd around the doors constrained him to stop.

After two or three ineffectual attempts to get through the bustle, he retreated a little behind the mob, at the moment when a chariot drew up, and a gentleman stepping out with two ladies, darted with them into the house. One glance was sufficient for Sobieski, who recognized his friend Pembroke Somerset, in full dress, gay and laughing. The heart of Thaddeus sprang to him at the sight; and forgetting his neglect, and his own misfortunes, he ejaculated—

"Somerset!"

Trembling with eagerness and emotion, he pressed through the crowd, and entered the passage at the instant a green door within shut upon his friend.

His disappointment was dreadful. To be so near Somerset, and to lose him, was more than he could sustain. His bounding heart recoiled, and the chill of despair running through his veins turned him faint. Leaning against the passage door, he took his hat off to give himself air. He scarcely had stood a minute in this situation, revolving whether he should follow

* The whole of this scene at the pawnbroker's is too true; the writer knows it from an eye and ear-witness.

his friend into the house or wait until he came out again, when a gentleman begged him to make way for a party of ladies that were entering. Thaddeus moved to one side; but the opening of the green door casting a strong light both on his face and the group behind, his eyes and those of the impertinent inquisitor of the Hummums met each other.

Whether the man was conscious that he deserved chastisement for his former insolence, and dreaded to meet it now, cannot be explained; but he turned pale, and shuffled by Thaddeus, as if he were fearful to trust himself within reach of his grasp. As for the count, he was too deeply interested in his own pursuit to waste one surmise upon him.

He continued to muse on the sight of Pembroke Somerset, which had conjured up ten thousand fond and distressing recollections; and with impatient anxiety, determining to watch till the performance was over, he thought of inquiring his friend's address of the servants; but on looking round for that purpose, he perceived the chariot had driven away.

Thus foiled, he returned to his post near the green door, which was opened at intervals by footmen passing and repassing. Seeing that the chamber within was a lobby, in which it would be less likely he should miss his object than if he continued standing without, he entered with the next person that approached; finding seats along the sides he sat down on the one nearest to the stairs.

His first idea was to proceed into the playhouse. But he considered the small chance of discovering any particular individual in so vast a building as not equal to the expense he must incur. Besides, from the dress of the gentlemen who entered the box-door, he was sensible that his greatcoat and round hat were not admissible.*

Having remained above an hour with his eyes invariably fixed on the stairs, he observed that some curious person, who had passed almost directly after his friend, came down the steps and walked out. In two minutes he was returning with a smirking countenance, when, his eyes accidentally falling on the count, (who sat with his arms folded, and almost hidden by the shadow of the wall,) he faltered in his step. Stretching out his neck towards him, the gay grin left his features; and exclaiming, in an impatient voice, "Confound him," he hastened once more into the house.

This rencontre with his Hummums' acquaintance affected

* A nearly full dress was worn at that time by ladies and gentlemen at the great theatres. And much respect has been lost to the higher classes by the gradual change.

Thaddeus as slightly as the former; and without annexing even a thought to his figure as it flitted by him, he remained watching in the lobby until half-past eleven. At that hour the doors were thrown open, and the company began to pour forth.

The count's hopes were again on his lips and in his eyes. With the first party who came down the steps, he rose; and planting himself close to the bottom stair, drew his hat over his face, and narrowly examined each group as it descended. Every set that approached made his heart palpitate. How often did it rise and fall during the long succession which continued moving for nearly half an hour!

By twelve the house was cleared. He saw the middle door locked, and, motionless with disappointment, did not attempt to stir, until the man who held the keys told him to go, as he was about to fasten the other doors.

This roused Thaddeus; and as he was preparing to obey, he asked the man if there were any other passage from the boxes.

"Yes," cried he; "there is one into Drury Lane."

"Then, by that I have lost him!" was the reply which he made to himself. And returning homewards, he arrived there a few minutes after twelve.

CHAPTER XVII.

THE MEETING OF EXILES.

"And they lifted up their voices and wept."

THADDEUS awoke in the morning with his heart full of the last night's rencontre. One moment he regretted that he had not been seen by his friend. In the next, when he surveyed his altered state, he was almost reconciled to the disappointment. Then, reproaching himself for a pride so unbecoming his principles and dishonorable to friendship, he asked, if he were in Somerset's place, and Somerset in his, whether he could ever pardon the morose delicacy which had prevented the communication of his friend's misfortunes, and arrival in the same kingdom with himself.

These reflections soon persuaded his judgment to what his

heart was so much inclined: determining him to inquire Pembroke's address of every one likely to know a man of Sir Robert Somerset's consequence, and then to venture a letter.

In the midst of these meditations the door opened, and Mrs. Robson appeared, drowned in tears.

"My dear, dear sir!" cried she, "my William is going. I have just taken a last look of his sweet face. Will you go down and say farewell to the poor child you loved so dearly?"

"No, my good madam," returned Thaddeus, his straying thoughts at once gathering round this mournful centre; "I will rather retain you here until the melancholy task be entirely accomplished."

With gentle violence he forced her upon a seat, and in silence supported her head on his breast, against which she unconsciously leaned and wept. He listened with a depressed heart to the removal of the coffin; and at the closing of the street door, which forever shut the little William from that house in which he had been the source of its greatest pleasure, a tear trickled down the cheek of Thaddeus; and the sobbings of the poor grandmother were audible.

The count, incapable of speaking, pressed her hand in his.

"Oh, Mr. Constantine!" cried she, "see how my supports, one after the other, are taken from me! first my son, and now his infant! To what shall I be reduced?"

"You have still, my good Mrs. Robson, a friend in Heaven, who will supply the place of all you have lost on earth."

"True, dear sir! I am a wicked creature to speak as I have done; but it is hard to suffer: it is hard to lose all we loved in the world!"

"It is," returned the count, greatly affected by her grief. "But God, who is perfect wisdom as well as perfect love, chooseth rather to profit us than to please us in his dispensations. Our sweet William has gained by our loss: he is blessed in heaven, while we weakly lament him on earth. Besides, you are not yet deprived of all; you have a grand-daughter."

"Ah, poor little thing! what will become of her when I die? I used to think what a precious brother my darling boy would prove to his sister when I should be no more!"

This additional image augmented the affliction of the good old woman; and Thaddeus, looking on her with affectionate compassion, exclaimed—

"Mrs. Robson, the same Almighty Being that protected me, the last of my family, will protect the orphan offspring of a woman so like the revered Naomi!"

Mrs. Robson lifted up her head for a moment. She had never before heard him utter a sentence of his own history; and what he now said, added to the tender solemnity of his manner, for an instant arrested her attention. He went on.

"In me you see a man who, within the short space of three months, has lost a grandfather, who loved him as fondly as you did your William; a mother, whom he saw expire before him, and whose sacred remains he was forced to leave in the hands of her murderers! Yes, Mrs. Robson, I have neither parents nor a home. I was a stranger, and you took me in; and Heaven will reward your family, in kind. At least, I promise that whilst I live, whatever be my fate, should you be called hence, I will protect your grand-daughter with a brother's care."

"May Heaven in mercy bless you!" cried Mrs. Robson, dropping on her knees. Thaddeus raised her with gushing eyes; having replaced her in a seat, he left the room to recover himself.

According to the count's desire, Mrs. Watts called in the evening, with an estimate of the expenses attending the child's interment. Fees and every charge collected, the demand on his benevolence was six pounds. The sum proved rather more than he expected, but he paid it without a demur, leaving himself only a few shillings.

He considered what he had done as a fulfilment of a duty so indispensible, that it must have been accomplished even by the sacrifice of his uttermost farthing. Gratitude and distress held claims upon him which he never allowed his own necessities to transgress. All gifts of mere generosity were beyond his power, and, consequently, in a short time beyond his wish; but to the cry of want and wretchedness his hand and heart were ever open. Often has he given away to a starving child in the street that pittance which was to purchase his own scant meal; and he never felt such neglect of himself a privation. To have turned his eyes and ears from the little mendicant would have been the hardest struggle; and the remembrance of such inhumanity would have haunted him on his pillow. This being the disposition of Count Sobieski, he found it more difficult to bear calamity, when viewing another's poverty he could not relieve, than when assailed himself by penury, in all its other shapes of desolation.

Towards night, the idea of Somerset again presented itself. When he fell asleep, his dreams repeated the scene at the play-house; again he saw him, and again he eluded his grasp.

His waking thoughts were not less true to their object;

and next morning he went to a quiet coffee-house in the lane, where he called for breakfast, and inquired of the master, "did he know the residence of Sir Robert Somerset?" The question was no sooner asked than it was answered to his satisfaction. The Court Guide was examined, and he found this address: "*Sir Robert Somerset, Bart., Grosvenor Square,—Somerset Castle, L—shire,——Deerhurst, W——shire.*"

Gladdened by the discovery, Thaddeus hastened home; and unwilling to affect his friend by a sudden appearance, with an overflowing heart he wrote the following letter:—

"To Pembroke Somerset, Esq., Grosvenor Square.

"Dear Somerset,

"Will the name at the bottom of this paper surprise you? Will it give you pleasure? I cannot suffer myself to retain a doubt! although the silence of two years might almost convince me I am forgotten. In truth, Somerset, I had resolved never to obtrude myself and my misfortunes on your knowledge, until last Wednesday night, when I saw you going into Drury Lane Theatre; the sight of you quelled all my resentment, and I called after you, but you did not hear. Pardon me, my dear friend, that I speak of resentment. It is hard to learn resignation to the forgetfulness of those we love.

"Notwithstanding that I lost the pocket-book in a battlefield which contained your direction, I wrote to you frequently at a venture; and yet, though you knew in what spot in Poland you had left Thaddeus and his family, I have never heard of you since the day of our separation. You must have some good reason for your silence; at least I hope so.

"Doubtless public report has afforded you some information relative to the destruction of my ever-beloved country! I bear its fate on myself. You will find me in a poor lodging at the bottom of St. Martin's Lane. You will find me changed in everything. But the first horrors of grief have subsided; and my dearest consolation in the midst of my affliction rises out of its bitterest cause: I thank Heaven, my revered grandfather and mother were taken from a consummation of ills which would have reduced them to a misery I am content to endure alone.

"Come to me, dear Somerset. To look on you, to press you in my arms, will be a happiness which, even in hope, makes my heart throb with pleasure.

"I will remain at home all day to-morrow, in the expectation of seeing you; meanwhile, adieu, my dear Somerset. You will find at No. 5 St. Martin's Lane your ever affectionate

"THADDEUS CONSTANTINE, COUNT SOBIESKI.

"*Friday noon.*

"*P. S.* Inquire for me by the name of Mr. Constantine."*

With the most delightful emotions, Thaddeus sealed this letter and gave it to Nanny, with orders to inquire at the post-office "when he might expect an answer?" The child returned with information that it would reach Grosvenor Square in an hour, and he could have a reply by three o'clock.

Three o'clock arrived, and no letter. Thaddeus counted the hours until midnight, but they brought him nothing but disappointment. The whole of the succeeding day wore away in the same uncomfortable manner. His heart bounded at every step in the passage; and throwing opon his room-door, he listened to every person that spoke, but no voice bore any resemblance to that of Somerset.

Night again shut in; and overcome by a train of doubts, in which despondence held the greatest share he threw himself on his bed, though unable to close his eyes.

Whatever be our afflictions, not one human creature who has endured misfortune will hesitate to aver, that of all the tortures incident to mortality, there are none like the rackings of suspense. It is the hell which Milton describes with such horrible accuracy; in its hot and cold regions, the anxious soul is alternately tossed from the ardors of hope to the petrifying rigors of doubt and dread. Men who have not been suspended between confidence and fear, in their judgment of a beloved friend's faithfulness, are ignorant of "the nerve whence agonies are born." It is when sunk in sorrow, when adversity loads us with divers miseries, and our wretchedness is completed by such desertion!—it is then we are compelled to acknowledge that, though life is brief, there are few friendships which have strength to follow it to the end. But how precious are those few! The are pearls above price!

Such were the reflections of the Count Sobieski when he arose in the morning from his sleepless pillow. The idea that the letter might have been delayed afforded him a faint hope, which he cherished all day, clinging to the expectation of seeing his friend before sunset. But Somerset did not appear; and

* The humble English home of Thaddeus Sobieski is now totally vanished, along with the whole row of houses of which it was one.

obliged to seek an excuse for his absence, in the supposition of his application having miscarried, Thaddeus determined to write once more, and to deliver the letter himself at his friend's door. Accordingly, with emotions different from those with which he had addressed him a few days before, he wrote these lines:—

"To Pembroke Somerset, Esq.,

"If he who once called Thaddeus Sobieski his friend has received a letter which that exile addressed to him on Friday last, this note will meet the same neglect. But if this be the first intelligence that tells Somerset his friend is in town, perhaps he may overlook that friend's change of fortune; he may visit him in his distress! who will receive him with open arms, at his humble abode in St. Martin's Lane.

"Sunday Evening, No. 5, St. Martin's Lane."

Thaddeus having sealed the letter, walked out in search of Sir Robert Somerset's habitation. After some inquiries, he found Grosvenor Square; and amidst the darkness of the night, was guided to the house by the light of the lamps and the lustres which shone through the open windows. He hesitated a few minutes on the pavement, and looked up. An old gentleman was standing with a little boy at the nearest window. Whilst the count's eyes were fixed on these two figures, he saw Somerset himself come up to the child, and lead it away towards a group of ladies.

Thaddeus immediately flew to the door, with a tremor over his frame which communicated itself to the knocker; for he knocked with such violence that the door was opened in an instant by half-a-dozen footmen at once. He spoke to one.

"Is Mr. Pembroke Somerset at home?"

"Yes," replied the man, who saw by his plain dress that he could not be an invited guest; "but he is engaged with company."

"I do not want to see him now," rejoined the count; "only give him that letter, for it is of consequence."

"Certainly, sir," replied the servant; and Thaddeus instantly withdrew.

He now turned homeward, with his mind more than commonly depressed. There was a something in the whole affair which pierced him to the soul. He had seen the house that contained the man he most warmly loved, but he had not been admitted within it. He could not forbear recollecting that when his gates opened wide as his heart to welcome Pembroke Somerset, how he had been implored by his then grateful friend to bring the palatine and the countess to England, "where his father would be proud to entertain them, as the preservers of his son." How different from these professions did he find the reality! Instead of seeing the doors widely unclose to receive him, he was allowed to stand like a beggar on the threshold; and he heard them shut against him, whilst the form of Somerset glided above him, even as the shadow of his buried joys.

These discomforting retrospections on the past, and painful meditations on the present, continued to occupy his mind, until crossing over from Piccadilly to Coventry Street, he perceived a wretched-looking man, almost bent double, accosting a party of people in broken French, and imploring their charity.

The voice and the accent being Sclavonian, arrested the ear of Thaddeus. Drawing close to the man, as the party proceeded without taking notice of the application, he hastily asked, "Are you a Polander?"

"Father of mercies!" cried the beggar, catching hold of his hand, "am I so blessed! have I at last met him?" and, bursting into tears, he leaned upon the arm of the count, who, hardly able to articulate with surprise, exclaimed—

"Dear, worthy Butzou! What a time is this for you and I to meet! But, come, you must go home with me."

"Willingly, my dear lord," returned he; "for I have no home. I begged my way from Harwich to this town, and have already spent two dismal nights in the streets."

"O, my country!" cried the full heart of Thaddeus.

"Yes," continued the poor old soldier; "it received its death wounds when Kosciusko and my honored master fell."

Thaddeus could not reply; but supporting the exhausted frame of his friend, who was hardly able to walk, after many pauses, gladly descried his own door.

The widow opened it the moment he knocked; and seeing some one with him, was retreating, when Thaddeus, who found from the silence of Butzou that he was faint, begged her to allow him to take his companion into her parlor. She instantly made way, and the count placed the now insensible old man in the arm-chair by the fire.

"He is my friend, my father's friend!" cried Thaddeus, looking at his pale and haggard face, with a strange wildness in his own features; "for heaven's sake give me something to restore him."

Mrs. Robson, in dismay, and literally having nothing better in the house, gave him a glass of water.

"That will not do," exclaimed he, still upholding the motionless body on his arm; "have you no wine? No anything? He is dying for want."

"None, sir; I have none," answered she, frightened at the violence of his manner. "Run, Nanny, and borrow something warming of Mrs. Watts."

"Or," cried Thaddeus, "bring me a bottle of wine from the nearest inn." As he spoke, he threw her the only half-guinea he possessed, and added, "Fly, for he may die in a moment."

The child flew like lightning to the Golden Cross, and brought the wine just as Butzou had opened his eyes, and was gazing at Thaddeus with a languid agony that penetrated his soul. Mrs. Robson held the water to his lips. He swallowed a little, then feebly articulated, "I am perishing for want of food."

Thaddeus had caught the bottle from Nanny, and pouring some of its contents into a glass, made him drink it. This draught revived him a little. He raised himself in his seat; but still panting and speechless, leaned his swimming head upon the bosom of his friend, who knelt by his side, whilst Mrs. Robson was preparing some toasted bread, with a little more heated wine, which was fortunately good sherry.

After much kind exertion between the good landlady and the count, they sufficiently recovered the poor invalid to enable them to support him up stairs to lie down on the bed. The drowsiness usually attendant on debility, aided by the fumes of the wine, threw him into an immediate and deep sleep.

Thaddeus seeing him at rest, thought it proper to rejoin Mrs. Robson, and by a partial history of his friend, acquaint her with the occasion of the foregoing scene. He found the good woman surprised and concerned, but no way displeased; and, in a few words, he gave her a summary explanation of the precipitancy with which, without her permission, he had introduced a stranger under her roof.

The substance of what he said related that the person up stairs had served with him in the army; that on the ruin of his country (which he could no longer conceal was Poland), the venerable man had come in quest of him to England, and in his journey had sustained misfortunes which had reduced him to the state she saw.

"I met him," continued he, "forlorn and alone in the street; and whilst he lives, I shall hold it my duty to protect him. I love him for his own sake, and I honor him for my grandfather's. Besides, Mrs. Robson," cried he, with additional energy, "before I left my country, I made a vow to my sovereign that wherever I should meet this brave old man, I would serve him to the last hour of his life. Therefore we must part no more. Will you give him shelter?" added he, in a subdued voice. "Will you allow me to retain him in my apartments?"

"Willingly, sir; but how can I accommodate him? he is already in your bed, and I have not one to spare."

"Leave that to me, best, kindest of women!" exclaimed the count: "your permission has rendered me happy."

He then wished her a good-night, and returning up stairs, wrapped himself in his dressing-gown, and passed the night by the little fire of the sitting-room.

CHAPTER XVIII.

THE VETERAN'S NARRATIVE.

Owing to comfortable refreshment and a night of undisturbed sleep, General Butzou awoke in the morning much recovered from the weakness which had subdued him the preceding day.

Thaddeus observed this change with pleasure. Whilst he sat by his bed, ministering to him with the care of a son, he dwelt with a melancholy delight on his revered features, and listened to his languid voice with those tender associations which are dear to the heart, though they pierce it with regretful anguish.

"Tell me, my dear general," said he, "for I can bear to hear it now—tell me what has befallen my unhappy country since I quitted it."

"Every calamity," cried the brave old man, shaking his head, "that tyranny could devise."

"Well, go on," returned the count, with a smile, which truly declared that the composure of his air was assumed; "we, who have beheld her sufferings, and yet live, need not fear hearing them described! Did you see the king before he left Warsaw?"

"No," replied Butzou; "our oppressors took care of that.

Whilst you, my lord, were recovering from your wounds in the citadel, I set off for Sachoryn, to join Prince Poniatowski. In my way thither I met some soldiers, who informed me that his highness, having been compelled to discharge his troops, was returning to support his royal brother under the indignities which the haughtiness of the victor might premeditate. I then directed my steps towards Sendomir, where I hoped to find Dombrowski, with still a few faithful followers; but here, too, I was disappointed. Two days before my arrival, that general, according to orders, had disbanded his whole party.* I now found that Poland was completely in the hands of her ravagers, and yet I prepared to return into her bosom; my feet naturally took that course. But I was agonized at every step I retrod. I beheld the shores of the Vistula, lined on every side with the allied troops. Ten thousand were posted on her banks, and eighteen thousand amongst the ruins of Praga and Villanow.

"When I approached the walls of Warsaw, imagine, my dear lord, how great was my indignation! How barbarous the conduct of our enemies! Batteries of cannon were erected around the city, to level it with the ground on the smallest murmur of discontent.

"On the morning of my arrival, I was hastening to the palace to pay my duty to the king, when a Cossack officer intercepted me, whom I formerly knew, and indeed kindly warned me that if I attempted to pass, my obstinacy would be fatal to myself and hazardous to his majesty, whose confinement and suffering were augmented in proportion to the adherents he retained amongst the Poles. Hearing this, I was turning away, overwhelmed with grief, when the doors of the audience chamber opened, and the Counts Potocki, Kilinski, and several others of your grandfather's dearest friends, were led forth under a guard. I was standing motionless with surprise, when Potocki, perceiving me, held forth his hand. I took it, and wringing it, in the bitterness of my heart uttered some words which I cannot remember, but my Cossack friend whispered me to beware how I again gave way to such dangerous remarks.

"'Farewell, my worthy general,' said Potocki, in a low voice; 'you see we are arrested. We loved Poland too faithfully, for her enemies: and for that reason we are to be sent prisoners

* Dombrowski withdrew into France, where he was soon joined by others of his countrymen; which little band, in process of time, by gradual accession of numbers, became what was afterwards styled the celebrated Polish legion, in the days of Napoleon; at the head of which legion, the Prince Poniatowski, so often mentioned in these pages, lost his life in the fatal frontier river his dauntless courage dared to swim. His remains were taken to Cracow, and buried near to the tomb of John Sobieski.

to St. Petersburg. Sharing the fate of Kosciusko, our chains are our distinction; such a collar of merit is the most glorious order which the imperial sceptre could bestow on a knight of St. Stanislaus.'

"'Sir, I cannot admit of this conversation,' cried the officer of the guard; and commanding the escort to proceed, I lost sight of these illustrious patriots, probably forever.*

"I understood, from the few Poles who remained in the citadel, that the good Stanislaus was to be sent on the same dismal errand of captivity, to Grodno, the next day. They also told me that Poland being no more, you had torn yourself from its bleeding remains, rather than behold the triumphant entry of its conqueror. This insulting pageant was performed on the 9th of November last. On the 8th, I believe you left Warsaw for England."

"Yes," replied the count, who had listened with a breaking heart to this distressing narrative; "and doubtless I saved myself much misery."

"You did. One of the magistrates described to me the whole scene, at which I would not have been present for the world's empire! He told me that when the morning arrived in which General Suwarrow, attended by the confederated envoys, was to make his public *entrée*, not a citizen could be seen that was not compelled to appear. A dead silence reigned in the streets; the doors and windows of every house remained so closed that a stranger might have supposed it to be a general mourning; and it was the bitterest sight which could have fallen upon our souls! At this moment, when Warsaw, I may say, lay dying at the feet of her conqueror, the foreign troops marched into the city, the only spectators of their own horrible tragedy. At length, with eyes which could no longer weep, the magistrates, reluctant, and full of indignation, proceeded to meet the victor on the bridge of Praga. When they came near the procession, they presented the keys of Warsaw on their knees."——

"On their knees!" interrupted Thaddeus, starting up, and the blood flushing over his face.

"Yes," answered Butzou, "on their knees."

"Almighty Justice!" exclaimed the count, pacing the room with emotion; "why did not the earth open and swallow them! Why did not the blood which saturated the spot whereon they

* The Potocki family at that time had still large possessions in the Crimean country of the Cossacks; for it had formerly belonged to the crown of Poland. And hence a kind of kindred memory lingered amongst the people: not disaffecting them from their new masters, but allowing a natural respect for the descendants of the old.

knelt cry out to them? O Butzou, this humiliation of Poland is worse to me than all her miseries!"

"I felt as you feel, my lord," continued the general, "and I expressed myself with the same resentment; but the magistrate who related to me that circumstance urged in excuse for himself and his brethren that such a form was necessary; and had they refused, probably their lives would have been forfeited."

"Well," inquired Thaddeus, resuming his seat, "but where was the king during this transaction?"

"In the castle, where he received orders to be present next day at a public thanksgiving, at which the inhabitants of Warsaw were also commanded to attend, to perform a *Te Deum*, in gratitude for the destruction of their country. Thank heaven! I was spared from witnessing this blasphemy; I was then at Sendomir. But the day after I had heard of it, I saw the carriage which contained the good Stanislaus guarded like a traitor's out of the gates, and that very hour I left the city. I made my way to Hamburgh, where I took a passage to Harwich. But when there, owing to excessive fatigue, one of my old wounds broke out afresh; and continuing ill a week, I expended all my money. Reduced to my last shilling, and eager to find you, I begged my way from that town to this. I had already spent two miserable days and nights in the open air, with no other sustenance than the casual charity of passengers, when Heaven sent you, my honored Sobieski, to save me from perishing in the streets."

Butzou pressed the hand of his young friend, as he concluded. Indignation still kept its station on the count's features.

The poor expatriated wanderer observed it with satisfaction, well pleased that this strong emotion at the supposed pusillanimity of his countrymen had prevented those bursts of grief which might have been expected from his sensitive nature, when informed that ruined Poland was not only treated by its ravagers like a slave, but loaded with the shackles and usage of a criminal.

Towards evening, General Butzou fell asleep. Thaddeus, leaning back in his chair, fixed his eyes on the fire, and mused with amazement and sorrow on what had been told him. When it was almost dark, and he was yet lost in reflection, Mrs. Robson gently opened the door and presented a letter. "Here, sir," said she, "is a letter which a servant has just left; he told me it required no answer."

Thaddeus sprang from his seat at sight of the paper, and almost catching it from her, his former gloomy cogitations dispersed before the hopes and fond emotions of friendship which now lit up in his bosom. Mrs. Robson withdrew. He looked at the superscription—it was the handwriting of his friend. Tearing it asunder, two folded papers presented themselves. He opened them, and they were his own letters, returned without a word. His beating heart was suddenly checked. Letting the papers fall from his hand, he dropped back on his seat and closed his eyes, as if he would shut them from the world and its ingratitude.

Unable to recover from his astonishment, his thoughts whirled about in a succession of accusations, surmises and doubts, which seemed for a few minutes to drive him to distraction.

"Was it really the hand of Somerset?"

Again he examined the envelope. It was; and the enclosures were his own letters, without one word of apology for such incomprehensible conduct.

"Could he make one? No," replied Thaddeus to himself. "Unhappy that I am, to have been induced to apply twice to so despicable a man! Oh, Somerset," cried he, looking at the papers as they lay before him; "was it necessary that insult should be added to unfaithfulness and ingratitude, to throw me off entirely? Good heavens! did he think because I wrote twice, I would persecute him with applications? I have been told this of mankind; but, that I should find it in him?"

In this way, agitated and muttering, and walking up and down the room, he spent another wakeful and cheerless night.

When he went down stairs next morning, to beg Mrs. Robson to attend his friend until his return, she mentioned how uneasy she was at having heard him most of the preceding night moving above her head. He was trying to account to her for his restlessness, by complaining of a headache, but she interrupted him by saying, "O no, sir; I am sure it is the hard boards you lie on, to accommodate the poor old gentleman. I am certain you will make yourself ill."

Thaddeus thanked her for her solicitude: but declaring that all beds hard, or soft, were alike to him, he left her more reconciled to his pallet on the floor. And with his drawings in his pocket, once more took the path to Great Newport Street.

Resentment against his fickle friend, and anxiety for the tranquillity of General Butzou, whose age, infirmities and sufferings threatened a speedy termination of his life, determined the count to sacrifice all false delicacy and morbid feelings, and to hazard another attempt at acquiring the means of affording those comforts to the sick veteran which his condition demanded. Happen how it would, he resolved that Butzow should never know the complete wreck of his property. He shuddered at loading him with the additional distress of thinking he was a burden on his protector.

Thaddeus passed the door of the printseller who had behaved so ill to him on his first application; and walking to the farthest shop on the same side, entered it. Laying his drawings on the counter, he requested the person who stood there to look at them. They were immediately opened; and the count, dreading a second repulse, or even more than similar insolence, hastily added—

"They are scenes in Germany. If you like to have them, their price is a guinea."

"Are you the painter, sir?" was the reply.

"Yes, sir. Do they please you?"

"Yes," answered the tradesman, (for it was the master,) examining them nearer; "there is a breadth and freedom in the style which is novel, and may take. I will give you your demand;" and he laid the money on the counter.

Rejoiced that he had succeeded where he had entertained no hope, Thaddeus, with a bow, was leaving the shop, when the man called after him, "Stay, sir!"

He returned, prepared to now hear some disparaging remark.

It is strange, but it is true, that those who have been thrust by misfortune into a state beneath their birth and expectations, too often consider themselves the objects of universal hostility. They see contempt in every eye, they suppose insult in every word; the slightest neglect is sufficient to set the sensitive pride of the unfortunate in a blaze; and, alas! how little is this sensibility respected by the rich and gay in their dealings with the unhappy! To what an addition of misery are the wretched exposed, meeting not only those contumelies which the prosperous are not backward to bestow, but those fancied ills which, however unfounded, keep the mind in a feverish struggle with itself, and an uttered warfare with the surrounding world!

Repeated insults infused into the mind of Sobieski much of this anticipating irritability; and it was with a very haughty step that he turned back to hear what the printseller meant to say.

"I only want to ask whether you follow this art as a profession?"

"Yes."

"Then I shall be glad if you can furnish me with six such drawings every week."

"Certainly," replied Thaddeus, pleased with the probability of thus securing something towards the support of his friend.

"Then bring me another half-dozen next Monday."

Thaddeus promised, and with a relieved mind took his way homeward.

Who is there in England, I repeat, who does not remember the dreadfully protracted winter of 1794, when the whole country lay buried in a thick ice which seemed eternal? Over that ice, and through those snows, the venerable General Butzou had begged his way from Harwich to London. He rested at night under the shelter of some shed or outhouse, and cooled his feverish thirst with a little water taken from under the broken ice which locked up the springs. The effect of this was a painful rheumatism, which fixed itself in his limbs, and soon rendered them nearly useless.

Two or three weeks passed over the heads of the general and his young protector, Thaddeus cheering the old man with his smiles, and he, in return, imparting the only pleasure to him which his melancholy heart could receive—the conviction that his attentions and affection were productive of comfort.

In the exercise of these duties, the count not only found his health gradually recover its tone, but his mind became more tranquil, and less prone to those sudden floods of regret which were rapidly sapping his life. By a strict economy on his part, he managed to pay the widow and support his friend out of the weekly profits of his drawings, which were now and then augmented by a commission to do one or two more than the stipulated number.

Thus, conversing with Butzou, reading to him when awake or pursuing his drawings when he slept, Thaddeus spent the time until the beginning of March.

One fine starlight evening in that month, just before the frost broke up, after painting all day, he desired little Nanny to take care of the general; and leaving his work at the print-seller's, he then proceeded through Piccadilly, intending to go as far as Hyde Park Corner, and return.

Pleased with the beauty of the night, he walked on, not remarking that he had passed the turnpike, until he heard a scream. The sound came from near the Park wall. He hurried along, and at a short distance perceived a delicate-looking woman struggling with a man, who was assaulting her in a very offensive manner.

Without a moment's hesitation, with one blow of his arm Thaddeus sent the fellow reeling against the wall. But whilst he supported the outraged person who seemed fainting, the man recovered himself, and rushing on her champion, aimed a stroke at his head with an immense bludgeon, which the count, catching hold of as it descended, wrenched out of his hand. The horrid oaths of the ruffian and the sobs of his rescued victim collected a mob; and then the villain, fearing worse usage, made off and left Thaddeus to restore the terrified female at his leisure.

As soon as she was able to speak, she thanked her deliverer, in a voice and language that assured him it was no common person he had befriended. But in the circumstance of her distress, all would have been the same to him;—a helpless woman was insulted; and whatever her rank might be, he thought she had an equal claim on his protection.

The mob dispersed; and finding the lady capable of walking, he begged permission to see her safe home.

"I thank you, sir," she replied, "and I accept your offer with gratitude. Besides, after your generous interference, it is requisite that I should account to you how a woman of my appearance came out at this hour without attendance. I have no other excuse to advance for such imprudence than that I have often done so with impunity. I have a friend whose husband, being in the Life-Guards, lives near the barracks. We often drink tea with each other; sometimes my servants come for me, and sometimes, when I am wearied and indisposed, I come away earlier and alone. This happened to-night; and I have to thank your gallantry, sir, for my rescue from the first outrage of the kind which ever assailed me."

By the time that a few more complimentary words on her side, and a modest reply from Thaddeus, had passed, they stopped before a house in Grosvenor Place.* The lady knocked at the door; and as soon as it was opened, the count was taking his leave, but she laid her hand on his arm, and said, in a voice of sincere invitation:

"No, sir; I must not lose the opportunity of convincing you that you have not succored a person unworthy of your kindness. I entreat you to walk in!"

* All this local scenery is changed. There is no turnpike gate now at the Hyde Park end of Piccadilly; neither is there a park wall. Splendid railings occupy its place; and two superb triumphal arches, in the fashion of France, one leading into the Park and the other leading towards Buckingham Palace, gorgeously fill the sites of the former plain, wayfaring, English turnpike-lodges.—1845.

Thaddeus was too much pleased with her manner not to accept this courtesy. He followed her up stairs into a drawing-room, where a young lady was seated at work.

"Miss Egerton," cried his conductress, "here is a gentleman who has this moment saved me from a ruffian. You must assist me to express my gratitude."

"I would with all my heart," returned she; "but your ladyship confers benefits so well, you cannot be at a loss how to receive them."

Thaddeus took the chair which a servant set for him, and, with mingled pleasure and admiration, turned his eyes on the lovely woman he had rescued. She had thrown off her cloak and veil, and displayed a figure and countenance full of dignity and interest.

She begged him to lay aside his great-coat, for she must insist upon his supping with her. There was a commanding softness in her manner, and a gentle yet unappealable decision in her voice, he could not withstand; and he prepared to obey, although he was aware the fashion and richness of the military dress concealed under his coat would give her ideas of his situation he could not answer.

The lady did not notice his hesitation, but, ringing the bell, desired the servant to take the gentleman's hat and coat. Thaddeus instantly saw in the looks of both the ladies what he feared.

"I perceive," said the elder, as she took her seat, "that my deliverer is in the army: yet I do not recollect having seen that uniform before."

"I am not an Englishman," returned he.

"Not an Englishman," exclaimed Miss Egerton, "and speak the language so accurately! You cannot be French?"

"No, madam; I had the honor of serving under the King of Poland."

"Then his was a very gallant court, I suppose," rejoined Miss Egerton, with a smile; "for I am sorry to say there are few about St. James's who would have taken the trouble to do what you have done by Lady Tinemouth."

He returned the young lady's smile. "I have seen too little, madam, of Englishmen of rank to show any gallantry in defending this part of my sex against so fair an accuser." Indeed, he recollected the officers in the Park, and the perfidy of Somerset, and thought he had no reason to give them more respect than their countrywomen manifested.

"Come, come, Sophia," cried Lady Tinemouth; "though

no woman has less cause to speak well of mankind than I have, I will not permit my countrymen to be run down *in toto.* I dare say this gentleman will agree with me, that it shows neither a candid nor a patriotic spirit." Her ladyship uttered this little rebuke smilingly.

"I dare say he will not agree with you, Lady Tinemouth. No gentleman yet, who had his wits about him, ever agreed with an elder lady against a younger. Now, Mr. gentleman!—for it seems the name by which we are to address you,—what do you say? Am I so very reprobate?"

Thaddeus almost laughed at the singular way she had chosen to ask his name; and allowing some of the gloom which generally obscured his fine eyes to disperse, he answered with a smile—

"My name is Constantine."

"Well, you have replied to my last question first; but I will not let you off about my sometimes bearish countrymen. I do assure you, the race of the Raleighs, with their footstep cloaks, is quite *hors de combat;* and so don't you think, Mr. Constantine, I may call them so, without any breach of good manners to them or duty to my country? For you see her ladyship hangs much upon a spinster's patriotism?"

Lady Tinemouth shook her head.

"O, Sophia, Sophia, you are a strange mad-cap."

"I don't care for that; I will have Mr. Constantine's unprejudiced reply. I am sure, if he had taken as long a time in answering your call as he does mine, the ruffian might have killed and eaten you too before he moved to your assistance. Come, may I not say they are anything but well-bred men?"

"Certainly. A fair lady may say anything."

"Positively, Mr. Constantine, I won't endure contempt! Say such another word, and I will call you as abominable a creature as the worst of them."

"But I am not a proper judge, Miss Egerton. I have never been in company with any of these men; so, to be impartial, I must suspend my opinion."

"And not believe my word!"

Thaddeus smiled and bowed.

"There, Lady Tinemouth," cried she, affecting pet, "take your champion to yourself; he is no *preux chevalier* for me?"

"Thank you, Sophia," returned her ladyship, giving her hand to the count to lead her to the supper-room. "This is the way she skirmishes with all your sex, until her shrewd humor transforms them to its own likeness."

"And where is the man," observed Thaddeus, "who would not be so metamorphosed under the spells of such a Circe?"

"It won't do, Mr. Constantine," cried she, taking her place opposite to him: "my anger is not to be appeased by calling me names; you don't mend the compliment by likening me to a heathen and a witch."

Lady Tinemouth bore her part in the conversation in a strain more in unison with the count's mind. However, he found no inconsiderable degree of amusement from the unreflecting volubility and giddy sallies of her friend; and, on the whole, spent the two hours he passed there with some perceptions of his almost forgotten sense of pleasure.

He was in an elegant apartment, in the company of two lovely and accomplished women, and he was the object of their entire attention and gratitude. He had been used to this in his days of happiness, when he was "the expectancy and rose of the fair state, the glass of fashion and the mould of form,—the observed of all observers!" and the re-appearance of such a scene awakened, with tender remembrances, an associating sensibility which made him rise with regret when the clock struck eleven.

Lady Tinemouth bade him good-night, with an earnest request that he would shortly repeat his visit; and they parted, mutually pleased with each other.

CHAPTER XIX.

FRIENDSHIP A STAFF IN HUMAN LIFE.

PLEASED as the count was with the acquaintance to which his gallantry had introduced him, he did not repeat his visit for a long time.

A few mornings after his meeting with Lady Tinemouth, the hard frost broke up. The change in the atmosphere produced so alarming a relapse of the general's rheumatic fever, that his friend watched by his pillow ten days and nights. At the end of this period he recovered sufficiently to sit up and read or to amuse himself by registering the melancholy events of the last campaigns in a large book, and illustrating it with plans of the battles. The sight of this volume would have distressed Thaddeus, had he not seen that it afforded comfort to the poor veteran, whom it transported back into the scenes on which he delighted to dwell; yet he would often lay down his pen, shut the book, and weep like an infant.

The count left him one morning at his employment, and strolled out, with the intention of calling on Lady Tinemouth. As he walked along by Burlington House, he perceived Pembroke Somerset, with an elderly gentleman, of a very distinguished air, leaning on his arm. They approached him from Bond Street.

All the blood in the count's body seemed rushing to his heart. He trembled. The ingenuous smile on his friend's countenance, and his features so sweetly marked with frankness, made his resolution falter.

"But proofs," cried he to himself, "are absolute!" and turning his face to a stand of books that was near him, he stood there until Somerset had passed. He went past him, speaking these words—

"I trust, father, that ingratitude is not his vice."

"But it is yours, Somerset!" murmured Thaddeus, while for a moment he gazed after them, and then proceeded on his walk.

When his name was announced at Lady Tinemouth's, he found her with another lady, but not Miss Egerton. Lady Tinemouth expressed her pleasure at this visit, and her surprise that it had been so long deferred.

"The pain of such an apparent neglect of your ladyship's goodness," replied he, "has been added to my anxiety for the declining health of a friend, whose increased illness is my apology."

"I wish," returned her ladyship, her eyes beaming approbation, "that all my friends could excuse their absence so well!"

"Perhaps they might if they chose," observed the other lady, "and with equal sincerity."

Thaddeus understood the incredulity couched under these words. So did Lady Tinemouth, who, however, rejoined, "Be satisfied, Mr. Constantine, that I believe you."

The count bowed.

"Fie, Lady Tinemouth!" cried the lady; "you are partial: nay, you are absurd; did you ever yet hear a man speak truth to a woman?"

"Lady Sara!" replied her ladyship, with one of those arch glances which seldom visited her eyes, "where will be your vanity if I assent to this?"

"In the moon, with man's sincerity."

Thaddeus paid little attention to this dialogue. His thoughts, in spite of himself, were wandering after the figures of Somerset and his father.

Lady Tinemouth, whose fancy had not been quiet about him since his prompt humanity had introduced him to her acquaintance, observed his present absence without noticing it. Indeed, the fruitful imagination of Sophia Egerton had not lain still. She declared, "he was a soldier by his dress, a man of rank from his manners, an Apollo in his person, and a hero from his gallantry!"

Thus had Miss Egerton described him to Lady Sara Ross; "and," added she, "what convinces me he is a man of fashion, he has not been within these walls since we told him we should take it as a favor."

Lady Sara was eager to see this handsome stranger; and having determined to drop in at Lady Tinemouth's every morning until her curiosity was gratified, she was not a little pleased when she heard his name announced.

Lady Sara was married; but she was young and of great beauty, and she liked that its power should be acknowledged by others besides her husband. The instant she beheld the Count Sobieski, she formed the wish to entangle him in her flowery chains. She learnt, by his pale countenance and thoughtful air, that he was a melancholy character; and above all things, she sighed for such a lover. She expected to receive from one of his cast a rare tenderness and devotedness; in short, a fervent and romantic passion!—the fashion of the day ever since the extravagant French romances, such as Delphine and the like, came in; and this unknown foreigner appeared to her to be the very creature of whom her fancy had been in search. His abstraction, his voice and eyes, the one so touching and the other so neglectful of anything but the ground, were irresistible, and she resolved from that moment (in her own words) "to make a set at him."

Not less pleased with this second view of her acquaintance than she had been at the first, Lady Tinemouth directed her discourse to him, accompanied by all that winning interest so endearing to an ingenuous heart. Lady Sara never augured well to the success of her fascinations when the countess addressed any of her victims; and therefore she now tried every means in her power to draw aside the attention of the count. She played with her ladyship's dog; but that not succeeding, she determined to strike him at once with the full graces of her figure. Complaining of heat, she threw off her large green velvet mantle, and rising from her chair, walked towards the window.

When she looked round to enjoy her victory, she saw that this manœuvre had failed like the rest, for the provoking countess was still standing between her and Thaddeus. Almost angry, she flung open the sash, and putting her head out of the window, exclaimed, in her best-modulated tones:

"How d'ye do?"

"I hope your ladyship is well this fine morning!" was answered in the voice of Pembroke Somerset.

Thaddeus grew pale, and the countess feeling the cold, turned about to ask Lady Sara to whom she was speaking.

"To a pest of mine," returned she gayly; and then, stretching out her neck, resumed: "but where, in the name of wonder, Mr. Somerset, are you driving with all that travelling apparatus?"

"To Deerhurst: I am going to take Lord Avon down. But I keep you in the cold. Good-morning!"

"My compliments to Sir Robert. Good-by! good-by!" waving her white hand until his curricle vanished from sight; and when she turned round, her desires were gratified, for the elegant stranger was standing with his eyes fixed on that hand. But had she known that, for any cognizance they took of its beauty, they might as well have been fixed on vacancy, she would not have pulled down the window, and reseated herself with such an air of triumph.

The count took his seat with a sigh, and Lady Tinemouth did the same.

"So that is the son of Sir Robert Somerset?"

"Yes," replied Lady Sara; "and what does your ladyship think of him? He is called very handsome."

"You forget that I am near-sighted," answered the countess; "I could not discriminate his features, but I think his figure fine. I remember his father was a singularly-admired man, and celebrated for taste and talents."

"That may be," resumed Lady Sara, laughing, and anxious to excite some emotion of rivalry in the breast of Thaddeus. "I am sure I ought not to call in question his talents and taste, for he has often wished that fate had reserved me for his son." She sighed while she spoke, and looked down.

This sigh and gesture had more effect upon her victim than all her exhibited personal charms. So difficult is it to break the cords of affection and habit. Anything relating to Pembroke Somerset could yet so powerfully interest the desolate yet generous Sobieski, as to stamp itself on his features. Besides, the appearance of any latent disquietude, where all seemed splendor and vivacity, painfully reminded him of the checkered lot of man. His eyes were resting upon her ladyship, full of a tender commiseration, pregnant with compassion for her, himself, and all the world, when she raised her head. The meeting of such a look from him filled her with agitation. She felt something strange at her heart. His eyes seemed to have penetrated to its inmost devices. Blushing like scarlet, she got up to hide an embarrassment not to be subdued; and hastily wishing the countess a good-morning curtseyed to him and left the room.

Her ladyship entered her carriage with feelings all in commotion. She could not account for the confusion which his look had occasioned; and half angry at a weakness so like a raw, inexperienced girl, she determined to become one of Lady Tinemouth's constant visitors, until she should have brought him (as she had done most of the men in her circle) to her feet.

These were her ladyship's resolutions, while she rolled along towards St. James's Place. But she a little exceeded the fact in the statement of her conquests; for notwithstanding she could have counted as many lovers as most women, yet few of them would have ventured the folly of a kneeling petition. In spite of her former unwedded charms, these worthy lords and gentlemen had, to a man. adopted the oracle of the poet—

> "Love, free as air, at sight of human ties,
> Spreads his light wings, and in a moment flies."

They all professed to adore Lady Sara; some were caught by her beauty, others by her *éclat*, but none had the most distant wish to make this beauty and *éclat* his own legal property. For she had no other property to bestow.

The young Marquis of Severn seemed serious towards her ladyship during the first year of his appearance at court; but at the end of that time, instead of offering her his hand, he married the daughter of a rich banker.

Lady Sara was so incensed at this disappointment, that, to show her disdain of her apostate lover, she set off next day for Gretna Green, with Horace Ross, a young and early celebrated commander in the navy, whose honest heart had been some time sueing to her in vain. He was also nephew to the Earl of Wintown. They were married, and her ladyship had the triumph of being presented as a bride the same day with the Marchioness of Severn.

When the whirlwind of her resentment subsided, she began most dismally to repent her union. She loved Captain Ross as little as she had loved Lord Severn. She had admired the rank and fashion of the one, and the profound adoration of the other had made a friend of her vanity. But now that her revenge was gratified, and the homage of a husband ceased to excite the envy of her companions, she grew weary of his attentions, and was rejoiced when the Admiralty ordered him to take the command of a frigate bound to the Mediterranean.

The last fervent kiss which he imprinted on her lips, as she breathed out the cold "Good-by, Ross; take care of yourself!" seemed to her the seal of freedom; and she returned into her dressing-room, not to weep, but to exult in the prospect of a thousand festivities and a thousand captives at her feet.

Left at an early age without a mother, and ignorant of the duties of a wife, she thought that if she kept her husband and herself out of Doctor's Commons, she should do no harm by amusing herself with the heart of every man who came in her way. Thus she hardly moved without a train of admirers. She had already attracted every one she deemed worthy of the trouble, and listened to their compliments, and insolent presumptions, until she was wearied of both. In this juncture of *ennui*, Miss Egerton related to her the countess's recontre with the gallant foreigner.

As soon as she heard he was of rank, (for Miss Egerton was not backward to affirm the dreams of her own imagination,) she formed a wish to see him, and when, to her infinite satisfaction, he did present himself, in her eyes he exceeded everything that had been described. To secure such a conquest, she thought, would not only raise the envy of the women, but put the men on the alert to discover some novel and attractive way of proving their devotion.

Whilst Lady Sara was meditating on her new conquest, the count and Lady Tinemouth remained in their *tete-à-tete.* Her ladyship talked to him on various subjects; but he answered ill upon them all, and sometimes very wide of the matter. At last, conscious that he must be burdensome, he arose, and, looking paler and more depressed than when he entered, wished her a good-morning.

"I am afraid, Mr. Constantine, you are unwell."

Like most people who desire to hide what is passing in their minds, Thaddeus gladly assented to this, as an excuse for a taciturnity he could not overcome.

"Then," cried her ladyship, "I hope you will let me know where to send to inquire after your health."

Thaddeus was confounded for a moment; then, returning into the room, he took up a pen, which lay on the table, and said,

"I will write my address to a place where any of your ladyship's commands may reach me; but I will do myself the honor to repeat my call very soon."

"I shall always be happy to see you," replied the countess, while he was writing; "but before I engage you in a promise of which you may afterwards repent, I must tell you that you will meet with dull entertainment at my house. I see very little company; and were it not for the inexhaustible spirits of Miss Egerton, I believe I should become a complete misanthrope."

"Your house will be my paradise!" exclaimed the count, with an expressiveness to the force of which he did not immediately attend.

Lady Tinemouth smiled.

"I must warn you here, too," cried she. "Miss Egerton must not be the deity of your paradise. She is already under engagements."

Thaddeus blushed at being mistaken, and wished to explain himself.

"You misunderstand me, madam. I am not insensible to beauty; but upon my word, at that moment I had nothing else in my thoughts than gratitude for your ladyship's kindness to an absolute stranger."

"That is true, Mr. Constantine: you are an absolute stranger, if the want of a formal introduction and an ignorance of your family constitute that title. But your protection introduced you to me; and there is something in your appearance which convinces me that I need not be afraid of admitting you into the very scanty number of my friends."

Thaddeus perceived the delicacy of Lady Tinemouth, who wished to know who he was, and yet was unwilling to give him pain by a question so direct that he must answer it. As she now proposed it, she left him entirely to his own discretion; and he determined to satisfy her very proper curiosity, as far as he could without exposing his real name and circumstances.

The countess, whose benevolent heart was deeply interested in his favor, observed the changes of his countenance with an anxious hope that he would be ingenuous. Her solicitude did not arise from any doubts of his quality and worth, but she wished to be enabled to reply with promptness to the inquisitive people who might see him at her house.

"I hardly know," said Thaddeus, "in what words to express my sense of your ladyship's generous confidence in me; and that my character is not undeserving of such distinction, time, I trust, will prove." He paused for a moment, and then resumed: "For my rank, Lady Tinemouth, it is now of little consequence to my comfort; rather, perhaps, a source of mortification; for——" he hesitated, and then proceeded, with a faint color tinging his cheek: "exiles from their country, if they would not covet misery, must learn to forget; hence I am no other than Mr. Constantine; though, in acknowledgment of your ladyship's goodness, I deem it only just that I should not conceal my real quality from you.

"My family was one of the first in Poland. Even in banishment, the remembrance that its virtues were as well known as its name, affords some alleviation to the conviction that when my country fell, all my property and all my kindred were involved in the ruin. Soon after the dreadful sealing of its fate, I quitted it, and by the command of a dying parent, who expired in my arms, sought a refuge in this island from degradations which otherwise I could neither repel nor avoid."

Thaddeus stopped; and the countess, struck by the graceful modesty with which this simple account was related, laid her hand upon his.

"Mr. Constantine, I am not surprised at what you have said. The melancholy of your air induced me to suspect that you were not happy, and my sole wish in penetrating your reserve was to show you that a woman can be a sincere friend."

Tears of gratitude glistened in the count's eyes. Incapable of making a suitable reply, he pressed her hand to his lips. She rose; and willing to relieve a sensibility that delighted her, added, "I will not detain you longer: only let me see you soon."

Thaddeus uttered a few inarticulate words, whose significancy conveyed nothing, but all he felt was declared in their confusion. The countess's eloquent smile showed that she comprehended their meaning; and he left the room.

CHAPTER XX.

WOMAN'S KINDNESS.

On the count's return home, he found General Butzou in better spirits, still poring over his journal. This book seemed to be the representative of all which had ever been dear to him. He dwelt upon it and talked about it with a doating eagerness bordering on insanity.

These symptoms, increasing from day to day, gave his young friend considerable uneasiness. He listened with pain to the fond dreams which took possession of the poor old man, who delighted in saying that much might yet be done in Poland when he should be recovered, and they be enabled to return together to Warsaw, and stimulate the people to resume their rights.

Thaddeus at first attempted to prove the emptiness of these schemes; but seeing that contradiction on this head threw the general into deeper despondency, he thought it better to affect the same sentiments, too well perceiving that death would soon terminate these visions with the venerable dreamer's life.

Accordingly, as far as lay in the count's power, he satisfied all the fancied wants of his revered friend, who on every other subject was perfectly reasonable; but at last he became so absorbed in this chimerical plot, that other conversation, or his meals, seemed to oppress him with restraint.

When Thaddeus perceived that his company was rather irksome than a comfort to his friend, he the more readily repeated his visits to Lady Tinemouth. She now looked for his appearance at least once a day. If ever a morning and an evening passed away without his appearance, he was sure of being scolded by Miss Egerton, reproached by the countess, and frowned at by Lady Sara Ross. In defiance of all other engagements, this lady contrived to drop in every night at Lady Tinemouth's. Her ladyship was not more surprised at this sudden attachment of Lady Sara to her house than pleased with her society. She found she could lay aside in her little circle that tissue of affectation and fashion which she wore in public, and really became a charming woman.

Though Lady Sara was vain, she was mistress of sufficient sense to penetrate with tolerable certainty into the characters of her acquaintance. Most of the young men with whom she had hitherto associated having lived from youth to manhood amongst those fashionable assemblies where individuality is absorbed in the general mass of insipidity, she saw they were frivolous, though obsequious to her, or, at the best, warped in taste, if not in principle ; and the fascinations she called forth to subdue them were suited to their objects—her beauty, her thoughtless, or her caprice. But, on the reverse, when she formed the wish to entangle such a man as Thaddeus, she soon discovered that to engage his attention she must appear in the unaffected graces of nature. To this end she took pains to display the loveliness of her form in every movement and position ; yet she managed the action with so inartificial and frank an air, that she seemed the only person present who was unconscious of the versatility and power of her charms. She conversed with good sense and propriety. In short, she appeared completely different from the gay, ridiculous creature he had seen some weeks before in the countess's drawing-room.

He now admired both her person and her mind. Her winning softness, the vivacity of Miss Egerton, and the kindness of the countess, beguiled him many an evening from the contemplation of melancholy scenes at his humble and anxious home.

One night it came into the head of Sophia Egerton to banter him about his military dress. "Do, for heaven's sake, my dear Don Quixote," cried she, "let us see you out of your rusty armor! I declare I grow frightened at it. And I cannot but think you would be merrier out of that customary suit of solemn black!"

This demand was not pleasing to Thaddeus, but he good-humoredly replied, "I knew not till you were so kind as to inform me that a man's temper depends on his clothes."

"Else, I suppose," cried she, interrupting him, "you would have changed yours before? Therefore, I expect you will do as I bid you now, and put on a Christian's coat against you next enter this house."

Thaddeus was at a loss what to say; he only bowed; and the countess and Lady Sara smiled at her nonsense.

When they parted for the night, this part of the conversation passed off from all minds but that of Lady Tinemouth. She had considered the subject, but in a different way from her gay companion. Sophia supposed that the handsome Constantine wore the dress of his country because it was the most becoming. But as such a whim did not correspond with the other parts of his character, Lady Tinemouth, in her own mind, attributed this adherence to his national habit to the right cause.

She remarked that whenever she wished him to meet any agreeable people at her house, he always declined these introductions under the plea of his dress, though he never proposed to alter it. This conduct, added to his silence on every subject which elated to the public amusements about town, led her to conclude, that, like the banished nobility of France he was encountering the various inconveniences of poverty in a foreign land. She hoped that he had escaped its horrors; but she could not be certain, for he always shifted the conversation when it too closely referred to himself.

These observations haunted the mind of Lady Tinemouth, and made her anxious to contrive some opportunity in which she might have this interesting Constantine alone, and by a proper management of the discourse, lead to some avowal of his real situation. Hitherto her benevolent intentions had been frustrated by various interruptions at various times. Indeed, had she been actuated by mere curiosity, she would longago have resigned the attempt as fruitless; but pity and esteem kept her watchful until the very hour in which her considerate heart was fully satisfied.

One morning, when she was writing in her cabinet, a servant informed her that Mr. Constantine was below. Pleased at this circumstance, she took advantage of a slight cold that affected her; and hoping to draw something out of him in the course of a *tete-à-tete*, begged he would favor her by coming into her private room.

When he entered, she perceived that he looked more pensive than usual. He sat down by her, and expressed his concern at her indisposition. She sighed heavily, but remained silent. Her thoughts were too much occupied with her kind plan to immediately form a reply. She had determined to give him a cursory idea of her own unhappiness, and thus, by her confidence, attract him.

"I hope Miss Egerton is well?" inquired he.

"Very well, Mr. Constantine. A heart at ease almost ever keeps the body in health. May she long continue as happy as at this period, and never know the disappointments of her friend!"

He looked at the countess.

"It is true, my dear sir," continued she. "It is hardly

probable that the mere effect of thirty-seven years could have made the inroads on my person which you see: but sorrow has done it; and with all the comforts you behold around me, I am miserable. I have no joy independent of the few friends which Heaven has preserved to me; and yet," added she, "I have another anxiety united with those of which I complain; some of my friends, who afford me the consolation I mention, deny me the only return in my power, the office of sharing their griefs."

Thaddeus understood the expression of her ladyship's eye and the tenderness of her voice as she uttered these words. He saw to whom the kind reproach was directed, and he looked down confused and oppressed.

The countess resumed.

"I cannot deny what your countenance declares; you think I mean you. I do, Mr. Constantine. I have marked your melancholy; I have weighed other circumstances; and I am sure that you have many things to struggle with besides the regrets which must ever hang about the bosom of a brave man who has witnessed the destruction of his country. Forgive me, if I give you pain," added she, observing his heightening color. "I speak from real esteem; I speak to you as I would to my own son were he in your situation."

"My dearest madam!" cried Thaddeus, overcome by her benevolence, "you have judged rightly; I have many things to struggle with. I have a sick friend at home, whom misfortune hath nearly bereft of reason, and whose wants are now so complicated and expensive, that never till now did I know the complete desolation of a man without a country or a profession. For myself, Lady Tinemouth, adversity has few pangs; but for my friend, for an old man whose deranged faculties have forgotten the change in my affairs, he who leans on me for support and comfort,—it is this that must account to your ladyship for those inconsistencies in my manner and spirits which are so frequently the subject of Miss Egerton's raillery

Thaddeus, in the course of this short and rapid narrative, gradually lowered the tone of his voice, and at the close covered his face with his hand. He had never before confided the history of his embarrassments to any creature; and he thought (notwithstanding the countess's solicitations) he had committed an outrage on the firmness of his character by having in any way acknowledged the weight of his calamities.

Lady Tinemouth considered a few minutes, and then addressed him.

"I should ill repay this generous confidence, my noble young friend, were I to hesitate a moment in forming some plan which may prove of service to you. You have told me no more, Mr. Constantine, than I suspected. And I had something in view." Here the countess stopped, expecting that her auditor would interrupt her. He remained silent, and she proceeded: "You spoke of a profession, of an employment."

"Yes, madam," returned he, taking his hands from his eyes; "I should be glad to engage in any profession or employment you would recommend."

"I have little interest," answered her ladyship, "with people in power; therefore I cannot propose anything which will in any degree suit with your rank; but the employment that I have in view, several of the most illustrious French nobility have not disdained to execute."

"Do not fear to mention it to me," cried the count, perceiving her reluctance; "I would attempt anything that is not dishonorable, to render service to my poor friend."

"Well, then, would you have any objection to teach languages?"

Thaddeus immediately answered, "Oh, no! I should be happy to do so."

"Then," replied she, greatly relieved by the manner in which he received her proposal, "I will now tell you that about a week ago I paid a visit to Lady Dundas, the widow of Sir Hector Dundas, the rich East Indian director. Whilst I was there, I heard her talking with her two daughters about finding a proper master to teach them German. That language has become a very fashionable accomplishment amongst literary ladies; and Miss Dundas, being a member of the Blue-stocking Club,* had declared her resolution to make a new translation of Werter. Lady Dundas expressed many objections against the vulgarity of various teachers whom the young ladies proposed, and ended with saying that unless some German gentleman could be found, they must remain ignorant of the language. Your image instantly shot across my mind; and deeming it a favorable opportunity, I told her ladyship that if she could wait a few days, I would sound a friend of mine, who I knew, if he would condescend to take the trouble, must be the most eligible person imaginable. Lady Dundas and the girls gladly left the affair to me, and I now propose it to you."

* Such was the real name given at the time to Mrs. Montague's celebrated literery parties, held at her house in Portman Square. The late venerable Sir William Pepys was one of their last survivors.

"And I," replied he, "with a thousand thanks, accept the task."

"Then I will make the usual arrangements," returned her ladyship, "and send you the result."

After half an hour's further conversation, Lady Tinemouth became more impressed with the unsophisticated delicacy and dignity of the count's mind; and he, more grateful than utterance could declare, left his respects for Miss Egerton, and took his leave.

CHAPTER XXI.

FASHIONABLE SKETCHES FROM THE LIFE.

NEXT morning, whilst Thaddeus was vainly explaining to the general that he no longer possessed a regiment of horse, which the poor old man wanted him to order out, to try the success of some manœuvres he had been devising, little Nanny brought in a letter from Slaughter's Coffee-house, where he had noted Lady Tinemouth to direct it to him.* He opened it, and found these contents:—

"My dear Sir,

"So anxious was I to terminate the affair with Lady Dundas, that I went to her house last night. I affirmed it as a great obligation that you would undertake the trouble to teach her daughters; and I insist that you do not, from any romantic ideas of candor, invalidate what I have said. I know the world too well not to be convinced of the truth of Dr. Goldsmith's maxim,—'If you be poor, do not seem poor, if you would avoid insult as well as suffering.'

"I told Miss Dundas that you had undertaken the task solely at my persuasion, and that I could not propose other terms than a guinea for two lessons. She is rich enough for any expense, and made no objection to my demand; besides, she presented the enclosed, by way of entrance-money. It is customary. Thus I have settled all preliminaries, and you are to commence your first lesson on Monday, at two o'clock. But before then, pray let me see you.

"Cannot you dine with us on Sunday? A sabbath privilege! to speak of good is blameless. I have informed Miss

* This respectable hotel still exists, near the top of St. Martin's Lane.—1845.

Egerton of as much of the affair as I think necessary to account for your new occupation. In short, gay in spirits as she is, I thought it most prudent to say as little to her and to Lady Sara as I have done to the Dundases; therefore, do not be uneasy on that head.

"Come to-morrow, if not before, and you will give real pleasure to your sincere friend,

"ADELIZA TINEMOUTH.

"SATURDAY MORNING, GROSVENOR PLACE."

Truly grateful to the active friendship of the countess, and looking at the general, who appeared perfectly happy in the prosecution of his wild schemes, Thaddeus inwardly exclaimed, "By these means I shall at least have it in my power to procure the assistance which your melancholy state my revered friend, requires."

On opening the enclosed, which her ladyship mentioned, he found it to be a bank note for ten pounds. Both the present and its amount gave him pain: not having done any service yet to the donor, he regarded the money more as a gift than as a bond of engagement. However, he found that this delicacy, with many other painful repugnances, must at this moment be laid aside; and, without further self-torment, he consigned the money to the use for which he felt aware the countess had wished it to be applied, namely, to provide himself with an English dress.

During these various reflections, he did not leave Lady Tinemouth's letter unanswered. He thanked her sincerely for her zeal, but declined dining with her the next day, on account of leaving his poor friend so long alone; though he promised to come in the evening when he should be retired to rest.

This excuse was regretted by none more than Lady Sara Ross, who, having heard from Lady Tinemouth that she expected Mr. Constantine to dinner on a Sunday, invited herself to be one of the party. She had now seen him constantly for nearly a month, and found, to her amazement, that in seeking to beguile him, she had only ensnared herself. Every word he uttered penetrated to her heart; every glance of his eyes shook her frame like electricity.

She had now no necessity to affect softness. A young and unsuspected passion had stolen into her bosom, and imparted to her voice and countenance all its subtle power to enchant and to subdue. Thaddeus was not insensible to this gentle fascination; for it appeared to his ingenuous nature to be unconsciously shown, and from under "veiled lids." He looked on her as indeed a lovely woman, who, with a touching delicacy, he observed, often tried to stifle sigh after sigh, which, fluttering, rose to her silent lips. Thus, as silently remarking her, he became deeply interested in her; for he believed her yearning heart then thought of her gallant husband, far, far at sea. So had been his conclusion when he first noticed these demonstrations of an inward unuttered sensibility. But in a little while afterwards, when those veiled lids were occasionally raised, and met his compassionate gaze, she mistook the nature of its expression; and her responsive glance, wild with ecstacy, returned him one that darted astonishment, with an appalling dread of his meaning, through his every vein. But on his pillow the same night, when he reflected on what he had felt on receiving so strange a look from a married woman, and one, too, whom he believed to be a virtuous one! he could not, he would not, suppose it meant anything to him; and ashamed of even the idea having entered his head, he crushed it at once, indignant at himself. Though, whenever he subsequently met her at Lady Tinemouth's, he could not help, as if by a natural impulse, avoiding the encountering of her eyes.

In the course of conversation at dinner, on the day Thaddeus had been expected by Lady Tinemouth, in a tone of pleasure she mentioned that she had conferred a great favor on her young cousins, the Misses Dundas, by having prevailed on Mr. Constantine to undertake the trouble of teaching them German. Lady Sara could not conceal her vexation, nor her wonder at Lady Tinemouth's thinking of such a thing; and she uttered something like angry contempt at acquiescence, while inwardly she hated her former old friend for having made the proposal.

Miss Egerton laughed at the scrape into which Lady Tinemouth had brought his good nature, and declared she would tell him next time she saw him what a mulish pair of misses he had presumed to manage.

It was the youngest of these misses that excited Lady Sara's displeasure. Euphemia Dundas was very pretty; she had a large fortune at her disposal; and what might not such united temptations effect on the mind of a man exposed every day to her habitual flirtation? Stung with jealousy, Lady Sara caught at a slight intimation of his possibly coming in before the evening should close. Rallying her smiles, she resolved to make one more essay on his relapsed insensibility, before she beheld him enter scenes so likely to extinguish her hopes. Hopes of what? She never allowed herself to inquire. She knew that she never had loved her husband, that now she detested him, and was devoted to another. To be assured of a reciprocal passion from that other, she believed was the extent of her wish. Thinking that she held her husband's honor safe as her life, she determined to do what she pleased with her heart. Her former admirers were now neglected; and, to the astonishment and admiration of the graver part of her acquaintance, she had lately relinquished all the assemblies in which she had so recently been the brightest attraction, to seclude herself by the domestic fireside of the Countess of Tinemouth.

Thus, whilst the world were admiring a conduct they supposed would give a lasting happiness to herself and to her husband, she was cherishing a passion which might prove the destruction of both.

On Sunday evening, Thaddeus entered Lady Tinemouth's drawing-room just as Miss Egerton seated herself before the tea equipage. At sight of him she nodded her head, and called him to sit by her. Lady Tinemouth returned the grateful pressure of his hand. Lady Sara received him with a palpitating heart, and stooped to remove something that seemed to incommode her foot; but it was only a feint, to hide the blushes which were burning on her cheek. No one observed her confusion. So common is it for those who are the constant witnesses of our actions to be the most ignorant of their expression and tendency.

Thaddeus could not, in spite of himself, be so uninformed, and he gladly obeyed a second summons from the gay Sophia, and drew his chair close to hers.

Lady Sara observed his motions with a pang she could not conceal; and pulling her seat as far from the opposite side as possible, began in silence to sip her tea.

"Ye powers of gallantry!" suddenly exclaimed Miss Egerton, pushing away the table, and lifting her eye-glass to her eye, "I declare I have conquered! Look, Lady Tinemouth; look, Lady Sara! If Mr. Constantine does not better become this English dress than his Polish horribles did him, drown me for a witch!"

"You see I have obeyed you, madam," returned Thaddeus smiling.

"Ah! you are in the right. Most men do that cheerfully. when they know they gain by the bargain. Now, you look like a Christian man; before, you always reminded me of some stalking hero in a tragedy."

"Yes," cried Lady Sara, forcing a smile; "and now you have given him a striking resemblance to George Barnwell!"

Sophia, who did not perceive the sarcasm couched under this remark, good-humoredly replied:

"May be so, Lady Sara; but I don't care for his black suit: obedience was the thing I wanted, and I have it in the present appearance."

"Pray, Lady Tinemouth," asked her ladyship, seeking to revenge herself on his alacrity to obey Miss Egerton, "what o'clock is it? I have promised to be at Lady Sarum's concert by ten."

"It is not nine," returned the countess; "besides, this is the first time I have heard of your engagement. I hoped you would have spent all the evening with us."

"No," answered Lady Sara, "I cannot." And ringing the bell, she rose.

"Bless me, Lady Sara!" cried Miss Egerton, "you are not going? Don't you hear that it is little more than eight o'clock?"

Busying herself in tying her cloak, Lady Sara affected not to hear her, and told the servant who opened the door to order her carriage.

Surprised at this precipitation, but far from guessing the cause, Lady Tinemouth requested Mr. Constantime to see her ladyship down stairs.

"I would rather not," cried she, "in a quick voice; and darting out of the room, was followed by Thaddeus, who came up with her just as she reached the street door. He hastened to assist her into the carriage, and saw by the light of the flambeaux her face streaming with tears. He had already extended his hand, when, instead of accepting it, she pushed it from her, and jumped into the carriage, crying in an indignant tone, "To Berkeley Square." He remained for a few minutes looking after her; then returned into the house, too well able to translate the meaning of all this petulance.

When he reascended the stairs, Lady Tinemouth expressed her wonder at the whimsical departure of her friend; but as Thaddeus (who was really disturbed) returned a vague reply, the subject ended.

Miss Egerton, who hardly thought two minutes on the same thing, sent away the tea-board, and, sitting down by him, exclaimed,—

"Mr. Constantine, I hold it right that no man should be thrown into a den of wild creatures without knowing what sort of animals he must meet there. Hence, as I find you have undertaken the taming of that *ursa major* Lady Dundas, and her pretty cubs, I must give you a taste of their quality. Will you hear me?"

"Certainly."

"Will you attend to my advice?

"If I like it."

"Ha!" replied she, returning his smile with another; "that is just such an answer as I would have made myself, so I won't quarrel with you. Lady Tinemouth, you will allow me to draw your kinsfolks' pictures?"

"Yes, Sophia, provided you don't make them caricatures. Remember, your candor is at stake; to-morrow Mr. Constantine will judge for himself."

"And I am sure he will agree with me. Now, Lady Dundas, if you please! I know your ladyship is a great stickler for precedence."

Lady Tinemouth laughed, and interrupted her—

"I declare, Sophia, you are a very daring girl. What do you not risk by giving way to this satirical spirit?"

"Not anybody's love that I value, Lady Tinemouth: *you* know that I never daub a fair character; Mr. Constantine takes me on your credit; and if you mean Charles Montresor, he is as bad as myself, and dare not for his life have any qualms."

"Well, well, proceed," cried her ladyship; "I will not interrupt you again."

"Then," resumed she, "I must begin with Lady Dundas. In proper historical style, I shall commence with her birth, parentage, and education. For the first, my father remembers her when she was *damoiselle a'honneur* to Judge Sefton's lady at Surat, and soon after her arrival there, this pretty Abigail by some means captivated old Hector Dundas, (then governor of the province,) who married her. When she returned in triumph to England, she coaxed her foolish husband to appropriate some of his rupee riches to the purchase of a baronetage. I suppose the appellation *Mistress* put her in mind of her ci-devant abigailship; and in a fond hour he complied, and she became *My Lady*. That over, Sir Hector had nothing more obliging to do in this world but to clear her way to perhaps a coronet. He was so good as to think so himself: and, to add to former obligations, had the civility to walk out of it; for one night, whether he had been dreaming of his feats in India, or of a review of his grand entry into his governorship palace, I cannot affirm, but he marched out of his bed room window and broke his neck. Ever since that untoward event, Lady Dundas has exhibited the finest parties in town. Everybody goes to see her, but whether in compliment to their own taste or to her silver muslins, I don't know; for there are half a dozen titled ladies of her acquaintance who, to my certain knowledge, have not bought a ball-dress this twelvemonth. Well, how do you like Lady Dundas?"

"I do not like your sketch," replied Thaddeus, with an unconscious sigh.

"Come, don't sigh about my veracity," interrupted Miss Egerton; "I do assure you I should have been more correct had I been more severe; for her Indian ladyship is as ill-natured as she is ill-bred, and is as presumptuous as ignorant; in short she is a fit mamma for the delectable Miss Dundas, whose description you shall have in two questions. Can you imagine Socrates in his wife's petticoats? Can you imagine a pedant, a scold, and a coquette in one woman? If you can, you have a foretaste of Diana Dundas. She is large and ugly, and thinks herself delicate and handsome; she is self-willed and arrogant, and believes herself wise and learned; and, to sum up all, she is the most malicious creature breathing."

"My dear Sophia," cried Lady Tinemouth, alarmed at the effect such high coloring might have on the mind of Thaddeus; "for heaven's sake be temperate! I never heard you so unbecomingly harsh in my life."

Miss Egerton peeped archly in her face.

"Are you serious, Lady Tinemouth? You know that I would not look unbecoming in your eyes. Besides, she is no real relation of yours. Come, shake hands with me, and I will be more merciful to the gentle Euphemia, for I intend that Mr. Constantine shall be her favorite. Won't you?" cried she, resigning her ladyship's hand. Thaddeus shook his head. "I don't understand your Lord Burleigh nods; answer me in words, when I have finished: for I am sure you will delight in the zephyr smiles of so sweet a fairy. She is so tiny and so pretty, that I never see her without thinking of some gay little trinket, all over precious stones. Her eyes are two diamond sparks, melted into lustre; and her teeth, seed pearl, lying between rubies. So much for the casket; but for the quality of the jewel within, I leave you to make the discovery."

Miss Egerton having run herself out of breath, suddenly stopped. Seeing that he was called upon to say something, Thaddeus made an answer which only drew upon him a new volley of raillery. Lady Tinemouth tried to avert it, but she failed; and Sophia continued talking with little interruption until the party separated for the night.

CHAPTER XXII.

HONORABLE RESOURCES OF AN EXILE.

Now that the count thought himself secure of the means of payment, he sent for a physician, to consult him respecting the state of the general. When Dr. Cavendish saw and conversed with the venerable Butzou, he gave it as his opinion that his malady was chiefly on the nerves, and had originated in grief.

"I can too well suppose it," replied Thaddeus.

"Then," rejoined the physician, "I fear, sir, that unless I know something of its cause, my visits will prove almost useless."

The count was silent. The doctor resumed—

"I shall be grieved if his sorrows be of too delicate a nature to be trusted with a man of honor; for in these cases, unless we have some knowledge of the springs of the derangement, we lose time, and perhaps entirely fail of a cure. Our discipline is addressed both to the body and the mind of the patient."

Thaddeus perceived the necessity of compliance, and did so without further hesitation.

"The calamities, sir, which have occasioned the disorder of my friend need not be a secret: too many have shared them with him; his sorrows have been public ones. You must have learnt by his language, Dr. Cavendish, that he is a foreigner and a soldier. He held the rank of general in the King of Poland's service. Since the period in which his country fell, his wandering senses have approximated to what you see."

Dr. Cavendish paused for a moment before he answered the count; then fixing his eyes on the veteran, who was sitting at the other end of the room, constructing the model of a fortified town, he said—

"All that we can do at present, sir, is to permit him to follow his schemes without contradiction, meanwhile strengthening his system with proper medicines, and lulling its irritation by gentle opiates. We must proceed cautiously, and I trust in Heaven that success will crown us at last. I will order something to be taken every night."

When the doctor had written his prescription, and was preparing to go, Thaddeus offered him his fee; but the good Cavendish, taking the hand that presented it, and closing it on the guinea, "No, my dear sir," said he; "real patriotism is too much the idol of my heart to allow me to receive payment when I behold her face. Suffer me, Mr. Constantine, to visit you and your brave companion as a friend, or I never come again."

"Sir, this generous conduct to strangers—"

"Generous to myself, Mr. Constantine, and not to strangers; I cannot consider you as such, for men who devote themselves to their country must find a brother in every honest breast. I will not hear of our meeting on any other terms." *

Thaddeus could not immediately form a reply adequate to the sentiment which the generous philanthropy of the doctor awakened. Whilst he stood incapable of speaking, Cavendish, with one glance of his penetrating eye, deciphered his countenance, and giving him a friendly shake by the hand, disappeared.

The count took up his hat; and musing all the way he went on the unexpected scenes we meet in life,—disappointment where we expected kindness, and friendship where no hope could arise,—he arrived at the door of Lady Dundas, in Harley Street.

He was instantly let in, and with much ceremony ushered into a splendid library, where he was told the ladies would attend him. Before they entered, they allowed him time to examine its costly furniture, its glittering book-cases, bird-cages, globes, and reading-stands, all shining with burnished gilding; its polished plaster casts of the nine muses, which stood in nine recesses about the room, draperied with blue net, looped up with artificial roses; and its fine cut-steel Grecian stove, on each side of which was placed, on sandal-wood pedestals, two five-feet statues of Apollo and Minerva.

Thaddeus had twice walked round these fopperies of learning, when the door opened, and Lady Dundas, dressed in a morning wrapper of Indian shawls, waddled into the apartment. She neither bowed nor curtseyed to the count, who was standing when she entered, but looking at him from head to foot, said as she passed, "So you are come;" and ringing the bell, called to the servant in no very soft tones, "Tell Miss Dundas the person Lady Tinemouth spoke of is here." Her ladyship then sat down in one of the little gilded chairs, leaving Thaddeus still standing on the spot where he had bowed to her entrance.

* This generous man is no fictitious character, the original being Dr. Blackburne, late of Cavendish Square; but who, since the above was written, has long retired from his profession, passing a revered old age in the beautiful neighborhood of our old British classic scenes, the Abbey of Glastonbury.

"You may sit down," cried she, stirring the fire, and not deigning to look at him; "for my daughter may not choose to come this half-hour."

"I prefer standing," replied the count, who could have laughed at the accuracy of Miss Egerton's picture, had he not prognosticated more disagreeableness to himself from the ill manners of which this was a specimen.

Lady Dundas took no further notice of him. Turning from her bloated countenance, (which pride as well as high living had swollen from prettiness to deformity,) he walked to a window and stationed himself there, looking into the street, until the door was again opened, and two ladies made their appearance.

"Miss Dundas," cried her ladyship, "here is the young man that is to teach you German."

Thaddeus bowed; the younger of the ladies curtseyed; and so did the other, not forgetting to accompany such condescension with a toss of the head, that the effect of undue humility might be done away.

Whilst a servant was setting chairs round a table, on which was painted the Judgment of Hercules, Lady Dundas again opened her lips.

"Pray, Mr. Thingumbob, have you brought any grammars, and primers, and dictionaries, and syntaxes with you?"

Before he had time to reply in the negative, Miss Dundas interrupted her mother.

"I wish, madam, you would leave the arrangement of my studies to myself. Does your ladyship think we would learn out of any book which had been touched by other people? Thomas," cried she to a servant, "send Stephens hither."

Thaddeus silently contemplated this strange mother and daughter, whilst the pretty Euphemia paid the same compliment to him. During his stay, he ventured to look once only at her sylph-like figure. There was an unreceding something in her liquid blue eyes, when he chanced to meet them, which displeased him; and he could not help seeing that from the instant she entered the room she had seldom ceased staring in his face.

He was a little relieved by the maid putting the books on the table. Miss Dundas, taking her seat, desired him to sit down by her and arrange the lessons. Lady Dundas was drawing to the other side of Thaddeus, when Euphemia, suddenly whisking round, pushed before her mother, and exclaimed—

"Dear mamma! you don't want to learn!" and squeezed

herself upon the edge of her mother's chair, who, very angrily getting up, declared that rudeness to a parent was intolerable from such well-bred young women, and left the room.

Euphemia blushed at the reproof more than at her conduct; and Miss Dundas added to her confusion by giving her a second reprimand. Thaddeus pitied the evident embarrassment of the little beauty, and to relieve her, presented the page in the German grammar with which they were to begin. This had the desired effect; and for an hour and a half they prosecuted their studies with close attention.

Whilst the count continued his directions to her sister, and then turned his address to herself, Miss Euphemia, wholly unseen by him, with a bent head was affecting to hear him, though at the same time she looked obliquely through her thick flaxen ringlets, and gazing with wonder and admiration on his face as it inclined towards her, said to herself, "If this man were a gentleman, I should think him the most charming creature in the world."

"Will your task be too long, madam?" inquired Thaddeus; "will it give you any inconvenience to remember?"

"To remember what?" asked she, for in truth she had neither seen what he had been pointing at nor heard what he had been saying.

"The lesson madam, I have just been proposing."

"Show it to me again, and then I shall be a better judge."

He did as he was desired, and was taking his leave, when she called after him:

"Pray, Mr. Constantine, come to-morrow at two. I want you particularly."

The count bowed and withdrew.

"And what do you want with him to-morrow, child?" asked Miss Dundas; "you are not accustomed to be so fond of improvement."

Euphemia knew very well what she was accustomed to be fond of; but not choosing to let her austere sister into her predilection for the contemplation of superior beauty, she merely answered, "You know, Diana, you often reproach me for my absurd devotion to novel-reading, and my repugnance to graver books; now I want at once to be like you, a woman of great erudition: and for that purpose I will study day and night at the German, till I can read all the philosophers, and be a fit companion for my sister."

This speech from Euphemia (who had always been so declared an enemy to pedantry as to affirm that she learnt German merely because it was the fashion) would have awakened Miss Dundas to some suspicion of a covert design, had she not been in the habit of taking down such large draughts of adulation, that whenever herself was the subject, she gave it full confidence. Euphemia seldom administered these doses but to serve particular views; and seeing in the present case that a little flattery was necessary, she felt no compunction in sacrificing sincerity to the gratification of caprice. Weak in understanding, she had fed on works of imagination, until her mind loathed all kinds of food. Not content with devouring the elegant pages of Mackenzie, Radcliffe, and Lee, she flew with voracious appetite to sate herself on the garbage of any circulating library that fell in her way.

The effects of such a taste were exhibited in her manners. Being very pretty, she became very sentimental. She dressed like a wood nymph, and talked as if her soul were made of love and sorrow. Neither of these emotions had she ever really felt; but in idea she was always the victim of some ill-fated passion, fancying herself at different periods in love with one or other of the finest young men in her circle.

By this management she kept faithful to her favorite principle that "love was a want of her soul!" As it was the rule of her life, it ever trembled on her tongue, ever introduced the confession of any new attachment, which usually happened three times a-year, to her dear friend Miss Arabella Rothes. Fortunately for the longevity f their mutual friendship, this young lady lived in an ancient house, forty miles to the north of London. This latter circumstance proved a pretty distress for their pens to descant on; and Arabella remained a most charming sentimental writing-stock, to receive the catalogue of Miss Euphemia's lovers; indeed, that gentle creature might have matched every lady in Cowley's calendar with a gentleman. But every throb of her heart must have acknowledged a different master. First, the fashionable sloven, Augustus Somers, lounged and sauntered himself into her good graces; but his dishevelled hair, and otherwise neglected toilette, not exactly meeting her ideas of an elegant lover, she gave him up at the end of three weeks. The next object her eyes fell upon, as most opposite to her former fancy, was the charming Marquis of Inverary. But here all her arrows failed, for she never could extract from him more than a "how d'ye do?" through the long lapse of four months, during which time she continued as constant to his fine figure, and her own folly, as could have fallen to the lot of any poor despairing damsel.

However, my lord was so cruel, so perfidious, as to allow several opportunities to pass in which he might have declared his passion; and she told Arabella, in a letter of six sheets, that she would bear it no longer.

She put this wise resolution in practice, and had already played the same game with half a score, (the last of whom was a young guardsman, who had just ridden into her heart by managing his steed with the air of a "feathered Mercury," one day in Hyde Park,) when Thaddeus made his appearance before her.

The moment she fixed her eyes on him, her inflammable imagination was set in a blaze. She forgot his apparent subordinate quality in the nobleness of his figure; and one or twice that evening, while she was flitting about, the sparkling cynosure of the Duchess of Orkney's masquerade, her thoughts hovered over the handsome foreigner.

She viewed the subject first one way and then another, and, in her ever varying mind, "he was everything by turns, and nothing long;" but at length she argued herself into a belief that he must be a man of rank from some of the German courts, who having seen her somewhere unknown to herself, had fallen in love with her, and so had persuaded Lady Tinemouth to introduce him as a master of languages to her family that he might the better appreciate the disinterestedness of her disposition.

This wild notion having once got into her head, received instant credence. She resolved, without seeming to suspect it, to treat him as his quality deserved, and to deliver sentiments in his hearing which should charm him with their delicacy and generosity.

With these chimeras floating in her brain, she returned home, went to bed, and dreamed that Mr. Constantine had turned out to be the *Duc d'Enghien*, had offered her his hand, and that she was conducted to the altar by a train of princes and princesses, his brothers and sisters.

She woke the next morning from these deliriums in an ecstasy, deeming them prophetic; and, taking up her book, began with a fluttering attention to scan the lesson which Thaddeus had desired her to learn.

CHAPTER XXIII.

"What are these words? These seeming flowers? Maids to call them, 'Love in idleness.'"

The following day at noon, as the Count Sobieski was crossing Cavendish Square to keep his appointment in Harley Street, he was met by Lady Sara Ross. She had spoken with the Misses Dundas the night before, at the masquerade, where discovering the pretty Euphemia through the dress of Eloisa, her jealous and incensed heart could not withstand the temptation of hinting at the captivating Abelard she had selected to direct her studies. Her ladyship soon penetrated into the situation of Euphemia's heated fancy, and drew from her, without betraying herself, that she expected to see her master the following day. Stung to the soul, Lady Sara quitted the rooms, and in a paroxysm of disappointment, determined to throw herself in his way as he went to her rival's house.

With this hope, she had already been traversing the square upwards of half an hour, attended by her maid, when her anxious eye at last caught a view of his figure proceeding along Margaret Street. Hardly able to support her tottering frame, shaken as it was with contending emotions, she accosted him first: for he was passing straight onward, without looking to the right or the left. On seeing her ladyship, he stopped, and expressed his pleasure at the meeting.

"If you *really* are pleased to meet me," said she, forcing a smile, "take a walk with me round the square. I want to speak with you."

Thaddeus bowed, and she put her arm through his, but remained silent for a few minutes, in evident confusion. The count recollected it must now be quite two. He knew the awkwardness of making the Misses Dundas wait; and notwithstanding his reluctance to appear impatient with Lady Sara, he found himself obliged to say—

"I am sorry I must urge your ladyship to honor me with your commands, for it is already past the time when I ought to have been with the Misses Dundas."

"Yes," cried Lady Sara, angrily, "Miss Euphemia told me as much; but, Mr. Constantine, as a friend, I must warn you against her acts, as well as against those of another lady, who would do well to correct the boldness of her manner."

"Whom do you mean, madam?" interrogated Thaddeus, surprised at her warmth, and totally at a loss to conjecture to whom she alluded.

"A little reflection would answer you," returned she, wishing to retreat from an explanation, yet stimulated by her double jealousy to proceed: "she may be a good girl, Mr. Constantine, and I dare say she is; but a woman who has promised her hand to another ought not to flirt with you. What business had Miss Egerton to command you to wear an English dress? But she must now see the danger of her conduct, by your having presumed to obey her."

"Lady Sara!" exclaimed the count, much hurt at this speech, "I hardly understand you; yet I believe I may venture to affirm that in all which you have just now said, you are mistaken. Who can witness the general frankness of Miss Egerton, or listen to the candid manner with which she avows her attachment to Mr. Montresor, and conceive that she possesses any thoughts which would not do her honor to reveal? And for myself," added he, lowering the tone of his voice, "I trust the least of my faults is presumption. It never was my character to presume on any lady's condescension; and if dressing as she approved be deemed an instance of that kind, I can declare, upon my word, had I not found other motives besides her raillery, my appearance should not have suffered a change."

"Are you sincere, Mr. Constantine?" cried Lady Sara, now smiling with pleasure.

"Indeed I am, and happy if my explanation have met with your ladyship's approbation."

"Mr. Constantine," resumed she, "I have no motive but one in my discourse with you,—friendship." And casting her eyes down, she sighed profoundly.

"Your ladyship does me honor."

"I would have you to regard me with the same confidence that you do Lady Tinemouth. My father possesses the first patronage in this country, I therefore have it a thousand times more in my power than she has to render you a service."

Here her ladyship overshot herself; she had not calculated well on the nature of the mind she wished to ensnare.

"I am grateful to your generosity," replied Thaddeus; "but on this head I must decline your kind offices. Whilst I consider myself the subject of one king, though he be in a prison, I cannot accept of any employment under another who is in alliance with his enemies."

Lady Sara discovered her error the moment he had made

his answer; and, in a disappointed tone, exclaimed, "Then you despise my friendship!"

"No, Lady Sara; it is an honor far beyond my merits; and my gratitude to Lady Tinemouth must be doubled when I recollect that I possess such honor through her means."

"Well," cried her ladyship, "have that as you will; but I expect, as a specimen of your confidence in me, you will be wary of Euphemia Dundas. I know she is artful and vain; she finds amusement in attracting the affections of men; and then, notwithstanding her affected sensibility, she turns them into a subject for laughter."

"I thank your ladyship," replied the count; "but in this respect I think I am safe, both from the lady and myself."

"How," asked Lady Sara, rather too eagerly, "is your heart?"——She paused and looked down.

"No, madam!" replied he, sighing as deeply as herself: but with his thoughts far from her and the object of their discourse; "I have no place in my heart to give to love. Besides, the quality in which I appear at Lady Dundas's would preclude the vainest man alive from supposing that such notice from any lady there to him could be possible. Therefore, I am safe, though I acknowledge my obligation to your ladyship's caution."

Lady Sara was satisfied with the first part of this answer. It declared that his heart was unoccupied; and, as he had accepted her proffered friendship, she doubted not, when assisted by more frequent displays of her fascinations, she could destroy its lambent nature, and in the end light up in his bosom a similar fire to that which consumed her own.

The unconscious object of all these devices began internally to accuse his vanity of having been too fanciful in the formation of suspicions which on a former occasion he had believed himself forced to admit. Blushing at a quickness of perception his contrition now denominated folly, he found himself at the bottom of Harley Street.

Lady Sara called her servant to walk nearer to her; and telling Thaddeus she should expect him the next evening at Lady Tinemouth's, wished him good-morning.

He was certain that he must have stayed at least half an hour beyond the time when he ought to be with the sisters. Anticipating very haughty looks, and perhaps a reprimand, he knocked at the door, and was again shown into the library. Miss Euphemia was alone.

He offered some indistinct excuse for having made her wait; but Euphemia, with good-humored alacrity, interrupted him.

"O pray, don't mind; you have made nobody wait but me, and I can easily forgive it; for mamma and my sister chose to to go out at one, it being May-day, to see the chimney-sweepers dine at Mrs. Montague's.* They did as they liked, and I preferred staying at home to repeat my lesson."

Thaddeus, thanking her for her indulgence, sat down, and taking the book, began to question her. Not one word could she recollect. She smiled.

"I am afraid, madam, you have never thought of it since yesterday morning."

"Indeed, I have thought of nothing else: you must forgive me. I am very stupid, Mr. Constantine, at learning languages; and German is so harsh—at least to my ears! Cannot you teach me any other thing? I should like to learn of you of all things, but do think of something else besides this odious jargon! Cannot you teach me to read poetry elegantly?—Shakspeare, for instance; I doat upon Shakspeare!"

"That would be strange presumption in a foreigner?"

"No presumption in the least," cried she; "if you can do it, pray begin! There is Romeo and Juliet."

Thaddeus pushed away the book with a smile.

"I cannot obey. I understand Shakspeare with as much ease as you, madam, will soon do Schiller, if you apply; but I cannot pretend to read the play aloud."

"Dear me, how vexatious!—but I must hear you read something. Do, take up that Werter. My sister got it from the Prussian ambassador, and he tells me it is sweetest in its own language."

The count opened the book.

"But you will not understand a word of it."

"I don't care for that; I have it by heart in English; and if you will only read his last letter to Charlotte, I know I can follow you in my own mind."

To please this whimsical little creature, Thaddeus turned to the letter, and read it forward with a pathos natural to his voice and character. When he came to an end and closed the volume, the cadence of his tones, and the lady's memory, did ample justice to her sensibility. She looked up, and smiling through her watery eyes, which glittered like violets wet with

* This was a gay spectacle, and a most kind act to these poor children, who thus once a-year found themselves refreshed and happy. They resorted to the green court-yard of Mrs. Montague's house every May-day, about one o'clock, dressed in their gala wreaths, and sporting with their brushes and shovels, where they found a good dinner, kind words from their hostess and her guests, and each little sweep received a shilling at parting. On the death of Mrs. Montague, this humane and pleasurable spectacle ceased.

dew, drew out her perfumed handkerchief, and wiping them, said—

"I thank you, Mr. Constantine. You see by this irrepressible emotion that I feel Goethe, and did not ask you a vain favor."

Thaddeus bowed, for he was at a loss to guess what kind of a reply could be expected by so strange a creature.

She continued—

"You are a German, Mr. Constantine. Did you ever see Charlotte?"

"Never, madam."

"I am sorry for that; I should have liked to have heard what sort of a beauty she was. But don't you think she behaved cruelly to Werter? Perhaps you knew him?"

"No, madam; this lamentable story happened before I was born."

"How unhappy for him! I am sure you would have made the most charming friends in the world! Have you a friend, Mr. Constantine."

The count looked at her with surprise. She laughed at the expression of his countenance.

"I don't mean such friends as one's father, mother, sisters and relations: most people have enough of them. I mean a tender, confiding friend, to whom you unbosom all your secrets: who is your other self—a second soul! In short, a creature in whose existence you forget your own!"

Thaddeus followed with his eyes the heightened color of the fair enthusiast, who, accompanying her rhapsody with action expressive as her words, had to repeat her question, "Have you such a friend?" before he found recollection to answer her in the negative.

The count, who had never been used to such extravagant behavior in a woman, would have regarded Miss Euphemia Dundas as little better than insane had he not been prepared by Miss Egerton's description; and he now acquiesced in the young lady's desire to detain him another hour, half amused and half wearied with her aimless and wild fancies. But here he was mistaken. Her fancies were not aimless; his heart was the game she had in view, and she determined a desperate attack should make it her own, in return for the deep wounds she had received from every tone of his voice, whilst reading the Sorrows of Werter.

CHAPTER XXIV.

LADY TINEMOUTH'S BOUDOIR.

THADDEUS spent nearly a fortnight in the constant exercise of his occupations. In the forepart of each day, until two, he prepared those drawings by the sale of which he was empowered every week to pay the good Mrs. Robson for her care of his friend. And he hoped, when the ladies in Harley Street should think it time to defray any part of their now large debt to him, he might be enabled to liquidate the very long bill of his friend's apothecary. But the Misses Dundas possessed too much money to think of its utility; they used it as counters; for they had no conception that to other people it might be the purchaser of almost every comfort. Their comforts came so certainly, they supposed they grew of necessity out of their situation, and their great wealth owned no other commission than to give splendid parties and buy fine things. Their golden shower being exhaled by the same vanity by which it had been shed, they as little regarded its dispersion as they had marked its descent.

Hence, these amiable ladies never once recollected that their master ought to receive some weightier remuneration for his visits than the honor of paying them; and as poets say the highest honors are achieved by suffering, so these two sisters, though in different ways, seemed resolved that Thaddeus should purchase his distinction with adequate pains.

Notwithstanding that Miss Dundas continued very remiss in her lessons, she unrelentingly required the count's attendance, and sometimes, not in the most gentle language, reproached him for a backwardness in learning she owed entirely to her own inattention and stupidity. The fair Diana would have been the most erudite woman in the world could she have found any fine-lady path to the temple of science; but the goddess who presides there being only to be won by arduous climbing, poor Miss Dundas, like the indolent monarch who made the same demand of the philosophers, was obliged to lay the fault of her own slippery feet on the weakness of her conductors.

As Thaddeus despised her most heartily, he bore ill-humor from that quarter with unshaken equanimity. But the pretty

Euphemia was not so easily managed. She had now completely given up her fanciful soul to this prince in disguise, and already began to act a thousand extravagances. Without suspecting the object, Diana soon discovered that her sister was in one of her love fits. Indeed she cared nothing about it; and leaving her to pursue the passion as she liked, poor Euphemia, according to her custom when laboring under this whimsical malady, addicted herself to solitude. This romantic taste she generally indulged by taking her footman to the gate of the green in Cavendish Square, where he stood until she had performed a pensive saunter up and down the walk. After this she returned home, adjusted her hair in the Madonna fashion, (because Thaddeus had one day admired the female head in a Holy Family, by Guido, over the chimney-piece,) and then seating herself in some becoming attitude, usually waited, with her eyes constantly turning to the door, until the object of these devices presented himself. She impatiently watched all his motions and looks whilst he attended to her sister; and the moment that was done, she ran over her own lessons with great volubility, but little attention. Her task finished, she shut the books, and employed the remainder of the time in translating a number of little mottoes into German, which she had composed for boxes, baskets, and other frippery.

One day, when her young teacher was, as usual, tired almost beyond endurance with making common sense out of so much nonsense, Euphemia observed that Diana had removed to the other end of the room with the Honorable Mr. Lascelles. To give an *éclat* to her new studies, Miss Dundas had lately opened her library door to morning visitors; and seeing her sister thus engaged, Euphemia thought she might do what she wished without detection. Hastily drawing a folded paper from her pocket, she desired Thaddeus to take it home, and translate it into the language he liked best.

Surprised at her manner, he held it in his hand.

"Put it in your pocket," added she, in a hurrying voice, "else my sister may see it, and ask what it is!"

Full of wonder, he obeyed her; and the little beauty, having executed her scheme, seemed quite intoxicated with delight. When he was preparing to withdraw, she called to him, and asked when he should visit Lady Tinemouth.

"This evening, madam."

"Then," returned she, "tell her ladyship I shall come and sit half-an-hour with her to-night; and here," added she, running up to him, "present her that rose, with my love." Whilst she put it into his hand, she whispered in a low voice, "and you will tell me what you think of the verses I have given you."

Thaddeus colored and bowed. He hurried out of the house into the street, as if by that haste he could have gotten out of a dilemma to which he feared all this foolish mystery might be only the introduction.

Though of all men in the world he was perhaps the least inclined to vanity, yet he must have been one of the most stupid had he not been convinced by this time of the dangerous attachment of Lady Sara. Added to that painful certainty he now more than dreaded a similar though a slighter folly in Miss Euphemia.

Can a man see himself the daily object of a pair of melting eyes, hear everlasting sighs at his entrance and departure, day after day receive tender though covert addresses about disinterested love, can he witness all this, and be sincere when he affirms it is the language of indifference? If that be possible, the Count Sobieski has no pretensions of modesty. He comprehended the "discoursing" of Miss Euphemia's "eye;" also the tendency of the love-sick mottoes which, under various excuses, she put into his hand; and with many a pitying smile of contempt he contemplated her childish absurdity.

A few days prior to that in which she made this appointment with Thaddeus, she had presented to him another of her posies, which ran thus: "Frighted love, like a wild beast, shakes the wood in which it hides."

Thaddeus almost laughed at the oddity of the conceit.

"Do, dear Mr. Constantine," cried she, "translate it into the sweetest French you can; for I mean to have it put into a medallion, and to give it to the person whom I most value on earth!"

There was something so truly ridiculous in the sentence, that, reluctant to allow even Miss Euphemia to expose herself so far, he considered a moment how he should make anything so bad better, and then said, "I am afraid I cannot translate it literally; but surely, madam, you can do it yourself!"

"Yes; but I like your French better than mine; so pray oblige me."

He had done the same kind of thing a hundred times for her, and, without further discussion, wrote as follows:—

"L'amour tel qu'une biche blessée, se trahit lui-même par sa crainte, qui fait remuer le feuillage qui le couvre."

"Bless me, how pretty!" cried she, and immediately put it into her bosom.

To this unlucky addition of the words *se trahit lui-meme* Thaddeus was indebted for the present of the folded paper. The ever-working imagination of Euphemia had seized the inserted thought as a delicate avowal that he was the wounded deer he had substituted in place of the wild beast; and as soon as he arrived at home, he found the fruits of her mistake in the packet she had given with so much secrecy.

When he broke the seal, something dropped out and fell on the carpet. He took it up, and blushed for her on finding a gold medallion, with the words he had altered for Miss Euphemia engraved on blue enamel. With a vexed haste he next looked at the envelope; it contained a copy of verses, with this line written at the top:

"To him who will apply them."

On perusing them, he found them to be Mrs. Phillips's beautiful translation of that ode of Sappho which runs—

"Blest as the immortal gods is he,
The friend who fondly sits by thee,
And hears and sees thee all the while
Softly speak and sweetly smile!

"'Twas this deprived my soul of rest,
And rais'd such tumults in my breast:
For while I gazed, in transport tost,
My breath was gone, my voice was lost.

"My bosom glow'd; the subtle flame
Ran quick through all my vital frame;
O'er my dim eyes a darkness hung;
My ears with hollow murmurs rung.

"In dewy damps my limbs were chill'd;
My blood with gentle horrors thrill'd:
My feeble pulse forgot to play;
I fainted, sunk and died away!

"EUPHEMIA.

Thaddeus threw the verses and the medallion together on the table, and sat for a few minutes considering how he could extricate himself from an affair so truly farcical in itself, but which might be productive of a very distressing consequence to him.

He was thinking of at once giving up the task of attending either of the sisters, when his eyes falling on the uncomplaining but melancholy features of his poor friend, he exclaimed, "No; for thy sake, gallant Butzou, I will brave every scene, however abhorrent to my heart."

Well aware, from observation on Miss Euphemia, that the seeming tenderness which prompted an act so wild and unbecoming originated in mere caprice, he did not hesitate in determining to return the things in as handsome a manner as possible, and by so doing, at once crush the whole affair. He felt no pain in forming those resolves, because he saw that not one impulse of her conduct sprung from her heart. It was a whim raised by him to-day, which might be superseded by another to-morrow.

But how different was the case with regard to Lady Sara! Her uncontrolled nature could not long brook the restraints of friendship. Every attention he gave to Lady Tinemouth, every civility he paid to Miss Egerton, or to any other lady whom he met at the countess's, went like a dagger to her soul; and whenever she could gain his ear in private, she generally made him sensible of her misery, and his own unhappiness in being its cause, by reproaches which too unequivocally proclaimed their source.

He now saw that she had given way to a reprehensible and headstrong passion; and, allowing for the politeness which is due to the sex, he tried, by an appearance of the most stubborn coldness, and an obstinate perversity in shutting his apprehension against all her speeches and actions, to stem a tide that threatened her with ruin.

Lady Tinemouth at least began to open her eyes to the perilous situation of both her friends. Highly as she esteemed Thaddeus, she knew not the extent of his integrity. She had lived too long near the circle of the heir apparent, and had seen too many men from the courts of the continent, to place much reliance on the firmness of a single and unattached young man when assailed by rank, beauty and love.

Alarmed at what might be the result of her observations, and fearing to lose any time, she had that very evening in which she expected Thaddeus to supper drawn out of Lady Sara the unhappy state of her heart.

The dreadful confession was made by her ladyship, with repeated showers of tears, and in paroxysms of agony which pierced the countess to the soul.

"My dear Lady Sara," cried she, "for heaven's sake, remember your duty to Captain Ross!"

"I shall never forget it," exclaimed her ladyship, shaking her head mournfully, and striking her breast with her clenched hand, "I never look on the face of Constantine that I do not execrate from my heart the vows which I have sworn to Ross;

but I have bound myself his property, and though I hate him, whatever it may cost me, I will never forget that my faith and honor are my husband's."

With a countenance bathed in tears, Lady Tinemouth put her arms round the waist of Lady Sara, who now sat motionless, with her eyes fixed on the fire.

"Dear Lady Sara! that was spoken like yourself. Do more; abstain from seeing Mr. Constantine."

"Don't require of me that?" cried she; "I could easier rid myself of existence. He is the very essence of my happiness. It is only in his company that I forget that I am a wretch."

"This is obstinacy, my dear Lady Sara! This is courting danger."

"Lady Tinemouth, urge me no more. Is it not enough?" continued she, sullenly, "that I am miserable? Would you drive me to desperation? If there be danger; you brought me into it."

"I! Lady Sara?"

"Yes, you, Lady Tinemouth; you introduced him to me."

"But you are married! Singularly attractive and amiable as indeed he is, could I suppose——"

"Nonsense!" cried her ladyship, interrupting her; "you know that I am married to a mere sailor, more in love with his ugly ship than with me! But it is not because Constantine is so handsome that I like him. No; though no human form can come nearer to perfection, yet it was not that: it was you. You and Sophia Egerton were always telling me of his bravery; what wealth and honors he had sacrificed in the service of his country; how nobly he succored the distresses of others; how heedless he was of his own. This fired my imagination and won my heart. No; it was not his personal attractions: I am not so despicable!"

"Dear Lady Sara, be calm!" entreated the countess, completely at a loss how to manage a spirit of such violence. "Think, my dear friend, what horrors you would experience if Mr. Constantine were to discover this predilection, and presume upon it! You know where even the best men are vulnerable."

The eyes of Lady Sara sparkled with pleasure.

"Why, surely, Lady Sara!" exclaimed Lady Tinemouth, doubtingly.

"Don't fear me, Lady Tinemouth; I know my own dignity too well to do anything disgraceful; yet I would acquire the knowledge that he loves me at almost any price. But he is cold," added she: "he is a piece of obstinate petrefaction, which Heaven itself could not melt!"

Lady Tinemouth was glad to hear this account of Thaddeus; but ere she could reply, the drawing-room door opened, and Miss Euphemia Dundas was announced.

When the little beauty expressed her amazement at not seeing Mr. Constantine, Lady Sara gave her such a withering look, that had her ladyship's eyes been Medusan, poor Euphemia would have stood there forever after, a stone statue of disappointment.

CHAPTER XXV.

THE COUNTESS OF TINEMOUTH'S STORY.

MEANWHILE the count, having seen Dr. Cavendish, and received a favorable opinion of his friend, wrote the following note to Miss Euphemia:—

"TO MISS EUPHEMIA DUNDAS.

"Mr. Constantine very much admires the taste of Miss Euphemia Dundas in her choice of the verses which she did him the honor of requesting he would translate into the most expressive language, and to the utmost of his abilities he has obeyed her commands in Italian, thinking that language the best adapted to the versification of the original.

"Mr. Constantine equally admires the style of the medallion which Miss E. Dundas has condescended to enclose for his inspection, and assures her the letters are correct."

Having sealed his note, and seen the general in bed, with little Nanny seated by him to watch his slumbers, Thaddeus pursued his way to Grosvenor Place.

When he entered Lady Tinemouth's drawing-room, he saw that his young *inamorata* had already arrived, and was in close conversation with the countess. Lady Sara, seated alone on a sofa, inwardly upbraided Constantine for what she thought an absolute assignation with Euphemia.

Her half-resentful eyes, yet dewed with the tears which her discourse with Lady Tinemouth had occasioned, sought his averted face, while he looked at Miss Dundas with evident surprise and disgust. This pleased her: and the more so as he only bowed to her rival, shook the countess by the hand, and then turning, took his station beside herself on the sofa.

She would not trust her triumphant eyes towards Lady Tinemouth, but immediately asked him some trifling question. At the same moment Euphemia tapped him on the arm with her fan, and inquired how it happened that she had arrived first.

He was answering Lady Sara. Euphemia impatiently repeated her demand, "How did it happen that I arrived first?"

"I suppose, madam," replied he, smiling, "because you were so fortunate as to set out first. But had I been so happy as to have preceded you, the message and present with which I was honored would have been faithfully delivered, and I hope your ladyship will permit me to do it now," said he, rising, and taking Euphemia's rose from his button, as he approached the countess; "Miss Euphemia Dundas had done me the honor to make me the bearer of sweets to the sweet; and thus I surrender my trust." He bowed, and put the flower into Lady Tinemouth's hand, who smiled and thanked Euphemia. But the little beauty blushed like her own rose; and murmuring within herself at the literal apprehension of her favorite, whom she thought as handsome as Cimon, and as stupid too, she flirted her fan, and asked Miss Egerton whether she had read Charlotte Smith's last delightful novel.

The evening passed off more agreeably to Thaddeus than he had augured on his entrance. Lady Sara always embarrassed and pained him; Miss Euphemia teased him to death; but to-night the storm which had agitated the breast of her ladyship having subsided into thoughtfulness, it imparted so abstracted an air to her ever-lovely countenance, that, merely to elude communication with Euphemia, he remained near her, and by paying those attentions which, so situated, he could not avoid, he so deluded the wretched Lady Sara, as to subdue her melancholy into an enchanting softness which to any other man might have rendered her the most captivating woman on earth.

The only person present who did not approve this change was Lady Tinemouth. At every dissolving smile of her Circean ladyship, she thought she beheld the intoxicating cup at the lips of Thaddeus, and dreaded its effect. Euphemia was too busily employed repeating some new poems, and too intensely dreaming of what her tutor might say on the verses and medallion in his possession, to observe the dangerous ascendency which the superior charms of Lady Sara might acquire over his heart. Indeed, she had no suspicion of finding a rival in her ladyship; and when a servant announced the arrival of her mother's coach, and she saw by her watch that it was twelve o'clock, she arose reluctantly, exclaiming,

"I dare say some plaguing people have arrived who are to stay with us, else mamma would not have sent for me so soon."

"I call it late," said Lady Sara, who would not lose an opportunity of contradicting her; "so I will thank you, Mr. Constantine," addressing herself to him, "to hand me to my coach at the same time."

Euphemia bit her lip at this movement of her ladyship, and followed her down stairs, reddening with anger. Her carriage being first, she was obliged to get into it, but would not suffer the servant to close the door until she had seen Lady Sara seated in hers; and then she called to Mr. Constantine to speak with her.

Lady Sara leaned her head out of the window. While she saw the man she loved approach Lady Dundas's carriage, she, in her turn, bit her lips with vexation.

"Home, my lady?" asked the servant, touching his hat.

"No; not till Miss Dundas's coach drives on.

Miss Euphemia desired Thaddeus to step in for a moment, and he reluctantly obeyed.

"Mr. Constantine!" cried the pretty simpleton, trembling with expectation, as she made room for him beside her, "have you opened the paper I gave you?"

"Yes, madam," returned he, holding the door open, and widening it with one hand, whilst with the other he presented his note, "and I have the honor, in that paper, to have exe cuted your commands."

Euphemia caught it eagerly; and Thaddeus immediately leaping out, wished her a good-night, and hurried back into the house. Whilst the carriages drove away, he ascended to the drawing-room, to take leave of the countess.

Lady Tinemouth, seated on the sofa, was leaning thoughtfully against one of its arms when he re-entered. He approached her.

"I wish you a good-night, Lady Tinemouth."

She turned her head.

"Mr. Constantine, I wish you would stay a little longer with me! My spirits are disturbed, and I am afraid it will be near morning before Sophia returns from Richmond. These rural balls are sad, dissipated amusements!"

Thaddeus laid down his hat and took a seat by her side.

"I am happy, dear Lady Tinemouth, at all times to be with you; but I am sorry to hear that you have met with any thing to discompose you. I was afraid when I came in that something disagreeable had happened; your eyes——"

"Alas! if my eyes were always to show when I have been weeping, they might ever be telling tales!" Her ladyship passed her hand across them, while she added, "We may think on our sorrows with an outward air of tranquillity, but we cannot always speak of them without some agitation."

"Ah, Lady Tinemouth!" exclaimed the count, drawing closer to her; "could not even your generous sympathizing heart escape calamity?"

"To cherish a sympathizing heart, my young friend," replied she, "is not a very effectual way to avoid the pressure of affliction. On the reverse, such a temper extracts unhappiness from causes which would fail to extort even a sigh from dispositions of less susceptibility. Ideas of sensibility and sympathy are pretty toys for a novice to play with; but change those wooden swords into weapons of real metal, and you will find the points through your heart before you are aware of the danger—at least, I find it so. Mr. Constantine, I have frequently promised to explain to you the reason of the sadness which so often tinges my conversation; and I know not when I shall be in a fitter humor to indulge myself at your expense, for I never was more wretched, never stood more in need of the consolations of a friend."

She covered her face with her handkerchief, and remained so for some time. Thaddeus pressed her hand several times, and waited in respectful silence until she recommenced.

"Forgive me, my dear sir; I am very low to-night—very nervous. Having encountered two or three distressing circumstances to-day, these tears relieve me. You have heard me speak of my son, and of my lord; yet I never collected resolution to recount how we were separated. This morning I saw my son pass my window; he looked up; but the moment I appeared, he turned away and hastened down the street. Though I have received many stronger proofs of dislike, both from his father and himself, yet slight as this offence may seem, it pierced me to the soul. O, Mr. Constantine, to know that the child to whom I gave life regards me with abhorrence, is dreadful—is beyond even the anxious partiality of a mother either to excuse or to palliate!"

"Perhaps, dear Lady Tinemouth, you misjudge Lord Harwold; he may be under the commands of his father, and yet yearn to show you his affection and duty."

"No, Mr. Constantine; your heart is too good even to guess what may be the guilt of another. Gracious Heaven! am I obliged to speak so of my son!—he who was my darling! —he who once loved me so dearly! But hear me, my dear sir; you shall judge for yourself, and you will wonder that I am now alive to endure more. I have suffered by him, by his father, and by a dreadful woman, who not only tore my husband and children from me, but stood by till I was beaten to the ground. Yes, Mr. Constantine, any humane man would shudder as you do at such an assertion; but it is too true. Soon after Lady Olivia Lovel became the mistress of my lord, and persuaded him to take my son from me, I heard that the poor boy had fallen ill through grief, and lay sick at his lordship's house in Hampshire. I heard he was dying. Imagine my agonies. Wild with distress, I flew to the park lodge, and, forgetful of anything but my child, was hastening across the park, when I saw this woman, this Lady Olivia, approaching me, followed by two female servants. One of them carried my daughter, then an infant, in her arms; and the other, a child of which this unnatural wretch had recently become the mother. I was flying towards my little Albina, to clasp her to my heart, when Lady Olivia caught hold of my arm. Her voice now rings in my ears. 'Woman!' cried she, 'leave this place, there are none here to whom you are not an object of abhorrence.'

"Struggling to break from her, I implored to be permitted to embrace my child; but she held me fast, and, regardless of my cries, ordered both the women to return into the house. Driven to despair, I dropped on my knees, conjuring her, by her feelings as a mother, to allow me for one moment to see my dying son, and that I would promise, by my hopes of everlasting happiness, to cherish her child as my own should it ever stand in need of a friend. The horrid woman only laughed at my prayers, and left me in a swoon. When I recovered, the first objects I beheld were my lord and Lady Olivia standing near me, and myself in the arms of a man-servant, whom they had commanded to carry me outside the gate. At the sight of my husband, I sprang to his feet, when with one dreadful blow of his hand he struck me to the ground. Merciful Providence! how did I retain my senses! I besought this cruel husband to give me a second blow, that I might suffer no more.

"'Take her out of my sight,' cried he · 'she is mad.'

"I was taken out of his sight, more dead than alive, and led by his pitying servants to an inn, where I was afterwards confined for three weeks with a brain fever. From that hour I have never had a day of health."

Thaddeus was shocked beyond utterance at this relation. The paleness of his countenance being the only reply he made, the anguished narrator resumed.

"I have gone out of order. I proposed to inform you clearly of my situation, but the principal outrage of my heart rose immediately to my lips. I will commence regularly, if I can methodize my recollection.

"The Earl of Tinemouth married me from passion: I will not sanctify his emotions by the name of affection; though," added she, forcing a smile, "these faded features too plainly show that of all mankind, I loved but him alone. I was just fifteen when he came to visit my father, who lived in Berkshire. My father, Mr. Cumnor, and his father, Lord Harwold, had been friends at college. My lord, then Mr. Stanhope, was young, handsome, and captivating. He remained the autumn with us, and at the end of that period declared an affection for me which my heart too readily answered. About this time he received a summons from his father, and we parted. Like most girls of my age, I cherished an unconquerable bashfulness against admitting any confidant to my attachment; hence my parents knew nothing of the affair until it burst upon them in the cruelest shape.

"About two months after Mr. Stanhope's departure, a letter arrived from him, urging me to fly with him to Scotland. He alleged as a reason for such a step that his grandfather, the Earl of Tinemouth, insisted on his forming a union with Lady Olivia Lovel, who was then a young widow, and the favorite niece of the most powerful nobleman in the kingdom. Upon this demand, he confessed to the earl that his affections were engaged. His lordship, whose passions were those of a madman, broke into such horrible execrations of myself and my family, that Mr. Stanhope, himself, alas! enraged, intemperately swore that no power on earth should compel him to marry so notorious a woman as Lady Olivia Lovel, nor to give me up. After communicating these particulars, he concluded with repeating his entreaties that I would consent to marry him in Scotland. The whole of this letter so alarmed me, that I showed it to my parents. My father answered it in a manner befitting his own character, but that only irritated the impetuous passions of my lover. In the paroxysm of his rage, he flew to the earl his grandfather, upbraided him with the ruin of his happiness, and so exasperated the old man, that he drew his sword upon him; and had it not been for the interference of his father, Lord Harwold, who happened to enter at the moment, a most fatal catastrophe might have ensued. To end the affair at once, the latter, whose gentle nature embraced the mildest measures, obtained the earl's permission to send Mr. Stanhope abroad.

"Meanwhile I was upheld by my revered parent, who is now no more, in firmly rejecting my lover's entreaties for a private marriage. And as his grandfather continued resolutely deaf to his prayers or threats, he was at length persuaded by his excellent father to accompany some friends to France.

"At the end of a few weeks Mr. Stanhope began to regard them as spies on him; and after a violent quarrel, they parted, no one knowing to what quarter my lover directed his steps. I believe I was the first who heard any tidings of him. I remember well; it was in 1773, about four-and-twenty years ago, that I received a letter from him. Oh! how legibly are these circumstances written on my memory! It was dated from Italy, where, he told me, he resided in complete retirement, under the assumed name of Sackville."

At this name, with every feature fixed in dismay, Thaddeus fell back on the sofa.

The countess caught his hand.

"What is the matter? You are ill? What is the matter?"

The bolt of indelible disgrace had struck to his heart. It was some minutes before he could recover; but when he did speak, he said, "Pray go on, madam; I am subject to this. Pray forgive me, and go on; I shall become better as you proceed."

"No, my dear friend; I will quit my dismal story at present, and resume it some other time."

"Pray continue it now," rejoined Thaddeus; "I shall never be more fit to listen. Do, I entreat you."

"Are you sincere in your request? I fear I have already affected you too much."

"No; I am sincere: let me hear it all. Do not hold back anything which relates to that stain to the name of Englishman, who completed his crimes by rendering you wretched!"

"Alas! he did," resumed her ladyship; "for when he returned, which was in consequence of the Earl of Tinemouth's death, my father was also dead, who might have stood between me and my inclinations, and so preserved me from many succeeding sorrows. I sealed my fate, and became Stanhope's wife.

"The father of my husband was then Earl of Tinemouth; and as he had never been averse to our union, he presented me with a cottage on the banks of the Wye, where I passed three delightful years, the happiest of womankind. My husband, my mother, and my infant son formed my felicity; and greatly I prize it—too greatly to be allowed a long continuance!

"At the end of this period, some gay friends paid us a visit. When they returned to town, they persuaded my lord to be of the party. He went; and from that fatal day all my sufferings arose.

"Lord Harwold, instead of being with me in a fortnight, as he had promised, procrastinated his absence under various excuses from week to week, during which interval my Albina was born. Day after day I anticipated the delight of putting her into the arms of her father; but, what a chasm! she was three months old before he appeared; and ah! how changed. He was gloomy to me, uncivil to my mother, and hardly looked at the child."

Lady Tinemouth stopped at this part of her narrative to wipe away her tears. Thaddeus was sitting forward to the table, leaning on his arm, with his hand covering his face. The countess was grateful for an excess of sympathy she did not expect; and taking his other hand, as it lay motionless on his knee, "What a consolation would it be to me," exclaimed she, "durst I entertain a hope that I may one day behold but half such pity from my own son!"

Thaddeus pressed her hand. He did not venture to reply; he could not tell her that she deceived herself even here; that it was not her sorrows only which so affected him, but the remembered agonies of his own mother, whom he did not doubt the capricious villany of this very earl, under the name of Sackville (a name that had struck like a death-bolt to the heart of Thaddeus when he first heard his mother utter it), had devoted to a life of uncomplaining but ceaseless self-reproach. And had he derived his existence from such a man—the reprobate husband of Lady Tinemouth! The conviction humbled him, crushed him, and trod him to the earth. He did not look up, and the countess resumed:

"It would be impossible, my dear sir, to describe to you the gradual changes which assured me that I had lost the heart of my husband. Before the end of the winter he left me again, and I saw him no more until that frightful hour in which he struck me to the ground.

"The good earl came into Monmouthshire about six weeks after I parted with my lord. I was surprised and rejoiced to see my kind father-in-law; but how soon were my emotions driven into a different course! He revealed to me that during Lord Harwold's first visit to town he had been in the habit of spending entire evenings with Lady Olivia Lovel.

"'This woman,' added he, 'is the most artful of her sex. In spite of her acknowledged dishonor, you well know my deceased father would gladly have married her to my son; and now it seems, actuated by revenge, she resents Lord Harwold's refusal of her hand by seducing him from his wife. Alas! I am too well convinced that the errors of my son bear too strict a resemblance to those of his grandfather. Vain of his superior abilities, and impatient of contradiction, flattery can mould him to what it pleases. Lady Olivia had discovered these weak points in his character; and, I am informed, she soon persuaded him that you impose on his affection by detaining him from the world; and, seconded by other fascinations, my deluded son has accompanied her into Spain.'

"You may imagine, Mr. Constantine, my distraction at this intelligence. I was like one lost; and the venerable earl, fearing to trust me in such despair out of his sight, brought me and my children with him to London. In less than four months afterwards, I was deprived of this inestimable friend by a paralytic stroke. His death summoned the new earl to England. Whilst I lay on a sick bed, into which I had been thrown by the shock of my protector's death, my lord and his mistress arrived in London.

"They immediately assumed the command of my lamented father-in-law's house, and ordered my mother to clear it directly of me. My heart-broken parent obeyed, and I was carried in a senseless state to a lodging in the nearest street. But when this dear mother returned for my children, neither of them were permitted to see her. The malignant Lady Olivia, actuated by an insatiable hatred of me, easily wrought on my frantic husband (for I must believe him mad) to detain them entirely. A short time after this, that dreadful scene happened which I have before described.

"Year succeeded year, during which time I received many cruel insults from my husband, many horrible ones from my son; for I had been advised to institute a suit against my lord, in which I only pleaded for the return of my children. I lost my cause, owing, I hope, to bad counsel, not the laws of my country. I was adjudged to be separated from the earl, with a maintenance of six hundred a-year, which he hardly pays. I was tied down never to speak to him, nor to his son nor his daughter. Though this sentence was passed, I never acknowledged its justice, but wrote several times to my children. Lord Harwold, who is too deeply infected with his father's cruelty, has either returned my letters unopened or with insulting replies. For my daughter, she keeps an undeviating silence; and I have not even seen her since the moment in which she was hurried from my eyes in Tinemouth Park.

"In vain her brother tries to convince me that she detests me. I will not believe it; and the hope that, should I survive her father, I may yet embrace my child, has been, and will be, my source of maternal comfort until it be fulfilled, or I bury my disappointment in the grave."

Lady Tinemouth put her handkerchief to her eyes, which were again flowing with tears. Thaddeus thought he must speak, if he would not betray an interest in her narrative, which he determined no circumstance should ever humble him to reveal. Raising his head from his hand, he unconsciously discovered to the countess his agonized countenance.

"Kind, affectionate Constantine! surely such a heart as thine never would bring sorrow to the breast of a virtuous husband! You could never betray the self-deluded Lady Sara to any fatal error!"

Lady Tinemouth did not utter these thoughts. Thaddeus rose from his seat.

"Farewell, my honored friend!" said he; "may Heaven bless you and pardon your husband!"

Then grasping her hand, with what he intended should be a pressure of friendship, but which his internal tortures rendered almost intolerable, he hastened down stairs, opened the outward door, and got into the street.

Unknowing and heedless whither he went, with the steps of a man driven by the furies, he traversed one street and then another. As he went along, in vain the watchmen reminded him by their cries that it was past three o'clock: he still wandered on, forgetting that it was night, that he had any home, any destination.

His father was discovered!—that father of whom he had entertained a latent hope, should they ever meet, that he might produce some excuse for having been betrayed into an act disgraceful to a man of honor. But when all these filial dreams were blasted by the conviction that he owed his being to the husband of Lady Tinemouth, that his mother was the victim of a profligate, that he had sprung from a man who was not merely a villain, but the most wanton, the most despicable of villains, he saw himself bereft of hope and overwhelmed with shame and horror.

Full of reflections which none other than a son in such circumstances can conceive, he was ost amidst the obscure alleys of Tottenham Court Yard, when loud and frequent cries recalled his attention. A quantity of smoke, with flashes of light, led him to suppose that they were occasioned by a fire; and a few steps further the awful spectacle burst upon his sight.

It was a house from the windows of which the flames were breaking out in every direction, whilst a gathering concourse of people were either standing in stupefied astonishment or uselessly shouting for engines and assistance.

At the moment in which he arrived, two or three naked wretches just escaped from their beds, were flying from side to side, making the air echo with their shrieks.

"Will nobody save my children?" cried one of them, approaching Thaddeus, and wringing her hands in agony; "will nobody take them from the fire?"

"Where shall I seek them?" replied he.

"Oh! in that room," exclaimed she, pointing; "the flames are already there; they will be burnt! they will be burnt!"

The poor woman was hurrying madly forward, when the count stopped her, and giving her in charge of a bystander, cried: "Take care of this woman, if possible, I will save her children." Darting through the open door, in defiance of the smoke and danger, he made his way to the children's room, where, almost suffocated by the sulphurous cloud that surrounded him, he at last found the bed; but it contained one child only. This he instantly caught up in his arms, and was hastening down the stairs, when the cries of the other from a distant part of the building made him hesitate; but thinking it better to secure one than to hazard both by lingering, he rushed into the street just as a post-chaise had stopped to inquire the particulars of the accident. The carriage-door being open, Thaddeus, seeing ladies in it, without saying a word, threw the sleeping infant into their laps, and hastened back into the house, where he hoped to rescue the other child before the fire could increase to warrant despair.

Th flames having now made dreadful progress, his face, hands, and clothes were scorched by their fury as he flew from the room, following the shrieks of the child, who seemed to change its situation with every exertion that he made to reach

At length, when every moment he expected the house would sink under his feet, as a last attempt he directed his steps along a passage he had not before observed, and to his great joy beheld the object of his search flying down a back staircase. The boy sprung into his arms; and Thaddeus, turning round, leaped from one landing-place to another, until he found him self again in the street, surrounded by a crowd of people.

He saw the poor mother clasp this second rescued child to her breast; and whilst the spectators were loading her with congratulations, he slipped away unseen, and proceeded homewards, with a warmth at his heart which made him forget, in the joy of a benevolent action, that petrifying shock which had been occasioned by the vices of one too nearly allied to his being to be hated without horror.

CHAPTER XXVI.

THE KINDREDSHIP OF MINDS.

When Thaddeus awoke next morning, he found himself more refreshed, and freer from the effects of the last night's discovery, than he could have reasonably hoped. The presence of mind and activity which the fire called on him to exert, having forced his thoughts into a different channel, had afforded his nerves an opportunity to regain some portion of their usual strength. He could now reflect on what he had heard without suffering the crimes of another to lay him on the rack. The reins were again restored to his hand, and neither agitation nor anxiety showed themselves in his face or manner.

Though the count's sensibility was very irritable, and when suddenly excited he could not always conceal his emotion, yet he possessed a power of look which immediately repressed the impertinence of curiosity or insolence. Indeed, this mantle of repulsion proved to be his best shield; for never had man more demands on the dignity of his soul to shine out about his person.

Not unfrequently has his sudden appearance in the study-room at Lady Dundas's at once called a natural glow through the ladies' rouge, and silenced the gentlemen, when he has happened to enter while Miss Dundas and half-a-dozen other beaux and belles have been ridiculing Euphemia on the absurd civilities she paid to her language-master!

The morning after the fire, a little bevy of these fashionable butterflies were collected in this way at one corner of Miss Dundas's Hercules table, when, during a moment's pause, "I hope, Miss Beaufort," cried the Honorable Mr. Lascelles, "I hope you don't intend to consume the brightness of your eyes over this stupid language?"

"What language, Mr. Lascelles?" inquired she; "I have this moment entered the room, and I don't know what you are talking about."

"Good Lud! that is very true," cried he; "I mean a shocking jargon, which a shocking penseroso man teaches to these ladies. We want to persuade Miss Euphemia that it spoils her mouth."

"You are always misconceiving me, Mr. Lascelles," interrupted Miss Dundus, impatiently; "I did not advance one word against the language; I merely remonstrated with Phemy against her preposterous attentions to the man we hire to teach it."

"That was what I meant, madam," resumed he, with a low bow.

"You meant what, sir?" demanded the little beauty, contemptuously; "but I need not ask. You are like a bad mirror, which from radical defect always gives false reflections."

"Very good, efaith, Miss Euphemia! I declare, sterling wit! It would honor Sheridan, or your sister."

"Mr. Lascelles," cried Euphemia, more vexed than before, "let me tell you such impertinence is very unbecoming a gentleman."

"Upon my soul, Miss Euphemia!"

"Pray allow the petulant young lady to get out of her airs, as she has, I believe, got out of her senses, without our help!" exclaimed Miss Dundas; "for I declare I know not where she picked up these vile democratic ideas."

"I am not a democrat, Diana," answered Euphemia, rising from her seat; "and I won't stay to be abused, when I know it is all envy, because Mr. Constantine happened to say that I have a quicker memory than you have."

She left the room as she ended. Miss Dundas, ready to storm with passion, but striving to conceal it, burst into a violent laugh, and turning to Miss Beaufort, said: "You now see, my dear Mary, a sad specimen of Euphemia's temper; yet I hope you won't think too severely of her, for, poor thing, she has been spoilt by us all."

"Pray, do not apologize to me in particular!" replied Miss

aufort; "but, to be frank, I think it probable she would have shown her temper less had that little admonition been given in private. I doubt not she has committed something wrong, yet——"

"Yes, something very wrong," interrupted Miss Dundas, reddening at this rebuke; "both Mr. Lascelles and Lord Berrington there——"

"Don't bring in my name, I pray, Miss Dundas," cried the viscount, who was looking over an old edition of Massinger's plays; you know I hate being squeezed into squabbles."

Miss Dundas dropped the corners of her mouth in contempt, and went on.

"Well, then, Mr. Lascelles, and Miss Poyntz, here, have both at different times been present when Phemy has conducted herself in a very ridiculous way towards a young man Lady Tinemouth sent here to teach us German. Can you believe it possible that a girl of her fashion could behave in this style without having first imbibed some very dangerous notions? I am sure I am right, for she could not be more civil to him if he were a gentleman." Miss Dundas supposed she had now set the affair beyond controversy, and stopped with an air of triumph. Miss Beaufort perceived that her answer was expected.

"I really cannot discover anything in the matter so very reprehensible," replied she. "Perhaps the person you speak of may have the qualifications of a gentleman; he may be above his situation."

"Ah! above it, sure enough!" cried Lascelles, laughing boisterously at his own folly. He is tall enough to be above everything, even good manners; for notwithstanding his plebeian calling, I find he doesn't know how to keep his distance."

"I am sorry for that, Lascelles," cried Berrington, measuring the puppy with his good-natured eye; "for these Magog men are terrible objects to us of meaner dimensions! 'A substitute shines brightly as a king until a king be by,'"

"Why, my lord, you do not mean to compare me with such a low fellow as this? I don't understand Lord Berrington——"

"Bless me, gentlemen!" cried Miss Dundas, frightened at the angry looks of the little honorable; "why, my lord, I thought you hated squabbles?"

"So I do, Miss Dundas," replied he, laying down his book and coming forward; "and upon my honor, Mr. Lascelles," added he, smiling, and turning towards the coxcomb, who stood nidging his head with anger by Miss Beaufort's chair,—"upon my honor, Mr. Lascelles, I did not mean to draw any parallel between your person and talents and those of this Mr. ———, I forget his name, for truly I never saw him in my life; but I dare swear no comparison can exist between you."

Lascelles took the surface of this speech, and bowed, whilst his lordship, turning to Miss Beaufort, began to compliment himself on possessing so fair an ally in defence of an absent person.

"I never have seen him," replied she; "and what is more, I never heard of him, till on entering the room Mr. Lascelles arrested me for my opinion about him. I only arrived from the country last night, and can have no guess at the real grounds of this ill-judged bustle of Miss Dundas's regarding a man she styles despicable. If he be so, why retain him in her service? and, what is more absurd, why make a person in that subordinate situation the subject of debate amongst her friends?"

"You are right, Miss Beaufort, returned Lord Berrington; but the eloquent Miss Dundas is so condescending to her friends, she lets no opportunity slip of displaying her sceptre, both over the republic of words and the empire of her mother's family."

"Are not you severe now, Lord Berrington? I thought you generous to the poor tutor!"

"No; I hope I am just on both subjects. I know the lady and it is true that I have seen nothing of the tutor; but it is natural to wield the sword in favor of the defenceless, and I always consider the absent in that light."

Whilst these two conversed at one end of the room, the other group were arraigning the presumption of the vulgar, and the folly of those who gave it encouragement.

At a fresh burst of laughter from Miss Dundas, Miss Beaufort mechanically turned her head; her eye was arrested by the appearance of a gentleman in black, who was standing a few paces within the door. He was regarding the party before him with that lofty tranquillity which is inseparable from high rank, when accompanied by a consciousness of as high inward qualities. His figure, his face, and his air contained that pure simplicity of contour which portrays all the graces of youth with the dignity of manhood.

Miss Beaufort in a moment perceived that he was unobserved; rising from her seat, she said, "Miss Dundas, here is a gentleman."

Miss Dundas looked round carelessly.

"You may sit down, Mr. Constantine."

"Is it possible!" thought Miss Beaufort, as he approached, and the ingenuous expression of his fine countenance was directed towards her; "can this noble creature have been the subject of such impertinence!"

"I commend little Phemy's taste!" whispered Lord Berrington, leaving his seat. "Ha! Miss Beaufort, a young Apollo?"

"And not in disguise!" replied she in the same manner, just as Thaddeus had bowed to her; and, with "veiled lids," was taking up a book from the table: not to read, but literally to have an object to look on which could not insult him.

"What did Miss Dundas say was his name?" whispered the viscount.

"Constantine, I think."

"Mr. Constantine," said the benevolent Berrington, "will you accept this chair?"

Thaddeus declined it. But the viscount read in the "proud humility" of his bow that he had not always waited, a dependent, on the nods of insolent men and ladies of fashion; and, with a good-humored compulsion, he added, "pray oblige me for by that means I shall have an excuse to squeeze into the *Sultane*, which is so 'happy as to bear the weight of Beaufort!'"

Though Miss Beaufort was almost a stranger to his lordship, having seen him only once before, with her cousin in Leicestershire, she smiled at this unexpected gallantry, and in consideration of the motive, made room for him on the sofa.

Offence was not swifter than kindness in its passage to the heart of Thaddeus, who, whilst he received the viscount's chair, raised his face towards him with a look beaming such graciousness and obligation, that Miss Beaufort turned with a renewed glance of contempt on the party. The next instant they left the study.

The instant Miss Dundas closed the door after her, Lord Berrington exclaimed, "Upon my honor, Mr. Constantine, I have a good mind to put that terrible pupil of yours into my next comedy! Don't you think she would beat Katharine and Petruchio all to nothing? I declare I will have her."

"In *propria persona*, I hope?" asked Miss Beaufort, with a playful smile. Lord Berrington answered with a gay sally from Shakspeare.

The count remained silent during these remarks, though he fully appreciated the first civil treatment which had greeted him since his admission within the doors of Lady Dundas. Miss Euphemia's attentions owned any other source than benevolence.

Miss Beaufort wished to relieve his embarrassment by addressing him; but the more she thought, the less she knew what to say; and she had just abandoned it as a vain attempt, when Euphemia entered the room alone. She curtseyed to Thaddeus, and took her place at the table. Lord Berrington rose.

"I must say good-by, Miss Euphemia; I will not disturb your studies. Farewell, Miss Beaufort!" added he, addressing her, and bending his lips to her hand. "Adieu! I shall look in upon you to-morrow. Good-morning, Mr. Constantine!"

Thaddeus bowed to him, and the viscount disappeared.

"I am surprised, Miss Beaufort," observed Euphemia, pettishly (her temper not having subsided since her sister's lecture), "how you can endure that coxcomb!"

"Pardon me, Euphemia," replied she; "though I did not exactly expect the ceremony his lordship adopts in taking leave, yet I think there is a generosity in his sentiments which deserves a better title."

"I know nothing about his sentiments, for I always run away from his conversation. A better title! I declare you make me laugh. Did you ever see such fantastical dressing? I vow I never meet him without thinking of Jemmy Jessamy, and the rest of the gossamer beaux who squired our grandmothers!"

"My acquaintance with Lord Berrington is trifling," returned Miss Beaufort, withdrawing her eyes from the pensive features of the count, who was sorting the lessons; "yet I am so far prepossessed in his favor, that I see little in his appearance to reprehend. However, I will not contest that point, as perhaps the philanthropy I this morning discovered in his heart, the honest warmth with which he defended an absent character, after you left the room, might render his person as charming in my eyes as I certainly found his mind."

Thaddeus had not for a long time heard such sentiments out of Lady Tinemouth's circle; and he now looked up to take a distinct view of the speaker.

In consequence of the established mode, that the presiding lady of the house is to give the tone to her guests, many were the visitors of Miss Dundas whose faces Thaddeus was as ignorant of when they went out of the library as when they came in. They took little notice of him; and he, regarding them much less, pursued his occupation without evincing a greater consciousness of their presence than what mere ceremony demanded.

Accordingly, when in compliance with Lord Berrington's politeness he received his chair, and saw him remove to a sofa beside a very beautiful woman, in the bloom of youth, Thaddeus supposed her manner might resemble the rest of Miss Dundas's friends, and never directed his glance a second time to her figure. But when he heard her (in a voice that was melody itself) defend his lordship's character, on principles which bore the most honorable testimony to her own, his eyes were riveted on her face.

Though a large Turkish shawl involved her fine person, a modest grace was observable in its every turn. Her exquisitely moulded arm, rather veiled than concealed by the muslin sleeve that covered it, was extended in the gentle energy of her vindication. Her lucid eyes shone with a sincere benevolence, and her lips seemed to breathe balm while she spoke. His soul startled within itself as if by some strange recognition that agitated him, and drew him inexplicably towards its object. It was not the beauty he beheld, nor the words she uttered, but he did not withdraw his fixed gaze until it encountered an accidental turn of her eyes, which instantly retreated with a deep blush mantling her face and neck. She had never met such a look before, except in an occasional penetrating glance from an only cousin, who had long watched the movements of her heart with a brother's care.

But little did Thaddeus think at that time who she was, and how nearly connected with that friend whose neglect has been a venomed shaft unto his soul!

Mary Beaufort was the orphan heiress of Admiral Beaufort, one of the most distinguished officers in the British navy. He was the only brother of the now lamented Lady Somerset, the beloved mother of Pembroke Somerset, so often the eloquent subject of his discourse in the sympathizing ear of Thaddeus Sobieski! The admiral and his wife, a person also of high quality, died within a few months after the birth of their only child, a daughter, having bequeathed her to the care of her paternal aunt; and to the sole guardianship of that exemplary lady's universally-honored husband, Sir Robert Somerset, baronet, and M. P for the county. When Lady Somerset's death spread mourning throughout his, till then, happy home, (which unforeseen event occurred hardly a week before her devoted son returned from the shores of the Baltic,) a double portion of Sir Robert's tenderness fell upon her cherished niece.

In her society alone he found any consolation for his loss. And soon after Pembroke's arrival, his widowed father, relinquishing the splendid scenes of his former life in London, retired into the country, sometimes residing at one family seat, sometimes at another, hoping by change of place to obtain some alleviating diversion from his ever sorrow-centred thoughts.

Sir Robert Somerset, from the time of his marriage with the accomplished sister of Admiral Beaufort to the hour in which he followed her to the grave, was regarded as the most admired man in every circle, and yet more publicly respected as being the magnificent host and most munificent patron of talent, particularly of British growth, in the whole land. Besides, by his own genius as a statesman, he often stood a tower of strength in the senate of his country; and his general probity was of such a stamp, that his private friends were all solicitous to acquire the protection of his name over any important trusted interests for their families. For instance, the excellent Lord Avon consigned his only child to his guardianship, and his wealthy neighbor, Sir Hector Dundas, made him sole trustee over the immense fortunes of his daughters.

This latter circumstance explains the intimacy between two families, the female parts of which might otherwise have probably seldom met.

On Sir Robert Somerset's last transient visit to London, (which had been only on a call of business, on account of his minor charge, Lord Avon,) Lady Dundas became so urgent in requesting him to permit Miss Beaufort to pass the ensuing season with her in town, that he could not, without rudeness, refuse. In compliance with this arrangement, the gentle Mary, accompanied by Miss Dorothy Somerset, a maiden sister of the baronet's, quitted Deerhurst to settle themselves with her importunate ladyship in Harley Street for the remainder of the winter—at least the winter of fashion ! which, by a strange effect of her magic wand, in defiance of grassy meadows, leafy trees, and sweetly-scented flowers, extends its nominal sceptre over the vernal months of April, May, and even the rich treasures of "resplendent June."

The summer part of this winter Miss Beaufort reluctantly consented should be sacrificed to ceremony, in the dust and heat of a great city ; and if the melancholy which daily increased upon Sir Robert since the death of his wife had not rendered her averse to oppose his wishes, she certainly would have made objections to the visit.

During the journey, she could not refrain from drawing a

comparison to Miss Dorothy between the dissipated insipidity of Lady Dundas's way of life and the rationality as well as splendor of her late lamented aunt's.

Lady Somerset's monthly assemblies were not the most elegant and brilliant parties in town, but her weekly *conversazi-ones* surpassed everything of the kind in the kingdom. On these nights her ladyship's rooms used to be filled with the most eminent characters which England could produce. There the young Mary Beaufort listened to pious divines of every Christian persuasion. There she gathered wisdom from real philosophers; and in the society of our best living poets, amongst whom were those leaders of our classic song, Rogers and William Southey, and the amiable Jerningham, cherished an enthusiasm for all that is great and good. On these evenings Sir Robert Somerset's house reminded the visitor of what he had read or imagined of the school of Athens. He beheld not only sages, soldiers, statesmen, and poets, but intelligent and amiable women. And in this rare assembly did the beautiful Mary imbibe that steady reverence for virtue and talent which no intermixture with the ephemera of the day could ever after either displace or impair.

Notwithstanding this rare freedom from the chains with which her merely fashionable friends would have shackled her mind, Miss Beaufort possessed too much judgment and delicacy to flash her liberty in their eyes. Enjoying her independence with meekness, she held it more secure. Mary was no declaimer, not even in the cause of oppressed goodness or injured genius. Aware that direct opposition often incenses malice, she directed the shaft from its aim, if it were in her power, and when the attempt failed, strove by respect or sympathy to heal the wound she could not avert. Thus, whatever she said or did bore the stamp of her soul, whose leading attribute was modesty. By having learned much, and thought more, she proved in her conduct that reflection is the alchemy which turns knowledge into wisdom.

Never did she feel so much regret at the shrinking of her powers from coming forth by some word or deed in aid of offended worth, as when she beheld the foreign stranger, so noble in aspect, standing under the overbearing insolence of Miss Dundas's parasites. But she perceived that his dignified composure rebounded their darts upon his insulters, and respect took the place of pity. The situation was new to her; and when she dropped her confused eyes beneath his unexpected gaze, she marvelled within herself at the ease with which she had just taken up the cause of Lord Berrington, and the difficulty she had found to summon one word as a repellant to the unmerited attack on the man before her.

Euphemia cared nothing about Lord Berrington: to her his faults or his virtues were alike indifferent; and forgetting that civility demanded some reply to Miss Beaufort's last observation, or rather taking advantage of the tolerated privilege usurped by many high-bred people of being ill-bred, when and how they pleased, she returned to Thaddeus, and said with a forced smile—

"Mr. Constantine, I don't like your opinion upon the ode I showed to you; I think it a very absurd opinion; or perhaps you did not understand me rightly?"

Miss Beaufort took up a book, that her unoccupied attention might not disturb their studies.

Euphemia resumed, with a more natural dimple, and touching his glove with the rosy points of her fingers, said,

"You are stupid at translation."

Thaddeus colored, and sat uneasily; he knew not how to evade this direct though covert attack.

"I am a bad poet, madam. Indeed, it would be dangerous even for a good one to attempt the same path with Sappho and Phillips."

Euphemia now blushed as deeply as the count, but from another motive. Opening her grammar, she whispered, "You are either a very dull or a very modest man!" and, sighing, began to repeat her lesson.

While he bent his head over the sheet he was correcting, she suddenly exclaimed, "Bless me, Mr. Constantine, what have you been doing? I hope you don't read in bed! The top of your hair is burnt to a cinder! Why, you look much more like one who has been in a fire than Miss Beaufort does."

Thaddeus put his hand to his head.

"I thought I had brushed away all marks of a fire, in which I really was last night."

"A fire!" interrupted Miss Beaufort, closing her book: "was it near Tottenham Court Road?"

"It was, madam," answered he, in a tone almost as surprised as her own.

"Good gracious!" cried Euphemia, exerting her little voice, that she might be heard before Miss Beaufort could have time to reply; "then I vow you are the gentleman who Miss Beaufort said ran into the burning house, and, covered with flames, saved two children from perishing!"

"And I am so happy as to meet one of the ladies," replied he, turning with an animated air to Miss Beaufort, "in you, madam, who so humanely assisted the poor sufferers, and received the child from my arms?"

"It was indeed myself, Mr. Constantine," returned she, a tear swimming over her eye, which in a moment gave the cue to the tender Euphemia. She drew out her handkerchief; and whilst her pretty cheeks overflowed, and her sweet voice was rendered sweeter by an emotion raised by ten thousand delightful fancies, she took hold of Miss Beaufort's hand.

"Oh! my lovely friend, wonder not that I esteem this brave Constantine far beyond his present station!"

Thaddeus drew back. Miss Beaufort looked amazed; but Euphemia had mounted her romantic Pegasus, and the scene was too sentimental to close.

"Come here, Mr. Constantine," cried she, extending her other hand to his. Wondering where this folly would terminate, he gave it to her, when, instantly joining it with that of Miss Beaufort, she pressed them together, and said, "Sweet Mary! heroic Constantine! I thus elect you the two dearest friends of my heart. So charmingly associated in the delightful task of compassion, you shall ever be commingled in my faithful bosom."

Then putting her handkerchief to her eyes, she walked out of the room, leaving Miss Beaufort and the count, confused and confounded, by the side of each other. Miss Beaufort, suspecting that some extravagant fancy had taken possession of the susceptible Euphemia towards her young tutor, declined speaking first. Thaddeus, fixing his gaze on her downcast and revolving countenance, perceived nothing like offended pride at his undesigned presumption. He saw that she was only embarrassed, and after a minute's hesitation, broke the silence.

"I hope that Miss Beaufort is sufficiently acquainted with the romance of Miss Euphemia's character to pardon the action, unintentional on my part, of having touched her hand? I declare I had no expectation of Miss Euphemia's design."

"Do not make any apology to me, Mr. Constantine," returned she, resuming her seat; "to be sure I was a little electrified by the strange situation in which her vivid feelings have just made us actors. But I shall not forego my claim on what she promised—your acquaintance."

Thaddeus expressed his high sense of her condescension.

"I am not fond of fine terms," continued she, smiling; "but I know that time and merit must purchase esteem. I can engage for the first, as I am to remain in town at least three months; but for the last, I fear I shall never have the opportunity of giving such an earnest of my desert as you did last night of yours."

Footsteps sounded on the stairs. Thaddeus took up his hat, and bowing, replied to her compliment with such a modest yet noble grace, that she gazed after him with wonder and concern. Before he closed the door he again bowed. Pleased with the transient look of a soft pleasure which beamed from his eyes, through whose ingenuous mirrors every thought of his soul might be read, she smiled a second adieu and as he disappeared, left the room by another passage.

CHAPTER XXVI..

SUCH THINGS WERE.

WHEN the count appeared the succeeding day in Harley Street, Miss Beaufort introduced him to Miss Dorothy Somerset as the gentleman who had so gallantly preserved the lives of the children at the hazard of his own.

Notwithstanding the lofty tossings of Miss Dundas's head, the good old maid paid him several encomiums on his intrepidity; and telling him that the sufferers were the wife and family of a poor tradesman, who was then absent in the country, she added, "But we saw them comfortably lodged before we left them; and all the time we stayed, I could not help congratulating myself on the easy compliance of Mary with my whims. I dislike sleeping at an inn; and to prevent it then, I had prevailed on Miss Beaufort to pursue our road to town even through the night. It was lucky it happened so, for I am certain Mary will not allow these poor creatures a long lament over the wreck of their little property."

"How charmingly charitable, my lovely friend!" cried Euphemia; "let us make a collection for this unfortunate woman and her babes. Pray, as a small tribute, take that from me!" She put five guineas into the hand of the glowing Mary.

The ineffable grace with which the confused Miss Beaufort laid the money on her aunt's knee did not escape the observation of Thaddeus; neither did the unintended approbation of his eye pass unnoticed by its amiable object.

When Lady Tinemouth was informed that evening by the count of the addition to the Harley Street party, she was delighted at the news, saying she had been well acquainted with Miss Dorothy and her neice during the lifetime of Lady Somerset, and would take an early day to call upon them. During this part of her ladyship's discourse, an additional word or two had unfolded to her auditor the family connection that had subsisted between the lady she regretted and his estranged friend. And when the countess paused, Thaddeus, struck with a forgiving pity at this intelligence, was on the point of expressing his concern that Pembroke Somerset had lost so highly-prized a mother; but recollecting that Lady Tinemouth was ignorant of their ever having known each other, he allowed her to proceed without a remark.

"I never have been in company with Sir Robert's son," continued the countess; "it was during his absence on the Continent that I was introduced to Lady Somerset. She was a woman who possessed the rare talent of conforming herself to all descriptions of people; and whilst the complacency of her attentions surpassed the most refined flattery, she commanded the highest veneration for herself. Hence you may imagine my satisfaction in an acquaintance which it is probable would never have been mine had I been the happy Countess of Tinemouth, instead of a deserted wife. Though the Somersets are related to my lord, they had long treated him as a stranger; and doubly disgusted at his late behavior, they commenced a friendship with me, I believe, to demonstrate more fully their detestation of him. Indeed, my husband is a creature of inconsistency. No man possessed more power to attract friends than Lord Tinemouth, and no man had less power to retain them; as fast as he made one he offended the other, and has at last deprived himself of every individual out of his own house who would not regard his death as a fortunate circumstance."

"But, Lady Somerset," cried Thaddeus, impatient to change a subject every word of which was a dagger to his heart, "I mean Miss Dorothy Somerset, Miss Beaufort——"

"Yes," returned her ladyship; "I see, kind Mr. Constantine, your friendly solicitude to disengage me from retrospections so painful! Well, then, I knew and very much esteemed the two ladies you mention; but after the death of Lady Somerset, their almost constant residence in the country has greatly prevented a renewal of this pleasure. However, as they are now in town, I will thank you to acquaint them with my intention to call upon them in Harley Street. I remember always thinking Miss Beaufort a very charming girl."

Thaddeus thought her more. He saw that she was beautiful; he had witnessed instances of her goodness, and the reccollection filled his mind with a complacency the more tender, since it had so long been a stranger to his bosom; and again he felt the strange emotion which had passed over his heart at their first meeting. But further observations were prevented by the entrance of Miss Egerton and Lady Sara Ross.

"I am glad to see you, Mr. Constantine," cried the lively Sophia, shaking hands with him: "you are the very person I have been plotting against."

Lady Tinemouth was uneasy at the care with which Lady Sara averted her face, well knowing that it was to conceal the powerful agitation of her features, which always took place at the sight of Thaddeus.

"What is your plot, Miss Egerton?" inquired he; "I shall consider myself honored by your commands, and do not require a conspiracy to entrap my obedience."

"That's a good soul! Then I have only to apply to you, Lady Tinemouth. Your ladyship must know," cried she, "that as Lady Sara and I were a moment ago driving up the Haymarket, I nodded to Mr. Coleman, who was coming out of the playhouse. He stopped, I pulled the check-string, and we had a great deal of confab out of the window. He tells me a new farce is to come out this day week, and he hoped I would be there! 'No,' said I, 'I cannot, for I am on a visit with that precise body, the Countess of Tinemouth, who would not, to save you and all your generation, come into such a mob.' 'Her ladyship shall have my box,' cried he; 'for I would not for the world lose the honor of your opinion on the merits of my farce.' 'To be sure not!' cries I; so I accepted his box, and drove off, devising with Lady Sara how to get your ladyship as our chaperon and Mr. Constantine to be our beau. He has just promised; so dear Lady Tinemouth, don't be inflexible!"

Thaddeus was confounded at the dilemma into which his ready acquiescence had involved his prudence. The countess shook her head.

"Now I declare, Lady Tinemouth," exclaimed Miss Egerton, "this is an absolute stingy fit! You are afraid of your purse! You know this private box precludes all awkward meetings, and you can have no excuse."

"But it cannot preclude all awkward sights," answered her ladyship. "You know, Sophia, I never go into public, for fear of being met by the angry looks of my lord or my son."

"Disagreeable people!" cried Miss Egerton, pettishly; "I wish some friendly whirlwind would take your lord and son out of the world together."

"Sophia!" retorted her ladyship, with a grave air.

"Rebuke me, Lady Tinemouth, if you like; I confess I am no Serena, and these trials of temper don't agree with my constitution. There," cried she, throwing a silver medal on the table, and laughing in spite of herself: "there is our passport; but I will send it back, and so break poor Coleman's heart."

"Fie! Sophia," answered her ladyship, patting her half-angry cheeks; "would you owe to your petulance what was denied to your good humor?"

"Then your ladyship will go!" exclaimed she, exultingly. "You have yielded; these sullens were a part of my stratagem, and I won't let you secede."

Lady Tinemouth thought this would be a fair opportunity to show one of the theatres to her young friend, without involving him in expense or obligation, and accordingly she gave her consent.

"Do you intend to favor us with your company, Lady Sara?" asked the countess, with a hope that she might refuse.

Lady Sara, who had been standing silently at the window, rather proudly answered—

"Yes, madam, if you will honor me with your protection."

Lady Tinemouth was the only one present who understood the resentment which these words conveyed; and, almost believing that she had gone too far, by implying suspicion, she approached her with a pleading anxiety of countenance. "Then, Lady Sara, perhaps you will dine with me? I mean to call on Miss Dorothy Somerset, and would invite her to be of the party."

Lady Sara curtseyed her acceptance of the invitation, and, smiling, appeared to think no more of the matter. But she neither forgot it nor found herself able to forgive Lady Tinemouth for having betrayed her into a confidence which her own turbulent passions had made but too easy. She had listened unwillingly to the reasonable declaration of the countess, that her only way to retreat from an error which threatened criminality was to avoid the object.

"When a married woman," observed her ladyship, in that confidential conference, "is so unhappy as to love any man besides her husband, her only safety rests in the resolution to quit his society, and to banish his image whenever it obtrudes."

Lady Sara believed herself incapable of this exertion, and hated the woman who thought it necessary. By letter and conversation Lady Tinemouth tried to display in every possible light the enormity of giving encouragement to such an attachment, and ended with the unanswerable climax—the consideration of her duty to Heaven.

Of this argument Lady Sara knew little. She never reflected on the true nature of religion, though she sometimes went to church, repeated the prayers, without being conscious of their spirit; and when the coughing, sneezing, and blowing of noses which commonly accompany the text subsided, she generally called up the remembrance of the last ball, or an anticipation of the next assembly, to amuse herself until the prosing business was over. From church she drove to the Park, where, bowling round the ring, or sauntering in the gardens, she soon forgot that there existed in the universe a Power of higher consequence to please than her own vanity—and the admiration of the spectators.

Lady Sara would have shuddered at hearing any one declare himself a deist, much more an atheist; but for any influence which her nominal belief held over her desires, she might as well have been either. She never committed an action deserving the name of premeditated injury, nor went far out of her way to do her best friend a service,—not because she wanted inclination, but she ceased to remember both the petitioner and his petition before he had been five minutes from her sight. She had read as much as most fine ladies have read: a few histories, a few volumes of essays, a few novels, and now and then a little poetry comprised the whole range of her studies; these, with morning calls and evening assemblies, occupied her whole day. Such had been the routine of her life until she met the once "young star" of Poland, Thaddeus Sobieski, in an unknown exile, an almost nameless guest, at Lady Tinemouth's, which event caused a total revolution in her mind and conduct.

The strength of Lady Sara's understanding might have credited a better education; but her passions bearing an equal power with this mental vigor, and having taken a wrong direction, she neither acknowledged the will nor the capability to give the empire to her reason. When love really entered her heart, its first conquest was over her universal vanity; she surrendered all her admirers, in the hope of securing the admiration of Thaddeus; its second victory mastered her discretion;

she revealed her unhappy affection to Lady Tinemouth, and more than hinted it to himself. What had she else to lose? She believed her honor to be safer than her life. Her *honor* was the term. She had no conception, or, at best, a faint one, that a breach of the marriage vow could be an outrage on the laws of Heaven. The word sin had been gradually ignored by the oligarchy of fashion, from the hour in which Charles the Second and his profligate court trod down piety with hypocrisy; and in this day the new philosophy has accomplished its total outlawry, denouncing it as a rebel to decency and the freedom of man.

Thus, the Christian religion being driven from the haunts of the great, pagan morality is raised from that prostration where, Dagon-like, it fell at the feet of the Scriptures, and is again erected as the idol of adoration. Guilt against Heaven fades before the decrees of man; his law of ethics reprobates crime. But crime is only a temporal transgression, in opposition to the general good; it draws no consequent punishment heavier than the judgment of a broken human law, or the resentment of the offended private parties. Morality neither promises rewards after death nor denounces future chastisement for error. The disciples of this independent doctrine hold forth instances of the perfectibility of human actions, produced by the unassisted decisions of human intellect on the limits of right and wrong. They admire virtue, because it is beautiful. They practice it, because it is heroic. They do not abstain from the gratification of an intemperate wish under the belief that it is sinful, but in obedience to their reason, which rejects the commission of a vicious act because it is uncomely. In the first case, God is their judge; in the latter, themselves. The comparison need only be proposed, to humble the pride that made it necessary. How do these systematizers refine and subtilize? How do they dwell on the principle of virtue, and turn it in every metaphysical light, until their philosophy rarifies it to nothing! Some degrade, and others abandon, the only basis on which an upright character can stand with firmness. The bulwark which Revelation erected between the passions and the soul is levelled first; and then that instinctive rule of right which the modern casuist denominates the citadel of virtue falls of course.

By such gradations the progress of depravity is accomplished; and the general leaven having worked to Lady Sara's mind on such premises, (though she might not arrange them so distinctly,) she deduced that what is called conjugal right is a mere establishment of man, and might be extended or limited by him to any length he pleased. For instance, the Turks were not content with one wife, but appropriated hundreds to one man; and because such indulgence was permitted by Mohammed, no other nation presumed to call them culpable.

Hence she thought that if she could once reconcile herself to believe that her own happiness was dearer to her than the notice of half a thousand people to whom she was indifferent; that only in their opinion and the world's her flying to the protection of Thaddeus would be crime;—could she confidently think this, what should deter her from instantly throwing herself into the arms of the man she loved?"*

"Ah!" cried the thus self-deluded Lady Sara, one night, as she traversed her chamber in a paroxysm of tears; "what are the vows I have sworn? How can I keep them? I have sworn to love, to honor Captain Ross; but in spite of myself, without any action of my own, I have broken both these oaths. I cannot love him; I hate him; and I cannot honor the man I hate. What have I else to break? Nothing. Ny nuptial vow is as completely annihilated as if I had left him never to return. How?" cried she, after a pause of some minutes, "how shall I know what passes in the mind of Constantine? Did he love me, would he protect me, I would brave the whole universe. Oh, I should be the happiest of the happy!"

Fatal conclusion of reflection! It infected her dreaming and her waking fancy. She regarded everything as an enemy that opposed her passion; and as the first of these enemies, she detested Lady Tinemouth. The countess's last admonishing letter enraged her by its arguments; and, throwing it into the fire with execrations and tears, she determined to pursue her own will, but to affect being influenced by her ladyship's counsels.

The Count Sobieski, who surmised not the hundredth part of the infatuation of Lady Sara, began to hope that her ardent manner had misled him, or that she had seen the danger of such imprudence.

Under these impressions, the party for the theatre was settled; and Thaddeus, after sitting an hour in Grosvenor Place, returned to his humble home, and attendance on his venerated friend.

* Such were the moral tactics for human conduct at the commencement of this century. But, thanks to the patience of God, he has given a better spirit to the present age,—to its philosophy an admirable development of the wisdom and beneficence of his works, instead of the former metaphysical vanities and contradictory bewilderments of opinions concerning the divine nature and the elements of man, which, as far as a demon-spirit could go, had plunged the created world, both physically and morally, into the darkness of chaos again. The Holy Scriptures are now the foundation studies of our country, and her ark is safe.—1845.

CHAPTER XXVIII.

MARY BEAUFORT AND HER VENERABLE AUNT.

THE addition of Miss Dorothy Somerset and Miss Beaufort to the morning group at Lady Dundas's imparted a less reluctant motion to the before tardy feet of the count, whenever he turned them towards Harley Street.

Miss Dorothy readily supposed him to have been better born than he appeared; and displeased with the treatment he had received from Miss Dundas and her guests, behaved to him herself with the most gratifying politeness.

Aunt Dorothy (for that was the title by which every branch of the baronet's family addressed her) was full twenty years the senior of her brother, Sir Robert Somerset. Having in her youth been thought very like the famous and lovely Mrs. Woffington, she had been considered the beauty of her time, and, as such, for ten years continued the reigning belle. Nevertheless, she arrived at the age, of seventy-two without having been either the object or the subject of a fervent passion.

Possessing a fine understanding, a refined taste, and fine feelings, by some chance she had escaped love. It cannot be denied that she was much admired, much respected, and much esteemed, and that she received two or three splendid proposals from men of rank. Some of those men she admired, some she respected, and some she esteemed, but not one did she love, and she successively refused them all. Shortly after their discharge, they generally consoled themselves by marrying other women, who, perhaps, wanted both the charms and the sense of Miss Somerset; yet she congratulated them on their choice, and usually became the warm friend of the happy couple.

Thus year passed over year; Miss Somerset continued the esteemed of every worthy heart, though she could not then kindle the embers of a livelier glow in any one of them; and at the epoch called a *certain age*, she found herself an old maid, but possessing so much good humor and affection towards the young people about her, she did not need any of her own to mingle in the circle.

This amiable old lady usually took her knitting into the library before the fair students; and whenever Thaddeus entered the room, (so natural is it for generous natures to sympathize,) his eyes first sought her venerable figure; then glancing around to catch an assuring beam from the lovely countenance of her niece, he seated himself with confidence.

The presence of these ladies operated as a more than sufficient antidote to the disagreeableness of his situation. To them he directed all the attention that was not required by his occupation; he heard them only speak when a hundred others were talking; he saw them only when a hundred others were in company.

In addition to this pleasant change, Miss Euphemia's passion assumed a less tormenting form. She had been reading Madame d'Arblay's Camilla; and becoming enamored of the delicacy and pensive silence of the interesting heroine, she determined on adopting the same character; and at the same time taking it into her ever-creative brain that Constantine's coldness bore a striking affinity to the caution of Edgar Mandelbert, she wiped the rouge from her pretty face, and prepared to "let concealment, like a worm in the bud, feed on her damask cheek."

To afford decorous support to this fancy, her gayest clothes were thrown aside, to make way for a negligence of apparel which cost her two hours each morning to compose. Her dimpling smiles were now quite banished. She was ever sighing, and ever silent, and ever lolling and leaning about; reclining along sofas, or in some disconsolate attitude, grouping herself with one of the marble urns, and sitting "like Patience on a monument smiling at grief."

Thaddeus preferred this pathetic whim to her former Sapphic follies; it afforded him quiet, and relieved him from much embarrassment.

Every succeeding visit induced Miss Beaufort to observe him with a more lively interest. The nobleness yet humility with which he behaved towards herself and her aunt, and the manly serenity with which he suffered the insulting sarcasms of Miss Dundas, led her not merely to conceive but to entertain many doubts that his present situation was that of his birth.

The lady visitors who dropped in on the sisters' studies were not backward in espousing the game of ridicule, as it played away a few minutes, to join in a laugh with the "witty Diana." These gracious beings thought their sex gave them privilege to offend; but it was not always that the gentlemen durst venture beyond a shrug of the shoulder, a drop of the lip, a wink of the eye, or a raising of the brows. Mary observed with contempt that they were prudent enough not to exercise even these specimens of a mean hostility except when its noble object had turned his back, and regarding him with increased admiration, she was indignant, and then disdainful, at the envy which actuated these men to treat with affected scorn him whom they secretly feared.

The occasional calls of Lady Tinemouth and Miss Egerton stimulated the cabal against Thaddeus. The sincere sentiment of equality with themselves which these two ladies evinced by their behavior to him, and the same conduct being adopted by Miss Dorothy and her beautiful niece, besides the evident partiality of Euphemia, altogether inflamed the spleen of Miss Dundas, and excited her *coterie* to acts of the most extravagant rudeness.

The little phalanx, at the head of which was the superb Diana, could offer no real reason for disliking a man who was not only their inferior, but who had never offended them even by implication. It was a sufficient apology to their easy consciences that "he gave himself such courtly airs as were quite ridiculous—that his presumption was astonishing. In short, they were all idle, and it was exceedingly amusing to lounge a morning with the rich Dundases and hoax Monsieur."

Had Thaddeus known one fourth of the insolent derision with which his misfortunes were treated behind his back, perhaps even his friend's necessity could not have detained him in his employment. The brightness of a brave man's name makes shadows perceptible which might pass unmarked over a duller surface. Sobieski's delicate honor would have supposed itself sullied by enduring such contumely with toleration. But, as was said before, the male adjuncts of Miss Dundas had received so opportune a warning from an accidental knitting of the count's brow, they never after could muster temerity to sport their wit to his face.

These circumstances were not lost upon Mary; she collected them as part of a treasure, and turned them over on her pillow with the jealous examination of a miser. Like Euphemia, she supposed Thaddeus to be other than he seemed. Yet her fancy did not suppose him gifted with the blood of the Bourbons; she merely believed him to be a gentleman; and from the maternal manner of Lady Tinemouth towards him, she suspected that her ladyship knew more of his history than she chose to reveal.

Things were in this state, when the countess requested that Miss Dorothy would allow her niece to make one in her party to the Haymarket Theatre. The good lady having consented,

Miss Beaufort received the permission with pleasure; and as she was to sup in Grosvenor Place, she ventured to hope that something might fall from her hostess or Miss Egerton which would throw a light on the true situation of Mr. Constantine.

From infancy Miss Beaufort had loved with enthusiasm all kinds of excellence. Indeed, she esteemed no person warmly whom she did no think exalted by their virtues above the common race of mankind. She sought for something to respect in every character; and when she found anything to greatly admire, her ardent soul blazed, and by its own pure flame lit her to a closer inspection of the object about whom she had become more than usually interested.

In former years Lady Somerset collected all the virtue and talent in the country around her table, and it was now found that they were not brought there on a vain errand. From them Miss Beaufort gathered her best lessons in conduct and taste, and from them her earliest perceptions of friendship. Mary was the beloved pupil and respected friend of the brightest characters in England; and though some of them were men who had not passed the age of forty, she never had been in love, nor had she mistaken the nature of her esteem so far as to call it by that name. Hence she was neither afraid nor ashamed to acknowledge a correspondence she knew to be her highest distinction. But had the frank and innocent Mary exhibited half the like attentions which she paid to these men in one hour to the common class of young men through the course of a month, they would have declared that the poor girl was over head and ears in love with them, and have pitied what they would have justly denominated her folly. Foolish must that woman be who would sacrifice the most precious gift in her possession—her heart—to the superficial graces or empty blandishments of a self-idolized coxcomb!

Such a being was not Mary Beaufort; and on these principles she contemplated the extraordinary fine qualities she saw in the exiled Thaddeus with an interest honorable to her penetration and her heart.

When Miss Egerton called with Lady Sara Ross to take Miss Beaufort to the Haymarket, Mary was not displeased at seeing Mr. Constantine step out of the carriage to hand her in. During their drive, Miss Egerton informed her that Lady Tinemouth had been suddenly seized with a headache, but that Lady Sara had kindly undertaken to be their chaperon, and had promised to return with them to sup in Grosvenor Place.

Lady Sara had never seen Mary, though she had frequently heard of her beauty and vast fortune. This last qualification her ladyship hoped might have given an unmerited *éclat* to the first; therefore when she saw in Miss Beaufort the most beautiful creature she had ever beheld, nothing could equal her surprise and vexation.

The happy lustre that beamed in the fine eyes of Mary shone like a vivifying influence around her; a bright glow animated her cheek, whilst a pleasure for which she did not seek to account bounded at her heart, and modulated every tone of her voice to sweetness and enchantment.

"Syren!" thought Lady Sara, withdrawing her large dark eyes from her face, and turning them full of dissolving languor upon Thaddeus; "here are all thy charms directed!" then drawing a sigh, so deep that it made her neighbor start, she fixed her eyes on her fan, and never looked up again until they had reached the playhouse.

The curtain was raised as the little party seated themselves in the box.

"Can anybody tell me what the play is?" asked Lady Sara.

"I never thought of inquiring," replied Sophia.

"I looked in the newspaper this morning," said Miss Beaufort, "and I think it is called *Sighs*,—a translation from a drama of Kotzebue's."

"A strange title!" was the general observation. When Mr. Suett, who personated one of the characters, began to speak, their attention was summoned to the stage.

On the entrance of Mr. Charles Kemble in the character of Adelbert, the count unconsciously turned pale. He perceived by the dress of the actor that he was to personate a Pole; and alarmed at the probability of seeing something to recall recollections which he had striven to banish, his agitation did not allow him to hear anything that was said for some minutes.

Miss Egerton was not so tardy in the use of her eyes and ears; and stretching out her hand to the back of the box, where Thaddeus was standing by Lady Sara's chair, she caught hold of his sleeve.

"There, Mr. Constantine!" cried she; "look at Adelbert! that is exactly the figure you cut in your outlandish gear two months ago."

Thaddeus bowed with a forced smile, and glancing at the stage, replied—

"Then, for the first time in my life, I regret having followed a lady's advice; I think I must have lost by the change."

"Yes," rejoined she, "you have lost much fur and much embroidery, but you now look much more like a Christian."

The substance of these speeches was not lost on Mary, who continued with redoubling interest to mark the changes his countenance underwent along with the scene. As she sat forward, by a slight turn of the head she could discern the smallest fluctuation in his features, and they were not a few. Placing himself at the back of Lady Sara's chair, he leaned over, with his soul set in his eye, watching every motion of Mr. Charles Kemble.

Mary knew, by some accidental words from Lady Tinemouth, that Constantine was a Polander, and the surmise she had entertained of his being unfortunate received full corroboration at the scene in which Adelbert is grossly insulted by the rich merchant. During the whole of it, she scarcely dared trust her eyes towards Constantine's flushed and agitated face.

The interview between Adelbert and Leopold commenced. When the former was describing his country's miseries with his own, Thaddeus unable to bear it longer, unobserved by any but Mary, drew back into the box. In a moment or two afterwards Mr. Charles Kemble made the following reply to an observation of Leopold's, that "poverty is no dishonor."

"Certainly none to me! To Poland, to my struggling country, I sacrificed my wealth, as I would have sacrificed my life if she had required it. My country is no more; and we are wanderers on a burdened earth, finding no refuge but in the hearts of the humane and virtuous."

The passion and force of these words could not fail of reaching the ears of Thaddeus. Mary's attention followed them to their object, by the heaving of whose breast she plainly discovered the anguish of their effect. Her heart beat with increased violence. How willingly would she have approached him, and said something of sympathy, of consolation! but she durst not; and she turned away her tearful eye, and looked again towards the stage.

Lady Sara now stood up, and hanging over Mary's chair, listened with congenial emotions to the scene between Adelbert and the innocent Rose. Lady Sara felt it all in her own bosom; and looking round to catch what was passing in the count's mind, she beheld him leaning against the box, with his head inclined to the curtain of the door. "Mr. Constantine!" almost unconsciously escaped her lips. He started, and discovered by the humidity on his eyelashes why he had withdrawn. Her ladyship's tears were gliding down her cheeks. Miss Egerton, greatly amazed at the oddness of this closet scene, turned to Miss Beaufort, who a moment before having caught a glimpse of the distressed countenance of the count, could only bow her head to Sophia's sportive observation.

Who is there that can enter into the secret folds of the heart and know all its miseries? Who participate in that joy which dissolves and rarifies man to the essence of heaven? Soul must mingle with soul, and the ethereal voice of spirits must speak before these things can be comprehended.

Ready to suffocate with the emotions she repelled from her eyes, Mary gladly affected to be absorbed in the business of the stage, (not one object of which she now saw), and with breathless attention lost not one soft whisper which Lady Sara poured into the ear of Thaddeus.

"Why," asked her ladyship, in a tremulous and low tone, "why should we seek ideal sorrows, when those of our own hearts are beyond alleviation? Happy Rose!" sighed her ladyship. "Mr. Constantine," continued she, "do not you think that Adelbert is consoled, at least, by the affection of that lovely woman?"

Like Miss Beaufort, Constantine had hitherto replied with bows only.

"Come," added Lady Sara, laying her soft hand on his arm, and regarding him with a look of tenderness, so unequivocal that he cast his eyes to the ground, while its sympathy really touched his heart. "Come," repeated she, animated by the faint color which tinged his cheek; "you know that I have the care of this party, and I must not allow our only *cavalier* to be melancholy."

"I beg your pardon, Lady Sara," returned he, gratefully pressing the hand that yet rested on his arm; "I am not very well. I wish that I had not seen this play."

Lady Sara sunk into the seat from which she had risen. He had never before taken her hand, except when assisting her to her carriage; this pressure shook her very soul, and awakened hopes which rendered her for a moment incapable of sustaining herself or venturing a reply.

There was something in the tones of Lady Sara's voice and in her manner far more expressive than her words: mutual sighs which breathed from her ladyship's bosom and that of Thaddeus, as they sat down, made a cold shiver run from the head to the foot of Miss Beaufort. Mary's surprise at the meaning of this emotion caused a second tremor, and with a palpitating heart she asked herself a few questions.

Could this interesting young man, whom every person of sense appeared to esteem and respect, sully his virtues by participating in a passion with a married woman? No; it was impossible.

Notwithstanding this decision, so absolute in his exculpation, her pure heart felt a trembling, secret resolve, "even for the sake of the honor of human nature," (she whispered to herself), to observe him so hereafter as to be convinced of the real worth of his principles before she would allow any increase of the interest his apparently reversed fate had created in her compassionate bosom.

What might be altogether the extent of that "reversed fate," she could form no idea. For though she had heard, in common with the rest of the general society, of the recent "melancholy fate of Poland!" she knew little of its particulars, politics of every kind, and especially about foreign places, being an interdicted subject in the drawing-rooms of Sir Robert Somerset. Therefore the simply noble mind of Mary thought more of the real nobility that might dwell in the soul of this expatriated son of that country than of the possible appendages of rank he might have left there.

With her mind full of these reflections, she awaited the farce without observing it when it appeared. Indeed, none of the party knew anything about the piece (to see which they had professedly come to the theatre) excepting Miss Egerton, whose ever merry spirits had enjoyed alone the humor of Totum in the play, and who now laughed heartily, though unaccompanied, through the ridiculous whims of the farce.

Nothing that passed could totally disengage the mind of Thaddeus from those remembrances which the recent drama had aroused. When the melting voice of Lady Sara, in whispers, tried to recall his attention, by a start only did he evince his recollection of not being alone. Sensible, however, to the kindness of her motive, he exerted himself; and by the time the curtain dropped, he had so far rallied his presence of mind as to be able to attend to the civility of seeing the ladies safe out of the theatre.

Miss Egerton, laughing, as he assisted her into the carriage, said, "I verily believe, Mr. Constantine, had I glanced round during the play, I should have seen as pretty a lachrymal scene between you and Lady Sara as any on the stage. I won't have this flirting! I declare I will tell Captain Ross——"

She continued talking; but turning about to offer his service to Miss Beaufort, he heard no more.

Miss Beaufort, however self-composed in thought, felt strangely: she felt cold and reserved; and undesignedly she appeared what she felt. There was a grave dignity in her air, accompanied with a collectedness and stillness in her before animated countenance, which astonished and chilled Thaddeus, though she had bowed her head and given him her hand to put her into the coach.

On their way home Miss Egerton ran over the merits of the play and farce; rallied Thaddeus on the "tall Pole," which she threatened should be his epithet whenever he offended her; and then, flying from subject to subject, talked herself and her hearers so weary, that they internally rejoiced when the carriage stopped in Grosvenor Place.

After they had severally paid their respects to Lady Tinemouth, who, being indisposed, was lying on the sofa, she desired Thaddeus to draw a chair near her.

"I want to learn," said she, "what you think of our English theatre?"

"Prithee, don't ask him!" cried Miss Egerton, pouring out a glass of water; "we have seen a tremendous brother Pole of his, who I believe has 'hopped off' with all his spirits! Why, he has been looking as rueful as a half-drowned man all the night; and as for Lady Sara, and I could vow Miss Beaufort, too, they have been two Niobes—'all tears.' So, good folks, I must drink better health to you, to save myself from the vapors."

"What is all this, Mr. Constantine?" asked the countess, addressing Thaddeus, whose eyes had glanced with a ray of delighted surprise on the blushing though displeased face of Miss Beaufort.

"My weakness," replied he, commanding down a rising tremor in his voice, and turning to her ladyship; "the play relates to a native of Poland, one who, like myself, an exile in a strange land, is subjected to sufferings and contumelies the bravest spirits may find hard to bear. Any man may combat misery; but even the most intrepid will shrink from insult. This, I believe, is the sum of the story. Its resemblance in some points to my own affected me; and," added he, looking gratefully at Lady Sara, and timidly towards Miss Beaufort, "if these ladies have sympathized with emotions against which I strove, but could not entirely conceal, I owe to it the sweetest consolation now in the power of fate to bestow."

"Poor Constantine!" cried Sophia Egerton, patting his head with one hand, whilst with the other she wiped a tear from her always smiling eye, "forgive me if I have hurt you. I like you vastly, though I must now and then laugh at you; you know I hate dismals, so let this tune enliven us all!" and flying to her piano, she played and sang two or three merry airs, till the countess commanded her to the supper-table.

At this most sociable repast of the whole day, cheerfulness seemed again to disperse the gloom which had threatened the circle. Thaddeus set the example. His unrestrained and elegant conversation acquired new pathos from the anguish that was driven back to his heart; like the beds of rivers, which infuse their own nature with the current, his hidden grief imparted an indescribable interest and charm to all his sentiments and actions.*

Mary now beheld him in his real character. Unmolested by the haughty presence of Miss Dundas, he became unreserved, intelligent, and enchanting. He seemed master of every subject talked on, and discoursed on all with a grace which corroborated her waking visions that he was as some bright star fallen from his sphere.

With the increase of Miss Beaufort's admiration of the count's fine talents, she gradually lost the recollection of what had occupied her mind relative to Lady Sara; and her own beautiful countenance dilating into confidence and delight, the evening passed away with chastened pleasure, until the little party separated for their several homes.

Lady Tinemouth was more than ever fascinated by the lovely Miss Beaufort. Miss Beaufort was equally pleased with the animation of the countess; but when she thought on Thaddeus, she was surprised, interested, absorbed.

Lady Sara Ross's reflections were not less delightful. She dwelt with redoubled passion on that look from the count's eyes, that touch of his hand, which she thought were signs of a reciprocal awakened flame. Both actions were forgotten by him the moment after they were committed; yet he was not ungrateful; but whilst he acknowledged her generous sympathy at that time, he could not but see that she was straying to the verge of a precipice which no thoroughly virtuous woman should ever venture to approach.

He found a refuge from so painful a meditation in the idea of the ingenuous Mary, on whose modest countenance virtue

* When this was written, (in the year 1804,) domestic hours were earlier; and the "supper hour" had not then dissipation and broken rest for a consequence.

seemed to have "set her seal." Whilst recollecting the pitying kindness of her voice and looks, his heart owned the empire of purity, and in the contemplation of her unaffected excellence, he the more deplored the witcheries of Lady Sara, and the dangerous uses to which her impetuous feelings addressed them.

CHAPTER XXIX.

HYDE PARK.

NEXT morning, when Thaddeus approached the general's bed to give him his coffee, he found him feverish, and his mind more than usually unsettled.

The count awaited with anxiety the arrival of the benevolent Cavendish, whom he expected. When he appeared, he declared his increased alarm. Dr. Cavendish having felt the patient's pulse, expressed a wish that he could be induced to take a little exercise. Thaddeus had often urged this necessity to his friend, but met with constant refusals. He hopelessly repeated the entreaty now, when, to his surprise and satisfaction, the old man instantly consented.

Having seen him comfortably dressed, (for the count attended to these minutiæ with the care of a son,) the doctor said they must ride with him to Hyde Park, where he would put them out to walk until he had made a visit to Piccadilly, whence he would return and take them home.

The general not only expressed pleasure at the drive, but as the air was warm and balmy, (it being about the beginning of June,) he made no objection to the proposed subsequent walk.

He admired the Park, the Serpentine River, the cottage on its bank, and seemed highly diverted by the horsemen and carriages in the ring. The pertinence of his remarks afforded Thaddeus a ray of hope that his senses had not entirely lost their union with reason ; and with awakened confidence he was contemplating what might be the happy effects of constant exercise, when the general's complaints of weariness obliged him to stop near Piccadilly Gate, and wait the arrival of the doctor's coach.

He was standing against the railing, supporting Butzou, and

with his hat in his hand shading his aged friend's face from the sun, when two or three carriages driving in, he met the eyes of Miss Euphemia Dundas, who pulling the check-string, exclaimed, "Bless me, Mr. Constantine! Who expected to see you here? Why, your note told us you were confined with a sick friend."

Thaddeus bowed to her, and still sustaining the debilitated frame of the general on his arm, advanced to the side of the coach. Miss Beaufort, who now looked out, expressed her hope that his invalid was better.

"This is the friend I mentioned," said the count, turning his eyes on the mild features of Butzou; "his physician having ordered him to walk, I accompanied him hither."

"Dear me! how ill you look, sir," cried Euphemia, addressing the poor invalid; "but you are attended by a kind friend."

"My dear lord!" exclaimed the old man, not regarding what she said, "I must go home. I am tired; pray call up the carriage."

Euphemia was again opening her mouth to speak, but Miss Beaufort, perceiving a look of distress in the expressive features of Thaddeus, interrupted her by saying, "Good-morning! Mr. Constantine. I know we detain you and oppress that gentleman, whose pardon we ought to beg." She bowed her head to the general, whose white hairs were blowing about his face, as he attempted to pull the count towards the pathway.

"My friend cannot thank you, kind Miss Beaufort," cried Thaddeus, with a look of gratitude that called the brightest roses to her cheeks; "but I do from my heart!"

"Here it is! Pray, my dear lord, come along!" cried Butzou. Thaddeus, seeing that his information was right, bowed to the ladies, and their carriage drove off.

Though the wheels of Lady Dundas's coach rolled away from the retreating figures of Thaddeus and his friend, the images of both occupied the meditations of Euphemia and Miss Beaufort whilst, *tete-à-tete* and in silence, they made the circuit of the Park.

When the carriage again passed the spot on which the subject of their thoughts had stood, Mary almost mechanically looked out towards the gate.

"Is he gone yet?" asked Euphemia, sighing deeply.

Mary drew in her head with the quickness of conscious guilt; and whilst a color stained her face, which of itself might have betrayed her prevarication, she asked, "Who?"

"Mr. Constantine," replied Euphemia, with a second sigh. "Did you remark, Mary, how gracefully he supported that sick old gentleman? Was it not the very personification of Youth upholding the fainting steps of Age? He put me in mind of the charming young prince, whose name I forget, leading the old Belisarius."

"Yes," returned Mary ashamed of the momentary insincerity couched in her former uncertain replying word, "Who?" yet still adding, while trying to smile, "but some people might call our ideas enthusiasm."

"So all tell me," replied Euphemia; so all say who neither possess the sensibility nor the candor to allow that great merit may exist without being associated with great rank. Yet," cried she, in a more animated tone, "I have my doubts, Mary, of his being what he seems. Did you observe the sick gentleman call him *My lord?*"

"I did," returned Mary, "and I was not surprised. Such manners as Mr. Constantine's are not to be acquired in a cottage."

"Dear, dear Mary!" cried Euphemia, flinging her ivory arms round her neck; "how I love you for these words! You are generous, you think nobly, and I will no longer hestitate to —to—" and breaking off, she hid her head in Miss Beaufort's bosom.

Mary's heart throbbed, her cheeks grew pale, and almost unconsciously she wished to stop the tide of Miss Dundas's confidence.

"Dear Euphemia!" answered she, "your regard for this interesting exile is very praiseworthy. But beware of ——." She hesitated; a remorseful twitch in her own breast stayed the warning that was rising to her tongue; and blushing at a motive she could not at the instant assign to friendship, selfishness, or to any interest she would not avow to herself, she touched the cheek of Euphemia with her quivering lips.

Euphemia had finished the sentence for her, and raising her head, exclaimed, "What should I fear in esteeming Mr. Constantine? Is he not the most captivating creature in the world! And for his person! Oh, Mary, he is so beautiful, that when the library is filled with the handsomest men in town, the moment Constantine enters, their reign is over. I compare them with his godlike figure, and I feel as one looking at the sun; all other objects appear dim and shapeless."

"I hope," returned Mary,—pressing her own forehead with her hand, her head beginning to ache strangely,—"that Mr.

Constantine does not owe your friendship to his fine person. I think his mental qualities are more deserving of such a gift."

"Don't look so severe, dear Mary!" cried Miss Dundas, observing her contracting brow; "are you displeased with me?"

Mary's displeasure was at the austerity of her own words, and not at her auditor. Raising her eyes with a smile, she gently replied, "I do not mean, my dear girl, to be severe; but I would wish, for the honor of our sex, that the objects which attract either our love or our compassion should have something more precious than mere exterior beauty to engage our interest."

"Well, I will soon be satisfied," cried Euphemia, in a gayer tone, as they drove through Grosvenor Gate; "we all know that Constantine is sensible and accomplished: he writes poetry like an angel, both in French and Italian. I have hundreds of mottoes composed by him; one of them, Mary, is on the work-box I gave you yesterday; and, what is more, I will ask him to-morrow why that old gentleman called him *My lord?* If he be a lord!" exclaimed she.

"What then?" inquired the eloquent eyes of Mary.

"Don't look so impertinent, my dear," cried the now animated beauty: "I positively won't say another word to you today."

Miss Beaufort's headache became so painful, she rejoiced when Euphemia ceased and the carriage drew up to Lady Dundas's door.

A night of almost unremitted sleep performed such good effects on the general condition of General Butzou, that Dr. Cavendish thought his patient so much better as to sanction his hoping the best consequences from a frequent repetition of air and exercise. When the drive and walk had accordingly been repeated the following day, Thaddeus left his friend to his maps, and little Nanny's attendance, and once more took the way to Harley Street.

He found only Miss Dundas with her sister in the study. Mary (against her will, which she opposed because it was her will) had gone out shopping with Miss Dorothy and Lady Dundas.

Miss Dundas left the room the moment she had finished her lessons.

Delighted at being *tete-à-tete* with the object of her romantic fancies, Euphemia forgot that she was to act the retreating character of Madame d'Arblay's heroine; and shutting her book the instant Diana disappeared, all at once opened her attack on his confidence.

To her eager questions, which the few words of the general had excited, the count afforded no other reply than that his poor friend knew not what he said, having been a long time in a state of mental derangement.

This explanation caused a momentary mortification in the imaginative Euphemia; but her busy mind was nimble in its erection of airy castles, and she rallied in a moment with the idea that "he might be more than a lord." At any rate, let him be what he may, he charmed her; and he had much ado to parry the increasing boldness of her speeches, without letting her see they were understood.

"You are very diffident, Mr. Constantine," cried she, looking down. "If I consider you worthy of my friendship, why should *you* make disqualifying assertions?"

"Every man, madam," returned Thaddeus, bowing as he rose from his chair, "must be diffident of deserving the honor of your notice."

"There is no man living," replied she, "to whom I would offer my friendship but yourself."

Thaddeus bit his lip; he knew not what to answer. Bowing a second time, he stretched out his hand and drew his hat towards him. Euphemia's eyes followed the movement.

"You are in a prodigious haste, Mr. Constantine!"

"I know I intrude, madam; and I have promised to be with my sick friend at an early hour."

"Well, you may go, since you are obliged," returned the pretty Euphemia, rising, and smiling sweetly as she laid one hand on his arm and put the other into her tucker. She drew out a little white leather *souvenir*, marked on the back in gold letters with the words, "*Toujours cher;*" and slipping it into his hand, "There, receive that, *monsignor*, or whatever else you may be called, and retain it as the first pledge of Euphemia Dundas's friendship."

Thaddeus colored as he took it; and again having recourse to the convenient reply of a bow, left the room in embarrassed vexation.

There was an indelicacy in this absolutely wooing conduct of Miss Euphemia which, notwithstanding her beauty and the softness that was its vehicle, filled him with the deepest disgust. He could not trace real affection in her words or manner; and that any woman, instigated by a mere whim, should lay aside the maidenly reserves of her sex, and actually court his regard, surprised whilst it impelled him to loathe her.

They who adopt Euphemia's sentiments,—and, alas! there are some,—can be little aware of the conclusion which society infer from such intemperate behavior. The mistaken creature who, either at the impulsion of her own disposition or by the influence of example, is induced to despise the guard of modesty, literally "forsakes the guide of her youth," and leaves herself open to every attack which man can devise against her. By levelling the barrier raised by nature, she herself exposes the stronghold of virtue, and may find, too late for recovery, that what modesty has abandoned is not long spared by honor.

Euphemia's affected attachment suggested to Thaddeus a few unpleasant recollections respecting the fervent and unequivocal passion of Lady Sara. Though guilty, it sprung from a headlong ardor of disposition which formed at once the error and its palliation. He saw that love was not welcomed by her (at least he thought so) as a plaything, but struggled against as with a foe. He had witnessed her tortures: he pitied them, and to render her happy, would gladly have made any sacrifice short of his conscience. Too well assured of being all the world to Lady Sara, the belief that Miss Euphemia liked him only from idleness, caprice, and contradiction, caused him to repay her overtures with decided contempt.

When he arrived at home, he threw on his table the pocket-book whose unambiguous motto made him scorn her, and almost himself for being the object of such folly. Looking round his humble room, whose wicker-chairs, oil-cloth floor, and uncurtained windows announced anything but elegance: "Poor Euphemia!" said he; "how would you be dismayed were the indigent Constantine to really take you at your word, and bring you home to a habitation like this!"

CHAPTER XXX.

INFLUENCES OF CHARACTER.

THE recital of the preceding scene, which was communicated to Miss Beaufort by Euphemia, filled her with still more doubting thoughts.

Mary could discover no reason why the old gentleman's mental derangement should dignify his friend with titles he had never borne. She remarked to herself that his answer to Euphemia was evasive; she remembered his emotion and apology on seeing Mr. C. Kemble in Adelbert; and uniting with these facts his manners and acquirements, so far beyond the charges of any subordinate rank, she could finally retain no doubt of his being at least well born.

Thus this mysterious Constantine continued to occupy her hourly thoughts during the space of two months, in which time she had full opportunity to learn much of a character with whom she associated almost every day. At Lady Tinemouth's (one of whose evening guests she frequently became) she beheld him disencumbered of that armor of reserve which he usually wore in Harley Street.

In the circle of the countess, Mary saw him welcomed like an idolized being before whose cheering influence all frowns and clouds must disappear. When he entered, the smile resumed its seat on the languid features of Lady Tinemouth; Miss Egerton's eye lighted up to keener archness; Lady Sara's Circassian orbs floated in pleasure; and for Mary herself, her breast heaved, her cheeks glowed, her hands trembled, a quick sigh fluttered in her bosom; and whilst she remained in his presence, she believed that happiness had lost its usual evanescent property, and become tangible, to hold and press upon her heart.

Mary, who investigated the cause of these tremors on her pillow, bedewed it with delicious though bitter tears, when her alarmed soul whispered that she nourished for this amiable foreigner "a something than friendship dearer."

"Ah! is it come to this?" cried she, pressing down her saturated eyelids with her hand. "Am I at last to love a man who, perhaps, never casts a thought on me? How despicable shall I become in my own eyes!"

The pride of woman puts this charge to her taken heart—that heart which seems tempered of the purest clay, and warmed with the fire of heaven; that tender and disinterested heart asks as its appeal—What is love? Is it not an admiration of all that is beautiful in nature and in the soul? Is it not a union of loveliness with truth? Is it not a passion whose sole object is the rapture of contemplating the supreme beauty of this combined character?

"Where, then," cried the enthusiastic Mary, "where is the shame that can be annexed to my loving Constantine? If it be honorable to love delineated excellence, it must be equally [illegible] to love it when embodied in a human shape. Such it is in

Constantine; and if love be the reflected light of virtue, I may cease to arraign myself of that which otherwise I would have scorned. Therefore, Constantine," cried she, raising her clasped hands, whilst renewed tears streamed over her face, "I will love thee! I will pray for thy happiness, though its partner should be Euphemia Dundas."

Mary's eager imagination would not allow her to perceive those obstacles in the shapes of pride and prudence, which would stand in the way of his obtaining Euphemia's hand; its light showed to her only a rival in the person of the little beauty; but from her direct confidence she continued to retreat with abhorrence.

Had Euphemia been more deserving of Constantine, Miss Beaufort believed she would have been less reluctant to hear that she loved him. But Mary could not avoid seeing that Miss E. Dundas possessed little to ensure connubial comfort, if mere beauty and accidental flights of good humor were not to be admitted into the scale. She was weak in understanding, timid in principle, absurd in almost every opinion she adopted; and as for love, true, dignified, respectable love, she knew nothing of the sentiment.

Whilst Miss Beaufort meditated on this meagre schedule of her rival's merits, the probability that even such a man as Constantine might sacrifice himself to flattery and to splendor stung her to the soul.

The more she reflected on it, the more she conceived it possible. Euphemia was considered a beauty of the day; her affectation of refined prettiness pleased many, and might charm Constantine: she was mistress of fifty thousand pounds, and did not esteem it necessary to conceal from her favorite the empire he had acquired. Perhaps there was generosity in this openness? If so, what might it not effect on a grateful disposition? or, rather, (her mortified heart murmured in the words of her aunt Dorothy,) "how might it not operate on the mind of one of that sex, which, at the best, is as often moved by caprice as by feeling."

Mary blushed at her adoption of this opinion; and, angry with herself for the injustice which a lurking jealousy had excited in her to apply to Constantine's noble nature, she resolved, whatever might be her struggles, to promote his happiness, though even with Euphemia, to the utmost of her power.

The next morning, when Miss Beaufort saw the study door opened for her entrance, she found Mr. Constantine at his station, literally baited between Miss Dundas and her honorable lover. At such moments Mary appeared the kindest of the kind. She loved to see Constantine smile; and whenever she could produce that effect, by turning the spleen of these polite sneerers against themselves, his smiles, which ever entered her heart, afforded her a banquet for hours after his departure.

Mary drew out her netting, (which was a purse for Lady Tinemouth,) and taking a seat beside Euphemia, united with her to occupy his attention entirely, that he might not catch even one of those insolent glances which were passing between Lascelles and a new visitant, the pretty lady Hilliars.

This lady seemed to take extreme pleasure in accosting Thaddeus by the appellation of "Friend," "My good man," "Mr. What's-your-name," and similar squibs of insult, with which the prosperous assail the unfortunate. Such random shots they know often inflict the most galling wounds.

However, "Friend," "My good man," and "Mr. What's-your-name,' disappointed this lady's small artillery of effect. He seemed invulnerable both to her insolence and to her affectation; for to be thought a wit, by even Miss Dundas's emigrant tutor, was not to be despised; though at the very moment in which she desired his admiration, she supposed her haughtiness had impressed him with a proper sense of his own meanness and a high conception of her dignity.

She jumped about the room, assumed infantine airs, played with Euphemia's lap-dag, fondled it, seated herself on the floor and swept the carpet with her fine flaxen tresses; but she performed the routine of captivation in vain. Thaddeus recollected having seen this pretty full-grown baby, in her peculiar character of a profligate wife, pawning her own and her husband's property; he remembered this, and the united shafts of her charms and folly fell unnoticed to the ground.

When Thaddeus took his leave, Miss Beaufort, as was her custom, retired for an hour to read in her dressing-room, before she directed her attention to the toilet. She opened a book, and ran over a few pages of Madame de Staël's Treatise on the Passions; but such reasoning was too abstract for her present frame of mind, and she laid the volume down.

She dipped her pen in the inkstand. Being a letter in debt to her guardian, she thought she would defray it now. She accomplished "My dear uncle," and stopped. Whilst she rested on her elbow, and, heedless of what she was doing, picked the feather of her quill to pieces, no other idea offered itself than the figure of Thaddeus sitting "severe in youthful beauty!" and surrounded by the contumelies with which the unworthy hope to disparage the merit they can neither emulate nor overlook.

Uneasy with herself, she pushed the table away, and, leaning her cheek on her arm, gazed into the rainbow varieties of a beaupot of flowers which occupied the fireplace. Even their gay colors appeared to fade before her sight, and present to her vacant eye the form of Thaddeus, with the melancholy air which shaded his movements. She turned round, but could not disengage herself from the spirit that was within her; his half-suppressed sighs seemed yet to thrill in her ear and weigh upon her heart.

"Incomparable young man!" cried she, starting up, "why art thou so wretched? Oh! Lady Tinemouth, why have you told me of his many virtues? Why have I convinced myself that what you said is true? Oh! why was I formed to love an excellence which I never can approach?"

The natural reply to these self-demanded questions suggesting itself, she assented with a tear to the whisperings of her heart—that when cool, calculating reason would banish the affections, it is incapable of filling their place.

She rang the bell for her maid.

"Marshall, who dines with Lady Dundas to-day?"

"I believe, ma'am," replied the girl, "Mr. Lascelles, Lady Hilliars, and the Marquis of Elesmere."

"I dislike them all three!" cried Mary, with an impatience to which she was little liable; "dress me how you like: I am indifferent to my appearance."

Marshall obeyed the commands of her lady, who, hoping to divert her thoughts, took up the poems of Egerton Brydges. But the attempt only deepened her emotion, for every line in that exquisite little volume "gives a very echo to the seat where love is throned!"

She closed the book and sighed. Marshall having fixed the last pearl comb in her mistress's beautiful hair, and observing that something was wrong that disquieted her, exclaimed, "Dear ma'am, you are so pale to-day! I wish I might put on some gayer ornaments!"

"No," returned Mary, glancing a look at her languid features; "no, Marshall: I appear as well as I desire. Any chance of passing unnoticed in company I dislike is worth retaining. No one will be here this evening whom I care to please."

She was mistaken; other company had been invited besides those whom the maid mentioned. But Miss Beaufort continued from seven o'clock until ten, the period at which the ladies left the table, the annoyed victim of the insipid and pert compliments of Lord Elesmere.

Sick of his subjectless and dragging conversation, she gladly followed Lady Dundas to the drawing-room, where, opening her knitting case, she took her station in a remote corner.

After half an hour had elapsed, the gentlemen from below, recruited by fresh company, thronged in fast; and, notwithstanding it was styled a family party, Miss Beaufort saw many new faces, amongst whom she observed an elderly clergyman, who was looking about for a chair. The yawning Lascelles threw himself along the only vacant sofa, just as the reverend gentleman approached it.

Miss Beaufort immediately rose, and was moving on to another room, when the coxcomb, springing up, begged permission to admire her work; and, without permission, taking it from her, pursued her, twisting the purse around his fingers and talking all the while.

Mary walked forward, smiling with contempt, until they reached the saloon, where the Misses Dundas were closely engaged in conversation with the Marquis of Elesmere.

Lascelles, who trembled for his Golconda at this sight, stepped briskly up. Miss Beaufort, who did not wish to lose sight of her purse whilst in the power of such a Lothario, followed him, and placed herself against the arm of the sofa on which Euphemia sat.

Lascelles now bowed his scented locks to Diana in vain; Lord Elesmere was describing the last heat at Newmarket, and the attention of neither lady could be withdrawn.

The beau became so irritated by the neglect of Euphemia, and so nettled at her sister's overlooking him, that assuming a gay air, he struck Miss Dundas's arm a smart stroke with Miss Beaufort's purse; and laughing, to show the strong opposition between his broad white teeth and the miserable mouth of his lordly rival, hoped to alarm him by his familiarity, and to obtain a triumph over the ladies by degrading them in the eyes of the peer.

"Miss Dundas," demanded he, "who was that quiz of a man in black your sister walked with the other day in Portland Place?'

"Me!" cried Euphemia, surprised.

"Ay!" returned he; "I was crossing from Weymouth Street, when I perceived you accost a strange-looking person—a courier from the moon, perhaps! You may remember you sauntered with him as far as Sir William Miller's. I would have joined you, but seeing the family standing in the balcony, I did not wish them to suppose that I knew anything of such queer company."

"Who was it, Euphemia?" inquired Miss Dundas, in a severe tone.

"I wonder he affects to be ignorant," answered her sister angrily; "he knows very well it was only Mr. Constantine."

"And who is Mr. Constantine?" demanded the marquis. Mr. Lascelles shrugged his shoulders.

"E'faith, my lord! a fellow whom nobody knows—a teacher of languages, giving himself the airs of a prince—a writer of poetry, and a man who will draw you, your house or dogs, if you will pay him for it."

Mary's heart swelled.

"What, a French emigrant?" drawled his lordship, dropping his lip; "and the lovely Euphemia wishes to soothe his sorrows."

"No, my lord," stammered Euphemia, "he is—he is——"

"What!" interrupted Lascelles, with a malicious grin. "A wandering beggar, who thrusts himself into society which may some day repay his insolence with chastisement! And for the people who encourage him, they had better beware of being themselves driven from all good company. Such confounders of degrees ought to be degraded from the rank they disgrace. I understand his chief protectress is Lady Tinemouth; his second, Lady Sara Ross, who, by way of *passant le temps*, shows she is not quite inconsolable at the absence of her husband."

Mary, pale and trembling at the scandal his last words insinuated, opened her lips to speak, when Miss Dundas (whose angry eyes darted from her sister to her lover) exclaimed, "Mr. Lascelles, I know not what you mean. The subject you have taken up is below my discussion; yet I must confess, if Euphemia has ever disgraced herself so far as to be seen walking with a schoolmaster, she deserves all you have said."

"And why might I not walk with him, sister?" asked the poor culprit, suddenly recovering from her confusion, and looking pertly up; "who knew that he was not a gentleman?"

"Everybody, ma'am," interrupted Lascelles; "and when a young woman of fashion condescends to be seen equalizing herself with a creature depending on his wits for support, she is very likely to incur the contempt of her acquaintance and the censure of her friends."

"She is, sir," said Mary, holding down her indignant heart and forcing her countenance to appear serene; "for she ought to know that if those men of fashion, who have no wit to be either their support or ornament, did not proscribe talents from their circle, they must soon find 'the greater glory dim the less.'"

"True, madam," cried Lord Berrington, who, having entered during the contest, had stood unobserved until this moment; "and their gold and tinsel would prove but dross and bubble, if struck by the Ithuriel touch of Merit when so advocated."

Mary turned at the sound of his philanthropic voice, and gave him one of those glances which go immediately to the soul.

"Come, Miss Beaufort," cried he, taking her hand; "I see the young musician yonder who has so recently astonished the public. I believe he is going to sing. Let us leave this discordant corner, and seek harmony by his side."

Mary gladly acceded to his request, and seating herself a few paces from the musical party, Berrington took his station behind her chair.

When the last melting notes of "From shades of night" died upon her ear, Mary's eyes, full of admiration and transport, which the power of association rendered more intense, remained fixed on the singer. Lord Berrington smiled at the vivid expression of her countenance, and as the young Orpheus moved from the instrument, exclaimed, "Come, Miss Beaufort, I won't allow you quite to fancy Braham the god on whom

Enamored Clitie turned and gazed! *

Listen a little to my merits. Do you know that if it were not for my timely lectures, Lascelles would grow the most insufferable gossip about town? There is not a match nor a divorce near St. James's of which he cannot repeat all the whys and wherefores. I call him Sir Benjamin Backbite; and I believe he hates me worse than Asmodeus himself."

"Such a man's dislike," rejoined Mary, "is the highest encomium he can bestow. I never yet heard him speak well of any person who did not resemble himself."

* This accomplished singer and composer still lives—one of the most admired ornaments of the British orchestra.—1845.

"And he is not consistent even there," resumed the viscount: "I am not sure I have always heard him speak in the gentlest terms of Miss Dundas. Yet, on that I cannot quite blame him; for, on my honor, she provokes me beyond any woman breathing."

"Many women," replied Mary, smiling, "would esteem that a flattering instance of power."

"And, like everything that flatters," returned he, "it would tell a falsehood. A shrew can provoke a man who detests her. As to Miss Dundas, notwithstanding her parade of learning, she generally espouses the wrong side of the argument; and I may say with somebody, whose name I have forgotten, that any one who knows Diana Dundas never need be at a loss for a woman to call impertinent."

"You are not usually so severe, my lord!"

"I am not usually so sincere, Miss Beaufort," answered he; "but I see you think for yourself, therefore I make no hesitation in speaking what I think—to you."

His auditor bowed her head sportively but modestly. Lady Dundas at that moment beckoned him across the room. She compelled him to sit down to whist. He cast a rueful glance at Mary, and took a seat opposite to his costly partner.

"Lord Berrington is a very worthy young man," observed the clergyman to whom at the beginning of the evening Miss Beaufort had resigned her chair; "I presume, madam, you have been honoring him with your conversation?"

"Yes," returned Mary, noticing the benign countenance of the speaker; "I have not had the pleasure of long knowing his lordship, but what I have seen of his character is highly to his advantage."

"I was intimate in his father's house for years," rejoined the gentleman: "I knew this young nobleman from a boy. If he has faults, he owes them to his mother, who doated on him, and rather directed his care to the adornment of his really handsome person than to the cultivation of talents he has since learned to appreciate."

"I believe Lord Berrington to be very sensible, and, above all, very humane," returned Miss Beaufort.

"He is so," replied the old gentleman; "yet it was not till he had attained the age of twenty-two that he appeared to know he had anything to do in the world besides dressing and attending on the fair sex. His taste produced the first, whilst the urbanity of his disposition gave birth to the latter. When Berrington arrived at his title, he was about five-and-twenty.

Sorrow for the death of his amiable parents, who died in the same month, afforded him leisure to find his reason. He discovered that he had been acting a part beneath him, and he soon implanted on the good old stock those excellent acquirements which you see he possesses. In spite of his regeneration," continued the clergyman, casting a good-humored glance on the dove-colored suit of the viscount, "you perceive that first impressions will remain. He loves dress, but he loves justice and philanthropy better."

"This eulogy, sir," said Mary, "affords me real pleasure. May I know the name of the gentleman with whom I have the honor to converse?"

"My name is Blackmore," returned he.

"Dr. Blackmore?"

"The same."

He was the same Dr. Blackmore who had been struck by the appearance of the Count Sobieski at the Hummums, but had never learned his name, and who, being a rare visitor at Lady Dundas's, had never by chance met a second time with the object of his compassion.

"I am happy," resumed Miss Beaufort, "in having the good fortune to meet a clergyman of whom I have so frequently heard my guardian, Sir Robert Somerset, speak with the highest esteem."

"Ah!" replied he, "I have not seen him since the death of his lady; I hope that he and his son are well!"

"Both are perfectly so now," returned she, "and are together in the country!"

"You, madam, I suppose are my lady's niece, the daughter of the brave Admiral Beaufort?"

"I am, sir."

"Well, I rejoice at this incident," rejoined he, pressing her hand; "I knew your mother when she was a lovely girl. She used to spend her summers with the late Lady Somerset, at the castle. It was there I had the honor of cultivating her friendship."

"I do not remember ever having seen my mother," replied the now thoughtful Mary. Dr. Blackmore observing the expression of her countenance, smiled kindly, and said, "I fear I am to blame here. This is a somewhat sad way of introducing myself. But your goodness must pardon me," continued he; "for I have so long accustomed myself to speak what I think to those in whom I see cause to esteem, that sometimes, as now I undesignedly inflict pain."

"Not in this case," returned Miss Beaufort. "I am always pleased when listening to a friend of my mother, and particularly so when he speaks in her praise."

The breaking up of the card-tables prevented further conversation. Lord Berrington again approached the sofa where Mary sat, exclaming, as he preceived her companion, "Ah! my good doctor; have you presented yourself at this fair shrine? I declare you eccentric folk may dare anything. Whilst you are free, Miss Beaufort," added he turning to her, "adopt the advice which a good lady once gave me, and which I have implicitly followed: 'When you are young, get the character of an oddity, and it seats you in an easy chair for life.'"

Mary was interrupted in her reply by a general stir amongst the company, who, now the cards were over, like bees and wasps were swarming about the room, gathering honey or stinging as they went.

At one the house was cleared; and Miss Beaufort threw herself on the pillow, to think, and then to dream of Thaddeus.

CHAPTER XXXI.

THE GREAT AND THE SMALL OF SOCIETY.

If it be true what the vivid imaginations of poets have frequently asserted, that when the soul dreams, it is in the actual presence of those beings whose images present themselves to their slumbers, then have the spirit, of Thaddeus and Mary been often commingled at the hour of midnight; then has the young Sobieski again visited his distant country, again seen it victorious, again knelt before his sainted parents.

From such visions as these did Thaddeus awake in the morning, after having spent the preceding evening with Lady Tinemouth.

He had walked with her ladyship in Hyde Park till a late hour. By the mild light of the moon, which shone brightly through the still, balmy air of a midsummer night, they took their way along the shadowy bank of the Serpentine.

There is a solemn appeal to the soul in the repose of nature that "makes itself be felt." No syllable from either Thaddeus or the countess for some time broke the universal silence. Thaddeus looked around on the clear expanse of water, overshaded by the long reflection of the darkening trees; then raising his eyes to that beautiful planet which has excited tender thoughts in every feeling breast since the creation of the world, he drew a deep sigh. The countess echoed it.

"In such a night as this," said Thaddeus, in a low voice, as if afraid to disturb the sleeping deity of the place, "I used to walk the ramparts of Villanow with my dear departed mother, and gaze on that lovely orb; and when I was far from her, I have looked at it from the door of my tent, and fancying that her eyes were then fixed on the same object as mine, I found happiness in the idea."

A tear stole down the cheek of Thaddeus. That moon yet shone brightly; but his mother's eyes were closed in the grave.

"Villanow!" repeated the countess, in a tone of tender surprise; "surely that was the seat of the celebrated Palatine of Masovia! You have discovered yourself, Constantine! I am much mistaken if you be not his grandson, the young, yet far-famed, Thaddeus Sobieski?"

Thaddeus had allowed the remembrances pressing on his mind to draw him into a speech which had disclosed to the quick apprehension of the countess what his still too sensitive pride would forever have concealed.

"I have indeed betrayed my secret," cried he, incapable of denying it; "but, dear lady Tinemouth, as you value my feelings, never let it escape your lips. Having long considered you as my best friend, and loved you as a parent, I forgot, in the recollection of my beloved mother, that I had withheld any of my history from you."

"Mysterious Providence!" exclaimed her ladyship, after a pause, in which ten thousand admiring and pitying reflections thronged on her mind: "is it possible? Can it be the Count Sobieski, that brave and illustrious youth of whom every foreigner spoke with wonder? Can it be him that I behold in the unknown, unfriended Constantine?"

"Even so," returned Thaddeus, pressing her hand. "My country is no more. I am now forgotten by the world, as I have been by fortune. I have nothing to do on the earth but to fulfil the few duties which a filial friendship has enjoined, and then it will be a matter of indifference to me how soon I am laid in its bosom."

"You are too young, dear Constantine, (for I am still to

call you by that name,) to despair of happiness being yet reserved for you."

"No, my dear Lady Tinemouth, I do not cheat myself with such hope; I am not so importunate with the gracious Being who gave me life and reason. He bestowed upon me for awhile the tenderest connections—friends, rank, honors, glory. All these were crushed in the fall of Poland; yet I survive. I sought resignation only, and I have found it. It cost me many a struggle; but the contest was due to the decrees of that all-wise Creator who gave my first years to happiness."

"Inestimable young man!" cried the countess, wiping the flowing tears from her eyes; "you teach misfortune dignity! Not when all Warsaw rose in a body to thank you, not when the king received you in the senate with open arms, could you have appeared to me so worthy of admiration as at this moment, when, conscious of having been all this, you submit to the direct reverse, because you believe it to be the will of your Maker! Ah! little does Miss Beaufort think, when seated by your side, that she is conversing with the youthful hero whom she has so often wished to see!"

"Miss Beaufort!" echoed Thaddeus, his heart glowing with delight. "Do you think she ever heard of me by the name of Sobieski?"

"Who has not?" returned the countess; "every heart that could be interested by heroic virtue has heard and well remembers its glorious struggles against the calamities of your country. Whilst the newspapers of the day informed us of these things, they noticed amongst the first of her champions the Palatine of Masovia, Kosciusko, and the young Sobieski. Many an evening have I passed with Miss Dorothy and Mary Beaufort, lamenting the fate of that devoted kingdom."

During this declaration, a variety of indeed happy emotions agitated the mind of Thaddeus, until, recollecting with a bitter pang the shameless ingratitude of Pembroke, when all those glories were departed from him, and the cruel possibility of being recognized by the Earl of Tinemouth as his son, he exclaimed, "My dearest madam, I entreat that what I have revealed to you may never be divulged. Miss Beaufort's friendship would indeed be happiness; but I cannot purchase even so great a bliss at the expense of memories which are knit with my life."

"How?" cried the countess; "is not your name, and all its attendant ideas, an honor which the proudest man might boast?"

Thaddeus pressed her hand to his heart.

"You are kind—very kind! yet I cannot retract. Confide, dear Lady Tinemouth, in the justice of my resolution. I could not bear cold pity; I could not bear the heartless comments of people who, pretending to compassion, would load me with a heavy sense of my calamities. Besides, there are persons in England who are so much the objects of my aversion, I would rather die than let them know I exist. Therefore, once again, dear Lady Tinemouth, let me implore you to preserve my secret."

She saw by the earnestness of his manner that she ought to comply, and without further hesitation promised all the silence he desired.

This long moonlight conversation, by awakening all those dormant remembrances which were cherished, though hidden in the depths of his bosom, gave birth to that *mirage* of imagination which painted that night, in the rapid series of his tumultuous dreams, the images of every being whom he had ever loved, or now continued to regard with interest.

Proceeding next morning towards Harley Street, he mused on what had happened; and pleased that he had, though unpremeditatedly, paid the just compliment of his entire confidence to the uncommon friendship of the countess, he arrived at Lady Dundas's door before he was sensible of the ground he had passed over, and in a few minutes afterwards was ushered into his accustomed purgatory.

When the servant opened the study-door, Miss Euphemia was again alone. Thaddeus recoiled, but he could not retreat.

"Come in, Mr. Constantine," cried the little beauty, in a languid tone; "my sister is going to the riding-school with Mr. Lascelles. Miss Beaufort wanted me to drive out with her and my mother, but I preferred waiting for you."

The count bowed; and almost retreating with fear of what might next be said, he gladly heard a thundering knock at the door, and a moment after the voice of Miss Dundas ascending the stairs.

He had just opened his books when she entered, followed by her lover. Panting under a heavy riding-habit, she flung herself on a sofa, and began to vilify "the odious heat of Pozard's odious place;" then telling Euphemia she would play truant to-day, ordered her to attend to her lessons.

Owing to the warmth of the weather, Thaddeus came out this morning without boots; and it being the first time the exquisite proportion of his figure had been so fully seen by any of the present company excepting Euphemia, Lascelles, bursting with an emotion which he would not call envy, measured the count's graceful limb with his scornful eyes; then declaring he was quite in a furnace, took the corner of his glove and waving it to and fro, half-muttered, "Come gentle air."

"The fairer Lascelles cries!" exclaimed Euphemia, looking off her exercise.

"What! does your master teach you wit?" drawled the coxcomb, with a particular emphasis.

Thaddeus, affecting not to hear, continued to direct his pupil.

The indefatigable Lascelles having observed the complacence with which the count always regarded Miss Beaufort, determined the goad should fret; and drawing the knitting out of his pocket which he had snatched the night before from Mary, he exclaimed, "'Fore heaven, here is my little Beaufort's purse!"

Thaddeus started, and unconsciously looking up, beheld the well-known work of Mary dangling in the hand of Lascelles. He suffered pangs unknown to him; his eyes became dim; and hardly knowing what he saw or said, he pursued the lesson with increased rapidity.

Finding that his malice had taken effect, with a careless air the malicious puppy threw his clumsy limbs on the sofa, which Miss Dundas had just quitted to seat herself nearer the window, and cried out, as in a voice of sudden recollection:

"By the bye, that Miss Mary Beaufort, when she chooses to be sincere, is a staunch little Queen Bess."

"You may as well tell me," replied Miss Dundas, with a deriding curl of her lip, "that she is the Empress of Russia."

"I beg your pardon!" cried he, and raising his voice to be better heard, "I do not mean in the way of learning. But I will prove in a moment her creditable high-mightiness in these presumptuous times, though a silly love of popularity induces her to affect now and then a humble guise to some people beneath her. When she gave me this gewgaw," added he, flourishing the purse in his hand, "she told me a pretty tissue about a fair friend of hers, whose music-master, mistaking some condescension on her part, had dared to press her snowy fingers while directing them towards a tender chord on her harp. You have no notion how the gentle Beaufort's blue eyes blazed up while relating poor Tweedledum's presumption!"

"I can have a notion of anything these boasted meek young ladies do when thrown off their guard," haughtily returned his contemptuous auditress, "after Miss Beaufort's violent sally of impertinence to you last night."

"Impertinence to me!" echoed the fop, at the same time dipping the end of the knitting into Diana's lavender-bottle, and dabbing his temples; "she was always too civil by half. I hate forward girls."

Thaddeus shut the large dictionary which lay before him with a force that make the puppy start, and rising hastily from his chair, with a face all crimson, was taking his hat, when the door opened, and Mary appeared.

A white-chip bonnet was resting lightly on the glittering tresses which waved over her forehead, whilst her lace-shade, gently discomposed by the air, half veiled and half revealed her graceful figure. She entered with a smile, and walking up to the side of the table where Thaddeus was standing, inquired after his friend's health. He answered her in a voice unusually agitated. All that he had been told by the countess of her favorable opinion of him, and the slander he had just heard from Diana's lover, were at once present in his mind.

He was yet speaking, when Miss Beaufort, casually looking towards the other side of the room, saw her purse still acting the part of a handkerchief in the hand of Mr. Lacelles.

"Look, Mr. Constantine," said she, gayly tapping his arm with her parasol, "how the most precious things may be degraded! There is the knitting you have so often admired, and which I intended for Lady Tinemouth's pocket, debased to do the office of Mr. Lascelles's napkin."

"You gave it to him, Miss Beaufort," cried Miss Dundas; "and after that, surely he may use it as he values it!"

"If I could have given it to Mr. Lascelles, madam, I should hardly have taken notice of its fate."

Believing what her lover had advanced, Miss Dundas was displeased at Mary for having, by presents, interfered with any of her danglers, and rather angrily replied, "Mr. Lascelles said you gave it to him; and certainly you would not insinuate a word against his veracity?"

"No, not insinuate," returned Miss Beaufort, "but affirm, that he has forgotten his veracity in this statement."

Lascelles yawned. "Lord bless me, ladies, how you quarrel! You will disturb Monsieur?"

"Mr. Constantine," returned Mary, blushing with indignation, "cannot be disturbed by nonsense."

Thaddeus again drew his hat towards him, and bowing to his lovely champion, with an expression of countenance which he little suspected had passed from his heart to his eyes, he was preparing to take his leave, when Euphemia requested him to inform her whether she had folded down the right pages for the next exercise. He approached her, and was leaning over her chair to look at the book, when she whispered, "Don't be hurt at what Lascelles says; he is always jealous of anybody who is handsomer than himself."

Thaddeus dropped his eyelids with a face of scarlet; for on meeting the eyes of Mary, he saw that she had heard this intended comforter as well as himself. Uttering a few incoherent sentences to both ladies, he hurried out of the room.

CHAPTER XXXII.

THE OBDURACY OF VICE—THE INHUMANITY OF FOLLY.

THE Count Sobieski was prevented paying his customary visit next morning in Harley Street by a sudden dangerous increase of illness in the general, who had been struck at seven o'clock by a fit of palsy.

When Dr. Cavendish beheld the poor old man stretched on the bed, and hardly exhibiting signs of life, he pronounced it to be a death-stroke. At this remark, Thaddeus, turning fearfully pale, staggered to a seat, with his eyes fixed on the altered features of his friend. Dr. Cavendish took his hand.

"Recollect yourself, my dear sir! Happen when it may, his death must be a release to him. But he may yet linger a few days."

"Not in pain, I hope!" said Thaddeus.

"No," returned the doctor; "probably he will remain as you now see him, till he expires like the last glimmer of a dying taper."

The benevolent Cavendish gave proper directions to Thaddeus, also to Mrs. Robson, who promised to act carefully as nurse; and then with regret left the stunned count to the melancholy task of watching by the bedside of his last early friend.

Thaddeus now retained no thought that was not riveted to the emaciated form before him. Whilst the unconscious invalid struggled for respiration, he listened to his short and convulsed breathing with sensations which seemed to tear the strings of his own breast. Unable to bear it longer, he moved to the fire-side, and seating himself, with his pallid face and aching head supported on his arm, which rested on a plain deal table, he remained; meeting no other suspension from deep and awe-struck meditation than the occasional appearance of Mrs. Robson on tiptoes, peeping in and inquiring whether he wanted anything.

From this reverie, like unto the shadow of death, he was aroused next morning at nine o'clock by the entrance of Dr. Cavendish. Thaddeus seized his hand with the eagerness of his awakened suspense. "My dear sir, may I hope——"

Not suffering him to finish with what he hoped, the doctor shook his head in gentle sign of the vanity of that hope, and advanced to the bed of the general. He felt his pulse. No change of opinion was the consequence, only that he now saw no threatenings of immediate dissolution.

"Poor Butzou!" murmured Thaddeus, when the doctor withdrew, putting the general's motionless hand to his quivering lips; "I never will leave thee! I will watch thee, thou last relic of my country! It may not be long ere we lie side by side."

With anguish at his heart, he wrote a few hasty lines to the countess; then addressing Miss Dundas, he mentioned as the reason for his late and continued absence the danger of his friend.

His note found Miss Dundas attended by her constant shadow, Mr. Lascelles, Lady Hilliars, and two or three more fine ladies and gentlemen, besides Euphemia and Miss Beaufort, who, with pensive countenances, were waiting the arrival of its writer.

When Miss Dundas took the billet off the silver salver on which her man presented it, and looked at the superscription, she threw it into the lap of Lascelles.

"There," cried she, "is an excuse, I suppose, from Mr. Constantine, for his impertinence in not coming hither yesterday. Read it, Lascelles."

"'Fore Gad, I wouldn't touch it for an earldom!" exclaimed the affected puppy, jerking it on the table. "It might affect me with the hypochondriacs. Pray, Phemy, do you peruse it."

Euphemia, in her earnestness to learn what detained Mr. Constantine, neglected the insolence of the request, and hastily breaking the seal, read as follows:

"Mr. Constantine hopes that a sudden and dangerous disorder which has attacked the life of a very dear friend with whom he resides will be a sufficient appeal to the humanity of the Misses Dundas, and obtain their pardon for his relinquishing the honor of attending them yesterday

"Dear me!" cried Euphemia, piteously; "how sorry I am! I dare say it is that white-haired old man we saw in the park. You remember, Mary, he was sick?"

"Probably," returned Miss Beaufort, with her eyes fixed on the agitated handwriting of Thaddeus.

"Throw the letter into the street, Phemy!" cried Miss Dundas, affecting sudden terror; "who knows but what it is a fever the man has got, and we may all catch our deaths."

"Heaven forbid!" exclaimed Mary, in a voice of real alarm; but it was for Thaddeus—not fear of any infection which the paper might bring to herself.

"Lascelles, take away that filthy scrawl from Phemy. How can you be so headstrong, child?" cried Diana, snatching the letter from her sister and throwing it from the window. "I declare you are sufficient to provoke a saint."

"Then you may keep your temper, Di," returned Euphemia, with a sneer; "you are far enough from that title."

Miss Dundas made a very angry reply, which was retaliated by another; and a still more noisy and disagreeable altercation might have taken place had not a good-humored lad, a brother-in-law of Lady Hilliars, in hopes of calling off the attention of the sisters, exclaimed, "Bless me, Miss Dundas, your little dog has pulled a folded sheet of paper from under that stand of flowers! Perhaps it may be of consequence."

"Fly! Take it up, George!" cried Lady Hilliars; "Esop will tear it to atoms whilst you are asking questions."

After a chase round the room, over chairs and under tables, George Hilliars at length plucked the devoted piece of paper out of the dog's mouth; and as Miss Beaufort was gathering up her working materials to leave the room, he opened it and cried, in a voice of triumph, "By Jove, it is a copy of verses!"

"Verses!" demanded Euphemia, feeling in her pocket, and coloring; "let me see them."

"That you sha'n't," roared Lascelles, catching them out of the boy's hand; "if they are your writing, we will have them."

"Help me, Mary!" cried Euphemia, turning to Miss Beaufort; "I know that nobody is a poet in this house but myself. They must be mine, and I will have them."

"Surely, Mr. Lascelles," said Mary, compassionating the poor girl's anxiety, "you will not be so rude as to detain them from their right owner?"

"Oh! but I will," cried he, mounting on a table to get out of Euphemia's reach, who, half crying, tried to snatch at the paper. "Let me alone, Miss Phemy. I will read them; so here goes it."

Miss Dundas laughed at her sister's confused looks, whilst Lascelles prepared to read in a loud voice the following verses. They had been hastily written in pencil by Thaddeus a long time ago; and having put them, by mistake, with some other papers into his pocket, he had dropped them next day, in taking out his handkerchief at Lady Dundas's. Lascelles cleared his throat with three hems, then raising his right hand with a flourishing action, in a very pompous tone began—

"Like one whom Etna's torrent fires have sent
Far from the land where his first youth was spent;
Who, inly drooping on a foreign shore,
Broods over scenes which charm his eyes no more:
And while his country's ruin wakes the groan,
Yearns for the buried hut he called his own.
So driv'n, O Poland! from thy ravaged plains,
So mourning o'er thy sad and but loved remains,
A houseless wretch, I wander through the world,
From friends, from greatness, and from glory hurl'd!

"Oh! not that each long night my weary eyes
Sink into sleep, unlull'd by Pity's sighs;
Not that in bitter tears my bread is steep'd—
Tears drawn by insults on my sorrows heap'd;
Not that my thoughts recall a mother's grave—
Recall the sire I would have died to save,
Who fell before me, bleeding on the field,
Whilst I in vain opposed the useless shield.
Ah! not for these I grieve! Though mental woe,
More deadly still, scarce Fancy's self could know!
O'er want and private griefs the soul can climb,—
Virtue subdues the one, the other Time:
But at his country's fall, the patriot feels
A grief no time, no drug, no reason heals.

"Mem'ry! remorseless murderer, whose voice
Kills as it sounds; who never says, Rejoice!
To my deserted heart, by joy forgot;
Thou pale, thou midnight spectre, haunt me not!
Thou dost but point to where sublimely stands
A glorious temple, reared by Virtue's hands,
Circled with palms and laurels, crown'd with light,
Darting Truth's piercing sun on mortal sight:
Then rushing on, leagued fiends of hellish birth
Level the mighty fabric with the earth!
Slept the red bolt of Vengeance in that hour
When virtuous Freedom fell the slave of Power!
Slumber'd the God of Justice! that no brand
Blasted with blazing wing the impious band!
Dread God of Justice! to thy will I kneel,
Though still my filial heart must bleed and feel;
Though still the proud convulsive throb will rise,
When fools my country's wrongs and woes despise;

When low-soul'd Pomp, vain Wealth, that Pity gives,
Which Virtue ne'er bestows and ne'er receives,—
That Pity, stabbing where it vaunts to cure,
Which barbs the dart of Want, and makes it sure.
How far removed from what the feeling breast
Yields boastless, breathed in sighs to the distress'd!
Which whispers sympathy, with tender fear,
And almost dreads to pour its balmy tear.
But such I know not now! Unseen, alone,
I heave the heavy sigh, I draw the groan;
And, madd'ning, turn to days of liveliest joy,
When o'er my native hills I cast mine eyes,
And said, exulting—"Freemen here shall sow
The seed that soon in tossing gold shall glow!
While Plenty, led by Liberty, shall rove,
Gay and rejoicing, through the land they love;
And 'mid the loaded vines, the peasant see
His wife, his children, breathing out,—'We're free!'
But now, O wretched land! above thy plains,
Half viewless through the gloom, vast Horror reigns,
No happy peasant, o'er his blazing hearth,
Devotes the supper hour to love and mirth;
No flowers on Piety's pure altar bloom;
Alas! they wither now, and strew her tomb!
From the Great Book of Nations fiercely rent,
My country's page to Lethe's stream is sent—
But sent in vain! The historic Muse shall raise
O'er wronged Sarmatia's cause the voice of praise,—
Shall sing her dauntless on the field of death,
And blast her royal robbers' bloody wrath!"

"It must be Constantine's!" cried Euphemia, in a voice of surprised delight, while springing up to take the paper out of the deriding reader's hand when he finished.

"I dare say it is," answered the ill-natured Lascelles, holding it above his head. "You shall have it; only first let us hear it again, it is so mighty pretty, so very lackadaisical!"

"Give it to me!" cried Euphemia, quite angry.

"Don't, Lascelles," exclaimed Miss Dundas, "the man must be a perfect idiot to write such rhodomontade."

"O! it is delectable!" returned her lover, opening the paper again; "it would make a charming ditty! Come, I will sing it. Shall it be to the tune of 'The Babes in the Wood,' or 'Chevy Chase,' or 'The Beggar of Bethnal Green?"

"Pitiless, senseless man!" exclaimed Mary, rising from her chair, where she had been striving to subdue the emotions with which every line in the poem filled her heart.

"Monster!" cried the enraged Euphemia, taking courage at Miss Beaufort's unusual warmth; "I will have the paper."

"You shan't," answered the malicious coxcomb; and raising his arm higher than her reach, he tore it in a hundred pieces. "I'll teach pretty ladies to call names!"

At this sight, no longer able to contain herself, Mary rushed out of the room, and hurrying to her chamber, threw herself upon the bed, where she gave way to a paroxysm of tears which shook her almost to suffocation.

During the first burst of her indignation, her agitated spirit breathed every appellation of abhorrence and reproach on Lascelles and his malignant mistress. Then wiping her flowing eyes, she exclaimed, "Yet can I wonder, when I compare Constantine with what they are? The man who dares to be virtuous beyond others, and to appear so, arms the self-love of all common characters against him."

Such being her meditations, she excused herself from joining the family at dinner, and it was not until evening that she felt herself at all able to treat the ill-natured group with decent civility.

To avoid spending more hours than were absolutely necessary in the company of a woman she now loathed, next morning Miss Beaufort borrowed Lady Dundas's sedan-chair, and ordering it to Lady Tinemouth's, found her at home alone, but evidently much discomposed.

"I intrude on you, Lady Tinemouth!" said Mary, observing her looks, and withdrawing from the offered seat.

"No, my dear Miss Beaufort," replied she, "I am glad you are come. I assure you I have few pleasures in solitude. Read that letter," added she, putting one into her hand: "it has just conveyed one of the cruelest stabs ever offered by a son to the heart of his mother. Read it, and you will not be surprised at finding me in the state you see."

The countess looked on her almost paralyzed hands as she spoke; and Miss Beaufort taking the paper, sat down and read to herself the following letter:

"To the Right Honorable the Countess of Tinemouth.

"Madam,

"I am commissioned by the earl, my father, to inform you that if you have lost all regard for your own character, he considers that some respect is due to the mother of his children; therefore he watches your conduct.

"He has been apprized of your frequent meetings, during these many months past, in Grosvenor Place, and at other people's houses, with an obscure foreigner, your declared lover.

The earl wished to suppose this false, until your shameless behavior became so flagrant, that he esteems it worthy neither of doubt nor indulgence.

"With his own eyes he saw you four nights ago alone with this man in Hyde Park. Such demonstration is dreadful. Your proceedings are abominable; and if you do not, without further parley, set off either to Craighall, in Cornwall, or to the Wolds, you shall receive a letter from my sister as well as myself, to tell the dishonored Lady Tinemouth how much she merits her daughter's contempt, added to that of her brother

"HARWOLD."

Mary was indeed heart-struck at the contents of this letter, but most especially at the accusation which so distinctly pointed out the innocent object of her already doubly-excited pity. "Oh! why these persecutions," cried her inward soul to heaven, "against an apparently obscure but noble, friendless stranger?" Unable to collect her thoughts to make any proper remarks whatever on the letter to Lady Tinemouth, she hastily exclaimed, "It is indeed horrible; and what do you mean to do, my honored friend?"

"I will obey my lord!" returned the countess, with a meek but firm emphasis. "My last action will be in obedience to his will. I cannot live long; and when I am dead, perhaps the earl's vigilance may be satisfied; perhaps some kind friend may then plead my cause to my daughter's heart. One cruel line from her would kill me. I will at least avoid the completion of that threat, by leaving town to-morrow night."

"What! so soon? But I hope not so far as Cornwall?"

"No," replied her ladyship; "Craighall is too near Plymouth; I determine on the Wolds. Yet why should I have a choice? It is almost a matter of indifference to what spot I am banished—in what place I am to die; anywhere to which my earthly lord would send me, I shall be equally remote from the sympathy of a friend."

Miss Beaufort's heart was oppressed when she entered the room! Lady Tinemouth's sorrows seemed to give her a license to weep. She took her ladyship's hand, and with difficulty sobbed out this inarticulate proposal:—"Take me with you, dear Lady Tinemouth! I am sure my guardian will be happy to permit me to be with you, where and how long you please."

"My dear young friend," replied the countess, kissing her tearful cheek, "I thank you from my heart; but I cannot take so ungenerous an advantage of your goodness as to consign your tender nature to the harassing task of attending on sorrow and sickness. How strangely different may even amiable dispositions be tempered! Sophia Egerton is better framed for such an office. Kind as she is, the hilarity of her disposition does not allow the sympathy she bestows on others to injure either her mind or her body."

Mary interrupted her. "Ah! I should be grieved to believe that my very aptitude to serve my friends will prove the first reason why I should be denied the duty. It is only in scenes of affliction that friendship can be tried, and declare its truth. If Miss Egerton were not going with you, I should certainly insist on putting my affection to the ordeal.'

"You mistake, my sweet friend," returned her ladyship; "Sophia is forbidden to remain any longer with me. You have overlooked the postscript to Lord Harwold's letter, else you must have seen the whole of my cruel situation. Turn over the leaf."

Miss Beaufort re-opened the sheet, and read the following few lines, which, being written on the interior part of the paper, had before escaped her sight:—

"Go where you will, it is our special injunction that you leave Miss Egerton behind you. She, we hear, has been the ambassadress in this intrigue. If we learn that you disobey, it shall be worse for you in every respect, as it will convince us, beyond a possibility of doubt, how uniform is the turpitude of your conduct."

Lady Tinemouth grasped Miss Beaufort's hand when she laid the matricidal letter back upon the table. "And that is from the son for whom I felt all a mother's throes—all a mother's love!—Had he died the first hour in which he saw the light, what a mass of guilt might he not have escaped! It is he," added she, in a lower voice, and looking wildly round, "that breaks my heart. I could have borne his father's perfidy; but insult, oppression, from my child! Oh, Mary, may you never know its bitterness!"

Miss Beaufort could only answer with her tears.

After a pause of many minutes, in which the countess strove to tranquillize her spirits, she resumed in a more composed voice.

"Excuse me for an instant, my dear Miss Beaufort; I must write to Mr. Constantine. I have yet to inform him that my absence is to be added to his other misfortunes."

With her eyes now raining down upon the paper, she took up a pen, and hastily writing a few lines was sealing them when Mary, looking up, hardly conscious of the words which escaped her, said, with inarticulate anxiety, "Lady Tinemouth, you know much of that noble and unhappy young man?" Her eyes irresolute and her cheek glowing, she awaited the answer of the countess, who continued to gaze on the letter she held in her hand, as if in profound thought; then all at once raising her head, and regarding the now downcast face of her lovely friend with tenderness, she replied, in a tone which conveyed the deep interest of her thoughts:—

"I do, Miss Beaufort; but he has reposed his griefs in my friendship and honor, therefore I must hold them sacred."

"I will not ask you to betray them," returned Mary, in a faltering voice; "yet I cannot help lamenting his sufferings, and esteeming the fortitude with which he supports his fall."

The countess looked steadfastly on her fluctuating countenance. "Has Constantine, my dear girl, hinted to you that he ever was otherwise than as he now appears?"

Miss Beaufort could not reply. She would not trust her lips with words, but shook her head in sign that he had not. Lady Tinemouth was too well read in the human heart to doubt for an instant the cause of her question, and consequent emotion. Feeling that something was due to an anxiety so disinterested, she took her passive hand, and said, "Mary, you have guessed rightly. Though I am not authorized to tell you the real name of Mr. Constantine, nor the particulars of his history, yet let this satisfy your generous heart, that it can never be more honorably employed than in compassionating calamities which ought to wreath his young brows with glory."

Miss Beaufort's eyes streamed afresh, whilst her exulting soul seemed ready to rush from her bosom.

"Mary!" continued the countess, warmed by the recollection of his excellence, "you have no need to blush at the interest which you take in this amiable stranger! Every trial of spirit which could have tortured youth or manhood has been endured by him with the firmness of a hero. Ah, my sweet friend," added the countess, pressing the hand of the confused Miss Beaufort, who, ashamed, and conscious that her behavior betrayed how dearly she considered him, had covered her face with her handkerchief, "when you are disposed to believe that a man is as great as his titles and personal demands seem to assert, examine with a nice observance whether his pretensions be real or artificial. Imagine him disrobed of splendor and struggling with the world's inclemencies. If his character cannot stand this ordeal, he is only a vain pageant, inflated and garnished; and it is reasonable to punish such arrogance with contempt. But on the contrary, when, like Constantine, he rises from the ashes of his fortunes in a brighter blaze of virtue, then, dearest girl," cried the countess, encircling her with her arms, "it is the sweetest privilege of loveliness to console and bless so rare a being."

Mary raised her weeping face from the bosom of her friend, and clasping her hands together with trepidation and anguish, implored her to be as faithful to her secret as she had proved herself to Constantine's. "I would sooner die," added she, "than have him know my rashness, perhaps my indelicacy! Let me possess his esteem, Lady Tinemouth! Let him suppose that I only *esteem* him! More I should shrink from. I have seen him beset by some of my sex; and to be classed with them—to have him imagine that my affection is like theirs!—I could not bear it. I entreat you, let him respect me!"

The impetuosity, and almost despair, with which Miss Beaufort uttered these incoherent sentences penetrated the soul of Lady Tinemouth with admiration. How different was the spirit of this pure and dignified love to the wild passion she had seen shake the frame of Lady Sara Ross.

They remained silent for some time.

"May I see your ladyship to-morrow?" asked Mary, drawing her cloak about her.

"I fear not," replied the countess, "I leave this house to-morrow morning."

Miss Beaufort rose; her lips, hands, and feet trembled so that she could hardly stand. Lady Tinemouth put her arm round her waist, and kissing her forehead, added, "Heaven bless you, my sweet friend! May all the wishes of your innocent heart be gratified!"

The countess supported her to the door. Mary hesitated an instant; then flinging her snowy arms over her ladyship's neck, in a voice scarcely audible, articulated, "Only tell me, does he love Euphemia?"

Lady Tinemouth strained her to her breast. "No, my dearest girl; I am certain, both from what I have heard him say and observed in his eyes, that did he dare to love any one, *you* would be the object of his choice."

How Miss Beaufort got into Lady Dundas's sedan-chair she had no recollection, so completely was she absorbed in the recent scene. Her mind was perplexed, her heart ached; and she arrived in Harley Street so much disordered and unwell as to oblige her to retire immediately to her room, with the excuse of a violent pain in her head.

CHAPTER XXXIII.

PASSION AND PRINCIPLE.

THIS interview induced Lady Tinemouth to destroy the note she had written to Thaddeus, and to frame another, better calculated to produce comfort to all parties. What she had declared to Mary respecting the state of the count's affections was sincere.

She had early pierced the veil of bashfulness with which Miss Beaufort overshadowed, when in his presence, that countenance so usually the tablet of her soul. The countess easily translated the quick receding of her eye whenever Thaddeus turned his attention towards her, the confused reply that followed any unexpected question from his lips, and, above all, the unheeded sighs heaved by her when he left the room, or when his name was mentioned during his absence. These symptoms too truly revealed to Lady Tinemouth the state of her young friend's bosom.

But the circumstances being different, her observations on Thaddeus were not nearly so conclusive. Mary had absolutely given the empire of her happiness, with her heart, into his hands. Thaddeus felt that his ruined hopes ought to prevent him laying his at her feet, could he even be made to believe that he had found any favor in her sight! and regarding her as a being beyond his reach, he conceived no suspicions that she entertained one dearer thought of him than what mere philanthropy could authorize.

He contemplated her unequalled beauty, graces, talents and virtues with an admiration bordering on idolatry! yet his heart flew from the confession that he loved her; and it was not until reason demanded of his sincerity why he felt a pang on seeing Mary's purse in the hands of Mr. Lascelles, that with a glowing cheek he owned to himself that he was jealous: that although he had not presumed to elevate one wish towards the possession of Miss Beaufort, yet when Lascelles flaunted her name on his tongue, he found how deep would be the wound in his peace should she ever give her hand to another than himself!

Confounded at this discovery of a passion the seeds of which he supposed had been crushed by the weight of his misfortunes and the depths of his griefs, he proceeded homewards in a trance of thought, not far differing from that of the dreamer who sinks into a harassing slumber, and, filled with terror, doubts whether he be sleeping or awake.

The sudden illness of General Butzou having put these ideas to flight, Thaddeus was sitting on the bedside, with his anxious thoughts fixed on the pale spectacle of mortality before him, when Nanny brought in a letter from the countess. He took it, and going to the window, read with mingled feelings the following epistle:—

"TO MR. CONSTANTINE.

"I know not, my dear count, when I shall be permitted to see you again: perhaps never on this side of the grave!

"Since Heaven has denied me the tenderness of my own children, it would have been a comfort to me might I have continued to act a parent's part by you. But my cruel lord, and my more cruel son, jealous of the consolation I meet in the society of my few intimate friends, command me to quit London; and as I have ever made it a rule to conform to their injunctions to the furthest extent of my power, I shall go.

"It pierces me to the soul, my dear son! (allow my maternal heart to call you by that name) it distresses me deeply that I am compelled to leave the place where you are, and the more that I cannot see you before my departure, for I quit town early to-morrow.

"Write to me often, my loved Sobieski; your letters will be some alleviation to my lot during the fulfilment of my hard duty.

"Wear the enclosed gold chain for my sake; it is one of two given me a long time ago by Miss Beaufort. If I have not greatly mistaken you, the present will now possess a double value in your estimation: indeed it ought. Sensibility and thankfulness being properties of your nature, they will not deny a lively gratitude to the generous interest with which that amiable and noble young woman regards your fate. It is impossible that the avowed Count Sobieski (whom, a year ago, I remember her animated fancy painted in colors worthy of his actions) could excite more of her esteem than I know she has bestowed on the untitled Constantine.

"She is all nobleness and affection. For, although I am sensible that she would leave much behind her in London to regret, she insists on accompanying me to the Wolds. Averse to transgress so far on her goodness, I firmly refused her offer until this evening, when I received so warm and urgent a letter from her disinterested, generous heart, that I could no longer withhold my grateful assent.

"Indeed, this lovely creature's active friendship proves of high consequence to me now, situated as I am with regard to a new whim of the earl's. Had she not thus urged me, in obedience to my lord's commands I should have been obliged to go alone, he having taken some wild antipathy to Miss Egerton, whose company he has interdicted. At any rate, her parents would not have allowed me her society much longer, for Mr. Montresor is to return this month.

"I shall not be easy, my dear count, until I hear from you. Pray write soon, and inform me of every particular respecting the poor general. Is he likely to recover?

"In all things, my loved son, in which I can serve you, remember that I expect you will refer yourself to me as to a mother. Your own could hardly have regarded you with deeper tenderness than does your affectionate and faithful

"ADELIZA TINEMOUTH.

"GROSVENOR PLACE, *Thursday, midnight.*

"Direct to me at Harwold Place, Wolds, Lincolnshire."

Several opposite emotions agitated the mind of Thaddeus whilst reading this epistle,—increased abhorrence of the man whom he believed to be his father, and distress at the increase of his cruelty to his unhappy wife! Yet these could neither subdue the balmy effect of her maternal affection towards himself nor wholly check the emotion which the unusual mentioning of Miss Beaufort's name had caused his heart to throb. He read the sentence which contained the assurance of her esteem a third time.

"Delicious poison!" cried he, kissing the paper; "if adoring thee, lovely Mary, be added to my other trials, I shall be resigned! There is sweetness even in the thought. Could I credit all which my dear lady Tinemouth affirms, the conviction that I possess one kind solicitude in the mind of Miss Beaufort would be ample compensation for ——"

He did not finish the sentence, but sighing profoundly, rose from his chair.

"For anything, except beholding her the bride of another!" was the sentiment with which his heart swelled. Thaddeus had never known a selfish wish in his life; and this first instance of his desiring that good to be unappropriated which he might not himself enjoy, made him start.

"There is an evil in my breast I wotted not of!" Dissatisfied with himself at this, he was preparing to answer her ladyship's letter, when turning to the date, he discovered that it had been written on Thursday night, and in consequence of Nanny's neglect in not calling at the coffee-house, had been delayed a day and a half before it reached him.

His disappointment at this accident was severe. She was gone, and Miss Beaufort along with her.

"Then, indeed, I am unfortunate. Yet this treasure!" cried he, fondly clasping the separated bracelet in his hand; "it will, indeed, be a representative of both—honored, beloved—to this deserted heart!"

He put the chain round his neck, and, with a true lover-like feeling, thought that it warmed the heart which mortification had chilled; but the fancy was evanescent, and he again turned to watch the fading life of his friend.

During the lapse of a few days, in which the general appeared merely to breathe, Thaddeus, instead of his attendance, despatched regular notes of excuse to Harley Street. In answer to these, he commonly received little tender billets from Euphemia, the strain of which he seemed totally to overlook, by the cold respect he evinced in his continued diurnal apologies for absence.

This young lady was so full of her own lamentations over the trouble which her elegant tutor must endure in watching his sick friend, that she never thought it worth while to mention in her notes any creature in the house excepting herself, and her commiseration. Thaddeus longed to inquire about Miss Beaufort; but the more he wished it, the greater was his reluctance to write her name.

Things were in this situation, when one evening, as he was reading by the light of a solitary candle in his little sitting-room, the door opened, and Nanny stepped in, followed by a female wrapped in a large black cloak. Thaddeus rose.

"A lady, sir," said Nanny, curtseying.

The moment the girl withdrew, the visitor cast herself into a chair, and sobbing aloud, seemed in violent agitation. Thaddeus, astonished and alarmed, approached her, and, though she was unknown, offered her every assistance in his power.

Catching hold of the hand which, with the greatest respect, he extended towards her, she instantly displayed to his dismayed sight the features of Lady Sara Ross.

"Merciful Heaven!" exclaimed he, involuntarily starting back.

"Do not cast me off, Constantine!" cried she, clasping his arm, and looking up to him with a face of anguish; "on you alone I now depend for happiness—for existence!"

A cold damp stood on the forehead of her auditor.

"Dear Lady Sara, what am I to understand by this emotion; has anything dreadful happened? Is Captain Ross——"

Lady Sara shuddered, and still grasping his hand, answered with words every one of which palsied the heart of Thaddeus. "He is coming home. He is now at Portsmouth. O, Constantine! I am not yet so debased as to live with him when my heart is yours."

At this shameful declaration, Thaddeus clenched his teeth in agony of spirit; and placing his hand upon his eyes, to shut her from his sight, he turned suddenly round and walked towards another part of the room.

Lady Sara followed him. Her cloak having fallen off, now displayed her fine form in all the fervor of grief and distraction. She rung her fair and jewelled arms in despair, and with accents rendered more piercing by the anguish of her mind, exclaimed, "What! You hate me? You throw me from you? Cruel, barbarous Constantine! Can you drive from your feet the woman who adores you? Can you cast her who is without a home into the streets?"

Thaddeus felt his hand wet with her tears. He fixed his eyes upon her with almost delirious horror. Her hat being off, gave freedom to her long black hair, which, falling in masses over her figure and face, gave such additional wildness to the imploring and frantic expression of her eyes, that his distracted soul felt reeling within him.

"Rise, madam! For Heaven's sake, Lady Sara!" and he stooped to raise her.

"Never!" cried she, clinging to him—"never! till you promise to protect me. My husband comes home to-night, and I have left his house forever. You—you!" exclaimed she, extending her hand to his averted face; "Oh, Constantine! you have robbed me of my peace! On your account I have flown from my home. For mercy's sake, do not abandon me!"

"Lady Sara," cried he, looking in desperation around him, "I cannot speak to you in this position! Rise, I implore you!"

"Only," returned she, "only say that you will protect me! —that I shall find shelter here! Say this, and I will rise and bless you forever."

Thaddeus stood aghast, not knowing how to reply. Terror-struck at the violent lengths to which she seemed determined to carry her unhappy and guilty passion, he in vain sought to evade this direct demand. Lady Sara, perceiving the reluctance and horror of his looks, sprang from her knees, while in a more resolute voice she exclaimed, "Then, sir, you will not protect me? You scorn and desert a woman whom you well know has long loved you?—whom, by your artful behavior, you have seduced to this disgrace!"

The count, surprised and shocked at this accusation, with gentleness, but resolution, denied the charge.

Lady Sara again melted into tears, and supporting her tottering frame against his shoulder, replied, in a stifled voice, "I know it well: I have nothing to blame for my wretched state but my own weakness. Pardon, dear Constantine, the dictates of my madness! Oh! I would gladly owe such misery to any other source than myself!"

"Then, respected lady," rejoined Thaddeus, gaining courage from the mildness of her manner, "let me implore you to return to your own house!"

"Don't ask me," cried she, grasping his hand. "O, Constantine! if you knew what it was to receive with smiles of affection a creature whom you loathe, you would shrink with disgust from what you require. I detest Captain Ross. Can I open my arms to meet him, when my heart excludes him forever? Can I welcome him home when I wish him in his grave?"

Sobieski extricated his hand from her grasp. Her ladyship perceived the repugnance which dictated this action, and with renewed violence ejaculated, "Unhappy woman that I am! to hate where I am loved! to love where I am hated! Kill me. Constantine!" cried she, turning suddenly towards him, and sinking down on a chair, "but do not give me such another look as that!"

"Dear Lady Sara," replied he, seating himself by her side, "what would you have me do? You see that I have no proper means of protecting you. I have no relations, no friends to receive you. You see that I am a poor man. Besides, your character——"

"Talk not of my character!" cried she: "I will have none that does not depend on you! Cruel Constantine! you will not understand me. I want no riches, no friends, but yourself. Give me *your* home and *your* arms," added she, throwing herself in an agony on his bosom, "and beggary would be paradise! But I shall not bring you poverty; I have inherited a fortune since I married Ross, on which he has no claim."

Thaddeus now shrunk doubly from her. Why had she not

felt a sacred spell in that husband's name? He shuddered, and tore himself from her clinging arms. Holding her off with his hand, he exclaimed, in a voice of mental agony, "Infatuated woman! leave me, for his honor and your own peace."

"No, no!" cried she, hoping she had gained some advantage over his agitated feelings, and again casting herself at his feet, exclaimed, "Never will I leave this spot till you consent that your home shall be my home; that I shall serve you forever!"

Thaddeus pressed his hands upon his eyes, as if he would shut her from his sight. But with streaming tears she added, while clasping his other hand to her throbbing bosom, "Exclude me not from those dear eyes! reject me not from being your true wife, your willing slave!"

Thaddeus heard this, but he did not look on her, neither did he answer. He broke from her, and fled, in a stupor of horror at his situation, into the apartment where the general lay in a heavy sleep.

Little expecting to see any one but the man she loved, Lady Sara rushed in after him, and was again wildly pressing towards her determined victim, when her eyes were suddenly arrested by a livid, and, she thought, dead face of a person lying on the bed. Fixed to the spot, she stood for a moment; then putting her spread hand on her forehead, uttered a faint cry, and fell soul-struck to the floor.

Having instant conviction of her mistake, Thaddeus eagerly seized the moment of her insensibility to convey her home. He hastily went to the top of the stairs, called to Nanny to run for a coach, and then returning to the extended figure of Lady Sara, lifted her in his arms and carried her back to the room they had left.

By the help of a little water, he restored her to a sense of existence. She slowly opened her eyes; then raising her head, looked round with a terrified air, when her eye falling on the still open door of the general's room, she caught Thaddeus by the arm, and said, in a shuddering voice, "Oh! take me hence."

Whilst she yet spoke, the coach stopped at the door. The count rose, and attempted to support her agitated frame on his arm; but she trembled so, he was obliged to almost carry her down stairs.

When he placed her in the carriage, she said, in a faint tone, "You surely will not leave me?"

Thaddeus made no reply; then desiring Nanny to sit by the general until his return, which should be in a few minutes, and having stepped into the coach, Lady Sara snatched his hand, while in dismayed accents she quickly said,

"Who was that fearful person?"

"Alas! the revered friend whose long illness Lady Tinemouth has sometimes mentioned in your presence."

Lady Sara shuddered again, but with a rush of tears, while she added imploringly, "Then, whither are you going to take me?"

"You shall again, dear Lady Sara," replied he, "return to a guiltless and peaceful home."

"I cannot meet my husband," cried she, wringing her hands; "he will see all my premeditated guilt in my countenance. O! Constantine, have pity on me! Miserable creature that I am! It is horrible to live without you! It is dreadful to live with him! Take me not home, I entreat you!"

The count took her clasped hands in his, saying,

"Reflect for a moment. Lady Tinemouth's eulogiums on our first acquaintance taught me to honor you. I believe that when you distinguished me with any portion of your regard, it was in consequence of virtues which you thought I possessed."

"Indeed, you do me justice!" cried she, with renewed energy.

He continued, feeling that he must be stern in words as well as in purpose if he would really rescue her from herself. "Think, then, should I yield to the influence of your beauty, and sink your respected name to a level with those"—and he pointed to a group of wretched women assembled at the corner of Pall-Mall. "Think, where would be the price of your innocence? I being no longer worthy of your esteem, you would hate yourself; and we should continue together, two guilty creatures, abhorring each other, and justly despised by a virtuous world."

Lady Sara sat as one dumb, and did not inarticulate any sound—except the groan of horror which had shot through her when she had glanced at those women—until the coach stopped in James's Place.

"Go in with me," were all the words she could utter, while, pulling her veil over her face, she gave him her hand to assist her down the steps.

"Is Captain Ross arrived?" asked Thaddeus of a servant, who, to his great joy, replied in the negative. During the drive, he had alarmed himself by anticipating the disagreeable suspicions which might rise in the mind of the husband should he see his wife in her present strange and distracted state

When Thaddeus seated Lady Sara in her drawing-room, he offered to take a respectful leave; but she laid one hand on his arm, whilst with the other she covered her convulsed features, and said, "Constantine, before you go, before we part, perhaps eternally, O! tell me that you do not, even now, hate me!—that you do not hate me!" repeated she, in a firmer tone; "I know too well how deeply I am despised."

"Cease, ah, cease these vehement self-reproaches!" returned he, tenderly replacing her on the sofa. "Shame does not depend on possessing passions, but in yielding to them. You have conquered yours, dear Lady Sara; and in future I must respect and love you like a sister of my heart."

"Noble Constantine! there is no guile in thee," exclaimed she, straining his hand to her lips. "May Heaven bless you wherever you go!"

He dropped on his knees, imprinted on both her hands a true brother's sacred kiss, and, hastily rising, was quitting the room without a word, when he heard, in a short, low sound from her voice, "O, why had I not a mother, a sister, to love and pity me! Should I have been such a wretch as now?"

Thaddeus turned from the door at the tone and substance of this apparently unconsciously uttered apostrophe. She was standing with her hands clasped, and her eyes fixed on the ground. By an irresistible impulse he approached her. "Lady Sara," said he, with a tender reverence in his voice, "there is penitence and prayer to a better Parent in those words! Look up to Him, and He will save you from yourself, and bless you in your husband."

She did raise her eyes at this adjuration, and without one earthward glance at her young monitor in their movement to the heaven she sought. Neither did she speak, but pressed, with an unutterable emotion, the hand which now held hers, while his own heart did indeed silently re-echo the prayer he saw in her upward eyes. Turning gently away, he glided, in a suffusion of grateful tears, out of the apartment.

CHAPTER XXXIV.

REQUIESCAT IN PACE.

The dream-like amazement which enveloped the count's faculties after the preceding scene was dissipated next morning by the appearance of Dr. Cavendish. When he saw the general, he declared it to be his opinion that, in consequence of his long and tranquil slumbers, some favorable crisis seemed near. "Probably," added he, "the recovery of his intellects. Such phenomena in these cases often happen immediately before death."

"Heaven grant it may in this!" ejaculated Thaddeus; "to hear his venerable voice again acknowledge that I have acted by him as became the grandson of his friend, would be a comfort to me."

"But, sir," replied the kind physician, touching his burning hand, "you must not forget the cares which are due to your own life. If you wish well to the general during the few days he may have to live, you are indispensably obliged to preserve your own strength. You are already ill, and require air. I have an hour of leisure," continued he, pulling out his watch; "I will remain here till you have taken two or three walks round St. James's Park. It is absolutely necessary; in this instance I must take the privilege of friendship, and insist on obedience."

Seeing the benevolent Cavendish would not be denied, Thaddeus took his hat, and with harassed spirits walked down the lane towards Charing Cross.

On entering Spring Garden gate, to his extreme surprise the first objects that met his sight were Miss Euphemia Dundas and Miss Beaufort.

Euphemia accosted him with ten thousand inquiries respecting his friend, besides congratulations on his own good looks.

Thaddeus bowed; then smiling faintly, turned to the blushing Mary, who, conscious of what had passed in the late conversation between herself and Lady Tinemouth, trembled so much that, fearing to excite the suspicion of Euphemia by such tremor, she withdrew her arm, and walked forward alone, tottering at every step.

"I thought, Miss Beaufort," said he, addressing himself to her, "that Lady Tinemouth was to have had the happiness of your company at Harwold Park?"

"Yes," returned she, fearfully raising her eyes to his face, the hectic glow of which conveyed impressions to her different from those which Euphemia expressed; "but to my indescribable alarm and disappointment, the morning after I had written to fix my departure with her ladyship, my aunt's foot caught in the iron of the stair-carpet as she was coming down stairs, and throwing her from the top to the bottom, broke her leg. I could not quit her a moment during her agonies; and the surgeons having expressed their fears that a fever might ensue, I was obliged altogether to decline my attendance on the countess."

"And how is Miss Dorothy?" inquired Thaddeus, truly concerned at the accident.

"She is better, though confined to her bed," replied Euphemia, speaking before her companion could open her lips, "and, indeed, poor Mary and myself have been such close nurses, my mother insisted on our walking out to-day."

"And Lady Tinemouth," returned Thaddeus, again addressing Miss Beaufort, "of course she went alone?"

"Alas, yes!" replied she; "Miss Egerton was forced to join her family in Leicestershire."

"I believe," cried Euphemia, sighing, "Miss Egerton is going to be married. Hers has been a long attachment. Happy girl! I have heard Captain Ross say (whose lieutenant her intended husband was) that he is the finest young man in the navy. Did you ever see Mr. Montresor?" added she, turning her pretty eyes on the count.

"I never had that pleasure."

"Bless me! that is odd, considering your intimacy with Miss Egerton. I assure you he is very charming."

Thaddeus neither heard this nor a great deal more of the same trifling chit-chat which was slipping from the tongue of Miss Euphemia, so intently were his eyes (sent by his heart) searching the downcast but expressive countenance of Miss Beaufort. His soul was full; and the fluctuations of her color, with the embarrassment of her step, more than affected him.

"Then you do not leave town for some time, Miss Beaufort?" inquired he; "I may yet anticipate the honor of seeing——" he hesitated a moment, then added in a depressed tone—"your aunt, when I next wait on the Misses Dundas."

"Our stay depends entirely on her health," returned she

striving to rally herself; "and I am sure she will be happy to find you better; for I am sorry to say I cannot agree with Euphemia in thinking you look well."

"Merely a slight indisposition," replied he, "the effect of an anxiety which I fear will too soon cease in the death of its cause. I came out now for a little air, whilst the physician remains with my revered friend."

"Poor old gentleman!" sighed Mary; "how venerable was his appearance the morning in which we saw him in the Park! What a benign countenance!"

"His countenance," replied Thaddeus, his eyes turning mournfully towards the lovely speaker, "is the emblem of his character. He was the most amiable of men."

"And you are likely to lose so interesting a friend; dear Mr. Constantine, how I pity you!" While Euphemia uttered these words, she put the corner of her glove to her eye.

The count looked at her, and perceiving that her commiseration was affectation, he turned to Miss Beaufort, who was walking pensively by his side, and made further inquiries respecting Miss Dorothy. Anxious to be again with his invalid, he was preparing to quit them, when Mary, as with a full heart she curtseyed her adieu, in a hurried and confused manner, said—"Pray, Mr. Constantine, take care of yourself. You have other friends besides the one you are going to lose. I know Lady Tinemouth, I know my aunt——" She stopped short, and, covered with blushes, stood panting for another word to close the sentence; when Thaddeus, forgetting all presence but her own, with delighted precipitancy caught hold of the hand which, in her confusion, was a little extended towards him, and pressing it with fervor, relinquished it immediately; then, overcome by confusion at the presumption of the action, he bowed with agitation to both ladies, and hastened through the Friary passage into St. James's Street.

"Miss Beaufort!" cried Euphemia, reddening with vexation, and returning a perfumed handkerchief to her pocket, "I did not understand that you and Mr. Constantine were on such intimate terms!"

"What do you mean, Euphemia?"

"That you have betrayed the confidence I reposed in you," cried the angry beauty, wiping away the really starting tears with her white lace cloak. "I told you the elegant Constantine was the lord of my heart; and you have seduced him from me! Till you came, he was so respectful, so tender, so devoted! But I am rightly used! I ought to have carried my secret to the grave."

In vain Miss Beaufort protested; in vain she declared herself ignorant of possessing any power over even one wish of Constantine's. Euphemia thought it monstrous pretty to be the injured friend and forsaken mistress; and all along the Park, and up Constitution-hill, until they arrived at Lady Dundas's carriage, which was waiting opposite Devonshire-wall, she affected to weep. When seated, she continued her invectives. She called Miss Beaufort ungenerous, perfidious traitor to friendship, and every romantic and disloyal name which her inflamed fancy could devise; till the sight of Harley Street checked her transports, and relieved her patient hearer from a load of impertinence and reproach.

During this short interview, Thaddeus had received an impulse to his affections which hurried them forward with a force that neither time nor succeeding sorrows could stop nor stem.

Mary's heavenly-beaming eyes seemed to have encircled his head with love's purest halo. The command, "Preserve yourself for others besides your dying friend," yet throbbed at his heart; and with ten thousand rapturous visions flitting before his sight, he trod in air, until the humble door of his melancholy home presenting itself, at once wrecked the illusion, and offered sad reality in the person of his emaciated friend.

On the count's entrance to the sick chamber, Doctor Cavendish gave him a few directions to pursue when the general should awake from the sleep into which he had been sunk for so many hours. With a heart the more depressed from its late unusual exaltation, Thaddeus sat down at the side of the invalid's bed for the remainder of the day.

At five in the afternoon, General Butzou awoke. Seeing the count, he stretched out his withered hand, and as the doctor predicted, accosted him rationally.

"Come, dear Sobieski! Come nearer, my dear master."

Thaddeus rose, and throwing himself on his knees, took the offered hand with apparent composure. It was a hard struggle to restrain the emotions which were roused by this awful contemplation—the return of reason to the soul on the instant she was summoned into the presence of her Maker!

"My kind, my beloved lord!" added Butzou, "to me you have indeed performed a Christian's part; you have clothed, sheltered and preserved me in your bosom. Blessed son of my most honored master!"

The good old man put the hand of Thaddeus to his lips. Thaddeus could not speak.

"I am going, dear Sobieski," continued the general, in a

lower voice, "where I shall meet your noble grandfather, your mother, and my brave countrymen; and if Heaven grants me power, I will tell them by whose labor I have lived, on whose breast I have expired."

Thaddeus could no longer restrain his tears.

"Dear, dear general!" exclaimed he, grasping his hand; "my grandfather, my mother, my country! I lose them all again in thee! O! would that the same summons took me hence!"

"Hush!" returned the dying man; "Heaven reserves you, my honored lord, for wise purposes. Youth and health are the marks of commission:* *you* possess them, with virtues which will bear you through the contest. *I* have done; and my merciful Judge has evinced his pardon of my errors by sparing me in my old age, and leading me to die with you."

Thaddeus pressed his friend's hand to his streaming eyes, and promised to be resigned. Butzou smiled his satisfaction; then closing his eyelids, he composed himself to a rest that was neither sleep nor stupor, but a balmy serenity, which seemed to be tempering his lately recovered soul for its immediate entrance on a world of eternal peace.

At nine o'clock his breath became broken with quick sighs. The count's heart trembled, and he drew closer to the pillow. Butzou felt him; and opening his eyes languidly, articulated, "Raise my head."

Thaddeus put his arm under his neck, and lifting him up, reclined him against his bosom. Butzou grasped his hands, and looking gratefully in his face, said, "The arms of a soldier should be a soldier's death-bed. I am content."

He lay for a moment on the breast of the almost fainting Thaddeus; then suddenly quitting his hold, he cried, "I lose you, Sobieski! But there is——" and he gazed fixedly forward.

* I cannot but pause here, in revising the volume, to publicly express the emotion (grateful to Heaven) I experienced on receiving a letter quoting these words, many, many years ago. It was from the excellent Joseph Fox, the well-known Christian philanthropist of our country, who spent both his fortune and his life in establishing and sustaining several of our best charitable and otherwise patriotic institutions. And once, when some of his anxious friends would gladly have persuaded him to grant himself more personal indulgences, and to labor less in the then recently-begun plans for national education, he wrote "to the author of Thaddeus of Warsaw," and, quoting to her those words from the work, declared "they were on his heart! and he would, with the blessing of God, perform what he believed to be his commission to the last powers of his youth and health."

This admirable man has now been long removed to his heavenly country—to the everlasting dwelling-place of the just made perfect. And such recollections cannot but make an historical novel-writer at least feel answerable for more, in his or her pages, than the purposes of mere amusement. They guide by examples. Plutarch, in his lives of Grecian and Roman Worthies, taught more effectually the heroic and virtuous science of life than did all his philosophical works put together.

"I am here," exclaimed the count, catching his motionless hand. The dying general murmured a few words m e, and turning his face inward, breathed his last sigh on the bosom of his last friend.

For a minute Sobieski continued incapable of thought or action. When he recovered recollection, he withdrew from his melancholy station. Laying the venerable remains back on the bed, he did not trust his rallied faculties with a second trial, but hastening down stairs, was met by Mrs. Robson.

"My dear madam," said he, "all is over with my poor friend. Will you do me the kindness to perform those duties to his sacred relics which I cannot?"

Thaddeus would not allow any person to watch by his friend's coffin besides himself. The meditations of this solitary night presented to his sound and sensible mind every argument rather to induce rejoicing than regret that the eventful life of the brave Butzou was terminated.

"Yes, illustrious old man!" cried he, gazing on his marble features; "if valor and virtue be the true sources of nobility, thou surely wast noble! Inestimable defender of Stanislaus and thy country! thou hast run a long and bright career; and though thou art fated to rest in the humble grave of poverty, it will be embalmed by the tears of Heaven—it will be engraven on my heart."

Thaddeus did not weep whilst he spoke. Nor did he weep when he beheld the mold of St. Paul's, Covent Garden, close from his view the last remains of his friend. It began to rain. The uncovered head of the officiating minister was wet; and so was that of a little delicate boy, in a black cloak, who stood near, holding the aged rector's hat during the service. As the shower descended faster, Dr. Cavendish put his arm through the count's to draw him away, but he lingered an instant, looking on the mold while the sexton piled it up. "Wretched Poland!" sighed he; "how far from thee lies one of thy bravest sons!" The words were breathed in so low a murmur, that none heard them except the ear of Heaven! and that little boy, whose gaze had been some time fixed on Thaddeus, and whose gentle heart never forgot them.

Dr. Cavendish, regarding with redoubled pity the now doubly desolated exile in this last resignation of his parental friend to a foreign grave, attempted to persuade him to return with him to dinner. He refused the kind invitation, alleging, with a faint smile, that under every misfortune he found his best comforter in solitude

Respecting the resignation and manliness of this answer, Doctor Cavendish urged him no further; but expressing his regret that he could not see him again until the end of the week, as he was obliged to go to Stanford next day on a medical consultation, he shook hands with him at the door of Mrs. Robson and bade him farewell.

Thaddeus entered his lonely room, and fell on his knees before the "ark of his strength,"—the Holy Book, that had been the gift of his mother. The first page he opened presented to him the very words which had poured consolation into his sad heart, from the lips of the venerable clergyman when he met him on his entrance into the church-porch before the coffin of his friend!

"I am the resurrection and the life, saith the Lord. He that believeth in me, though he were dead, yet shall he live; and whosoever liveth, and believeth in me, shall never die."

After reading this, how truly did the young mourner feel that "Death had lost its sting—the grave its victory."

CHAPTER XXXV.

DEEP ARE THE PURPOSES OF ADVERSITY.

NEXT morning, when the Count Sobieski unfolded the several packets of papers which were put into his hands by little Nanny, he laid them one after the other on the table, and sighing heavily, said to himself, "Now comes the bitterness of poverty! Heaven only knows by what means I shall pay these heavy charges."

Mere personal privations, induced by his fallen fortunes, excited little uneasiness in the mind of Thaddeus. As he never had derived peculiar gratification from the enjoyment of a magnificent house, splendid table, and numerous attendants, he was contented in the field, where he slept on the bare ground, and snatched his hasty meals at uncertain intervals. Watching, rough fare, and other hardships were dust in the path of honor; he had dashed through them with light and buoyant spirits; and he repined as little at the actual wants of his forlorn state in exile, until, compelled by friendship to contract demands which he could not defray, he was plunged at once into the full horrors of poverty and debt.

He looked at the amount of the bills. The apothecary's was twelve pounds; the funeral fifteen. Thaddeus turned pale. The value of all that he possessed would not produce one half of the sum; besides, he owed five guineas to his good landlady, for numerous little comforts procured for his deceased friend.

"Whatever be the consequence," cried he, "that excellent woman shall not suffer by her humanity! If I have to part with the last memorial of those who were so dear, she shall be repaid."

He scarcely had ceased speaking, when Nanny re-entered the room, and told him the apothecary's young man and the undertaker were both below, waiting for answers to their letters. Reddening with disgust at the unfeeling haste of these men, he desired Nanny to say that he could not see either of them to-day, but would send to their houses to-morrow."

In consequence of this promise, the men made their bows to Mrs. Robson (who too well guessed the reason of this message), and took their leave.

When Thaddeus put the pictures of his mother and the palatine, with other precious articles, into his pocket, he could not forbear an internal invective against the thoughtless meanness of the Misses Dundas, who had never offered any further liquidation of the large sum they now stood indebted to him than the trifling note which had been transmitted to him, prior to his attendance, through the hands of Lady Tinemouth.

Whilst his necessities reproached them for this illiberal conduct, his proud heart recoiled at making a request to their charity; for he had gathered from the haughty demeanor of Miss Diana that what he was entitled to demand would be given, not as a just remuneration for labor received, but as alms of humanity to an indigent emigrant.

"I would rather perish," cried he, putting on his hat, "than ask that woman for a shilling."

When the count laid his treasure on the table of the worthy pawnbroker, he desired to have the value of the settings of the pictures, and the portraits themselves put into leather cases. With the other little things, there were a pair of gold spurs, the peculiar insignia of his princely rank, which the palatine himself had buckled on his grandson's heels on mounting his noble charger for his first field. There was a peculiar pang in parting with these—a sort of last relic of what he had been! But there was no alternative: all that had any intrinsic value must pass from him.

Having examined the setting of the miniatures, and the

gold of the other trinkets, with that of the spurs (which their hard service had something marred), Mr. Burket declared, on the word of an honest man, that he could not give more than fifteen pounds.

With difficulty Thaddeus stifled as torturing a sigh as ever distended his breast, whilst he said,

"I will take it. I only implore you to be careful of the things, trifling as they are; circumstances with which they were connected render them valuable to me to redeem."

"You may depend on me, sir," replied the pawnbroker, presenting him the notes and acknowledgment.

When Thaddeus took them, Mr. Burket's eye was caught by the ring on his finger.

"That ring seems curious? If you won't think me impertinent, may I ask to look at it?"

The count pulled it off, and forcing a smile, replied, "I suppose it is of little jewel value. The setting is slight, though the painting is fine."

Burket breathed on the diamonds. "If you were to sell it," returned he, "I don't think it would fetch more than three guineas. The diamonds are flawed, and the emeralds would be of little use, being out of fashion here; as for the miniature, it goes for nothing."

"Of course," said Thaddeus, putting it on again; "but I shall not part with it." While he drew on his glove, Mr. Burket asked him "whether the head were not intended for the King of Poland?"

The count, surprised, answered in the affirmative.

"I thought so," answered the man; "it is very like two or three prints which I had in my shop of that king."* Indeed, I believe I have them somewhere now: these matters are but a nine-day's wonder, and the sale is over."

His auditor did not clearly comprehend him, and he told him so.

"I meant nothing," continued he, "to the disparagement of the King of Poland, or of any other great personage who is much the subject of conversation. I only intended to say that everything has its fashion. The ruin of Poland was the fashionable topic for a month after it happened; and now nobody minds it—it is forgotten."

Thaddeus, in whose bosom all its miseries were written,

* The author has a very correct likeness of this memorable king, copied from an original miniature; and it is not one of the least valued portraits in a little room which contains those of several other heroes of different countries,—friends and gallant foes.

with a clouded brow bowed to the remarks of Mr. Burket, and in silence quitted the shop.

Having arrived at home, he discharged his debt to the worthy Mrs. Robson; then entering his room, he laid the remainder of his money on the bills of the two claimants. It was unequal to the demands of either; yet, in some measure to be just to both, he determined on dividing it between them, and to promise the liquidation of the rest by degrees.

Surely he might hope that, even should the Misses Dundas entirely forget his claims on them, he could, in the course of time make drawings sufficient to discharge the residue of the debt; but he was not permitted to put this calculation to the trial.

When he called on the apothecary, and offered him only half his demand, the man refused it with insolence, insisting upon having the whole then, "or he would make him pay for it!" Unused to the language of compulsion and vulgarity, the count quitted the shop saying "he was at liberty to act as he thought fit." With no very serene countenance, he entered the undertaker's warehouse. This man was civil; to him Thaddeus gave the entire sum, half of which the apothecary had rejected with so much derision. The undertaker's politeness a little calmed the irritated feelings of the count, who returned home musing on the vile nature of that class of mankind who can with indifference heap insult upon distress.

Judging men by his own disposition, he seldom gave credence to the possibility of such conduct. He had been told of dastardly spirits, but never having seen them, and possessing no archetype within his own breast of what he heard, the repeated relation passed over his mind without leaving an impression. He had entered the world filled with animating hopes of virtue and renown. He was virtuous; he became powerful, great, and renowned. Creation seemed paradise to his eyes; it was the task of adversity to teach him a different lesson of mankind. Not less virtuous, not less great, his fortunes fell: he became poor. The perfidy, the hard-heartedness of man, made and kept him friendless. When he wanted succor and consolation, he found the world peopled by a race too mean even to bear the stamp of the devil.

Whilst Sobieski was employed next morning at his drawing, Mrs. Robson sent Nanny to say that there were two strange-looking men below who wanted to speak with him. Not doubting they were messengers from the apothecary, he desired the girl to show them up stairs. When they entered his room, the count rose. One of the men stepped forward, and laying a slip of paper on the table, said, "I arrest you, sir, at the suit of Messrs. Vincent and Jackson, apothecaries!"

Thaddeus colored; but suppressing his indignant emotion, he calmly asked the men whither they were going to take him?

"If you like," replied one of them, "you may be well enough lodged. I never heard a word against Clement's in Wych Street."

"Is that a prison?" inquired Thaddeus.

"No, not exactly that, sir," answered the other man, laughing. "You seem to know little of the matter, which, for a Frenchman, is odd enough; but mayhap you have never a lock-upd-house in France, since ye pulled down the bastile! Howsoever, if you pay well, Mr. Clements will give you lodgings as long as you like. It is only poor rogues who are obligated to go to Newgate; such gemmen as you can live as ginteely in Wych Street as at their own houses."

There was such an air of derision about this fellow while he spoke, and glanced around the room, that Thaddeus, sternly contracting his brows, took no further notice of him, but, turning towards his more civil companion, said:

"Has this person informed me rightly? Am I going to a prison, or am I not? If I do not possess money to pay Mr. Jackson, I can have none to spend elsewhere."

"Then you must go to Newgate!" answered the man, in as surly a tone as his comrade's had been insolent.

"I'll run for a coach, Wilson," cried the other, opening the room door.

"I will not pay for one," said Thaddeus, at once comprehending the sort of wretches into whose custody he had fallen; "follow me down stairs. I shall walk."

Mrs. Robson was in her shop as he passed to the street. She called out, "You will come home to dinner, sir?"

"No," replied he; "but you shall hear from me before night."

"The men, winking at each other, sullenly pursued his steps down the lane. In the Strand, Thaddeus asked them which way he was to proceed?"

"Straight on," cried one of them; "most folks find the road to a jail easy enough."

Involved in thought, the count walked forward, unmindful of the stare which the well-known occupation of his attendants attracted towards him. When he arrived at Somerset House, one of the men stepped up to him, and said, "We are now nearly opposite Wych Street. You had better take your mind again, and go there instead of Newgate. I don't think your honor will like the debtor's hole."

Thaddeus, coldly thanking him, repeated his determination to be led to Newgate. But when he beheld the immense walls, within which he believed he should be immured for life, his feet seemed rooted to the ground; and when the massive doors were opened and closed upon him, he felt as if suddenly deprived of the vital spring of existence. A mist spread over his eyes, his soul shuddered, and with difficulty he followed the men into the place where his commitment was to be ratified. Here all the proud energies of his nature again rallied round his heart.

The brutal questions of the people in office, re-echoed by taunts from the wretches who had brought him to the prison, were of a nature so much beneath his answering, that he stood perfectly silent during the business; and when dismissed, without evincing any signs of discomposure, he followed the turnkey to his cell.

One deal chair, a table, and a miserable bed, were all the furniture it contained. The floor was paved with flags, and the sides of the apartment daubled with disclored plaster, part of which, having been peeled off by the damp, exposed to view large spaces of the naked stones.

Before the turnkey withdrew he asked Thaddeus whether he wanted anything?

"Only a pen, ink, and paper."

The man held out his hand.

"I have no money," replied Sobieski.

"Then you get nothing here," answered the fellow, pulling the door after him.

Thaddeus threw himself on the chair, and in the bitterness of his heart exclaimed, "Can these scoundrels be Christians?—can they be men?" He cast his eyes round him with the wildness of despair. "Mysterious Heaven, can it be possible that for a few guineas I am to be confined in this place for life? In these narrow bounds am I to waste my youth, my existence? Even so; I cannot, I will not, degrade the spirit of Poland by imploring assistance from any native of a land in which avarice has extinguished the feelings of humanity."

By the next morning, the first paroxysm of indignation having subsided, Thaddeus entertained a cooler and more reasonable opinion of his situation. He considered that though he was a prisoner, it was in consequence of debts incurred in behalf of a friend whose latter hours were rendered less wretched by such means. Notwithstanding "all that man could do unto him," he had brought an approving conscience to lighten the gloom of his dungeon; and resuming his wonted serenity, he continued to distance the impertinent freedom of his jailers by a calm dignity, which extorted civility and commanded respect.

CHAPTER XXXVI.

AN ENGLISH PRISON.

SEVERAL days elapsed without the inhabitants of Harley Street hearing any tidings of Thaddeus.

Miss Dundas never bestowed a thought on his absence, except when, descanting on her favorite subject, "the insolence of dependent people," she alleged his daring to withdraw himself as an instance. Miss Euphemia uttered all her complaints to Miss Beaufort, whom she accused of not being satisfied with seducing the affections of Mr. Constantine, but she must also spirit him away, lest by remorse he should be induced to renew his former devotion at the shrine of her tried constancy.

Mary found these secret conferences very frequent and very teasing. She believed neither the count's past devoirs to Euphemia nor his present allegiance to herself. With anxiety she watched the slow decline of every succeeding day, hoping that each knock at the door would present either himself or an apology for his absence.

In vain her reason urged the weakness and folly of giving way to the influence of a sentiment as absorbing as it was unforeseen. "It is not his personal graces," murmured she, whilst her dewy eyes remained riveted on the floor; "they have not accomplished this effect on me! No; matchless as he is, though his countenance, when illumined by the splendors of his mind, expresses consummate beauty, yet my heart tells me I would rather see all that perfection demolished than lose one beam of those bright charities which first attracted my esteem. Yes, Constantine!" cried she, rising in agitation, "I could adore thy virtues were they even in the bosom of deformity. It is these that I love; it is these that are thyself! it is thy noble, godlike soul that so entirely fills my heart, and must forever!"

She recalled the hours which, in his society, had glided so swiftly by to pass in review before her. They came, and her tears redoubled. Neither his words nor his looks had been kinder to her than to Miss Egerton or to Lady Sara Ross. She remembered his wild action in the park: it had transported her at the moment; it even now made her heart throb; but she ceased to believe it intended more than an animated expression of gratitude.

An adverse apprehension seemed to have taken possession of her breast. In proportion to the vehemence of Miss Euphemia's reproaches (who insisted on the passion of Thaddeus for Mary), she the more doubted the evidence of those delightful emotions which had rushed over her soul when she found her hand so fervently pressed in his.

Euphemia never made a secret of the tenderness she professed; and Miss Beaufort having been taught by her own heart to read distinctly the eyes of Lady Sara, the result of her observations had long acted as a caustic on her peace; it had often robbed her cheeks of their bloom, and compelled her to number the lingering minutes of the night with sighs. But her deep and modest flame assumed no violence; removed far from sight, it burnt the more intensely.

Instead of over-valuing the fine person of Thaddeus, the encomiums which it extorted, even from the lips of prejudice, occasioned one source of her pain. She could not bear to think it probable that the man whom she believed, and knew, to be gifted with every attribute of goodness and of heroism, might one day be induced to sacrifice the rich treasure of his mind to a creature who would select him from the rest merely on account of his external superiority.

Such was the train of Mary's meditations. Covering her face with her handkerchief, she exclaimed in a tender and broken voice, "Ah, why did I leave my quiet home to expose myself to the vicissitudes of society? Sequestered from the world, neither its pageants nor its mortifications could have reached me there. I have seen thee, matchless Constantine! Like a bright planet, thou has passed before me!—like a being of a superior order! And I never, never can debase my nature to change that love. Thy image shall follow me into solitude—shall consecrate my soul to the practice of every virtue! I will emulate thy excellence, when, perhaps, thou hast forgotten that I exist."

The fit of despondence which threatened to succeed this last melancholy reflection was interrupted by the sudden entrance of Euphemia. Miss Beaufort hastily rose, and drew her ringlets over her eyes.

"O, Mary!" cried the little beauty, holding up her pretty hands, "what do you think has happened?"

"What?" demanded she in alarm, and hastening towards the door; "anything to my aunt?"

"No, no," answered Euphemia, catching her by the arm; "but could my injured heart derive satisfaction from revenge, I should now be happy. Punishment has overtaken the faithless Constantine."

Miss Beaufort looked aghast, and grasping the back of the chair to prevent her from falling, breathlessly inquired what she meant?

"Oh! he is sent to prison," cried Euphemia, not regarding the real agitation of her auditor (so much was she occupied in appearing overwhelmed herself), and wringing her hands, she continued, "That frightful wretch Mr. Lascelles is just come in to dinner. You cannot think with what fiendish glee he told me that several days ago, as he was driving out of town, he saw Mr. Constantine, with two bailiffs behind him, walking down Fleet Street! And, besides, I verily believe he said he had irons on."

"No, no!" ejaculated Mary, with a cry of terror, at this *ad libitum* of Euphemia's; "what can he have done?"

"Bless me!" returned Euphemia, staring at her pale face; "why, what frightens you so? Does not everybody run in debt, without minding it?"

Miss Beaufort shook her head, and looking distractedly about, put her hand to her forehead. Euphemia, determining not to be outdone in "tender woe," drew forth her handkerchief, and putting it to her eyes, resumed in a piteous tone—

"I am sure I shall hate Lascelles all my life, because he did not stop the men and inquire what jail they were taking him to? You know, my dear, you and I might have visited him. It would have been delightful to have consoled his sad hours! We might have planned his escape."

"In irons!" ejaculated Mary, raising her tearless eyes to heaven.

Euphemia colored at the agonized manner in which these words were reiterated, and rather confusedly replied, "Not absolutely in irons. You know that is a metaphorical term for captivity."

"Then he was not in irons?" cried Miss Beaufort, seizing her hand eagerly: "for Heaven's sake, tell me he was not in irons?"

"Why, then," returned Euphemia, half angry at being obliged to contradict herself, "if you are so dull of taste, and cannot understand poetical language, I must tell you he was not."

Mary heard no further, but even at the moment, overcome by a revulsion of joy, sunk, unable to speak, into the chair.

Euphemia, supposing she had fainted, flew to the top of the stairs, and shrieking violently, stood wringing her hands, until Diana and Lady Dundas, followed by several gentlemen, hastened out of the saloon and demanded what was the matter? As Euphemia pointed to Miss Beaufort's dressing-room, she staggered, and sinking into the arms of Lord Elesmere, fell into the most outrageous hysterics. The marquis, who had just dropped in on his return from St. James's, was so afraid of the agitated lady's tearing his point-lace ruffles, that, in almost as trembling a state as herself, he gladly shuffled her into the hands of her maid; and scampering down stairs, as if all Bedlam were at his heels, sprung into his *vis-à-vis*, and drove off like lightning.

When Miss Beaufort recovered her scattered senses, and beheld this influx of persons entering her room, she tried to dispel her confusion, and rising gently from her seat, while supporting herself on the arm of Miss Dorothy's maid, thanked the company for their attention and withdrew into her chamber.

Meanwhile, Euphemia, who had been carried down into the saloon, thought it time to raise her lily head and utter a few incoherent words. The instant they were breathed, Miss Dundas and Mr. Lascelles, in one voice, demanded what was the matter?

"Has not Mary told you?" returned her sister, languidly opening her eyes.

"No," answered Lascelles, rubbing his hands with delighted curiosity; "come, let us have it."

Euphemia, pleased at this, and loving mystery with all her heart, waved her hand solemnly, and in an awful tone replied, "Then it passes not my lips."

"What, Phemy!" cried he, "you want us to believe you have seen a ghost? But you forget, they don't walk at midday."

"Believe what you like," returned she, with an air of consequential contempt; "I am satisfied to keep the secret."

Miss Dundas burst into a provoking laugh; and calling her the most incorrigible little idiot in the world, encouraged Lascelles to fool her to the top of his bent. Determining to gratify his spleen, if he could not satisfy his curiosity, this witless coxcomb continued the whole day in Harley Street, for the mere pleasure of tormenting Euphemia. From the dinner hour until twelve at night, neither his drowsy fancy nor wakeful malice could find one other weapon of assault than the stale jokes of mysterious chambers, lovers incognito, or the silly addition of two Cupid-struck sweeps popping down the chimney to pay their addresses to the fair friends. Diana talked of Jupiter with his thunder; and patting her sister under the chin, added, "I cannot doubt that Miss Beaufort is the favored Semelé; but, my dear, you over-acted your character? As confidant, a few tears were enough when your lady fainted." During these attacks, Euphemia reclined pompously on a sofa, and not deigning a reply, repelled them with much conceit and haughtiness.

Miss Beaufort remained above an hour alone in her chamber before she ventured to go near her aunt. Hurt to the soul that the idle folly of Euphemia should have aroused a terror which had completely unveiled to the eyes of that inconsiderate girl the empire which Thaddeus held over her fate, Mary, overwhelmed with shame, and arraigning her easy credulity, threw herself on her bed.

Horror-struck at hearing he was led along the streets in chains, she could have no other idea but that, betrayed into the commission of some dreadful deed, he had become amenable to the laws, and might suffer an ignominious death. Those thoughts having rushed at once on her heart, deprived her of self-command. In the conviction of some fatal rencontre, she felt as if her life, her honor, her soul, were annihilated. And when, in consequence of her agonies, Euphemia confessed that she had in this last matter told a falsehood, the sudden peace to her soul had for an instant assumed the appearance of insensibility.

Before Miss Beaufort quitted her room, various plans were suggested by her anxiety and inexperience, how to release the object of her thoughts. She found no hesitation in believing him poor, and perhaps rendered wretchedly so by the burden of that sick friend, who, she suspected, might be a near relation. At any rate, she resolved that another sun should not pass over her head and shine on him in a prison. Having determined to pay his debts herself, she next thought of how she might manage the affair without discovering the hand whence the assistance came. Had her aunt been well enough to leave the house, she would not have scrupled unfolding to her the recent calamity of Mr. Constantine. But well aware that Miss Dorothy's maidenly nicety would be outraged at a young woman appearing the sole mover in such an affair, she conceived herself obliged to withhold her confidence at present, and to decide on prosecuting the whole transaction alone.

In consequence of these meditations, her spirits became less discomposed. Turning towards Miss Dorothy Somerset's apartments, she found the good lady sipping her coffee.

"What is this I have just heard, my dear Mary? Williams tells me you have been ill!"

Miss Beaufort returned her aunt's gracious inquiry with an affectionate kiss; and informing her that she had only been alarmed by an invention of Miss Euphemia's, begged that the subject might drop, it being merely one out of the many schemes which she believed that young lady had devised to render her visit to London as little pleasant as possible.

"Ah!" replied Miss Dorothy, "I hope I shall be well enough to travel in the course of a few days. I can now walk with a stick; and upon my word, I am heartily tired both of Lady Dundas and her daughters."

Mary expressed similar sentiments; but as the declaration passed her lips, a sigh almost buried the last word. Go when she would, she must leave Constantine behind; leave him without an expectation of beholding him more—without a hope of penetrating the thick cloud which involved him, and with which he had ever baffled any attempt she had heard to discover his birth or misfortunes. She wept over this refinement on delicacy, and "loved him dearer for his mystery."

When the dawn broke next morning, it shone on Miss Beaufort's yet unclosed eyes. Sleep could find no languid faculty in her head whilst her heart was agitated with plans for the relief of Thaddeus. The idea of visiting the coffee-house to which she knew the Misses Dundas directed their letters, and of asking questions about a young and handsome man, made her timidity shrink.

"But," exclaimed she, "I am going on an errand which ought not to spread a blush on the cheek of prudery itself. I am going to impart alleviation to the sufferings of the noblest creature that ever walked the earth!"

Perhaps there are few persons who, being auditors of this speech, would have decided quite so candidly on the supera-

-tive by which it was concluded. Mary herself was not wholly divested of doubt about the issue of her conduct; but conscious that her motive was pure, she descended to the breakfast-room with a quieter mind than countenance.

Never before having had occasion to throw a gloss on her actions, she scarcely looked up during breakfast. When the cloth was removed, she rose suddenly from her chair, and turning to Miss Dorothy, who sat at the other end of the parlor, with her foot on a stool, said in a low voice, "Good-by, aunt! I am going to make some particular calls; but I shall be back in a few hours." Luckily, no one observed her blushing face whilst she spoke, nor the manner in which she shook hands with the old lady and hurried out of the room.

Breathless with confusion, she could scarcely stand when she arrived in her own chamber; but aware that no time ought to be lost, she tied on a long, light silk cloak, of sober gray, over her white morning-dress, and covering her head with a straw summer bonnet, shaded by a black lace veil, hesitated a moment within her chamber-door—her eyes filling with tears, drawn from her heart by that pure spirit of truth which had ever been the guardian of her conduct! Looking up to heaven, she sunk on her knees, and exclaimed with impetuosity, "Father of mercy! thou only knowest my heart! Direct me, I beseech thee! Let me not commit anything unworthy of myself nor of the unhappy Constantine—for whom I would sacrifice my life, but not my duty to thee!"

Reassured by the confidence which this simple act of devotion inspired, she took her parasol and descended the stairs. The porter was alone in the hall. She inquired for her servant.

"He is not returned, madam,"

Having foreseen the necessity of getting rid of all attendants, she had purposely sent her footman on an errand as far as Kensington.

"It is of no consequence," returned she to the porter, who was just going to propose one of Lady Dundas's men. "I cannot meet with anything disagreeable at this time of day, so I shall walk alone."

The man opened the door; and with a bounding heart Mary hastened down the street, crossed the square, and at the bottom of Orchard Street stepped into a hackney-coach, which she ordered to drive to Slaughter's Coffee-house, St. Martin's Lane.

She drew up the glasses and closed her eyes. Various

thoughts agitated her anxious mind whilst the carriage rolled along; and when it drew up at the coffee-house, she involuntarily retreated into the corner. The coach-door was opened.

"Will you alight, ma'am?"

"No; call a waiter."

A waiter appeared; and Miss Beaufort, in a tolerably collected voice, inquired whether Mr. Constantine lived there?

"No, ma'am."

A cold dew stood on her forehead; but taking courage from a latent and last hope, she added, "I know he has had letters directed to this place."

"Oh! I beg your pardon, ma'am!" returned the man recollecting himself; "I remember a person of that name has received letters from hence, but they were always fetched away by a little girl."

"And do you not know where he lives?"

"No, ma'am," answered he; "yet some one else in the house may: I will inquire."

Miss Beaufort bowed her head in token of acknowledgment, and sat shivering with suspense until he returned, followed by another man.

"This person, ma'am," resumed he, "says he can tell you."

"Thank you, thank you!" cried Mary; then, blushing at her eagerness, she stopped and drew back into the carriage.

"I cannot for certain," said the man, "but I know the girl very well by sight who comes for the letters; and I have often seen her standing at the door of a chandler's shop a good way down the lane. I think it is No. 5, or 6. I sent a person there who came after the same gentleman about a fortnight ago. I dare say he lives there."

Miss Beaufort's expectations sunk again, when she found that she had nothing but a dare say to depend on; and giving half-a-crown to each of her informers, she desired the coachman to drive as they would direct him.

While the carriage drove down the lane, with a heart full of fears she looked from side to side, almost believing she should know by intuition the house which had contained Constantine. When the man checked his horses, and her eyes fell on the little mean dwelling of Mrs. Robson, she smothered a deep sigh.

"Can this be the house in which Constantine has lived? How comfortless! And should it not," thought she, as the man got off the box to inquire, "whither shall I go for information?"

The appearance of Mrs. Robson, and her immediate affirmative to the question, "Are these Mr. Constantine's lodgings?" at once dispelled this last anxiety. Encouraged by the motherly expression of the good woman's manner, Mary begged leave to alight. Mrs. Robson readily offered her arm, and with many apologies for the disordered state of the house, led her up stairs to the room which had been the count's house.

Mary trembled; but seeing that everything depended on self-command, with apparent tranquillity she received the chair that was presented to her, and turning her eyes from the books and drawings which told her so truly in whose apartment she was, she desired Mrs. Robson, who continued standing, to be seated. The good woman obeyed. After some trepidation, Mary asked where Mr. Constantine was? Mrs. Robson colored, and looking at her questioner for some time, as if doubting what to say, burst into tears.

Miss Beaufort's ready eyes were much inclined to flow in concert; but subduing the strong emotions which shook her, she added, "I do not come hither out of impertinent curiosity. I have heard of the misfortunes of Mr. Constantine. I am well known to his friends."

"Dear lady!" cried the good woman, grasping at any prospect of succor to her benefactor: "if he has friends, whoever they are, tell them he is the noblest, most humane gentleman in the world. Tell them he has saved me and mine from the deepest want; and now he is sent to prison because he cannot pay the cruel doctor who attended the poor dead general."

"What! is his friend dead?" ejaculated Mary, unable to restrain the tears which now streamed over her face.

"Yes," replied Mrs. Robson; "poor old gentleman! he is dead, sure enough; and, Heaven knows, many have been the dreary hours the dear young man has watched by his pillow! He died in that room."

Miss Beaufort's swimming eyes would not allow her to discern objects through the open door of that apartment within which the heart of Thaddeus had undergone such variety of misery. Forming an irresistible wish to know whether the deceased were any relation of Constantine, she paused a moment to compose the agitation which might betray her, and then asked the question.

"I thought, ma'am," replied Mrs. Robson, "you said you knew his friends?"

"Only his English ones," returned Mary, a little confused at the suspicion this answer implied; "I imagined that this old gentleman might have been his father or an uncle, or——"

"O no," interrupted Mrs. Robson, sorrowfully; "he has neither father, mother nor uncle in the wide world. He once told me they were all dead, and that he saw them die. Alas! sweet soul! What a power of griefs he must have seen in his young life! But Heaven will favor his at last; for thought he is in misfortune himself, he has been a blessing to the widow and the orphan!"

"Do you know the amount of his debts?" asked Miss Beaufort.

"Not more than twenty pounds," returned Mrs. Robson, "when they took him out of this room, a week ago, and hurried him away without letting me know a word of the matter. I believe to this hour I should not have known where he was, if that cruel Mr. Jackson had not come to demand all that Mr. Constantine left in my care. But I would not let him have it. I told him if my lodger had filled my house with bags of gold, *he* should not touch a shilling; and then he abused me, and told me Mr. Constantine was in Newgate."

"In Newgate!"

"Yes, madam. I immediately ran there, and found him more able to comfort me than I was able to speak to him."

"Then be at rest, my good woman," returned Miss Beaufort, rising from her chair; "when you next hear of Mr. Constantine, he shall be at liberty. He has friends who will not sleep till he is out of prison."

"May Heaven bless you and them, dear lady!" cried Mrs. Robson, weeping with joy; "for they will relieve the most generous heart alive. But I must tell you," added she, with recollecting energy, "that the costs of the business with raise it to some pounds more. For that wicked Jackson, getting frightened to stand alone in what he had done, went and persuaded poor weak-minded Mr. Watson, the undertaker, to put in a detainer against Mr. Constantine for the remainder of his bill. So I fear it will be full thirty pounds before his kind friends can release him."

Mary replied, "Be not alarmed: all shall be done." While she spoke, she cast a wistful look on the drawings on the bureau; then withdrawing her eyes with a deep sigh, she descended the stairs. At the street-door she took Mrs. Robson's hand, and not relinquishing it until she was seated in the coach, pressed it warmly, and leaving within it a purse of twenty guineas, ordered the man to return whence he came.

Now that the temerity of goi' g herself to learn the particulars of Mr. Constantine's fate had been achieved, determined as she was not to close her eyes whilst the man whom she valued above her life remained a prisoner and in sorrow, she thought it best to consult with Miss Dorothy respecting the speediest means of compassing his emancipation.

In Oxford Road she desired the coachman to proceed to Harley Street. She alighted at Lady Dundas's door, paid him his fare, and stepped into the hall before she perceived that a travelling-carriage belonging to her guardian had driven away to afford room for her humble equipage.

"Is Sir Robert Somerset come to town?" she hastily inquired of the porter.

"No, madam; but Mr. Somerset is just arrived."

The next minute Miss Beaufort was in the drawing-room, and clasped within the arms of her cousin.

"Dear Mary!"—"Dear Pembroke!" were the first words which passed between these two affectionate relatives.

Miss Dorothy, who doted on her nephew, taking his hand as he seated himself between her and his cousin, said, in a congratulatory voice, "Mary, our dear boy has come to town purposely to take us down."

"Yes, indeed," rejoined he; "my father is moped to death for want of you both. You know I am a sad renegade! Lord Avon and Mr. Loftus have been gone these ten days to his lordship's aunt's in Bedfordshire; and Sir Robert is so completely weary of solitude, that he has commanded me"—bowing to the other ladies—"to run off with all the fair inhabitants of this house sooner than leave you behind."

"I shall be happy at another opportunity to visit Somerset Hall," returned Lady Dundas; "but I am constrained to spend this summer in Dumbartonshire. I have not yet seen the estate my poor dear Sir Hector bought of the Duke of Dunbar."

Pembroke offered no attempt to shake this resolution. In the two or three morning calls he had formerly made with Sir Robert Somerset on the rich widow, he saw sufficient to make him regard her arrogant vulgarity with disgust; and for her daughters, they were of too artificial a stamp to occupy his mind any longer than with a magic-lantern impression of a tall woman with bold eyes, and the prettiest yet most affected little fairy he had ever beheld.

After half an hour's conversation with this family group, Miss Beaufort sunk into abstraction. During the first month of Mary's acquaintance with Thaddeus, she did not neglect to mention in her correspondence with Pembroke having met with a very interesting and accomplished emigrant, in the capacity of a tutor at Lady Dundas's. But her cousin, in his replies, beginning to banter her on pity being allied to love, she had gradually dropped all mention of Constantine's name, as she too truly found by what insensible degrees the union had taken place within her own breast. She remembered these particulars, whilst a new method of accomplishing her present project suggested itself; and determining (however extraordinary her conduct might seem) to rest on the rectitude of her motives, a man being the most proper person to transact such a business with propriety, she resolved to engage Pembroke for her agent, without troubling Miss Dorothy about the affair.

So deeply was she absorbed in these reflections, that Somerset, observing her vacant eye fixed on the opposite window, took her hand with an arch smile, and exclaimed.

"Mary! What is the matter? I hope, Lady Dundas, you have not suffered any one to run away with her heart? You know I am her cousin, and it is my inalienable right."

Lady Dundas replied that young ladies best know their own secrets.

"That may be, madam," rejoined he; "but I won't allow Miss Beaufort to know anything that she does not transfer to me. Is not that true, Mary?"

"Yes," whispered she, coloring; "and the sooner you afford me an opportunity to interest you in one, the more I shall be obliged to you."

Pembroke pressed her hand in token of assent; and a desultory conversation continuing for another half-hour, Miss Beaufort, who dreaded the wasting one minute in a day so momentous to her peace, sat uneasily until her aunt proposed retiring to her dressing-room a while, and requested Pembroke to assist her up stairs.

When he returned to the drawing-room, to his extreme satisfaction he found all the party were gone to prepare for their usual drives, excepting Miss Beaufort, who was standing by one of the windows, lost in thought. He approached her, and taking her hand—

"Come, my dear cousin," said he, "how can I oblige you?"

Mary struggled with her confusion. Had she loved Thaddeus less, she found she could with greater ease have related the interest which she took in his fate. She tried to speak distinctly, and she accomplished it, although her burning cheek and downcast look told to the fixed eye of Pembroke what she vainly attempted to conceal.

"You can, indeed, oblige me! You must remember a Mr. Constantine! I once mentioned him to you in my letters.

"I do, Mary. You thought him amiable!"

"He was the intimate friend of Lady Tinemouth," returned she, striving to look up; but the piercing expression she met from the eyes of Somerset, beating hers down again, covered her face and neck with deeper blushes. She panted for breath.

"Rely on me," said Pembroke, pitying her embarrassment, whilst he dreaded that her gentle heart had indeed become the victim of some accomplished and insidious foreigner—"rely on me, my beloved cousin: consider me as a brother. If you have entangled yourself——"

Miss Beaufort guessed what he would say, and interrupting him, added, with a more assured air, "No, Pembroke, I have no entanglements. I am going to ask your friendly assistance in behalf of a brave and unfortunate Polander." Pembroke reddened and she went on. "Mr. Constantine is a gentleman. Lady Tinemouth tells me he has been a soldier, and that he lost all his possessions in the ruin of his country. Her ladyship introduced him here. I have seen him often, and I know him to be worthy the esteem of every honorable heart. He is now in prison, in Newgate, for a debt of about thirty pounds, and I ask you to go and release him. That is my request—my secret; and I confide in your discretion that you will keep it even from him."

"Generous, beloved Mary!" cried Pembroke, pressing her hand; "it is thus you always act. Possessed of all the softness of thy sex, dearest girl," added he, still more affectionately, "nature has not alloyed it with one particle of weakness!"

Miss Beaufort smiled and sighed. If to love tenderly, to be devoted life and soul to one being, whom she considered as the most perfect work of creation, be weakness, Mary was the weakest of the weak; and with a languid despondence at her heart, she was opening her lips to give some directions to her cousin, when the attention of both was arrested by a shrill noise of speakers talking above stairs. Before the cousins had time to make an observation, the disputants descended towards the drawing-room, and bursting open the door with a violent clamor, presented the enraged figure of Lady Dundas followed by Diana, who, with a no less swollen countenance, was scolding vociferously, and dragging forward the weeping Euphemia.

"Ladies! ladies!" exclaimed Somerset, amazed at so extraordinary a scene; "what has happened?"

Lady Dundas lifted up her clenched hand in a passion.

"A jade!—a hussy!" cried her vulgar ladyship, incapable of articulating more.

Miss Dundas, still grasping the hands of her struggling sister, broke out next, and turning furiously towards Mary, exclaimed, "You see, madam, what disgrace your ridiculous conduct to that vagabond foreigner has brought on our family! This bad girl has followed your example, and done worse—she has fallen in love with him!"

Shocked, and trembling at so rude an accusation, Miss Beaufort was unable to speak. Lost in wonder, and incensed at his cousin's goodness having been the dupe of imposition, Pembroke stood silent, whilst Lady Dundas took up the subject.

"Ay," cried she, shaking her daughter by the shoulder, "you little minx! if your sister had not picked up these abominable verses you chose to write on the absence of this beggarly fellow, I suppose you would have finished the business by running off with him! But you shall go down to Scotland, and be locked up for months. I won't have Sir Hector Dundas's family disgraced by a daughter of mine."

"For pity's sake, Lady Dundas," said Pembroke, stepping between her shrewish ladyship and the trembling Euphemia, "do compose yourself. I dare say your daughter is pardonable. In these cases, the fault in general lies with our sex. We are the deluders."

Mary was obliged to reseat herself; and in pale attention she listened for the reply of the affrighted Euphemia, who, half assured that her whim of creating a mutual passion in the breast of Thaddeus was no longer tenable, without either shame or remorse she exclaimed, "Indeed, Mr. Somerset, you are right; I never should have thought of Mr. Constantine if he had not teased me every time he came with his devoted love."

Miss Beaufort rose hastily from her chair. Though Euphemia colored at the suddenness of this motion, and the immediate flash she met from her eye, she went on: "I know Miss Beaufort will deny it, because she thinks he is in love with her; but indeed, indeed, he has sworn a thousand times on his knees that he was a Russian nobleman in disguise, and adored me above every one else in the world."

"Villain!" cried Pembroke, inflamed with indignation at his double conduct. Afraid to read in the expressive countenance of Mary her shame and horror at this discovery, he turned his eyes on her with trepidation; when, to his surprise, he beheld her standing perfectly unmoved by the side of the sofa from which she had arisen. She advanced with a calm step towards Euphemia, and taking hold of the hand which concealed her face whilst uttering this last falsehood, she drew it away.

and regarding her with a serene but penetrating look, she said: "Euphemia! you well know that you are slandering an innocent and unfortunate man. You know that never in his life did he give you the slightest reason to suppose that he was attached to you; for myself, I can also clear him of making professions to me. Upon the honor of my word, I declare," added she, addressing herself to the whole group, "that he never breathed a sentence to me beyond mere respect. By this last deviation of Euphemia from truth, you may form an estimate how far the rest she has alleged deserves credit."

The young lady burst into a vehement passion of tears.

"I will not be browbeaten and insulted, Miss Beaufort!" cried she, taking refuge in noise, since right had deserted her. "You know you would fight his battles through thick and thin, else you would not have fallen into fits yesterday when I told you he was sent to jail."

This last assault struck Mary motionless; and Lady Dundas, lifting up her hands, exclaimed, "Good la! keep me from the forward misses of these times! As for you, Miss Euphemia," added she, seizing her daughter by the arm, "you shall leave town to-morrow morning. I will have no more tutoring and falling in love in my house; and for you, Miss Beaufort," turning to Mary, (who, having recovered herself, stood calmly at a little distance,) "I shall take care to warn Miss Dorothy Somerset to keep an eye over your conduct."

"Madam," replied she, indignantly, "I shall never do anything which can dishonor either my family or myself; and of that Miss Dorothy Somerset is too well assured to doubt for an instant, even should calumny be as busy with me as it has been injurious to Mr. Constantine."

With the words of Mrs. Robson suddenly reverberating on her heart, "He has no father, no mother, no kindred in this wide world!" she walked towards the door. When she passed Mr. Somerset, who stood bewildered and frowning near Miss Dundas, she turned her eyes on her cousin, full of the effulgent pity in her soul, and said, in a collected and decisive voice, "Pembroke, I shall leave the room; but, remember, I do not release you from your engagement."

Staggered by the open firmness of her manner, he looked after her as she withdrew, and was almost inclined to believe that she possessed the right side of the argument. Malice did not allow him to think so long. The moment the door closed on her, both the sisters fell on him pell-mell; and the prejudiced illiberality of the one, supported by the ready falsehoods of the other, soon dislodged all favorable impressions from the mind of Somerset, and filled him anew with displeasure.

In the midst of Diana's third harangue, Lady Dundas having ordered Euphemia to be taken to her chamber, Mr. Somerset was left alone, more incensed than ever against the object of their invectives, whom he now considered in the light of an adventurer, concealing his poverty, and perhaps his crimes, beneath a garb of lies. That such a character, by means of a fine person and a few meretricious talents, could work himself into the confidence of Mary Beaufort, pierced her cousin to the soul; and as he mounted the stairs with an intent to seek her in her dressing-room, he almost resolved to refuse obeying her commands.

When he opened the room-door, he found Miss Beaufort and his aunt. The instant he appeared, the ever-benevolent face of Miss Dorothy contracted into a frown.

"Nephew," cried she, "I shall not take it well of you if you give stronger credence to the passionate and vulgar assertions of Lady Dundas and her daughters than you choose to bestow on the tried veracity of your cousin Mary."

Pembroke was conscious that if his countenance had been a faithful transcript of his mind, Miss Beaufort did not err in supposing he believed the foreigner to be a villain. Knowing that it would be impossible for him to relinquish his reason into what he now denominated the partial hands of his aunt and cousin, he persisted in his opinion to both the ladies, that their unsuspicious natures had been rendered subservient to knavery and artifice.

"I would not, my dear madam," said he, addressing Miss Dorothy, "think so meanly of your sex as to imagine that such atrocity can exist in the female heart as could give birth to ruinous and unprovoked calumnies against an innocent man. I cannot suspect the Misses Dundas of such needless guilt, particularly poor Euphemia, whom I truly pity. Lady Dundas forced me to read her verses, and they were too full of love and regret for this adventurer to come from the same breast which could wantonly blacken his character. Such wicked inconsistencies in so young a woman are not half so probable as that you, my dear aunt and cousin, have been deceived.

"Nephew," returned the old lady, "you are very peremptory. Methinks a little more lenity of opinion would better become your youth! I knew nothing of this unhappy young man's present distress until Miss Beaufort mentioned it to me; but before she breathed a word in his favor, I had conceived a very high respect for his merits. From the first hour in which I saw him, I gathered by his deportment that he must be a gentleman, besides a previous act of benevolent bravery, in rescuing at the hazard of his own life two poor children from a house in flames—in all this I saw he must have been born far above his fortunes. I thought so; I still think so; and, notwithstanding all that the Dundasses may choose to fabricate, I am determined to believe the assertions of an honest countenance."

Pembroke smiled, whilst he forced his aunt's reluctant hand into his, and said, "I see, my dear madam, you are bigoted to the idol of your own fancy! I do not presume to doubt this Mr. Constantine's lucky exploits, nor his enchantments; but you must pardon me if I keep my senses at liberty. I shall think of him as I could almost swear he deserves, although I am aware that I hazard your affection by my firmness." He then turned to Mary, who, with a swelling and distressed heart, was standing by the chimney. "Forgive me, my dearest cousin," continued he, addressing her in a softened voice, "that I am forced to appear harsh. It is the first time I ever dissented from you; it is the first time I ever thought you prejudiced!"

Miss Beaufort drew the back of her hand over her glistening eyes. All the tender affections of Pembroke's bosom smote him at once, and throwing his arms around his cousin's waist, he strained her to his breast, and added, "Ah! why, dear girl, must I love you better for thus giving me pain? Every way my darling Mary is more estimable. Even now, whilst I oppose you, I am sure, though your goodness is abused, it was cheated into error by the affectation of honorable impulses and disasters!"

Miss Beaufort thought that if the prudence of reserve and decorum dictated silence in some circumstances, in others a prudence of a higher order would justify her in declaring her sentiments. Accordingly she withdrew from the clasping arms of Mr. Somerset, and whilst her beautiful figure seemed to dilate into more than its usual dignity, she mildly replied:

"Think what you please, Pembroke; I shall not contend with you. Mr. Constantine is of a nature not to be hidden by obscurity; his character will defend itself; and all that I have to add is this, I do not release you from your promise. Could a woman transact the affair with propriety, I would not keep you to so disagreeable an office; but I have passed my word to myself that I will neither slumber nor sleep till he is out of prison." She put a pocket-book into Pembroke's hand, and added, "Take that, my dear cousin; and without suffering a syllable to transpire by which he may suspect who served him, accomplish what I have desired, acting by the memorandum you will find within."

"I will obey you, Mary," returned he; "but I am sorry that such rare enthusiasm was not awakened by a worthier object. When you see me again, I hope I shall be enabled to say that your ill-placed generosity is satisfied."

"Fie, nephew, fie!" cried Miss Dorothy; "I could not have supposed you capable of conferring a favor so ungraciously."

Pained at what he called the obstinate infatuation of Miss Beaufort, and if possible more chagrined by what he considered the blind and absurd encouragement of his aunt, Mr. Somerset lost the whole of her last reprimand in his hurry to quit the room.

Disturbed, displeased, and anxious, he stepped into a hackney-coach; and ordering it to drive to Newgate, called on the way at Lincoln's Inn, to take up a confidential clerk of his father's law-agent there, determining by his assistance to go through the business without exposing himself to any interview with a man whom he believed to be an artful and unprincipled villain.

CHAPTER XXXVII.

"Calumny is the pastime of little minds, and the venomed shaft of base ones."

THE first week of the count's confinement was rendered in some degree tolerable by the daily visits of Mrs. Robson, who, having brought his drawing materials, enabled him, through the means of the always punctual printseller, to purchase some civility from the brutal and hardened people who were his keepers. After the good woman had performed her diurnal kindness, Thaddeus did not suffer his eyes to turn one moment on the dismal loneliness of his abject prison, but took up his pencil to accomplish its daily task, and when done, he opened some one of his books, which had also been brought to him, and so sought to beguile his almost hopeless hours,—hopeless with regard to any human hope of ever re-passing those incarcerating walls. For who was there but those who had put him there who could now know even of his existence?

The elasticity and pressing enterprise of soul inherent in youth renders no calamity so difficult to be borne as that which fetters its best years and most active virtues under the lock of any captivity. Thaddeus felt this benumbing effect in every pulse of his ardent and energetic heart. He retraced all that he had been. He looked on what he was. Though he had reaped glory when a boy, his "noon of manhood," his evening sun, was to waste its light and set in an English prison.

At short and distant intervals such melancholy reveries gave place to the pitying image of Mary Beaufort. It sometimes visited him in the day—it always was his companion during the night. He courted her lovely ideal as a spell that for a while stole him from painful reflections. With an entranced soul he recalled every lineament of her angel-like face, every tender sympathy of that gentle voice which had hurried him into the rashness of touching her hand. One moment he pressed her gold chain closer to his heart, almost believing what Lady Tinemouth had insinuated; the next, he would sigh over his credulity, and return with despondent though equally intense love to the contemplation of her virtues, independent of himself.

The more he meditated on the purity of her manners, the elevated principles to which he could trace her actions, and, above all, on the benevolent confidence with which she had ever treated him (a man contemned by one part of her acquaintance, and merely received on trust by the remainder), the more he found reasons to regard that character with his grateful admiration. When he drew a comparison between Miss Beaufort and most women of the same quality whom he had seen in England and in other countries, he contemplated with delighted wonder that spotless mind which, having passed through the various ordeals annexed to wealth and fashion, still bore itself uncontaminated. She was beautiful, and she did not regard it; she was accomplished, but she did not attempt a display; what she acquired from education, the graces had so incorporated with her native intelligence, that the perfection of her character seemed to have been stamped at once by the beneficent hand of Providence.

Never were her numberless attractions so fascinating to Thaddeus as when he witnessed the generous eagerness with which, forgetful of her own almost unparalleled talents, she pointed out merit and dispensed applause to the deserving.

Miss Beaufort's nature was gentle and benevolent; but it wsa likewise distinguishing and animated. Whilst the count saw that the urbanity of her disposition made her politeness universal, he perceived that neither rank, riches nor splendor, when alone, could extract from her bosom one spark of that lambent flame which streamed from her heart, like fire to the sun, towards the united glory of genius and virtue.

He dwelt on her lovely, unsophisticated character with an enthusiasm bordering on idolatry. He recollected that she had been educated by the mother of Pembroke Somerset; and turning from the double remembrance with a sigh fraught with all the bitterness and sweetness of love, he acknowledged how much wisdom (which includes virtue) gives spirit and immortality to beauty. "Yes," cried he, "it is the fragrance of the flower, which lives after the bloom is withered."

From such reflections of various hues Thaddeus was one evening awakened by the entrance of the chief jailer into his cell. His was an unusual visit. He presented a sealed packet to his prisoner, saying he brought it from a stranger, who, having paid the debts and costs for which he was confined, and all the prison dues, had immediately gone away, leaving that packet to be instantly delivered into the hand of Mr. Constantine.

While Thaddeus, scarcely crediting the information, was hastily opening the packet, hoping it might throw some light on his benefactor, the jailer civilly withdrew. But the breaking of the seal discovered a blank cover only, save these words, in a handwriting unknown to him—"You are free!"—and bank of England notes to the amount of fifty pounds.

Overwhelmed with surprise, gratitude to Heaven, and to this generous unknown, he sank down into his solitary chair, and tried to conjecture who could have acted the part of such a friend, and yet be so careful to conceal that act of friendship.

He had seen sufficient proofs of a heedless want of benevolence in Miss Euphemia Dundas to lead him to suppose that she could not be so munificent, and solicitous of secrecy. Besides, how could she have learned his situation? He thought it was impossible; and that impossibility compelled an erratic hope of his present liberty having sprung from the goodness of Miss Beaufort to pass by him with a painful swiftness.

"Alas!" cried he, starting from his chair, "it is the indefatigable spirit of Lady Sara Ross that I recognize in this deed! The generous but unhappy interest which she yet takes in my fate has discovered my last misfortune, and thus she seeks to relieve me!"

The moment he conceived this idea, he believed it; and taking up a pen, with a grateful though disturbed soul he addressed to her the following guarded note :—

"To the Right Honorable Lady Sara Ross.

"An unfortunate exile, who is already overpowered by a sense of not having deserved the notice which Lady Sara Ross has deigned to take of his misfortunes, was this day liberated from prison in a manner so generous and delicate, that he can ascribe the act to no other than the noble heart of her ladyship.

"The object of this bounty, bending under a weight of obligations which he cannot repay, begs permission to re-enclose the bills which Lady Sara's agent transmitted to him; but as the deed which procures his freedom cannot be recalled, with the most grateful emotions he accepts that new instance of her ladyship's goodness."

Thaddeus was on the point of asking one of the turnkeys to send him some trusty person to take this letter to St. James Place, when, recollecting the impropriety of making any inmate of Newgate his messenger to Lady Sara, he was determining to remove immediately to St. Martin's Lane, and thence dispatch his packet to his generous friend, when Mrs. Robson herself was announced by his turnkey, who, as customary, disappeared the moment he had let her in. She hastened forward to him with an animated countenance, and exclaimed, before he had time to speak, "Dear sir, I have seen a dear, sweet lady, who has promised me not to sleep till you are out of this horrid place!"

The suspicions of the count, that his benefactress was indeed Lady Sara Ross, were now confirmed. Seating his warm-hearted landlady in the only chair his apartment contained, to satisfy her humility, he took his station on the table, and then said: "The lady has already fulfilled her engagement. I am free, and I only wait for a hackney-coach—which I shall send for immediately—to take me back to your kind home."

At this assurance the delighted Mrs. Robson, crying and laughing by turns, did not cease her ejaculations of joy until the turnkey, whom he had recalled to give the order for the coach, returned to say that it was in readiness.

He took up his late prisoner's small portmanteau, with the drawing-materials, &c., which had been brought to him during his incarceration; and Thaddeus, with a feeling as if a band of iron had been taken from his soul, passed through the door of his cell; and when he reached the greater portal of Newgate, where the coach stood, he gave the turnkey a liberal *douceur*, and handing Mrs. Robson into the vehicle, stepped in after her, full of thankfulness to Heaven for again being permitted to taste the wholesome breeze of a free atmosphere.

They drove quickly on, and from the fullness of his thoughts, little passed between the count and his happy companion till they alighted at her door and he had re-entered his humble apartment. But so true is it that advantages are only appreciated by comparison, when he looked around, he considered it a palace of luxury, compared to the stifling dungeon he had left. "Ah!" cried Mrs. Robson, pointing to a chair, "there is the seat in which that dear lady sat—sweet creature! If I had known I durst believe all she promised, I would have fallen on my knees and kissed her feet for bringing back your dear self!"

"I thank you, my revered friend!" replied Thaddeus, with a grateful smile and a tear at so ardent a demonstration of her maternal affection. "But where is little Nanny, that I may shake hands with her?" It being yet early in the evening, he was also anxious, before the probable retiring time of Lady Sara into her dressing-room to prepare for dinner should elapse, to dispatch his letter to her; and he inquired of his still rejoicing landlady "whether she could find him a safe porter to take a small packet of importance to St. James's Place, and wait for an answer?"

The good woman instantly replied that "Mrs. Watts, her neighbor, had a nephew at present lodging with her, a steady man, recently made one of the grooms in the King's Mews, and as this was the customary hour of his return from the stables, she was sure he would be glad to do the service." While the count was sealing his letter, Mrs Robson had executed her commission, and re-entered with young Watts. He respectfully received his instructions from Thaddeus, and withdrew to perform the duty.

Nanny had also appeared, and welcomed her grandmother's beloved lodger with all those artless and animated expressions of joy which are inseparable from a good and unsophisticated heart.

The distance between the royal precincts of St. James's and the unostentatious environs of St. Martin's church being very short, in less than half an hour the count's messenger returned with the wished-for reply. It was with pain that he opened it, for he saw, by the state of the paper, that it had been blotted with tears. He hurriedly took out the re-enclosed bills, with a flushed cheek, and read as follows:—

"I cannot be mistaken in recognizing the proud and high-minded Constantine in the lines I hold in my hand. Could anything have imparted to me more comfort than your generous belief that there is indeed some virtue left in my wretched and repentant heart, it would have arisen from the consciousness of having been the happy person who succored you in your distress. But no: that enjoyment was beyond my deserving. The bliss of being the lightener of your sorrows was reserved by Heaven for a less criminal creature. I did not even know that you were in prison. Since our dreadful parting, I have never dared to inquire after you; and much as it might console me to serve one so truly valued, I will not insult your nice honor by offering any further instance of my friendship than what will evince my soul's gratitude to your prayers and my acquiescence with the commands of duty.

"My husband is here, without perceiving the ravages which misery and remorse have made in my unhappy heart. Time, perhaps, may render me less unworthy of his tenderness; at present, I detest myself.

"I return the bills; you may safely use them, for they never were mine.

"S. R."

The noble heart of Thaddeus bled over every line of this letter. He saw that it bore the stamp of truth which did not leave him a moment in doubt that he owed his release to some other hand. Whilst he folded it up, his grateful suspicions next lighted on Lady Tinemouth. He had received one short letter from her since her departure, mentioning Sophia's stay in town to meet Mr. Montresor, and Miss Beaufort's detention there, on account of Miss Dorothy's accident, and closing with the intelligence of her own arrival at the Wolds. He was struck with the idea that, as he had delayed answering this letter in consequence of his late embarrassment, she must have made inquiries after him; that probably Miss Egerton was the lady who had visited Mrs. Robson, and finding the information true had executed the countess's commission to obtain his release.

According to these suppositions, he questioned his landlady about the appearance of the lady who had called. Mrs. Robson replied, "She was of an elegant height, but so wrapped up, I could neither see her face nor her figure, though I am certain, from the softness of her voice, she must be both young and handsome. Sweet creature! I am sure she wept two or three times. Besides, she is the most charitable soul alive, next to you, sir; for she gave me a purse with twenty guineas, and she told me she knew your honor's English friends."

This narration substantiating his hope of Lady Tinemouth's being his benefactress, that the kind Sophia was her agent, and the gentleman who defrayed the debt Mr. Montresor, he felt easier under an obligation which a mysterious liberation would have doubled. He knew the countess's maternal love for him. To reject her present benefaction, in any part, would be to sacrifice gratitude to an excessive and haughty delicacy. Convinced that nothing can be great that it is great to despise, he no longer hestitated to accept Lady Tinemouth's bounty, but smothered in his breast the embers of a proud and repulsive fire, which, having burst forth in the first hour of his misfortunes, was ever ready to consume any attempt that might oppress him with the weight of obligation.

Being exhausted by the events of the day, he retired at an early hour to his grateful devotions and to his pillow, where he found that repose which he had sought in vain within the gloomy and (he supposed) ever-sealed walls of his prison.

In the morning he was awakened by the light footsteps of his pretty waiting-maid entering the front room. His chamber-door being open, he asked her what the hour was? She replied nine o'clock; adding that she had brought a letter, which one of the waiters from Slaughter's Coffee-house had just left, with information that he did so by the orders of a footman in a rich livery.

Thaddeus desired that it might be given to him. The child obeyed, and quitted the room. He saw that the superscription was in Miss Dundas's hand; and opening it with pleasure,—because everything interested him which came from the house which contained Mary Beaufort,—to his amazement and consternation he read the following accusations:—

"To Mr. Constantine.

"Sir,

"By a miraculous circumstance yesterday morning, your deep and daring plan of villany has been discovered to Lady D—— and myself. The deluded victim, whom your arts and falsehoods would have seduced to dishonor her family by con-meeting herself with a vagabond, has at length seen through her error, and now detests you as much as ever your insufferable presumption could have hoped she would distinguish you with her regard. Thanks be to Heaven! you are completely exposed. This young woman of fashion (whose name I will not trust in the same page with yours) has made a full confession of your vile seductions, of her own reprehensible weakness, in ever having deigned to listen to so low a creature. She desires me to assure you that she hates you, and commands you never again to attempt the insolence of appearing in her sight. Indeed this is the language of every soul in this house, Lady D—— Miss D——, S——, Miss B——, besides that of

"D—— D——,

"HARLEY STREET."

Thaddeus read this ridiculous letter twice before he could perfectly comprehend its meaning. In a paroxysm of indignation at the base subterfuge under which he did not doubt Euphemia had screened some accidental discovery of her absurd passion, he hastily threw on his clothes, and determined, though in defiance of Miss Dundas's mandates, to fly to Harley Street, and clear himself in the eyes of Miss Beaufort and her venerable aunt.

Having flown rather than walked, he arrived in sight of Lady Dundas's house just as a coachful of her ladyship's maids and packages drove from the door. Hurrying up the step, he asked the porter if Miss Dorothy Somerset were at home.

"No," replied the man; "she and Miss Beaufort, with Miss Dundas and Mr. Somerset, went out of town this morning by eight o'clock; and my lady and Miss Euphemia, about an hour ago, set off for Scotland, where they mean to stay all the summer."

At this information, which seemed to be the sealing of his condemnation with Mary, the heart of Thaddeus was pierced to the core. Unacquainted until this moment with the torments attending the knowledge of being calumniated, he could scarcely subdue the tempest in his breast, when forced to receive the conviction that the woman he loved above all the world now regarded him as not merely a villain, but the meanest of villains.

He returned home indignant and agitated. The probability that Pembroke Somerset had listened to the falsehood of Euphemia, without suggesting one word in defence of him who once was his friend, inflicted a pang more deadly than the rest

Shutting himself within his apartment, tossed and tortured in soul, he traversed the room. First one idea occurred and then another, until he resolved to seek redress from the advice of Lady Tinemouth. With this determination he descended the stairs, and telling Mrs. Robson he should leave London the ensuing day for Lincolnshire, begged her not to be uneasy on his account, as he went on business, and would return in a few days. The good woman almost wept at this intelligence, and prayed Heaven to guard him wherever he went.

Next morning, having risen at an early hour, he was collecting his few articles of wardrobe to put into his cloak-bag for his meditated short visit, when going to open one of the top drawers in his chamber, he found it sealed, and observed on the black wax the impress of an eagle. It was a large seal. Hardly crediting his eyes, it appeared to be the armorial eagle of Poland, surmounted by its regal crown. Nay, it seemed an impression of the very seal which had belonged to his royal ancestor, John Sobieski, and which was appended to the watch of his grandfather when he was robbed of it on his first arrival in England.

Thaddeus, in a wondering surprise, immediately rang the bell, and Mrs. Robson herself came up stairs. He hurriedly but gently inquired "how the drawer became not only locked as he had left it, but fastened with such a seal?"

Mrs. Robson did not perceive his agitation, and simply replied, "While his honor was in that horrid place, and after the attempt of Mr. Jackson to get possession of his property, she had considered it right to so secure the drawer, which she believed contained his most valuable pictures, and the like. So, having no impression of her own big enough, she went and bought a bunch of tarnished copper-seals she had seen hanging in the window of a huckster's shop at the corner of an ally hard by, one of them appearing about the size she wanted. The woman of the shop told her she had found them at the bottom of a tub of old iron, sold to her a while ago by a dustman; and as, to be sure, they were damaged and very dirty, she would not ask more than a couple of shillings for the lot, and would be glad to get rid of them!"

"So, sir," continued Mrs. Robson, with a pleased look, "I gave the money, and hastened home as fast as I could, and with Mrs. Watts by my side to witness it, you see I made all safe which I thought you most cared for."

"You are very thoughtful for me, kindest of women!" returned Thaddeus, with grateful energy; "but let me see the seals—for it is possible I may recognize in the one of this impression, indeed, a relic precious to my memory!"

Mrs. Robson put her hand into her pocket, and instantly gave them to him. There were three, one large, two small, and strung together by a leather thong. The former massive gold chain was no longer their link, and the rust from the iron had clouded the setting; but a glance told Sobieski they were his! He pressed them to his heart, whilst with glistening eyes he turned away to conceal his emotion. His sensible landlady comprehended there was something more than she knew of in the recognition (he never having told her of the loss of his watch, when he had saved her little grandchild from the plunging horses in the King's Mews;) and from her native delicacy not to intrude on his feelings, she gently withdrew unobserved, and left him alone.

About half an hour afterwards, when she saw her beloved lodger depart in the stage-coach that called to take him up, her eyes followed the wheels down the lane with renewed blessings.

His long journey passed not more in melancholy reveries against the disappointing characters he had met in revered England than in affectionate anticipations of the moment in which he should pour out his gratitude to the maternal tenderness of Lady Tinemouth, and learn from her ingenuous lips how to efface from the minds of Miss Dorothy Somerset and her angel-like niece the representations, so dishonoring, torturing, and false, which had been heaped upon him by the calumnies of the family in Harley Street.

CHAPTER XXXVIII.

ZEAL IS POWER.

THE porter at Lady Dundas's had been strictly correct in his account respecting the destination of the dispersed members of her ladyship's household.

Whilst Pembroke Somerset was sullenly executing his forced act of benevolence at Newgate, Miss Dundas suddenly took into her scheming head to compare the merits of Somerset's rich expectancy with the penniless certainty of Lascelles. She considered the substantial advantages which the wife of a wealthy baronet would hold over the thriftless *cara sposa* of a man owning no other estate than a reflected lustre from the coronet of an elder brother. Besides, Pembroke was very handsome—Lascelles only tolerably so; indeed, some women had presumed to call him "very plain." But they were "stupid persons," who, not believing the *metempsychosis* doctrine of the tailor and his decorating adjuncts, could not comprehend that although a mere human creature can have no such property, a man of fashion may possess an *elixir vitæ* which makes age youth, deformity beauty, and even transforms vice into virtue.

In spite of recollection, which reminded Diana how often she had contended that all Mr. Lascelles' teeth were his own; that his nose was not a bit too long, being a fac-simile of the feature which reared its sublime curve over the capricious mouth of his noble brother, the Earl of Castle Conway—notwithstanding all this, the Pythagorean pretensions of fashion began to lose their ascendency; and in the recesses of her mind, when Miss Dundas compared the light elegance of Pembroke's figure with the heavy limbs of her present lover, Pembroke's dark and ever-animated eyes with the gooseberry orbs of Lascelles, she dropped the parallel, and resolving to captivate the heir of Somerset Castle, admitted no remorse at jilting the brother of Castle Conway.

To this end, before Pembroke's return from Newgate, Diana had told her mother of her intention to accompany Miss Dorothy to the baronet's, where she would remain until her ladyship should think Euphemia might be trusted to rejoin her in town. Neither Miss Dorothy nor Miss Beaufort liked this arrangement; and next morning, with an aching heart, the latter prepared to take her seat in the travelling equipage which was to convey them all into Leicestershire.

After supper, Pembroke coldly informed his cousin of the success of her commands—that Mr. Constantine was at liberty. This assurance, though imparted with so ungracious an air, laid her head with less distraction on her pillow, and as she stepped into Sir Robert's carriage next day, enabled her with more ease to deck her lips with smiles. She felt that the penetrating eyes of Mr. Somerset were never withdrawn from her face. Offended with his perverseness, and their scrutiny, she tried to baffle their inspection. She attempted gayety, when she gladly would have wept. But when the coach mounted the top of Highgate Hill, and she had a last view of that city which contained the being whose happiness was the sole object of her thoughts and prayers, she leaned out of the window to hide a tear she could not repress; feeling that another and another would start, she complained of the dust, and pulling her veil over her eyes, drew back into the corner of the carriage. The trembling of her voice and hands during the performance of this little artifice too well explained to Pembroke what was passing in her mind. At once dispelling the gloom which shrouded his own countenance, he turned towards her with compassionate tenderness in his words and looks; he called her attention by degrees to the happy domestic scene she was to meet at the Castle; and thus gradually softening her displeasure into the easy conversation of reciprocal affection, he rendered the remainder of their long journey less irksome.

When, at the end of the second day, Miss Beaufort found herself in the old avenue leading to the base of the hill which sustains the revered walls of Somerset's castellated towers, a mingled emotion took possession of her breast; and when the carriage arrived at the foot of the highest terrace, she sprang impatiently out of it, and hastening up the stone stairs into the front hall, met her uncle at the door of the breakfast-parlor, where he held out his arms to receive her.

"My Mary! My darling!" cried he, embracing her now wet cheek, and straining her throbbing bosom to his own. "Why, my dear love," added he, almost carrying her into the room, "I am afraid this visit to town has injured your nerves! Whence arises this agitation?"

She knew it had injured her peace; and now that the flood-gates of her long-repelled tears were opened, it was beyond her power, or the soothings of her affectionate uncle, to stay them. A moment afterwards her cousin entered the room, followed by Miss Dorothy and Miss Dundas. Miss Beaufort hastily rose, to conceal what she could not check. Kissing Sir Robert's hand, she asked permission to retire, under the pretence of regaining those spirits which had been dissipated by the fatigues of her journey.

In her own chamber she did indeed struggle to recover herself. She shuddered at the impetuosity of her emotions when once abandoned of their reins, and resolved from this hour to hold a stricter control over such betrayals of her ill-fated, devoted heart.

She sat in the window of her apartment, and looking down the extensive vale of Somerset, watched the romantic meanderings of its shadowed river, winding its course through the domains of the castle, and nourishing the roots of those immense oaks which for many a century had waved their branches over its stream. She reflected on the revolution which had taken place in herself since she walked on its banks the evening that preceded her visit to London. Then she was free as the air, gay as the lark; each object was bright and lovely in her eyes; hope seemed to woo her from every green slope, every remote dingle. All nature breathed of joy, because her own breast was the abode of gladness. Now, all continued the same, but she was changed. Surrounded by beauty, she acknowledged its presence; the sweetness of the flowers bathed her senses in fragrance; the setting sun, gilding the height, shed a yellow glory over the distant hills; the birds were hailing the falling dew which spangled every leaf. She gazed around, and sighed heavily, when she said to herself, "Even in this paradise I shall be wretched. Alas! my heart is far away! My soul lingers about one I may never more behold!—about one who may soon cease to remember that such a being as Mary Beaufort is in existence. He will leave England!" cried she, raising her hands and eyes to the glowing heavens. "He will live, he will die, far, far from me! In a distant land he will wed another, whilst I shall know no wish that strays from him."

Whilst she indulged in these soliloquies, she forgot both Sir Robert and her resolution, until he sent her maid to beg, if she were better, that she would come down and make tea for him. At this summons she dried her eyes, and with assumed serenity descended to the saloon, where the family were assembled. The baronet having greeted Miss Dundas with an hospitable welcome, seated himself between his sister and his son; and whilst he received his favorite beverage from the hands of his beloved niece, he found that comfort once more re-entered his bosom.

Sir Robert Somerset was a man whose appearance alone attracted respect. His person bore the stamp of dignity, and his manners, which possessed the exquisite polish of travel, and of society in its most refined courts, secured him universal esteem. Though little beyond fifty, various perplexing situations having distressed his youth, had not only rendered his hair prematurely gray, but by clouding his once brilliant eyes with thoughtfulness, marked his aspect with premature old age and melancholy. The baronet's entrance into town life had been celebrated for his graceful vivacity; he was the animating spirit of every party, till an inexplicable metamorphosis suddenly took place. Soon after his return from abroad, he had married Miss Beaufort (a woman whom he loved to adoration), when, strange to say, excess of happiness seemed to change his nature and give his character a deep tinge of sadness. After his wife's death, the alteration in his mind produced still more extraordinary effects, and showed itself more than once in all the terrors of threatened mental derangement.

His latest attack of the kind assailed him during the last winter, under the appearance of a swoon, while he sat at breakfast reading the newspaper. He was carried to bed, and awoke in a delirium which menaced either immediate death or the total extinction of his intellects. However, neither of these dreads being confirmed, in the course of several weeks, to the wonder of everybody, he recovered much of his health and his sound mind. Notwithstanding this happy event, the circumstances of his danger so deeply affected his family, that he ceased not to be an object of the most anxious attention. Indeed, solicitude did not terminate with them : the munificence of his disposition having spread itself through every county in which he owned a rood of land, as many prayers ascended for the repose of his spirit as ever petitioned Heaven from the mouths of "monkish beadsmen" in favor of power and virtue.

Since the demise of Lady Somerset, this still-admired man drew all his earthly comfort from the amiable qualities of his son Pembroke. Sometimes in his livelier hours, which came "like angel visits, few and far between," he amused himself with the playfulness of the little Earl of Avon, the pompous erudition of Mr. Loftus, (who was become his young ward's tutor), and with giving occasional entertainments to the gentry in his neighborhood.

Of all the personages contained within this circle (which the hospitality of Sir Robert extended to a circumference of fifty miles,) the noble family of Castle Granby, brave, patriotic, and accomplished, with female beauty at its head,

> "Fitted to move in courts or walk the shade,
> With innocence and contemplation joined,"

were held in the highest and most intimate appreciation ; while many of the numerous titled visitants who attended the celebrated and magnificent Granby hunt were of too convivial notoriety to be often admitted within the social home-society of either Castle Granby or Somerset Castle, the two cynosure mansions which, now palace-like, crest with their peaceful groves the summits of those two promontory heights whereon in former times they stood in fortress strength, the guardians of each opening pass into that spacious and once important belligerent vale!

Amongst the less-esteemed frequenters of the chase was a devoted Nimrod, Sir Richard Shafto, who every season fixed himself and family at a convenient hunting-lodge near the little town of Grantham, with his right worthy son and heir, who by calling at Somerset Castle soon after the arrival of its guests, caused a trifling change in its arrangements. When Dick Shafto (as all the grooms in the stables familiarly designated him) was ushered into the room, he nodded to Sir Robert, and, turning his back on the ladies, told Pembroke he had ridden to Somerset "on purpose to *bag* him for Woodhill Lodge."

"Upon my life," cried he, "if you don't come, I will cut and run. There is not a creature but yourself within twenty miles to whom I can speak—not a man worth a sixpence. I wish my father had broken his neck before he accepted that confounded embassy, which encumbers me with the charge of my old mother!"

After this dutiful wish, which brought down a weighty admonition from Miss Dorothy, the young gentleman promised to behave better, provided she would persuade Pembroke to accompany him to the Lodge. Mr. Somerset did not show much alacrity in his consent; but to rid his family of so noisy a guest, he rose from his chair, and acquiescing in the sacrifice of a few days to good nature, bade his father farewell, and gave orders for a ride to Grantham.

As soon as the gentlemen left the saloon, Miss Dundas ran up stairs, and from her dressing-room window in the west tower pursued the steps of their horses as they cantered down the winding steep into the high road. An abrupt angle of the hill hiding them from her view, she turned round with a toss of the head, and flinging herself into a chair, exclaimed, "Now I shall be bored to death by this prosing family! I wish his boasted hunter had run away with Shafto before he thought of coming here!"

In consequence of the temper which engendered the above no very flattering compliment to the society at the Castle, Miss Dundas descended to the dining-room with sulky looks and a chilling air. She ate what the baronet laid on her plate with an indolent appetite, cut her meat carelessly, and dragged the vegetables over the table-cloth. Miss Dorothy colored at this indifference to the usual neatness of her damask covers; but Miss Dundas was so completely in the sullens, that, heedless of any other feelings than her own, she continued to pull and knock about the things just as her ill-humor dictated.

The petulance of this lady's behavior did not in the least assimilate with the customary decorum of Sir Robert's table; and when the cloth was drawn, he could not refrain from expressing his concern that Somerset Castle appeared so little calculated to afford satisfaction to a daughter of Lady Dundas. Miss Dundas attempted some awkward declaration that she never was more amused—never happier.

But the small credit Sir Robert gave to her assertion was fully warranted the next morning by the ready manner in which she accepting a casual invitation to spend the ensuing day and night at Lady Shafto's. Her ladyship called on Miss Dorothy, and intended to have a party in the evening, invited the two young ladies to return with her to Woodhill Lodge, and be her guests for a week. Miss Beaufort, whose spirits were far from tranquillized, declined her civility; but with a gleam of pleasure she heard it accepted by Miss Dundas, who departed with her ladyship for the Lodge.

Whilst the enraptured Diana, all life and glee, bowled along with Lady Shafto, anticipating the delight of once more seating herself at the elbow of Pembroke Somerset, Mary Beaufort, relieved from a load of ill-requited attentions, walked out into the park, to enjoy in solitude the "sweet sorrow" of thinking on the unhappy and far-distant Constantine. Regardless of the way, her footsteps, though robbed of elasticity by nightly watching and daily regret, led her beyond the park, to the ruined church of Woolthorpe, its southern boundary. Her eyes were fixed on the opposite horizon. It was the extremity of Leicestershire; and far, far behind those hills was that London which contained the object dearest to her soul. The wind seemed scarcely to breathe as it floated towards her; but it came from that quarter, and believing it laden with every sweet which love can fancy, she threw back her veil to inhale its balm, then, blaming herself for such weakness, she turned, blushing, homewards and wept at what she thought her unreasonably tenacious passion.

The arrival of Miss Dundas at the Lodge was communicated to the two young men on their return from traversing half the country in quest of game. The news drew an oath from Shafto, but rather pleased Somerset, who augured some amusement from her attempts at wit and judgment. Tired to death, and dinner being over when they entered, with ravenous appetites they devoured their uncomfortable meal in a remote room; then throwing themselves along the sofas, yawned and slept for nearly two hours.

Pembroke waking first, suddenly jumped on the floor, and shaking his disordered clothes, exclaimed, "Shafto! get up. This is abominable! I cannot help thinking that if we spend one half of our days in pleasure and the other in lolling off its fatigues, we shall have passed through life more to our shame than our profit!"

"Then you take the shame and leave me the profit," cried his companion, turning himself round: "so good-night to you!"

Pembroke rang the bell. A servant entered.

"What o'clock is it?"

"Nine, sir."

"Who are above?"

"My lady, sir, and a large party of ladies."

"There, now!" cried Shafto, yawning and kicking out his legs. "You surely won't go to be bored with such maudlin company?"

"I choose to join your mother," replied Pembroke. "Are there any gentlemen, Stephen?"

"One sir: Doctor Denton."

"Off with you!" roared Shafto; "what do you stand jabbering there for? You won't let me sleep. Can't you send away the fellow, and go look yourself?"

"I will, if you can persuade yourself to rise off that sofa and come with me."

"May Lady Hecate catch me if I do! Get about your business, and leave me to mine."

"You are incorrigible, Shafto," returned Pembroke, as he closed the door.

He went up stairs to change his dress, and before he gained the second flight, he resolved not to spend another whole day in the company of such an ignorant, unmannerly cub.

On Mr. Somerset's entrance into Lady Shafto's drawing-room, he saw many ladies, but only one gentleman, who was, the before-mentioned Dr. Denton—a poor, shallow-headed, parasitical animal. Pembroke having seen enough of him to despise his pretensions both to science and sincerity, returned his wide smirk and eager inquiries with a ceremonious bow, and took his seat by the side of the now delighted Miss Dundas The vivid spirits of Diana, which she now strove to render peculiarly sparkling, entertained him. When compared with the insipid sameness of her ladyship, or the coarse ribaldry of her son, the mirth of Miss Dundas was wit and her remarks wisdom.

"Dear Mr. Somerset!" cried she, "how good you are to

break this sad solemnity. I vow, until you showed your face, I thought the days of paganism were revived, and that lacking men, we were assembled here to celebrate the mysteries of the *Bona Dea.*"

"Lacking men!" replied he, smiling; "you have overlooked the assiduous Doctor Denton?"

"O, no; that is a chameleon in man's clothing. He breathes air, he eats air, he speaks air; and a most pestilential breath it is. Only observe how he is pouring its fumes into the ear of yonder sable statue."

Pembroke directed his eyes as Miss Dundas desired him, and saw Dr. Denton whispering and bowing before a lady in black. The lady put up her lip: the doctor proceeded; she frowned: he would not be daunted; the lady rose from her seat, and slightly bending her head, crossed the room. Whilst Mr. Somerset was contemplating her graceful figure, and fine though pale features, Miss Dundas touched his arm, and smiling satirically, repeated in an affected voice—

"Hail, pensive nun! devout and holy!
Hail, divinest Melancholy!"

"If she be Melancholy," returned Pembroke, "I would forever say

"Hence, unholy Mirth, of Folly born!"

Miss Dundas reddened. She never liked this interesting woman, who was not only too handsome for competition, but possessed an understanding that would not tolerate ignorance or presumption. Diana's ill-natured impertinence having several times received deserved chastisement from that quarter, she was vexed to the soul when Pembroke closed his animated response with the question, "Who is she?"

Rather too bitterly for the design on his heart, Miss Dundas iterated his words, and then answered, "Why, she is crazed. She lives in a place called Harrowby Abbey, at the top of that hill," continued she, pointing through the opposite window to a distant rising ground, on which the moon was shining brightly; "and I am told she frightens the cottagers out of their wits by her midnight strolls."

Hardly knowing how to credit this wild account, Pembroke asked his informer if she were serious.

"Never more so. Her eyes are uncommonly wild."

"You must be jesting," returned he; "they seem perfectly reasonable."

Miss Dundas laughed. "like Hamlet's, they 'know not seems, but have that within which passeth show!' Believe me, she is mad enough for Bedlam; and of that I could soon convince you. I wonder how Lady Shafto thought of inviting her; she quite stupefied our dinner."

"Well," cried Pembroke, "if those features announce madness, I shall never admire a look of sense again."

"Bless us," exclaimed Miss Dundas, "you are wonderfully struck! Don't you see she is old enough to be your mother?"

"That may be," answered he, smiling; "nevertheless she is one of the most lovely women I ever beheld. "Come, tell me her name."

"I will satisfy you in a moment," rejoined Diana; "and then away with your rhapsodies! She is the very Countess of Tinemouth, who brought that vagabond foreigner to our house who would have run off with Phemy!"

"Lady Tinemouth!" exclaimed Pembroke; "I never saw her before. My ever-lamented mother knew her whilst I was abroad, and she esteemed her highly. Pray introduce me to her!"

"Impossible," replied Diana, vexed at the turn his curiosity had taken; "I wrote to her about the insidious wretch, and now we don't speak."

"Then I will introduce myself," answered he. He was moving away, when Miss Dundas caught his arm, and by various attempts at badinage and raillery, held him in his place until the countess had made her farewell curtsey to Lady Shafto, and the door was closed.

Disappointed by this manœuvre, Pembroke re-seated himself; and wondering why his aunt and cousin had not heard of Lady Tinemouth's arrival at Harrowby, he determined to wait on her next day. Regardless of every word which the provoked Diana addressed to him, he remained silent and meditating, until the loud voice of Shafto, bellowing in his ear, made him turn suddenly round. Miss Dundas tried to laugh at his reverie, though she knew that such a flagrant instance of inattention was death to her hopes; but Pembroke, not inclined to partake in the jest, coolly asked his bearish companion what he wanted?

"Nothing," cried he, "but to hear you speak! Miss Dundas tells me you have lost your heart to yonder grim countess? My mother wanted me to gallant her up the hill; but I would see her in the river first!"

"Shafto!" answered Pembroke, rising from his chair, "you cannot be speaking of Lady Tinemouth?"

"Efaith I am," roared he; "and if she be such a scamp as to live without a carriage, I won't be her lackey for nothing. The matter of a mile is not to be tramped over by me with no pleasanter companion than an old painted woman of quality."

"Surely you cannot mean," returned Pembroke, "that her ladyship was to walk from this place?"

"Without a doubt," cried Shafto, bursting into a hoarse laugh; "you would be clever to see my Lady Stingy in any other carriage than her clogs.

Irritated at the malice of Miss Dundas, and despising the vulgar illiberality of Shafto, without deigning a reply, Pembroke abruptly left the room, and hastening out of the house, ran, rather than walked, in hopes of overtaking the countess before she reached Harrowby.

CHAPTER XXXIX.

THE VALE OF GRANTHAM.—BELVOIR.

PEMBROKE crossed the little wooden bridge which lies over the Witham; he scoured the field; he leaped every stile and gate in his way, and at last gained the enclosure that leads to the top of the hill, where he descried a light moving, and very rightly conjectured it must be the lantern carried by the countess's attendant. Another spring over the shattered fence cleared all obstacles, and he found himself close to Lady Tinemouth, who was leaning on the arm of a gentleman. Pembroke stopped at this sight. Supposing she had been met by some person belonging to the neighborhood, whose readier gallantry now occupied the place which Miss Dundas had prevented him from filling, he was preparing to retreat, when Lady Tinemouth happening to turn her head, imagined, from the hesitating embarrassment of his manner, that he was a stranger, who had lost his way, and accosted him with that inquiry.

Pembroke bowed in some confusion, and related the simple fact of his having heard that she had quitted Lady Shafto's house without any guard but the servant, and that the moment he learned the circumstance he had hurried out to proffer his services. The countess not only thanked him for such attention, but, constrained by a civility which at that instant she could have wished not to have been necessary, asked him to walk forward with her to the abbey, and partake of some refreshment.

"But," added she, "though I perfectly recollect having seen another gentleman in Lady Shafto's room besides Doctor Denton, I have not the honor of knowing your name."

"It is Somerset," returned Pembroke; "I am the son of that Lady Somerset, who, during the last year of her life, had the happiness of being intimate with your ladyship."

Lady Tinemouth expressed her pleasure at this meeting; and turning to the gentleman who was walking in silence by her side, said, "Mr. Constantine, allow me to introduce to you the cousin of the amiable Miss Beaufort."

Thaddeus, who had too well recognized the voice of his false friend in the first accents he addressed to the countess, with a swelling heart bent his head to the cold salutation of Somerset. Hearing that her ladyship's companion was the same Constantine whom he had liberated from prison, Pembroke was stimulated with a desire to take the perhaps favorable occasion to unmask his double villany to Lady Tinemouth; and conceiving a curiosity to see the man whose person and meretricious qualities had blinded the judgment of his aunt and cousin, he readily obeyed the second invitation of the countess, and consented to go home and sup with her.

Meanwhile, Thaddeus was agitated with a variety of emotions. Every tone of Pembroke's voice, reminding him of happier days, pierced his heart, whilst a sense of his ingratitude awakened all the pride and indignation of his soul. Full of resentment, he determined that, whatever might be the result, he would not shrink from an interview, the anticipation of which Pembroke (who had received from himself an intimation of the name he had assumed) seemed to regard with so much contemptuous indifference.

Not imagining that Somerset and the count had any personal knowledge of each other, Lady Tinemouth begged the gentlemen to accompany her into the supper-parlor. Pembroke, with inconsiderate, real indifference, passed by Thaddeus to give his hand to the countess. Thaddeus was so shocked at this instance of something very like a personal affront, that, insulted in every nerve, he was obliged to pause a moment in the hall, to summon coolness to follow him with a composed step and dispassionate countenance. He accomplished this conquest over himself, and taking off his hat, entered the room. Lady Tinemouth began to congratulate herself with many kind expressions on his arrival. The eyes of Pembroke fixed themselves on the calm but severe aspect of the man before him; he stood by the table with such an air of noble greatness, that the candid heart of Pembroke Somerset soon whispered to himself, "Sure nothing ill can dwell in such a breast!"

Still his eyes followed him, when he turned round, and when he bent his head to answer the countess, but in a voice so low that it escaped his ear. Pembroke was bewildered. There was something in the features, in the mien of this foreigner, so like his friend Sobieski! But then Sobieski was all frankness and animation; his cheek bloomed with the rich coloring of youth and happiness; his eyes flashed pleasure, and his lips were decked with smiles. On the contrary, the person before him was not only considerably taller, and of more manly proportions, but his face was pale, reserved, and haughty; besides, he did not appear even to recollect the name of Somerset; and what at once might destroy the supposition, his own was simply Constantine.

These reasonings having quickly passed through the mind of Pembroke, they left his heart unsatisfied. The conflict of his doubts flushed his cheeks; his bosom beat; and keeping his searching and ardent gaze riveted on the man who was either his friend or his counterpart, on Lady Tinemouth turning away to lay her cloak down, the eyes of the young men met. Thaddeus turned paler than before. There is an intelligence in the interchange of looks which cannot be mistaken; it is the communication of souls, and there is no deception in their language. Pembroke flew forward, and catching hold of his friend's hand, exclaimed in an impetuous voice, "Am I right? Are you Sobieski?"

"I am," returned Thaddeus, almost inarticulate with emotion, and hardly knowing what to understand by Somerset's behavior.

"Gracious heaven!" cried he, still grasping his hand; "can you have forgotten your friend Pembroke Somerset?"

The ingenuous heart of Thaddeus acknowledged the words and manner of Pembroke to be the language of truth. Trusting that some mistake had involved his former conduct, he at once cast off suspicion, and throwing his arms around him, strained him to his breast and burst into tears.

Lady Tinemouth, who during this scene stood mute with surprise, now advanced to the friends, who were weeping on each other's necks, and taking a hand of each, "My dear

Sobieski," cried she, "why did you withhold the knowledge of this friendship from me? Had you told me that you and Mr. Somerset were acquainted, this happy meeting might have been accomplished sooner."

"Yes," replied Pembroke, turning to the countess, and wiping away the tears which were trembling on his cheek; "nothing could have given me pain at this moment but the conviction that he who was the preserver of my life, and my most generous protector, should in this country have endured the most abject distress rather than let me know it was in my power to be grateful."

Thaddeus took out his handkerchief, and for a few moments concealed his face. The countess looked on him with tenderness; and believing he would sooner regain composure were he alone with his friend, she stole unobserved out of the room.

Pembroke affectionately resumed: "But I hope, dear Sobieski, you will never leave me more. I have an excellent father, who, when he is made acquainted with my obligations to you and your noble family, will glory in loving you as a son."

Having subdued "the woman in his heart," Thaddeus raised his head with an expression in his eyes far different from that which had chilled the blood of Pembroke on their first encounter.

"Circumstances," said he, "dear Somerset, have made me greatly injure you. A strange neglect on your side, since we separated at Villanow, gave the first blow to my confidence in your friendship. Though I lost your direct address, I wrote to you often, and yet you persevered in silence. After having witnessed the destruction of all that was dear to me in Poland, and then of Poland itself, when I came to England I wished to give your faithfulness another chance. I addressed two letters to you. I even delivered the last at your door myself, and I saw you in the window when I sent it in."

"By all that is sacred," cried Pembroke, vehemently, and amazed, "I never saw any letter from you! I wrote you many. I never heard of those you mention. Indeed, I should even now have been ignorant of the palatine's and your mother's cruel fate had it not been too circumstantially related in the newspapers."

"I believe you," returned Thaddeus, drawing an agonizing sigh at the dreadful picture which the last sentence recalled. "I believe you; though at the time of which I speak, I thought otherwise, for both my last letters were re-enclosed to me in a blank cover, directed as if by your hand, and brought by a servant, with a message that there was no answer."

"Amazing!" exclaimed Somerset; "there must be some horrible treachery! Can it be that some lurking foreign spy got amongst my servants at Dantzic, and has been this traitor ever since? Oh, Thaddeus!" cried he, abruptly interrupting himself, and grasping his hand, "I would have flown to you, had it been to meet death, instead of the greatest joy Heaven could bestow upon me. But why did you not come in yourself? then no mistake could have happened! Oh, why did you not come in?"

"Because I was uncertain of your sentiments. My first letter remained unnoticed; and my heart, dear Somerset," added he, pressing his hand, "would not stoop to solicitation."

"Solicitation!" exclaimed Pembroke, with warmth; "you have a right to demand my life! But there is some deep villany in this affair; nothing else could have carried it through. Oh, if anybody belonging to me have dared to open these letters—Oh, Sobieski!" cried he, interrupting himself, "how you must have despised me!"

"I was afflicted," returned Thaddeus, "that the man whom my family so warmly loved could prove so unworthy; and afterwards, whenever I met you in the streets, which I think was more than once or twice, I confess that to pass you cut me to the heart."

"And you have met me?" exclaimed Pembroke, "and I not see you; I cannot comprehend it."

"Yes," answered Thaddeus; "and the first time was going into the playhouse. I believe I called after you."

"Is it not now ten months since?" returned Pembroke. "I remember very well that some one called out my name in a voice that seemed known to me, while I was handing Lady Calthorpe and her sister into the porch. I looked about, but not seeing any one I knew, I thought I must have been mistaken. But why, dear Sobieski, why did you not follow me into the theatre?"

Thaddeus shook his head and smiled languidly. "My poverty would not permit," replied he; "but I waited in the hall until every body left the house, in hopes of intercepting you as you passed again."

Pembroke sprung from his chair at these words, and with vehemence exclaimed, "I see it! That hypocrite Loftus is at the bottom of it! He followed me into the theatre; he must have seen you, and his cursed selfishness was alarmed. Yes;

it is no foreign traitor! it must be he! He would not allow me to return that way. When I said I would, he told me a thousand lies about the carriages coming round; and I, believing him, went out by another door. I will tax him of it to his face!"

"Who is Mr. Loftus?" inquired Thaddeus, surprised at his friend's suspicion; "I do not know the man."

"What!" returned Pembroke, "don't you remember that Loftus is the name of my scoundrel tutor who persuaded me to volunteer against Poland? To screen his baseness I have brought all this upon myself."

"Now I recollect it," replied Thaddeus; "but I never saw him."

"Yet I am not less certain that I am right," replied Somerset. "I will tell you my reasons. After I quitted Villanow, you may remember I was to meet him at Dantzic. Before we left the port, he implored, almost on his knees, that in pity to his mother and sisters, whom he said he supported out of his salary, I would refrain from incensing my parents against him by relating any circumstance of our visit to Poland. The man shed tears as he spoke; and, like a fool, I consented to keep the secret till the Vicar of Somerset (a poor soul, still ill of dropsy) dies, and he be in possession of the living. When we landed in England, I found the cause of my sudden recall had been the illness of my dear mother. But Heaven denied me the happiness of beholding her again; she had been buried two days before I reached the shore." Pembroke paused a moment, and then resumed: "For near a month after my return, I could not quit my room; on my recovery, I wrote both to you and to the palatine. But I still locked up your names within my heart, the old rector being yet in existence. I repeated my letters at least every six weeks during the first year of our separation, though you persisted in being silent. Hurt as I was at this neglect, I believed that gratitude demanded some sacrifices from pride, and I continued to write even till the spring following. Meanwhile the papers of the day teemed with Sobieski's actions—Sobieski's fame; and supposing that increasing glory had blotted me out of your memory, I resolved thenceforth to regard our friendship as a dream, and never to speak of it more."

Confounded at this double misapprehension, Thaddeus with a glowing countenance expressed his regret for having doubted his friend, and repeating the assurance of having been punctual to his promise of correspondence, even when he dreamed him inconstant, acknowledged that nothing but a premeditated scheme could have effected so many disappointments.

"Ay," returned Pembroke, reddening with awakened anger; "I could swear that Mr. Loftus has all my letters in his bureau at this moment! No house ever gave a man a better opportunity to play the rogue in than ours. It is a custom with us to lay our letters every morning on the hall-table, whence they are sent to the office; and when the post arrives they are spread out in the same way, that their several owners may take them as they pass to breakfast. From this arrangement I cannot doubt the means by which Mr. Loftus, under the hope of separating us forever, has intercepted every letter to you and every letter from you. I suppose the wretch feared I might become impatient, and break my engagement if our correspondence were allowed. He trembled lest the business should be blown before the rector died, and he, in consequence, lose both the expected living and his present situation about Lord Avon. A villain! for once he has judged rightly. I will unmask him to my father, and show him what it is to purchase advancement at the expense of honor and justice."

Thaddeus, who could not withhold immediate credit to these evidences of chicanery, tried to calm the violence of his friend, who only answered by insisting on having his company back with him to Somerset Castle.

"I long to present you to my father," cried he. "When I tell him who you are, of your kindness to me, how rejoiced will he be! How happy, how proud to have you his guest; to show the grandson of the Palatine of Masovia the warm gratitude of a Briton's heart! Indeed, Sobieski, you will love him, for he is generous and noble, like your inestimable grandfather. Besides," added he, smiling with a sudden recollection, "there is my lovely cousin, Mary Beaufort, who I verily believe will fly into your arms!"

The blood rushed over the cheeks of Thaddeus at this speech of his friend, and suppressing a bitter sigh, he shook his head.

"Don't look so like an infidel," resumed Somerset. "If you have any doubts of possessing her most precious feelings, I can put you out of your suspense by a single sentence! When Lady Dundas's household, with myself amongst them (for little did I suspect I was joining the cry against my friend), were asserting the most flagrant instances of your deceit to Euphemia, Mary alone withstood the tide of malice, and compelled me to release you."

"Gracious Providence!" cried Thaddeus, catching Pem

broke's hand, and looking eagerly and with agitation in his face; "was it you who came to my prison? Was it Miss Beaufort who visited my lodgings?"

"Indeed it was," returned his friend, "and I blush for myself that I quitted Newgate without an interview. Had I followed the dictates of common courtesy, in the fulfilment of my commission, I should have seen you; and then, what pain would have been spared my dear cousin! What a joyful surprise would have awaited myself!"

Thaddeus could only reply by pressing his friend's hand. His brain whirled. He could not decide on the nature of his feelings; one moment he would have given worlds to throw himself at Miss Beaufort's feet, and the next he trembled at the prospect of meeting her so soon.

"Dear Sobieski!" cried Pembroke, "how strangely you receive this intelligence! Is it possible such sentiments from Mary Beaufort can be regarded by a soul like yours with coldness?"

"O no!" cried the count, his fine face flushed with emotion. "I adore Miss Beaufort. Her virtues possess my whole heart. But can I forget that I have only that heart to offer? Can I forget that I am a beggar?—that even now I exist on her bounty?" The eyes of Thaddeus, and the sudden tremor which shook his frame, finished this appeal to his fate.

Pembroke found it enter his soul. To hide its effect, he threw himself on his friend's breast, and exclaimed, "Do not injure me and my father by such thoughts. You are come, dearest Sobieski, to a second home. Sir Robert Somerset will consider himself ennobled in supplying the place of your lamented grandfather—in endowing you like a son! Oh, Thaddeus, you must be my cousin, dear as a brother, as well as my friend!"

Thaddeus replied with an agitated affection as true as that of the generous speaker. "But," added he, "I must not allow the noble heart of my now regained Somerset to believe that I can live a dependent on any power but the Author of my being. Therefore, if Sir Robert Somerset will assist me to procure some unobtrusive way of acquiring my own support in the simplicity I wish, I shall thank him from my soul. In no other way my kindest friend, can I ever be brought to tax the munificence of your father."

Pembroke colored at this, and exclaimed, in a voice of distress and displeasure, "Sobieski! what can you mean? Do you imagine that ever my father or myself can forget that you were little less than a prince in your own country?—that when in so high a station you treated me like a brother; that you preserved me even when I lifted my arm against your life. Can we be such monsters as to forget all this, or to think that we act justly by you in permitting you to labor for your bread? No, Thaddeus; my very soul spurns the idea. Your mother sheltered me as a son; and I insist that you allow my father to perform the same part by you! Besides, you shall not be idle; you may have a commission in the army, and I will follow you."

The count pressed the hand of his friend, and looking gratefully but mournfully in his face, replied, "Had I a hundred tongues, my generous Pembroke, I could not express my sense of your friendship; it is indeed a cordial to my heart; it imparts to me an earnest of happiness which I thought had fled forever. But it shall not allure me from my principles. I am resolved not to live a life of indolent uselessness; and I cannot, at this period, enter the British army. No," added he, emotion elevating his tone and manner; "rather would I toil for subsistence by the sweat of my brow than be subjected to the necessity of acting in concert with those ravagers who destroyed my country! I cannot fight by the side of the allied powers who dismembered it! I cannot enlist under the allies! I will not be led out to devastation! Mine was, and ever shall be, a defensive sword; and should danger threaten England, I would be as ready to withstand her enemies as I ardently, though ineffectually, opposed those of unhappy Poland."

Pembroke recognized the devoted soul of Thaddeus of Warsaw in this lofty burst of enthusiasm; and aware that his father's munificence and manner of conferring it would go further towards removing these scruples than all his own arguments, he did not attempt to combat a resolution which he knew he could not subdue, but tried to prevail with him to become his guest until something could be arranged to suit his wishes.

With an unuttered emotion at the thought of meeting Miss Beaufort, Thaddeus had just consented to accompany Somerset to the Castle, after Sir Robert had been apprized of his coming, when the countess's old and faithfully-attached manservant entered, and respectfully informed her guests that his lady, not willing to disturb their conversation, had retired to her room for the night, but that beds were prepared for them in the Abbey, and she hoped to meet both friends at her breakfast-table in the morning. The honest man then added, "It was now past eleven o'clock; and after their honors had partaken of their yet untasted refreshment, he would be ready to attend them to their chambers."

Pembroke started up at this, and shaking his friend warmly by the hand, bade him, he said, "a short farewell;" and hastening down the hill, arrived at the gate of the Wold Lodge just at the turn of midnight.

At an early hour the next morning he gave orders to his groom, wrote a slight apology to Shafto for his abrupt departure, and, mounting his fleet horse, galloped away full of delight towards Somerset Castle.

CHAPTER XL.

SOMERSET CASTLE.

BUT Sobieski did not follow the attentive domestic of his maternal friend to the prepared apartment in the Abbey. He asked to be conducted back through the night-shadowed grounds to the little hotel he had seen early in the evening on his approach to the mansion. It stood at the entrance of the adjoining village, and under its rustic porch he had immediately entered, to engage a lodging beneath its humble sign, "The Plough," for the few days of his intended visit to Lady Tinemouth. A boy had been his guide, and bearer of his small travelling-bag, from the famous old Commandery inn, the "Angel," at Grantham, where the Wold diligence had set him down in the afternoon at the top of the market-place of that memorable town of ancient chivalry, to find his way up to the occasional rural palace cells on Harrowby Hill, of the same doughty and luxurious knights who were now lying, individually forgotten, in their not only silent but unknown graves, there not being a trace of them amongst the chapel ruins of the Abbey, nor below the hill, on the sight of the old Commandery church at Grantham.

"Ah, transit mundi!" exclaimed Thaddeus to himself, with a calmed sigh, as he thought on those things, while resting under the modest little portal of the hotel, whose former magnificence, when a hermit cell, might still be discernible in a few remaining remnants of the rich Gothic lintel yet mingling with the matted straw and the clinging ivy of the thatch.

"What art thou, world, and thine ambitions?" again echoed in silence from the heart of Thaddeus. "Though yet so young, I have seen thee in all thy phases which might wean me from this earth. But there are still some beings dear to me in the dimmed aspect, that seem to hold my hopes to this transitory and yet too lovely world." He was then thinking of his restored friend Pembroke Somerset, and of her whose name had been so fondly uttered by him, as a possible bond of their still more intimate relationship. He tried to quell the wild hope this recollection waked in his bosom, and hurried from the little parlor of the inn, where Lady Tinemouth's old servant had left him, to seek repose in his humbly-prepared chamber.

At sight of its white-robed bed and simple furniture, and instantly conscious to the balmy effects of the sweet freshness that breathed around him, where no perfume but that of flowers ever entered, his agitated feelings soon became soothed into serenity, and within a quarter of an hour after he had laid his grateful head on that quiet pillow, he had sunk to a sleep of gentle peace with man and Heaven.

Next morning, when the countess met her gladly re-welcomed guest at the breakfast-table, she expressed surprise and pleasure at the scene of the preceding night, but intimated some mortification that he had withheld any part of his confidence from her. Sobieski soon obtained her pardon, by relating the manner of his first meeting with Mr. Somerset in Poland, and the consequent events of that momentous period.

Lady Tinemouth wept over the distressful fate that marked the residue of his narrative with a tenderness which yet more endeared her to his soul. But when, in compliance with his inquiries, she informed him how it happened that he had to seek her at Harrowby Abbey, when he supposed her to be on the Wolds, it was his turn to pity, and to shudder at his own consanguinity with Lord Harwold.

"Indeed," added the countess, wishing to turn from the painful subject, "you must have had a most tedious journey from Harwold Park to Harrowby, and nothing but my pleasure could exceed my astonishment when I met you last night on the hill."

Thaddeus sincerely declared that travelling a few miles further than he intended was no fatigue to him; yet, were it otherwise, the happiness which he then enjoyed would have acted as a panacea for worse ills, could he have seen her looking as well as when she left London.

Lady Tinemouth smiled. "You are right, Sobieski. I am worse than when I was in town. My solitary journey to Harwold oppressed me; and when my son sent me orders to leave it, because his father wanted the place for the autumnal months, his capricious cruelty seemed to augment the hectic of my distress. Nevertheless, I immediately obeyed, and in augmented disorder, arrived here last week. But how kind you were to follow me! Who informed you of the place of my destination?—hardly any of Lady Olivia's household?"

"No," returned Thaddeus; "I luckily had the precaution to inquire at the inn on the Wolds where the coach stopped, what part of Lord Tinemouth's family were at the Park; and when I heard that the earl himself was there, my next question was, "Where, then, was the countess?" The landlord very civilly told me of your having engaged a carriage from his house a day or two before, to carry you to one of his lordship's seats within a few miles of Somerset Castle. Hence, from what I heard you say of the situation of Harrowby, I concluded it must be the Abbey, and so I sought you at a venture."

"And I hope a happy issue," replied she, "will arise from your wanderings! This rencontre with so old a friend as Mr. Somerset is a pleasing omen. For my part, I was ignorant of the arrival of the family at the Castle until yesterday morning, and then I sent off a messenger to apprize my dear Miss Beaufort of my being in her neighborhood. To my great disappointment, Lady Shafto found me out immediately; and when, in compliance with her importunate invitation, I walked down to an early dinner with her yesterday, little did I expect to meet the amiable cousin of our sweet friend. So delightful an accident has amply repaid me for the pain I endured in seeing Miss Dundas at the Lodge; an insolent and reproachful letter which she wrote to me concerning you has rendered her an object of my aversion."

Thaddeus smiled and gently bent his head. "Since, my dear Lady Tinemouth, her groundless malice and Miss Euphemia's folly have failed in estranging either your confidence or the esteem of Miss Beaufort from me, I pardon them both. Perhaps I ought to pity them; for is it not difficult to pass through the brilliant snares of wealth and adulation and emerge pure as when we entered them? Unclouded fortune is, indeed, a trial of spirits; and how brightly does Miss Beaufort rise from the blaze! Surrounded by splendor, homage and indulgence, she is yet all nature, gentleness and virtue!"

The latter part of this burst of heart he uttered rapidly, the nerves of that heart beating full at every word.

The countess, who wished to appear cheerful, rallied him on the warmth of his expressions; and observing that "the day was fine, invited him to walk out with her througn the romantic, though long-neglected, domains of the Abbey.

Meanwhile, the family at Somerset were just drawn round the breakfast-board, when they were agreeably surprised by the sudden entrance of Pembroke. During the repast Miss Beaufort repeated the contents of the note she had received the preceding day from Lady Tinemouth, and requested that her cousin would be kind enough to drive her in his curricle that morning to Harrowby.

"I will, with pleasure," answered he. "I have seen her ladyship, and even supped with her last night."

"How came that?" asked Miss Dorothy.

"I shall explain it to my father, whenever he will honor me with an audience," returned her happy nephew, addressing the baronet with all the joy of his heart looking out at his eyes. "Will you indulge me, dear sir, by half an hour's attention?"

"Certainly," replied Sir Robert; "at present I am going into my study to settle my steward's books, but the moment I have finished, I will send for you."

Miss Dorothy walked out after her brother, to attend her aviary, and Miss Beaufort, remaining alone with her cousin, made some inquiries about the countess's reasons for coming to the Abbey. "I know nothing about them," replied he, gayly, "for she went to bed almost the instant I entered the house. Too good to remain where her company was not wanted, she left me to enjoy a most delightful *tete-à-tete* with a dear friend, from whom I parted nearly four years ago. In short, we sat up the whole night together, talking over past scenes—and present ones too, for, I assure you, you were not forgotten."

"I! what had I to do with it?" replied Mary, smiling. "I cannot recollect any dear friend of yours whom you have not seen these four years."

"Well, that is strange!" answered Pembroke; "he remembers you perfectly; but, true to your sex, you affirm what you please, though I know there is not a man in the world I prefer before him."

Miss Beaufort shook her head, laughed, and sighed; and withdrawing her hand from his, threatened to leave him if he would not be serious.

"I am serious," cried he. "Would you have me *swear* that I have seen him whom you most wish to see?"

She regarded the expression of his countenance with a momentary emotion; taking her seat again, she said, "You can have seen no one that is of consequence to me; whoever your friend may be, I have only to congratulate you on a meeting which affords you so much delight."

Pembroke burst into a joyous laugh at her composure.

"So cold!" cried he—"so cautious! Yet I verily believe you would participate in my delights were I to tell you who he is. However, you are such a skeptic, that I wont hint even one of the many fine things he said of you."

She smiled incredulously.

"I could beat you, Mary," exclaimed he, "for this oblique way of saying I am telling lies! But I will have my revenge on your curiosity; for on my honor I declare," added he, emphatically, "that last night I met with a friend at Lady Tinemouth's who four years ago saved my life, who entertained me several weeks in his house, and who has seen and adores you! 'Tis true; true, on my existence! And what is more, I have promised that you will repay these weighty obligations by the free gift of this dear hand. What do you say to this, my sweet Mary?"

Miss Beaufort looked anxious at the serious and energetic manner in which he made those assertions; even the sportive kiss that ended the question did not dispel the gravity with which she prepared to reply.

Pembroke perceiving her intent, prevented her by exclaiming, "Cease, Mary, cease! I see you are going to make a false statement. Let truth prevail, and you will not deny that I am suing for a plighted faith? You will not deny who it was that softened and subdued your heart? You cannot conceal from me that the wanderer Constantine possesses your affections?"

Amazed at so extraordinary a charge from her hitherto always respectful as well as fraternally affectionate cousin, she reddened with pain and displeasure. Rising from her seat, and averting her tearful eyes, she said, "I did not expect this cruel, this ungenerous speech from you, Pembroke! What have I done to deserve so rude, so unfeeling a reproach?"

Pembroke threw his arm round her. "Come," said he, in a sportive voice; "don't be tragical. I never meant to reproach you, Mary. I dare say if you gave your heart, it was only in return for his. I know you are a grateful girl; and I verily believe you won't find much difference between my friend the young Count Sobieski and the forlorn Constantine."

A suspicion of the truth flashed across Miss Beaufort's mind. Unable to speak, she caught hold of her cousin's hands, and looking eagerly in his face, her eyes declared the question she would have asked.

Pembroke laughed triumphantly. A servant entering to tell him that Sir Robert was ready, he strained her to his breast and exclaimed, "Now I am revenged! Farewell! I leave you to all the pangs of doubt and curiosity!" He then flew out of the room with an arch glance at her agitated countenance, and hurried up stairs.

She clasped her trembling hands together as the door closed on him. "O, gracious Providence!" cried she, "what am I to understand by this mystery, this joy of my cousin's? Can it be possible that the illustrious Sobieski and my contemned Constantine are the same person?" A burning blush overspread her face at the expression *my* which had escaped her lips.

Whilst the graces, the sweetness, the dignity of Thaddeus had captivated her notice, his sufferings, his virtues, and the mysterious interests which involved his history, in like manner had fixed her attention had awakened her esteem. From these grounds the step is short to love. "When the mind is conquered, the heart surrenders at discretion." But she knew not that she had advanced too far to retreat, until the last scene at Dundas House, by forcing her to defend Constantine against the charge of loving her, made her confess to herself how much she wished the charge were true.

Poor and lowly as he seemed, she found that her whole heart and life were wrapped in his remembrance; that his worshipped idea was her solace; her most precious property the dear treasure of her secret and sweetest felicity, It was the companion of her walks, the monitor of her actions. Whenever she planned, whenever she executed, she asked herselt, how would Constantine consider this? and accordingly did she approve or condemn her conduct, for she had heard enough from Mrs. Robson to convince her that piety was the sure fountain of his virtues.

When she had left London, and so far separated from this idol of her memory, such was the impression he had stamped on her heart; he seemed ever present. The shade of Laura visited the solitude of Vaucluse; the image of Constantine haunted the walks of Somerset. The loveliness of nature, its leafy groves and verdant meadows, its blooming mornings and luxuriant sunsets, the romantic shadows of twilight or the soft glories of the moon and stars, as they pressed beauty and sentiment upon her heart, awoke it to the remembrance of Constantine; she saw his image, she felt his soul, in every object. Subtile and undefinable is that ethoreal chord which unites our tenderest thought, with their chain of association!

Before this conversation, in which Pembroke mentioned the name of Constantine with so much badinage and apparent familiarity, he never heard him spoken of by Mary or his aunt without declaring a displeasure nearly amounting to anger. Hence, when she considered his now so strangely altered tone, Miss Beaufort necessarily concluded that he had seen, in the person of him she most valued, the man whose public character she had often heard him admire, and who, she now doubted not, had at some former period given him some private reason for calling him his friend. Before this time, she more than once had suspected, from the opinions which Somerset occasionally repeated respecting the affairs of Poland, that he could only have acquired so accurate a knowledge of its events by having visited the country itself. She mentioned her suspicion to Mr. Loftus: he denied the fact; and she had thought no more on the subject until the present ambiguous hints of her cousin conjured up these doubts anew, and led her to suppose that if Pembroke had not disobeyed his father so far as to go to Warsaw, he must have met with the Count Sobieski in some other realm. The possibility that this young hero, of whom fame spoke so loudly, might be the mysterious Constantine, bewildered and delighted her. The more she compared what she had heard of the one with what she had witnessed in the other, the more was she reconciled to the probability of her ardent hope. Besides, she could not for a moment retain a belief that her cousin would so cruelly sport with her delicacy and peace as to excite expectations that he could not fulfil.

Agitated by a suspense which bordered on agony, with a beating heart she heard his quick step descending the stairts. The door opened, and Pembroke, flying into the room, caught up his hat. As he was darting away again, unable to restrain her impatience, Miss Beaufort with an imploring voice ejaculated his name. He turned, and displayed to her amazed sight a countenance in which no vestige of his former animation could be traced. His cheek was flushed, and his eyes shot a wild fire that struck to her heart. Unconscious what she did, she ran up to him; but Pembroke, pushing her back, exclaimed, "Don't ask me any questions, if you would not drive me to madness."

"O Heaven!" cried she, catching his arm, and clinging to him, while the eagerness of his motion dragged her into the hall. "Tell me! Has anything happened to my guardian—to your friend—to Constantine?"

"No," replied he, looking at her with a face full of desperation; "but my father commands me to treat him like a villain."

She could hardly credit her senses at this confirmation that Constantine and Sobieski were one. Turning giddy with the tumultuous delight that rushed over her soul, she staggered back a few paces, and leaning against the open door, tried to recover breath to regain the room she had left.

Pembroke, having escaped from her grasp, ran furiously down the hill, mounted his horse, and forbidding any groom to attend him, galloped towards the high road with the impetuosity of a madman. All the powers of his soul were in arms. Wounded, dishonored, stigmatized with ingratitude and baseness, he believed himself to be the most degraded of men.

It appeared that Sir Robert Somerset had long cherished a hatred to the Poles, in consequence of some injury he affirmed he had received in early youth from one of that nation. In this instance his dislike was implacable; and when his son set out for the continent, he positively forbade him to enter Poland. Notwithstanding his remembrance of this violated injunction, when Pembroke joined the baronet in his library, he did it with confidence. With a bounding heart and animated countenance, he recapitulated how he had been wrought upon by his young Russian friends to take up arms in their cause and march into Poland. At these last words his father turned pale, and though he did not speak, the denunciation was on his brow.

Pembroke, who expected some marks of displeasure, hastened to obliterate his disobedience by narrating the event which had introduced not only the young Count Sobieski to his succor, but the consequent friendship of the whole of that princely family.

Sir Robert still made no verbal reply, but his countenance deepened in gloom; and when Pembroke, with all the pathos of a deep regret, attempted to describe the death of the palatine, the horrors which attended the last hours of the countess, and the succeeding misery of Thaddeus, who was now in England, no language can paint the frenzy which burst at once from the baronet. He stamped on the ground, he covered his face with his clenched hands; then turning on his son with a countenance no longer recognizable, he exclaimed with fury, "Pembroke! you have outraged my commands! Never will I pardon you if that young man ever blast me with his sight."

"Merciful Heaven!" cried Pembroke, thunderstruck at a violence which he almost wished might proceed from real madness: "surely something has agitated my father! What can this mean?"

Sir Robert shook his head, whilst his teeth ground against

each other. "Don't mistake me," replied he, in a firm voice. "I am perfectly in my senses. It depends on *you* that I continue so. You know my oath against all of that nation! and, I repeat again, if you ever bring that young man into my presence, you shall never see me more."

A cold dew overspread the body of Pembroke. He would have caught his father's hand, but he held it back. "O sir," said he, "you surely cannot intend that I shall treat with ingratitude the man who saved my life?"

Sir Robert did not vouchsafe him an answer, but continued walking up and down the room, until, his hesitation increasing at every step, he opened the door of an interior apartment and retired, bidding his son remain where he left him.

The horror-struck Pembroke waited a quarter of an hour before his father re-entered. When he did appear, the deep gloom of his eye gave no encouragement to his son, who, hanging down his head, recoiled from speaking first. Sir Robert approached with a composed but severe countenance, and said, "I have been seeking every palliation that your conduct might admit, but I can find none. Before you quitted England, you knew well my abhorrence of Poland. One of that country many years ago wounded my happiness in a way I shall never recover. From that hour I took an oath never to enter its borders, and never to suffer one of its people to come within my doors. Rash, disobedient boy! You know my disposition, and you have seen the emotion with which this dilemma has shaken my soul! But be it on your own head that you have incurred obligations which I cannot repay. I will not perjure myself to defray a debt contracted against my positive and declared principles. I never will see this Polander you speak of; and it is my express command, on pain of my eternal malediction, that you break with him entirely."

Pembroke fell into a seat. Sir Robert proceeded.

"I pity your distress, but my resolution cannot be shaken. Oaths are not to be broken with impunity. You must either resign him or resign me. We may compromise your debt of gratitude. I will give you deeds to put your friend in possession of five hundred pounds a-year for life forever; nay, I would even double it to give you satisfaction; but from the hour in which you tell him so, you must see him no more."

Sir Robert was quitting the room, when Pembroke, starting from his chair, threw himself in agony on his knees, and catching by the skirt of his father's coat, implored him for God's sake to recall his words; to remember that he was affixing everlasting dishonor on his son! "Remember, dear sir!" cried he, holding his struggling hand, "that the man to whom you offer money as a compensation for insult is of a nature too noble to receive it. He will reject it, and spurn me; and I shall know that I deserve his scorn. For mercy's sake, spare me the agony of harrowing up the heart of my preserver—of meeting reproach from his eyes!"

"Leave me!" cried the baronet, breaking from him; "I repeat, unless you wish to incur my curse, do as I have commanded."

Thus outraged, thus agonised, Pembroke had appeared before the eyes of his cousin Mary more like a distracted creature than a man possessed of his senses. Shortly after his abrupt departure, her apprehension was petrified to a dreadful certainty of some cruel ruin to her hopes, by an order she received in the handwriting of her uncle, commanding her not to attempt visiting Lady Tinemouth whilst the Count Sobieski continued to be her guest, and under peril of his displeasure never to allow that name to pass her lips.

Hardly knowing whither he went, Pembroke did not arrive at the ruined aisle which leads to the habitable part of the Abbey until near three o'clock. He inquired of the groom that took his horse whether the countess and Mr. Constantine were at home. The man replied in the affirmative, but added, with a sad countenance, he feared neither of them could be seen.

"For what reason?" demanded Somerset.

"Alas! sir," replied the servant, "about an hour ago my lady was seized with a violent fit of coughing, which ended in the rupture of a blood-vessel. It continued to flow so long, that Mr. Constantine told the apothecary, whom he had summoned, to send for a physician. The doctor is not yet arrived, and Mr. Constantine won't leave my lady."

Though Mr. Somerset was truly concerned at the illness of the countess, the respite it afforded him from immediately declaring the ungrateful message of Sir Robert gave him no inconsiderable degree of ease. Somewhat relieved by the hope of being for one day spared the anguish of displaying his father in a disgraceful light, he entered the Abbey, and desired that a maid-servant might be sent to her ladyship's room to inform his friend that Mr. Somerset was below.

In a few minutes the girl returned with the following lines on a slip of paper:

"TO PEMBROKE SOMERSET, ESQ.

"I am grieved that I cannot see my dear Somerset to-day! I fear my revered friend is on her death-bed. I have sent for Dr. Cavendish, who is now at Stanford; doubtless you know he is a man of the first abilities. If human skill can preserve her, I may yet have hopes; but her disorder is on the lungs and in the heart, and I fear the stroke is sure. I am now sitting by her bedside, and writing what she dictates to her husband, her son, and her daughter. Painful, you may believe, is the task! I cannot, my dear Somerset, add more than my hope of seeing you soon, and that you will join in prayers to Heaven for the restoration of my inestimable friend, with your faithful and affectionate

"SOBIESKI."

"Alas! unhappy, persecuted Sobieski!" thought Pembroke, as he closed the paper; "to what art thou doomed! Some friends are torn from thee by death; others desert thee in the hour of trouble."

He took out his pencil to answer this distressing epistle, but he stopped at the first word; he durst not write that his father would fulfil any one of those engagements which he had so largely promised; and throwing away the pencil and the paper, he left a verbal declaration of his sorrow at what had happened, and an assurance of calling next day. Turning his back on a house which he had left on the preceding night with so many joyful hopes, he remounted his horse, and, melancholy and slow, rode about the country until evening,—so unwilling was he to return to that home which now threatened him with the frowns of his father, the tears of Mary Beaufort, and the miserable reflections of his own wretched heart.

CHAPTER XLI.

THE MATERNAL HEART.

DOCTOR Cavendish having been detained beyond his expected time with his invalid friend at Stanford, was happily still there, and set off for Harrowby the instant Mr. Constantine's messenger arrived, and before midnight alighted at the Abbey.

When he entered Lady Tinemouth's chamber he found her supported in the arms of Thaddeus, and struggling with a second rupture of her lungs. As he approached the bed, Thaddeus turned his eyes on him with an expression that powerfully told his fears. Dr. Cavendish silently pressed his hand; then taking from his pocket some styptic drops, he made the countess swallow them, and soon saw that they succeeded in stopping the hemorrhage.

Thaddeus and her physician remained by the side of the patient sufferer until ten in the morning, when she sunk into a gentle sleep. Complete stillness being necessary to continue this repose, the good doctor proposed leaving the maid to watch by her ladyship, and drawing the count out of the room, descended the stairs.

Mr. Somerset had been arrived half an hour, and met them in the breakfast parlor. After a few kind words exchanged between the parties, they sat down with dejected countenances to their melancholy meal. Thaddeus was too much absorbed in the scene he had left to take anything but a dish of coffee.

"Do you think Lady Tinemouth is in imminent danger?" inquired Pembroke of the doctor.

Dr. Cavendish sighed, and turning to Thaddeus, directed to him the answer which his friend's question demanded. "I am afraid, my dear Mr. Constantine," said he, in a reluctant voice, "that you are to sustain a new trial! I fear she cannot live eight-and-forty hours."

Thaddeus cast down his eyes and shuddered, but made no reply. Further remarks were prevented by a messenger from the countess, who desired Mr. Constantine's immediate attendance at her bedside. He obeyed. In half an hour he returned, with the mark of tears upon his cheek.

"Dearest Thaddeus!" cried Pembroke, "I trust the countess is not worse? This threatened new bereavement is too much: it afflicts my very heart." Indeed it rent it; for Pembroke could not help internally acknowledging that when Sobieski should close the eyes of Lady Tinemouth, he would be paying the last sad office to his last friend. That dear distinction he durst no longer arrogate to himself. Denied the fulfilment of its duties, he thought that to retain the title would be an assumption without a right.

Thaddeus drew his hand over his again filling eyes. "The countess herself," said he, "feels the truth of what Dr. Cavendish told us. She sent for me, and begged me, as I loved her, or would wish to see her die in peace, to devise some means for bringing her daughter to the Abbey to-night. As for Lord Harwold, she says his behavior since he arrived at manhood has been of a nature so cruel and unnatural, that she would not draw on herself the misery, nor on him the added guilt, of a refusal; but with regard to Lady Albina, who has been no sharer in those barbarities, she trusts a daughter's heart might be prevailed on to seek a last embrace from a dying parent. It is this request," continued he, ' that agitates me. When she pictured to me, with all the fervor of a mother, her doating fondness for this daughter, (on whom, whenever she did venture to hope, all those hopes rested;) when she wrung my hand, and besought me, as if I had been the sole disposer of her fate, to let her see her child before she died, I could only promise every exertion to effect it, and with an aching heart I came to consult you."

Dr. Cavendish was opening his lips to speak, but Somerset, in his eagerness to relieve his friend, did not perceive it, and immediately answered, "This very hour I will undertake what you have promised. I know Lord Tinemouth's family are now at the Wolds. It is only thirty miles distant; I will send a servant to have relays of horses ready. My curricle, which is now at the door, will be more convenient than a chaise; and I will engage to be back before to-morrow morning. Write a letter, Thaddeus," added he, "to Lady Albina; tell her of her mother's situation; and though I have never seen the young lady, I will give it into her own hand, and then bring her off, even were it in the face of her villanous father."

The pale cheeks of Sobieski flushed with a conscious scarlet. Turning to Dr. Cavendish, he requested him, as the most proper person, to write to Lady Albina, whilst he would walk out with his friend to order the carriage. Pembroke was thanked for his zeal, but it was not by words; they are too weak vehicles to convey strong impressions. Thaddeus pressed his hand, and accompanied the action with a look which spoke volumes. The withered heart of Pembroke expanded under the animated gratitude of his friend. Receiving the letter, he sprang into his seat, and, until he lost sight of Harrowby Hill, forgot how soon he must appear to that friend the most ungrateful of men.

It was near six in the evening before Mr. Somerset left his curricle at the little inn which skirts the village of Harthorpe. He affected to make some inquiries respecting the families in the neighborhood; and his host informed him that the ladies of the earl's family were great walkers, passing almost the whole of the day in the grounds. The measures to be adopted were now obvious. The paling belonging to Lord Tinemouth's park was only a few yards distant; but fearful of being observed, Pembroke sought a more obscure part. Scaling a wall which was covered by the branches of high trees, he found his way to the house through an almost impassable thicket.

He watched nearly an hour in vain for the appearance of Lady Albina, whose youth and elegance, he thought, would unequivocally distinguish her from the rest of the earl's household. Despairing of success, he was preparing to change his station, when he heard a sound among the dry leaves, and the next moment a beautiful young creature passed the bush behind which he was concealed. The fine symmetry of her profile assured him that she must be the daughter of Lady Tinemouth. She stooped to gather a china-aster. Knowing that no time should be lost, Pembroke gently emerged from his recess, but not in so quiet a manner as to escape the ear of Lady Albina, who instantly looking round, screamed, and would have fled, had he not thrown himself before her, and exclaimed, "Stay, Lady Albina! For heaven's sake, stay! I come from your mother!"

She gazed fearfully in his face, and tried to release her hand, which he had seized to prevent her flight.

"Do not be alarmed," continued he; "no harm is intended you. I am the son of Sir Robert Somerset, and the friend of your mother, who is now at the point of death. She implores to see you this night (for she has hardly an hour to live) to hear from your own lips that you do not hate her."

Lady Albina trembled dreadfully, and with faded cheeks and quivering lips replied, "Hate my mother! Oh, no! I have ever dearly loved her!"

A flood of tears prevented her speaking further; and Pembroke, perceiving that he had gained her confidence, put the doctor's letter into her hand. The gentle heart of Lady Albina bled at every word which her almost blinded eyes perused. Turning to Pembroke, who stood contemplating her lovely countenance with the deepest interest, she said, "Pray, Mr. Somerset, take me now to my mother. Were she to die before I arrive, I should be miserable for life. Alas! alas! I have never been allowed to behold her!—never been allowed to visit London, because my father knew that I believed my poor mother innocent, and would have seen her, had it been possible."

Lady Albina wept violently while she spoke, and giving her hand to Pembroke, timidly looked towards the house, and added, "You must take me this instant. We must hasten away, in case we should be surprised. If Lady Olivia were to know that I have been speaking with anybody out of the family, I should be locked up for months."

Pembroke did not require a second cammand from his beautiful charge. Conducting her through the unfrequented paths by which he had entered, he seated her in his curricle, and whipping his horses, set off, full speed, towards the melancholy goal of his enterprise.

CHAPTER XLII.

HARROWBY ABBEY.

WHILST the two anxious travellers were pursuing their sad journey, the inhabitants of the Abbey were distracted with apprehension lest the countess might expire before their arrival. Ever since Lady Tinemouth received information that Mr. Somerset was gone to the Wolds, hope and fear agitated her by turns, till, wearied out with solicitude and expectation, she turned her dim eyes upon Thaddeus, and said, in a languid voice, "My dear friend, it must be near midnight. I shall never see the morning; I shall never in this world see my child. I pray you, thank Mr. Somerset for all the trouble I have occasioned; and my daughter—my Albina! O father of mercies!" cried she, holding up her clasped hands, "pour all thy blessings upon her head! She never wilfully gave this broken heart a pang!"

The countess had hardly ended speaking when Thaddeus heard a bustle on the stairs. Suspecting that it might be the arrival of his friend, he made a sign to Dr. Cavendish to go and inquire. His heart beat violently whilst he kept his eye fixed on the door, and held the feeble pulse of Lady Tinemouth in his hand. The doctor re-entered, and in a low voice whispered, "Lady Albina is here."

The words acted like magic on the fading senses of the countess. With preternatural strength she started from her pillow, and catching hold of Sobieski's arm with both hers, cried, "O give her to me whilst I have life."

Lady Albina appeared, led in by Pembroke, but instantly quitting his hand, with an agonizing shriek she rushed towards the bed, and flung herself into the extended arms of her mother. Those arms closed on her, and the head of the countess rested on her bosom.

Dr. Cavendish perceived by the struggles of the young lady that she was in convulsions; and taking her off the bed, he consigned her to Pembroke and his friend, who, between them, carried her into another apartment. He remained to assist the countess.

Albina was removed; but the eyes of her amiable and injured mother were never again unclosed: she had breathed her last sigh, in grateful ecstasy, on the bosom of her daughter; and Heaven had taken her spotless soul to Himself.

Being convinced that the countess was indeed no more, the good doctor left her remains in charge of the women; and repairing to the adjoining room, found Lady Albina yet senseless in the arms of his two friends. She was laid on a sofa, and Cavendish was pouring some drops into her mouth, when he descried Thaddeus gliding out of the room. Desirous to spare him the shock of suddenly seeing the corpse of one whom he loved so truly, he said, "Stop, Mr. Constantine! I conjure you, do not go into the countess's room!"

The eyes of Thaddeus turned with emotion on the distressed face of the physician; one glance explained what the doctor durst not speak. Faintly answering, "I will obey you," he hurried from the apartment.

In the count's silent descent from Lady Albina's room to the breakfast-parlor, he too plainly perceived by the tears of the servants that he had now another sorrow to add to his mournful list. He hastened from participation in their clamorous laments, almost unseen, into the parlor, and shutting the door, threw himself into a chair; but rest induced thought, and thought subdued his soul. He started from his position; he paced the room in a paroxysm of anguish; he would have given worlds for one tear to relieve his oppressed heart. Ready to suffocate, he threw open a window and leaned out. Not a star was visible to light the darkness. The wind blew freshly, and with parched lips he inhaled it as the reviving breath of Heaven.

He was sitting on the window-seat, with his head leaning against the casement, when Pembroke entered unobserved; walking up to him, he laid his hand upon his arm, and ejaculated in a tremulous voice, "Thaddeus, dear Thaddeus!"

Thaddeus rose at the well-known sounds: they reminded him that he was not yet alone in the world; for his soul had been full of the dying image of his own mother. Clasping Somerset in his arms, he exclaimed, "Heaven has still reserved thee, faithful and beloved, to be my comforter! In thy friendship and fond memories," he added, with a yet heaving breast, "I shall find tender bonds of the past still to endear me to this world."

Pembroke received the embrace of his friend; he felt his tears upon his cheek; but he could neither return the one nor sympathize with the other. The conviction that he was soon to sever that cord, that he was to deprive the man who had preserved his life of the only stay of his existence, and abandon him to despair, struck to his soul. Grasping the hand of his friend, he gazed on his averted and dejected features with a look of desperate horror. "Sobieski," cried he, "whatever may happen, never forget that I swear I love you dearer than my life! And when I am forced to abandon my friend, I shall not be long of abandoning what will then be worthless to me."

Not perceiving the frenzied look which accompanied this energetic declaration, Thaddeus gave no other meaning to the words than a renewed assurance of his friend's affection.

The entrance of Dr. Cavendish disturbed the two young men, to whom he communicated the increased indisposition of Lady Albina.

"The shock she has received," said he, "has so materially shaken her frame, I have ordered her to bed and administered an opiate, which I hope will procure her repose; and you, my dear sir," added he, addressing the count, "you had better seek rest! The stoutest constitution might sink under what you have lately endured. Pray allow Mr. Somerset and myself to prevail with you, on our accounts, if not on your own, to retire for half an hour!"

Thaddeus, in disregard of his personal comfort, never infringed on that of others; he felt that he could not sleep, but he knew it would gratify his benevolent friends to suppose that he did; and accordingly he went to a room, and throwing himself on a bed, lay for an hour, ruminating on all that had passed.

There is an omnipresence in thought, or a celerity producing nearly the same effect, which brings within the short space of a few minutes the images of many foregoing years. In almost the same moment, Thaddeus reflected on his strange meeting with the countess; the melancholy story; her forlorn death-bed; the fatal secret that her vile husband and son were his father and brother; and that her daughter, whom his warm heart acknowledged as a sister, was with him under the same roof, and, like him, the innocent inheritor of her father's shame.

Whilst these multifarious and painful meditations were agitating his perturbed mind, Dr. Cavendish found repose on a couch; and Pembroke Somerset, resolving once more to try the influence of entreaty on the hitherto generous spirit of his father, with mingled hope and despondence commenced a last attempt to shake his fatal resolution, in the following letter:

"TO SIR ROBERT SOMERSET, BART, SOMERSET CASTLE.

"I have not ventured into the presence of my dear father since he uttered the dreadful words which I would give my existence to believe I had never heard. You denounced a curse upon me if I opposed your will to have me break all connection with the man who preserved my life! When I think on this, when I remember that it was from *you* I received a command so inexplicable from one of your character, so disgraceful to mine, I am almost mad; and what I shall be should you, by repeating your injunctions, force me to obey them, Heaven only knows! but I am certain that I cannot survive the loss of my honor; I cannot survive the sacrifice of all my principles of virtue which such conduct must forever destroy.

"Oh, my father! I conjure you, reflect, before, in compliance with an oath it was almost guilt to make, you decree your only son to everlasting shame and remorse. Act how I will, I shall never be happy more. I cannot live under your malediction; and should I give up my friend, my conscience will reproach me every instant of my existence. Can I draw the breath which he prolonged and cease to remember that I have abandoned him to want and misery? It were vain to flatter myself that he will condescend to escape either by the munificence which you offer as a compensation for my friendship. No; I cannot believe that his sensible and independent nature is so changed; circumstances never had any power over the nobility of his soul.

"Misfortune, which threw the Count Sobieski on the bounty of England, cannot make him appear otherwise in my eyes than as the idol of Warsaw, whose smile was honor and whose friendship conferred distinction.

"Though deprived of the splendor of command; though the eager circle of friends no longer cluster round him; though a stranger in this country, and without a home; though, in place of an equipage and retinue, he is followed by calamity and neglect, yet, in my mind, I still see him in a car of triumph: I see not only the opposer of his nation's enemies, but the vanquisher of his own desires. I see the heir of a princely house, who, when mankind have deserted him, is yet encompassed by his virtues. I see him, though cast out from a hardened and unjust society, still surrounded by the lingering spirits of those who were called to better worlds!

"And this is the man, my dear father, (whom I am sure, had he been of any other country than Poland, you would have selected from all other men to be the friend and example of your son),—this is he whom you command me to thrust away.

"I beseech you to examine this injunction! I am now writing under the same roof with him; it depends on you, my ever-revered father, whether I am doing so for the last time; whether this is the last day in which your son is to consider himself a man of honor, or whether he is henceforth to be a wretch overwhelmed with shame and sorrow!

"I have not yet dared to utter one word of your cruel orders to my unhappy friend. He is now retired to seek some rest, after the new anguish of having witnessed the almost sudden death of Lady Tinemouth. Should I have to tell him that he is to lose me too—but I cannot add more. Your own heart, my father, must tell you that my soul is on the rack until I have an answer to this letter."

"Before I shut my paper, let me implore you on my knees, whatever you may decide, do not hate me; do not load my breaking heart with a parent's curse! Whatever I may be, however low and degraded in my own eyes, still, that I sacrificed what is most precious to me, to my father, will impart the only consolation which will then have power to reach your dutiful and afflicted son.

"P. Somerset.

"Harrowby Abbey, two o'clock in the morning."

Dr. Cavendish remained in a profound sleep, whilst Pembroke, with an aching heart having written the above letter, and dispatched it by a man and horse, tried to compose himself to half an hour's forgetfulness of life and its turmoils; but he found his attempts as ineffectual as those of his friend.

Thaddeus had found no repose on his restless pillow. Reluctant to disturb the doctor and Somerset, who, he hoped.

having less cause for regret, were sleeping tranquilly, he remained in bed; but he longed for morning. To his fevered nerves, any change of position, with movement, seemed better than where he was, and with some gleams of pleasure he watched the dawn, and the rising of the son behind the opposite hill. He got up, opened the window to inhale the air, and looking out, saw a man throw himself off a horse, which was all in foam, and enter the house.

Surprised at this circumstance, he descended to the parlor to make inquiry, and met the man in the hall, who, being Pembroke's messenger, had returned express from the Castle, bearing an order from Sir Robert (who was taken alarmingly ill) that his son must come back immediately.

Dismayed with this new distress, Mr. Somerset, on its instant information, pressed the count so closely to his breast when he bade him farewell, that a more suspicious person might have apprehended it was a final parting; but Thaddeus discerned nothing more in the anguish of his friend's countenance than fear for the safety of Sir Robert; and fervently wishing his recovery, he bade Pembroke remember that should more assistance be necessary, Dr. Cavendish would remain at the Abbey until Lady Albina's return to the Wolds.

Mr. Somerset being gone, towards noon, when the count was anxiously awaiting the appearance of the physician from the room of the new invalid, he was disappointed by the abrupt entrance of two gentlemen. He rose, and with his usual courtesy to strangers, inquired their business? The elder of the men, with a fierce countenance and a voice of thunder, announced himself to be the Earl of Tinemouth, and the other his son.

"We are come," said he, standing at a haughty distance—"we are come to carry from this nest of infamy Lady Albina Stanhope, whom some one of her mother's paramours—perhaps you, sir—dared to steal from her father's home yesterday evening. And I am come to give you, sir, who I guess to be some fugitive vagabond! the chastisement your audacity deserves."

With difficulty the Count Sobieski suppressed the passions which were rising in his breast. He turned a scornful glance on the person of Lord Harwold (who, with an air of insufferable derision, was coolly measuring his figure through an eye-glass); and then, replying to the earl, said, in a firm voice, "My lord, whoever you suppose me to be, it matters not; I now stand in the place of Lady Tinemouth's confidential friend.

and to my last gasp I will prove myself the defender of her injured name."

"Her lover!" interrupted Lord Harwold, turning on his heel.

"Her defender, sir!" repeated Thaddeus, with a tremendous frown; "and shame and sorrow will pursue that son who requires a stranger to supply his duty."

"Wretch!" cried the earl, forgetting his assumed loftiness, and advancing passionately towards Thaddeus, with his stick held up; "how dare you address such language to an English nobleman?"

"By the right of nature, which holds her laws over all mankind," returned Thaddeus, calmly looking on the raised stick. "When an English nobleman forgets that he is a son, he deserves reproach from his meanest vassal."

"You see, my lord," cried Harwold, sliding behind his father, "what we bring on ourselves by harboring these democratic foreigners! Sir," added he, addressing himself to Thaddeus, "your dangerous principles shall be communicated to Government. Such traitors ought to hanged."

Sobieski eyed the enraged little lord with contempt; and turning to the earl, who was again going to speak, he said, in an unaltered tone, "I cannot guess, Lord Tinemouth, what is the reason of this attack on me. I came hither by accident; I found the countess ill; and, from respect to her excellent qualities, I remained with her until her eyes were closed forever. She desired to see her daughter before she died,—what human heart could deny a mother such a request?—and Pembroke Somerset, her kinsman, undertook to bring Lady Albina to the Abbey.

"Pembroke Somerset!" echoed the earl. "A pretty guard for my daughter, truly! I have no doubt that he is just such a fellow as his father—just such a person as yourself! I am not to be imposed upon. I know Lady Tinemouth to have been a disgrace to me, and you to be that German adventurer on whose account I sent her from London."

Shocked at this calumny on the memory of a woman whose fame from any other mouth came as unsullied as purity itself, Thaddeus gazed with horror at the furious countenance of the man whom he believed to be his father. His heart swelled: but not deigning to reply to a charge as unmanly as it was false, he calmly took out of his pocket two letters which the countess had dictated to her husband and her son.

Lord Harwold tore his open, cast his eyes over the first

words, then crumpling it in his hand, threw it from him, exclaiming, "I am not to be frightened either by her arts or the falsehoods of the fellows with whom she dishonored her name."

Thaddeus, no longer master of himself, sprang towards this unnatural son, and seized his arm with an iron grasp. "Lord Harwold!" cried he, in a dreadful voice, "were it not that I have some mercy on you for that parent's sake, to whom, like a parricide, you are giving a second death by such murderous slander, I would resent her wrongs at the hazard of your worthless life!"

"My lord! my lord!" cried the trembling Harwold, quaking under the gripe of Thaddeus, and shrinking from the terrible brightness of his eye,—"my lord! my lord, rescue me!"

The earl, almost suffocated with rage, called out, "Ruffian! let go my son!" and again raising his arm, aimed a blow at the head of Thaddeus, who, wrenching the stick out of the foaming lord's hand, snapped it in two, and threw the pieces out of the open window.

Lord Harwold took this opportunity to ring the bell violently, on which summons two of his servants entered the room.

"Now, you low-born, insolent scoundrel," cried the disarmed earl, stamping with his feet, and pointing to the men who stood at the door; "you shall be turned by the neck and heels out of this house. Richard, James, collar that fellow instantly."

Thaddeus only extended his arm to the men (who were looking confusedly on each other), and calmly said, "If either of you attempt to obey this command of your lord, you shall have cause to repent it."

The men retreated. The earl repeated his orders.

"Rascals! do as I command you, or instantly quit my service. I will teach you," added he, clenching his fist at the count, who stood resolutely and serenely before him, "I will teach you how to behave to a man of high birth."

The footmen were again deterred from approaching by a glance from the intimidating eyes of Thaddeus, who, turning with stern dignity to the storming earl, said, "You can teach me nothing about high birth that I do not already know. Could it be of any independent benefit to a man, then had I not received the taunts and insults which you have dared to cast upon me."

At that moment Dr. Cavendish, having heard a bustle, made

his appearance. Amazed at the sight of two strangers, who, from their enraged countenances and the proud elevation with which Thaddeus was standing between them, he rightly judged to be the earl and his son, he advanced towards his friend, intending to support him in the attack which he saw was menaced by the violent gestures of these visitors.

"Dr. Cavendish," said Thaddeus, speaking to him as he approached, "your name must be a passport to the confidence of any man; I therefore shall gratify the husband of my ever-lamented friend by quitting this house; but I delegate to you the office with which she entrusted me. I leave you in charge of her sacred remains, and of the jewels which you will find in her apartment. She desired that half of them might be given, with her blessing, to her daughter, and the other half, with her pardon, to her son."

"Tell me, Dr. Cavendish," cried the earl, as Thaddeus was passing him to leave the room, "who is that insolent fellow? By heaven, he shall smart for this!"

"Ay, that he shall," rejoined Lord Harwold, "if I have any interest with the Alien-office."

Dr. Cavendish was preparing to speak, when Thaddeus, turning round at this last threat of the viscount, said, "If I did not know myself to be above Lord Harwold's power, perhaps he might provoke me to treat him according to his deserts; but I abjure resentment, while I pity his delusions. For you, my lord," "added he, addressing the earl with a less calm countenance, "there is an angel in heaven who pleads against the insults you have uninquiringly and unjustly heaped upon an innocent man!"

Thaddeus disappeared from the apartment while uttering the last word; hastening from the house and park, he stopped near the brow of the hill, at the porch of his lately peaceful little hotel. The landlady was a sister of John Jacobs, the faithful servant of his lamented friend, and who was then watching the door of the neglected chamber in which the sacred remains of his dear mistress lay, as he would have guarded her life, had the foes who had now destroyed it been still menacing its flickering flame. The worthy couple were also attached to that benevolent lady, and with sad looks, but respectful welcoming, they saw Mr. Constantine re-enter their humble home, and assured him of its retirement as long as he might wish to abide in the neighborhood of the Abbey. Any prospect of repose promised elysium to him; and with harassed and torn nerves he took possession of his apartment, which looked down the road that led from the old monastic structure o tne town of Grantham. The rapidity of the recent events bewildered his senses, like the illusions of a dream. He had seen his father, his sister, his brother; and most probably he had parted from them forever!—at least, he hoped he should never again be tortured with the sight of Lord Tinemouth or his son.

"How," thought he, whilst walking up and down his solitary parlor, "could the noble nature of my mother love such a man? and how could he have held so long an empire over the pure heart he has just now broken."

He could nowhere discern, in the bloated visage and rageful gestures of the earl, any of that beauty of countenance or grace of manners which had alike charmed Therese Sobieski and the tender Adeliza.

Like those hideous chasms which are dug deep in the land by the impetuous sweep of a torrent, the course of violent passions leaves vast and irreparable traces on the features and in the soul. So it was with Lord Tinemouth.

"How legibly does vice or virtue," ejaculated Thaddeus, "write itself on the human face! The earl's might once have been fine, but the lineaments of selfishness and sin have degraded every part of him. Mysterious Providence! Can he be my father—can it be his blood that is now running in my veins? Can it be his blood that rises at this moment with detestation against him?"

Before the sun set, Sobieski was aroused from these painful soliloquies by still more painful feelings. He saw from his window a hearse driving at full speed up the road that ascended to the Abbey, and presently return at a slower pace, followed by a single black coach.

"Inhuman men!" exclaimed he, while pursuing with his eyes the tips of the sable plumes as the meagre cavalcade of mourners wound down the hill; could you not allow this poor corse a little rest? Must her persecution be extended to the grave? Must her cold relics be insulted, be hurried to the tomb without reverence—without decency?"

The filial heart that uttered this thought also of his own injured mother, and shrunk with horror at this climax of the earl's barbarity. Dr. Cavendish entered with a flushed countenance. He spoke indignantly of the act he still saw from the window, which he denounced as a sacrilege against the dead. "Not four-and-twenty hours since," cried he, "she expired! and she is hurried into the cold bosom of the earth, like a criminal, or a creature whose ashes a moment above ground might spread a pestilence. Oh, how can that sweet victim, Lady Albina, share such peccant blood?"

Thaddeus, whose soul had just writhed under a similar question with regard to himself, could little bear the repetition, and interrupted the good physician by tenderly inquiring how she had borne that so abrupt removal of her mother's remains.

"With mute anguish," returned Dr. Cavendish, in a responding, calmer voice of pity; "and though I had warned her father that the shock of so suddenly tearing his daughter from such beloved relics might peril her own life, he continued obdurate; and putting her into his travelling chariot in a state of insensibility, along with her maid, in a few minutes afterwards I saw him set off in a hired post-chaise, accompanied by his detestable son, loaded with more than one curse, muttered by the honest rustics. Only servants followed in that mourning coach."

In the midst of this depressing conversation a courier arrived from Stamford to Dr. Cavendish, recalling him immediately to return thither, the invalid there having sustained an alarming relapse. The good doctor, sincerely reluctant to quit Thaddeus (whom he still knew by no other name than Constantine), ordered the dispatch-chaise to the hotel door. When it was announced, he shook hands with the now lonely survivor of his departed friend in this stranger land, requested that he might hear from him before he left that part of the country for London again, and bidding him many cordial adieus, continued to look out of the back window of the carriage, until the faint light of the moon and the receding glimmer of the village candles finally hid the little spot that yet contained this young and sadly-stricken exile from his lingering eyes.

CHAPTER XLIII.

THE OLD VILLAGE HOTEL.

FOR the first time during many nights, Thaddeus slept soundly; but his dreams were disturbed, and he awoke from them at an early hour, unrefreshed and in much fever.

The simple breakfast which his attentive host and hostess set before him was scarcely touched. Their nicely-dressed dinner met with the same fate. He was ill, and possessed neither appetite nor spirits to eat. The good people being too civil to intrude upon him, he sat alone in his window from eight o'clock (at which hour he had arisen) until the cawing of the rooks, as they returned to the Abbey-woods, reminded him of the approach of evening. He was uneasy at the absence of Somerset, not so much on his own account, as on that of Sir Robert, whose increased danger might have occasioned this delay; however, he hoped otherwise. Longing earnestly for a temporary sanctuary under his friend's paternal roof, in the quiet of its peace and virtues, he trusted that the sympathy of Pembroke, the only confidant of his past sorrows, would tend to heal his recent wounds (though the nature of the most galling, he felt, must ever remain unrevealed even to him!) and so fit him, should it be required, to yet further brave the buffets of an adverse fate. Nor was Miss Beaufort forgotten. If ever one idea more than another sweetened the bitterness of his reflections, it was the remembrance of Mary Beaufort. Whenever her image rose before him—whether he were standing in the lonely day with folded arms, in vacant gaze on the valley beneath, or when lying on his watchful pillow he opened his aching eyes to the morning light—still, as her angel figure presented itself to his mind, he did indeed sigh, but it was a sigh laden with balm; it did not tear his breast like those which had been wrung from him by the hard hand of calamity and insult. It was the soft breath of a hallowed love, which makes man dream of heaven, while he feels sinking to an early grave. Thaddeus felt it delightful to recollect how she had looked on him that day in Hyde Park, when she "bade him take care of his own life, while so devoted to that of his dying friend!" and how she "blessed him in his task," with a voice of tenderness so startlingly sacred to his soul in its accents, that in remembering her words now, when so near the moment of his again seeing and hearing her, his soul expanded towards her, agitated, indeed, but soothed and comforted.

"Sweet Mary!" murmured he, "I shall behold thee once more; I shall again revive under thy kind smile! Oh, it is happiness to know that I owe my liberty to thee, though I may not dare to tell thee so! Yet my swelling heart may cherish the dear consciousness, and, bereaved though I am of all I formerly loved, be indeed blessed while on earth with the heaven-bestowed privilege of loving thee, even in silence and forever! Alas! alas! a man without kindred or a country dare not even wish thee to be his!" A sigh from the depths of his soul closed this soliloquy.

The sight of Pembroke riding through the field towards the

little inn, recalled the thoughts of Sobieski to that dear friend alone. He went out to meet him. Mr. Somerset saw him, and putting his horse to a brisk canter, was at his side in a few minutes. Thaddeus asked anxiously about the baronet's health. Pembroke answered with an incoherency devoid of all meaning. Thaddeus looked at him with surprise, but from increased anxiety forbore to repeat the question. They walked towards the inn; still Pembroke did not appear to recover himself, and his evident absence of mind and the wild rambling of his eyes were so striking, that Thaddeus could have no doubt of some dreadful accident.

As soon as they had entered the little parlor, his friend cast himself into a chair, and throwing off his hat, wiped away the perspiration which, though a cold October evening, was streaming down his forehead. Thaddeus endured a suspense which was almost insupportable.

"What is the direful matter, dear Pembroke? Is any we honor, and love, ill unto death?" His pale face showed that he apprehended it, and he thought it might be Mary.

"No, no," returned Pembroke; "everybody is well, excepting myself and my father, who, I verily believe, has lost his senses; at any rate he will drive me mad."

The manner in which this reply was uttered astonished Thaddeus so much, that he could only gaze with wonder on the convulsed feature of his friend. Pembroke observed his amazement, and laying his hand on his arm, said, "My dear, dear Sobieski! what do I not owe to you? Good Heaven! how humbled am I in your sight! But there is a Power above who knows how intimately you are woven with every artery of this heart."

"I believe it, my kind Pembroke," cried Thaddeus, yet more alarmed than before; "tell me what it is that distresses you? If my counsel or my sympathy can offer anything to comfort or assist you, you know I am your own."

Pembroke burst into tears, and covering his streaming eyes with his handkerchief, exclaimed, "I am indeed distressed—distressed even beyond your comfort. Oh! how can I speak it! You will despise my father! You will spurn me!"

"Impossible!" cried Thaddeus with energy, though his flushed cheek and fainting heart immediately declared that he had anticipated what he must hear.

"I see," cried Pembroke, regarding the altered features of his friend with a glance of agony—"I see that you think it is possible that my father can sink me below my own contempt."

The benumbing touch of ingratitude ran through the veins of Thaddeus; his frame was chilled—was petrified; but his just affection and calmed countenance proclaimed how true a judgment he had passed on the whole. He took the burning hand of Mr. Somerset in his own, and, with a steady and consoling voice, said, "Assure yourself, dear Pembroke, whatever be the commands of your father, I shall adhere to them. I cannot understand by these generous emotions that he objects to receive me as your friend. Perhaps," added he,—a flash of suspicion gleaming through his mind,—"perhaps Miss Beaufort may have perceived the devotedness of my heart, and disdaining my——"

"Hush, for Heaven's sake!" cried Pembroke, starting from his chair; "do not implicate my poor cousin! Do not add to her disappointment the misery that you suspect her! No, Thaddeus," continued he, in a calmer tone; "Mary Beaufort loves you: she confessed it in an agony of grief on my bosom, just before I came away; and only through her I dare ever expect to meet forgiveness from *you*. In spite of my father, you may marry her. She has no curse to dread; she need not sacrifice all that is most precious in her sight to the obstinate caprice of criminal resentment."

"A curse!" reiterated Thaddeus. "How is this!—what have I done, to deserve such hatred from your father?"

"Oh! nothing," cried Pembroke—"nothing. My father never saw you. My father thanks you for all that you have done for me; but it is your country that he hates. Some Polander, years back, injured him; and my father took a fatal oath against the whole nation. He declares that he cannot, he will not, break it, were he by so doing to save his own life, or even mine; for, (Heaven forgive me!) I was this morning wrought up to such frenzy, that I threatened to destroy myself rather than sacrifice my gratitude and honor to his cruel commands! Nay, to convince you that his is no personal enmity to yourself, he ordered me to give you writings which will put you in possession of an independence forever. I have them with me."

All the pride of his princely house rose at once in the breast of Thaddeus. Though full of indignation at this insult of Sir Robert's, he regarded the averted face of his friend with compassion, whilst in a firm voice he rejected the degrading compromise.

"Tell your father," added he, addressing Pembroke, in a tone which even his affection could not soften from a command, "that my absence is not to be bought with money, nor my friendship so rewarded."

Pembroke covered his burning face with his hands. This sight at once brought down the haughty spirit of Sobieski, who continued in gentler accents, "Whatever be the sentiments of Sir Robert Somerset, they shall meet with due attention from me. He is your father, therefore I respect him; but he has put it out of his power to oblige me: I cannot accept his bounty. Though your heart, my dearest Pembroke, is above all price, yet I will make it a sacrifice to your duty." And by so doing put the last seal on my misfortunes, was the meaning of the heavy sigh which accompanied his last words.

Pembroke traversed the room in an agony. "Merciful Providence!" cried he, wringing his clasped hands, "direct me! Oh, Thaddeus, if you could read my tortured heart, you would pity me; you would see that this affair is tearing my soul from my body. What am I to do? I cannot, I will not, part with you forever."

Thaddeus, with a calm sadness, drew him to a seat. "Be satisfied," said he, "that I am convinced of your affection. Whatever may happen, this assurance will be sufficient to give me comfort; therefore, by that affection, I entreat you, dear Pembroke, not to bring regret to me, and reproach on yourself, by disobeying in any way the will of your father in this matter! If we separate for life, remember, my beloved friend, that the span of our existence here is short; we shall meet again in a happier world—perhaps more blest, for having immolated our wishes to hard duty in this."

"Cease, Sobieski, cease!" cried Pembroke; "I can draw no consolation from this reasoning. It is not duty to obey a hatred little short of distraction; and if we now separate, I feel that I never shall know peace again. Good Heaven! what comfort can I find when you are exposed to all the indignities which the world levels against the unfortunate? Can I indulge in the luxuries of my father's house when I know that you have neither a home nor subsistence? No, Thaddeus, I am not such a villain. I will not give you up, though my father should load me with curses. I trust there is a just Power above who would avert them."

Perceiving that argnment would not only be fruitless, but might probably incense his friend's irritated nature to the commission of some rash action, Thaddeus pretended to overlook the frantic gesture and voice which terminated this speech, and assuming a serene air, replied: "Let this be the subject of a future conversation. At present I must conjure you, by the happiness of us both, to return to the Castle. You know my message to Sir Robert. Present my respects to your aunt; and," added he, after an agitated pause, "assure Miss Beaufort that whilst I have life, her goodness, her sometimes remembrance, will be——"

Pembroke interrupted him. "Why these messages, dear Thaddeus? Do not suppose, though I fulfil my father's orders to return to Somerset to-night, that it is our separation. Gracious Heaven! Is it so easy to part forever?"

"Not forever! Oh, no," replied Thaddeus, grasping his hand; "we shall see each other again; only, meanwhile, repeat those, alas! inadequate messages to your aunt and cousin. Go, my dear Pembroke, to your father; and may the Lord of Heaven bless you!"

The last words were spoken in almost a stifled voice, as he opened his arms and strained his friend to his breast.

"I shall see you to-morrow," cried Pembroke; "on no other condition will I leave you now."

Thaddeus made no further answer to this demand (which he determined should never be granted) than a second embrace. Pembroke went out of the room to order his horse; then, returning, he stood at the door, and holding out his hand to the count, repeated, "Farewell till to-morrow." Thaddeus pressed it warmly, and he disappeared.

The outward gate closed after his friend, but Sobieski remained on the seat into which he had thrown himself. He did not venture to move, lest he should by chance catch a second glance of Pembroke from the window. Now that he was gone, he acknowledged the full worth of what he had relinquished. He had resigned a man who loved him; one who had known and revered his ever-lamented grandfather, and his mother—the only one with whom he could have discoursed of their virtues! He had severed the link which had united his present state with his former fortunes! and throwing his arms along a table that stood near him, he leaned his aching head upon them, and in idea followed with a bleeding heart the progress and reception of his friend at the Castle.

The racking misery which tortured the mind of Mr. Somerset was not borne with equal resignation. Conscious of his having inflicted fresh wounds on the breast of his truest friend, his spirits were so ill adapted t any conversation, that he was pleased rather than disappointea when he found the supper-room at the Castle quite vacant, and only one cover on the table awatting his arrival.

He asked a few questions of the servants, who informed him that it was past twelve o'clock, and that Sir Robert, who had become worse, had retired to bed early in the evening.

"And where are my aunt and cousin?" demanded Pembroke.

One of the men replied that, in consequence of Miss Beaufort having been taken suddenly indisposed, both the ladies left the saloon before eleven. Pembroke readily guessed the cause of her disorder; he too truly ascribed it to Mary's anxiety respecting the reception which the noble Sobieski would give to his disgraceful proposition. Sighing bitterly, he said no more but went to his chamber.

The restless state of his mind awoke Mr. Somerset by times. Anxious for the success of an application which he intended to make to his beloved cousin, whose pure and virgin heart he believed did indeed here sympathize with his own, he traversed the terrace for an hour before he was summoned to breakfast. The baronet continuing too ill to leave his room, the ladies only were in the parlor when he entered. Miss Dorothy, who had learned the particulars of the late events from her niece, longed to ask Pembroke how his noble friend would act on her brother's so strange and lamentable conduct —conduct so unlike himself in any other circumstance of gratitude in his life. But every time she moved her lips to inquire, her nephew's inflamed eyes and wan countenance made her fear to venture on the subject. Mary sat in mute dejection, watching the agitation of his features; and when he rose to quit the room, still in silence, she looked wistfully towards him. Pembroke turned at the same moment, and holding out his hand to her, said, "Come, Mary: I want to say something to you. Will you walk with me on the terrace?"

With a beating heart Miss Beaufort took his arm, and proceeded without a word until they ascended the stone steps and reached the terrace. A mutual deep-drawn sigh was the first opening to a conversation on which the souls of both hung. Pembroke was the first who spoke.

"My dear Mary," cried he, "you are now my sole dependence. From what I told you yesterday of my father's inflexibility, we can have no hope of his relenting: indeed, after what has passed, I could not flatter myself that Thaddeus Sobieski would now submit to any obligation at his hands. Already he has refused, with all the indignation I expected, Sir Robert's offer of an annuity. My dear cousin, how can I exist and yet witness this my best friend in distress, and living without the succor of my friendship? Heaven knows, this cannot be the case, for I would sooner perish than venture to insult the man my father has treated so ill with any pecuniary offers from me! Therefore, dear girl, it is on you alone that I depend. With his whole soul, as our marriage service says, Thaddeus 'worships you;' you love him! In a few days you will become of age. You will be your own mistress. Marry him, my beloved cousin," cried Pembroke, pressing her hand to his lips, "and relieve my heart from a load of misery! Be generous, my sweet Mary," added he, supporting her now trembling frame against his breast; "act up to your noble nature, and offer him, by me, that hand which his calamities and disinterestedness preclude him from wooing himself."

Miss Beaufort, hardly able to articulate, replied, "I would give him all that I possess could it purchase him one tranquil hour. I would serve him forever could I do it and be unknown? but——"

"O, do not hesitate!—do not doubt!" interrupted Pembroke. "To serve your friends, I know you are capable of the most extraordinary exertions. I know there is nothing within the range of possibility that your generous disposition would not attempt; then, my beloved Mary, dare to be what you are, by having the magnanimity to act as you know you ought—by offering your hand to him. Show the noble Sobieski that you really deserve the devotion of a hero's heart—deserves to be his consolation, who, in losing his mother, lost an angel like yourself."

"Dear Pembroke," replied Miss Beaufort, wiping the gliding tears from her burning cheek, "after the confession which you drew from me yesterday, I will not deny that to be this to your friend would render me the happiest of created beings; but I cannot believe what your sanguine affection tells me. I cannot suppose, situated as I was at Lady Dundas's, surrounded by frivolous and contemptible society, that he could discover anything in me to warrant such a vanity. Every way embarrassed as I was, disliking my companions, afraid of my own interest in him, a veil was drawn over my mind, through which he could neither judge of my good nor bad qualities. How, then, can I flatter myself, or do the Count Sobieski so great an injury, as to imagine that he could conceive any preference for so insignificant a being as I must have appeared?"

It was some time before Pembroke could shake this prepossession of a sincere humility from Miss Beaufort's mind. But after having set in every possible light the terms with which his friend had spoken of her, he at length convinced her of what her heart so earnestly wished to believe—that the love of Sobieski was indeed hers.

Mr. Somerset's next achievement was to overcome her scruples against sanctioning him with the commission he was bent on communicating to Thaddeus. But from the continual recurrence of her apprehensions, that the warm affection of her cousin had too highly colored the first part of his representation, this latter task was not more easy to accomplish than the former.

In vain she remonstrated, in vain she doubted, in vain demurred. Pembroke would not be denied. He saw her heart was with him; and when with faltering lips she assented to the permission, which he almost extorted, she threw her arms round his neck, and implored him, "by all he loved and honored, to be careful of her peace; to remember that she put into his charge all that was most precious to woman—the modesty of her sex and her own self-esteem!"

Delighted at this consent, notwithstanding he received it through the medium of many tears, he fondly and gratefully pressed her to his bosom, uttering his own soul's fervent conviction of a future domestic happiness to them all. Having stood till he saw her re-enter the house from a door on the terrace, he mounted his horse and set off on the spur towards Harrowby Hill.

CHAPTER XLIV.

LETTERS OF FAREWELL.

WHEN Thaddeus recovered from the reverie into which he fell on the departure of Mr. Somerset, he considered how he might remove out of a country in which he had only met with and occasioned distress.

The horrid price that Pembroke's father had set on the continuance of his son's friendship with a powerless exile was his curse. Whatever might have been the injury any individual of now annihilated Poland could, in its palmy days of independence, and sometimes pride, inflict on this implacable Englishman, of a nature that appeared to have blinded him to even human feeling, Thaddeus felt so true an indignation against such cruel injustice, and so much of a contrary sentiment towards the noble son of this hard parent, that he determined to at once relieve the warring mind of Pembroke of any further conflict on his account by immediately quitting England. Averse to a second interview with a friend so justly beloved, which could only produce them new pangs, he resolved on instant preparations—that another morn should not rise upon him in the neighborhood of Somerset Castle. Taking up a pen, with all the renewed loneliness of his fate brooding on his heart, he wrote two letters.

One he addressed to Mr. Somerset, bidding him that farewell which he confessed he could never take. As he wrote, his hand trembled, his bosom swelled, and he hastily shut his eyelids, to withhold his tears from showing themselves on the paper. His emotion, his grief, were driven back, were concealed, but the tenderness of his soul flowed over the letter. He forgave Pembroke's father for Pembroke's sake; and in spite of their personal disunion, he vowed that no earthly power should restrain his love from following the steps of his friend, even into the regions of eternity. He closed his melancholy epistle with informing Mr. Somerset that, as he should quit not only England directly, but Europe, any search after him which his generons nature might dictate would be in vain.

Though Thaddeus Sobieski would have disdained a life of dependence on the greatest potentate of the world; though he rejected with the same sincerity a similar proposal from his friend, and despised the degrading offer of Sir Robert, yet he did not disparage his dignity, not infringe on the disinterested nature of friendship, when he retained the money which Pembroke had conveyed to him in prison. Thaddeus never acted but from principle. His honorable and penetrating mind knew exactly at what point to draw the tender thread of delicacy—the cord of independence. But pride and independence were with him distinct terms. Receiving assistance from a friend and leaning on him wholly for support have different meanings. He accepted the first with gratitude; he would have thought it impossible to live and endure the last. Indeed Thaddeus would have considered himself unworthy to confer a benefit if he had not known how to receive one. But had not Pembroke told him "the whole gift was Mary Beaufort's?" And what were his emotions then? They were full of an ineffable sense of happiness inexplicable to himself. Mary Beaufort was the donor, and it was bliss to have it so, and to know it was so. With these impressions again throbbing at his heart, he began a short letter to her, which he felt must crush that heart forever.

"TO MISS BEAUFORT.

"My faculties lose their power when I take up my pen to address, for the first and the last time, Miss Beaufort. I hardly know what I would say—what I ought to say; I dare not venture to write all that I feel. But have you not been my benefactress? Did you not assert my character and give me liberty when I was calumniated and in distress? Did you not ward from me the scorn of unpitying folly? Did you not console me with your own compassion? You have done all this; and surely you will not despise the gratitude of a heart which you have condescended to sooth and to comfort. At least I cannot leave England forever without imploring blessings on the head of Miss Beaufort, without thanking her on my knees, on which I am writing, for that gracious and benign spirit which discovered a breaking heart under the mask of serenity, which penetrated through the garb of poverty and dependence, and saw that the condemned Constantine was not what he seemed! Your smiles, Miss Beaufort, your voice speaking commiseration, were my sweetest consolations during those heavy months of bitterness which I endured at Dundas House. I contemplated you as a pitying angel, sent to reconcile me to a life which had already become a burden. These are the benefits which Miss Beaufort has bestowed on a friendless exile; these are the benefits which she has bestowed on me! and they are written on my soul. Not until I go down into the grave can they be forgotten. Ah! not even then, for when I rise again, I shall find them still registered there.

"Farewell, most respected, most dear, most honored! My passing soul seems in those words. O, may the Father of heaven bless with his almighty care her whose name will ever be the first and the last in the prayer of the far distant

"THADDEUS CONSTANTINE SOBIESKI.

"HARROWBY VILLAGE, MIDNIGHT."

When he had finished this epistle, with a tremulous hand he consigned it to the same cover that contained his letter to Somerset. Then writing a few lines to the worthy master of the inn, (the brother-in-law of the faithful servant of his late lamented maternal friend,) saying that a sudden occasion had required his immediate departure at that untimely hour, he enclosed a liberal compensation in gold for the attentive services of both the honest man and his warm-hearted wife. Having sealed each packet, he disposed them so on the table that they might be the first things seen on entering the room.

He had fixed on deep night as the securest time for commencing unobserved his pedestrian tour. The moon was now full, and would be a sufficient guide, he thought, on his solitary way. He had determined to walk to London by the least public paths; meaning to see kind Mrs. Robson, and bid her a grateful farewell before he should embark, probably never to return, for America.

He had prepared his slender baggage before he sat down to write the two letters which had cost him so many pangs; compressed within a light black leather travelling-bag, he fastened it over his shoulders by its buckled straps, in the manner of a soldier's knapsack. He then put the memorandum-book which contained his "world's wealth," now to be carefully husbanded, into a concealed pocket in the breast of his waistcoat, feeling, while he pressed it down upon his heart, that his mother's locket and Miss Beaufort's chain kept guard over it.

"Ah!" cried he, as he gently closed the low window by which he leaped into the garden: "England, I leave thee forever, and within thee all that on this earth had been left to me to love. Driven from thee! Nay, driven as if I were another Cain, from the face of every spot of earth that ever had been or would be dear to me! Oh, woe to them who began the course. And thou, Austria, ungrateful leader in the destruction of the country which more than once was thy preserver!—could there be any marvel that the last of the Sobieskis should perish with her? What accumulated sins must rest on thy head, thou seducer of other nations into the spoliation and dismemberment of the long-proved bulwark of Christendom? Assuredly, every hasty sigh that rebels in the breasts of Poland's outcast sons against the mystery of her doom will plead against thee at the judgment-seat of Heaven!"

He went on at a rapid pace through several fields, his heart and soul full of those remembrances, and the direful echoes to them he had met in England. Stopping a moment at the boundary-gate of the Harrowby domains,—the property of a disgraceful owner of a name that might have been his, had not his nobler mother preserved to him that of Sobieski,—he stretched out his arms to the heavens, over which a bleak north-west wind was suddenly collecting dark and spreading clouds, and exclaimed, in earnest supplication, "Oh, righteous Power of Mercy! in thy chastening, grant me fortitude to bear with resignation to thy will the miseries I may yet have to encounter

Ah!" added he, his heart melting as the images presented themselves even as visions to his soul, "teach me to forget what I have been. Teach me to forget that on this dreadful October night twelve months ago I clasped the dying body of my revered grandfather in these arms!"

He could not speak further. Leaning his pale face against the gate, he remained for a few minutes dissolved in all a son's sorrow; then, recovering himself by a sudden start, he proceeded with hurried steps through the further extending meadows until they conducted him by a short village-lane into the high road.

It was on the 10th of October, 1795, that the Count Sobieski commenced this lonely and melancholy journey. It was the 10th of October in the preceding year that he found the veteran palatine bleeding to death in the midst of a heap of slain. The coincidence of his renewed banishment and present consequent mental sufferings with those of that fatal period powerfully affected him, recalling, in the vivid colors of an actual existence, scenes and griefs which the numerous successive events he had passed through had considerably toned down into dream-like shades.

But now, when memory, by one unexpected stroke, had once conjured up the happy past of his early life and its as early blighting, true to her nature, she raised before his mind's eye every hope connected with it and his present doom, till, almost distracted, he quickened his speed. He then slackened it; he quickened it again; but nothing could rid him of those successive images which seem to glide around him like mournful apparitions of the long-lamented dead.

When the dawn broke and the sun rose, he found himself advanced several miles on the south side of Ponton Hill. The spiry aisles of Harrowby Abbey were discernible through the mist, and the towers of Somerset Castle, from their height and situation, were as distinctly seen as if he had been at their base. Neither of these objects were calculated to raise the spirits of Thaddeus. The sorrows of the countess, whose eyes he so recently had closed, and the treatment which he afterwards received from the man to whom he owed his life, were recollections which made him turn from the Abbey with a renewed pang and fix his eyes on Somerset. He looked towards its ivied battlements with all the regret and all the tenderness which can overflow a human heart. Under that roof he believed the eyes of his almost, indeed, worshipped Mary were sealed in sleep; and in an instant his agitated soul addressed her as if she had been present.

"Farewell, most lovely, most beloved! The conviction that it is to ensure the peace of my now only friend on earth, my faithful Pembroke, that I resign the hope of ever beholding thee again in this life, will bring me one comfort, at least, in my barren exile!"

Thus communing with his troubled spirit, he walked the whole day on his way to London. Totally absorbed in meditation, he did not remark the gaze of curiosity which followed his elegant yet distressed figure as he passed through the different towns and villages. Musing on the past, the present, and the future, he neither felt hunger nor thirst, but, with a fixed eye and abstracted countenance, pursued his route until night and weariness overtook him near a cross-road, far away from any house.

Thaddeus looked around and above. The sky was then clear and glittering with stars; the moon, shining on a branch of the Ouse which divides Leicestershire from Northamptonshire, lit the green heath which skirted its banks. He wished not for a more magnificent canopy; and placing his bag under his head, he laid himself down beneath a hillock of furze, and slept till morning.

When he awoke from a heavy sleep, which fatigue and fasting had rendered more oppressive than refreshing, he found that the splendors of the night were succeeded by a heavy rain, and that he was wet through. He arose with stiffness in his limbs, pain in his head, and a dimness over his eyes, with a sense of weakness which almost disabled him from moving. He readily judged that he had caught cold; and every moment feeling himself grow worse, he thought it necessary to seek some house where he might procure rest and assistance.

Leaning on his closed umbrella, which, in his precarious circumstances of travelling, he used in preference to a walking-stick, and no longer able to encumber himself with even the light load of his bag, he cast it amongst the brambles near him. Thinking, from the symptoms he felt, that he might not have many more hours to endure the ills of life, he staggered a few yards further. No habitation appeared; his eyes soon seemed totally obscured, and he sunk down on a bank. For a minute he attempted to struggle with the cold grasp of death, which he believed was fastening on his heart.

"And are my days to be so short?—are they to end thus?" was the voice of his thoughts,—for he was speechless. "Oh! thou merciful Providence, pardon my repining, and those who have brought me to this! My only Father, hear me!"

These were the last movements of his soundless lips, whilst his blood seemed freezing to insensibility. His eyelids were closed, and pale, and without sign of animation, he lay at the foot of a tree nigh which he had dropped.

He remained a quarter of an hour in this dead-like state before he was observed; at length, a gentleman who was passing along that road, on his way to his country-seat in the neighborhood, thought he perceived a man lying amongst the high grass a little onward on the heath. He stopped his carriage instantly, though driven by four spirited horses, and ordering one of the outriders to alight, bade him examine whether the object in view were living or dead.

The servant obeyed; and presently returning with an affrighted countenance, he informed his master that "it was the body of a young man, who, by his dress, appeared to be a gentleman; and being quite senseless, he supposed he had been waylaid and murdered by footpads." The features of the benevolent inquirer immediately reflected the alarm of his informant. Ordering the chariot door to be opened, he took in his, hand a bottle of medicine, (which, from his own invalid states was his carriage companion,) and, stepping out, hastened to the side of the apparently lifeless Thaddeus.

By this time all the servants were collected round the spot. The master himself, whilst he gazed with pity on the marble features of the stranger, observed with pleasure that he saw no marks of violence. Supposing that the present accident might have been occasioned by a fit, and thinking it possible to recall life, he desired that the unfortunate person's neck-cloth might be unloosened, and removing his hat, he contrived to pour some drops into his mouth. Their warmth renewed pulsation to the heart, for one of the men, who was stooping, declared that it beat under his hand. When the benevolent gentleman was satisfied of the truth of this report, he bade his servants place the poor traveller in his carriage; having only another mile or two to go, he said he hoped his charge might be restored at the end of so short a drive.

Whilst the postilions drove rapidly towards the house, the cold face of Thaddeus rested on the bosom of his benefactor, who continued to chafe his temples with eau de Cologne until the chariot stopped before the gates. The men carried the count into the house, and leaving him with their master and a medical man, who resided near, other restoratives were applied which in a short time restored him to consciousness. When he was recalled to recollection, and able to distinguish objects, he saw that he was supported by two gentlemen, and in a spacious chamber.

Gratitude was an active virtue in the soul of Thaddeus. At the moment of his awakening from that sleep which, when it fell upon him, he believed would last until time should be lost in eternity, he pressed the hands of those who held his own, not doubting but that they were the good Samaritans who had preserved him from perishing.

The younger of the gentlemen, perceiving, by the animated lustre which spread over his patient's eyes, that he was going to speak, put his hand on his lips, and said, "Pardon me, sir! you must be mute! Your life at present hangs on a thread; the slightest exertion might snap it. As all you want is rest and resuscitation to supply some great loss which the vital powers have sustained, I must require that you neither speak nor be spoken to until I give permission. Meanwhile, be satisfied, sir, that you are in the kindest hands. This gentleman," added he, (pointing to his friend, who bore the noble presence of high rank,) "saw you on the heath, and brought you to his house, where you now are."

Thaddeus bowed his head to them both in sign of obedience and gratitude, and the elder, with a kind bend of his mild eyes, in silence left the room.

CHAPTER XLV.

DEERHURST.

NEXT morning, when the seal was taken off the lips of the object of their care, he expressed in grateful terms his deep sense of the humanity which had actuated both the gentleman to take so generous an interest in his fate.

"You owe no thanks to me," replied the one who had enjoined and released him from silence, and who was now alone with him; "I am only the agent of another. Yet I do not deny that, in obeying the benevolent orders of Sir Robert Somerset, I have frequent opportunities of gratifying my own heart."

Thaddeus was so confounded at this discovery that he could not speak, and the gentleman proceeded.

"I am apothecary to Sir Robert's household, and as my

excellent employer has been long afflicted with an ill state of health, I live in a small Lodge at the other end of the park. He is the boast of the county: the best landlord and the kindest neighbor. All ranks of people love him; and when he dies, (which his late apoplectic fits make it too probable may be soon,) both poor and rich will lose their friend. Ill as he was this morning, when I told him you were out of danger, he expressed a pleasure which did him more good than all my medicines."

Not considering the wildness of the question, Thaddeus hastily demanded, "Does he know who I am?"

The honest apothecary stared at the look and tone with which these words were delivered, and then replied, "No, sir; is there any reason to make you wish that he should not?"

"Certainly none," replied Thaddeus, recollecting himself; "but I shall be impatient until I have an opportunity of telling him how grateful I am for the goodness he has shown to me as a stranger."

Surprised at these hints, (which the count, not considering their tendency, allowed to escape him,) the apothecary gathered sufficient from them, united with the speaker's superior mien, to make him suppose that his patient was some emigrant of quality, whom Sir Robert would rejoice in having served. These surmises and conclusions having passed quickly through the worthy gentleman's brain, he bowed his head with that respect which the generous mind is proud to pay to nobility in ruins, and resumed:

"Whoever you may be, sir, a peasant or a prince, you will meet with British hospitality from the noble owner of this mansion. The magnificence of his spirit is equalled by the goodness of his heart; and I am certain that Sir Robert will consider as fortunate the severe attack which, bringing him from Somerset for change of air, has afforded him an opportunity of serving you."

Thaddeus blushed at the strain of this speech. Readily understanding what was passing in the mind of the apothecary, he hardly knew what to reply. He paused for a moment, and then said, "All you have declared, sir, in praise of Sir Robert Somerset I cannot doubt is deserving. I have already felt the effects of his humanity, and shall ever remember that my life was prolonged by his means; but I have no pretensions to the honor of his acquaintance. I only wish to see him, that I may thank him for what he has done; therefore, if you will permit me to rise this evening, instead of to-morrow morning, you will oblige me."

To this request the apothecary gave a respectful yet firm denial, and went down stairs to communicate his observations to his patron. When he returned, he brought back a request to his patient from the baronet, even as a personal consideration for his host's solicitude concerning him, to remain quietly in the perfect repose of his closed chamber until next day; then it might be hoped Sir Robert would find him sufficiently recovered to receive his visit without risk. To this Sobieski could not but assent, in common courtesy, as well as in grateful feeling; yet he passed in anything but repose the rest of the day, and the anxiety which continued to agitate him while reflecting that he was receiving these obligations from his implacable enemy so occupied and disturbed him, that he spent a sleepless night. The dawn found his fever much augmented; but no corporeal sufferings could persuade him to defer seeing the baronet and immediately leaving his house. Believing, as he did, that all this kindness would have been withheld had his host known on whom he was pouring such benefits, he thought that every minute which passed over him while under Sir Robert's roof inflicted a new outrage on his own respect and honor.

To this end, then, as soon as Mr. Middleton, the apothecary, retired to breakfast, Thaddeus rose from his bed, and was completely dressed before he returned. He had effected this without any assistance, for he was in possession of his travelling-bag. One of the outriders having discerned it amongst the herbage, while the others were busied in carrying its helpless owner to the carriage, he had picked it up, and on the arrival of the party at home, delivered it to the baronet's valet to convey to the invalid gentleman's chamber, justly considering that he would require its contents.

When Mr. Middleton re-entered the apartment, and saw his patient not only risen from his bed, but so completely dressed, he expostulated on the rashness of what he had done, and augured no less than a dangerous relapse from the present increased state of his pulse. Thaddeus, for once in his life, was obstinate, though civilly so; and desiring a servant to request that Sir Robert would indulge him with an audience for a few minutes alone in his library, he soon convinced Mr. Middleton that his purpose was not to be shaken.

The baronet returning his compliments, and saying that he should be happy to see his guest, the still anxious apothecary offered him his assistance down stairs. Thaddeus needed no help, and gratefully declined it. The exertion necessary to be summoned for this interview imparted as much momentary strength to his frame as to his mind, and though his color was heightened, he entered the library with a firm step.

Sir Robert met him at the door, and, shaking him by the hand with a warm assurance of pleasure at so rapid a restoration, would have led him to a seat; but Thaddeus only supported himself against the back of it with his hand, whilst in a steady voice he expressed the most earnest thanks for the benefits he had received; then pausing, and casting the proud lustre of his eyes to the ground, lest their language should tell all that he thought, he continued, "I have only to regret, Sir Robert, that your benevolence has been lavished on a man whom you regard with abhorrence. I am the Count Sobieski, that Polander whom you commanded your son to see no more. Respecting even the prejudices of my friend's parent, I was hastening to London, meaning to set sail for America with the first ship, when I swooned on the road. I believe I was expiring. Your humanity saved me; and I now owe to gratitude, as well as to my own satisfaction, the fulfilment of my determination. I shall leave Deerhurst immediately, and England as soon as I am able to embark."

Thaddeus with a second bow, and not quite so firm a step, without venturing a glance at what he supposed must be the abashed or the enraged looks of Pembroke's father, was preparing to quit the room, when Sir Robert, with a pale and ghastly countenance, exclaimed, "Stop!"

Thaddeus looked round, and struck by the change in his preserver's appearance, paused in his movement. The baronet, incapable of saying more, pointed to a chair for him to sit down; then sinking into another himself, took out his handkerchief, and wiping away the large drops which stood on his forehead, panted for respiration. At last, with a desperate kind of haste, he said.

"Was your mother indeed Therese Sobieski?"

Thaddeus, still more astonished, replied in the affirmative. Sir Robert threw himself back on the chair with a deep groan. Hardly knowing what he did, the count rose from his seat and advanced towards him. On his approach, Sir Robert stretched out his hand, and, with a look and tone of agony, said, "Who was your father?" He then, without waiting for a reply, covered his convulsed features with his handkerchief. The baronet's agitation, which now shook him like an earthquake, became contagious. Thaddeus gazed at him with a palsying uncertainty in his heart; laying his hand on his bewildered brain, he answered, "I know not; yet I fear I must believe him to be the Earl of Tinemouth. But here is his picture." With an almost disabling tremor he unclasped it from his neck where his mother's last blessing had placed it, and touching the spring which held it in its little gold case in the manner of a watch, he gave it open to Sir Robert, who had started from his seat at the name of the earl. The moment the baronet's eyes rested on the miniature, he fell senseless upon the chair.

Thaddeus, hardly more alive, sprinkled some water on his face, and with throbbing temples and a bleeding heart stood in wordless expectation over him. Such excessive emotion told him that something more than Sir Robert's hatred of the Polanders had stimulated his late conduct. Too earnest for an explanation to ring for assistance, he rejoiced to see, by the convulsion of the baronet's features and the heaving of his chest, that animation was returning. In a few minutes he opened his eyes, but when he met the anxious gaze of Thaddeus, he closed them as suddenly. Rising from his seat, he staggered against the chimney-piece, exclaiming, "Oh God, direct me!"

Thaddeus, whose conjectures were now wrought almost to wildness, followed him, and whilst his exhausted frame was ready to sink to the earth, he implored him to speak.

"Sir Robert," cried he, "if you know anything of my family, if you know anything of my father, I beseech you to answer me. Or only tell me: am I so wretched as to be the son of Lord Tinemouth?"

The violence of the count's emotions during this agonizing address totally overcame him; before he finished speaking, his limbs withdrew their support, and he dropped breathless against the side of the chair.

Sir Robert turned hastily round. He saw him sunk, like a beautiful flower, bruised and trampled on by the foot of him who had given it root. Unable to make any evasive reply to this last appeal of virtue and of nature, he threw himself with a burst of tears upon his neck, and exclaimed, "Wretch that I have been! Oh, Sobieski! I am thy father. Dear, injured son of the too faithful Therese!"

The first words which carried this avowal to the heart of Thaddeus deprived it of motion, and when Sir Robert expected to receive the returning embrace of his son, he found him senseless in his arms.

The cries of the baronet brought Mr. Middleton and the servants into the room. When the former saw the state of the count, and perceived the agonized position of his patron, (who was supporting and leaning over his son,) the honest man declared that he expected nothing less from the gentleman's disobedience of his orders. The presence of the servants having recalled Sir Robert's wandering faculties, he desired them to remove the invalid with the greatest care back to his chamber. Following them in silence, when they had laid their charge on the bed, he watched in extreme but concealed suspense till Mr. Middleton once more succeeded in restoring animation to his patient.

The moment the count unclosed his eyes, they fixed themselves on his father. He drew the hand which held his to his lips. The tears of paternal love again bathed the cheeks of Sir Robert; he felt how warm at his heart was the affection of his deserted son. Making a sign for Mr. Middleton to leave the room, who obeyed, he bent his streaming eyes upon the other hand of Thaddeus, and, in a faltering voice, "Can you pardon me?"

Thaddeus threw himself on his father's bosom, and wept profusely; then raising Sir Robert's clasped hands to his, whilst his eloquent eyes seemed to search the heavens, he said, "My dear, dear mother loved you to her latest hour; and I have all my mother's heart. Whatever may have been his errors, I love and honor my father."

Sir Robert strained him to his breast. After a pause, whilst he shook the tears from his venerated cheeks, he resumed—"Certain, my dear son, that you require repose, and assured that you will not find it until I have offered some apology for my unnatural conduct, I will now explain the circumstances which impelled my actions, and drew distress upon that noble being, your mother."

Sir Robert hesitated a moment to recover breath, and then, with the verity of a grateful penitence, commenced.

"Keep your situation," added he, putting down Thaddeus, who at this opening was raising himself, "I shall tell my melancholy story with less pain if your eyes be not upon me. I will begin from the first."

The baronet, with frequent agitated pauses, proceeded to relate what may be more succinctly expressed as follows: Very early in life he had attached himself to Miss Edith Beaufort, the only sister of the late Admiral Beaufort, who at that time was pursuing his chosen brave career as post-captain in the British navy. By the successive deaths of their parents, they had been left young to the guardianship of Sir Fulke Somerset and their maternal aunt, his then accomplished lady: she and their deceased mother, the Lady Grace Beaufort, having been sisters—the two celebrated beautiful daughters of Robert Earl Studeley of Warwick.

Sir Fulke's family by the amiable twin of the Lady Grace were Robert (who afterwards succeeded him) and Dorothy his only daughter. But he had a son by a former marriage with the brilliantly-endowed widow of a long-resident governor in the East, who having died on his voyage home to England, on her landing she found herself the sole inheritrix of his immense wealth. She possessed charms of person as well as riches, and as soon as "her weeds" could be laid aside, she became the admired wife of the "gay and gallant" Sir Fulke Somerset. Within the twelve subsequent months she presented him with a son and heir, soon to be her own too; for though she lived three or four years after his birth, her health became so delicate that she never bore another child, but gradually declined, and ultimately expired while apparently in a gentle sleep.

Sir Fulke mourned his due time "in the customary suit of solemn black;" but he was a man of a lofty and social spirit, by no means inclined to be disconsolate, and held "a fair helpmate" to be an indispensable appendage to his domestic state. In this temper, (just before the election of a new parliament, when contending interests were running very close,) he obtained the not less eagerly disputed hand of Lady Arabella Studeley, whose elder sister (as has been mentioned) had made a magnificent marriage, only a year or two before, with John of Beaufort, the lord of the noble domain of Beaufort in the Weald of Kent—a lineal endowment from his princely ancestor, John of Gaunt. This illustrious pair dwelt on the land, like its munificent owners in the olden times, revered and beloved; and they were the parents of their two equally-honored representatives—Guy, afterwards Admiral Beaufort, and Edith, who subsequently became the adored wife of her also tenderly-beloved cousin, Robert Somerset.

But before that fondly-anticipated event took place, the young lover had to pass through a path of thorns, some of which pierced him to the end. From his childhood to manhood, he saw little of Algernon, his elder brother, who always seemed to him more like an occasional brilliant phantom, alighting amongst them, than a dear member of the family coming delightedly to cheer and to share his paternal home. Algernon was either at Eaton school, or at one of the universities, or travelling somewhere on the continent; and at all these places, or from them all, he became the enchanted theme of every tongue. Mean while, Robert—though, perhaps, equally endowed by nature, yet certainly of a milder radiance—was the object of so apprehensive a solicitude in his gentle mother's breast for the purity as well as the intellectual accomplishments of her son, that she obtained Sir Fulke's reluctant consent to his being brought up in what is called "a home education;" that is, under the especial personal care of the best private tutors, and which were found, to the great credit of her judgment. He showed an ardent devotedness to his studies; and though, like his mother, he was one of the mildest of human beings in his dealings with those around him, yet his aspirations towards high attainments were as energetic as they were noiseless, and ever on steady wing soaring upward. Robert Somerset was then unconsciously forming himself for what he afterwards became—the boast of the country of his birth, the glory of England, to whose prosperity he dedicated all his noble talents, showing what it is to be a true English country gentleman. Being alike "the oak or laurel" of "Old England's fields and groves,"

> "With sickle or with sword,
> Or bardic minstrelsy!

he was permitted to pass a term or two at Oxford, where he acquitted himself with honor, particularly in the classics, to the repeated admiration of their then celebrated professor, the late Thomas Warton. But the young student was also fond of rural pursuits and domestic occupations. He lived mostly at home, enjoying the gentle solace of elegant modern literature and the graces of music, with the ever blameless delights of an accomplished female society, at the head of which his revered mother had presided, accompanied by his lively sister Dorothy and the sweet Edith Beaufort, whom he had gradually learned to love like his own soul. His heart became yet more closely knit to her when his beloved parent died, which sad event occurred about a year after the death of Edith's own mother, who on her widowhood had continued to live more with her sister, Lady Arabella Somerset, than at her bereaved home. Edith's filial sorrow was renewed in the loss of her maternal aunt, and her tenderest sympathy reciprocated the tears of her son. Their hearts blended together in those tears, and both felt that "they were comforted"

Time did not long pass on before the happy Robert communicated their mutual attachment to his father, petitioning for his consent to woo for the hand of her whose heart he had already gained. But the baronet, in some surprise at what he heard, refused to give his sanction to any such premature engagement, first, on account of the applicant's "extreme youth;" and second, being a younger scion of his house," it might not be deemed well of in the world should he, the guardian of his niece and her splendid fortune, show so much haste to bestow her on his comparatively portionless son. The baronet, with some of his parliamentary acumen, drew another comparison, which touched the disappointed lover with a feeling almost of despair. He compared what he denominated his romantic fancies for "woods and wilds," and book-worm pursuits in the old crypts of the castle or the college, with the distinguished consideration held by his travelled brother in courts and councils, whether abroad or at home, closing the parallel by telling him "to follow Algernon's example, and become more like a man of some account amongst men before he dared pretend to to a hand of so much importance as that of the heiress of Beaufort."

Robert was standing silent and dismayed, as one struck by a thunder-flash, when his brother (who had been only a month arrived from a long revisit to the two Sicilies) suddenly entered his father's library, as Sir Fulke had again resumed his discourse with even more severity. At sight of the animated object of his contrasting eulogy, he instantly described to his new auditor what had been mutually said, and referred the subject to him.

"Romance, indeed! whether in merry Sherwood, with hound and horn, or with gentle dames in bower and hall, you have had enough of, my brother," replied the gay-spirited traveller. "Neither men nor women like philandering after deer or doe, or a lady's slipper, beyond the greenwood season. So I say, for the glory of your manhood up and away! Abroad, abroad! My father is right. That is the only ground for such a race and guerdon as you aspire to. I admire your taste, and not less your ambition, my brave boy. Do not thwart him, Sir Fulke," added he, to the baronet, who began to frown: "let him enter the lists with the boldest of us; faint heart never won fair lady! So, forward, Robert! and give me another sweet sister to love and to cherish as I do our blithe little Dora."

At this far from unwelcome advice, Robert smiled and sighed; but the smile swallowed up the sigh, for his soul kindled with hope. His father smiled also; the cloud of a stern authority had passed from his brow, and before that now perfectly reconciled party rose, it was decided that Robert should make immediate preparations for commencing a regulated course of continental travels, the route to be drawn out by his brother, and his expenses in the tour to be liberally supplied by his father. The length of the probation was not then thought on, at least not mentioned. Shortly afterwards, when Robert hastened from the library to communicate what had passed to the beloved object of the discussion, he left his father and his brother together to think and to plan all the rest for him.

But Edith Beaufort wept when she heard of the separation; her heart failed within her. For since her first coming under the roof of her guardian uncle, she had never been without seeing her brother-like cousin beyond a few days or weeks at most. He was now going to be banished (and, it was asserted, for her sake too) into far distant countries, and for an indefinite period—months, perhaps years. And these saddening thoughts made her weep afresh, though silently; for her full-flowing tears were soft and noiseless, like the heart from whence they sprung. Robert, with all his now sanguine expectations, sought to cheer her, but in vain. She felt an impression, that should he go, they would never meet again. But she did not betray that feeling to him; yet the infection of her despondency, by its continuance, so wrought on his own consequent depressed spirits, that when his father announced to him that his absence must be for two or three years at least, he ventured to remonstrate, beseeching that it might be limited to the shorter term of two years. The baronet derided the proposal, with many words of contempt towards the urgent pleader. Robert withheld from disclosing to the too often hard mind of his father that the proposition he so scorned had originated in the tender bosom of Edith Beaufort, and Sir Fulke's sarcasm fell so thick on the bending head of his son, that at last the insulted feelings of the generous lover became so indignant at the little confidence placed in the real manliness of his character, which had hitherto been found ever present when actually called for, that his heart began to swell to an almost uncontrollable exasperation, and while struggling to master himself from uttering the disrespectful retort risen to his lips, his brother again accidentally entered the room, and by giving Robert the moment to pause, happily rescued his tottering duty from that regretful offence.

As soon as Algernon appeared, the baronet resumed his sarcastic tone, in a rapid recapitulation of Robert's retrograde request. Algernon again took up the cause of his brother, and, with his usual tact, gained the victory, by the dexterous gayety with which he pleaded for the young noviciate in all the matters for which he was to be sent so far afield to learn. At last the conference ended by Sir Fulke agreeing to a proposition from his eldest son,—that the time for this foreign tutelage might possibly expire within the second year, should the results invoked by the ambitious passion of his youngest born be in any fair progress to fulfilment.

In little more than a week after this final arrangement, every preparation was finished for the wildly-contemplated tour. Robert had taken a heart-plighting adieu from his beloved Edith. But by his father's positive injunction, there was no engagement for a hereafter actual plighting of hands made between them. Yet their eloquent eyes, transparent through their mutual tears, vowed it to each other, and with silent prayers for his indeed early return, they parted.

When taking leave of his father, and receiving his directions relative to a correspondence with his family, permission was peremptorily denied him to hold any with his cousin Edith. He had learned enough lately to avoid all supplications to the paternal quarter, if he would not invite scorn as well as to receive disappointment. But Algernon whispered to him "that nobody should remain wholly *incognita* to him in that house while he dipped pen in any one of the three hundred and sixty-five inkhorns under its awful towers!" Robert then bowed his farewell with a flushed cheek and grave respect to his father, but gratefully separated from his brother with a warm pressure of the hand. The old household servants blessed him as he passed through the hall, and in a few minutes he found himself seated in the family post-chaise and four that was to convey him from the home of his youth and happy innocence, and, alas! to return to it "an altered man."

When he reached Dover to embark, he fell in with the present Earl of Tinemouth, then Mr. Stanhope, sent abroad on a similar errand with himself. But Stanhope's was to forget a mistress—Somerset's to merit the one he sought. The two young men were kinsfolk by birth, and they now felt themselves so in severing from their parents. Stanhope was in high wrath against his, and he soon rekindled the already excited mind of Somerset to a responsive demonstration of resentment. They determined to show that "they were not such boys as to submit any further in passive obedience to the stern authority dominating over them." Sir Fulke's particular charge against his son was a "womanish softness, unworthy his loftier sex!" "Show him," cried Stanhope, that "you have the hardihood of a true man by an immediate act of independence. Let us travel together, kinsmen as we are, change our names, and let no one in England know anything about us during our tour except the two dear women on whose accounts we are thus transported!"

With these views they landed in France, gave themselves out to be brothers (which a certain resemblance in their persons corroborated), and called themselves Sackville. Agreeably amused with the novelties presented to them at almost every step of their tour from gay Paris to sentimental Italy, they proceeded pretty amicably until they reached Naples. There Mr. Stanhope involved himself in an intrigue with the only daughter of an old British officer, who had retired to that climate for his health. Somerset remonstrated on the villany of seducing an innocent girl, when he knew his heart and hand were pledged to another. Stanhope, enraged at finding a censor in a compan on whom he had considered to be as headstrong as himself, ended the argument by drawing his sword, and if the servants of the hotel had not interfered, the affray would probably have terminated with one of their lives. Since that hour they never met. Mr. Stanhope fled from his shame and his bleeding friend, and, fearful of consequences, took temporary refuge in one of the Aonian Isles, not daring to proceed any further against the innocence of the poor officer's daughter, who had been thus rescued from becoming his victim!

When recovered from his wound, Robert Somerset (by some strange infatuation still retaining the name of Sackville) proceeded to Florence, in which interesting city, for works of art, ancient and modern, and the graces of classic society, determining to stay some time, he rather sought than repelled the civilities of the inhabitants. Here he became acquainted with the palatine, and the lovely Countess Therese, his daughter, Her beauty pleased his taste; her gentle virtues and exquisite accomplishments affected both his heart and mind; and he often gazed on her with tenderness, when his fidelity to Edith Beaufort only meant him to convey a look of grateful admiration. The palatine honored England, and was prepared to esteem her sons wherever he might meet them; and very soon he became so attached to this apparently lonely young traveller. that he invited him to all the excursions he and his daughter made into the adjoining states, whether visiting them by the romantic scenery of the land-roads, or coasting the beautiful bays of the sublime shores on either side of those parts of the Mediterranean.

In the midst of this intimacy, as if she were aware of a friendship so hostile to his cousin's love, he suddenly ceased to receive any remembrance-messages from her to him, in the two last letters from his brother,—for he had never allowed himself to so brave his father's parting commands as to write to her himself. Desperate with jealousy of some unknown object supplanting him, he was on the point of setting off for home, to judge with his own eyes, when a large packet from England was put into his hands. On opening it he found a letter from Edith, on which his surprised and eager gaze had immediately fixed. Without looking on any of the rest, he broke the seal, and read, astounded by the contents, "that having for some time been led to consider the probable consequences to him, both from his father's better judgment and the ultimate opinion of the world, should he and she continue their pertinacious adherence to their childish attachment, she had tried to wean both him and herself from so rebellious a folly towards her revered guardian, his honored father; and trusting that the gradual shortening of her cousin-like messages to him, through his brother's letters, must have had the effect intended, she now had permission to write one herself to him, to convince him at once of the unreasonableness and danger of all such premature entanglements. For," she added, "soon after his departure, a journey to town had taught her to know her own heart. She learned to feel that it was still at her disposal; and time did not long pass after she returned to the country before, having compared the object of her awakened taste with that of her former delusion, she persuaded her own better judgment to set a generous example to her ever-dear cousin Robert, by marrying where that judgment now pointed. And so, with the full consent of Sir Fulke (who she well knew had been totally averse to her marriage with his youngest son), she had yielded to the long love of his brother, which had been struggling in his manly bosom many agonizing months against his persistent fidelity to Robert, but whose sister she hoped to shortly become, as his affectionate Edith—then Somerset."

Having read this extraordinary epistle to the end, so monstrous in the character of its sentiments and its language, when compared with all he had hitherto known of the pure and simple mind from which it came, a terrible revulsion seized on his own, and, almost maddened with horror at every name in that letter, he foreswore his family forever! Hastening, as for one drop of heaven's dew upon his burning brain, to seek Therese Sobieski, he found her alone, and though without such aim when he rushed so frenzied into her presence, he besought her "to heal a miserable and broken heart, which could only be saved to endure any continuance of life by an acknowledgment that she loved him!" Alas! the avowal was too soon wrung from that tender and noble spirit! and yielding to a paroxysm of a rash and blinding revenge, he hurried her to a neighboring convent and secretly married her.

This most unrighteous act perpetrated, he in vain sought tranquillity. He was now stung within by a constant sense of increasing guilt. Before this act he was the injured party—injured by those in whom he had confided his dearest earthly happiness; and he could raise his head in conscious truth, though all his fondest hopes had been wrecked by their falsehood. But now he was the betrayer of a young and innocent heart, which had implicitly trusted in him. And he had insulted with a base and treacherous ingratitude, by that act of deceit, without excuse, the honor of her father, whose generous confidence had also been implicitly placed in him. But the effects of these scorpion reproaches in his bosom were not less destructive of her peace than of his own. He saw that his wedded Therese was unweariedly anxious to soothe the mysterious wanderings of his mind with her softest tenderness. But his thoughts were, indeed, far from her, ever hovering over the changed image of his so lately adored Edith—ever agonizing over the lightness of a conduct so unlike her former virgin delicacy, so unlike the clinging vows she breathed to him in their hour of boding separation!—ever execrating the perfidy of his brother, which had brought on him this distracting load of guilt and woe!

In this temper of alienation from all the world, a second packet from England was put into his hand. Again he saw Edith's writing; but he dropped it unopened, in horror of the signature he anticipated would be appended to it. Roused by resentment towards him whose name he believed she then bore, he tore asunder the wax of a letter from his father, which was sealed with black. His eyes were speedily riveted to it. Sir Fulke, in the language of deep contrition, confessed a train of deception that petrified his son. He declared, with bitter invectives against himself, that all which had been communicated to that unhappy son relating to Edith and her intended marriage with Algernon had been devised by that unkind brother, and his no less unnatural father, for the treacherous purpose of that marriage. Devoted to ambition for his own sake, as well as for that of his favorite son, Sir Fulke owned that he had from the first of Edith Beaufort's becoming his ward resolved on her union in due time with Algernon, in order to endow him, in addition to his own rich inheritance, with all the political influence attendant on the vast estate to which she was heiress, and so build up the family, in the consideration of government, to any pitch of coroneted rank their high-reaching parent might choose to reclaim.

With many prayers for pardon from Heaven and the cruelly-injured Robert, the wretched father acknowledged that this confession was wrung from him by the sudden death of his eldest son, who having been thrown off his horse on a heap of stones in the high-road, after three days of severe bodily and mental suffering, now lay a sadly-disfigured corpse, under the vainly mourning blazonry of his house, in the darkened hall of his ancestors. The disconsolate narrator then added, "that in contrite repentance his son had conjured him, with his dying breath, to confess the falsehood of all that had passed to the grossly-abused Robert;" amongst which, was Algernon turning to the account of his own designs every confidence imparted to him by his brother, in his *incognito* movements, and awakened intimacy with the noble Sarmatian family at Florence. And from these unsuspected sources, this false friend and kinsman had contrived to throw out hints of his brother's reported sliding heart to the shrinking object of his own base and perfidious passion. At last, believing Robert to be unfaithful, she sunk into a depression of spirits which Sir Fulke thought would be easy to work to an assent, in mere reckless melancholy, to the union he sought. With that object, and to break the knot at once by a trenchant blow on Robert's side, Algernon forged that letter in Edith Beaufort's handwriting which had announced so unblushingly her preparations for an immediate marriage with the eldest son.

"But," continued Sir Fulke, "death has put an end to this unnatural rivalry. And my poor girl, undeceived in her opinion of you, longs to see you, and to give you that hand which your ill-fated brother and infatuated father so unjustly detained from you. You are now my only son, the only prop of my house, the only comfort of my old age! My son, do not abandon to his remorse and sorrow your only parent."

On receipt of this packet, in a consternation of amazement, and a soul divided between rekindled love in all its fires and pity and honor towards her he had betrayed before the altar of heaven, Robert Somerset sacrificed both to his imperious passion. He adored the woman on whose account he had left the country, and though every tie, sacred and just, bound him to the tender and faithful wife he must forsake to regain that idol, he at once consigned her to the full horrors of desertion and hastened to England.

"Disgraceful to relate!" ejaculated Sir Robert, putting his hand over his face, "I married Edith Beaufort, while in our deepest mourning, but at Somerset, as the place farthest from general notice. My father, eager to efface as fast as possible from my mind and hers all recollection of his past conduct towards us, had prepared everything splendid, though private for our union; and in her blissful, restored possession, I forgot for a while Therese and her agonies. But when my dear Pembroke first saw the light, when I pressed him to my heart, it seemed as if in the same instant a dagger pierced it. When I would have breathed a blessing over him, the conviction struck me that I durst not—that I had deluded the mother who gave him birth, and that at some future period he might have cause to curse the author of his existence.

"Well," continued the baronet, wiping his forehead, "though the birth of this boy conjured up the image of your mother, to haunt me day and night, I never could summon moral courage to inquire of her destiny after I had left her. When the troubles of Poland commenced, what a dreadful terror seized me! The successes of their allied enemies, and the consequent distress and persecution of the chief nobility, overwhelmed me with apprehension. I knew not but that many, like the *noblesse* of France, might be forced to abandon their country; and the bare idea of meeting your grandfather, or the injured Therese, in England, precipitated me into a nervous state that menaced my life. I became abstracted and seriously ill, was forbidden all excitements; hence easily avoided the sight of newspapers; and, on the plea you have heard, my family were withheld from speaking on any public subjects that manifestly gave me pain. But I could not prevent the tongues of our visitors from discoursing on a theme which at that period interested every thinking mind. I heard of the valiant Kosciusko, the good Stanislaus, and the palatine Sobieski, with his brave grandson, spoken of in the same breath. I durst not surmise who this grandson was; I dared not ask—I dreaded to know.

"At length," added the agitated father, quickening his voice, "the idol of my heart—she for whom I had sacrificed my all of human probity, perhaps my soul's eternal peace—died in my arms. Where could a wretch like me turn for consolation? I had forfeited all right to it from Heaven or earth.

But at last a benignant spirit seemed to breathe on me, and I bent beneath the stroke with humility; for I embraced it as the just chastisement of a crime which till then, even in the midst of my married felicity, had often pressed on my dearest feelings like the hand of death. I repeat, I bore this chastening trial with the resignation I have described. But when, two years afterwards, my eye fell by accident upon the name of Sobieski in one of the public papers, I could not withdraw it; my sight was fascinated as if by a rattle-snake. In one column I read how bravely the palatine fell, and in the next the dreadful fate of his daughter. She was revenged!" cried Sir Robert, eagerly grasping the hand of Thaddeus, who could not restrain the groan that burst from his breast. "For nearly three months I was deprived of that reason which had abused her noble nature.

"When I recovered my senes," continued he, in a calmer tone, "and found I had so fatally suffered the time of any restitution to her to go by, I began to torture my remorseful heart because that I had not, immediately on the death of my too much loved Edith, hastened to Poland, and besought Therese's pardon from her ever-generous heart. But this vivid approach to a sincere repentance was soon obliterated by the consideration that, the Countess Sobieski having had a prior claim to my name, such restitution on my part must have illegitimatized my darling Pembroke, his dying mother's fondest bequeathment to a father's arms.

"It was this fearful conviction," exclaimed Sir Robert, a sudden horror, indeed, distracting his before affectionate eye, "that caused all my barbarian cruelty. When my dear and long-believed only son described the danger from which you had rescued him, when he told me that Therese had fostered him with a parent's tenderness, I was probed to the heart. But when he added that the young Count Sobieski was now an alien from his country, and relying on my friendship for a home, my terror was too truly manifested. Horror drove all natural remorse from my soul. I thought an avenging power had sent my deserted child to discover his father, to claim his rights, and to publish me as a disgrace to the name I had stolen from him. And when I saw my innocent Pembroke, even to his knees, petitioning for the man who I believed had come to undo him, I became almost deranged. May the Lord of mercy pardon the fury of that derangement! For under that temper," added he, putting the trembling hand of Thaddeus to his streaming eyes, "I drove my first-born to be a wanderer on the face of the earth, not for his own crimes, but for those of his father; and Heaven justly punished in the crime the sin of my injustice. When I thought that evidence of my shame was divided from me by an insuperable barrier, when I believed that the ocean would soon separate me from my fears, a righteous Providence brought thee before me, forlorn and expiring. It was the son of Therese Sobieski I had exposed to such wretchedness. It was the cherished of her heart I had delivered to the raging elements! Oh, Thaddeus, my son," cried he, "can I be forgiven for all this, in this world or in the next?"

"Oh, my father!" returned Thaddeus, with a modest, but a pathetic energy, "I am thy son! thy happy son, in such acknowledgment! Therefore no longer upbraid yourself. Did you not act, as by a sacred impulse, a father's part to me when you knew me not? You raised my dying head from the earth and laid it on your bosom. O, my father! He who brought us so together in his own appointed time, chasteneth every son whom he receiveth, and has thus proved his love and pardon to your contrite heart, both on earth and in heaven, by the nature of your chastisement and the healing balm at its close!"

At the end of this interview, so interesting and vital to the happiness of both these newly-united parties, father and son, Sir Robert motioned his blessing to that son by laying his hand gently on his head, while the parental tears flowed on that now dear forehead—for he could not then speak. He immediately withdrew, to leave Thaddeus to repose, and himself to retire to pour out his grateful spirit in private.

CHAPTER XLVI.

THE SPIRIT OF PEACE.

At dawn on the morning following the preceding eventful but happy conference, Sir Robert, painfully remembering the frantic grief of Pembroke on finding that Sobieski had not only withdrawn himself from Harrowby, but had adjured England forever, and still feeling the merited bitterness of the reproaches which his inexplicable commands, dishonoring to his son, had provoked from that only too-long-preferred offspring of his idolized Edith,—which reproaches, unknowingly so inflicted by the desperation of their utterer, had driven the guilty father to seek a temporary refuge from them, if not from his own accusing conscience, under the then solitary roof of one of his country seats in the adjacent county,—yet somewhat relieved, as by the immediate mercy of Heaven, from the load of his misery, he eagerly wrote by the auspicious beams of the rising sun a few short lines to Pembroke, telling him that "a providential circumstance had occurred since they parted, which he trusted would finally reconcile into a perfect peace all that had recently passed so distressingly between them; therefore he, his ever tenderly-affectioned father, requested him to join him alone, and without delay, at Deerhurst."

This duty done to one beloved child, he then turned to anticipate a second converse to his comfort with the other.

That sickness which is the consequence of mental suffering usually vanishes with its cause. Long before the dinner-hour of this happy day, Thaddeus, refreshed by the peaceful and lengthened sleep from which he awoke late in the morning, rose as if with a renewed principle of life. Quitting his room, he met his glad father in the passage-gallery, who instantly conducted him into a private room, where that now tranquillized parent soon brought him to relate, with every sentence a deepening interest, the rapid incidents of his brief but eventful career. The voice of fame had already blazoned him abroad as "the plume of war, with early laurels crowned;" but it was left to his own ingenuous tongue to prove, in all the modest simplicity of a perfect filial confidence, that the most difficult conflicts are not those which are sustained on the battle-field.

Sir Robert listened to him with affection, admiration, and delight,—ah, with what pride in such a son! He was answering the heartfelt detail with respondent gratefulness to that Almighty Power which had shed on his transgressing head such signal "signs of heavenly amnesty!" when the door opened, and a servant announced that Mr. Somerset was in the library.

Thaddeus started up with joy in his countenance; but Sir Robert gently put him down again. "Remain here, my son," said he, "until I apprize your brother how nearly you are related to him. Yonder door leads into my study; I will call you when he is prepared."

The moment Sir Robert joined Pembroke, he read in his pale and haggard features how much he needed the intelligence he was summoned to hear. Mr. Somerset bowed coldly but respectfully on his father's entrance, and begged to be honored with his commands.

"They are what I expect will restore to you your usual looks and manner, my dear son," returned the baronet; "so attend to me."

Pembroke listened to his father's narrative with mute and, as it proceeded, amazed attention. But when the name of Therese Sobieski was mentioned as that of the foreign lady whom he had married and deserted, the ready apprehension of his breathless auditor conceiving the remainder yet unuttered by the agitated narrator, Sir Robert had only to confirm, though in a hardly audible voice, the eager demand of his son, "Was Thaddeus Sobieski indeed his brother?" and while hearing the reply, unable to ask another question, he looked wildly from earth to heaven, as if seeking where he might yet be found.

"O, my father!" cried he, "what have you done? Where is he? For what have you sacrificed him?"

"Hear me to an end," rejoined the baronet. He then, in as few words as possible, repeated the subsequent events of the recent meeting.

Pembroke's raptures were now as high as his despair had been profound. He threw himself on his father's breast; he asked for his friend, his brother, and begged to be conducted to him. Sir Robert did no more than open the intervening door, and in one instant the brothers were locked in each other's arms.

The transports of the young men for a long while denied them words; but their eyes, their tears, and their united hands imparted to each breast a consciousness of mutual love unutterable, not even to be expressed by those looks which are indeed the heralds of the soul.

Sir Robert wept like an infant whilst contemplating these two affectionate brothers; in a faltering voice he exclaimed, "How soon may these plighted hands be separated by inexorable law! Alas, Pembroke, you cannot be ignorant that I buy this son at a terrible price from you!"

At this speech the blood rushed over the cheek of the ingenuous Pembroke; but Thaddeus, turning instantly to Sir Robert, said, with an eloquent smile.

"On this head I trust that neither my father nor my brother will entertain one thought to trouble them. Had I even the inclination to act otherwise than right, my revered grandfather has put it out of my power to claim or to bear any other name than that of Sobieski. He made me swear never to change it; and, as I hope to meet him hereafter," added he, with solemnity,

"I will obey him. Therefore, my beloved father, in secret only can I enjoy the conviction that I am your son, and Pembroke's brother. Yet the happiness I receive with the knowledge of being so will ever live here, will ever animate my heart with gratitude to Heaven and to you."

"Noble son of the sainted Therese!" cried Sir Robert; "I do not deserve thee!"

"How shall I merit your care of my honor, of my dearest feelings?" exclaimed Pembroke, grasping the hand of his brother. "I can do nothing, dearest Thaddeus; I am a bankrupt in the means of evincing what is passing in my soul. My mother's chaste spirit thanks you from my lips. Yet I will not abuse your generosity. Though I retain the name of Somerset, it shall only be the name; the inheritance entailed on my father's eldest son belongs to you."

Whilst Thaddeus embraced his brother again, he calmly and affectionately replied that he would rather encounter all the probable evils from which his father's benevolence had saved him, than rob his brother of any part of that inheritance, "which," he earnestly added, "I sincerely believe, according to the Providence of Heaven, is your just due."

Sir Robert, with abhorrence of himself and admiration of his sons, attempted to stop this noble contention by proposing that it should be determined by an equal division of the family property.

"Not so, my father," returned Thaddeus, steadfastly, but with reverence; "I can never admit that the title of Somerset should sacrifice one jot of its inherited accustomed munificence by making any such alienation of its means."

And then the ingenuous son of Therese Sobieski proceeded, in the same modest but firm tone, to remind his father that "though the laws of the national church wherein he had married her would have given their son every right over any inheritance from either parent which belonged to Poland, yet as no opportunity had subsequently occurred for repeating the sacred ceremony by the laws of his father's church, her son could make no legal claim whatever on a rood of the Somerset lands in England."

Sir Robert, with unspeakable emotion, clasped the hand of his first-born when he had made, and with such tender delicacy, this conclusive remark, and which, indeed, had never presented itself to his often distractedly apprehensive mind, either before or after the death of Pembroke's mother; even had it done so, it would not have afforded any quiet to his soul from the internal orm gnawing there. His act had been guilt towards Therese Sobieski and her confiding innocence. And it was not the discovery of any omitted legislative ordinance that could have satisfied the accusing conscience in his own bosom, hourly calling out against him. But the heaven-consecrated son of that profaned marriage had found the reconciling point—had poured in the healing balm; and the spirit of his father was now at peace.

In cordial harmony, therefore, with this generous opinion, so opportunely expressed by the sincere judgment of the last of the house of Sobieski, when so united to that of Somerset, and with a corresponding simplicity of purpose, interwoven by the sweet reciprocity of mutual confidence, the remainder of the evening passed pleasantly between the happy father and his no less happy sons.

Sir Robert dispatched a letter next day to his sister, to invite her and his beloved Mary to join the home party at Deerhurst without delay. Pembroke rejoiced in this prospective relief to the minds of his aunt and cousin, being well aware that he had left them in a state of intense anxiety, not only on account of the baronet's strange conduct,—which had not been explicable in any way to their alarmed observations,—but on account of himself, whose mind had appeared from the time of his father's incensed departure in a state verging on derangement. On the instant of his return from the deserted hotel, while passing Mary, whom he accidently met in his bewildered way to Sir Robert's room, he had exclaimed to her, "I have not seen Sobieski! he is gone! and your message is not delivered." From the time of that harrowing intimation, he had constantly avoided even the sight of his cousin or his aunt. Yet before he quitted the Castle to obey his father's new commands, he had summoned courage to enter Mary's boudoir, where she sat alone. Not trusting himself to speak, he put the letter which Thaddeus had written to her into her hand, and disappeared, not daring to await her opening what he knew to be a last farewell.

He had guessed aright; for from the moment in which her trembling hand had broken the seal and she had read it to the end, bathed in her tears, it lay on her mourning heart, whether she waked or slept, till her silent grief was roused to share her thoughts with a personal exertion, welcome to that despondent heart. It was Sir Robert's invitation for her own and her aunt's immediate removal to their always favorite Deerhurst! because far from the gay world, and ever devoted to quite domestic enjoyments.

But before this summons had arrived, and early in the morning of the same day, Lady Albina Stanhope, more dead than alive in appearance, had reached Somerset Castle in a post-chaise, accompanied by her maid alone, to implore the protection of its revered owner against the most terrible evils that could be inflicted by an unnatural parent on a daughter's heart—that of being compelled to be a party in a double outrage on the memory of her mother, by witnessing the marriage of her father, by special license, to Lady Olivia Lovel, that very evening, in the Harwold great hall, and herself to commit the monstrous act of being married to a nephew of that profligate woman. To avoid such horrors, she had flown for refuge to the only persons she knew on earth likely to shield her from so great an infamy.

Soon after this disclosure, to which the sister and niece of the beneficent Sir Robert Somerset—whom she had hoped to find at the Castle—had listened with the tenderest sympathy, his letter to Miss Dorothy was delivered to the venerable lady. Mary and their fatigued guest were seated together on the sofa; and the seal, without apology, from the receiver's anxious haste to learn what it might contain of her brother's health, was instantly broken. A glance removed every care. Reading it aloud to both her young auditors, at every welcome word the bosom of the amazed Miss Beaufort heaved with increasing astonishment, hope, and gratitude, while beneath the veil of her clustered ringlets her eyes shed the tribute of happy tears to heaven—to that heaven alone her virgin spirit breathed the emotions of her reviving heart. The good old lady was not backward in demonstrating her wonderings. Surprised at her brother's rencontre with Thaddeus, but more at his avowal of obligations to any of that nation about which he had always proclaimed an aversion, she was so wrapped in bewilderment yet delight at the discovery, that her ever cheerful tongue felt nothing loathe to impart to the attentively-listening Albina—who had recognized in the names of Constantine and Thaddeus those of her lamented mother's most faithful friend—all that she knew of his public as well as his private character since she had known him by that of Sobieski also.

Sir Robert's letter informed his sister "that a providential circumstance had introduced Pembroke's friend, the Count Sobieski, to his presence, when, to his astonishment and unutterable satisfaction, he discovered that this celebrated young hero (though one of a nation against which he had so often declared his dislike, but which ungenerous prejudice he now abjured!) was the only remaining branch of a family from whom, about twenty-five years ago, while in a country far distant equally from England or Poland, he had received many kindnesses. He had contracted an immense debt, under peculiarly embarrassing circumstances to himself, when then an alien from his father's confidence. And his benefactor in this otherwise inextricable dilemma was the Palatine of Masovia, the world-revered grandfather of the young Count Sobieski. And," he added, "in some small compensation for the long-unredeemed pecuniary part of this latter obligation, (the fulfilment of which certain adverse events on the continent had continued to prevent), he had besought and obtained permission from the young count, now in England, to at once set at rest his past anxieties to settle an affair of so much importance, by signing over to him, as the palatine's heir and representative, the sole property of his (Sir Robert's) recently-purchased new domain —the house and estates of Manor Court, nearly adjoining to those of Deerhurst, on the Warwick side. The rent-roll might be about five thousand pounds per annum. And there, in immediate right of possession, the noble descendant of his munificent friend would resume his illustrious name, and embrace, with a generous esteem of this country's national character, a lasting home and filiation in England!"

Sir Robert closed this auspicious letter (which he had striven, however, to write in such a manner as not to betray the true nature of the parental feelings which dictated it) with a playful expression of his impatience to present to his sister and niece "their interesting *emigré* in a character which reflected so much honor on their discernment."

The impatience was indeed shared, though in different degrees and forms, by the whole little party—the soul of one in it totally absorbed. But owing to some insurmountable obstacles, occasioning delays, by the exhausted state of the overwrought Lady Albina; and notwithstanding the necessity of getting on as fast as possible, to be out of the reach of the enraged earl, should he have missed and traced his daughter to Somerset Castle, the fugitives could not start till late in the afternoon of that day, and it was an hour or more past midnight before they arrived at Deerhurst.

The family, in no small disappointment, had given them up for the night, and had retired to their rooms. Miss Dorothy, who would not suffer her brother to be disturbed, sent the two young ladies to their chambers, and was crossing, on tiptoe, the long picture-gallery to her own apartment, when a door opening, Pembroke, in his dressing-gown and slippers, looked out on hearing the stealthy step. She put forth her hand to him with delight, and in a low voice congratulated him on the change in Sir Robert's mind, kissed his cheek, and told him to prepare for another pleasant surprise in the morning. Smiling with these words, she bade him good-night, and softly proceeded to her chamber.

Pembroke had thought so little of his ever-merry aunt's lively promise, that she saw him one of the latest in entering the breakfast-parlor, he not having hastened from his usual breezy early walk over the neighboring downs, where Thaddeus had been his companion. Miss Dorothy gayly reproached her nephew for his undutiful lack of curiosity; while Mary, with a glowing cheek, received the glad embrace of her cousin, who gently whispered to her, "Now I shall see together the two beings I most dearly love! Oh! the happiness contained in that sight!" Mary's vivid blush had not subsided when the entrance of Thaddeus, and his agitated bow, overspread her neck and brow with crimson. A sudden dimness obscured her faculties, and she scarcely heard the animated words of Sir Robert, whilst presenting him to her as the Count Sobieski, the beloved grandson of one who had deserved the warmest place in his heart! Whatever he was, the lowly Constantine or the distinguished Sobieski, she was conscious that he was lord of hers; and withdrawing her hand confusedly from the timid and thrilling touch of him she would have willingly lingered near forever, she glided towards an open casement, where the fresh air helped to dispel the faintness which had seized her.

After Miss Dorothy, with all the urbanity of her nature, had declared her welcome to the count, she put away the coffee that was handed to her by Pembroke, and said, with a smile, "Before I taste my breakfast, I must inform you, Sir Robert, that you have a guest in this house you little expect. I forbade Miss Beaufort's saying a word, because, as we are told, 'the first tellers of unwelcome news have but a losing office;' *vice versâ*, I hoped for a gaining one, therefore preserved such a profitable piece of intelligence for my own promulgation. Indeed, I doubt whether it will not win me a pair of gloves from some folks here," added she, glancing archly on Pembroke, who looked round at this whimsical declaration. "Suffice it to say, that yesterday morning Lady Albina Stanhope, looking like a ghost, and her poor maid, scared almost out of her wits, arrived in a hack-chaise at Somerset Castle, and besought our protection. Our dear Mary embraced the weeping young creature, who, amidst many tears, recapitulated the injuries she had suffered since she had been torn from her mother's remains at the Abbey. The latest outrage of her cruel father was his intended immediate marriage with the vile Lady Olivia Lovel, and his commands that Lady Albina should the same evening give her hand to that bad woman's nephew. Ill as she was when she received these disgraceful orders, she determined to prevent the horror of such double degradation by instantly quitting the house; 'and,' added she, 'whither could I go? Ah! I could think of none so likely to pity the unhappy victim of the wickedness I fled from as the father of the kind Mr. Somerset. He had told me we were relations; I beseech you, kind ladies, to be my friends!' Certain of your benevolence, my dear brother," continued Miss Dorothy, "I stopped this sweet girl's petition with my caresses, and promised her a gentler father in Sir Robert Somerset."

"You did right, Dorothy," returned the baronet; "though the earl and I must ever be strangers, I have no enmity to his children. Where is this just-principled young lady?"

Miss Dorothy informed him that, in consequence of her recent grief and ill treatment, she had found herself too unwell to rise with the family; but she hoped to join them at noon.

Pembroke was indeed deeply interested in this intelligence. The simple graces of the lovely Albina had on the first interview touched his heart. Her sufferings at Harrowby, and the sensibility which her ingenuous nature exhibited without affectation or disguise, had left her image on his mind long after they parted. He now gave the reins to his eager imagination, and was the first in the saloon to greet her as his lovely kinswoman.

Sir Robert Somerset welcomed her with the warmth of a parent, and the amiable girl wept in happy gratitude.

During this scene, Miss Beaufort, no longer able to bear the restraint of company nor even the accidental encountering of his eyes whose presence, dear as it was, oppressed and disconcerted her, walked out into the park. Though it was the latter end of October, the weather continued fine. A bright sun tempered the air, and gilded the yellow leaves, which the fresh wind drove before her into a thousand glittering eddies. This was Mary's favorite season. She ever found its solemnity infuse a sacred tenderness into her soul. The rugged form of Care seemed to dissolve under the magic touch of sweet Nature. Forgetful of the world's anxieties, she felt the tranquillising spirit of soothing melancholy that shades the heart of sorrow with a veil which might well be called the twilight of the mind; and the entranced soul, happy in its dream, half closes its bright eye, reluctant to perceive that such bland repose is pillowed on the shifting clouds.

Such were the reflections of Miss Beaufort, after her disturbed thoughts had tossed themselves, in a sea of doubts, regarding any possible interest she might possess in the breast of Sobieski. She recalled the hours they had passed together; they agitated but did not satisfy her heart. She remembered Pembroke's vehement declaration that Thaddeus loved her; but then it was Pembroke's declaration, not his! and the circumstances in which it had been made were too likely to mislead the wishes of her cousin. And then Sobieski's farewell letter! It was noble—grateful; but where appeared the glowing, soul-pervading sentiment that consumed her life for him? Exhausted by the anguish of this suspense, she resolved to resign her future fate to Providence. Turning her gaze on the lovely objects around, she soon found the genius of the season absorb her wholly. Her cheeks glowed, her eyes became humid, and casting their mild radiance on the fading flowers beneath, she pursued her way through a cloud of fragrance. It was the last breath of the expiring year. Love is full of imagination. Mary easily glided from the earth's departing charms to her own she thought waning beauty; the chord once touched, every note vibrated, and hope and fear, joy and regret, again dispossessed her lately-acquired serenity.

CHAPTER XLVII.

AN AVOWAL.

After some little time, Lady Albina, having missed Miss Beaufort, expressed a wish to walk out in search of her, and the two brothers offered their attendance. But before her ladyship had passed through the first park, she complained of fatigue. Pembroke urged her to enter a shepherd's hut close by, whilst the Count Sobieski would proceed alone in quest of his cousin.

With a beating heart Thaddeus undertook this commission.

Hastening along the nearest dell with the lightness of a young hunter, he mounted the heights, descended to the glades, traversed one woody nook and then another, but could see no trace of Miss Beaufort. Supposing she had returned to the house, he was slackening his pace to abandon the search, when he caught a glimpse of her figure as she turned the corner of a thicket leading to a terrace above. In an instant he was at her side, and with his hat in his hand, and a glowing cheek, he repeated his errand.

Mary blushed, faltered, and became strangely alarmed at finding herself alone with him. Though he now stood before her in a quality which she ever believed was his right, the remembrance of what had passed between them in other circumstances confounded and overwhelmed her. When Constantine was poor and unfriended, it seemed a sacred privilege to pity and to love him. When the same Constantine appeared as a man of rank, invested with a splendid fortune and extensive fame, she felt lost—annihilated. The cloud which had obscured, not extinguished, his glory was dispersed. He was that Sobieski whom she had admired unseen; he was that Constantine whom she had loved unknown; he was that Sobieski, that Constantine, whom, seen and known, she now, alas! loved almost to adoration!

Oppressed by the weight of these emotions, she only bowed to what he said, and gathering her cloak from the winds which blew it around her, was hurrying with downward eyes to the stairs of the terrace, when her foot slipped, and she must have fallen, had not Thaddeus caught her in his ready arm. She rose with a blushing face, and the color did not recede when she found that he had not relinquished her hand. Her heart beat violently, her head became giddy, her feet lost their power. Finding that, after a slight attempt to withdraw her hand, he still held it fast, though in a trembling grasp, and nearly overcome by inexplicable distress, she turned away her face to conceal its confusion.

Thaddeus saw all this, and with a fluttering hope, instead of surrendering the hand he had retained, he made it a yet closer prisoner by clasping it in both his. Pressing it earnestly to his breast, he said in a hurried voice, whilst his earnest eyes poured all their beams upon her averted cheek, "Surely Miss Beaufort will not deny me the dearest happiness I possess—the privilege of being grateful to her?"

He paused: his soul was too full for utterance; and raising Mary's hand from his heart to his lips, he kissed it fervently. Almost fainting, Miss Beaufort leaned her head against a tree of the thicket where they were standing. The thought of the confession which Pembroke had extorted from her, and dreading that its fullness might have been imparted to him, and that all this was rather the tribute of gratitude than of love, she waved her other hand in sign for him to leave her.

Such extraordinary confusion in her manner palsied the warm and blissful emotions of the count. He, too, began to blame the sanguine representation of his friend; and fearing that he had offended her, that she might suppose he presumed on her kindness, he stood for a moment in silent astonishment; then dropping on his knee, (hardly conscious of the action,) declared in an agitated voice his sense of having given this offence; at the same time he ventured to repeat, with equally modest energy, the soul-devoted passion he had so long endeavored to seal up in his lonely breast.

"But forgive me!" added he, with increased earnestness; "forgive me, in justice to your own virtues. In what has just passed, I feel I ought to have only expressed thanks for your goodness to an unfortunate exile; but if my words or manner have obeyed the more fervid impulse of my soul, and declared aloud what is its glory in secret, blame my nature, most respected Miss Beaufort, not my presumption. I have not dared to look steadily on any aim higher than your esteem."

Mary knew not how to receive this address. The position in which he uttered it, his countenance when she turned to answer him, were both demonstrative of something less equivocal than his speech. He was still grasping the drapery of her cloak, and his eyes, from which the wind blew back his fine hair, were beaming upon her full of that piercing tenderness which at once dissolves and assures the soul.

She passed her hand over her eyes. Her soul was in a tumult. She too fondly wished to believe that he loved her to trust the evidence of what she saw. His words were ambiguous, and that was sufficient to fill her with uncertainty. Jealous of that delicacy which is the parent of love, and its best preserver, she checked the overflowings of her heart, and whilst her concealed face streamed with tears, conjured him to rise. Instinctively she held out her hand to assist him. He obeyed; and hardly conscious of what she said, she continued—

"You have done nothing, Count Sobieski, to offend me. I was fearful of my own conduct—that you might have supposed—I mean, unfortunate appearances might lead you to imagine that I was influenced—was so forgetful of myself——

"Cease, madam! Cease, for pity's sake!" cried Thaddeus, starting back, and dropping her hand. Every motion which faltered on her tongue had met an answering pang in his breast.

Fearing that he had set his heart on the possession of a treasure totally out of his reach, he knew not how high had been his hope until he felt the depth of his despair. Taking up his hat, which lay on the grass, with a countenance from which every gleam of joy was banished, he bowed respectfully, and in a lower tone continued: "The dependent situation in which I appeared at Lady Dundas's being ever before my eyes, I was not so absurd as to suppose that any lady could then notice me from any other sentiment than humanity. That I excited this humanity, where alone I was proud to awaken it, was, in these hours of dejection, my sole comfort. It consoled me for the friends I had lost; it repaid me for the honors which were no more. But that is past! Seeing no further cause for compassion, you deem the delusion no longer necessary. Since you will not allow me an individual distinction in having attracted your benevolence, though I am to ascribe it all to a charity as diffused as effective, yet I must ever acknowledge with the deepest gratitude that I owe my present home and happiness to Miss Beaufort. Further than this, I shall not—I dare not—presume."

These words shifted all the count's anguish to Mary's breast. She perceived the offended delicacy which actuated each syllable as it fell; and fearful of having lost everything by her cold and what might appear haughty reply, she opened her lips to say what might better explain her meaning; but her heart failing her, she closed them again, and continued to walk in silence by his side. Having allowed the opportunity to escape, she believed that all hopes of exculpation were at an end. Not daring to look up, she cast a despairing glance at Sobieski's graceful figure, as he walked, equally silent, near her. His arms were folded, his hat pulled over his forehead, and his long dark eyelashes, shading his downward eyes, imparted a dejection to his whole air which wrapped her weeping heart round and round with regretful pangs. "Ah!" thought she, "though the offspring of but one moment, they will prey on my peace forever."

At the turning of a little wooded knoll, the mute and pensive pair heard the sound of some one on the other side, approaching them through the dry leaves. In a minute after Sir Robert Somerset appeared.

Whilst his father advanced smiling towards him, Thaddeus

attempted to dispel the gloom of his countenance, but not succeeding, he bowed abruptly to the agitated Mary, and hastily said, "I will leave Miss Beaufort in your protection, sir, and go myself to see whether Lady Albina be recovered from her fatigue."

"I thought to find you all together," returned Sir Robert; "where is her ladyship?"

"I left her with Pembroke, in a hut by the river," said Thaddeus, and bowing again, he hurried away, whilst his father called after him to return in a few minutes, and accompany him in a walk.

The departure of Sobieski, when he had come expressly to attend her to Lady Albina, nearly overwhelmed Miss Beaufort's before-exhausted spirits. Hardly knowing whether to remain or retreat, she was attempting the latter, when her guardian caught her hand.

"Stay, Mary!" cried he; "you surely would not leave me alone?"

Miss Beaufort's tears had gushed over her eyes the moment her back was turned, and as Sir Robert drew her towards him, to his extreme amazement he saw that she was weeping. At a sight so unexpected, the smile of hilarity left his lips. Putting his arm tenderly round her waist, (for now that her distress had discovered itself, her emotion became so great that she could hardly stand,) he inquired in a kindly manner what had affected her.

She answered by sobs only, until finding it impossible to break away from her uncle's arms, she hid her face in his bosom and gave vent to the full tide of her tears.

Recollecting the strange haste in which Thaddeus had hurried from them, and remembering Miss Beaufort's generosity to him in town, followed by her succeeding melancholy, Sir Robert at once united these circumstances with her present confusion, and conceiving an instantaneous suspicion of the reality, pressed her with redoubled affection to his bosom.

"I fear, my dearest girl," said he, "that something disagreeable has happened between you and the Count Sobieski. Perhaps he has offended you? perhaps he has found my sweet Mary too amiable?"

Alarmed at this supposition, after a short struggle she answered, "O no, sir! It is I who have offended him. He thinks I pride myself on the insignificant services I rendered to him in London."

This reply convinced the baronet that he had not been premature in his judgment, and, with a new-born delight springing in his soul, he inquired why she thought so? Had she given him any reason to believe so?

Mary trembled at saying more.—Dreading that every word she might utter would betray how highly she prized the count's esteem, she faltered, hesitated, stopped. Sir Robert put the question a second time, in different terms.

"My loved Mary," said he, seating her by him on the trunk of a fallen tree, "I am sincerely anxious that you and this young nobleman should regard each other as friends. He is very dear to me; and you cannot doubt, my sweet girl, my affection for yourself. Tell me, therefore, the cause of this little misunderstanding."

Miss Beaufort took courage at this speech. Drying her glowing eyes, though still concealing them with a handkerchief, she replied in a firmer voice, "I believe, sir, the fault lies totally on my side. The Count Sobieski met me on the terrace, and thanked me for what I had done for him. I acted very weakly; I was confused. Indeed I knew not what he said; but he fell upon his knees, and I became so disconcerted, so frightened at the idea of his having attributed my conduct to indelicacy, or forwardness, that I answered something which offended him, and I am sure he now thinks me unfeeling and proud."

Sir Robert kissed her throbbing forehead, as she ended this rapid and hardly-articulated explanation.

"Tell me candidly, my dearest Mary!" rejoined the baronet, "can you believe that a man of Sobieski's disposition would bend his knee to a woman whom he did not both respect and love? Simple gratitude, my dear girl, is not so earnest. You have said enough to convince me, whatever may be your sentiments, that you are the mistress of his fate; and if he should mention it to me, may I describe to him the scene which has now passed between us? May I tell him that its just inference would requite his tenderness with more than your thanks and best wishes?"

Miss Beaufort, who believed that the count must now despise her, looked down to conceal the wretchedness which spoke through her eyes, and with a half-suppressed sigh, answered, "I will not deny that I deeply esteem the Count Sobieski. I admired his character before I saw him, and when I did see him, although ignorant that it was he, the impression seemed the same. Yet I never aspired to any place in his heart, or even his remembrance: I could not have the presumption.

Therefore, my dear uncle," added she, laying her trembling hand on his arm, "I beseech you, as you value my feelings, my peace of mind, never to breathe a syllable of my weakness to him. I think," added she, clasping her hands with energy, and forgetting the force of her expression, "I would sooner suffer death than lose his respect."

"And yet," inquired Sir Robert, "you will at some future period give your hand to another man?"

Mary, who did not consider the extent of this insidious question, answered with fervor, "Never! I never can be happier than I am," added she, with breathless haste. Seeing, by the smile on Sir Robert's lips, that far more had been declared by her manner than her words intended, and fearful of betraying herself further, she begged permission to retire to the house.

The baronet took her hand, and reseating her by him, continued, "No, my Mary; you shall not leave me unless you honestly avow what your sentiments are towards the Count Sobieski. You know, my sweet girl, that I have tried to make you regard me as a father—to induce you to receive from my love the treble affection of your deceased parents and my lamented wife. If her dear niece do not deny this, she cannot treat me with reserve."

Miss Beaufort was unable to speak. Sir Robert proceeded:

"I will not overwhelm your shrinking delicacy by repeating the inquiry whether I have mistaken the source of your recent and present emotion; only allow me to bestow some encouragement on the count's attachment, should he claim my services in its behalf."

Mary drew her uncle's hand to her lips, and whilst her dropping tears fell upon it, she threw herself, like a confiding child, on her knees, and replied in a timid voice: "I should be a monster of ingratitude could I hide anything from you, my dearest sir, after this goodness! I confess that I do regard the Count Sobieski more than any being on earth. Who could see and know him and think it possible to become another's?"

"And you shall be his, my darling Mary!" cried the baronet, mingling his own blissful tears with hers. "I once hoped to have contrived an attachment between you and Pembroke, but Heaven has decreed it better. When you and Thaddeus are united, I shall be happy; I may then die in peace."

Miss Beaufort sighed heavily. She could not yet quite participate in her uncle's rapture. She thought that she had insulted and disgusted the count by her late behavior, beyond his excuse, and was opening her lips to urge it again, when the object of their conversation appeared at a short distance, coming towards them.

Full of renewed trepidation, she burst from the baronet's hand, and taking to flight, left her uncle to meet Sobieski alone.

Sir Robert's anxious question on the same subject received a more rapid reply from Thaddeus than had proceeded from the reluctant Miss Beaufort. The animated gratitude of Sobieski, the ardent yet respectful manner with which he avowed her eminence in his heart above all other women, convinced the baronet that Mary's retreating delicacy had misinformed her. A complete explanation was the consequence ; and Thaddeus, who had not been more sanguine in his hopes than was his lovely mistress in hers, now allowed the clouds over his so lately darkened eyes to disappear.

Impatient to see these two beings, so dear to his soul, repose confidently in each other's affection, the moment Sir Robert returned to the house, he asked his sister for Miss Beaufort. Miss Dorothy replied that she had seen her about half an hour ago retire to her own apartments ; the baronet, therefore, sent a servant to beg that she would meet him in the library.

This message found her in a paroxysm of distress. She reproached herself for her imprudence, her temerity, her unwomanly conduct, in having given away her heart to a man who she again began to torment herself by believing had never desired it. She remembered that her weakness, not her sincerity, had betrayed this humiliating secret to Sir Robert ; and nearly distracted, she lay on the bed, almost hoping that she was in a miserable dream, when her maid entered with the baronet's commands.

Disdaining herself, and determining to regain some portion of her own respect by steadily opposing all her uncle's deluding hopes, with an assumed serenity she arrived at the study-door. She laid her hand on the lock, but the moment it yielded to her touch, all her firmness vanished. Trembling, and pale as death, she appeared before him.

Sir Robert, having supported her to a chair, with the most affectionate and tender expressions of paternal exultation repeated to her the sum of his conversation with the count. Mary was almost wild at this discourse. So inconsistent and erratic is the passion of love, when it reigns in woman's breast, she forgot in an instant the looks and voice of Thaddeus ; she forgot her terror of having forfeited his affection by her affected coldness alone; and dreading that the first proposal of their union had proceeded from her uncle, she buried her agitated face in her hands, and exclaimed, "O sir! I fear that you have made me forever hateful in my own eyes and despicable in those of the Count Sobieski!"

Sir Robert looked on her emotion with a smiling but a pitying gaze, reading in all the unaffected apprehensive modesty of that noble maiden's heart.

"Well," cried he, in a gentle raillery of tone, "my own beloved one! if thy guardian uncle cannot prevail over this wayward fancifulness, so unlike his ingenuous Mary's usual fair dealing with the truth of others, I must call in even a better-accredited pleader, and shall then leave my object, the balance of justice and mercy, in equally beloved hands."

While he spoke, he rose and opened a door that led to an adjoining room. Miss Beaufort would have flown through another had not Sir Robert suddenly stood in her way. He threw his arm about her, and turning round, she saw the count, who had entered, regarding her with an anxiety which covered her before pale features with blushes.

His father bade him come near. Sobieski obeyed, though with a step that expressed how reluctant he was to oppress the woman he so truly loved. Mary's face was now hidden in her uncle's bosom. Sir Robert put her trembling hand into that of his son, who, dropping on his knee, said, in an agitated voice, "Honored, dearest Miss Beaufort! may I indulge myself in the idea that I am blessed with your regard?"

She could not reply, but whispered to her uncle, "Pray, sir, desire him to rise! I am overwhelmed."

"My sweet Mary!" returned the baronet, pressing her to his breast, "this is no time for deception on either side. I know both your hearts. Rise, Thaddeus," said he to the count, whilst he locked both their hands within his. "Take him, Mary! Receive from your guardian his most precious gift—my matchless and injured son."

The abruptness of the first part of this speech might have shocked her exhausted spirits to insensibility, had not the extraordinary assertion at its end, and Sir Robert's audible sobs, aroused and surprised her.

"Your son!" exclaimed she; "what do you mean, my uncle?"

"Thaddeus will explain all to you," returned he. "May Heaven bless you both!"

Mary was too much astonished to think of following her agitated uncle out of the room. She sunk on a seat, and turning her gaze full of amazement towards the count, seemed to ask an explanation. Thaddeus, who still retained her passive hand, pressed it warmly to his heart; and whilst his effulgent eyes were beaming on her with joyous love, he imparted to her a concise but impressive narrative of his relationship with Sir Robert. He touched with short yet deep enthusiasm, with more than one tearful pause, on the virtues of his mother; he acknowledged the unbounded gratitude which was due to that God who had so wonderfully conducted him to find a parent and a home in England, and with renewed pathcs of look and manner ratified the proffer which Sir Robert had made of his heart and hand to her who alone on this earth had reminded him of that angelic parent. "I have seen her beloved face, luminous in purity and tender pity, reflected in yours, ever-honored Miss Beaufort, when your noble heart, more than once, looked in compassion on her son. And I then felt, with a wondering bewilderment, a sacred response in my soul, though I could not explain it to myself. But since then that sister spirit of my mother has often whispered it as if direct from heaven."

Mary had listened with uncontrollable emotion to this interesting detail. Her eyes overflowed: their ingenuous language, enforced by the warm blood which glowed on her cheek, did not require the medium of words to declare what was passing in her mind. Thaddeus gazed on her with a certainty of bliss which penetrated his soul until its raptures almost amounted to pain. The heart may ache with joy; neither sighs nor language could express what passed in his mind. He held her hand to his lips; his other arm fell unconsciously round her waist, and in a moment he found that he had pressed her to his breast. His heart beat violently. Miss Beaufort rose instantaneously from her chair; but her pure nature needed no disguise. She looked up to him, whilst her blushing eyes were shedding tears of delight, and said in a trembling voice: "Tell my dear uncle that Mary Beaufort glories in the means by which she becomes his daughter."

She moved to the door. Thaddeus, whose full tide of transport denied him utterance, only clasped her hands again to his lips and bosom; then, relinquishing them, he suffered her to quit the room.

CHAPTER XLVIII.

A FAMILY PARTY.

The magnificent establishment which this projected union offered to Sobieski seemed to heal the yet bleeding conscience of Sir Robert Somerset. Although he had acquiesced in the count's generous surrender of the family-inherited honors, his heart remained still ill at ease. Every dutiful expression from his long-neglected son at times had stung him with remorse. But Miss Beaufort's avowed and returned affection at once removed the lingering accuser from his bosom. Mistress of immense wealth, her hand would not only put the injured Thaddeus in possession of the pure delights which only a mutual sympathy can bestow, but would enable his munificent spirit to again exert itself in the worthy disposal of an almost princely fortune.

Such meditations having followed the now tranquillized baronet to his pillow, they brought him into the breakfast-parlor next day full of that calm pleasure which promises a steady continuance. The happy family were assembled. Miss Dorothy saluted her brother, whose brightened eye declared that he had something pleasant to communicate; and he did not keep her in suspense. With the first cup of coffee the good lady poured out, his grateful heart unburdened itself of the delightful tidings that ere many months, perhaps weeks, he had reason to hope Miss Beaufort would give her hand to the Count Sobieski. Pembroke was the only hearer who did not evince surprise at this announcement. Every one else had been kept uninformed, on the especial injunction of Sir Robert, who desired its knowledge to be withheld till he had completed some necessary preliminaries in his mind. But Thaddeus, by the permission of the happy parent, during a long and interesting conversation in his library, which passed between the father and his new-found son, immediately after the latter's blissful parting with his then heart-affianced Mary, had hastened to his brother, and retiring with him to his little study, there communicated, in full and enraptured confidence, the whole events of the recent mutual explanations.

During Sir Robert's animated disclosure, Mary's blushing yet grateful eyes sought a veil in a branch of geranium which she held in her trembling hand.

Miss Dorothy rose from her chair; her smiling tears spoke more than her lips when she pressed first her niece and then the Count Sobieski in her venerable arms.

"Heaven bless you both!" cried she. "This marriage will be the glory of my age."

Miss Beaufort turned from the embrace of her aunt to meet the warm congratulations of Pembroke. Whilst he kissed her burning cheek, he whispered, loud enough for every one to hear, "And why may I not brighten in my good aunt's triumph? Attempt it, dear Mary! If you can persuade my father to allow me to make myself as happy with Lady Albina Stanhope as you will render Sobieski, I shall forever bless you!"

Lady Albina colored and looked down. Sir Robert took her hand with pleased surprise. "Do you, my lovely guest—do you sanction what this bold boy has just said?"

Lady Albina made no answer; but, blushing deeper than before, cast a sidelong glance at Pembroke, as if to petition his support. He was at her side in an instant; then seriously and earnestly entreating his father's consent to an union with their gentle kinswoman (whose approbation he had obtained the preceding day in the shepherd's hut), he awaited with anxiety the sounds which seemed faltering on Sir Robert's lips

The baronet, quite overcome by his ever-beloved Pembroke having, like his brother, disposed of his heart so much to his own honor, found himself unable to say what he wished. Joining the hands of the two young people in silence, he hurried out of the room. He ascended to the library, where kneeling down, he returned devout thanks to that "all-gracious Being who had crowned one so unworthy with blessings so conspicuous."

Thaddeus, no less than his father, remembered the hand which, having guided him through a sharply-beset wilderness of sorrow, had in so short a term conducted him to an Eden of bliss. Long afterwards, when years had passed over his happy head, and his days became dedicated to various important duties, public and private, attendant on his station in life and the landed power he held in his adopted country, never did he forget that he was "only a steward of the world's Benefactor!" The sense of whose deputy he was gave to his heart a grateful conviction that in whatever spot he might be so placed, he was to consider it as his country!—the Canaan of his commission.

Before the lapse of a week, it became expedient that Sir Robert should hasten the marriage of Pembroke with Lady Albina, or be forced by law to yield her to the demands of her father. After much search, Lord Tinemouth had discovered that his daughter was under the protection of Sir Robert Somerset. Inflamed with rage and revenge, he sent to order her immediate return, under pain of an instantaneous appeal to the courts of judicature.

Too well aware that her nonage laid her open to the realization of this threat, Lady Albina fell into the most alarming swoonings on the first communication of the message. Sir Robert urged that in her circumstances no authority could be opposed to the earl's excepting that of a husband's; and on this consideration she complied with his arguments and the prayers of her lover, to directly give that power into the hands of Pembroke.

Accordingly, with as little delay as possible, accompanied by Miss Dorothy and the enraptured Mr. Somerset, the terrified Lady Albina commenced her journey to Scotland, that being the only place where, in her situation, the marriage could be legally solemnized. A clerical friend of the baronet's, who dwelt just over the borders, could perform the rite with every proper respect.

Whilst these young runaways, chaperoned by an old maiden aunt, were pursuing their rapid flight across the Tweed, Sir Robert sent his steward to London to prepare a house near his own in Grosvenor Square for the reception of the bridal pair. During these necessary arrangements, a happy fortnight elapsed at Deerhurst—thrice happy to Mary, because its tranquil hours imparted to her long-doubting heart "a sober certainty of that waking bliss" which had so often animated with hope the visions of her imagination, when contemplating the mystery of such a mind as that of Thaddeus having been destined to the humble lot in which she had found him. Morning, noon, and evening the loving companion of the Count Sobieski, she saw with deepened devotedness that the brave and princely virtues did not reign alone in his bosom. Their full lustre was rendered less intense by the softening shades of those gentler amenities which are the soothers and sweeteners of life. His breast seemed the residence of love—of a love that not only infused a warmer existence through her soul, but diffused such a light of benevolence over every being within its influence, that all appeared happy who caught a beam of his eye—all enchanted who shared the magic of his smile. Under what different aspects had she seen this man! Yet how consistent! At the first period of their acquaintance, she beheld him, like that glorious orb which her ardent fancy told her he resembled, struggling with the storm, or looking dimmed, yet unmoved, through the clouds which obscured his path; but now, like the radiant sun of summer amidst a splendid sky, he seemed to stand the source of light, and love, and joy.

Thus did the warm fancy and warmer heart of Mary Beaufort paint the image of her lover; and when Sir Robert received intelligence that the Scottish party had arrived in town, and were impatient for the company of the beloved inhabitants of Deerhurst, while preparing to revisit the proud and gay world, she confessed that some embers of human pride did sparkle in her own bosom at the anticipation of witnessing the homage which they who had despised the unfriended Constantine would pay to the declared and illustrious Sobieski.

The news of Lady Albina's marriage infuriated the Earl of Tinemouth almost to frenzy. Well assured that his withholding her fortune would occasion no vexation to a family of Sir Robert Somerset's vast possessions, he gave way to still more vehement bursts of passion, and in a fit of impotent threatening embarked with all his household to spend the remainder of the season on his much-disregarded estates in Ireland.

This abrupt departure of the earl caused Lady Albina little uneasiness. His unremitted cruelty, her brother's indifference, and the barbed insults of Lady Olivia Lovel, now the earl's wife, rankled too deeply in the daughter's bosom to leave any filial regret behind. Considering their absence a suspension of pain rather than a punishment, she did not stain the kiss which she imprinted on the revered cheek of her new parent with one tear to the memory of her unnatural father.

Whilst all was splendor and happiness in Grosvenor Square. Thaddeus did not forget the excellent Mrs. Robson. He hastened to St. Martin's Lane, where the good woman received him with open arms. Nanny hung, crying for joy, upon his hand, and sprung rapturously about his neck when he told her he was now a rich man, and that she and her grandmother should live with him forever. "I am going to be married, my dear Mrs. Robson," said he; "that ministering angel who visited you when I was in prison was sent to wipe away the tears from my eyes." Drying the cheek of his weeping landlady, while he spoke, with his own handkerchief, he continued:—"She commanded me not to leave you until you had assured me that you will brighten our happiness by taking possession of a pretty cottage close to her house in Kent. It is within Beaufort Park, and there my Mary and myself will visit you continually."

"Blessed Mr. Constantine!" cried the worthy woman, pressing his hand; "myself, my Nanny, we are yours;—take us where you please, for wherever you go, there will the Almighty's hand lead us, and there will his right hand hold us."

The count rose and turned to the window; his heart was full, and he was obliged to take time to recover himself before he could resume the conversation. He saw her twice after this; and on the day of her departure for Kent, to await in her own new home his and his Mary's arrival there, he put into her hand the first quarterly payment of an annuity which would henceforward afford her every comfort, and raise her to that easy rank in society which her gentle manners and rare virtues were so admirably fitted to adorn. Neither did he neglect Mr. Burket. It was not in his nature to allow any one who served him to pass unrewarded. He called on him on the last day he visited St. Martin's Lane, (when Mrs. Watts, too, shared his bounty,) and having repaid him with a generosity which astonished the good money-lender, he took back his sword, and the venerated old seals he had left with Mrs. Robson to get repaired by the same honest hand; also the other precious relics he had had refitted to their original settings, and pressing them mournfully yet gratefully to his breast, re-entered Sir Robert's carriage to drive home. What bliss to his heart was in that word?

Next day Thaddeus directed his steps to Dr. Cavendish's. He found his worthy friend at home, who received him with kindness. But how was that kindness increased to transport when Thaddeus told him, with a smiling countenance, that he was the very Sobieski about whose wayward fate he had asked so many ill-answered questions. The delighted doctor embraced him with an ardor which spoke better than language his admiration and esteem. His amazement having subsided, he was discoursing with animated interest on events at once so fatal and so glorious to Sobieski, when a gentleman was announced by the name of Mr. Hopetown. He entered; and Dr. Cavendish at the same time introducing Thaddeus as the Count Sobieski, Mr. Hopetown fixed his eyes upon him with an expression which neither of the friends could comprehend. A little disconcerted at the merchant's seeming rudeness, the good doctor attempted to draw off the steadiness of his gaze by asking how long he had been in England.

"I left Dantzic," replied he, "about three weeks ago; and I should have been in London five days since, but a favorite horse of mine, which I brought with me, fell sick at Harwick, and I waited until he was well enough to travel.'

Whilst he spoke he never withdrew his eyes from the face of Thaddeus, who at the words Dantzic and horse recollected his faithful Saladin; almost hoping that this Mr. Hopetown might prove to be the Briton to whom he had consigned the noble animal, he took a part in the conversation by inquiring of the merchant whether he were a resident of Dantzic.

"No, your excellency," replied he; "I live within a mile of it. Several years ago I quitted the smoke and bustle of the town to enjoy fresh air and quiet."

"Last year," rejoined Sobieski, "I passed through Dantzic on my way to England. I believe I saw your house, and remarked its situation. The park is beautiful."

"And I am indebted, count," resumed the merchant, "to a nobleman of your country for its finest ornament: I mean the very horse I spoke of just now. He was sent to me one morning, with a letter from his brave owner, requesting me to give him shelter in my park. He is the most beautiful animal I ever beheld. Unwilling to leave behind so valuable a deposit, when I came to England I brought him with me."

"Poor Saladin!" cried Thaddeus, his heart overflowing with remembrance; "how glad I shall be to see thee!"

"What! was the horse yours?" asked Dr. Cavendish, surprised at this apostrophe.

"Yes," returned Thaddeus, "he was mine! and I owe to Mr. Hopetown a thousand thanks for his generous acquiescence with the prayers of an unfortunate stranger."

"No thanks to me, Count Sobieski. The moment I entered this room, I recollected you to be the same Polish officer I had observed on the beach at Dantzic. When I described your figure to the man who brought the horse, he said it was the same who gave him the letter. I could not learn your excellency's name; but I hoped one day or other to have the pleasure of meeting you again, and of returning Saladin into your hands in as good condition as when he came to mine."

Tears started into the eyes of Thaddeus.

"That horse, Mr. Hopetown, has carried me through many a bloody field; he alone witnessed my last adieu to the bleeding corpse of my country! I shall receive him again as an old and dear friend; but to his kind protector, how can I ever demonstrate the whole of my gratitude?" *

* The love of Thaddeus to his horse has had some resemblances in the author's knowledge in yet more recent times. It seems to belong to the brave heart of every country in our civilized Europe, as well as in that of the wild Arab of the desert, to companion itself with his war-steed as with a friend or brother. I knew more than one gallant man who wept over the doom of his old charger when shot in the lines near Corunna; and another, of

"To have had it in my power to serve the Count Sobieski is a privilege of itself," returned Mr. Hopetown. "I am proud of that distinction; to be called the friend of a man who all the world honors will be a title which John Hopetown may be proud of."

Before the worthy merchant took his leave, he promised Thaddeus to send Saladin to Grosvenor Square that evening, and accepted his invitation to meet him and Dr. Cavendish the following day at dinner at Mr. Somerset's.

CHAPTER XLIX.

"If I forget thee, O Jerusalem, let my right hand forget her cunning."

LADY Albina Somerset's arrival in London was greeted by the immediate visits of all the persons in town who had been esteemed by the late Countess of Tinemouth, or on intimate terms with the baronet's family. It was not the gay season for the metropolis. Amongst the earliest names that appeared at her door were those of Lord Berrington, the Hon. Captain and Mrs. Montresor, and the Rev. Dr. Blackmore. Under any circumstances, either in the country or in town, Mr. Somerset and his young bride did not propose opening their gates to more general acquaintances until Miss Beaufort and the count were married, and both bridal parties had been presented at court in the spring. To this little select group of friends who were to assemble round Mr. Somerset's table on the appointed day, Thaddeus informed him, with frank pleasure, that he had taken the liberty of adding Dr. Cavendish and Mr. Hopetown of Dantzic.

Lady Albina received the two strangers with graceful hospitality. The affianced Mary, with an equally blushing grace, presented her hand to the generous protector of Saladin, accompanying the action with a modest acknowledgment of her

the same and other fields, who can never mention without turning pale the name of his faithful and beloved horse Columbus, who had carried him through various dangers on the South American continent, and at last perished by his side during a tremendous storm at sea, when no exertions of his master could save him. These are pangs of which only those who have the generous sensibility to feel them can have any idea. But they are true to the noble nature of which the inspired page speaks when it says, "The just man is merciful to his beast."—1822.

The benignant master of the regretted Columbian steed was the late Sir R. K. Porter, the lamented brother of the yet surviving writer of the preceding note.—1845.

interest in an animal so deservedly dear to the Count Sobieski. He had turned to meet Lord Berrington and the ever lively Sophia Egerton (now Mrs. Montresor), who both advanced to him at the same instant, to express their gratulations not only at seeing him again, but in a situation of happy promise, so consonant to his avowed rank and personal early fame.

Thaddeus replied to their felicitations with a smiling dignity, in that ingenuous manner peculiarly his own. He was not a little surprised when Dr. Blackmore soon after recognized him be the noble foreigner whose appearance had so much excited his attention, about a twelvemouth ago, at the Hummums, in Covent Garden. The count did not recollect the circumstance of having seen the good doctor there; but the venerable man recapitulated the scene in the coffee-room through which the count had passed, describing, with no little animation, "a pedantic-mannered person, dressed in black, and wearing spectacles (whose name he afterwards learned was Loftus), an M.A. of one of the colleges, who took the liberty to make some not very liberal remarks on the number of noble strangers then confiding themselves to the honorable sanctuary and sympathy of our country."

Pembroke could hardly hear the benevolent speaker to the end; stifling any audible expression of his re-awakened indignation, he whispered to the baronet, "My dear father! recent happy events have made us almost forget that villain's baseness; but I pray, let him not remain another week a blot upon our house's escutcheon."

"All shall be done as you wish," returned his father, in the same subdued tone; "but let us remember how much of that recent happiness the goodness of Providence hath brought out of this wretched man's offence. Were I extreme to mark what is done amiss, how could I abide the sentence that might be justly pronounced against myself? To-morrow we will talk over this matter, and settle it, I trust, with satisfaction to all parties."

Pembroke gratefully pressed his father's hand, and then, walking up the room, addressed Mrs. Montresor. In a few minutes her brave husband joined them. While talking of his late victorious and happily-completed homeward-bound voyage, he spoke with great regret of the threatened absence from England of his late colleague on the battle-field of the ocean, his old friend Captain Ross.

"How—whither is he going?" asked his wife, in a tone of interest.

Montresor replied, "The ill state of Lady Sara's health requires a milder air, and poor Ross means to take her without loss of time to Italy. I met him this morning, in despair about the suddenness of some alarming symptoms."

Thaddeus too well divined that this increased indisposition owed its rise to his recent return to town, and inwardly petitioning Heaven that absence and her husband's devoted tenderness might complete her cure, he could not repress a sigh, wrung from his respectful pity towards her, in this deep bosom-struggle with herself.

No one present except the future partner of his own heart marked the transient melancholy which passed over his countenance. She, who had suspected the unhappy Lady Sara's attachment, loved Thaddeus, if possible, still dearer for the compassion he bestowed on the meek penitence of the unhappy victim of a passion often as inscrutable as destructive.

When the party descended to dinner, Miss Dorothy, who sat next to the Count Sobieski, rallied him upon the utter desertion of one of his most pertinacious allies or adversaries—she did not know which to call the fair delinquent. "For admiring or detesting seemed quite the same to some ladies, so they did but show their power of mischief over any poor mortal man they found in their way!"

This strange attack, though uttered in perfect good humor by the lively old lady, following so closely the information relative to Lady Sara Ross, summoned a fervid color into the count's face; he looked surprised, and rather confused, at the revered speaker, who soon gayly related what she had been told that morning by her milliner, of "Miss Euphemia Dundas being on the point of marriage with a young Scotch nobleman in Berwickshire; and in proof, her elegant informant, Madame de Maradon, was making the bridal *trousseau*."

"So much the better for all straight-going people, *ma chere tante*," cried Pembroke; "little Phemy was no contemptible assailant either way. Besides," added he, turning airily to his own gentle bride, "you, my young lady, may congratulate yourself on the same good hope. I hear that an old turf-comrade of mine is going to take her loving sister off my hands. Come, Lord Berrington, you must verify my report, for I learned it from you."

His lordship smiled, and answered in the affirmative, adding that a friend of his in Lincolnshire, had written to him as most amusing news, "That the most worthy Orson, heir of all the lands, tenements, stables, and kennels of the doughty Sir

Helerand Shafto, of that ilk, and twenty ilks besides north of the Humber, had been discovered by the wonderful occult penetration possessed by the exceedingly blue sorceress-lady, Miss Diana Dundas (of as many ilks north of the Tweed), to be no Orson at all; but her very veritable Valentine, to whom she was now preparing to give her fair and golden-garnished hand in the course of the forthcoming month; that is, when the season of hunting and shooting is past and gone, and the chase-wearied pair may turn themselves, with their blown horses and hounds, to a little wholesome rustication in their homestead fields."

"I would not be their companion for Nebuchadnezzar's crown!" reiterated Pembroke, laughing.

Sobieski, not suppressing the smile that played on his lip at the whimsical description given by Lord Berrington's correspondent, wished the nuptials happy, as far as the parties could comprehend the feeling. The viscount in return protested that their Polish friend "was more generous than just in such a benediction."

"I vow to heaven," cried his lordship, "that I never knew people the aim of whose lives seemed so bent on sly mischief as those two sisters. Euphemia, pretty as she is, is better known by her skill in tormenting than by her beauty. And as for the poor squire Diana has conjured into matrimony, I have little doubt of his future baited fate when she springs her dogs of war upon that petted deer!"

"Ah, poor fool!" exclaimed Mrs. Montresor, "I warrant he will not escape the punishment he merits, for stepping between the goddess and her delectable Endymion, Lascelles."

"Quarter for an old acquaintance!" whispered Miss Beaufort, in a beseeching voice.

"She does not deserve it of you!" returned the lady, pursuing her ridiculous game, until both Miss Dorothy and Sir Robert petitioned for mercy from so fair a judge.

Thaddeus, who possessed not the disposition to exult in the misconduct or mischances of any one who had injured him, felt this part of the conversation the least pleasant on that happy day, and to change its strain, he, in his turn, whispered to his father "to prevail on Lady Albina to indulge his friend Mr. Hopetown by singing a few passages from that beautiful ballad of the Scottish borders, 'Chevy Chase,' which had so delighted their own family party the preceding evening."

He did not ask this "charmed resource" from his own betrothed, because it was only at the close of that very preceding evening he had for the first time heard her voice, "in sweetest melody," chanting forth the parting anthem for the night, "From the ends of the earth, I will call upon thee, O Lord," and with tones of a kindred pathos, too thrilling to a son's startled ear and memory, to be invoked again in a mixed company.

Strange, indeed, it might be, but it was a sacred balm to his soul when these recurring remembrances discovered to his heart in the young and lovely future partner of his life a bond of union with that angelic mother who had given him being; and perhaps this devoted filial heart alone could appreciate the joy, the comfort, the bliss of such a similitude! But in after days he shared those feelings with his father, bringing to his regretful bosom a soothing perception of the likeness.

Lady Albina instantly complied, casting a sweet glance at Sir Robert, who immediately led her to the piano-forte, followed by the Scottish merchant of the Baltic, whither the noble symphony of "The Douglas," "hound and horn," soon gathered the rest of the company. The remainder of the evening passed away delightfully in the awakened harmony. Mrs. Montresor joined Lady Albina in some touching Italian duets; Pembroke supported both ladies in a fine trio of Mozart's; Mr. Hopetown requested another favorite son of his country, "Auld Robin Gray," and himself repaid Lady Albina's kind assent by a magnificent voluntary on his part, "Scots wha hae wi' Wallace bled." Mary accompanied that well-known pibroch of "The Bruce" with a true responsive echo from her harp; but she declined singing herself, and when Thaddeus took the relinquished instrument from her hand, he pressed it with a silent tenderness, sweeter to her than could have been the plaudits of all the accomplished listeners around. That soft hand had stroked the branching neck of his recovered Saladin the same morning, and the happy master now marked his feeling of the gentle deed.

In the course of a few days, Pembroke's wishes with regard to Mr. Loftus were put into a train of fulfilment, Dr. Blackmore having undertaken to find a fitting tutor for the young Lord Avon, and in the interim would receive him into his own classical instruction, whenever it should be deemed proper to terminate his present holiday visit in Bedfordshire. But whilst Sir Robert had thus adjudged the guilty, he was careful not to expose him to fresh temptations, nor to suffer his crimes to implicate the innocent in its punishment. Hence, in pity to age and helplessness, he determined to settle two hundred pounds per annum on the wretched man's mother and sisters, who dwelt together in Wales. Shortly after, in consequence of his contrite confessions, "that all Mr. Somerset's allegations against him were too true," the humane father and son appointed one hundred pounds more to be paid yearly to the culprit himself, so that at least he might not be induced to lighten his honest labors for a suitable subsistence by renewed villanies. With reference to the benefice of Somerset, which had been the ill-sought price of this base pretender to sanctity and truth, Sir Robert decided on presenting it to the exemplary Dr. Blackmore whenever it should become vacant.

Meanwhile, the baronet's sojourn in town became indispensably prolonged, not only by the simple nature of the affairs that brought him thither, but by certain unlooked-for intricacies occurring in making a final adjustment of the various settlements and consequent conveyances to be effected on account of the two felicitous marriages in his family. During these lingering proceedings amongst the legal protectors of "soil and surety," Miss Beaufort remained the cherished and cheering guest of the already espoused pair, one of whom, indeed, still wore the garb of "a mourning bride," but all within was clad in the true white robe of nuptial purity and peace. Sobieski was the now no less privileged abiding inmate in the home and heart of Sir Robert Somerset. Increasing daily in favor with "good aunt Dorothy," the presiding mistress of his father's house, he soon became nearly as precious in her sight as had long been the pleasant society of her nephew Pembroke. And all this her ingenuous and affectionate nature avowed to Mary, in their frequent visits between the two houses, with a sort of delighted wonder at her heart's so prescient recognition of the new nephew her sweet niece was to bestow upon her. For it had not yet been revealed to her that Thaddeus did stand in that same tender relationship to her by a former marriage of her beloved brother with the lamented mother of the noble object of her cherished esteem. And what was the double joy of the blessed moment when that happy secret was confided to her bosom.

The last busy month of autumn in London had not only laid down its wearied head under the dark canopy of a murky atmosphere, lit with dimmed street-lamps to its slumbers, but its expected refreshment in the country did not offer much more agreeable materials for repose and vernal renovation. There were blustering winds strewing the recently green earth with beds of withered leaves of every foliage, stripped and fallen from the shivering woods above. And there were drenching rains, laying the lately pleasant fields in trackless swamps, and swelling the clear and gentle brooks into brawling floods, rending asunder the long-remembered rustic bridges which had hitherto linked the villages together, in convenient passages for wholesome relaxation or useful toil.

Such were the newspaper accounts from the country during the latter part of November; but there was seen a fairer prospect from the carriage windows of Sir Robert Somerset, when he and his gladdened party, one bright morning, on quitting the splashy environs of Hammersmith and Brentford, entered the broad expanse of Hounslow Heath, on their way into Warwickshire, and beheld its wide common covered with a fair carpet of spotless snow. Winter had then seriously, or, rather, smilingly, set in. It was the 10th of December; and the baronet, having signed and sealed all things necessary to transfer with perfect satisfaction himself and family (as was always his custom at this homeward season), now set forth to one or other of his ancient domains, to pass his Christmas in the bosom of an enlarged and a grateful domestic happiness. Thus, year after year, he diffused from each of those parental mansions that bounteous hospitality to high and low which he considered to be an especial duty in an English gentleman, whether in the character of "landlord" to noble guests and respected neighbors, or to wayfaring strangers passing by; or, while graciously mingling with his widely-established tenantry, or his equally regarded daily guests at this "holy festival," the virtuous, lowly peasantry, laborers on the land. Then smiled the cottager, with honest consciousness of yeoman worth, when seated in the great hall, under the eye of his munificent lord, who partook of the general feast. Then, too, did he smile when, at the head of his own little board, he sat with his children and humbler dependents, all furnished with ample Christmas fare by the baronet's still open hand.

When Thaddeus shared these primeval scenes of old England by the side of his British parent, (which festivities are still honorably preserved by some of its most ancient and noblest families,) they brought back to his heart those similar assemblages at Villanow and in Cracovia, where his revered grandfather, the palatine, had reigned prince and father over every happy breast.*

And happy were now the recollections of all who met at

* The writer remembers a similar scene to the above when she had the honor of dining along with her revered family, on a festival of harvest-home at Bushy Palace, when its royal owner, his late majesty, was Duke of Clarence. Himself moved through his rustic guests in the gracious manner described.

Deerhurst on this their first joyful Christmas season! Week after week glided along in the bland exercise of social duties, aided by the more homefelt enjoyments of sweet domestic affections, which gave a living grace to all that was said or done, and more intimately knit hearts together, never more to be divided.

But winter's howling blasts and sheltering halls, "where fireside comforts, taste, and gentle love, with soft amenities mingled into bliss," swiftly and fairer, changed their pleasant song, proclaiming in every brightening hue the hymn of nature—

> "These, as they change, Almighty Father!
> Are but the varied God! The rolling year
> Is full of Thee! Forth in the pleasing spring
> Thy beauty walks, thy tenderness and love;"

and in the first month of that genial season, when the young grass covers the downy hills with verdure, and the glowing branches of the trees bud with an infant foliage, the sun smiles in the heavens, and the pellucid streams reflect his glorious rays, the day was fixed by Sir Robert Somerset, and approved by the beloved objects of his then peculiar solicitude, in which his paternal hand should plight theirs together before the altar of eternal truth.

The solemnity was to be performed in the village church, which stood in the park of Deerhurst, and the Rev. Dr. Blackmore, who came over from his own private dwelling in Worcestershire, accompanied by his pupil, Lord Avon, was to perform the holy rite. No adjunct of the Roman Catholic ceremony (then the national church of Poland) was needful fully to legalize it. Thaddeus from his infancy had been reared in the Protestant faith, the faith of his mother, whose own mother was a daughter of the staunch Hussite race of the princely Zamoiski, who still professed that ancient, simple creed of their country. It was also the national faith of him who had given Therese's son being; therefore, to the same pure doctrine of Christianity had she dedicated his deserted child; and should they ever meet again, she believed it must be before the throne of Divine Mercy; and there she trusted to present their solitary offspring with the sacred words—"Here I am, Lord, and the child thou didst give me."

But to return to the marriage-day itself. The hour having arrived in which the soul-devoted Mary Beaufort was to resign herself and her earthly happiness into the power of the only man to whom, having once beheld and known him, she could ever have committed them, she pronounced her vows at the sacred altar with unsteadiness of tongue but with a fixed heart. And when, after embracing all the fond kindred so long dear to her, and now to him, and having received their parting blessings within the walls of her ever-cherished home,—sweet, while familiar Deerhurst,—she was driven rapidly through its gates, while a mixed and awed emotion agitated her breast. But immediately she felt the supporting arm of her husband gently pressing her trembling form; and so, with all that husband's tender sympathy, the hours glided away unperceived, till the august towers of her own native domain appeared on the evening horizon, and soon afterwards she alighted at the mansion itself, having passed along a central avenue of ancient oaks amid the congratulatory cheers of a large assemblage of her tenantry on horseback and on foot, planted on each side, to bid a glad welcome to their "liege lady and her lord."

Within the great entrance of the baronial hall, which opened to her by the immediate raising of a massive brazen portcullis, the ancient insignia of the Beaufort name, she received the joyful obeisance of the old domestics of her honored parents, hailing her, their beloved daughter, with a humble ardor of affection that bathed her enraptured face with filial tears. Thaddeus felt the scene in his own recollective heart.

Next morning Mrs. Robson and the delighted Nanny (dressed in a white frock for the blissful occasion), on being brought into the countess's private saloon, threw themselves at the feet of their benefactors and sobbed forth their happiness. The still more happy Sobieski raised them in his arms, and, embracing both, accosted the old lady as he would have done a revered relative, and the affectionate little girl like an adopted child.

The same day the vicar of Beaufort, whose large rural parish extended from the Castle to several miles around, rode to the gate, and was announced by name (the Rev. Mr. Tillotson), to pay his pastoral duty to his future noble neighbors and sacred charge, the owners of the land.

"His is a good name," observed Mary, with a gracious smile; "it was borne by one of the brightest luminaries of our Protestant church, Archbishop Tillotson, whose works you will find in the family library, now your own. And his descendant, the revered late vicar, christened me in the dear old church of the adjacent village, to which we go to-morrow, Sunday. Oh, how much have I to bless Heaven for in that holy place!" she tenderly ejaculated. "You, kneeling by my side there—one faith, one heart, one death, one salvation. O, my husband, I am blessed indeed!"

"My Mary, in earth and heaven!" was his soul's response, and with the words he pressed her fervently-clasped hands with a hallowed emotion to his lips.

In a few minutes after this she led the way to the ancient library, tapestried with family portraits, and furnished with book-cases of every past generation. Thither the young vicar, a truly worthy successor to his pious father, had been conducted; and there, being introduced by the countess (who had seen him only once before) to her lord, they found him not merely a clergyman to be respected, but an accomplished general scholar and a polished man.*

Thus was Thaddeus, the long-cherished orphan of a broken paternal vow, by a wondrous providence established in his new British character—a husband, and an owner of large estates in the soil. And he soon became fully sensible to the double commission devolved upon himself. Whether as a son of Poland, in right of the life he had drawn from his mother's bosom, or as one equally claimed by England, in right of his paternal parent, he was well prepared to faithfully fulfil their relative duties, with a zeal to each respondent to the important privileges and blessings of so signal a lot. In two short preceding years he had indeed passed through a host of severe trials; but in all he had been supported by an Almighty hand, and under the same gracious trust he now looked forward to a long Sabbath of hallowed peace, and of grateful service to Him who bestowed it.

He had met it at Deerhurst, when under his father's roof; he maintained it at Beaufort, the seat of his most continuous residence; nor did he neglect its duties at Manor Court, Sir Robert's parental gift, and his own near neighborhood. And when the time came round for the family to revisit London, his pleasures there were of a character to correspond with his pursuits in the country, the happiness of others being the source of his own enjoyments.

* Over the gate-like arch of the library door had been erected, by a recent order from the gentlest hand now within its walls, a simple but exquisitely-carved escutcheon, showing the armorial bearing of the ancient and royal house of Sobieski—a crowned buckler, with the family motto, "God is the shield that covers me."

CHAPTER L.

"We are brethren!"

After the termination of the Count Sobieski's first Easter passed with the beloved of his soul in the home of her ancestors, they proceeded together to join Sir Robert Somerset, and their kind aunt Miss Dorothy, in Grosvenor Square, to become again his welcome guests, and always thereafter when in town, while Heaven prolonged their lives to renew the cherished re-union at each succeeding season.

Thus it was that, immediately subsequent to the holy festival, the now revered Lord of Beaufort cheerfully obeyed his father's summons to London, where he found Pembroke and Lady Albina already resettled in their former residence. Having ere long met the gratulatory calls of his metropolitan friends, he daily beheld his lovely bride—lovely in mind as in person—becoming more and more "the worshipped cynosure of neighboring eyes;" not only adorning the highest circles of society, but filling his home with all the ineffable charms of a wedded life, inspired by the gentle graces of domestic tenderness.

One balmy evening in May, when he and his young countess were driving out alone together, which they sometimes did, that she might have the delight of showing to him the varied rural environs of the great and gay royal city of England, the carriage, by her direction, took its course towards Primrose Hill, then crowned by a grove of "fair elm-trees," and clothed with a vesture of green sward, enamelled with wild flowers. Thence the light vehicle threaded a maze of shady lanes and pleasant field-paths, into a rustic, newly-made road, leading a little to the north of Covent Garden.*

Mary proposed stopping a few minutes in that magnificent general garden of the town, to purchase a bouquet of early roses, to present to Sir Robert on their return from their drive.

When the carriage drew up at the entrance of the great parterre, she stepped out to select them. Having quickly combined their fragrant beauties, she put the nosegay into the hand of one of the servants to place on the seat. Being nigh the church porch, she suddenly expressed a wish to her husband.

* All this has since become Regent's Park and its dependencies, whether streets or &c.

on whose arm she leaned, to walk through the church-yard, and that the carriage should meet them at the opposite gate.

Thaddeus, not being aware that this porch belonged to the church where his veteran friend had been buried, gave instant assent; and before he had time to make more than a few remarks on the pure religious architecture of the building, which he thought had attracted his tasteful bride to take a nearer view, she had led him unconsciously to the general's grave. But it was no longer the same as when Sobieski last stood by its side. A simple white marble tomb now occupied the place of its former long grass and yarrow. Surprised, he bent forward, and read with brimming eyes the following inscription:—

1795-6.

Stop, Traveller! Thou treadest on a Hero.

Here rest the mortal remains

of

LIEUTENANT-GENERAL BUTZOU,

Late of the Kingdom of Poland.

A faithful soldier to his Lord and to his country!

He sleeps in Faith and Hope!

Thaddeus for a moment felt as he did when he beheld those "mortal remains" laid there. But his own faith in that hope which consecrated this mortality to an immortal resurrection had then silently spread the balm of its full assurance over all those remembered pangs; and now, without speaking, he led his also pensive and tremulous companion to her carriage, where it awaited them, and seating her within it, clasped her to his breast. His tears, no longer restrained, poured those sweet pledges of a soul-felt approbation into her bosom that made it even ache with excess of happiness. But while the grateful voice of her husband was beginning to breathe its uttered thanks, he found the carriage stop again, in a street not far distant from the one they had just quitted. It drew up at the door of a handsome house, of an apparently contemporary structure with the church. It was the rectory of St. Paul's, Covent Garden and at its portal stood the reverend incumbent, evidently awaiting to receive his guests.

Thaddeus perceived him, and also the welcome of his position; so did his gentle wife, who with a blushing smile explained all the alterations he had observed on the respected grave, avowing that they had been done at her devoted wish, and were effected by the kind agency of that venerable man, the rector of the church, the Honorable Bruce Fitz-James. She then timidly added, (and how beautiful in that timidity!) she had something more to confess; she had ventured, after obtaining permission of the rector for the erection of the monument, to see it once during its progress, and then to promise him that on its completion her honored husband, the Count Sobieski, whose parental friend that noble dead had been, would, when she revealed her secret to him, pay a personal visit along with herself to her beneficent coadjutor, and duly express their united gratitude. She had scarcely spoken her rapid information, when its courteous object descended the portal to approach the carriage. His hat was taken off, and the snow-white hair, blown suddenly by a guest of wind across his benign brow, a little obscured his face, while he conducted the lady from the carriage up the steps of his door. But Sobieski found no difficulty in recognizing the time-blanched locks, which had been wetted by the weeping heavens in that hour of his lonely sorrow, whilst committing to the dust the remains of him whose sacred memorial he had just contemplated, raised by a wife's dear hand.

With these recollections had arisen the image of the pale, delicately-formed boy who had gazed so compassionately into his eyes while taking as he thought his last look at that humble grave; and with this bland recurrence came also the almost closing words of the solemn service, seeming again to proclaim to his heart, "I heard a voice from heaven, saying unto me, Write, From henceforth blessed are the dead who die in the Lord!"

With calmed feelings and perfectly recovered self-possession, Thaddeus now followed his beloved wife (his solace and his joy), led by her delighted host, into the bright-panelled parlor of the rectory, where the mutual introduction instantly took place.

The beneficent old man, with a polished sincerity, declared his high gratification at this visit from the Count Sobieski, brought to him by the gracious lady who so deservedly shared his illustrious name. Thaddeus, with his usual modest dignity, received the implied compliment, and expressed his just sense of the deep obligation conferred on him and his countess by the last consecrated rite to the memory of his most revered friend.

Mary was then seated on an old-fashioned silk-embroidered settee, opposite to the flower-latticed bay-window of the apartment. The rector, with a courteous bow, which in his youth would have been called graceful, as if confident of a permitted privilege, placed himself beside her, while observing to her lord, in reply to these unfeigned thanks, that, "the reported name alone of the veteran patriot who lay there had not ceased from the day of his interment to attract, shrine-like, the pilgrim feet of many persons to the spot who respected and bewailed the fate of Poland."

Sobieski's cheek flushed and his eye kindled at this testimony. To change a subject which he found wrought too powerfully on the recently-regained serenity of his mind, he affectionately inquired for the amiable boy he had seen take so touching an interest in the mournful errand to the church-yard on that ever-remembered day, and who, like a ministering seraph, had so guardingly watched the exposed head of his revered master, under the pitiless element then pouring down.

"He is my nephew," returned the rector, in a tone of tenderness: "Lord Edward Fitz-James. He is in delicate health; the youngest son of my eldest brother, the Marquis Fitz-James, who married late in life. Edward is, indeed, what he appears, a spirit of innocent, happy love, or of condoling commiseration, wherever his gentle footsteps move. And when I rejoin him this autumn, at his father's house in Scotland, and shall tell him that the never-forgotten chief mourner at that simple bier, with whom his own young tears fell in spontaneous sympathy, was the Count Sobieski—a kinsman of his own, whose character was already known to him in its youthful fame and by its honored name—what will be that meek child's exulting ecstasy!"

"A kinsman of that noble boy!" echoed Thaddeus, in surprise. "How may I flatter myself it can be so?"

Mary simultaneously uttered an amazed ejaculation of pleasure at the idea of any real relationship between that venerable man and herself; and he, with an answering look of kindred respect on both the astonished husband and his bride, replied to the former with the unstudied brevity of truth.

"A few sentences will explain it, for I consider it unnecessary to remind my present auditors of two great events in their respective countries. First, with regard to England; the change of royal succession in the Stuart line, from the branch of which James the Second was the head, to that of Brunswick—a backward step, originating in Elizabeth of Bohemia, the daughter of James the First, and therefore, the aunt of James the Second. At the height of these eventful circumstances, the offended sovereign retired with his exemplary queen and their infant son to the continent. There the royal boy continued to be styled, by his father's adherents, James Prince of Wales, but in the general world was usually known by the cognizance of the Chevalier St. George.

"This is the first link in our bracelet, noble lady!" observed the narrator, with a smile, and then proceeded. "I now advance to my second part, the crisis of which took place in Poland, about the same period. At the death of the great John Sobieski, King of Poland, the father of his people, there arose a deep-rooted conspiracy in certain neighboring states, jealous of his late power and glorious name, determining to undermine the accession of his family to the throne; and they found an apt soil to work on in a corresponding feeling ready to break out amongst some of the most influential nobles of the realm. Foreign and domestic revolutionists soon understand each other; and the dynasty of Sobieski being speedily overturned by the double treason of pretended friends and false allies, his three princely sons withdrew from occasioning the dire conflict of a civil war, two into distant lands, the other to the ancestral patrimony, in provinces far from the intrigues of ambition or the temptation of its treacherous lures.

"The two elder brothers, in a natural indignation against the popular ingratitude, took the expatriating destination. But Constantine, the youngest born, with the calm dignity of a son without other desired inheritance than the honor of such a parent, retired to the tranquil seclusion of the castled domain of Olesko, the ancient fortified palace of his progenitors, on the Polish border of Red Russia; and there, in philosophic quiet, he passed his blameless days with science and the arts, and in deeds of true Christian benevolence—the purport of his life. This respected seclusion was ultimately sweetly cheered when 'woman smiled" upon it, in the form of a fair daughter of a neighboring magnate in the adjacent province, whose noble retirement, sharing the same patriotic principles with those of Constantine, yielded to the young philosopher a lovely helpmate for him.

"Prince James, his eldest brother, had meanwhile married a sister of their early associate in arms, the brave Charles of Newburg, when under the royal banner of Sobieski, in the memorable field of Vienna. Alexander, the second son, also met with a distinguished bride in Germany. Both princes were accomplished and handsome men; but one of our countrymen, contemporary and family physician to the late king, familiarly describes them in his curious reminiscences, thus:—' His majesty possessed a fine figure; he was tall and graceful. The nobleness and elevation of his soul were deeply depicted in his countenance and air. Prince James is dark-complexioned, slender in person, and more like a Spaniard than a Pole; he is very social, courteous and liberal. Alexander is of more manly proportions, and of a true Sarmatian physiognomy. But Constantine is an exact likeness of the king, his father.' " *

"And such was my ever-revered grandsire, his only son!" responded the heart of Thaddeus, but he did not utter the words. Meanwhile, the enthusiastic historiographer of a period he was so seldom called to touch on proceeded without a pause.

"In process of time, one fair scion from this illustrious stock became engrafted on our former royal stem. I mean her highness the Lady Clementina, the daughter of Prince James of Poland, who, after his rejection of all foreign aid to re-establish him in his father's kingdom, had, like the abdicated monarch of England, gone about a resigned pilgrim, 'seeking a better country,' till the two families auspiciously met, to brighten each other's remainder of earthly sojourn at St. Germains, in France. Then came the 'sweet bindwith,' the royal maid, the Prince Sobieski's beauteous daughter, to give her nuptial hand to the only son of the exiled king; and so, most remarkably, was united the equally extraordinary destinies of the regal race of the heroic John Sobieski with that of our anointed warrior, Robert Bruce, in the person of his princely descendant, James Fitz-James, in diplomatic parlance styled the Chevalier de St. George; and from that blended blood, and by family connection, sprung from the same branching tree, I feel sanguinely confident that the claim I have set up for myself and gentle nephew, whose kindred spirit the warm heart of the Count Sobieski has already acknowledged, will not be deemed an old man's dream."

A short silence ensued.

Thaddeus had been riveted with an almost breathless attention to this part of the narrative, some of its public circumstances having found a dim recollection in his mind; but his apprehensive mother had always turned him aside from any line in his historical reading which might particularly engage his ever-wakeful interest to the chivalrous nation of his own never avowed parentage, and from which a father's desertion had expatriated him even before his birth. But now, how ample had been the atonement, the restitution, to this forsaken son?

* The writer of this note has seen a magnificent picture of that glorious king, a full length, the stature of life. It was nobly painted by an artist of the period.

Not being able to express any of the kindled feelings this narration had suggested, added to the daily increasing claims the blessing of such an atonement were hourly making on his best affections, he could only grasp the hand of the venerated speaker with a fervent pressure when he ceased. But Mary, irradiating smiles, the emanating light of her soul then at her Maker's feet, gently breathed her ardent felicitations at what she had just heard, which had indeed established her kindred with the venerated friend whose kindness had met her so unreservedly as a stranger.

When the little party so signally brought together, to become mutually entwined, as if already known to each other for years instead of minutes,—when they became composed, after the excited emotions of the disclosure had subsided, the reverend host, now considering the count and countess rather as young cousins to be honored than as guests to be entertained, conversed awhile more particularly with regard to the marquis and his family, and finally accepted, with declared pleasure, the earnest invitation of his gladly responsive new relatives to accompany them the following day, when they would call for him in their carriage, to dine with their dearest guardian and parental friend, Sir Robert Somerset.

"He is my Mary's maternal uncle," remarked Thaddeus, with a calm emphasis, "and has been to me as a father in this her adopted land. I found a brother, also, in his admirable son, Mr. Somerset, whom, with his young bride, you will meet to-morrow at Sir Robert's family table. Hence, my revered kinsman, you see what England still does in her kind bosom for a remnant of the race of Sobieski."

The appointed hour next day arrived. The count called for his friend, who was ready at the door of the rectory mansion, and, after much interesting conversation during the drive, conducted him into the presence of the baronet. Sir Robert greeted his guest in perfect harmony with the filial eloquence of Sobieski, in describing his adopted father's ever-gracious heart, and consequent benignant manners. Thaddeus had repeated to Sir Robert the revealments of yesterday's visit to the honorable and reverend rector of St. Paul's, which had so stirringly mingled with his own most cherished memories.

The cordial reception thus given to the revered narrator gratified him, as a full repayment for his imparted confidence of the day before, though he could not be aware of the real paternal fountain from which these warm welcomes flowed. But Thaddeus recognized it in every word, look, and act of his beloved father, and with his mother in his heart, he appreciated all.

Dr. Cavendish and Dr. Blackmore had been added to the party. Sincere esteem, with an ever-grateful recollection of the past, always spread the board of Sobieski for the former, whenever he might have leisure to enrich it with his highly intellectual store. Dr. Blackmore had arrived the preceding evening with Lord Avon, grown a fine youth, to pass a few days with his patron and friend, Sir Robert Somerset, on his way to transfer his noble charge to the tutorage of the fully competent, though young, vicar of Beaufort, Mr. Tillotson. Lord Avon was to reside in the vicarage, but would also possess the constant personal care of his friends at the Castle, and a home invitation to visit there, with his accomplished tutor, whenever it should be agreeable to Mr. Tillotson to bring him.

The rector of St. Paul's and the recently inducted rector of Somerset (whither he was proceeding after he should have deposited his young lordship at Beaufort) were respectively introduced to each other—worthy brethren in the pure church they were equally qualified to support and to adorn.

When dinner was announced, the Rev. Bruce Fitz-James received the hand of the cheerful Miss Dorothy to lead her down. She had given him a frank greeting of relationship on his being presented to her, as mistress of her brother's house, on his first entrance into the drawing-room. During the social repast, much elegant and intellectual conversation took place, and promises were solicited, both then and after the banquet, by the members of the family group from their several guests for visits at the seasons most pleasant to themselves, to Deerhurst, to Somerset, and to Beaufort. The venerable Fitz-James and his young nephew were particularly besought by Thaddeus and his Mary, who anticipated a peculiar delight in becoming intimately acquainted with that interesting boy. Lord Avon they hoped might prove a companionable attraction to the latter.

The invitations were cordially accepted, the paternal uncle of the young Lord Edward not doubting the ready approbation of his brother, the marquis. And it was arranged that both at Beaufort and at Deerhurst the whole of the baronet's family group should be assembled, including Mr. Somerset and his gentle lady, whose placid graces moved round his ever sparkling vivacity with a softly-tempering shade.

Thus, day after day, week after week, while continuing in town, time passed on in the alternate interchanges of domestic tranquillity and the active exercises of those duties to society in general, and to the important demands of public claims on the present stations of the several individuals on whom such calls were made.

Nor in the country, when returned to their separate dwelling-places, did the same happy and honorable routine cease its genial round. Pembroke's most stationary residence was Somerset Castle, his father's beneficent representative, whose favorite home was Deerhurst. And thus mutually endeared, and worthy of their Heaven-bestowed stewardship, we leave the family of Sir Robert Somerset.

We leave Thaddeus Sobieski, now one of its most beloved members, blessed in the fruition of every earthly good. The virtues, the muses, and the charities were the chosen guests at his abundant table. Poverty could not veil genius from his penetration, nor misfortune obscure the inborn light of its integrity. Though exiled from his native land, where his birth gave him dominion over rich territories, now in the hands of strangers, and a numerous happy people, now no more, he had not yet relinquished the love of empire. But it was not over principalities and embattled hosts that he desired to prolong the sceptre of command. He wished to reign in the soul. His throne was sought in the hearts of the good, the kind, the men of honest industry, and the unfortunate, on whom prosperity had frowned. In fact, the unhappy of every degree and nation found consolation, refuge, and repose within the sheltering domains of Beaufort. No eye looked wistfully on him to turn away disappointed; his smiles cheered the disconsolate, and his protecting arms warded off, when possible, the approach of new sorrows. "Peace was within his walls, and plenteousness within his palaces."

And when a few eventful months of the succeeding year had distinguished its course with the death of the imperious destroyer of Poland, and General Kosciusko (having been set at liberty by her generous successor, and honorably empowered to go whither he willed) had arrived in England on his way to the United States, he sought and found Thaddeus, his young comrade in the fields of Poland, and was hailed with the warmest welcome by that now indeed truly "comforted" brave and last representative of the noble race and name of the glory of his country, the more than once Gideon-shield of Christendom—John Sobieski.

"Ah, my chief!" cried he, while he clasped the veteran to his breast, "I am indeed favored above mortals. I see thee again, on whom I believed the gates of a ruthless prison had closed forever! I have all that remains of my country now within my arms. Kosciusko, my friend, my father, bless your son!"

Kosciusko did bless him, and embalmed the benediction with a shower of tears more precious than the richest unction that ever flowed on a royal head. They were drawn from a Christian soldier's heart—a true patriot and a hero.

Sobieski presented his lovely wife to this illustrious friend, and while he gratefully acknowledged the rare felicity of his ultimate fate, he owned that the retrospection of the past calamity, like a shade in a picture, gives to our present bliss greater force and brightness. But that such felicity was his, he could only ascribe to the gracious providence of God, who "trieth the spirit of man," and can bring him to a joy on earth even like unto a resurrection from the dead. And the conclusion is not even then; "there remaineth yet a better life, and a better country for those who trust in the Lord of earth and heaven!"

APPENDIX.

NOTES

CHIEFLY RELATING TO

GENERAL KOSCIUSKO.

NOTES

THE writer prefaces these notes with the following dedicatory tribute she inscribed to the memory of this illustrious chief in a former but subsequent edition, some years after the first publication of the work. It runs thus :—

THADDEUS OF WARSAW.

THIS TENTH EDITION IS HUMBLY AND AFFECTIONATELY INSCRIBED TO THE MEMORY OF THE LATE JUSTLY REVERED AND RENOWNED

General Thaddeus Kosciusko.

"The spirit of war between nation and nation, and between man and man in those nations, for public supremacy on the one side and private aggrandizement on the other, being still as much the character of the times as in the days when the preceding biographical tale of Poland was written, the author continues to feel the probable consequences of such a crisis in forming the future principles of manly British youth—a feeling which was the origin of the work itself.

"Its direct aim being to draw a distinguishing line between the spirit of true patriotism and that of ambitious public discontent,—between real glory, which arises from benefits bestowed, and the false fame of acquired conquests, which a leader of banditti has as much right to arrogate as would the successful invader of kingdoms,—the character of General Kosciusko, under these views, presented itself to the writer as the completest exemplar for such a picture.

"Enthusiasm attempted to supply the pencil of genius, and though the portraiture be imperfectly sketched, yet its author has been gratified by the sympathy of readers, not only of her own people, but of those of distant nations ; and that the principles of heroic virtue which she sought to inculcate in her narrative were pronounced by its great patriot subject, in a letter he addressed to herself, 'as worthy of his approbation and esteem,' seems, now that he is removed from all earthly influence, to sanction her paying that honest homage to his memory which delicacy forbade her doing while he lived.

"The first publication of this work was inscribed to a British hero, 'a land commander and a tar,' whose noble nature well deserved the title bestowed upon it by his venerable sovereign, George III., ('Cœur-de-Lion.') He, a brother in spirit, fully appreciated the character of Thaddeus Kosciusko, and the writer of this devoted tribute feels that she deepens the tints of honor on each name by thus associating them together. But may the tomb of the British hero be long in finding its place! That of the Polish patriot has already received its sacred deposit, and with the sincere oblation of a not quite stranger's heart, this poor offering is laid on the grave of him who fought for 'his country's freedom, laws, and native king;' who, when riches and a crown were proffered to himself by the then dictator of almost all Europe, declined both, because no price could buy the independence of an honest man.

"Such was General Kosciusko; such was the model of disinterestedness, of tempered valor, and of public virtue which his annalist sought to set forth in the foregoing pages; such was the man who honored their narrator with his approval and esteem! and in that last word she feels a privilege, but with due humility, to thus link some little memorial of herself to after times, by so uniting to the name of Thaddeus Kosciusko that of his humble but sincere aspirer to such themes,

"JANE PORTER.

"LONG-DITTON ON-THAMES, September, 1819."

Since the above inscription was first written and inscribed in the former edition, the brave and benign "Christian knight," the Cœur-de-Lion of our own times, has also been gathered to the tears of his country, and his monumental statue, as if standing on the victorious mount of St. Jean d'Acre, is now preparing to be set up, with its appropriate sacred trophies, in the great Naval Hall at Greenwich. It is understood that his mortal remains will be removed from the Pere la Chaise in Paris, where they now lie, to finally rest in St. Paul's Cathedral, where Nelson sleeps. Kosciusko's tomb is at Cracow, the ancient capital of Poland; and in the manner of its most ancient style of sepulchre, it appears an immense earthen tumulus, piled over the simple-mounded grave, which accumulating portions were severally borne to their hallowed place in the arms alone of each silent mourner, in a certain number of successive days, till the whole was raised into a grand pyramidal mass.

In looking back through the avenue of life to those periods the tale tells of, what events have occurred, public and private, to the countries and the individuals referred to in these memoranda! to persons of lofty names and excellence, both in our own and in other lands, mutually affected with admiration and regret for the virtues and the calamities described. It is an awful contemplation, and in sitting down in my now solitary chamber to its retrospection, I find that nearly half a century has passed since its transactions swept over Europe like a desolating blast. Then I wrote my little chronicle when the birthright independence of Poland was no more; when she lay in her ashes, and her mighty men were trodden into the dust; when the pall of death overspread the country, and her widows and her orphans wandered afar into the trackless wilderness of a barren world.

During this wide expatriation, some distinguished captives, who had fallen in the field, and were counted among the slain, having been found by the victors alive in their stiffened blood, were conveyed to various prisons; and along with these was discovered the justly feared, and not less justly deplored, General Kosciusko, who, though long unheard of by the lone wanderers of his scattered host, had been thus preserved by the supreme Lord of all, to behold again a remnant of his own brightened in hope, and comforted by the honoring sympathy of the good and brave in many nations.

Kosciusko was of noble birth, and early distinguished himself by his spirit and talents for the martial field. Indeed, owing to the belligeren position of Poland, situated in the midst of jealous and encroaching nations, arms was the natural profession of every gentleman in the kingdom, commerce and agriculture being the usual pursuits of the middle classes. But it happened, in the early manhood of Thaddeus Kosciusko, that the dangerous political Stromboli which surrounded his country, and often aroused an answering blaze in that since devoted land, slept in their fires; and Poland being at peace, her young military students, becoming desirous of practising their science in some actual campaign, resolved to try their strength across the Atlantic. Hearing of the war then just commenced between the British Colonies in America and the mother country, Kosciusko, as a deciding spirit amongst his ardent associates, brought them to this resolution. Losing no time, they embarked, passed over the wide ocean of the Western world, and landing safe and full of their object, offered their services to the army of independence. Having been readily accepted, and immediately applied to use, the extraordinary warrior talents of Kosciusko soon shone conspicuous, and were speedily honored by his being appointed special aide-de-camp to General Washington. His subsequent conduct in the camp and field was consonant to its beginning, and he became a distinguished general in rank and command long before his volunteered military services had terminated. When the war ended, in the peace of mutual concessions between the national parent and its children on a distant land, (a point that is the duty of all Christian states to consider, and to measure their ultimate conduct by,) the Poles returned to their own country, where they soon met circumstances which caused them to call forth their recently passed experience for her. But they had not departed from the newly-established American State without demonstrations of its warm gratitude; and Koscuisko, in particular, with his not less popular compatriot and friend, Niemcivitz, the soldier and the poet, bore away with them the pure esteem of the brave population, the sighs of private friendship, and the tears of an abiding regret from many fair eyes.

To recapitulate the memorable events of the threatened royal freedom of Poland, by the three formidable foreign powers confederated for its annihilation, and in repelling which General Kosciusko took so gallant a lead, is not here necessary to connect our memoranda concerning his unreceding struggles to maintain her political existence. They have already been sketched in the preceding little record of the actual scenes in which he and his equally devoted compeers held their indomitable resistance till the fatal issue. "Sarmatia lay in blood!" and the portion of that once great bulwark of civilized Europe was adjudged by the paricidal victors to themselves: a sentence like unto that passed on the worst of criminals was thus denounced against Christendom's often best benefactor, while the rest of Europe stood silently by, paralyzed or appalled, during the immediate execution of the noble victim.

But though dismembered and thrown out from the "map of nations" by the combination of usurping ambition and broken faith, and no longer to be regarded as one in its "proud cordon," Poland retained within herself (as has been well observed by a contemporary writer) "a mode of existence unknown till then in the history of the world—a domestic national vitality." Unknown, we may venture to say, except in one extraordinary yet easily and reverentially understood instance. We mean the sense of an integral national being, ever-living in the bosoms of the people of Israel, throughout all their different dispersions and captivities. And, perhaps, with respect to this principle of a moral, political, and filial life, still drawing its aliment from the inhumed heart of their mother-country, who, to them, "is not dead but sleepeth!" may be explained, in some degree, in reference to the above remark on the existing and individual feeling amongst the wanderers of Poland, by considering some of the best effects, latent in their "working together for good," in the deep experience of her ancient variously-constituted modes of civil government.

Under that of her early monarchs, the Piasts and their senate, she sat beneath an almost patriarchal sceptre, they being native and truly parental princes. John Sobieski was one of this description, by descent and just rule. Under the Jagellon dynasty, also sprung from the soil, she held a yet more generalizing constitutional code, after which she gradually adopted certain republican forms, with an elective king—a strange contradiction in the asserted object, a sound system for political freedom, but which, in fact, contained the whole alchemy of a nation's "anarchical life," and ultimately produced the entire destruction of the state. From the established date of the elective monarchy, the kingdom became an arena for every species of ambitious rivalry, and its sure consequences, the interference of foreign influences; and hence rapidly advanced the decline of the true independent spirit of the land, to stand in her laws, and in her own political strength; her own impartial laws, the palladium of the people and a native king the parental guardian of their just administration. But, in sad process of time, "strangers of Rome, of Gaul, and of other nations," in whose veins not a drop of Sclavonian blood flowed, found means to successively seat themselves on the throne of the Piasts, the Jagellons, and the Sobieskis, of ancient Sarmatia; and the revered fabric fell, as by an earthquake, to be registered no more amongst the kingdoms of the world.

The Early Education of Kosciusko and his Compatriots, with its subsequent Effects on the Principles of their Lives.

Though their country appeared thus lost to them, they felt its kingdom still in their minds—in the bosom of memory, in the consciousness of an ancestry of bravery and of virtue; and though the soil had passed away from the feet of those whose ancestors of "sword or share" had trod it as sons and owners, and it now holds no place for them but their fathers' graves, yet the root is deep in such planting, and the tree, though invisible to the world, is seen and nourished in the depths of their hearts by the dews of heaven.

The pages of universal history, sacred and profane, ancient and modern, when opened with the conviction that He who made the world governs it also, will best explain the *why* of these changes in the destiny of nations; and within half of the latter part of the last century, and the nearly half of the present, awful have been the pages to be read. Hence we may understand the vital influence of the objects of education with regard to the principles inculcated, whether with relation to individual interest or to the generalized consideration of a people as a commonwealth or a kingdom. A kingdom and a commonwealth may be considered the same thing, when the power of both people and king are limited by just laws, established by the long exercised wisdom of the nation, holding the whole powers of the state in equilibrium; and in this sense, meaning "a royal commonwealth," comprising, as in England, "kings, lords, and commons," it is generally believed is intended to be understood the term, "The republic of Poland, with its king."

The Polish nation, however, under all their dominions of government, usually partook something of the policies and manners of the then existing times. Yet they were always distinguished by a particular chivalry of character, a brave freedom from all foreign and domestic vassalage, and a generous disposition to respect and to assist the neighboring nations to maintain the same independence they themselves enjoyed. Though actual schools, or colleges, or written lore, might not originally have had much to do with it, the continued practice of old, well-formed customs held them in "the ways their fathers walked in," and they found them those of "pleasantness" and true honor. But the time came when literary dictation was to take the place of oral tradition, and of habitual imitative reverence of the past. Schools and colleges were instituted, teaching for doctrines the prevailing sentiments of the endowers, or of the instructors employed. During the reigns of the later sovereigns of the Jagellon dynasty, Sigismund I. and II., and that of their predecessor, John Sobieski, the principles of these seminaries might be considered sound. But soon after the death of the last-named monarch, when the latent mischief contained in the Utopian idea of the perfection of an always elective monarchy began to shake the stability of even the monarchy itself, certain of the public teachers evinced correspondent signs of this destructive species of freemasonry; and about the same period the Voltaire venom of infidelity against all the laws of God and man being poured throughout the whole civilized world, the general effect had so banefully reached the seats of national instruction in Poland, that several of the most venerated personages, whose names have already been commemorated in the preceding biographical story, congregated together to stem, by a counteracting current, the torrent where they saw it likely to overflow; to sap up its introduced sources, by obtaining the abolition of some of the most subtle and dangerous of the scholastic institutions, and the establishment of others in their room, on the sound foundation of moral and religious polity between men and nations.

The sole remaining princely descendants of the three just referred to, true patriot-monarchs, were the earliest awakened to resist the spirit of evil spreading amongst all classes in the nation. The Czartoryski and the Zamoyski race, both of the Jagellon line, and near kinsmen to the then newly-raised monarch to the Polish throne, Stanislaus Poniatowski, appeared like twin stars over the darkened field, and the whole aspect of the country seemed speedily changed. A contemporary writer bears record that "one hundred and twenty-seven provincial colleges were founded, perfected, and supported by them and their patriotic colleagues; while the University of Vilna was judiciously and munificently organized by its prince palatine Adam Czartoryski himself, and a statute drawn up which declared it "an open high-school from the supreme board of public education for all the Polish provinces." Herein was every science exalting to the faculties of man, and conducive to his sacred aspirations, seriously and diligently inculcated; and every principle of morality and religion, purifying to his mixed nature, and therefore calculated to establish him in the answering conduct, truth, justice, and loyal obedience to the hereditary revered laws of the nation, equally instilled, qualifying him to uphold them, and to defend their freedom from all offensive operations at home or abroad, intended to subvert the purity of their code or the integrity of their administration. Such was the import of the implied vow on entering the university.

Amongst the gallant youths brought up in such a school of public virtue was Thaddeus Kosciusko and the young Timotheus Niemcivitz, his friend from youth to age. Kosciusko, as has already been said, was of noble parentage; and to be the son of a Polish nobleman was to be born a soldier, and its practical education, with sabre and lance, his daily pastime. But military studies were included in these various colleges, and the friends soon became as mutually expert in arms as they ever after continued severally distinguished in the fields of their country with sword or lyre. Besides, neither of the young cavaliers passed quite away from their *alma mater* without having each received the completing accolade of "true knighthood" by the stroke of "fealty to honor!" from the inaugurating sunbeam of some lovely woman's eye. Such befell the youthful Kosciusko, one bright evening, in a large and splendid circle of "the beautiful and brave" at Vilna; and it never lessened its full rays in his chivalric heart, from that hour devoted to the angel-like unknown who had shed them on him, and who had seemed to doubly consecrate the ardors of his soul to his country—her country—the country of all he loved and honored upon earth.

How he wrought out this silent vow is a story of deep interest—equally faithful to his patriotic loyalty and to his ever-cherished love; and in some subsequent reminiscences of the hero, should the writer live to touch a Polish theme again, they may be related with additional honor to his memory.

Brief was the time after the preceding sealing scene of the young Kosciusko for his military vocation took place, before himself and his friend Niemcivitz—who had also received his "anointing spell," which he gayly declared came by more bright eyes than he would dare whisper to their possessors—made a joint arrangement to quit the study of arms, though thus cheered on by the Muses and the Graces, and at once enter the exercise in some actual field of rugged war. The newly-opened dispute between Great Britain and her colonies in North America seemed calculated for their honorable practice. Consulting some of their most respected friends, they speedily found means to cross the seas, and shared the first great campaign under Washington. The issue of that campaign, and those which followed it, need not be repeated here; suffice it to say, the hard-fought contest ended in a treaty of peace between the parent country and its contumacious offspring, in the year 1783, with England's acknowledgment of their independence, under the name of the United States of America.

The two gallant Poles returned to Europe, and onward to their own country, by a route tracked by former brave deeds; through France, Germany, and other lands, marked by the Gustavuses, the Montecuculi, the Turennes, the Condes, the Marlboroughs, the Eugenes, champions alike of national peace and national glory on those widely-extended plains and bulwarked frontiers, till the belligerent clouds of a still more threatening hostility than any of those repelled invasions were seen hovering luridly over their own beloved country. Warned thus, during their pleasant travel, of the coming events whose shadows seemed to rise on every side of Poland, in forms appalling to the luxurious, the avaricious, the indolently selfish, of every description in the land, but which only roused and nerved the hearts and arms of her two sons, courageous in the simplicity of their purpose—Poland's preservation! they hastened in that moment to her bosom.

The events of this her mortal struggle, in fast union with these faithful sons, and other filial hearts, commemorated in the foregoing narrative of Thaddeus Sobieski, need not be recapitulated here. It amply tells the fate of the great kingdom which had stood as with gates of brass, until the intestine rivalries of an elective monarchy—the worshipped idol alike of presumptuous private ambition and pretended patriotic liberality—the true masked priest of public anarchy—rent them asunder, and the watchful nations, ready for plunder and extended dominion, poured into them a flood like the rivers of Babylon, over all her walls and towers.

We have read that part of her bravest sons were swept away into distant lands; some to die in homeless exile, others to meet the honorable compassion and the cheering hopes of sympathy from a people like themselves, who had formerly fought the good fight for England's laws, liberties, and royal name in Europe. And some were shut up from the light of day in the fettered captivity of foreign prisons, until "the iron entered their souls." Amongst these noble captives were General Kosciusko and his faithful Achates, Niemcivitz, to whom might be justly applied the words of our bard of "The Seasons," affixed to the young brow of Sir Philip Sidney—

> "The plume of war, with early chaplets crown'd
> The hero's laurel with the poet's bays."

But the Emperor Paul, on his accession to the throne of the Czars, as has before been noted, was too generous a captor to hold in cage so sweet a singing bird and so noble a lion; and he gave them liberty, appending to the act, dearest to a free-born heart, an imperial donation to Kosciusko that might have furnished him with a golden argosy all over the world. But the wounded son of Poland declined it in a manner worthy her name, and with an ingenuous gratitude towards the munificent sovereign who had offered it not as a bribe for "golden opinions," but as a sincere tribute to high heroic virtue.

The writer of this note was informed of this fact many years ago, by a celebrated English banker, at that time at St. Petersburg, and corresponding between that city and London, with whom the imperial present had been lodged, and through whom General Kosciusko respectfully but decidedly declined its acceptance.

Then it was that, after halting a short time in England, he with his school and camp companion in so many changes, prepared a second crossing over the Atlantic, to revisit its victor President in his olive-grounds at Mount Vernon. But Niemcivitz had another errand. His roving Cupid had long settled its wing, and he eagerly sought to plight, before Heaven's altar in the church, the already sacred vow he had pledged to a fair daughter of that country while sharing the dangers of its battle-fields.

It was with great difficulty the portcullis of a friendship strong as death had been raised in old chivalric Kent, to allow departure to so dear and honored a guest as he, who their master had seen fall in his memorable wounds on the plain of Brzesc. But he promised to return again, should the same sweet cherub that sat up aloft on his first voyage to America steer back his little bark in safety; and then he trusted to be once more clasped to the bosom of Poland, in that of his most beloved friend, a dweller in England.*

Besides this cherished heir of his earliest remembrances, there were other friends of olden days who had welcomed him with gladdening recollections. Amongst these was the family of Vanderhorst, originally of the Spanish Netherlands, who, from religious rather than political motives, had transferred themselves from certain persecutions in that land during times of papal tyranny to the shelter of the British colonies on the Transatlantic shore, and who, on the separation of those colonies into independent states from the mother country, had removed, in relative grateful duties, to the governing land of their early refuge, and were now dwelling here in prosperity and happy repose, when General Kosciusko set his honored foot on its sea-girt and virtue-bulwarked coast. He was their former guest while at New York, and he readily accepted their eager invitation that he would revisit them in their new paternal country. At this period the head of the respected family resided at Bristol, in Queen's Square, (the Grosvenor Square of that opulent city,) and Mr. Vanderhorst inhabited one of the most superb mansions in it. General Kosciusko arrived at his worthy host's door on the 7th of June, 1797, and was greeted by the hearty embrace of his old friend and the blush-

* The portcullis, the gate, and the armorial crest of Beaufort has descended from the royal founder of the family, John of Gaunt, Duke of Lancaster.

ingly-presented cheeks of his two daughters, young and lovely, in their teens. Their brother, a fine youth, pressed the hand of his father's gallant and revered guest to his lips. Niemcivitz, meanwhile, with dew-like tear-drops glittering over his joyous smiles, greeted every one with the affectionate recognition of a heart that seemed to know only to love. The writer, for one, shall never forget those tears and smiles on that venerable but ever kindly face; yet it was only in his old age that I first knew him. But sweet sisters, whom I began to know in your bright bloom, I can never forget those charming looks of reciprocating welcome that sprang alone from the fulness of a good and truthful virgin heart. They are now before me, though the eyes which then beamed so ingenuously on the honored countenance of the Polish hero are closed in death; or rather, shall I say, re-opened on him in a fairer and never-closing light.

He spent a happy week in that bright circle, in which the present commemorator has often since moved, and heard members of it over and over again describe its happy scenes; sometimes the younger sister, my own especial friend; at other times the animated brother. The revered father has long been in his respected grave; and the elder sister, after an early marriage with an officer of distinction in the British army, breathed her last sigh in the island of Antigua, leaving an only child, a daughter, Cordelia Duncombe Taylor, a beautiful memorial of the surpassingly lovely mother and aunt from whom she is descended.

During the Bristol sojourn, brief as it was, numerous were the sincere votaries to simple-hearted public virtue who sought it to pay their homage to the modest hero within its hospitable walls. Rufus King, then diplomatic minister from the United States to Great Britain, and the accomplished Turnbull, by pen, pencil, and sword the celebrated compeer of General Washington in his fields of glory, was here also.

On the Polish chief's approach to the city becoming known, the above gentlemen, with its sheriffs, Penry and Edgar, and Colonel Sir George Thomas, commanding a regiment of dragoons in the vicinity, went out in procession to meet him, to give him honoring welcome to the British shores. Crowds of the neighboring gentry, in carriages or on horseback, thronged the cavalcade; and on each succeeding day, while he remained at Bristol, similar throngs of enthusiastic visitants congregated in the square to catch a moment's sight of him. The military band of the cavalry regiment attended every evening in the hall of Mr. Vanderhorst, to regale the honor-oppressed invalid with martial airs, from every land wherever a soldier's banner had waved.

But letters arrived from Mount Vernon. General Washington had become impatient for his expected guest, and the morning of his separation from his Bristol friends was fixed. The vessel in which he was to embark was inspected with scrupulous care; and from the state of some of his yet unhealed wounds, he was obliged to be conveyed from Queen's Square to the quay in a sedan-chair. Mr. Vanderhorst and his son preceded it on foot, and two military officers, Captains Whorwood and Ferguson, walked on each side, each with his helmet off and in his hand, resting them on the poles of the sedan as they moved along. The colonel and other personal friends of Mr. Vanderhorst, and admirers of his hero-guest, followed in the rear of the chair, and a respectful and self-organized rank and file of humbler station closed the procession to the water-side.

There he embarked in a lightly-manned boat, with a sail and rudder, a more precious freight than Cæsar and his fortunes; for the Roman general crossed a barrier-river to subvert his country—Thaddeus Kosciusko a stream of refuge, after having sacrificed his all, though in vain, to preserve the independence of his native land. And thus the welcomed coming speeded parting guest took a grateful leave of the party who escorted him. They had seen him comfortably placed in the boat, and when it had put off, he and Niemcivitz, uncapped, extended their handkerchiefs, fluttering in the breeze, to them and the other bystanders, as the little sail gave bosom to the wind, and the farewell of this salution was answered with the warm and brave-hearted cheers of old British custom, and the waving of hats, which propitious sounds echoed back from cliff to cliff of the superb St. Vincent rocks that rampart the keys of the Bristol Avon.

All along the river, as the bark proceeded down, it was met, when within sight of any of the numerous merchant villas that adorned its banks, by pretty pleasure-skiffs, bringing votive presents of fruits and flowers to the brave voyagers on board. And then, while the wounded and fatigued veteran, as he lay on his pallet on the deck, was only able to bow his head with a gracious accepting smile to the respectful messengers, Niemcivitz stood at the prow, his then bright locks dallying with the sweet zephyrs from the gardened shores, and spoke the general's and his own heartfelt thanks, in a language of poetry that best accorded with his own glowing and his chief's gallant feelings, and the generous *benedicite* of the fair donators.

Onward the little vessel sped, until it reached the American ship afloat in King's Road, to convey its two noble passengers to the new republic, just established in the western hemisphere. That the well-remembered aid-de-camp of its boasted hero, Washington, was received with warrior honors, need not be here described. He rested that night under the variegated flag streaming from the topmast head, which his own volunteer arm had assisted to place there; and he thought of Poland and of England till he glided into a gentle sleep, and dreamed of both. By the following letter it may be seen that his eyes were visited next day by a sweet vision, in real personal existence, of the same kind beings whose recollections alone had so blandly soothed his pillow on the surge.

"Letter from General Kosciusko, to —— Vanderhorst, Esq., &c., &c., &c. From the United States of America, No. 36 Queen's Square, Bristol.

"At sea," (but without further date; circumstances, however, establishing it to have been written on or about the 21st or 22d June, 1797.)

"Dear Sir:

"It is the subject for a drama only, where the actors can express with the action and words what may approach nearest to what was passed yesterday within us, that I try to write. We were highly pleased, it is true, and with uncommon satisfaction, to see the approach of your family in a boat to our ship. But how short was the duration of the pleasure! When separation took place, our hearts were melted in tears. And we were frightened at their return, with fears of what might happen to them upon a high sea in so small a boat. Every rising wave gave the greatest pain to our anxiety, and the extreme painfulness of our alarm even increased when we were so far off that we could not see them more.

"I must beg of you to give them a good reprimand. Their kind and sensible hearts passed the limits of safety for themselves, and gave us the most distressful emotions of soul. The sea was so rough, I am sure they must all be very sick. However, we send them the warmest thanks, with everlasting friendship and remembrance. Be pleased, also, to take for yourself our tender respects.

"Never shall I forget so kind reception of me in your

house, nor the attentions of your friends. I am sensible that I gave to you and your amiable family a great trouble; but your goodness will not acknowledge it, and by so doing, it more impresses my mind with the obligation, and with a true answering affection for your whole family.

"I am, dear sir, with friendship and esteem, your most thankful and most obedient servant,

"T. KOSCIUSKO."

"I can nothing add to the feelings of my worthy friend but that I wish to the respectable and beautiful family of Vanderhorst all the happiness that virtue and the most excellent qualities of the heart can deserve.

"J. NIEMCIVITZ."

"The fair deity—I mean Mister Cupid—desires his best compliments to you all."

This tender yet playful postscript from the young soldier votary of Cupid and the muse is evidently appended in the gayety of an affectionate heart, speeding to the land of his own lady-love, shortly to become his bride after his arrival, and which was so consummated. Kosciusko never swerved from his soul's loyalty to the bright Polish Laura of his cherished devotedness; and his subsequent correspondence, one of pure, unselfish friendship, with the youngest daughter of his venerable Anglo-American friend, lovely as she was pure, confided to her how faithful had been his heart's allegiance to the woman of his first and last vows. They had met during his track of early military fame, and had exchanged these vows. But blighting circumstances interfered, and they lived, and loved, but never met again.

The narrator of these little reminiscences might well, perhaps most agreeably, drop the curtain here; for strange and stirring incidents awaited the two friends on their return to Europe, after a rather prolonged sojourn amongst the animated hospitalities of a grateful people.

The homeward side of that curtain was wrought in mingled fabric, gold, silver, and various threaded yarns; and many were the different hands that threw the shuttles—emperors, kings, princes, friends, traitors; but above all, in the depth of mischief, the spirit of suspicion had steeped the web.

Such was the lurid appearance of the great drama of Europe when Kosciusko and Niemcivitz set foot again upon its shores. Death had thrown his pall over some in high places and others in low. But more cheering suns soon arose, to scare away the darkening shadows, and the patriot heroes' hopes ascended with them. How some were honored, some deceived in the observance, need not lengthen out our present pages; suffice it to say that there were stars then rising on the horizon which promised fairer elements.

It may be recollected that at the signing of the partition of Poland by the benumbed Senate, on the fatal day of its political decease, the young prince Adam Czartoryski, the eldest son of the justly-renowned and virtuous palatine of Vilna, who had been so signal a benefactor to his country by the endowment and reformation of its chief schools, was sent out a hostage to Russia, in seal of the then final resignation. His education had been noble, like the principles of those schools in the foundation of which the brave, illustrious and also erudite Lithuanian family of Krasinski had been eminent sharers.* The young prince's manners were equally noble with his principles, and not long in attracting the most powerful eyes in the empire. During the remainder of the reign of the Empress Catharine, she caused him to be treated with protective kindness, and on her demise he was instantly removed by the Emperor Paul from whatever surveillance had been left over him, into the imperial palace of St. Petersburg, where this justly-admired princely student of Vilna was to be the constant inmate and companion of the youthful Alexander, the eldest son and heir of the empire.

Their studies, their amusements, were shared together; and they soon became friends like brothers. About the same time, as has before been related, Paul had given freedom to General Kosciusko and his compatriot Niemcivitz. And still, after the death of that mysteriously-destined sovereign, a halcyon sky seemed to hold its bland aspects over Russia's Sclavonian sister people, ancient Sarmatia. But ere long the scene changed, and the "seething-pot" of a universal ambition, the crucible of nations, grasped by the hand of Napoleon, began again to darken the world's atmosphere.

* Count Valerian Krasinski, a distinguished son of this house, has long been an honored guest in England, and held in high literary respect for his veritable and admirable works, written in fine English: "The Times of Philip Augustus," and "The History of the Protestant Reformation in Poland." The writer of this note knows that he has in his possession some beautiful manuscript tales, descriptive of the manners of Poland; one called "Amoina," a most remarkable story; another, entitled, "My Grandmamma," full of interesting matter, written as a solace in occasional rests from severer literary occupations. And she laments that he has not yet allowed himself to be prevailed on to give any of these touching and elegant reminiscences to his English readers.

Kosciusko now looked on, sometimes with yet struggling hopes, then with well-founded convictions that "the doom was not yet spent;" and no more to be deluded one way or another, while such shifting grounds and sudden earthquakes were erupting the earth under his feet, like the prophet of old, boding worse things to come, he withdrew himself far into the solitudes of nature, into the wide yet noiseless temple of God, where the prayer of an honest man's heart might be heard and answered by that all-merciful and all-wise Being, who sometimes leaves proud men to themselves, to the lawless, headlong driving of their arrogant passions, to show them, in the due turn of events, what a vicious self-aggrandizing, abhorrent and despicable monster in human shape such a noble creature, when turned from the divine purpose of his creation, may become. To such contemplations, and to the repose of a mind and conscience at peace with itself, did the once, nay, ever-renowned hero of Poland, retire into the most sequestered mountains of Switzerland. A few friends, of the same closed accounts with the world, congregated around him; and there he dwelt several years, beloved and revered, as, indeed, he was wherever he planted his pilgrim staff.

He died at Soleure, in the house of a friend, Mr. Zeltner, in consequence of a fall from his horse while taking a solitary ride. He was buried there with every demonstration of respect in the power of the simple inhabitants to bestow. But the Emperor Alexander, on hearing of the event, would not allow remains so honorable to be divided from the land of their birth; and such high and sincere homage to the undaunted heroism and universally acknowledged integrity of the lamented dead found no difficulty in obtaining the distinguishing object sought, that of transferring his virtue-consecrated relics to the shrine of ancient Christian Poland, the city of Cracow, and there reinterring them in the great royal cemetery of the most revered patriots of the kingdom.

Years rolled on over the head and heart of the patriot and the bard, Niemcivitz, the ever "faithful Achates" of his friend and his country, even after, to his bereaved heart, he had survived both. He had also become a widower. His gentle and delicate wife went to revisit her native climate in the United States, but died there. On his return thence to Europe, the consolations of a fraternal friendship, in the bosoms of his noble countrymen, who had become adopted denizens of free and happy England, vainly sought to retain him with them. Sorrow in a breast of his temperament cannot find rest in any place. His shining locks, once likened to those of Hyperion, became frosted by an age of wandering as well as of sadness; and the till then joyous and ever-tender heart of the sweetest poet of Sclavonian birth breathed its last sigh in Paris, in the summer of 1841. It was on the first of June; and on the eighth of the month he was buried with military honors and all the distinguishing rites of the national church. The funeral service was performed by the Archbishop of Chalcidonia, with a large body of the clergy attending. A choir of fifty professors sung the mass, and more than a thousand persons thronged the procession—persons of all nations, of all creeds, religious or political, of every rank amongst men, of every mind, from the prince to the peasant, that understood the true value of genius when helmed by virtue, either on the land or on the wave; whether in the field or in the cabinet; in the student's closet, or in the duties of domestic home.

Such a man was Niemcivitz. So was he wept; so will he be remembered, proving, indeed, most convincingly, that there is a standard set up in men's hearts, if they would but look to it, which, whatever be their minor clashing opinions, shows that the truly great and good in this earth are all of one family in the estimation of pure intellect, the spiritual organ of all just estimation, which is, in fact, that of the kingdom of heaven—that kingdom which, if its laws to man were properly preserved and obeyed, would spread the shepherds' promised "peace and good-will to all mankind." But men may listen, approve, and admire, and yet withhold obedience. But why will the heirs of such a covenant, with sight and hearing, die from its inheritance?

Kosciusko and Niemcivitz were real appreciators of so rich a birthright in "the better country!" and now are gone to Him who purchased it by His most precious blood, to enter with Him forever into its peaceful and glorious rest.

J. P.

BRISTOL, SEPTEMBER, 1845.

www.ingramcontent.com/pod-product-compliance
Lightning Source LLC
Chambersburg PA
CBHW020501020726
47493CB00001B/131

* 9 7 8 1 4 3 4 4 1 6 9 0 2 *